James Becker spent over twenty years in the Royal Navy's Fleet Air Arm and ser██ ███ during the Falklands War. Throughout his career ████████████████ ████ overt operations in many of ████████████████████ ke Yemen, Northern Ireland and Russia. ██ ██ an accomplished combat pistol shot and has an abiding interest in ancient and medieval history. His previous novels, *The First Apostle*, *The Moses Stone* and *The Messiah Secret* also feature Chris Bronson. *The First Apostle* was one of the biggest selling eBooks of 2009.

Also by James Becker

THE FIRST APOSTLE
THE MOSES STONE
THE MESSIAH SECRET

and published by Bantam Books

THE NOSFERATU SCROLL

James Becker

BANTAM BOOKS
LONDON · TORONTO · SYDNEY · AUCKLAND · JOHANNESBURG

TRANSWORLD PUBLISHERS
61–63 Uxbridge Road, London W5 5SA
A Random House Group Company
www.transworldbooks.co.uk

THE NOSFERATU SCROLL
A BANTAM BOOK: 9780553825145

First published in Great Britain
in 2011 by Bantam Press
an imprint of Transworld Publishers
Bantam edition published 2011

A CIP catalogue record for this book
is available from the British Library.

Addresses for Random House Group Ltd companies outside the UK
can be found at: www.randomhouse.co.uk
The Random House Group Ltd Reg. No. 954009

The Random House Group Limited supports The Forest Stewardship Council
(FSC®), the leading international forest certification organisation. Our books
carrying the FSC label are printed on FSC® certified paper. FSC is the only forest
certification scheme endorsed by the leading environmental organisations,
including Greenpeace. Our paper procurement policy can be found at
www.randomhouse.co.uk/environment

Typeset in 11/14½pt Sabon by
Kestrel Data, Exeter, Devon.
Printed and bound by
CPI Group (UK) Ltd, Croydon, CR0 4YY.

4 6 8 10 9 7 5 3

To Sally.
For always and for everything.

Acknowledgements

No book is ever the work of just the author: it's invariably a team effort. In this case, the original spark came from the talented team at Transworld, and specifically from my dedicated and forceful editor there, Selina Walker. She liked the idea of Bronson and Angela mixing it with the undead, as a departure from their usual haunts of dusty caves, ancient manuscripts and clay tablets. My brilliant agent, Luigi Bonomi of LBA, liked the idea as well, and we all thought Venice was pretty much the ideal location for the story. Throughout the writing process they both offered invaluable insights and suggestions, all of which improved the book immeasurably.

Prologue

10 May 1741
Krumlov Zamek, Český Krumlov, Bohemia

'Open it.'

The torchlight gave the priest's face a haunting, almost satanic, quality, an impression reinforced by the chamber in which he was standing. It was a small underground room in the castle, located in the same part of the building as the cages that held the wolves. Four flickering torches were mounted in sconces, one on each wall, but they failed to drive away all the shadows.

A sturdy table stood in the centre of the room, and on it lay a large, ornate, black wooden coffin, the closed lid divided into two parts and hinged on one side, the other edges secured with screws. The coffin had arrived from the Schwarzenberg Palace in Vienna two days earlier and had immediately been carried into St George's Chapel in the castle. There, the upper section of the coffin had been opened to allow the mere handful of mourners who had appeared in the building to see the thin, white face of the body inside.

The princess had come home for the last time.

Masses for the immortal soul of Princess Eleonora Elisabeth Amalia Magdalena von Schwarzenberg had been held all over Bohemia, but few people made the journey to the vast castle – which wasn't a single structure at all, but a complex of huge yellow and grey stone buildings roofed with red tiles – that stood on the north bank of the Vltava River.

It was here that her burial was about to take place, and there were preparations – important preparations – to be made.

Four servants had carried the coffin down from St George's Chapel. Now, one of them moved forward in response to the priest's instruction and removed the hand-made iron screws that secured the upper part of the lid. His task done, he stepped back.

'No. Take all of them out,' the priest ordered.

The man looked surprised, but obediently removed the remaining fastenings that held down the lower section of the lid. As he worked, he glanced back at the priest, wondering why the man who'd so publicly shunned the princess while she was alive was now so concerned with her dead body.

The priest's name was Bohdan Řezník, the surname

meaning 'butcher', and in truth he looked as though he would be more at home in a bloodstained apron than in the plain, dark brown robes he habitually wore.

When the body of the Princess Eleonora Amalia had been delivered to the castle, one of the escort party had walked down into Krumlov town, found Řezník at his home and handed him a single folded sheet of parchment. The document bore three separate seals, one of them the distinctive double-headed eagle mark of Karel VI, King of Bohemia, the current ruler, and a member of the Habsburg dynasty, which had governed the country since 1526.

The instructions contained on the parchment were unambiguous, and made perfect sense to Řezník. He'd noted with satisfaction that his orders had been prepared by Dr Franz von Gerschstov, Eleonora Amalia's preferred physician, and a man whose other, less well-known, qualities struck a chord with Řezník.

The servant removed the final screw, and stepped back from the coffin once more, awaiting any further instructions the priest might issue.

'Swing back the lid,' the priest said, and watched as two of the servants did so, to reveal the whole interior of the coffin.

'Now leave me with her. You may return in half an hour.'

Only when the door of the small room had closed behind the men did the priest step forward. He walked across the flag-stoned floor to the coffin and looked down with distaste at the slight figure of Eleonora Amalia. Her hands were placed demurely on her breast, the right hand resting on the left, her wasted body clad in a long white dress, her small feet bare.

Řezník felt in the pocket of his habit and pulled out a folding knife with a black wooden handle. He'd spent several minutes the previous evening putting a fine edge on the dark steel blade.

He made the sign of the cross and muttered a prayer – not for the immortal soul of Eleonora, but for himself, asking for forgiveness and divine protection for the actions he now had to take. He lifted the princess's hands and lay her arms at her sides, then snapped open the knife. Řezník inserted the blade under the neckline of the dress and in a single fluid movement ran the knife all the way down to Eleonora's feet, slicing through the layers of material. Then he peeled aside the two cut halves of the dress and looked down at her naked body. The skin that had been so white in life was now mottled and discoloured, with livid brown and purple marks where the initial stages of decay had taken hold.

But that wasn't the most noticeable feature. What held Řezník's attention was the crudely stitched cut that ran from between the princess's small, wrinkled breasts down to her pubis.

Her nakedness offended him, but he had his instructions. His expression of distaste deepened as he again used his blade, this time to slice through each of the rough stitches that held the skin and flesh of her abdomen closed. Then he put down the knife, inserted his fingers into the wide incision and with little difficulty pulled apart the two sections of dead tissue. He was looking for one thing, one single object in the chest cavity, and in seconds he knew it wasn't there – which was as it should be. But Řezník had been ordered to make absolutely sure before the burial took place.

He nodded in satisfaction, wiped his hands on the front of his robe and stepped back from the open coffin. Then he walked across to one corner of the chamber, where another, much smaller and very plain wooden box was propped against the wall. Řezník was a strong man, and he picked up the box with little effort. He carried it across to the table, placed it next to the princess's coffin, and lifted off the lid.

Then he strode back to the wall of the chamber and picked up a leather bag, the contents of which clattered metallically as he carried it over to the table. He placed the bag on the floor, opened it and took out three substantial leather straps, which he positioned under the open box, spacing them equally along its length.

He reached into the larger casket, picked up the mortal remains of Eleonora Amalia and dropped the body unceremoniously into the smaller box. Before he placed the lid in position, he took a small vial of clear liquid from his pocket and sprinkled the contents over the corpse, muttering a prayer as he did so. Then he took a hammer and a handful of nails from his bag, and drove a dozen of them firmly through the box's lid, securely sealing it to the base. To complete the process, he knelt down and tightened each of the leather straps around it.

Řezník took a deep breath and then, grunting with the effort, he lifted up the small wooden box and manoeuvred it into the larger coffin. It would have been easier to wait until the servants returned, but his instructions had been clear – when they returned to the chamber, he was to have sealed the coffin for the last time. Nobody must ever know what he had done. He closed the lid and started replacing the screws.

When the servants knocked at the door a few minutes later, Řezník had finished securing the lid and was standing beside the coffin, waiting for them.

'We leave the castle at eight,' he said. 'Ensure that the carriage is ready and everything has been prepared by then.'

A few minutes before the appointed hour, Řezník strode into the castle courtyard. Night was already falling, and the expansive open space was in deep shadow, the only illumination coming from the fitful flames of the torches mounted along the walls.

A black-painted carriage, its doors bearing the device of the Schwarzenberg dynasty stood waiting in the centre of the courtyard. Two black mares were already hitched to it and tossing their heads impatiently in black-plumed headdresses. The driver, also dressed in black, stood beside the vehicle. As Řezník had instructed – his absolute authority conferred by the parchment he still carried – all of the castle's servants, wearing the darkest clothes they possessed, were standing silently on one side of the courtyard to bid their mistress a last farewell.

Řezník walked across to the carriage and looked into the rear section, behind the seats. The coffin was already in place, the gleaming black wood marred in two places by the leather straps that held it *in situ*, a precaution against the jolting the carriage would experience on the rough and unmade road that ran from the castle to the church of St Vitus, where the princess's body was destined to rest for all eternity. Řezník nodded in satisfaction: all his instructions had been followed to the letter. Finally, he clambered up on to the carriage, the driver joining him a few moments later.

For a couple of minutes nothing else happened, and then the castle clock struck eight. As the first peal of the bell echoed around the courtyard, the servants standing beside the large wooden gates stepped forward, released the bolts, and pulled them open. Only then did the driver tap the reins lightly across the broad backs of the two mares. Obediently, the horses stepped forward, their hooves clattering on the uneven stones of the courtyard, and the carriage began to move, creaking gently as it did so.

The funeral cortège, if that word could accurately be applied to only a single carriage containing two men and one corpse, passed through the wide gateway and out of the castle. The sight that greeted the two men outside the walls was both spectacular and sad: the road that wound away from the castle was lined on both sides by silent and unmoving figures, each holding aloft a flaming brand. Indeed, from the castle gates, it looked as if a thin double ribbon of fire was stretching out in front of the carriage, illuminating the final route that the princess's body would take.

Řezník glanced at the first few figures as the carriage drove slowly past them. Some of the torchbearers had been drawn from the local villagers, but the others, and perhaps the majority, were men and women of the cloth: monks and nuns who had been summoned by Řezník so that their piety and righteousness might lend a certain dignity – and protection – to the proceedings. Each of them bowed his or her head in respectful supplication as the carriage passed, and then made the sign of the cross.

And as the carriage trundled slowly past the silent ranks, the torchbearers extinguished their burning brands in metal water buckets which had been placed beside each of them specifically for that purpose. The moving end of the ribbon of fire marked the position of the carriage, while behind it darkness again reclaimed the land.

An impartial observer might have wondered at a funeral for a princess of the Schwarzenberg dynasty being conducted in such a manner. It was unusual enough that the presiding clergyman should be just a village priest rather than a bishop or some other high Church official, but even more surprising was the complete absence of a single member of the Schwarzenberg family, or any representatives from the other aristocratic families to which the Schwarzenbergs were linked or related. Even Eleonora Amalia's son Joseph was missing.

It was as if the only people who had any regard or respect or affection for the princess were the peasants and villagers of Krumlov itself, but even that impression was false. The local men and women lining the route and holding the torches aloft had been ordered to do so by Řezník, on pain of punishment.

About twenty minutes after leaving the castle, the carriage drew to a halt outside the open doors of the Church of St Vitus. Řezník climbed down from his seat and issued a series of instructions. The straps holding the coffin in place were released, and the heavy wooden box was hoisted on to the shoulders of six powerfully built monks. They carried the coffin into the church and placed it on a wooden trestle that had been prepared and positioned in front of the altar.

The service was short – about as brief as Řezník could make it – and almost all the pews in front of the pulpit were noticeably empty. The only people sitting in the church were wearing the habits of monks and nuns, summoned like the torchbearers before them. Once his duty was done, Řezník stepped down from the pulpit to supervise the actual burial.

As a Schwarzenberg, it might have been expected that the princess would be laid to rest in the family vault, in St Augustine's church in Vienna, but Eleonora had been denied that privilege. Instead, Řezník led the way into a small side chapel where a large section of the stone-flagged floor had already been removed and a deep grave dug, a grave that had been lined with a clay-based concrete. The six monks lowered the casket to the floor where three substantial ropes had been placed in readiness. Then they each seized the end of one of the ropes and lifted the coffin off the floor, moving awkwardly in the confined space around the grave, and manoeuvred the casket over the hole. Slowly they lowered the coffin into the waiting void.

Řezník murmured a few last prayers, and then ordered the handful of official mourners out of the church. The final rituals were to be witnessed by as small a number of people as possible.

Řezník stepped to one side of the chapel and picked up a crudely fashioned wooden ladder, which he carried over to the side of the grave and then lowered into it. He gestured to the monks, who silently descended into the pit. Řezník held a torch over the void so they could see what they were doing. Stacked along both sides of the grave were a number of heavy flat stones. Working under the priest's direction, the monks picked these up, two men to each stone, and placed them carefully on the flat top of the black wooden coffin, in a double layer.

Řezník inspected their work carefully from the top of

the grave, and ordered them to climb out again. Their next task required all the considerable strength the monks possessed. Řezník had already arranged for a rough wooden arch fitted with a heavy-duty pulley to be positioned inside the chapel to allow a single heavy slab to be laid across the top of the open grave to seal it completely. Even with this mechanical device to assist them, it still took almost half an hour before the slab was positioned to Řezník's satisfaction and, despite the cool evening air, the sweat was pouring off the faces of the six men.

But still they weren't finished. Řezník permitted them a short break to recover their strength, then supervised the disassembly of the wooden arch, the component pieces of which they stacked against the side wall of the chapel. Once that had been completed, he instructed them to drag three heavy sacks containing soil, taken from the cemetery outside the church, across to the slab that now covered the tomb. They upended the sacks and spread the contents into a single even layer over the slab.

Now, finally, the monks' work was almost over. They replaced the flagstones that had been removed to allow the hole to be dug, but left enough space directly over the grave for the gravestone itself, a slab that Řezník had had prepared by a stone mason in the village the previous day. Two of the monks picked up the stone and lowered it carefully into position.

Řezník stepped to the end of the gravestone and lowered his head in prayer for the last time, the six monks who had assisted him kneeling on the flagstone floor beside the tomb.

Moonlight speared in through one of the chapel's side windows and the beam played silently across the freshly cut and very simple inscription in the stone. The words made no mention of Eleonora Amalia's family name or her aristocratic status. It didn't even include the Schwarzenberg coat of arms. On the specific instructions of Řezník, who had himself simply been following the orders he had been given by the men who had prepared the parchment, the inscription simply listed the first name of the princess, and the date of her death:

Hier liget die arme sunderin Eleonora bittet fur sie. Obut die 5 Mai A1741.

With the body of Eleonora now safely consigned to the earth, Řezník had two more tasks to perform. The carriage was standing outside the church, the driver waiting for him. Řezník climbed up on to the vehicle and instructed the man to return to Krumlov Castle.

The gates were still wide open, but the courtyard was now virtually deserted. Only three men waited for Řezník's return and the orders they expected him to issue. The priest stepped down from the carriage and walked across to them.

The men were all wearing tunics that identified them as servants of the Schwarzenberg dynasty, and two of them were armed with short swords, the scabbards buckled to their belts. It was these two men that Řezník approached first.

'It's time,' he said. 'Do it now. Kill them all, and dump the bodies in the forest.'

The men nodded, turned on their heels and vanished inside the building.

Řezník turned to the third man. 'Show me the painting.'

The servant led Řezník into the castle and to a long gallery, at one end of which hung a life-size portrait of Eleonora. The priest stared at the princess's pale face for a few moments, his lip curling in disgust.

'Lift it down,' he ordered.

Once the painting was leaning against the wall, Řezník took his folding knife and opened it. He drove the point of the blade through the canvas to the left of the princess's head and hacked downwards in a vertical line. He repeated the operation on the right-hand side of the image as well, then sliced a horizontal line above the head to join the two cuts. He seized the flap of canvas that now fell forward, and started to cut along the last remaining side.

As his blade began cutting through the painted image of Eleonora's neck, the mournful howl of an animal echoed through the vast old building.

The man beside Řezník glanced round in alarm, but the priest ignored the interruption. He completed the final cut through the canvas and stepped back, holding the painted image of the princess's head in his left hand. He looked around and then stepped across to the nearest sconce in which a torch burned brightly. Taking it down, he held the flames to one corner of the square he'd removed from the painting. The canvas was heavy and the paint thick, and for a few seconds it merely smouldered. Then the fire took hold and it flared suddenly, the flames a kaleidoscopic mix of colours as the pigments in the paint were consumed by the heat. Řezník dropped the final corner of the canvas to the floor and watched as the last of the flames flickered and died.

'Are there any other pictures showing that woman?' he demanded. He couldn't even bring himself to speak her name.

'That was the last one. All the others have been destroyed.'

Řezník nodded in satisfaction. His work was done. The princess was buried in what amounted to an unmarked grave, and he had done his best to expunge all traces of her life, all reminders of her presence, from the castle.

Without a backwards glance, he walked out of the gallery and a few minutes later passed through the double gates that secured the courtyard of Krumlov Zamek. He knew he would never enter that cursed and wretched castle again.

He just hoped that he had done enough to stop the contagion before it took hold in the district.

*   *   *

But in that regard, Řezník was mistaken. Over the next few years he would officiate at nearly a dozen burials that would require him to use his peculiar and arcane knowledge, though none of these would involve another member of the aristocracy.

And on his own deathbed, nearly twenty years later, he would finally acknowledge the truth he had shied away from for all those years.

Because what happened in the months and years after the burial of Eleonora Amalia proved to him beyond doubt that she was not the source of the plague, as Řezník had always believed, but simply another victim.

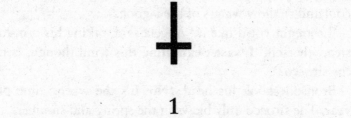

1

Present day

'This truly is a spectacular place,' Chris Bronson said, looking back at the city of Venice.

It was the first day of November, and he and Angela were standing side by side in the stern of a crowded *vaporetto* that was ferrying them from the Fondamente Nuove stop on Venice itself across the lagoon to the Isola di San Michele – the island of St Michael – to take part in the celebrations known unofficially as the Festival of the Dead.

There was a stiff breeze blowing from the south-east, sufficiently strong to create dozens of white horses that surged all around the vessel, but the boat carved an arrow-straight wake through the choppy waters. The lights of the city were just starting to pierce the late-afternoon gloom, a gloom made more pronounced by the patches of mist that were forming over the water. Venice looked almost like a huge and improbable cruise ship, floating silently in the cool and shallow waters of the lagoon.

'I thought you'd like it,' Angela said, taking his arm to steady herself. 'I wasn't expecting this wind though. Is it the sirocco?'

Bronson shook his head. 'No. It's the wrong time of year. The sirocco only blows in the spring and summer.'

'Well, I was hoping for a warm and balmy evening – a kind of last gasp of summer, if you like – but this feels more like the onset of winter.'

'It is November, you know.'

Angela shivered slightly. She was wearing a pair of black trousers (she'd guessed that a skirt would be much less practical for climbing in and out of *vaporettos* during the evening), a white blouse and a kind of woollen tunic that Bronson had incautiously referred to as a cardigan, only to receive a loud sigh at his manifest lack of fashion sense. Over this, she was wearing a midnight-blue silk coat. Bronson liked it: it brought out the colour of her eyes. He could see now that it couldn't be very warm.

Bronson had always regarded fashion as an easy way of separating large sums of money from gullible men – and even more gullible women – who were foolish enough to believe the rubbish spouted by the self-appointed fashion 'experts'. He invariably dressed for comfort and practicality, selecting a shirt by opening a drawer and picking up the one that lay on top of the others. He chose trousers, socks and underwear using the same simple and, to him, foolproof system. His only concessions to fashion were that he normally wore dark colours, usually blues and blacks, and had never owned a pair of white socks. This evening, he had chosen a dark check shirt, slightly faded blue jeans, and a pair of black trainers. And his leather jacket was proof against even the strongest wind the Adriatic could produce.

Angela buttoned her coat, and snuggled closer to Bronson. 'With your love of Italy, and all things Italian,' she murmured, 'I'm really surprised that you've never been to Venice before.'

'I know,' Bronson replied. 'For some reason, I've spent my time on the west side of the country. So I know Rome, Florence, Pisa and Naples really well, but this is the first time I've ever visited the Adriatic coast. And it really is stunning.'

It had all been Angela's idea. There had been an un-expected reduction in her workload at the British Museum, and for the first time since the start of her employment there she had found herself with almost nothing to do. She was a ceramics conservator, and spent most of her working day either trying to reassemble ancient pottery shards into something that resembled a recognizable vessel or writing reports and assessments for the benefit of other people who were trying to do pretty much the same thing.

And this lull in her workload had coincided neatly with the dates of Bronson's final week's leave for the year. Her ex-husband had planned to do little more than sit around at his home in Tunbridge Wells, watch a bit of television and, if he could summon the energy and enthusiasm, tackle a handful of DIY jobs that he knew needed doing. When Angela had suggested spending the week exploring Venice instead, Bronson had thought carefully about his choice for nearly a second and a half before agreeing to go with her. It was, he thought now as he put his arm round her, absolutely the right decision.

'OK,' he said, smiling down at her, 'you're the historian. So what, exactly, is the Festival of the Dead?'

Angela rested her head against his shoulder. 'Do you really want a history lesson?' she asked.

'I like hearing you talk, especially when you're talking about something that really interests you. And you know I'm never tired of hearing about Italy.'

'Actually, it's not really *Italian* history,' Angela began, 'because the date – the first of November – comes from a really old pagan festival, and is celebrated over most of Western Europe. Yesterday was, of course, the last day of October, or Halloween, which as everyone knows has always been associated with death and the supernatural. But what's less well known is that it's only ever been a kind of taster, a precursor, if you will, for the main event – Allhallows or Hallowmas, which is today.'

'I thought it was a kind of saints' day,' Bronson objected.

Angela nodded. 'If you talk to a Christian, especially an Anglican or Roman Catholic, he or she will tell you that today is All Saints' Day, a day that celebrates God and all his saints, both known and unknown, so the Church can cover all the bases. But it's a little more complicated than that, because the early Christian Church was desperate to try to stamp out all competing religions, especially all pagan rituals and celebrations. They couldn't simply ban pagan festivals because they feared that people would still observe them in secret, so they did the next best thing: they hijacked them.

'Some time in the early seventh century, Christians began celebrating All Saints' Day on the first of November. In 835 AD Pope Gregory IV officially authorized the festival, and it's been celebrated ever since. Allhallows was once one of the four greatest and most important festivals in the pagan calendar, but most Christians today have never heard of it, because the Church has done such a good job of changing the original purpose and meaning of the celebrations.

'And, just to ram home the fact that November the first was a Christian celebration, the Church also created another festival day on the second of the month – All Souls' Day, which is a celebration to help cleanse and purify the spirits of the dead. And you'll find similar crowds out on San Michele tomorrow, because the Venetians celebrate both days.'

'But surely the early Christians weren't celebrating death?'

Angela shook her head. 'No, not death, but the dead

themselves. Allhallows was intended to help people remember the dead, and to say prayers for the souls of the departed. Interestingly, it's not just in Western Europe that you find this kind of celebration. Over in Mexico they have a Day of the Dead, which is also on the second of November, and that's a kind of combination of an ancient Native American tradition and the Catholic All Souls' Day. The people there decorate their homes with fake skeletons, visit cemeteries to clean and tidy the graves of their deceased relatives, and even leave offerings of food and drink for various wandering spirits.'

'And I suppose the Venetian Festival of the Dead is something similar?' Bronson asked.

'Exactly, but over here they don't so much tend the graves as wander about the cemetery carrying lighted candles and chrysanthemums. Those flowers have become firmly associated with burial ceremonies in Italy, and it's a very bad idea to offer a bunch to anyone who's still alive. But, being Italy, it's become a social event, too, especially for locals – and because we're here in Venice, I thought it would be interesting to come along.'

'So we'll be spending the evening in a graveyard. How nice!' Bronson turned his back on the city they had left and looked ahead at the Isola di San Michele, colloquially known as the 'Island of the Dead' because it was simply a huge graveyard.

He'd read that the idea of using one of the islands in the Venetian lagoon as a graveyard dated back to 1807, when

Venice was conquered by Napoleon and was suffering under a French occupation that virtually bankrupted the city. Burial on Venice itself was deemed to be unsanitary, so the neighbouring island of San Cristoforo della Pace was selected for the task. When that proved inadequate in size, the narrow canal that separated San Cristoforo della Pace from the larger San Michele was filled in, during 1836, and the combined island became known simply as San Michele. For a very short period the island was also used as a prison, but afterwards reverted to solely being a graveyard, which still held some very famous corpses. The bodies of the dead were transported across to the island from Venice on special funeral gondolas.

The edge of San Michele lay only a couple of hundred yards from Venice itself, but the *vaporetto* stop was at the most northerly point of the island, right beside the Chiesa di San Michele, one of the earliest Renaissance churches in Venice. Bronson could see it now, its stark white Istrian stone standing out in the gloom, and marking it out from the mellow colours that characterized most Venetian architecture.

A couple of minutes later, the *vaporetto* was stationary alongside the jetty, and the gangway had been opened. The passengers surged off the vessel and started making their way towards the entrance. Bronson and Angela were in no particular hurry to leave the boat, so they waited in the stern until almost all the other passengers had left. Then they too stepped on to the jetty and followed the rest of the crowd who, noisy and gesticulating, seemed to be getting in the mood for the evening ahead.

'The wind's dropped, which is good news, but it's getting a bit murky,' Bronson said to Angela, pointing at the blanket of fog that was descending fast. They had seen patches of mist forming over the water after they'd left Venice, but what lay in front of them was more like a real peasouper. Within minutes, visibility was reduced to just a few yards, and they were glad that the path itself was visible, though the family in front of them were still making enough noise that following them was very easy.

Angela shivered again. 'You're right – it's quite spooky now. And this mist is exactly the right atmosphere for an evening in a graveyard.' She took a map of the island out of her pocket and smoothed it out.

'Well, as long as we can find our way back to the jetty and the boat I'm not bothered,' Bronson said. 'But I certainly wouldn't fancy spending the night out here. Do you see that kind of yellow glow in the mist over to the left of us? Shall we head towards it?'

Angela looked in that direction as well, and nodded. 'It's probably from all the candles people are carrying.'

They were now catching up with the people ahead, who had walked along the semicircular path that curved around in front of the church, and had then turned down another path that seemed to be leading in the opposite direction.

'Where are they going now?'

Angela looked down at the map. 'This path takes us

over towards the centre of the cemetery, and also towards some of the older areas. One slightly odd thing about this graveyard is that, these days, the bodies are removed after about ten years. They're buried in the usual way in the ground, with the grave marked by a slab or headstone, but because this graveyard serves the entire population of Venice, space is pretty limited. So once the body has been reduced to bones, it's exhumed and the skeleton stored in an ossuary, or bone box. Apparently, there's an exhumation timetable posted near the entrance.'

Most of the more modern graves they were passing displayed photographs of the occupants, and almost all of them had been decorated with fresh flowers, giving the graveyard a strangely colourful appearance despite the gloom.

Even through the fog, Bronson could tell that the cemetery was huge, a vast expanse of ground studded with ancient vaults and individual tombstones, some standing erect, others either deliberately placed flat on the earth or having presumably fallen at some point over the centuries.

Walking through one of the older parts of the cemetery, they paused at intervals to look at some of the inscriptions. These varied from the simple to the flowery: from just a name, date of birth and date of death, to elaborate verses written in Italian or even Latin, to glorify or justify the life that had ended.

Angela had been right about the source of the yellowish

glow. Almost every person they passed – and there seemed to be literally hundreds – was carrying a large candle, and the combined mass of tiny flames was giving the heavy mist a distinctly yellow or orange colour.

'So what do we do now?' Bronson asked.

'It's a shame we didn't think to bring any refreshments,' Angela replied, pointing at the people milling around them. Many were carrying bottles or flasks, and a few had even brought wicker picnic baskets with them, others clear plastic boxes containing food.

Angela had been absolutely right: it was obvious that Hallowmas or the Festival of the Dead was a major social and family event. Men, women and children were wandering around the graveyard, obviously determined to enjoy their evening in the somewhat unusual surroundings.

'Well, I've got a bar of chocolate in my pocket if you want to share that,' Bronson said, passing it over.

Angela snapped the bar in two and handed back one section. For a few moments they just stood there, enjoying their impromptu snack and soaking up the atmosphere.

'It's strange, isn't it?' Angela asked, after a minute or two, looking around at the noisy and cheerful crowds.

'What do you mean?'

'Here we are in a graveyard, walking above the decaying bones of hundreds or even thousands of long-dead citizens of Venice. This should be a place of sorrow or sombre reflection, but actually we're in the middle of a huge party.'

Bronson grinned at her. 'That just goes to show the importance of atmosphere. In those old Hammer films you used to be so fond of, the director would try to get the audience quivering expectantly just by showing them a couple of polystyrene tombstones with some fake mist swirling around them, while some suitably spooky music played in the background. And here we are, surrounded by the real thing, and everyone's really happy, laughing and joking. The dead aren't bothering them at all.'

But then, in the distance, they both heard a distant howl, the sound so faint that the animal – which Bronson presumed was an Alsatian or some other breed of large dog – clearly wasn't anywhere near the Isola di San Michele.

'What the hell was that?' Angela asked, her face white and strained in the darkness.

'It sounded like a hungry German shepherd,' Bronson suggested. 'But don't worry – it's a long way off and not about to rip out our throats.'

Angela laughed out loud, then stopped as the sound of a solid thump echoed from somewhere nearby, and a scream of pure, undiluted terror cut across the noise of the revelry with the awful finality of the fall of a guillotine blade.

THE ROSWELL SCROLL

✝

2

On the Island of the Dead, the mist was thick, and visibility was reduced to a matter of only a few yards. To complicate things further, it was difficult to identify the direction from which the first scream had come. But by now, Bronson and Angela were surrounded by people in a hurry, and who seemed to be moving south, towards the centre of the island. So Bronson and Angela headed in the opposite direction, to where they thought the commotion had occurred.

Moving aside to avoid the sea of people rushing straight towards them, they threaded their way between the tombstones and, moments later, found themselves facing a group of men and women who were standing in a rough circle, staring at one of the larger tombs.

Bronson's police training kicked in, despite the fact that he was about a thousand miles from his home beat. He switched to Italian and pulled out his British warrant card

– he knew it would mean absolutely nothing to anybody there, but it would give him a thin veneer of authority while he found out what had so alarmed everyone in the cemetery.

'Police. Let me through . . . Police officer,' he kept repeating, waving the warrant card like a talisman as he pushed his way through the unmoving crowd, Angela following just a few feet behind him.

Almost reluctantly the people parted to allow him passage. Unusually for any group of Italians, they were almost silent, staring in fascination at something on the ground in front of them. And then Bronson reached the middle of the group, and could see precisely what had sparked the general exodus from the area.

The Festival of the Dead was in some ways a misnomer. The revellers who travelled to the cemetery were not there to celebrate the dead, but rather to celebrate the lives and memories of friends and relatives who had passed away. Absolutely the last thing they actually expected to see in the cemetery was a body. But that was the sight which now confronted Bronson.

And it wasn't just any corpse.

'Fascinating,' Angela breathed as she stopped beside him and looked down at the tomb. 'Though I can't believe this was the cause of so much panic in the crowd.'

Bronson took a couple of steps forward to study the tomb.

It was clearly one of the older burial chambers in the

cemetery, an oblong stone box about four feet high and topped by a flat stone slab. The sides were carved with symbols or scenes, but the old stone had weathered so much that it was difficult to make out exactly what was depicted, while the slab on top bore faint and virtually illegible marks – presumably an ancient inscription that gave the name and date of death of the occupant.

Bronson didn't know exactly how it had happened, but one of the sides of the tomb had cracked into three pieces and then fallen out, and in doing so had dragged the upper slab of stone with it. That must have caused the sound they'd heard, he thought. And now, the previously sealed box was open to the elements, and the body inside exposed to view for the first time in what he guessed was at least a hundred years.

Unsurprisingly, the remains were mainly skeletal. Parts of the coffin had survived, but only as fragments of wood along both sides of the corpse. A few wisps of rotted cloth still clung to the long bones of the legs, and part of the rib cage was encased in leathery, dark brown skin. In short, the corpse looked almost exactly as one might expect a body to appear if it had been buried in a wooden coffin inside a sealed tomb for over a century. Except in two respects.

Above the rib cage the neck terminated in a single shattered vertebra. The head of the body which, like the rib cage, was still partially covered in skin, and even had a few tufts of white hair clinging to it, was positioned centrally between the bony feet. That was unusual enough in itself, but to add a further layer of the macabre to the scene, the mouth of the skull had been levered open and a thin half brick jammed firmly between the jaws.

For a few seconds, Bronson stared at the desiccated – and desecrated – corpse, then he glanced sideways at Angela. 'What did you mean when you said "fascinating"?' he asked.

'I'll explain later,' she said. 'This is something I've heard about and read about, but I never thought I'd actually get to see an example of it.'

She opened her handbag, pulled out a compact digital camera and started snapping pictures of the scene before them. She moved closer to the corpse, and took several shots of the severed neck and the head with its bizarre mutilation.

There was a further commotion behind them, and Bronson turned to see two uniformed *carabinieri* approaching. Behind him, Angela was still snapping away, recording the scene.

The two *carabinieri* looked closely into the open tomb. One of them crossed himself and muttered something that could have been a short prayer.

'Your name, please, signor?' the other officer asked.

Bronson pulled out his passport and gave it to him.

The officer wrote down Bronson's name and passport number, handed back the document, and then asked, in halting English, what he was doing in Venice. Bronson replied in fluent Italian that he was on holiday with a friend. They had heard shouts and screams from the vicinity of the tomb and had come to investigate. He also produced his warrant card and explained that he was a British police officer, and his former wife – the woman who was still taking pictures of the open tomb behind them – worked for the British Museum.

The policeman glanced at her. 'And why is she taking so many pictures of that skeleton?' he asked.

Bronson raised his voice slightly, and repeated the question to Angela, in English.

'It's not actually the bones I'm interested in,' she replied, 'but these pottery vessels in the tomb. They've been broken, but I think they were probably intact when they were put in beside her.'

'How do you know that the skeleton is female?' Bronson asked.

'The pelvis is fully exposed, and the male pelvis and female pelvis are very different in shape. This skeleton is definitely that of a woman.'

Bronson translated what she'd told him to the police officer.

'It's very strange, what's happened to that body,' the Italian said. 'Perhaps it was done by vandals, a couple of centuries ago.'

'What will you do with it?' Bronson asked.

'Eventually, I expect we'll bury it again, but for the moment we'll have to take it into custody. Our orders in this kind of circumstance are quite clear. It's the body of the human being, and because it's skeletal we will need to get a forensic pathologist out here to inspect the scene and ascertain its age. Then we'll transport it back to the mortuary for examination, just in case any kind of crime has been committed.'

'Well, whoever did that to her head is certainly guilty of a crime.'

Privately, Bronson thought that transporting the body to the local morgue was a complete waste of everyone's time and effort, but he fully understood the position of the *Carabinieri*. Police forces in Britain had similar regulations governing the handling of both corpses and skeletal remains. It was not unknown for murderers to conceal the bodies of their victims inside existing graves.

A few of the onlookers had started to drift away, many of them taking pictures of the tomb and its occupant as they left, but others, curious at the presence of two police officers beside an ancient open grave, were beginning to appear.

'I don't know if it would be of any help to you,' Bronson said, 'but my partner is an expert on pottery. If you have a problem dating the burial – if the inscription on the tomb can't be read, I mean – then she can probably help by analysing those pottery shards.'

'Thank you for the offer, Signor Bronson. Which hotel are you staying at?'

Bronson told him, as Angela finally finished her

photographic record and stepped forward to join him.

The second police officer was already speaking into his radio, organizing transport for the forensic pathologist from Venice out to the Isola di San Michele.

While they waited for the boat to arrive, Bronson and Angela provided the two *carabinieri* with brief written statements of their recollection of the events of the evening.

Almost half an hour passed before three new figures emerged from the mist, accompanied by one of the police officers who had gone to the *vaporetto* stop to wait for the boat. One carried a collapsible stretcher, another a black body bag and the third, a grey-haired, stooped man in his fifties, carried a large plastic equipment box. Quickly, they donned gloves, plastic overshoes and white coveralls. The older man – the pathologist, Bronson assumed – stepped forward and looked at the grave and the corpse from a few feet away. He gestured to one of the men who'd accompanied him to take a series of pictures, and stepped back to talk to the *carabinieri* who were still waiting by the grave. Then he moved forward again and examined the skeleton closely, before issuing further instructions and peeling off his protective clothing.

The two men with him transferred the remains of the corpse from the shattered tomb to the body bag, taking particular care with the head to ensure that the brick remained in place. They also removed all the pieces of broken pottery. Finally, they used torches to scan the interior of the tomb to make sure they hadn't missed any last small bones or fragments, placed the bag on the stretcher, and vanished in the direction from which they'd arrived, accompanied by both police officers.

'Is there anything else you want to see?' Bronson asked Angela, watching as the short procession vanished into the mist.

Angela shook her head. 'No. I think I've got enough. Those pottery shards are interesting and unusual, and I'd like to take a proper look at them, but in a laboratory, not out here on site. Actually, there was something much more interesting than them in that grave.' She patted her pocket, and smiled at him, her eyes shining. 'And unlike the pottery, which, of course, I had to leave in situ, I've got it with me.'

✝

3

Marietta Perini stepped off the *vaporetto* at the Accademia stop on the southern side of the Grand Canal and walked briskly north across the Ponte dell'Accademia towards central Venice. Her route took her through the dog-leg shape of the Campo San Vidal and on into the Campo San Stefano, one of the biggest squares in Venice, second only to the Piazza San Marco. Both squares were busy with people: old men with small dogs on leads, women with children in prams and pushchairs, Venetians returning home after work or just couples and families strolling around with each other. Church bells rang out across the Campo San Stefano, sending peals of sound across the open space, almost drowning out the buzz of conversation from the cafés and restaurants that lined the square.

Everywhere and in all directions, people walked and talked, arms flying in extravagant gestures as they illustrated some point they were trying to make.

Marietta paused for a few moments by the monument in the centre of the square. Known irreverently to Venetians as the *Cagalibri* or 'book-shitter', it commemorated the life of the nineteenth-century writer and ideologue Nicolò Tommaseo, his studious career represented by the large pile of books positioned just behind him, and which had given rise to the statue's nickname. As usual, there was a pigeon sitting on his head, and the colourful organic decoration that had been applied to the statue's head and shoulders suggested that this was a favourite perch for some of Venice's innumerable feathered residents.

Over to one side of the square was the reason Marietta had not continued straight across towards her destination. She had a weakness for ice cream, and just a few yards away was one of her favourite *gelaterias*. She glanced at her watch, checking she had enough time, then gave way to temptation, strolling across and choosing a large cornet, into which the smiling, dark-haired waiter inserted three balls of ice cream in her choice of flavours.

Then she walked on, taking small and delicious bites from the top of the cornet, and savouring each morsel, moving it around her mouth with her tongue before finally swallowing it. She moved slowly across the square, concentrating far more on what she was eating than on where she was going or on her surroundings.

Marietta was completely unaware that two men were following her, and had in fact picked her out even before she'd boarded the *vaporetto* at the Arsenale stop on the east side of Venice.

She wasn't a random target. The two men had been sent out that evening to find her, and her alone. One of them was holding a folded sheet of paper in his hand. On it was a full-face photograph of their quarry, plus her address, and details of the company for which she worked. And there was a very specific and compelling reason why she had been chosen.

As she left the Campo San Stefano, Marietta took one of the narrow streets to the right, and almost immediately the press of people reduced, and she found herself walking along with just a handful of other pedestrians.

Then she took another turning, moving further and further from the crowded thoroughfares and closer to her destination: her boyfriend's apartment near the centre of the old city. And only then did she wonder if the two men were following her.

Marietta didn't feel concerned, not at first. Venice was a crowded city and it was almost impossible to walk down most of the streets at any time of the day or night without finding other people there. But when she took another turning, and the men continued to follow her down this narrow – and conspicuously empty – street, she glanced behind her again and then quickened her pace.

Immediately, both men started running and in a few seconds they had caught up with her. One of them slammed Marietta back against a wall. She opened her mouth to scream, but then collapsed to the ground when the second man produced a black pistol-like object from his pocket, pressed it against her stomach and pulled the trigger. The taser sent a charge of over one hundred thousand volts through her body, rendering her senseless for a few minutes.

This was all the time the men needed. One of them swiftly applied a sticking plaster gag to her face and lashed her wrists together with plastic cable ties, while the other man unzipped the bulky bag he was carrying, and pulled out a folded lightweight carpet – an old, but still very effective, way of concealing a body. He dropped it flat on the ground and, working together, they rolled the girl's unconscious body into it. In moments, the bigger of the two men had hoisted the carpet on to his shoulder, and the two of them walked down the street towards one of the canals that penetrated central Venice from all sides. The other man took out a small mobile phone and spoke urgently into it.

When they reached the bank of the canal, they stopped and peered to their right, towards the junction with the encircling Grand Canal. A dark blue speedboat was heading towards them, a single figure at the controls. The vessel came to a halt at the landing stage in front of the two men. The driver climbed out, holding a mooring line which he wrapped around a vertical wooden post, and held the boat steady while the two men embarked in it. Then he released the rope and climbed back aboard himself, swung the boat around in a half circle and headed back the way he'd come.

The bundle in the carpet began moving, and one of the men unrolled it just enough to reveal the girl's terrified face. He held the taser in front of her eyes and squeezed the trigger. A vicious high-voltage spark leapt between the two electrodes with an audible crackle.

'Shut up and lie still,' he hissed in colloquial Italian, 'or I'll give you another dose of this.'

Then he flipped the end of the carpet back over Marietta's face.

'You need to be careful with that thing,' his companion murmured. 'Hit somebody too often with it and you can kill them. And we need her in prime condition.'

'I know, but all we need to do is keep her quiet until we get into the lagoon. Then she can scream and wriggle about all she wants to, because it won't make any difference.'

At that moment, the powerboat swung left into the Grand Canal and heeled over as the driver opened the throttle and increased speed.

4

Venice is a stunning and amazing place, Bronson thought, but it also has a lot of problems.

Possibly the most beautiful city in the world, it is spread over a total of one hundred and seventeen islands set in a shallow lagoon, and its population of around sixty thousand live in a maze of streets so confusing that even natives of the city can still get lost in them. And, although it possesses some of the most outstanding architectural jewels in Italy, arguably in the world, the vast majority are slowly and inexorably sinking into the mud of the lagoon as their wooden foundations yield to the enormous weight of masonry pressing down on them. Many buildings have been abandoned; many others will suffer the same fate without very extensive – and very expensive – renovation and recovery work.

It is perhaps therefore not surprising that hotels in Venice are a long way from being the cheapest in the world.

Angela had made the booking over the Internet, and had managed to find a small hotel tucked away in the Cannaregio district, to the north of central Venice, which wasn't charging anything like the rates demanded by some of the more central establishments. To be fair, the rooms were small and cramped, there was no lift, and the only views available from any room were of the walls of the adjacent buildings or the street outside. But, as she'd explained to Bronson, the whole point about being in Venice was to get out and see the city, not lounge around in a hotel bedroom all day, so in her opinion the views were much less important than the price.

They'd caught a *vaporetto* back to the Fondamente Nuove stop from the Isola di San Michele a few minutes after the two *carabinieri* had left with the pathologist, but Angela had stubbornly refused to show him what she'd taken from the grave until they reached the hotel.

The narrow streets were dark and silent as they walked towards their hotel, the only noise the lapping of the water in the canals beside them. There was something about the atmosphere Bronson didn't like, and it was a relief when he saw the lights of the hotel lobby shining brightly in front of them.

'Right, Angela,' Bronson said, once they were safely inside their room, 'what was it in the tomb that's got you so excited?'

'What we saw back there was the tomb of a vampire.'

For a few seconds, Bronson just stared at her. Then his

face creased into a smile, and he laughed. 'Of course it was,' he said. 'Now stop messing around and tell me what you really mean.'

Angela smiled back at him. 'I'm being perfectly serious,' she said. 'Or, to be absolutely exact, the people who broke into that tomb about a century and a half ago were being perfectly serious.'

'A vampire? But you and I both know that vampires don't exist. Just like werewolves and krakens and golems don't exist. They're the product of myth and legend, nothing more than that.'

'*We* know that, here and now in the twenty-first century. But it wasn't always that clear cut, you know.'

'But I thought Bram Stoker more or less invented the vampire myth when he wrote *Dracula* in, what, the late nineteenth century?'

'No,' Angela said. 'Nobody knows exactly when people first started believing in vampires, but it certainly predates the Middle Ages, and possibly dates back a lot further than that, maybe as early as the Assyrians. There's also some suspicion that vampire-like creatures were believed to exist in the countries surrounding the Mediterranean basin as early as five thousand BC, and one of the ancient Egyptian gods – Shezmu – had what you might call vampire-like habits. He was the old god of execution, slaughter, blood and wine, and often killed people by decapitating them, putting their heads in a wine press and drinking the blood that came out.'

She paused for a moment to collect her thoughts, then spoke again. 'If you search the literature, belief in vampires, or creatures that act in some way like vampires, seems to be endemic. Almost every culture, on every continent, has some kind of a legend of this type. And that includes places you wouldn't normally expect, like Australasia and China, and even Mexico and the Caribbean.

'And it wasn't actually Bram Stoker who first wrote about it. In eighteen sixteen, almost a century before Stoker, Lord Byron was holidaying near Lake Geneva with friends and suggested they each write a ghost story. Byron came up with the idea of a tale about a vampire and one of his friends, in fact his personal physician, a man named John Polidori, picked it up and expanded it. This was the first time a vampyre – he spelt the word with a "y" instead of an "i" – had appeared in a piece of fiction written in English. But nearly a century earlier, in seventeen thirty-two, the word "vampyre" had first appeared in print in Britain, but then the word was being used as a political symbol.'

'How come you know so much about vampires?' Bronson demanded.

Angela grinned at him. 'I read a lot,' she said. 'Anyway, what I was going to say was that even as late as the first millennium, the world was still a very mysterious place, and people were looking around for explanations for natural phenomena that we now understand perfectly. They still believed that prayers to a god or spirit, or even a sacrifice, were absolutely necessary to ensure the rising of the sun or a good harvest, and the end of winter was still greeted with relief and celebrations. That was the kind of climate in which belief in vampires first arose, when superstition and belief in supernatural events and beings were the norm, not the exception.'

'But a bloodsucking creature of the night? Where the hell did that come from?' Bronson objected.

'Nobody knows. It's been a part of the folklore of Europe, and especially of central Europe, since records began. But it's possible that this kind of creature was first assumed to exist as a reasonable explanation for something that otherwise made no sense.'

'Like what?'

'Post-mortem changes to a body, for instance. If for any reason a grave was opened a short while after the burial had taken place, the people who looked at the corpse wouldn't have understood what they were seeing. There might well be blood in and near the mouth, and the hair and nails would have grown, and the body would appear to be plump and well nourished. Medical science now knows exactly why these strange effects occur. After death, blood may be expelled from all orifices, not just the mouth, as a normal part of the decay process. The receding skin can make the hair and nails of the corpse appear longer, and the gases created by decomposition will bloat the body – you know that.'

Bronson nodded. As a policeman, he'd grown used to seeing corpses in varying stages of decay.

'Now put yourself in the position of somebody who's just opened a fresh grave. You see a corpse that looks well fed, with hair and nails growing, and with blood on the mouth and face. Knowing nothing about what is actually happening inside the dead body, the most reasonable explanation might be that the corpse isn't a corpse at all, and that somehow it's managing to escape from the grave at night and is feeding on the blood of living things, hence the blood around its mouth. And if somebody in the neighbourhood is suffering from anaemia or consumption or some other wasting disease, you might also conclude that that person was the victim. Even the unexplained deaths of cattle or sheep might be attributed to the actions of a vampire.

'And that's probably all it would take for the legend to be born. As far as I know, nobody knows exactly when belief in vampires first started, but it quickly spread all over Europe, and was concentrated in Hungary and the Slav countries in the early eighteenth century. It was probably those legends that Byron, and later Bram Stoker, picked up on. And we do know that the word "vampire" itself was derived from the Serbo-Croat word *vampir*, and it entered the English language through either French or German, probably also in the eighteenth century. It's also true that many of the other Slavik and middle European languages, like Bulgarian and Croatian, had very similar words to describe the same phenomenon. But the actual root of the word probably comes from the Old Russian word *upir*, which was first recorded in the eleventh century.'

'And what about crucifixes, garlic and a stake through the heart?' Bronson asked.

'You can thank Bram Stoker and *Dracula* for that,' Angela said, 'though I suppose the crucifix and the stake do make some kind of sense. A body arising from the grave to feed on the living is obviously demonic, and people might well think that such a creature would be frightened away by the symbol of the Christian religion. Driving a stake through the chest would destroy the heart and prevent it from circulating the blood, and that would kill the vampire as well. There's another theory that impaling it with a stake would pin the vampire's body to the earth and stop it moving.'

'And garlic?'

'I've no idea, but garlic was supposed to be a cure, or at least a preventative, for the plague, so there might be a link there. Actually, garlic's been renowned as a deterrent against vampires in almost every culture that has legends about the creatures, but nobody seems to know why that should be. And before you ask, I'm fairly certain that vampires being destroyed by sunlight, not being visible in a mirror and not casting a shadow are all either creations of Mr Stoker's imagination or embellishments added by later writers.'

'Are you saying that vampires were linked to the plague?' Bronson asked.

Angela nodded. 'At one time, almost everything was linked to the plague. The Black Death arrived in Europe in the middle of the fourteenth century, and nobody had the slightest idea what caused it. All they knew was that it was incredibly contagious, and that once you'd got it, it was effectively a death sentence. Wild theories abounded about the possible cause, everything from an unfavourable alignment of the planets to earthquakes that released foul air from the interior of the earth, and even a kind of ethnic cleansing orchestrated by aliens.'

'You're kidding.'

'I'm not. There were numerous reports of evil-looking, black-clad figures standing at the edges of towns waving a kind of wand that emitted a noxious fog, and anyone that the substance touched subsequently died of the plague. The accounts sound remarkably like descriptions of men wearing protective suits dispensing a chemical or biological weapon through some sort of pressurized dispersal system. Witnesses described the strangers as acting as if they were scything, swinging the wand from side to side, and it's actually that image which gave us the expression "the grim reaper".'

'Your breadth of knowledge never ceases to amaze me,' Bronson said.

Angela smiled at him. 'Well, history is my thing,' she said. 'It's the minutiae, the details, which have always fascinated me. In some countries, particularly in Germany and Switzerland, the Jews were blamed for the plague, and records show that there were several massacres in which they were rounded up and killed, sometimes by being burned alive. Religious zealots believed the plague had been sent by God, and for some time flagellation became a popular cure. Travelling bands of flagellants roamed Europe, flogging themselves in the name of God, and in many cases very efficiently helping to spread the plague at the same time.

'Perhaps the most common belief was that it was somehow caused by a miasma, by corrupted air, which harks back to that grim reaper image, and many of the preventative measures put in place were intended to combat this, to try to purify the air that people were breathing. So houses were washed with scented water, timber that was known to give off a pleasant smell, like juniper, was burned in fireplaces, and people carried garlic and vinegar to ward off the contagion. But, bizarrely, other people believed that the plague was spread by vampires, and extraordinary measures were taken to try to combat this.'

'So we've come full circle,' Bronson suggested. 'We're back to the woman in the grave.'

'Exactly,' Angela agreed. 'The death toll from the Black Death was simply enormous. For obvious reasons, no accurate figures have survived, but it's been conservatively estimated that in some towns where the plague took hold, as much as half, sometimes even two thirds, of the population died. This meant that individual burial of bodies was simply impossible. The dead were tossed into huge communal graves – plague pits. But for anyone suspected of being a vampire, special precautions had to be taken, to avoid the vampire feeding on the other victims buried alongside it in the pit. And perhaps the commonest preventative measure was to jam a brick between the vampire's jaws.

'Two or three years ago, right here in Venice, a plague pit was discovered and excavated, and one of the skulls from a female skeleton was recovered intact, with the brick still jammed into her mouth. That body dated from the sixteenth century, because although the Black Death was at its height in Europe in the fourteenth century, there were recurrences of the epidemic right up to the eighteenth century, and mass graves have been found that date from this whole period.'

'Do you think somebody believed that the woman in the grave we saw tonight on the Isola di San Michele was a vampire, and applied an ancient remedy to ensure that she would stay dead and buried? So why did they also cut off her head?'

'That was another traditional way of killing a vampire. Because they sucked blood from their victims, removing the head from the body would prevent them from feeding.'

'So in her case it was a kind of belt and braces – the brick in the mouth and decapitation.'

Angela nodded. 'Yes,' she said, 'but actually, it's a bit more complicated than that.'

'What do you mean?'

'According to legend, most vampires were heretics, criminals or victims of suicide, and in most cases such people would be denied burial in a Christian graveyard because of religious sensibilities. The tomb that cracked open was quite an expensive burial chamber and, as far as I could see, she was the only occupant. If she had been suspected of being a vampire in life, even if she came from a wealthy and aristocratic family, she would probably have been buried in an unmarked grave on unconsecrated ground. That's the first point.

'The other thing that struck me was that the vertebra in her neck had crumbled when it was smashed. I'm not a forensic pathologist, obviously, but that suggests to me that the body was already at least partially skeletonized when the head was removed.'

'So you think she was just buried in the usual way, and then several years later somebody decided that she might have been a vampire, cracked open the tomb, and did their best to ensure that she would stay there for eternity.'

'That makes sense,' Angela said, 'except for three things. Did you notice anything odd about the grave?'

'You mean apart from the decapitated body and the skull with the brick rammed into its jaw? No, not really.'

Angela sighed. 'Almost every tomb I looked at on that island had either a crucifix inscribed on the slab covering the grave or a separate stone cross standing at one end of it. That grave had neither, and that's unusual.'

Bronson looked puzzled, but didn't say anything.

'And the remains of those pottery jars we saw in the grave suggest something slightly different about the original burial,' Angela went on. 'I have a feeling that she probably *was* buried as a vampire, but by people who didn't find that concept in any way offensive, a kind of vampire cult, if you like.'

'Really?'

'Yes. I think those jars were deliberately smashed when the grave was opened later. Pottery was never normally placed inside Christian tombs, but if it had been, in a sealed environment, it should have remained intact. The fact that those jars – there were at least two of them – were broken suggests a deliberate act. And why would a pair of sealed pottery vessels be placed in a tomb? To me, the only thing that makes sense is that they were there for the benefit of the dead woman. And if they thought she was a vampire, they would probably have contained blood, most likely human blood. I'd love to get my hands on them and analyse what's left of the contents.'

'Are you serious?' Bronson asked, startled. 'A vampire cult?'

'They're not unknown,' Angela said, 'though I'm not aware of any operating in Venice around the time our woman was buried. The inscription on the lid of her tomb was badly weathered, but I did take a few pictures of it, and I'm pretty sure the year she died was eighteen twenty-five. At least that bit of the inscription was still legible.

And I'm guessing that the grave was opened again before the end of the nineteenth century, and that the ritual killing of the vampire inside it took place then.'

Bronson leaned back and stretched. The chair he was sitting in was cramped and really too small for him. 'It seems to me that you're deducing the existence of an entire – and pretty bizarre – secret society on the basis of a few bits of smashed pottery and one crumbled neck vertebra on a two-hundred-year-old skeleton.'

'No, there's something else.' Angela reached into her handbag, and pulled out a small, heavily discoloured black object, which appeared to be bound in leather. 'This was lying under the body,' she said. 'I think it was originally inside a wooden box, probably placed under the coffin, but over the centuries both the coffin and the box rotted away. I spotted what was left of the box underneath the skeleton, but when I touched it, the wood crumbled away to nothing and I saw this.'

'So now you're a grave robber,' Bronson said.

'I trained as an archaeologist,' Angela replied, 'and "archaeologist" is just a polite word for a tomb raider. It's what we do. And if I hadn't picked it up, it would have either been sealed up again in the grave or taken by some tourist who would have no idea what it was.'

'And what is it?'

'I think,' Angela said, 'it's a kind of diary.'

✝

5

The dark blue powerboat was speeding through the inky darkness of the Venetian night, heading south, past San Clemente, towards a small island situated some distance from its nearest neighbour.

This island only covered three or four acres, and was dominated by a large and impressive Venetian mansion, a five-storey edifice in grey stone that sat at its highest point. Directly below the house was a substantial stone-built jetty capable of berthing perhaps a dozen powerboats. At first sight, the jetty seemed ridiculously large, but the lagoon provided the only means of access to and from the property.

Four other vessels were already secured to the bollards that edged the jetty, but the driver of the blue powerboat had plenty of space to manoeuvre. He brought the boat alongside the landing stage, put the gearbox into reverse, and expertly stopped the vessel close enough for one of the other men to step ashore. In moments, both mooring lines were secured and the engine shut down.

The driver assisted his two passengers in manhandling the rolled carpet on to the jetty, where they lowered it to the ground.

'I think she can walk from here,' one of the men said, unrolling the carpet and pulling Marietta Perini to her feet. The man with the taser checked her wrists were still securely bound, ripped off her gag, then aimed the weapon at her and squeezed the trigger. The girl shrank back as the evil blue spark jumped from one electrode to the other with an audible crack.

'What do you want with me?' she said, her voice trembling with fear.

'You'll find out soon enough,' the man snapped. 'Now, do exactly what we tell you, or—' He triggered the taser again, then pointed towards the house. 'Go up there,' he ordered.

Marietta stared around her, at the small island with its grass-covered slopes, clumps of bushes and occasional small trees, and at the house itself. Beyond it lay the waters of the Venetian lagoon. Pockets of mist were drifting over the surface, driven by light breezes. She looked at the pitiless faces of the three men who had abducted her from the city of her birth. A surge of pure terror coursed through her body as she realized she was beyond help.

'I have a friend,' she said desperately. 'I was on my way to visit him. When I don't arrive, he'll call the police.'

The man with the taser smiled at her, but it was not a smile of amusement. 'I've no doubt he will, and I'm sure the *carabinieri* will make all the right noises and do their best to reassure him. But we left no clues, and nobody saw what we did. It's as if you simply vanished from the face of the earth. The police will never find us, or you. And even if they did,' he added, 'it wouldn't make any difference, because you're not the first.'

Marietta stared at him, and then she screamed, a cry of terror that stopped only when the last vestige of breath had been driven from her lungs.

'Feel better now? Get moving. We have people waiting for you.'

Marietta gasped for breath and stared round again, looking desperately for anything or anyone that might offer her some hope. But there was nothing.

6

'A diary? You mean a *vampire* diary?' Bronson asked. 'Are you serious?'

'I've only had a very quick look at it,' Angela said, 'but as far as I can tell it contains a list of dates and events, which is pretty much a definition of a diary, I suppose.'

'So what are these events? If they're written in Italian, you'll probably need my help to translate them.'

'Actually, I won't,' Angela said, 'unless you've added Latin to your repertoire of languages. At the time this burial originally took place, Latin was still being used as an international language, and it remained the language of classical scholarship right through the eighteenth and nineteenth centuries. Even today some documents and treatises are composed in Latin, and of course it's still the official written language of the Roman Catholic Church and the Vatican.'

She leaned forward and handed the book carefully to Bronson.

'Our woman was buried in the first half of the nineteenth century. If she came from an educated and aristocratic family, which she probably did if her tomb is anything to go by, she might well have spoken Italian or a local dialect in daily life, but she would certainly have been able to read Latin, and probably would have used it for all her letters and written communications. Frankly, I'd have been amazed if the language in the book was anything other than Latin.'

'So what have you translated so far?' Bronson asked.

'I haven't had time to do more than glance at a few of the pages. But I've already found several references to blood, to its healing and rejuvenating properties, and in a couple of places there are descriptions of rituals that seem to involve drinking blood. I really think this might be a vampire's diary.'

Bronson groaned. 'Does this mean that our sightseeing holiday is now going to be replaced by the two of us sitting in this hotel room translating a two-hundred-year-old diary, written by someone who thought she was a vampire?'

Angela grinned. 'Of course not. This is just a curio. Nobody knows we found it, and it's frankly of little or no interest to anybody except someone like me, or an historian specializing in that period of Italian or Venetian history. It's pretty fragile, so what I will do is scan the pages into my laptop so that the text will be preserved, even if the book falls to pieces. Then I'll take it back to London and work on it in my spare time. As far as I'm concerned, we continue with our holiday just like before.'

She looked across at Bronson. 'Speaking of which,' she added, 'isn't it about time we had something to eat? That bar of chocolate we shared on the island seems like a long time ago.'

Bronson glanced at his watch and nodded. 'You're absolutely right. I feel a bowl of spaghetti coming on. That family restaurant on the corner might still be open.'

'Good idea,' Angela said, standing up. 'I'll just nip down to reception and see if I can borrow their scanner, and then I'll be ready to go.'

7

Marietta Perini walked slowly towards the double wooden doors set into the front façade of the grey stone house. Her senses were acutely sharpened by the terror coursing through her, and she noticed that the ground-floor windows, on the right-hand side of the entrance door, were brightly illuminated. Through the old glass, she could see a pair of elegant chandeliers, brilliant clusters of cut glass studded with tiny electric lights. And she could also see figures in the room, perhaps three or four men in elegant evening clothes, moving about and talking and drinking.

She took another couple of steps towards the doors, then felt a tug on her arm.

'Not that way,' one of her captors snapped, pointing instead to a stone path that ran around the side of the house.

Marietta turned down the path, wondering about the scene she'd glimpsed inside the spacious salon. It looked to her like an upmarket reception, a social evening, or maybe even a group of wealthy men enjoying an aperitif before sitting down to a banquet.

But that didn't square with what was happening to her. The men who had abducted her in Venice were malevolent, evil, she was certain. Though it didn't make sense, perhaps they were nothing to do with the elegantly dressed men in the salon she was walking away from. Maybe the people inside the property could be her salvation?

Marietta took a deep breath and screamed her heart out, a shriek of agony and terror that bounced off the walls of the house.

As she had hoped, the sound clearly penetrated the windows of the lighted room and, as she looked back, all of the men turned to stare at her. A couple of them even walked across to the tall windows and looked out, straight at her.

One of her captors seized her and turned her to face the house, so the people inside could see her more clearly. The two well-dressed men by the window smiled at her, and one nodded approval. Then the man holding her started to laugh. In that instant, the terrified girl knew she was beyond any help, any hope of rescue.

She stared around her. Surely somewhere there was a place to hide, to get away from the three men behind her? But even if by some miracle she could manage to elude them, she would still be a prisoner on the island.

But she had to try.

Taking another deep breath, Marietta stepped off the path and ran for her life.

She heard a muttered curse, and then the sound of the men behind her. Almost immediately, one of them grabbed at her shoulder, but she ducked and swerved, and the man lost his grip.

Her bound wrists were a greater impediment than she'd expected, and in seconds she lost her footing on the uneven ground and tumbled sideways. Before she could even try to get to her feet again, the men reached her. Two of them grabbed her by the arms and pulled her upright.

'I told you what would happen,' said the man with the taser, his face dark with anger.

'Be careful,' one of the others warned. 'She needs to be unharmed.'

The man adjusted something on the taser, then took a step forward. 'Hold her still,' he instructed, menace in every syllable.

Marietta shrank back. 'No, please, no, don't,' she whispered.

The man looked into her eyes and smiled slightly as he rested the twin prongs on the thin material of her blouse.

Then he pulled the trigger.

Marietta had never felt such agony. It seemed as if every nerve ending in her body was on fire, or bathed in acid. She lurched backwards, and would have fallen but for the restraining hands of the other two men.

The man in front of her kept the trigger of the taser pressed for what felt like minutes, such was the pain surging through her, though in reality the current could only have flowed for a matter of one or two seconds, possibly even less than that. Finally, mercifully, the agony stopped, the men released her arms, and Marietta slumped to the ground.

They gave her a couple of minutes to recover her senses, then jerked her back on to her feet and marched her towards the rear of the house. This time they were taking no chances. One man walked on either side of Marietta, gripping her upper arm. There was no way she could free herself from their grasp even if she had had the energy or the strength to do so. In any case, the last charge from the taser had left her nerves jangling and screaming, and she knew that if her arms were released, she would probably not even be able to walk unaided. Running was out of the question.

The path ran beside the house, then curved around in a circle towards the back door of the building. Marietta assumed this was their destination, but instead she was led towards another, smaller structure hidden behind the house. It had also been solidly constructed of grey stone, and just one glance was enough to tell her that it had once been a small church or chapel. Most of the steeply pitched roof was missing, but all four walls were still standing, and looked to be in a reasonable state of repair. Strangely, even the old wooden church door was still in place, and

71

both the windows in the end wall contained stained-glass panels.

One of the men lifted the latch on the door and swung it open, the well-oiled old hinges making no sound. Marietta was pushed through the doorway into the open space beyond. Above her head, about half of the original supporting timbers for the roof were still in place, a dimly visible skeleton, showing black against the evening sky.

The men led her down what was once the church's central aisle, and across the space where the altar would have stood; a few broken slabs of stone were all that remained of the original structure. She was marched across to the far side of the building and shoved against the wall. The man behind her stepped over to one side, and Marietta briefly lost sight of him as the other two stood beside her, blocking her view. Then she heard a faint rumbling sound, and a section of the wall a few feet away from her swung open like a door. The third man reappeared, reached into the black opening in front of her, and clicked a switch. Naked bulbs sprang into life, illuminating a narrow spiral staircase that curved down to the right.

Marietta stopped dead. She'd always loathed cellars and any other sort of underground space. It wasn't just simple claustrophobia, though this was a part of it. She'd always thought that a cellar smelt like a tomb.

'Keep going,' one of the men ordered.

'No,' Marietta said.

She felt the twin prongs of the taser pressing into her back, and knew she would do anything to avoid suffering that pain again. Fighting back tears of terror and frustration in equal measure, she stumbled forward, and started down the stone staircase, the sound of her footsteps echoing off the walls.

It wasn't a long staircase – for obvious reasons, deep cellars were almost unknown in Venice and on its islands – and after about twenty steps the staircase ended at a flagstone floor. Again, one of the men clicked a switch and a single bright light came on at one end of the room, enabling Marietta to see her surroundings.

It was a long and wide cellar, possibly extending to exactly the same floor area as the ruined church building that stood above it. By the foot of the staircase was a cleared circular area, in the centre of which was a large oblong stone table, looking something like an altar. Marietta guessed that it was positioned directly below the broken altar in the church above. When she looked at it again, she realized that it wasn't a perfect oblong, because it had a small square extension in the middle of one of the two shorter sides, and at each corner a hole had been drilled through the stone. Behind that table was another table, also made of stone but much smaller.

Along one side of the cellar were four short stone walls which extended from the floor up to the low ceiling and created a line of small, open-fronted rooms that had possibly been used as storerooms originally. The three men led Marietta into the first of these and hustled her across to the back wall. There she saw a rough wooden bed covered by a thin mattress and, bolted firmly to the wall above it, a new steel ring. A single metal handcuff dangled from the ring on the end of a metal chain.

The men pushed Marietta on to the bed. One of them reached into his pocket and pulled out a small pair of pliers, which he used to sever the plastic ties holding her wrists together. The moment he did so, another man snapped the handcuff around her left wrist, chaining her to the wall. It didn't matter that there was no door to her room. She would not be leaving.

'Please, no,' Marietta shouted after the men as they walked away. 'Don't just leave me here. Please.'

Moments later the light clicked off, and she was left in the Stygian blackness and utter silence of the cellar.

For several minutes Marietta just sat motionless on the hard mattress, eyes wide, willing them to adapt to the dark, to allow her to see something, anything. She sought a glow, a chink of light – something, however small, to provide her with a frame of reference. But there was nothing. Not even the faintest scintilla of illumination penetrated the blackness.

She gave way, and for a few minutes sobbed out of fear and frustration, but then she started to pull herself together. She tried to slide the handcuff off her wrist, but it was clamped too tightly. She tugged on the chain attached to the ring in the wall, but it was new and strong, and the ring was completely immovable.

When she finally accepted that there was no way she could get free, she set about exploring her immediate surroundings. Before the light had been extinguished, she'd seen the wooden bed, but hadn't noticed anything else. Now, she walked to the limit of the chain, and then, with her right arm stretched out in front of her, she moved first left and then right, feeling her way through the blackness. All she found was empty space, and the cold and damp stone walls of her underground prison.

As she walked back to the wooden bed, her shoe hit something beneath it, and she bent down, her fingers probing. Moments later, she realized it was a metal bucket shoved under the bed, the purpose of which was fairly obvious. There was even a half-used roll of toilet paper on the floor beside it.

For a few minutes, she sat on the edge of the bed, trying to make sense of what had happened to her, and listening intently, alert for the slightest sound.

And then she heard a noise. Very faintly, and from somewhere at the far end of the cellar, it was like a distant whispering of several people, a sound which seemed to be getting slightly louder, though Marietta wasn't even sure of this.

'Who's there?' she yelled at last, in as strong and determined a voice as she could muster.

There was no response, except for a slight and temporary reduction in the volume of the sound, which then continued just as before.

Marietta listened again. What was it? Where could it be coming from?

With a sudden start she'd realized what it was.

And then she screamed.

8

The following morning, Bronson and Angela lingered over breakfast. Sitting at a corner table in the hotel's small dining room, surrounded by the remains of their meal, they were trying to decide where to visit next in Venice. They'd already been to some of the principal attractions in the centre of the city, and had spent an expensive but pleasant afternoon wandering around the Piazza San Marco, climbing to the top of the Campanile to take in the spectacular views which that vantage point offered. In fact, they both decided that they preferred the much smaller Piazzetta San Marco, the open space which lay on the south side of the piazza, near the Doge's Palace, and which served as a connection between the piazza and the waters of the Grand Canal.

'How about Murano?' Bronson suggested. 'Glass-making has always fascinated me. According to this guidebook, the demonstrations there are free, and that's not a word you normally associate with Venice.'

'That's this island here, isn't it?' Angela asked, pointing at the map in her own book.

Bronson nodded. 'Yes, though it's actually a group of six islands, not just one. And apparently there are lots of interesting little shops and boutiques there which you can have a root around in. We can take a number forty-one or forty-two *vaporetto* from the Fondamente Nuove stop, and it's not that far away – the next stop after San Michele, in fact.'

But a few moments later, it became obvious to both of them that they weren't going to be able to visit Murano or, at least, not that morning.

The dining-room door swung open, and the hotel receptionist peered inside. Spotting Bronson and Angela, she pointed them out to somebody waiting just outside. A moment later, two Italian police officers walked in, and crossed briskly to the table where they were sitting.

'Signor Bronson?' the first officer asked.

From the insignia on his uniform, Bronson guessed he was the equivalent of a sergeant, and the other man probably a constable. He nodded.

The officer pulled out a notebook, flipped through it until he found what he was looking for, and glanced at something written on the page.

'I understand you speak Italian,' he said, and Bronson nodded again. 'Where were you last night?'

'What?'

'I asked where you were last night,' the police officer repeated.

'I understood what you said,' Bronson said, 'but I don't know why you're asking me this.'

'There was an incident, and we are trying to establish the movements of anybody who might have been involved. It's routine.'

Bronson didn't like the sound of that. In his experience, whenever a policeman assured a suspect that a particular line of questioning was 'routine', it usually meant that it was anything but.

'What sort of incident?' he asked, deciding to play along. He knew he had absolutely nothing to worry about, whatever the 'incident' might be. 'I was here, in this hotel, after we got back from the Isola di San Michele. Then we went out for a late dinner, probably at about nine, and returned to the hotel just after eleven. We were in our room all night until about an hour ago, when we came down for breakfast.'

The *carabinieri* officer noted down Bronson's answer, then looked at him again. 'Can anyone substantiate your account, Signor Bronson?'

'I paid for the meal at the restaurant with a credit card,' he replied, 'so that will establish where I was between about nine and eleven. After that, Angela and I were together, and as far as I'm aware nobody else saw us after we came back to the hotel.'

The officer frowned, and Bronson could tell that his answers hadn't satisfied him.

'If you can tell me what incident you're talking about, and the time it took place, we might be able to help.'

The officer shrugged. 'There was a break-in at the mortuary last night, and some damage was done.'

'What's he saying, Chris?' Angela asked.

Bronson briefly translated what the officer had just told him.

'Somebody burgled the mortuary?' Angela sounded incredulous. 'Why on earth would anyone want to do that?'

'Was anything taken?' Bronson asked. 'And when did it happen?'

'We think the break-in occurred at about two or three in the morning. No valuables were stolen, as far as I know, apart from a camera.'

'Then I have no alibi,' Bronson said, 'except that my partner is a very light sleeper, and if I had got up and left the room, I'm sure she would have heard me. What damage was done?'

'You saw a corpse, I believe, on the Isola di San Michele, at the Cimitero Comunale?' Bronson nodded. 'Whoever broke into the mortuary removed its head, and scattered all the other bones and pieces of pottery, as if they were looking for something. And they stole an expensive digital camera.'

Bronson leaned forward. He'd guessed that it had to

be something to do with the events of the previous night; otherwise he could see no possible reason why the Italian police would want to question him.

'It wasn't us,' he said firmly. 'If you want to search our room, you're very welcome to do so. We've got nothing to hide, and absolutely no reason to steal an ancient skull or take a camera.'

The Italian officer shrugged again and closed his notebook with a snap. As he did so, his radio emitted a static-laden squeak, and he turned his head and pressed the transmit button to respond. For some reason the radio reception in the hotel wasn't particularly good, but despite that Bronson was able to make out a few phrases of the message that the *carabinieri* control room was passing. One in particular seized his attention: 'there's been another, but we've found this one'. Taken in isolation, this phrase seemed innocuous enough, but it clearly meant something more to the sergeant, who immediately gestured to his companion to leave the room.

'How long will you be staying in Venice?' he asked Bronson.

'For the rest of this week.'

'Good. We may need to speak to you again.'

'So what the hell was all that about?' Angela demanded, when they were once again on their own.

'I've no idea,' Bronson replied, 'but I intend to find out.'

'Where are you going?'

'I'm going to follow those two. Something's going on, and it must be linked to that corpse we saw in the cemetery last night.'

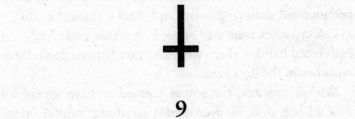

9

Marietta Perini woke with a yelp of fear as something brushed across her face. Her eyes snapped open. She rubbed desperately at her cheeks, but whatever had touched her – a fly or spider, or whatever it was – had disappeared. The rattle of the chain that secured her left wrist to the wall, and the impenetrable blackness that surrounded her, only confirmed her terror. The nightmare of her dreams was her living reality.

She ran her hands over her body, checking that no other insects were anywhere on her skin or clothes, because she now knew the source of the noise that had so alarmed her the previous night. It was the sound of dozens, maybe hundreds, of tiny pointed feet moving across the flagstone floor and along the walls. The cellar was alive with cockroaches.

She had screamed at the realization, and had immediately lifted her feet off the floor and on to the mattress, away from what she'd felt sure was a plague of insects heading towards her. And then she'd heard a louder, more pronounced scurrying noise, and she'd screamed again.

Cockroaches were bad enough, but that noise had then convinced her that there were also rats or mice down there with her in the darkness.

Within minutes, the sound seemed to have spread all around her, and she'd created a terrifying mental image of tens of thousands of cockroaches swarming on to the bed and all over her, and rats gnawing at her flesh. But actually, the reality had been considerably less traumatic. She'd continued hearing the insects and the rodents scurrying about, but not one creature had touched her or climbed on to the bed – yet.

She hadn't expected to sleep, because of her fear and loathing of the other residents of the cellar, but the air down there was cold, and eventually she'd pulled an old and smelly blanket – the only piece of bedding provided – over her, simply to keep warm. And within a few minutes she'd drifted off into a fitful sleep, from which she had awoken, shivering and terrified, at intervals during the night.

Marietta had no watch on her wrist, but she guessed it was mid-morning, and she was ravenously hungry and really thirsty. She'd had nothing to eat or drink since the previous afternoon, and her throat was parched and dry.

She consoled herself with the thought that if her captors had intended to kill her, they would probably already have done so. And that meant that they wanted her alive. But why? It couldn't be for ransom – her family wasn't rich, and she had no money of her own. There must be something else. And if they didn't want her to die, they would have to feed her.

Even as that thought gave her some slight comfort, she heard a grating and rumbling sound as the door at the top of the spiral staircase was opened, and the cellar lights snapped on.

Blinking in the harsh illumination, she stood up, shivering and waiting. Alone. And very frightened.

10

Bronson picked up the compact binoculars and small digital camera that he'd brought down from their room in readiness for their day of sight-seeing. He slipped both instruments into the pockets of his leather jacket.

'Are you sure about this, Chris?' Angela asked.

'I'm afraid so,' Bronson replied with a rueful smile. 'Look, while I'm out following those two *carabinieri*, maybe you could have a look at the pictures you took of the grave. See if anything strikes you as being odd, apart from the decapitated body and the brick, I mean. It might also be worth trying to find out the name of the woman in the grave.'

He glanced through the window at the street outside, where the two policemen had stopped for a few moments. Bending down, he kissed Angela lightly on the lips, and then strode across the dining room and walked out of the hotel.

The two *carabinieri* were on foot, of course – Venice being a car-free zone – and were walking north-east along the street from the hotel, turning right at the end, and then left. It looked to Bronson, who was following about fifty yards behind them and taking frequent glances at the street map of Venice he'd picked up at the airport, as if they were heading towards the edge of the lagoon. This suspicion was confirmed when the two men walked on to the jetty by the Fondamente Nuove *vaporetto* stop. There he saw a police launch waiting for them, the engine running and two other officers already on board.

Although Bronson guessed that he would look just like any other tourist in the anonymous throngs already crowding the streets, he hung back, waiting for the vessel to depart. As soon as the sergeant and constable were sitting down in the launch, the driver freed the mooring line and gunned the engine. Bronson took out his binoculars and watched the vessel and its passengers. Once it had cleared the other water traffic that was manoeuvring near the *vaporetto* stop, the boat swung round to the left and headed north-east, accelerating across the lagoon towards the northern end of the Isola di San Michele – in other words, pretty much as he'd expected.

About ten minutes later, shortly after the police launch had reached the jetty on the island, in fact, Bronson boarded a number forty-two *vaporetto* and began the same journey himself.

The Isola di San Michele was reasonably large, about

five hundred yards by four hundred yards, he guessed, and very popular with visitors to Venice, so he didn't anticipate any particular difficulty in remaining unobserved once he got there.

He stepped out of the *vaporetto* on to the jetty more or less in the middle of a group of German tourists, and headed towards the part of the cemetery where they'd found the broken tomb the previous evening.

That was his first surprise. The tomb was covered in a heavy green tarpaulin, which was lashed down and held in place with a couple of orange polypropylene ropes. Clearly the authorities had decided to shield the broken structure from prying eyes. And there was no sign of any police officers. Whatever the *carabinieri* had come over to the island to investigate, it was obviously nothing at all to do with that grave.

Bronson looked round the vast cemetery, and over to one side he finally spotted a handful of police officers clustered around another grave. Feeling somewhat like a ghoul, he headed that way himself, taking a circuitous route so as not to make his approach too obvious.

Standing at the edge of the group of tourists that had gathered at the site, Bronson pulled his camera from his pocket, held it unobtrusively by his side and aimed it in the general direction of all the activity. The camera was equipped with a powerful zoom lens and had both still and movie modes, so he pressed the button that would provide him with a video record of what was going on.

The *carabinieri* had erected a temporary screen on the far side of the new grave. This, like the broken grave of the previous night, was another stone box with a slab covering the top, but as far as Bronson could see, it was completely intact. Instead, the police officers' attention was directed towards the ground beside the tomb. As he watched, a man wearing a set of white waterproof overalls, cap, gloves and rubber boots, and carrying a large plastic toolbox, emerged from behind the screen. He paused for a moment to exchange a few words with a couple of the police officers, then walked over to a patch of grass on which several other cases had been left. Bronson had been involved with enough serious crimes to know what the man's job was, and then, as the white-clad figure turned slightly towards him, he recognized the man as the same forensic pathologist who'd travelled out to the island the previous night. And that, he knew, meant that another body had been discovered.

If any confirmation was needed, it followed just moments later, when two men dressed in civilian clothes, and carrying a black body bag and a collapsible stretcher, walked behind the screen.

A few minutes later they emerged, carrying a zipped body bag on the stretcher. Before they moved away, however, one of the policemen halted them with a gesture, and unzipped the bag just far enough to allow him to see the head of the victim.

Bronson lifted the camera higher, pressed the zoom

button and tried to get a close-up shot. A tumble of blonde hair filled the LCD screen, but it looked as if the face of the girl – and the victim was obviously a young woman – was invisible. Several of the tourists standing near him were also using their cameras, snapping away, and one of the *carabinieri* shouted angrily at them.

Bronson stepped back and tucked the camera into his pocket, a flush of embarrassment warming his cheek. He'd never liked the salacious attitude of the public – and especially of the British press – to accidents and crime, and he didn't much like the feeling of being on the other side of the crime-scene tape, of being one of the morbid spectators.

And, he admitted to himself, he was probably just wasting his time. He had no idea whether the girl who was being carried away from the tomb had died by accident or from some other cause. About the only thing he was sure of was that it had nothing to do with the ancient mutilated corpse they'd seen the previous evening.

Turning away, he walked quickly through the graveyard towards the Cimitero *vaporetto* stop. He would go back to Angela, he decided, and they would resume their holiday and try to forget all about the vampire's tomb and the dead girl he'd just seen.

But as the *vaporetto* cut through the waters of the lagoon, a part of what he'd overheard continued to nag at him. The radio broadcast to the sergeant had included the phrase 'there's been another'. This could only mean one thing: the blonde-haired girl hadn't had an accident; she had been the victim of foul play. And she hadn't been the first.

11

'Sit down,' the man holding the taser instructed.

Marietta knew she had to obey, so she nodded meekly and backed towards the bed.

'What do you want?' she asked, fighting to keep her voice level, to sound unafraid, despite the abject terror that had her nearly paralysed. She'd tried running, she'd tried fighting back; neither had done her any good at all. The memory of the bolts of electricity she'd endured from the taser still seared through her brain. She would do anything – almost anything – to avoid experiencing that agony again.

'You'll find out soon enough,' the man said, his voice indifferent, almost conversational. He gestured to the other man who'd accompanied him into the cellar, and who was carrying a laden tray. 'Breakfast,' he added shortly, and instructed his companion to place the tray on the floor well within Marietta's reach.

She eyed the food hungrily. She was absolutely famished, but for the moment she didn't move. She remembered reading somewhere that hostages – and to quiet her escalating terror she'd decided that she was, for whatever reason, a hostage – stood more chance of surviving their ordeal if they could establish some kind of rapport with their captors. With no other options, this seemed to be the only viable course of action she could take.

'What's your name?' she asked.

The man with the taser looked at her. 'My name is not important,' he said, 'and I don't think you'll be around long enough for us to become friends.'

His words, and the light, almost careless manner with which he said them, sent a chill through Marietta, but she forced a smile on to her face. 'My name's Marietta,' she said.

'I know. Marietta Perini,' the guard replied.

Marietta felt a lurch of despair. She'd rationalized that perhaps she resembled someone else, that she'd been snatched by mistake, and that once her captors realized their error, she'd be released unharmed. The guard's matter-of-fact statement meant that she'd been abducted for a specific reason, and she didn't like to think what this reason might be.

'Eat some food,' the guard instructed, pointing at the tray.

'When I've finished,' Marietta said, 'could I please wash?'

'I'll have a bucket of warm water brought down, with some soap and a towel. Anything else?'

'Yes. Can you please, please, leave the light on, at least while I'm eating? Just to keep the rats and insects away.'

The guard nodded, then he turned on his heel and walked out, his companion following.

The moment Marietta heard the cellar door slam shut, she picked up the tray of food and attacked it ravenously. There were bread rolls, butter and preserves, a small plate of ham and cheese, a large glass of water, a cup of black coffee, two cubes of sugar and a plastic container of milk. She needed the water more than anything else, and drank it all in moments, then slowed down, taking her time over the rest of the meal. She ate every scrap, then poured the milk in the coffee and drank that. She didn't put the sugar in the drink, but hid the cubes under the mattress, as a pathetic reserve, just in case they didn't bring her anything else to eat or drink for the rest of the day.

She scanned the tray for the last time, to see if there was anything she'd missed, or if there was anything on it that she could use as a weapon or a tool to try to free herself. But the only utensils she'd been given were a plastic knife, fork and spoon, and none of them would be of the slightest use to her. She replaced everything neatly on the tray, walked forward and put it down on the floor where it had been left.

About half an hour later, the guard reappeared, carrying, as he'd promised, a bucket of warm water, and with a towel draped over his arm.

Marietta sat silently on the bed as he lowered the bucket to the ground, and stepped forward to toss the towel on to the mattress beside her. Then he fished in his pocket and pulled out a small wrapped bar of soap – the kind found in budget hotels all over the world – and another small packet, both of which he placed on the towel.

'There's a toothbrush and toothpaste in that,' he said, as he backed away to pick up the breakfast tray.

'Can you untie me so that I can wash?' Marietta asked, even though she knew her request was futile.

The guard shook his head. 'Not a chance.'

In a couple of minutes, Marietta was alone again, but at least now she felt a little better. She'd eaten a decent breakfast, had enough to drink, and she was sure that once she'd washed her face and hands – and that was about all she was going to do – she'd feel a lot cleaner as well. And being able to clean her teeth was a bonus.

She dragged the bucket over to the bed and first brushed her teeth, while the water was still clean. Then she unbuttoned her blouse and slid it down her left arm and on to the metal chain so that it was out of her way. She unwrapped the soap and washed herself as best she could, her chained left wrist restricting her movements more than she had expected.

Then she retrieved her blouse and got dressed again. All

she could do then was lie on the bed and wait for whatever the day might bring.

At least the cellar light was still on, and she'd not seen any sign of the cockroaches that she'd heard the night before. They were still there, she knew that, because she could hear an occasional rustling sound from the walls, but for the moment the light seemed to be keeping them at bay.

There was another thing about her captors that surprised her. Despite the brutal way she'd been grabbed from the street in Venice, they had treated her quite well since she'd arrived on the island. She'd anticipated physical abuse, maybe even rape, but apart from being manhandled after they'd shocked her with the taser, none of them had so much as touched her.

But that wasn't all. What bothered her most was their air of superiority, of detachment. It was almost as if they felt they were above the law, as if they knew that the authorities wouldn't, or couldn't, touch them. She had the feeling that no matter what they subsequently did to her, none of the men believed they would suffer for it. And Marietta found this more frightening than her captivity itself.

Worse still, it suggested that she was a disposable asset in their eyes, a person of no consequence. Which meant that – short of a miracle – she was never going to get off the island alive.

12

A stocky, middle-aged man, his black hair showing the first subtle shadings of grey at the temples, walked out of the elegant building situated a short distance from the Piazza San Marco and turned north, heading for the Campo Santa Maria Formosa. It was a sensible place for a meeting, away from the more usual haunts of the tourists who still thronged the city, and with several cafés and bars were two men could sit together quietly and exchange confidences. In fact, Carlo Lombardi had not the slightest intention of saying very much at all: he was going to the square to receive information; important information, he hoped.

The call he'd taken in his office about a quarter of an hour earlier had been the first important break they'd received in the case – assuming, of course, that the man who had telephoned the police station really did know something of value about the multiple killings of young women that were currently plaguing the city.

Lombardi shook his head as he strode down the street, casting off his doubts. The caller was clearly well informed, because he had already mentioned one fact about the series of murders that had never been released to the press, or publicized in any way at all. Whoever he was – he'd told Lombardi to call him 'Marco', a common enough Italian name and almost certainly not his true identity – he had at least one piece of information that was known only to the perpetrators and the police. If he hadn't been involved in the killings himself, then it was at least probable that he had been a witness to them.

In any event, he was somebody that Lombardi, as the senior investigating officer in charge of the case, needed to talk to. 'Marco' had told Lombardi that he would only meet him alone and face-to-face in a public area, and the Campo Santa Maria Formosa had seemed as good a spot as any. And Lombardi was going there alone and on foot, as he'd been instructed, just in case the man was mounting surveillance of the streets between the police station and the square. But that didn't mean that their meeting would go unobserved.

Lombardi had already dispatched a dozen police officers to cover the eight or so exits from the Campo, and four more to position themselves with parabolic microphones and high-resolution still and video cameras in a couple of the buildings that lined the square, to record the meeting.

'Marco' would find it easy enough to get to the Campo and to the café he'd selected, but he would find it much more difficult to leave afterwards.

Lombardi's orders had been absolutely clear: the man he was going to meet was to be arrested as soon as he left the café.

The senior police officer didn't hurry as he walked up the Calle Drio La Chiesa, allowing his men plenty of time to get into position. He turned left past the Museo Guidi, still closed after proving too expensive to run, then right again, following the west bank of the canal towards the square.

Carlo Lombardi had been born in Venice and prided himself on knowing every street and alley and canal in the city, and he believed he'd covered every possible way out. He was quite certain that once 'Marco' walked into the Campo Santa Maria Formosa, he would only leave the square in handcuffs. And, at last, they might finally have a break in the case that had been both puzzling and alarming Venetian police officers for the previous two years.

He still remembered that dreadful afternoon when he'd responded to a call from one of his senior inspectors, and had travelled in a police launch out to the Isola di San Michele. He had stood over a shallow pit behind a line of trees and looked down on to the white and waxy naked body of a twenty-year-old girl, apparently dumped there only a few hours earlier. Her eyes had been wide open, though already discoloured by the action of insects, attracted by the faint smell of decomposition. As Lombardi had stared down at the body, he'd heard a faint buzzing sound, and then a couple of blowflies had emerged from the girl's open mouth, where they'd doubtless been laying eggs. Other flies were clustered around the left-hand side of her neck.

Lombardi had looked at the inspector, his eyes questioning, but the man had simply flapped a handkerchief beside the girl's neck to drive away the insects. And then he and Lombardi had stared down at the fatal wound, its edges raised and ragged, which marred the perfect white skin of the corpse.

The results of the subsequent autopsy hadn't been a surprise. The girl had died from loss of blood – exsanguination – which had pumped out of the wound on her neck. There was also clear evidence of restraints: the marks of ropes or straps around her wrists and ankles. And she'd been raped, raped violently, several times, her genital area marred by heavy bruising. The body had yielded no useful clues to suggest where the girl had died, or any indication of the identity of her killers. Despite the evidence of rape, traces of lubrication within her vagina meant that the rapist, or rapists, had used a condom; and the body appeared to have been thoroughly washed after death to remove any pubic hairs or other trace evidence.

The one slight oddity revealed at the post-mortem was the contents of the stomach. Very shortly before she died, the girl had ingested about a quarter of a litre of milk.

That in itself was unsurprising, but extensive bruising to the lips and the inside of her mouth suggested she might have been force-fed the liquid, which was unusual. But the analysis of the milk itself provided the biggest surprise, because the pathologist hadn't been able to identify the animal from which it came. All he could tell Lombardi was that it wasn't from a cow, sheep, goat or any other farmed animal he was aware of, nor even from a human female. It simply wasn't in the database.

There were, of course, a lot of animal species in which the female produced milk to nourish her offspring, and testing the samples removed from the dead girl's stomach against every possible mammal would have been a lengthy and very expensive process – and probably ultimately pointless. So Lombardi had told the pathologist not to bother, because it was already clear that the milk hadn't contained any form of drug, and had in no way contributed to the girl's death. It was just a curious anomaly.

Lombardi was quickly convinced that she had been the victim of a kind of ritualized murder, and he'd vowed there and then that he would bring the perpetrators – and there were obvious indicators that several men had been involved – to justice.

Since then, there had been other disappearances of young girls, usually between the ages of eighteen and twenty-five. Some of the bodies had been found, but in other cases the girls had simply vanished without trace. The recovered corpses bore the same indicators of a hideous death as the first corpse: evidence of multiple rape and exsanguination through severe wounds in the neck. And in every case, a small amount of the unidentifiable milk had been recovered from the victim's stomach.

Lombardi mused on this as he walked along beside the canal. As was so often the case with investigations into serious crimes, the Italian police had been plagued by the usual crop of nutters who wanted to confess to the murders, or to produce convincing – to them – evidence that the killer was the man next door or the Pope or the American President or even a visiting alien. They'd talked to most of them, just in case they were involved in some way, but they were quite satisfied that none of the people they'd interviewed had had anything to do with the crimes.

But the thing that had convinced Lombardi that 'Marco' could help him with the murders was the single sentence the man had said during his telephone conversation: 'I know about the milk.'

Nobody, apart from the pathologist and the senior *carabinieri* officers investigating the murders had been told what had been found in the victims' stomachs. Now they had a potential witness, or perhaps even a member of the group responsible for the killings, who was prepared to talk to them. This, Lombardi knew, could finally break the case wide open.

By now he was walking towards the end of the street. The last part of his journey – a right turn over one bridge and then an immediate left turn over another – would take him into the southern end of the Campo.

Then somebody grabbed his arm and swung him round, and Lombardi found himself looking into the hostile eyes of a man he was sure he'd never seen before.

'Who are you?' Lombardi demanded, casually loosening his jacket so that he could reach his pistol more easily.

The stranger smiled slightly and slid his hands into his jacket pockets. 'I'm Marco.'

'But we were supposed—' Lombardi began.

The other man shook his head. 'By now, you'll have plain-clothes officers and uniformed police forming a nice tight circle around the Campo, and probably a surveillance unit or two watching the café. If I walk into the square with you, I'll only leave it with my hands cuffed behind my back. And that's not a part of my plan at all.'

'And what is your plan, Marco?' Lombardi asked, relaxing slightly.

'You don't need to know that.' The man's voice was almost haughty, his manner arrogant, as if he were talking to an inferior. 'All I want to do is give you a message to take to your colleagues, because we think you're getting a little too close to us. And that must stop.'

'So what's the message?'

'This,' Marco replied. Shifting his right hand slightly, he pulled the trigger of the compact semi-automatic pistol he held concealed in his pocket.

The nine-millimetre bullet, fired at almost point-blank

range, ploughed through Lombardi's stomach, driving him on to the ground, his hands clutching at the wound. The sound of the shot echoed deafeningly around the street, and the few pedestrians in the vicinity stopped dead and stared in horror at the scene being played out in front of them.

Unhurriedly, Marco walked a couple of paces forward to where Lombardi lay writhing and screaming on the ground and looked down at him.

'You should have stuck to what you're good at,' he said, 'which is catching common criminals, and left us to get on with our important work.'

He pulled the pistol from his pocket, and almost casually fired two further shots into Lombardi's chest. Then he turned and strode away, tucking the pistol out of sight as he did so.

Behind him, Lombardi's legs twitched a couple of times in his death throes. And then he lay still.

13

'Any luck?' Bronson asked, opening the door to their hotel bedroom. It was early afternoon, and Angela was sitting near the window in the pale sunshine, frowning at her computer screen.

'That really depends on your definition of luck,' she said. 'Rather than trying to tackle the diary, which I thought might take me a while because my Latin is probably a bit rusty, I decided to do the easy bit first. I thought I'd start by trying to trace the family history of the woman in the grave.'

'And did you?'

'Well, you know that I photographed the slab that covered the tomb?' Bronson nodded: she'd photographed everything in sight the previous evening. 'When I looked at the pictures, even blown up on the screen of my laptop, almost the entire inscription is illegible. Absolutely the only thing I can make out for certain is the date of the burial, which was eighteen twenty-five, and I actually read that when we were in the cemetery last night.'

'That slab looked very badly weathered to me,' Bronson said. 'In fact, I suggested to one of the *carabinieri* officers that you might be able to assist with dating the grave by looking at those shards of pottery we saw in the tomb.'

Angela shook her head. 'No, you misunderstood me. The slab was weathered, I agree. That's not surprising, bearing in mind it's been sitting out there, exposed to the elements, for nearly two hundred years. But that wasn't why I can't read the name on the gravestone. The letters have actually been chipped off, probably with a hammer and chisel, because I can just about make out the marks of a steel tool on the stone.'

'You mean it's been vandalized?'

'Unless Venetian vandals are better equipped than their British counterparts, probably not. To me, this looks like a determined attempt to obliterate the name of the woman in the grave.'

'Could you make out any part of the inscription?' Bronson asked.

'I thought her surname began with the letter "P", but I couldn't even swear to this with what I found on the tomb. There's a short gap where none of the stone has been chipped away, which I assume was the space between her first name and her family name, and in one of my photographs you can just about see the upper half of the letter carved into the stone. But it could also be the letter "R", "B" or even a "D" – not much to go on.'

'Can I see it?'

Angela turned the laptop so that Bronson could see the screen easily.

The display showed a greyish stone, the surface marked with patches of lichen in faded reds and greens. On the right-hand side of the frame was a faint semicircular mark, barely visible, with a straight line on the left-hand side of it. It looked like the upper part of the letter 'P'. Above and around the marks, several parallel scratches could be seen.

Angela pointed at them. 'You can't see it terribly well in this picture,' she said, 'but that area is lower than the surrounding stone, and I think those marks were left by the chisel that hacked away that piece of stone.'

'So why didn't the person who did this chip off the rest of the letter?'

'They did,' Angela said shortly, 'or they tried to. Most inscriptions on masonry use a V-shaped cut to form the letters, and that was done here. The upper part of the letter was removed, and what we're seeing in this picture is the deepest cut made by the mason's chisel, the very bottom of the V-cut that formed the letter. This is the only picture that shows it, and I think that was just luck. The camera angle meant that the flash just managed to pick it out.'

Angela looked away from the screen and up at Bronson. 'And where did you get to? You've been gone for hours.'

'I know. Oddly enough, I went back to the Isola di San Michele. I followed those two *carabinieri* to the edge of the lagoon where there was a police launch waiting for them. I watched them head out to the island, then I hopped on a *vaporetto* and followed them.'

'They went back to the grave, you mean?'

'That was my assumption too, but they went to a different part of the cemetery because another body had been found there. A fresh corpse, I mean, not another old burial.'

Bronson explained to Angela what he'd seen, not mentioning the video and still images he'd taken at the scene, because he was, in truth, still a little embarrassed about what he'd done.

'So that's an entirely separate crime,' Angela said.

'Actually, I don't even know if it was a crime. All I saw was the body of a girl with long blonde hair being carted off, presumably for forensic examination and an autopsy. She could easily have been the victim of accidental death. All I saw, really, was her hair.'

'So the fact that her body was on the island, not far from the broken grave, is just a coincidence,' Angela said, looking sceptical. 'You think that the two incidents are entirely unconnected.'

Bronson paused. 'As far as I can tell, there's no link between the two apart from their location. But there is one thing that intrigues me, something I overheard when that police sergeant received the radio message.'

'I guessed you'd heard something when you decided to follow them.'

'The dispatcher, or whatever they're called in the *carabinieri*, said that "there's been another, but we've found this one". Then the two officers went straight out to the island. To me, that suggests young women have been disappearing, and only some of their bodies have been recovered.'

Angela sighed, got up from her chair and stretched. 'In other words, it rather looks as if there could be a serial killer operating here in Venice.' She turned to Bronson. 'And you want to investigate, don't you?'

Bronson stood up too and put his hands on her shoulders. 'I'm not going to get involved, I promise. I'm just interested in what's going on. Just like you're interested in that vampire diary or whatever it is.'

Angela smiled gently. 'Touché,' she murmured. 'So what are you going to do about it?'

'Nothing much. I thought I might just check the archives of the local newspaper and see if I can spot a pattern. That's all. And what about you?' he added. 'Have you got anywhere with that thing yet?'

Angela gestured towards the small black leather-bound volume lying on the desk next to her laptop.

'Not really. It's in pretty poor condition, as you might expect. I still think it was put in the grave underneath the coffin when the woman was buried. That makes the most sense, especially if the people who buried her,

her family or her friends, accepted her for what she was.'

'That she was a vampire, you mean?' Bronson said.

'Well, to be accurate, she was a woman who believed she was a vampire, which isn't exactly the same thing. But to honour her memory, as it were, they buried her diary with her, and those two small pottery jars as well. I still think they most likely contained blood, intended to sustain her. They probably just thought they were humouring her last wishes.'

'But later on, somebody took her claim to be a vampire a lot more seriously, and they had a very different attitude to her.'

'Exactly. It was someone who obviously believed absolutely in the vampire myth, and was probably appalled to think that the body of such a creature should be buried here in Venice. They went to enormous trouble to obliterate her name from the tomb, and to desecrate her body, to kill her off if she was a vampire, at the same time.'

'So what have you found in the diary?' Bronson asked.

'I've only had a quick look at some of the early pages,' Angela replied. 'But the exciting thing is that I now know her name, because on one of the first pages she's explained the purpose of the book. The translation of one phrase she wrote is "the record of the life of Carmelita Paganini", and that ties up with the remains of the letter "P" I deciphered on the slab over her grave. I also tried to see if the lengths of the obliterated words from the slab more or less matched that name, and they do.'

Bronson picked up the book and opened it carefully, but the closely written text meant nothing to him. It was obvious that Carmelita had used different types and colours of ink over the years, because on some pages the writing was as clear and sharp as if it had been done the day before, while on others the ink had faded to a grey or reddish shadow.

'Be careful with it, Chris,' Angela said, taking it back from him. 'It's very fragile.'

'I suppose you're using the scanned images,' he replied, 'because the writing on some of these pages is virtually illegible.'

'Oddly enough, because I could adjust the sensitivity of the scanner, the images in my laptop are a lot clearer than the original text. So, yes, I am working on the computer, and not from the book.'

Angela glanced at her watch. 'Why don't we go out for a bite of lunch now? And then I'll do a bit more work on the diary, and you can amuse yourself digging around in some newspaper's morgue, looking for clues, just like a real detective.'

'I am a real detective,' Bronson protested faintly, 'but that's a good idea. I'll just see if I can find out anything, just to satisfy my curiosity, and then we can forget about it. And tomorrow we'll go back on the sight-seeing trail.'

✝

14

'Officer down! Officer down!'

'Get an ambulance! Right now!'

The cries of shock and alarm rang through the Campo Santa Maria Formosa and the neighbouring streets. The officers who'd been deployed on the stake-out at the café were at the scene in seconds. But by then, the well-dressed assassin had vanished into the crowds, leaving behind his grisly handiwork.

Within minutes the area was swamped by police officers and paramedics, and two ambulance launches were moored in the canals closest to the scene of the shooting, their engines rumbling quietly. But the reality was that they were too late. They were all a lifetime too late.

Inspector Filippo Bianchi approached the scene at a run, his identity card held in his left hand for all to see.

'Who in God's name is it?' he shouted.

The uniformed *carabinieri* officer stationed some

distance from the scene swung round as the senior officer approached. He recognized him immediately, and shook his head. 'It's the chief inspector, sir,' he said. 'It's Lombardi.'

When he heard that name, Bianchi stopped in dismay. Around him, uniformed police officers, paramedics, technicians in civilian clothes and others wearing white coveralls milled about the scene. The obvious focus of their attention was the area right beside the edge of the canal. Temporary screens had already been erected in a rough square to protect the crime scene, and to hide the body from the curious glances of the Venetians and tourists who were passing down the opposite side of the canal, and looking over at the scene from boats and gondolas.

Inspector Bianchi was a solidly built man in his fifties, his fine aquiline features now darkly suffused with anger and disgust. As he walked closer to the body, several of the men nodded greetings, but none spoke to him. Their mood was clearly both subdued and very angry.

Carabinieri officers, like policemen everywhere, accept the inherent dangers of their job. They are on the frontline, the thin blue line that separates the criminal elements from the law-abiding citizens in their country. And in Italy there has always been the added menace and complication of the *Cosa Nostra*, the Mafia – the criminal organization that many maintain still holds the real power in the country. As many prominent officials have found to their cost over the years, Mafia godfathers are always prepared to remove –

permanently – anyone who they believe is getting in their way. Judges, politicians, and, of course, police officers, have all paid the ultimate price for their desire to uphold the rule of law.

But Carlo Lombardi had not been involved, as far as Bianchi knew, in any anti-Mafia operations, at least not in the five years he had known him. Lombardi was Venetian born and bred, had spent all his working life in the city, rising to become one of the most senior officers employed there. And most of this time, all he and his men had had to deal with was the usual spate of bag-snatching and pick-pocketing, as criminal elements at the very bottom of the ladder preyed upon Venice's annual influx of tourists. 'Bottom feeders' was the way Lombardi had usually referred to these criminals. They were an irritation, not a threat, and rarely targeted any of the local people.

And never, in Bianchi's experience, had any one of these 'bottom feeders' carried a firearm. But now, Chief Inspector Carlo Lombardi lay dead in the centre of the screened-off area, three bullet holes in his body, and his dark blood staining the old stones on which he lay.

A plain-clothes officer looked up as Bianchi came to a stop beside the feet of the dead man.

'A bad business, Filippo,' the officer said.

Bianchi nodded. 'What happened, Piero? Any witnesses?'

'He was executed, that's what happened,' Inspector Piero Spadaccino replied angrily. 'He was shot down in cold blood, right here in the middle of Venice. It looks like the first bullet hit his stomach, because of the position of his hands. And either of the second two in his chest would have been enough to kill him. The doctor thinks both those bullets probably went through his heart. I tell you, Filippo, this looks to me like a gangland killing.'

'Any witnesses?' Bianchi asked again.

Spadaccino nodded. 'Several,' he replied shortly. 'None of them saw the first shot, though they all heard it. A medium-calibre pistol, probably nine millimetre. That took Lombardi down, and they all turned to look. Then the killer walked over to him, lying here on the ground, said something to him, and then fired the other two shots. An execution; nothing more, nothing less.

'All the witnesses describe a man in a dark suit with black hair, dark eyes and a tanned complexion, no distinguishing features. About the only point of interest in the descriptions is that a couple of people said the man was very casual – no hurry, no sign of stress. He just walked over, shot the chief inspector and then walked away. One man told me he actually thought it was part of a film, and he spent a few seconds looking around to see where the cameras were. I've got my men taking full written statements from the witnesses now, and obviously we'll do follow-up questioning as well, but I don't think any of them will be able to give us a photofit for this guy, or pick him out of a line-up.'

Spadaccino paused, and he and Bianchi both looked

down at the crumpled figure lying on the stones between them.

'You worked with him, Filippo,' Spadaccino said softly. 'What the hell could he have got himself involved with that could lead to this? I mean, was he investigating organized crime?'

Bianchi shook his head. 'Not that I'm aware of.'

In fact, Inspector Bianchi had a very good idea who had ordered the assassination of his superior officer. The trouble was, if he said anything, the plan he was working on would probably come to nothing. And now the endgame was so close, he couldn't take that chance.

For the moment, all he could do was wait.

15

Bronson had visited various newspaper morgues in Britain over the years, and he was all too familiar with the unmistakable smell of musty newsprint that seemed to infuse such places, even those that had embraced modern technology to the extent of installing microfiche machines.

The Venice newspaper office had taken a step further into the twenty-first century, and had scanned all their previous copies into a series of hard drives that were accessible through a couple of PC terminals. The newspapers printed more than twenty years earlier had simply been scanned as images, and searching through those would be a laborious process, just like searching microfiche records. To find anything relevant amongst those copies would really require a fairly accurate date, so that the appropriate edition could be inspected.

But the articles and stories in the more recent newspapers

had been stored as text files, as well as images, which meant that Bronson was able to search for a specific word or phrase. He really had no clue when any other young women's disappearances had been reported – or even if there had been any such disappearances – but, because of this facility, he was able to carry out extensive and detailed searches without much difficulty.

The results were generated almost immediately, and he printed out the relevant stories as each one appeared on the screen in front of him. Within a matter of minutes, Bronson realized that there had been a spate of disappearances from Venice and the surrounding area, including a couple of girls who had been reported missing from the mainland. The only common factor, as far as he could tell, was that no trace of most of the young women had been found – in fact, only two bodies had turned up. It was as if the other girls had simply vanished.

The Italian police, of course, had been informed, and had carried out interviews with friends and relatives of the missing girls, but with no clues, and without any bodies to analyse and investigate, there was little they could do. It was even suggested that the girls might have become romantically involved with somebody, or that perhaps they had just run away.

These suggestions irritated and angered the parents involved, who all believed that, even if their daughters had eloped or run off, they would still have written or telephoned to confirm that they were alive. The continued lack of any form of communication from any of the young women was distressing for all concerned, but there was still little that the police could do, simply because they had nothing to go on.

Bronson totted up the total number of disappearances, and realized that at least a dozen girls had vanished over the previous eighteen months, six of them recently. Prior to that, there had been reports of a couple of women who had gone missing, but in both cases there appeared to be good reasons for them to have left their families. And both had later reappeared, alive and well. So unless there was something about these twelve girls that the journalists had failed to report, it looked very much to Bronson as if a serial abductor, who was almost certainly a serial killer as well, was operating in Venice. And operating with impunity.

This was interesting, but that was all, because Bronson knew that if he could deduce this from reading a handful of newspaper articles, the Italian police, who would have had access to those same articles plus all the other reports relating to the disappearances, must have come to exactly the same conclusion. And perhaps, if the body found in the cemetery on the Isola di San Michele was that of a girl who had disappeared – and a very recent edition of the local paper reported another disappearance the previous week – the police would now have plenty of clues to work with. In Bronson's experience, the dead could speak, and often produced a wealth of information about the manner in which they'd died, and sometimes a lot about their killers as well.

Almost as an afterthought, he did another search of the archives, this time looking for articles on a totally unrelated subject – the vandalizing of graves. He was somewhat surprised to discover that there was plenty of information in the back numbers of the newspaper about this as well. Again, he printed a series of articles so that he could read them at his leisure back to the hotel.

What he'd found surprised him so much that he decided to run a third search, which produced a single result. It had nothing whatsoever to do with Venice, but Bronson took a copy of this as well. You never knew, he thought, what information might prove valuable. Especially when it related to vampires.

16

'It'll be dark in three or four hours,' Angela objected. 'Are you sure you want to go back there again today?'

They were back in the hotel room, the newspaper printouts Bronson had obtained spread across the bed.

'I'm not bothered about the dead girls,' Bronson said. 'Investigating those disappearances is a police matter, without question. It's nothing to do with us. But these other stories I found, about the vandalized graves out on the island, are really interesting. I just thought I'd like to go over there and see what sort of damage had been done, and also find out the age of the tombs that had been targeted.'

'Why?' Angela was already putting on her boots, Bronson noted, and had selected a heavier coat for the journey across the water.

'It's your talk about a vampire cult that's got me interested. I was wondering if all the graves were from the nineteenth century, and if their occupants were all female. I'd also like to know if the tombs were opened, or if the vandals had sprayed graffiti on them, for instance. Was it genuine vandalism, or were the people involved trying to open the graves because they were looking for something?'

Angela smiled. 'Oddly enough, I want to go back to the Isola di San Michele as well, but for a completely different reason. While you were out, I translated some more of the Latin text in that book, and there's a reference in it that I'd like to look at.' She pointed at the black leather-bound book. 'In fact, there are several references to the same thing. According to that diary, somewhere in the grave-yard, in the "tomb of the twin angels", as the writer calls it, is the "answer". Now, I haven't got the slightest idea what she means, but I'd be very interested in finding out.'

'Right then,' Bronson said, zipping up his leather jacket. 'Let's go.'

A few minutes later they walked out of the hotel and turned north, towards the *vaporetto* stop. Angela had her handbag slung over her shoulder, while Bronson was carrying her laptop bag. She had insisted on taking her computer and the diary with them while they explored the cemetery, just in case she needed to refer back to the Latin text.

Ten minutes after they'd left, a man appeared at the recep-tion desk, produced identification that showed he was a senior *carabinieri* officer, and demanded to see the hotel register. He explained that it was just a routine check, as part of a confidential statistical analysis that the Venetian authorities were carrying out into hotel occupancy by non-Italian guests.

The receptionist handed over the register without comment.

The *carabinieri* officer made some notes, thanked the receptionist, and then left the building.

A little over half an hour after that, two middle-aged Italian men, both wearing business suits and carrying briefcases, marched straight into the hotel lobby, deep in conversation, and climbed the stairs to the upper levels. The receptionist didn't recognize them, but there were a number of new guests at the hotel, and he assumed that the men were new arrivals.

Once they were out of earshot of the reception desk, the two men fell silent. At the top of the stairs, they walked down a corridor and stopped outside one particular room. While one of them watched for any sign of movement, the other man removed a small jemmy from his briefcase, slid the point between the door and jamb, and gave a hard shove. Moments later, they were both inside.

They left the hotel about fifteen minutes later, still talking together and still carrying their briefcases. Again the receptionist ignored them.

✝

17

Without a watch, Marietta had no idea of the time, or even if it was day or night. She'd been given another tray of food about three or four hours ago, just bread, ham and cheese and a cup of coffee, which she presumed was her lunch. Since then she'd neither heard nor seen anyone or anything. Despite being terrified about her predicament, she was also thoroughly bored.

Her other problem was the cold. The cellar was obviously damp, the walls moist to the touch, and the very air chilled her bones. The only way she could keep warm was by sitting on the bed and wrapping the blanket around her.

Hours later, she heard the rumble of the cellar door opening again, and the guard reappeared with another tray, which he placed on the floor near her bed. A waft of even colder air seemed to swoop down the staircase, reducing the temperature in the cellar still further. Marietta guessed that it was already late afternoon, and the temperature was dropping.

She didn't move, didn't speak, just watched as he swapped the trays round and turned to leave. Then, as he started walking away towards the spiral staircase, Marietta heard a sound that chilled her even more than the cold of her surroundings. Through the open door to the ruined church above the cellar, she suddenly heard a loud and mournful howl.

Somehow she knew it wasn't a dog, an Alsatian or anything like that. There was something different about that noise, something that caused the hairs on the back of her neck to rise. It sounded almost primeval, an ancient human nightmare come terrifyingly to life.

And it was close – really close. Definitely somewhere on the island.

'What's that?' she demanded, as the guard continued to walk away from her.

He stopped, turned round and looked back at her, a malicious grin working its way across his face. 'Just one of our little pets,' he said. 'A playmate for you, perhaps, a bit later on.'

'But what is it?' she asked again. 'A wolf?'

'You'll find out,' the guard said. 'But if I were you, I wouldn't be in too much of a hurry to meet it.'

A few seconds later, the cellar door rumbled closed and Marietta was alone once more with her thoughts and fears.

At first, she ignored her meal and just sat on the bed, looking across the cellar to the base of the spiral staircase. Over and over again, in her mind, she replayed the sound she'd heard, and the guard's thinly veiled threat.

She was never going to escape from this island. She knew that with a kind of dull certainty that settled in her mind like a cold and heavy weight. There was no hope for her.

Marietta toppled onto her side, pulled the filthy blanket over her head, and let the tears flow.

18

It was late afternoon, and once again the Island of the Dead was shrouded in shadows as the sun sank slowly towards the western horizon.

'Let's start with your vandalized graves, Chris,' Angela suggested as they walked away from the *vaporetto* stop. 'What do the newspapers say about them?'

Bronson shrugged. 'Like most newspaper stories, they're heavy on sensation and light on details. According to the best report, two graves were interfered with on one night, and they were very close to each other, down at the southern end of the cemetery.'

'So let's make a start there, then.'

They walked between the ranks of tombs down to the south of the island, looking at the names on the graves as they passed them. Bronson spotted an area where most of the tombs appeared somewhat older than the majority.

'This report also says that one of the graves was over

127

four hundred years old,' he said. 'Those graves over there look pretty old to me.'

Despite the enormous number of tombs, it didn't take them that long to find the first of the two graves the newspaper claimed had been attacked by vandals. It was a similar structure to the one Angela had taken to calling the 'vampire's grave' – another stone box topped with a flat stone slab that bore the name and dates of the deceased entombed within.

'Here it is,' Bronson said. 'That's the name that they give in the paper.'

For a few moments they both stared at the structure in front of them.

'I don't know about you, Chris,' Angela said, 'but I don't see much evidence of damage. In fact, it looks untouched.'

'You're right.' Then Bronson noticed something, and pointed at the base of the slab covering the top of the grave. 'I think somebody lifted off that slab,' he said. 'Look, the cement holding it in place is fresh. You can see that clean line running all the way around it.'

Once he'd pointed it out, the new cement was very obvious. And when they found the second tomb, it was precisely the same story, except that on this grave the slab had obviously cracked when it had been levered off, and the repair work on the damaged slab also included a couple of metal pins to hold the two sections of it together.

'Well,' Bronson said, 'I think it's obvious that we're not

looking at the work of your average vandal here. Both of these graves were opened by people who were clearly searching for something, and I'll bet that if we located all the other tombs that have been attacked, we'd find the same thing. The other point that strikes me is that both of these graves date from the early nineteenth century, so they're about the same age as your vampire's tomb.'

'Which does make you wonder what, exactly, they were looking for,' Angela said. 'There's not likely to be a hell of a lot left inside a two-hundred-year-old tomb, unless the grave was sealed completely, or they used a lead coffin. Do you want to try to find any of the other graves mentioned in the newspaper stories, or are you satisfied with what you've seen here?'

'No, I'm happy that we know what happened, even if we don't know why. These graves were opened by people who were looking for something specific. Let's try to find the twin angels tomb you're interested in.'

'The book describes it as the "tomb of the twin angels", so presumably we're looking for a grave that's marked by a couple of carved stone angels,' Angela said, looking around at the mass of tombs that surrounded them. 'The problem is that the two most common symbols on all these graves are the crucifix and angels, single or multiple. I suppose we just have to hope that there's something very obvious about the one we're looking for.'

'And if we find it?' Bronson asked. 'Are you planning another session of grave robbing?'

'I'd just like to find the tomb to prove that my translation of the Latin is accurate. I mean, this is just an intellectual exercise, not a treasure hunt or anything like that.'

'Why don't we split up? That way we can cover more ground. Just make sure we don't get too far apart. We don't want to have to spend hours tramping around here looking for each other.'

'It's not that big a place, Chris,' Angela pointed out. 'And what we're looking for is quite specific. Because of the date of the diary, the tomb has to be dated no later than about eighteen hundred, maybe eighteen ten, and because the diary uses the expression "twin angels" every time the topic is mentioned, I think the carving will be of two identical angel figures, not just two different stone angels on the same grave.'

'OK,' Bronson said, and turned to his right. 'I'll head over this way.'

For the next hour or so, they both looked at a wide variety of graves, all of which exhibited some of the characteristics they were searching for. In all, they found over a dozen tombs that were about the right date, and which were decorated with the stone figures of angels.

But it wasn't until they looked in a section of the graveyard that appeared to be the most neglected, that Angela thought they might have found the one referred to in the diary.

In one corner of this area she spotted a sarcophagus-type tomb. Unlike most of the others they'd looked at, which had carved stone figures surmounting them, either as part of a heavily ornamented top slab or as a separate piece of monumental stone, this grave had a fairly plain slab covering the top of the sarcophagus, and there was no immediate sign of any angelic carvings. But then she looked at the foot and saw an incised carving that depicted two angels side by side, their limbs entwined, one virtually a mirror image of the other.

'Is this it?' Bronson asked, walking over in response to her wave.

'It's the most likely, I think. The two angels are identical, and it's obviously a really old grave.'

Angela stepped forward and looked at the letters and numbers on the top of the slab. The stone was quite badly weathered, but most of the inscription was just about legible.

'The date of the burial was July seventeen eighty-three,' she said. 'The name is a bit more difficult to read, but I think the surname is Delaca. I can't make out the first name at all, except that it begins with the letter "N".'

Angela took a notebook out of her handbag and recorded the information she'd found on the slab.

'I'll do a bit of research on the web,' she said, 'and maybe check one or two genealogy sites. I might be able to find out something about him or her.' She looked closely at the tomb, at the joints between the stones, and shook her head. 'It doesn't look to me as if anybody's touched this grave for decades, maybe even centuries. Perhaps the "answer" – or whatever Carmelita Paganini was referring to – isn't actually in the grave, but visible outside it.'

'You mean there might be something in the inscriptions themselves?' Bronson asked.

Angela nodded, took out her digital camera and took pictures of the tomb from every angle, trying to ensure that the images showed the inscriptions and symbols carved into the stone as clearly as possible.

'Are we finished here?' Bronson asked finally. It was being to get chilly and he didn't like the way the shadows were starting to lengthen between the graves.

'Yes. Let's go back to the hotel,' Angela replied. 'I'll do a bit more work on the translation when I have time, and see if I can find out anything else about this "answer" our diarist talks about.'

'And I suppose you can do that once we get back to England, so tomorrow we can start our holiday again?'

Angela nodded in agreement and laced her arm through his as they walked back towards the entrance to the cemetery.

They'd gone about fifty or sixty yards when Bronson suddenly stopped and looked around.

Angela looked at him enquiringly. 'What is it?'

'Can you smell something?'

'Sorry?'

'It's foul and unpleasant – and I have a horrible feeling I know what it is.'

For a second or two, Angela looked at him. 'We are standing in the middle of a graveyard,' she reminded him.

'I know. But even in a cemetery you shouldn't be able to smell a decomposing corpse. That's why bodies are buried in coffins – to keep everything inside.' Bronson glanced around. 'I think it's coming from over there,' he said, gesturing over to the right of the path they were following.

He stepped off the path and walked slowly through the graves. 'It's definitely stronger over here,' he called out.

'I can smell it now,' Angela confirmed, joining him.

The odour faded slightly as they passed a line of tombs, and they turned round to retrace their steps.

'That might be it,' Bronson suggested, pointing at an old grave. 'You see the corner of it? A section of the slab has broken off.'

They walked over to the sarcophagus-type structure that Bronson had indicated, and with every step they took, the smell grew stronger and more offensive. Angela took a handkerchief from her bag and pressed it against her nose, but it made little difference.

The stone box that comprised the grave was about eight or nine feet long, about four feet wide and roughly the same high. The slab covering the top had obviously cracked in one corner and that section of the stone had fallen on to the ground beside the tomb. Bronson stepped closer to the opening that had been created, then retreated.

He coughed a couple of times, trying to rid his lungs of the stench of decay, then turned back to Angela.

'I left my camera back at the hotel,' he said. 'Can I borrow yours?'

'You're going to photograph a rotting body?' Angela looked shocked.

'Don't you see? This is an old grave, so the body should have decayed into nothing years and years ago. Whatever is causing that smell is very recent. We've got two choices. Either we slide the slab off the top of the grave, which is something I really don't want to do, or I point your camera into the tomb through that hole in the corner and take a picture of the interior. If it's just a cat or some animal that's crawled in there to die, we can forget all about it. But if it's something else, we'll be able to tell exactly what it is from the image, and then, if we have to, we can make a call.'

'You think there's a fresh corpse in there, don't you?' Angela asked, and Bronson nodded. 'Right, here's my camera.'

Bronson took it from her, walked back to the tomb, aimed the lens through the hole, and pressed the shutter release. There was a sudden explosion of light as the flash was triggered. It took the camera a couple of seconds to process the image, and then a picture of the interior of the tomb appeared in full colour on the small LCD screen.

Bronson turned away from the tomb, and handed the camera back to Angela.

'Oh my God, Chris,' she whispered, her face turning pale.

Bronson nodded grimly, took his mobile phone from his pocket and dialled 112. They needed the emergency services, fast.

✝

19

'Signor Bronson, we meet again.' The *carabinieri* sergeant looked at Bronson appraisingly. 'You seem to be making something of a habit of being at the scene of desecrated tombs.'

'It's only happened twice,' Bronson objected.

'Apart from some simple vandalism over the past few years, there have only been two cases that I know of where graves in this cemetery have been desecrated. The first one was yesterday, just over there' – the sergeant pointed – 'and when two police officers arrived on the scene, the first person they spoke to was you. And now you've called us to report this one as well. That's two in two days, and the only common factor, Signor Bronson, seems to be you. That's what I call a habit.'

Behind the sergeant, about half a dozen police officers were in attendance, as well as numerous other people wearing civilian clothes – Bronson presumed they were scene-of-crime technicians, the pathologist and staff from the mortuary.

'In your call,' the sergeant referred to his notebook, 'you said there was a dead girl in the tomb.'

Bronson shook his head. 'No, I didn't,' he said. 'I actually told the operator there were three dead girls.'

'Three?'

Bronson nodded.

'So you looked into the grave?'

'As a matter of fact, I didn't. I haven't got a torch and I wouldn't have been able to see anything inside the tomb without one. Instead, I used a digital camera with an automatic flash.'

Bronson reached into his jacket pocket, pulled out Angela's camera, switched it on and found the photograph he had taken through the crack in the lid of the tomb.

The sergeant muttered something under his breath. The image was pin-sharp, and the flash had driven away the darkness inside the grave, and recorded for ever the appalling scene inside it.

Clearly visible in the picture were the stone base and sides of the tomb, and the remains of a very old coffin, most of the wood disintegrated and rotten. Mixed in with the wooden fragments were a few tattered scraps of cloth and, at one end of the grave, the leg bones of a human skeleton. But it wasn't this evidence of an ancient burial that had transfixed the sergeant. It was the three naked female bodies that were lying on top of the disintegrated coffin, one on top of the other, their corpses already bloated and discoloured as the disintegration of their tissues accelerated.

The sergeant looked at the picture on the LCD screen for a few moments longer, then handed the camera back to Bronson. He turned away and addressed the men who'd arrived in response to Bronson's call, issuing orders and instructions.

Temporarily dismissed, Bronson walked a few paces to where Angela sat on the ground, her back resting against a gravestone. He sat down beside her and took her hand. She looked pale and shaken by what she'd seen.

'Why did whoever killed those girls dump their bodies here?' she asked.

'That's easy. Where's the best place to hide a body?'

'In a graveyard?'

'Exactly. And that's what happened here. If the corner of that slab hadn't cracked and fallen off, they might never have been discovered.'

'So can we go home? Back to the hotel, I mean?' Angela asked.

Bronson shook his head. 'Not yet. We'll have to make statements, obviously, and my guess is that the investigating officers will want to speak to us before they'll let us leave.'

He looked across at the tomb, which was now isolated behind a perimeter of tape to prevent anyone approaching it. Several tripod-mounted floodlights had been positioned around the scene, illuminating the grave in the evening darkness. A technician, wearing white coveralls, latex gloves and with slip-on bootees covering his shoes, was standing just outside the tape, carrying a powerful digital camera. As Bronson watched, he shot at least a couple of dozen pictures of the grave from various angles, moving around the perimeter to do so. Then he ducked under the tape, took several close-up shots of the tomb from all sides, then finally stepped closer still and took several more shots of the interior through the gap in the slab.

'Why don't they just take the slab off the top?' Angela asked.

'They will do, of course, but first they'll want to gather as much information as they can about the scene. There might be footprints around the grave, though that's a bit unlikely on this surface. They'll want to dust the slab for fingerprints, and thoroughly examine the immediate vicinity of the tomb for any possible clues – objects the perpetrators might have dropped, fibres from their clothing, tool marks on the slab, all that kind of thing. They'll probably just be wasting their time, in my opinion, because they've no idea how many other people might have passed this way since the bodies were dumped here, and of course last night was the Festival of the Dead, when the number of living on the island probably outnumbered the dead.'

'You think those poor girls were left here before the festival yesterday, then?'

'Judging by the condition of their bodies, I do. And I think if there are any clues to be found they'll be inside the tomb, and probably on the corpses themselves. But until the officer who's been appointed to lead this investigation arrives here, they certainly won't open the grave.'

The *carabinieri* sergeant walked back to where Bronson and Angela were sitting, a uniformed constable following behind him.

'This officer will now take a written statement from you, Signor Bronson, and from your companion,' he said.

About ten minutes after Bronson had read and signed his own statement, and had translated into Italian Angela's much shorter statement – which basically corroborated what he had said – and she had signed it in her turn, another half-dozen men arrived at the scene, one of whom was immediately approached by the sergeant.

The two men talked together for a few minutes, then the sergeant pointed towards Bronson and Angela. The other man followed his glance, and nodded. Then he walked across to look closely at the tomb, the sergeant following. Even from where Bronson was sitting, perhaps twenty yards away from the tomb, the smell of putrefaction was unpleasantly strong, and he wasn't surprised at the expression of distaste on the senior officer's face as he moved forward to the hole in the slab and peered inside, a small but powerful torch in his hand. Then he stepped back and walked briskly away from the grave.

Bronson and Angela seemed to have been temporarily forgotten, and although Angela wanted to get back to the hotel, Bronson was keen to stay, at least for a few minutes more, and watch the recovery of the bodies. And, as he pointed out, they hadn't yet been told that they could leave.

The Italians were working in much the same way as English police officers would have done in the same circumstances. Once the tomb was opened, the photographer moved forward again to record the scene. He was followed by several of the investigating officers and a man Bronson thought was probably the pathologist. Only then was the first body lifted out of the grave and transferred immediately into a body bag.

Bronson used Angela's digital camera to record the operation.

'What are you doing?' she muttered in disapproval.

'I'm making a record of what's happening,' he replied. 'Just in case.'

'Just in case what?'

'I don't know, but this is a peculiar situation we're involved in, and having a photographic record seems to be a good idea.'

With the first body removed, more photographs were taken, and then the operation was repeated to lift out the second corpse, and then the third. Once all three body bags had been closed, the unpleasant smell began to dissipate, and several of the Italian officers removed their face masks. Further checks were run on the tomb, and it was carefully searched for any other possible clues.

'I'll ask the sergeant whether we can go now,' Bronson said at last.

With Angela beside him, he walked around the taped-off tomb and approached the investigating officers.

'Is there anything else you need from us?' Bronson asked in Italian.

The sergeant glanced towards the more senior *carabinieri* officer. 'Inspector Bianchi?'

The officer glanced at Bronson and Angela, looked as if he was going to speak, and then shook his head.

'You've both made statements,' the sergeant said, turning back to Bronson, 'and we know where you're staying, so that's it. Just try to keep away from graveyards for the rest of your time in the city. We really don't need any more bodies.'

'I'll try,' Bronson promised.

On the way out of the cemetery, they passed the vampire's tomb and Bronson noticed immediately that the position of the ropes had changed. Obviously the site had been disturbed.

Motioning Angela to wait, he stepped across to the grave and lifted the base of the tarpaulin so that he could see inside the tomb. The few bits of wood from the coffin that had survived the passage of time were scattered around. There was even evidence of digging in the soil around the grave, and marks on the stone that suggested it had been hit by some hard metallic object, perhaps a hammer or a chisel.

Bronson dropped the tarpaulin back into place, and then rejoined Angela.

'What is it?' she asked.

'Somebody has searched that tomb,' Bronson replied. 'And I think we both know what they were looking for.'

20

The hotel management had been most apologetic. They had no idea when the thief had broken into their room, or how he had managed to get past the reception desk without being challenged.

Actually, Bronson thought that getting past the receptionist desk would be the easiest part of the operation, but he hadn't said that to the duty manager who'd met them in the lobby with the unwelcome news.

They couldn't stay in their original room, obviously, because the door would no longer lock, or even close, so they'd been given a slightly larger room on the floor above instead.

The following morning, at breakfast, Angela was subdued, but clearly angry.

'Yesterday was horrible,' she announced, as they finished the meal. 'Do you really think that it was a random break-in?'

Bronson shook his head. 'No, and nor do you. I think most robberies in hotels are carried out by the staff, because they're the people who've got access to the room keys. Breaking down the door is rare, and it seems far too coincidental that our room was the only one in the building to be targeted.'

'So you think they were looking for the diary?'

'That seems the simplest explanation, yes.'

'So what are we going to do about it? Should we give the book to the police?'

'Definitely not. They've got their hands full, according to what I read in the local paper this morning. One of their most senior detectives was killed yesterday, gunned down in the street on his way to meet an informer. And in any case I'm not sure how interested the *carabinieri* would be in a two-hundred-year-old diary written by some woman who thought she was a vampire. In fact, I'm not sure why anybody, apart from perhaps a social historian, would have the slightest interest in it.' Bronson shook his head. 'But the reality is that somebody seems desperate to get their hands on it.'

'Do you think it could have anything to do with the bodies of those three poor girls you found in that tomb?'

'Frankly, no,' Bronson replied, 'apart from the coincidence of the two graves being quite close together. I don't see what link there could be between a woman who's been dead for two hundred years and a serial killer operating in Venice today.'

He drank the last of his coffee. 'So what would you like to do today?' he asked. 'And, before you tell me, we'll be sticking together. I'm not prepared to risk you being targeted because somebody wants that diary.'

'That's what I was going to suggest as well,' Angela said. 'We'll take the diary and my laptop with us again. And something else struck me about this attempted robbery—'

'I have a feeling I know what you're going to say,' Bronson interrupted. 'The only people who knew that we had been at the scene of that first vandalized tomb were the *carabinieri*. I talked to two of them in the cemetery that night, and then two other officers appeared here at the hotel the following morning. As far as I know, nobody outside the Venetian police force has any idea who we are or how we're involved.'

'Exactly. And that doesn't exactly fill me with confidence.' She sighed. 'I still wish I knew why somebody wants that diary.'

'I might have a theory about that as well,' Bronson said, and reached into his jacket pocket to pull out a folded sheet of paper. 'I found this story in the newspaper archives, in the international news pages. Apparently there was some kind of a road improvement scheme on the outskirts of a Czech town called Český Krumlov. When the workmen dug up a piece of land as part of their road-widening operation, they found an early eighteenth-century grave containing eleven bodies. That's not unusual, but what puzzled them was the way three of the corpses had been buried.'

'According to this article, bodies were usually laid to rest lying in an east-west direction, but these three had been positioned so that they lay from north to south. And one skeleton had been treated in exactly the same way as the body we saw in the grave on the Isola di San Michele: it had been decapitated, the skull placed between its legs, and a stone rammed into its mouth. All three of the skeletons had been pinned to the ground with heavy, flat stones, and another one had a hole in the left side of the chest directly above where the heart would have been, which was consistent with the sternum having been pierced by a sharp object. The article doesn't actually say that it was a wooden stake, but that's pretty obviously what they think did the damage.'

Angela nodded, staring at the picture that accompanied the story. 'It sounds like a typical vampire burial. Quite a few of these have been recorded, most often from places like Czechoslovakia and Hungary.'

'And there's an interesting postscript to the story you've got in your hand. In the last paragraph it says that they took the skeletons to Prague, but before the remains were transported, somebody broke into the building where they were being kept and stole several bones from each body. Someone seems to be collecting vampire relics – those bones in Czechoslovakia, the head from the grave here in Venice – and they're obviously after that diary as well.'

'You're talking like there's some kind of vampire con-spiracy,' Angela said, smiling.

'Well, it's the only explanation that seems to fit the facts. Look,' he leaned forward across the table, 'you and I both know that the vampire myth is exactly that – a myth. But I'm beginning to think that there are people right here, in this city, who not only think vampires were real creatures of flesh and blood, but who are actively trying to collect relics from them. And maybe they're even trying to become vampires themselves. It bothers me.'

'You and me both,' Angela said. 'You really think there are people who are that deluded?'

'Well, somebody's certainly collecting relics, and they're doing it now. That's unarguable.'

Angela shivered. 'I'm beginning to think that coming to Venice for a holiday was a really bad idea. We might have had a quieter time in Transylvania, the way things are going.'

Half an hour later, they left the hotel together, and made their way through the streets towards the city centre. They'd decided to walk first over to the Piazza San Marco, and then explore the Castello district, before picking up a *vaporetto* from the Celestia stop that would take them back to their hotel.

Bronson was very aware of their surroundings as they walked through the narrow streets of the Cannaregio area, but he saw nobody who concerned him.

They crossed over the Grand Canal into the Santa Croce district on the Ponte degli Scalzi, which literally translated as the 'bridge of the barefoot monks' and was one of only four bridges which spanned the *Canal Grande*. Suddenly, the door of one of the tall houses that lined the street was pushed open directly in front of them and a man stepped out. He was so close that Bronson and Angela had to step quickly over to the left to avoid walking into him. The man turned towards them, his face and voice full of apology.

But even as Bronson tried to wave aside the man's explanation, he was suddenly aware of two other figures emerging through the open doorway behind them. He reached out to try to protect Angela, but before he could pull her to him, something crashed into the side of his head, and he fell senseless to the ground.

✞

21

Marietta Perini stared in horror at the cockroach climbing up the wooden leg of her bed. It was almost the size of a rat, easily the biggest insect she had ever seen. She lay still, clutching the filthy blanket in both hands, paralysed with terror, because that was just the vanguard of the attack. From the other side of the bed, by the stained concrete wall, dozens of enormous insects were climbing up towards her. She could see their probing antennae above the edge of the mattress, could hear their feet scratching as they drew closer to her.

Then the first cockroach reached her feet and, with a sudden spurt, ran straight under the blanket, heading for her bare legs. She felt the insect's horny carapace rubbing along the side of her calf, felt the movements of its legs as it moved up her body, but she simply couldn't move an inch. Then a tidal wave of cockroaches swept across the edge of the mattress, heading straight towards her, and finally she found her voice.

She screamed, the noise echoing off the walls of the cellar, and suddenly found she could move. She threw the blanket from her body and jumped off the mattress on to the floor, the chain attached to her left wrist wrenching her arm back as she did so.

And then she woke up. For a few seconds she stood stock still, panting with terror, eyes wide as she stared around her, looking at the nightmare that had become her reality. There were no giant cockroaches, of course, but there were three or four of the insects scuttling about on her bed.

With an expression of disgust, Marietta flicked them off with the blanket, and checked the mattress and her clothing carefully before she got back on to the bed. She hadn't expected to sleep at all, her mind whirling with images of insects and rats, and whatever that nameless creature was that she'd heard howling the previous night, and what sleep she'd got had been restless and disturbed, punctuated by vivid and disturbing images.

Then her thoughts shifted, changing direction, and an image of her boyfriend's face swam into her mind. He would be worried sick about her. He had always been possessive, perhaps too possessive, forever wanting to know where she was, where she was going and who she was with. In the past she'd found it slightly irksome – she was, after all, a liberated Venetian woman – but right then she thanked her stars for Augusto's personality. He would, she knew, have tried to contact her, to call her mobile, when she hadn't arrived at his apartment that evening as they'd arranged. Then he would have called her parents, and after that he would have raised the alarm.

Somewhere out there, beyond the island, the search would already have begun. People – a lot of people – would be out looking for her by now, of that she was certain.

She thought of her parents, sitting in their small apartment at the north-western end of Venice, near the railway station, worrying about her, wondering where she was and – knowing them as she did – probably fearing the worst. More than anything else, she wished she could see them again, or at least talk to her mother one last time. But that, she knew, wasn't going to happen.

Tears sprang to her eyes, and she wiped them away angrily, because she'd just heard the cellar door rumble open. She didn't want to show any sign of weakness, of emotion, to her captors. It wouldn't make any difference to her fate, but keeping up her calm façade gave her something – some tiny bit of pride and strength – to hang on to.

One of the guards stepped into the cellar and walked across to her, a plastic tray in his hands.

'Why are you keeping me here?' Marietta asked, as the man lowered the tray to the floor and turned to walk away.

'You'll find out,' the guard snapped, as he'd done on

every previous occasion. But this time, as he turned to leave the cellar, he looked back towards her for the briefest of instants with something like pity in his eyes, and added a single bleak sentence that drove all other thoughts from her mind. 'You'll find out tonight, because we've just found the second one.'

✝

22

Bronson opened his eyes, and immediately closed them again against the glare of the sun. For a few seconds he had no idea where he was or why the side of his head ached so appallingly. When he lifted his arm to touch his skull, his hand came away red with blood. He levered himself up on to one elbow and opened his eyes again. For the first time, he became aware of a small group of people surrounding him, their faces grave with concern. Two men were kneeling on the ground beside him. One was repeatedly asking him something, while the other was trying to help him up into a sitting position.

Bronson reached again towards the injury on his head, then suddenly realized that he couldn't see Angela. This drove all other thoughts from his mind, and he staggered clumsily to his feet, staring around him.

'Gently, signor,' one of the men said. 'You've had a bad fall. We've called for an ambulance.'

But Bronson wasn't listening. Angela was nowhere in sight, and a sickening realization dawned on him: the men who had attacked him had taken her. He quickly took stock of his situation. He didn't know exactly how long he'd been unconscious, but it could only have been a matter of minutes.

'There were some men with me,' he said to the man standing closest to him, 'and a woman. Did you see where they went?'

'No. I only saw you lying on the street.'

Bronson stared at the building from which he'd seen the man emerge, seconds before he'd been attacked. Shaking off the restraining hands of one of the men, he walked somewhat shakily across to the door, and tried the handle, but it was locked. That, too, was unsurprising.

For a few seconds, Bronson tugged at the handle in impotent fury, and then his rational mind reasserted itself. The one place in Venice where Angela certainly wouldn't be was inside that building. He had no doubt his attackers had dragged her inside as soon as the assault had taken place, but she'd have been within its walls only long enough for them to subdue her, and then they'd have taken her to some other secure location. Both the streets and buildings in that part of Venice were narrow, and many of the houses ran from one street to another. By now, she could be in any building or even on a boat, heading for another part of the city or out to one of the islands.

'The ambulance boat will be here soon,' one of the men said. 'You need to have that wound examined.'

Bronson shook him off. His head ached, but already the bleeding seemed to have diminished, and he was fairly certain there was no serious damage. In any case, he had other priorities.

Until that moment, he had thought they'd been dealing with two unrelated sets of incidents. A person or group of people obviously wanted the vampire diary that Angela had lifted from the tomb on the Isola di San Michele, and there appeared to be a serial killer operating in Venice. Now the appalling possibility hit Bronson like a hammer blow: suppose, just suppose, that the serial killer and the man looking for vampire relics were one and the same.

And now Angela might be in his clutches.

Bronson knew that scenario didn't really make sense. Virtually all documented cases of serial killers showed quite clearly that they invariably worked alone, or at most as a pair. And the attack that had just occurred had involved three people – the decoy, the man who'd opened the door right in front of them and distracted Bronson, and then the two men who'd emerged from the building behind them.

The much more likely probability was that Angela had been grabbed because she had the diary, and once they'd taken that from her, the chances were that they'd let her go. Rationally, Bronson knew this made sense, but that didn't help calm his almost frantic worry for her safety.

Now that he was on his feet, and able to talk, several of the people in the group started to drift away. But a couple of the men remained behind. For the briefest of instants, Bronson wondered if they'd actually been a part of the attack, but then he dismissed the idea as ridiculous. If they had been, there was always the chance that he might recognize one of them.

Again, Bronson shrugged off their concerns. He needed to call the police and find Angela. The sound of an approaching ambulance siren on the canal galvanized him into action. He knew his head wound needed treating, but this was very much a secondary concern. He picked up the padded bag containing Angela's laptop – at least he still had that – which had dropped from his shoulder when he was attacked, and walked away from the scene as quickly as he could. The moment he was around the corner, he took his mobile phone out of his pocket and called the police.

Ninety minutes later, Bronson was at the *Ospedale Civile* – the local hospital in the Castello district – sitting on a hard chair, his hands gripping the arm rests, as a young Italian doctor closed the cut on the side of his head with metal clips. When he'd arrived at the hospital, his wound had been cleaned, the hair around it cut off and that section of his scalp shaved. A couple of shots of local anaesthetic had been pumped into the torn and bruised skin, and then the metal sutures applied. Stitches, apparently, were rarely used these days, the metal staples – at least, that's what they looked and felt like to Bronson – being the preferred way of closing up a wound.

The emergency operator had been more interested in the attack Bronson had suffered than in Angela's disappearance, but Bronson's insistence and concern had finally convinced her to connect him with an officer in the *carabinieri*. Bronson had given the man a brief description of Angela, and had explained the circumstances of the attack.

It helped that Bronson knew the ropes. He'd provided the best possible description he could of the man who had stepped out in front of them in the street. Unfortunately, though, he had only seen him for a matter of seconds, and his description – a man of medium height, average build, with dark hair, wearing glasses and dressed in a light grey suit – would probably fit several hundred men in Venice. And as for the men who had carried out the attack, he could offer no description at all, except for his impression that they were both about his height – around six feet tall – with dark hair.

Frankly, Bronson couldn't care less about the three men. His only interest in them was as a possible route to finding Angela. The officer, who'd met Bronson at the *Ospedale Civile* and ensured his injury had been attended to as quickly as possible, had taken careful note of his description of Angela, and had radioed it to the dispatcher for immediate dissemination to all *carabinieri* officers in Venice and on the mainland.

'We'll find her, Signor Bronson,' the officer said reassuringly, closing his notebook.

'I'm sure you'll try,' Bronson snapped. 'But what worries me is the number of young women who've vanished from the streets of Venice over the last few months, women who've left no trace, and who've never been seen again.'

The officer seemed surprised that Bronson knew what had been happening in the city.

'That isn't confidential information, is it?' Bronson said sharply. 'I checked the local newspaper archives, and about a dozen girls have disappeared over roughly the last eighteen months. And you can add another one to that total if you count the girl who vanished a couple of days ago, and one more if you include Angela. I want her found,' he added, his voice cracking with the strain, 'before some maniac dumps her body in a tomb on the Island of the Dead.'

The officer looked even more surprised. 'How do you know about that?' he asked.

'I was the one who found them,' Bronson said shortly. 'Now, you know precisely where and when my partner was abducted. I know Venice has a lot of buildings, and a hell of a lot of places where a person could be hidden, but it's also quite a small city. So please, please, do your best to find her for me.'

Bronson's eyes had suddenly filled with tears, and it wasn't just because of the doctor driving home the final staple into his scalp.

23

Marietta had barely touched the meal her captor had brought down for her at lunchtime. All she could think of were his last words. What lay in store for her that night? She felt physically sick with dread, her body numb with fear.

When the cellar door rumbled open some time later she absolutely knew that something out of the ordinary was going to happen. She still had no weapon to defend herself, nor any form of protection; all she could do was what she had done almost every time any of the men had entered the cellar: she sat very upright on the edge of the bed, staring towards the base of the spiral staircase, and waited to see who was coming towards her.

Whoever it was seemed to be carrying something heavy, because she could hear the confused sound of footsteps clattering down the stairs, rather than the measured tread she had grown accustomed to.

A sudden piercing scream, obviously a woman's, tore through the still air of the cellar, and Marietta jumped. Then she heard a cracking sound that had become only too familiar – the sound of a taser being discharged – and the scream ended as suddenly as it had begun.

Moments later, the guard and one of the other men who'd abducted her stepped into view, dragging the unconscious form of a young woman between them. Neither man so much as glanced towards Marietta as they hauled the body past the end of her open room.

Because of her restricted view, Marietta couldn't see where they took her, but the sounds she was hearing suggested they had entered the cell right next to her. There was a dull thud, which she presumed was the noise of the men dumping the unconscious girl on a bed, followed by a clanking sound and a click – the handcuff being secured around the girl's wrist.

After a few seconds, the two men reappeared, and the guard stopped for a moment at the entrance to Marietta's room.

'You've got company at last,' he said, an unpleasant sneer on his face. 'She's the one we've been waiting for. Now we can get started.'

24

For about twenty minutes after the men had left the cellar, the only sound Marietta could hear from the adjacent room was a dull moaning. The girl, whoever she was, had clearly reacted badly to being shocked by the taser, and was taking a long time to recover.

Eventually the girl's breathing grew more regular as the effects of the high-voltage current she'd experienced subsided, and Marietta could hear her starting to move around on the bed. She left it another couple of minutes, then called out to her.

'Who are you?' The girl's voice was tremulous, racked with fear and uncertainty.

'My name is Marietta Perini. Who are you?' She echoed the girl's question.

'I'm Benedetta Constanta. Where am I?'

'Didn't you see where they brought you?' Marietta asked.

'I was just outside my apartment when a man walked up and fired something at me. The next thing I knew, I was in some ruined church. I started fighting and struggling, and they shot me again.'

It sounded as if Benedetta had taken a lot longer to recover her senses than Marietta, or maybe the men who'd taken her had used a higher voltage in the weapon.

'They snatched me in just the same way as you, but I was conscious for most of the time,' Marietta said. 'We're on an island out in the lagoon, but I've no idea what it's called. It's not very big, and I think the only buildings on it are a house and the ruined church that you saw. We're in the cellar under that church.'

'But what do they want with us? Have they – you know – attacked you?'

Benedetta didn't use the word 'rape', but Marietta knew that was exactly what she was thinking.

'They haven't touched me,' she said, trying to keep her voice steady. 'They've fed me regularly, and brought me warm water and soap so I can wash. But the nights are the worst – it's very cold and dark, and I . . . I keep hearing things . . .'

'How long have you been here?'

'About two days. I think it's Wednesday today, and I was on my way to see my boyfriend in Venice on Monday evening when I was attacked.' Marietta wrapped her arms round herself to stop the shivering. 'He'll be wondering where I am. What happened—'

'What do they want from us?' Benedetta interrupted harshly.

Sitting on her bed on the other side of the old stone wall, Marietta shook her head. 'I don't have any idea,' she said, rubbing the tears from her eyes. Her voice broke as her mind vividly replayed the last words the guard had spoken. 'But I think we're going to find out very soon.'

25

Bronson had been discharged from the hospital, and was walking slowly back towards Cannaregio. He was conserving his strength, because the attack – both the physical assault and the sheer shock of the event – had left him feeling weak and unsteady.

And as he walked, he looked everywhere, desperately searching for some sign of Angela. He knew that what he was doing was essentially pointless, but he did it anyway. Whoever had snatched her, and whatever their motive, he was certain that she was now either hidden inside a building somewhere in the city or being held on one of the dozens of outlying islands. The chances of her still being somewhere on the streets of Venice itself were nil. But still he kept looking.

It took him well over an hour to get back to their hotel, because of his slow progress and the meandering route he'd taken. When he arrived and walked into the lobby, the receptionist gave him a somewhat startled look, her attention fixed on the white bandage and thick pad that covered one side of his head. Bronson ignored her and went slowly up the stairs.

He paused for a second in the corridor outside their room, hoping against all odds that somehow Angela had managed to escape and that she'd be waiting for him inside. But as he pushed open the door, he saw at once that the room was completely empty.

The rooms in that hotel didn't have mini-bars, and he knew that consuming alcohol wasn't a particularly good idea after what he'd been through that day, but at that moment all he really wanted was a good stiff drink. He put down the laptop bag, took another look round the room, locked the door and then walked back down the stairs to the hotel bar. He ordered a gin and tonic, and took the drink over to a corner table by one of the windows that offered a view of the street outside the hotel.

He took a long swallow of his drink, and gazed through the window at the pedestrians strolling by, at the Venetian businessmen mingling with the press of tourists, cameras raised to faces that were partially obscured by hats and sunglasses. Bronson stared at the throng, searching vainly for Angela.

After a few moments, he took out his mobile and stared at the screen for what felt like the hundredth time that day. There were no missed calls, no text messages.

His head told him that the Italian police would be doing

everything they could to find Angela, and that the only thing he would achieve by calling them would be to raise their level of irritation. His head knew this, but his heart didn't agree, and almost without thinking, he dialled the mobile number he'd been given – as a courtesy and simply because of his job – by the investigating officer.

The ensuing conversation was short and fairly brusque. Yes, all *carabinieri* officers in the area had been given a description of Angela and a copy of her passport photograph. Yes, an officer would leave Angela's passport at the hotel reception desk later that day. And, finally, yes, he would definitely be the first to know if and when they found a trace of her.

Bronson ended the call with a sense of immense frustration. He wasn't used to being on the other side of a police investigation, and the lack of any hard information was difficult to handle. He was sure that the Italian police were searching for Angela, but how many men had they deployed? Were they checking cars and trains leaving Venice? Had they detailed men to check the *vaporettos* and gondolas and the privately owned speedboats that buzzed up and down the canals and across the lagoon? Were they searching the outlying islands? He had no answers to any of these questions, and he knew that the *carabinieri* officer would refuse to tell him, just as he, Bronson, would be unwilling to answer similar questions from a member of the general public in Britain in the same circumstances.

He finished his drink and sat for a few moments, his

head in his hands. Then he roused himself. Getting drunk wouldn't help find Angela, and nor would moping around the hotel. Walking the streets looking for her would achieve nothing, because he knew she wouldn't be there. But he had to do something, something constructive, something that might help the police effort. He toyed with the idea of visiting some of the quieter canals, just in case the abductors hadn't yet smuggled her out of the city, but a moment's thought showed him that that idea would also be a waste of time. Venice wasn't that big a city, but there were miles of canals, and he wouldn't be able to cover more than one or two of them.

That started a new train of thought. One thing he could do was to ensure that he was as mobile as possible.

Standing up, he walked out of the bar, and across to the reception desk. The pretty dark-haired girl who'd checked them in was on duty, and gave him a welcoming smile as he walked across the lobby.

'Signor Bronson, what happened to your head?' she asked, looking with concern at the bandage around his skull.

'I had a bad fall, that's all,' he said, deciding not to tell the staff what had happened to Angela.

'Can I help you with something?'

'We'd like to explore the canals. Is it possible to hire a speedboat for three or four days?'

'Of course. It will take me a little while to arrange, because this is a popular time of year in Venice, and I may have to try several hire companies. Will you be taking the boat outside the city – into the lagoon, I mean?'

'I might do, yes. Does that make a difference?'

'Only to the type of boat. If you're going into the Lagoon you'll need one with a more powerful engine. Please leave it with me, Signor Bronson, and I'll see what I can find. Will tomorrow morning be soon enough?'

Bronson would have preferred to get his hands on a boat straight away, but he replied, 'Perfect. Thank you.'

He waited while the girl noted down details of his credit card, gave her a smile that was completely at odds with the inner turmoil he was feeling, then walked back up the stairs to their room. He hadn't done much, but already he felt better, simply knowing that by the morning he would be able to navigate his way around Venice reasonably quickly.

He lay down on the bed for a few minutes, his eyes wide open, staring at the ceiling. What could he achieve? he wondered. Yet again, he replayed the events of the day, trying to remember any clues or indications that might help the *carabinieri* narrow the search. But he came up with a blank.

Then something struck him. Because the gang of men had grabbed Angela, they would now have the vampire's diary in their possession. Could there possibly be any information contained within it that might suggest where they were likely to go next? If, for example, the diary mentioned another grave, and if the people who'd snatched

169

Angela were hunting for relics, he could suggest to the police that they could mount a watch on that location.

It was thin enough, but as far as Bronson could see, it was the only useful thing he could do.

He got up from the bed, took Angela's laptop out of its case, and plugged the power cable into the wall socket. Angela hadn't switched off the computer, and as soon as he opened the lid, the system resumed operating. A screensaver appeared, and when Bronson touched the space-bar to clear it, a dialogue box popped up requesting the input of a password. He hesitated for a few moments, then typed 'SealChart' into the space, and pressed the enter key. Angela always used the same password – the name of the church in Kent where they'd got married – and Bronson felt a sudden lump in his throat as the system accepted the password.

Angela, he thought. I can't lose you now, not after everything we've been through. I'm going to find you if it's the last thing I do.

✝

26

Marietta jumped as the dull rumble echoed through the cellar: she knew what that noise meant. She moved to the edge of the bed and sat there, waiting. This time it sounded as though more than one person was descending the stone spiral staircase.

'What is it?' Benedetta sounded terrified, and Marietta didn't feel much better.

'It's the door at the top of the stairs. Someone's coming,' she replied, not taking her eyes off the opening that marked the base of the staircase.

The sound of footsteps drew closer, and then two men stepped into view. Marietta could have wept with relief as she saw the guard approaching her carrying a towel and a metal bucket, the contents of which steamed slightly.

The guard went straight over to where Marietta sat, and placed the bucket on the floor in front of her.

'Wash yourself,' he instructed curtly, then turned and left.

The other man, who had presumably delivered a bucket and towel to Benedetta, followed him from the room.

'What do we do now?' Benedetta asked, her voice trembling with fear.

'We do what they tell us,' Marietta said.

Ten minutes later, the guards returned, carrying two bundles of white material, one of which they tossed onto Marietta's bed, the other one on to Benedetta's. One of the men removed a key from his pocket and the taser from another, and then stepped forward.

'Give me your left hand,' he said. 'I'm going to release your handcuff so you can get changed. If you try anything, you'll taste the taser again. Do you understand?'

Marietta nodded. 'Get changed into what?' she asked. 'What for?'

'You're to put on that white robe I've given you, ready for the ceremony. Take off all your other clothes. All of them – your underwear as well. And then wash your whole body again. You have to be clean.'

Releasing her handcuff, he stepped back. 'Now get on with it,' he snapped. 'We haven't got much time. The ceremony must begin on time.'

✝

27

Bronson was no further forward. He was unfamiliar with Latin, and had spent most of that time reading through Angela's translations of the pages of the diary, looking for something – anything – that might give him a clue about what had happened to her. He looked at the computer screen, his gaze unfocused, as he mentally relived the events of the previous two days, and the macabre mystery that they had become embroiled in. The desecrated tomb; the vampire's diary; the dead girl in the cemetery; the three corpses jammed into the grave; the burglary of their hotel room, and, finally, the attack on Bronson himself and Angela's abduction. Running through the sequence of events, two things immediately stood out.

First, the desecrated tomb and the vampire's diary were clearly important, very important, to somebody in Venice. The only reason, he was convinced, that he'd been attacked was so that the group of men could grab the diary, and they'd needed to get him out of the way first. But what he still didn't understand was why they had taken Angela as well.

Then he remembered his conversation with the *carabinieri* officer in the cemetery on San Michele. He'd mentioned to the Italian that Angela worked for the British Museum and, actually, that might provide some kind of a motive. Because of the burglary at the hotel, Bronson was fairly sure somebody in the Italian police force had leaked the information about where they were staying. Maybe her kidnappers had also learned that she was an archaeologist, and believed she could help them translate the text in the diary.

It was a stretch to reach that conclusion, but why else would anyone want to kidnap an English woman who spoke almost no Italian? Bronson immediately felt better, because it suggested an alternative to the only other reason why Angela had been kidnapped: that she'd been grabbed by a serial killer who was operating in Venice. And that was a possibility he simply wasn't prepared to face.

The second factor that seemed obvious to him now was that the Isola di San Michele, the Venetian Island of the Dead, was inextricably linked with what had been going on in the city.

This set Bronson thinking about the four dead girls whose bodies had been found in the cemetery, and he decided to take a look at the pictures he'd taken out on the island, to see if there were any visible clues on the corpses. As he transferred the images from his camera on to the laptop – Angela had already downloaded all the still images and video films from her digital camera on to the hard drive – he acknowledged the possibility that he'd been trying to avoid ever since the attack, that the girls had been killed by the same people who were accumulating the vampire relics.

Setting his misgivings aside, Bronson concentrated on the images that were now appearing on the screen of the laptop. When he'd taken the video film of the police recovering the body of the first girl on the island, he'd been trying to use the camera as inconspicuously as possible. The inevitable result was that the video was jerky and frequently didn't actually show the scene he'd been trying to capture.

He watched carefully as the two men emerged from behind the temporary screen carrying the body on a stretcher, and then saw a police officer step forward and unzip the body bag. The dead girl's tumble of blonde hair filled the screen as Bronson had used the camera's zoom lens to focus on her face. For the briefest of instants he saw her forehead, her open left eye – at the moment of death, the eyes don't close serenely the way they do in the movies, but remain open and staring – the side of her face, her cheek and part of her neck.

Something struck him about what he was seeing, and he wound the movie sequence back to the point just before the police officer unzipped the body bag. Then he ran it forward in slow motion. This helped clarify what he was seeing, but he still couldn't be certain. So he ran it again, this time advancing the video film frame by frame.

Three of the frames offered him the clearest possible view of the dead girl's face, and he examined each of them carefully, enlarging one particular section to study it more closely.

The girl's skin was marred, almost freckled, by dark marks, which Bronson guessed were either dried blood or earth from where her body had been dumped; the skin itself was mottled with the first signs of decomposition. But there were several marks that he didn't understand, but which filled him with unease.

Bronson closed down the video and searched the hard drive until he found the pictures that he'd taken with Angela's camera of their discovery of the three dead bodies in the cemetery and the subsequent events.

The first image he opened was the shot he'd taken through the hole in the slab over the grave. It was, by any standards, an extremely gruesome picture. The image showed the stone sides of the grave, the ancient coffin lying on the floor of the tomb, and the naked and decaying bodies of three young women dumped on top of it. Unsurprisingly, given the circumstance in which the picture had been taken, it was a little out of focus, and the flare of the automatic flash meant that some parts of the scene were so brightly lit that little or no detail was visible. But the upper corpse, the girl who'd been put in the grave last, was reasonably clear. Bronson enlarged the part of the picture that showed her head and neck, and studied it closely for some minutes. Then he sat back in his chair and shook his head. What he was seeing just didn't make any sense.

In both the images he enlarged, he'd found what looked like the same type of injury: on the sides of the girls' necks puncture marks stood out. He frowned. When any animal – a dog, a cat or a human being – bites, both the upper and lower jaws are involved. If it's small enough, the object being bitten will have marks on both sides.

The twin puncture wounds used by Hollywood directors to portray the bite of a vampire are impossible to make unless the vampire's mouth is capable of entirely encircling the neck of the victim, something that is at best extremely unlikely. In fact, any creature with jaws the approximate size and shape of the human mouth, whether equipped with oversized canine teeth or not, would leave bite marks on the side of a human neck completely unlike the neat twin puncture wounds of the classic vampire mythology.

The most likely shape of such a wound would probably be two semicircular marks made by the jaws, probably with deeper wounds where the longest teeth would have sunk into the flesh. And if the bite was delivered powerfully enough, quite probably the skin and flesh might be bitten through to leave an almost circular wound. And that, Bronson realized, was exactly what he was staring at in these photographs.

It looked to Bronson as if the people who were collecting vampire relics were far from the bunch of harmless nutters that he and Angela had assumed. Whoever they were, they'd clearly moved a long way beyond just collecting old books and ancient bones.

The girls in the cemetery might have been enthusiastic members of the group, for whom it had all gone badly wrong. But Bronson doubted it. He thought it was far more likely that they were innocent victims on whom the vampirists – for want of a better description – had been feasting.

The very idea was manifestly ridiculous, but Bronson couldn't doubt the evidence of his own eyes. And what he'd seen on those images lent a still greater urgency to his search for Angela, because he now had no doubt that she was in the clutches of a group of people who had killed at least four women already, and would presumably have no qualms about increasing that tally.

28

Getting washed when the only equipment to hand was a bucket of lukewarm water and a small bar of soap was difficult enough. Doing so standing up in front of a stranger – a man – who was staring at her body with unconcealed lust was one of the most unpleasant experiences of Marietta Perini's short life.

She began by trying her best to conceal her private parts from his gaze, but quickly realized that this was impossible. Eventually she just ignored him, never looked in his direction, and pretended that she was alone. When she'd finished and dried herself, the guard nodded his approval.

'Very good,' he said. 'Now put on the robe. Don't bother with any underwear. You're not going to need it.'

Shaking with fear, Marietta pulled the robe on over her head, then her captor snapped the handcuff back around her wrist, securing her to the wall of the cellar once again.

Then he walked out of the room to the adjoining cell, and repeated the operation with Benedetta, who initially refused point-blank to take off a single item of clothing. But her resistance ended moments later when the crackle of the taser told its own story. When she'd recovered she washed and put on the white robe, but Marietta could hear her sobbing in terror and fury as she did so.

As soon as Benedetta had finished dressing, the guard turned to leave the cellar. But before he could walk across to the foot of the stone spiral staircase, another sound intruded into the relative silence of the cellar. Somebody, or something, was coming down the steps, but the noise sounded more like a kind of slithering than footsteps.

Marietta stared across the flagstone floor, trying to see who it was. Then she noticed that the guard seemed incredibly uncomfortable, almost scared. He'd moved back until he was almost standing against the wall opposite and he, too, was staring fixedly towards the entrance to the cellar.

Then a figure entered the chamber. Clad in an all-enveloping black robe, the hood pulled forward to obscure his face, hands invisible in the long sleeves, the new arrival moved a few feet forward and stopped.

Marietta was immediately conscious of a sharp and unpleasant odour, and then a feeling, a sudden and completely irrational feeling, of abject terror. Never before had she felt that she was standing in the presence of such unremitting and undiluted evil. And she knew that, whoever it was, he was staring straight at her. She could feel his eyes, still invisible under the hood, roaming up and down her body.

The figure turned towards the guard and asked a question, his voice soft and sibilant, the words inaudible to the two girls. The guard took a couple of hesitant steps forward, pointed at Marietta and then spoke.

'That is the Perini girl, Master,' he said; 'the other one is Constanta. She has the strongest bloodline. Both are linked to Diluca.'

The figure looked back towards the two girls, and appeared to nod, although the large hood made it impossible to see a definite movement of his head. Then he glided – that was the word that sprang unbidden into Marietta's brain – across the floor and into Benedetta's cell. There was a sudden high-pitched scream, followed by the sound of terrified sobbing.

A few moments later, the figure reappeared, and Marietta caught a glimpse of his left hand as he moved past the open entrance to her cell. It was only fleeting, but just enough for her to see he had unusually long fingernails and white skin, mottled with age spots.

The figure pointed back to Benedetta's cell, and said something in his soft voice. The guard nodded, but didn't move until the hooded figure had crossed to the cellar doorway and vanished.

Marietta was the first to find her voice. 'Who was that?' she demanded.

'It's probably better that you don't know,' the guard said. 'It's better that no one knows.'

'Are you OK?' Marietta asked, as soon as he'd gone. 'What did that man do to you?'

For a few moments Benedetta didn't respond. Then she spoke again, her voice tremulous with fear and loathing.

'He just touched me, that was all. He ran his fingers down my cheek, but his hand was like ice, freezing cold, and his breath – his whole body – simply reeked.'

'I smelt something too,' Marietta said, shuddering at the recollection, 'but I didn't know what it was.'

'He smelt like rotting flesh, as if he had gangrene or some hideous disease. It was all I could do not to throw up when he got close to me. And before that, the guard stared at me the whole time I was getting washed. I've never been so terrified in my entire life.'

'That's all he did, though? He didn't do anything else to you, did he?'

'No. But I have a horrible feeling that all that's about to change. I think he's been told not to go near us, in case he sullies us. We've been saved for some kind of special event, haven't we? And it's going to happen tonight. Why else would we be told to wash and dress in this stupid out-fit? Oh, God, Marietta. I don't want to frighten you, but somehow I don't think we're going to see tomorrow.'

29

Angela came to slowly. Her head was throbbing, and when she tried to move her hands she couldn't. Unaccountably, they remained by her side, as if she was held by some kind of restraint. There was something tied around her thighs as well, and she could feel a pad or bandage wrapped round her head and covering her eyes.

She could sense people around her, could hear figures moving and talking in a language she didn't understand. For a few moments she assumed she must have had some kind of accident and was in hospital. That would explain the noises, certainly, but she had no recollection of how she'd got there.

What had happened to her? She remembered being in the hotel, remembered leaving the building and walking down the streets with Chris at her side. Then her memories became more confused. There had been a man, and a door suddenly opening right in front of them.

And then something else had happened but she couldn't clearly remember what. There had been other figures, men crowding around her, a dark room or maybe a passageway, then nothing.

Where was Chris? And where was she, come to that? Angela suddenly went cold as the realization finally dawned on her. She wasn't in any hospital. She was somewhere far, far worse.

The murmur of voices around her ebbed and flowed. The only thing she was sure about was that they were speaking Italian. She recognized the musical cadences of the language, if nothing else.

Then she felt hands doing something to the bandage that was wrapped around her head; and moments later the pad was lifted away from her face and she opened her eyes.

High above her was a white ceiling, decorated with elaborate cornices and mouldings, and with a large electric chandelier providing brilliant illumination. It was the kind of ceiling you might expect to find in the drawing-room of an English country house. But the one thing she was certain of was that she was a long way from England.

She seemed to be lying flat on her back on a wide sofa, her wrists tied with lengths of cord; and cord was wrapped around her upper thighs, too: a simple and effective way of immobilizing her. Standing in a rough circle around the sofa were about half a dozen well-dressed men, all looking at her and talking quietly together. Their expressions were neither hostile nor threatening: they simply looked down, regarding her as though she was a strange life-form they'd not previously encountered, which Angela found far more disturbing than blatant aggression would have been.

'Who are you?' Angela asked, her voice cracking with tension.

But the men just continued to look at her, with no hint of understanding in their faces.

Angela tried again. 'Where am I?'

'You're on an island in the Venetian lagoon,' a new voice replied in accented English, and the circle of men parted to admit another figure.

He was, like the other men in the room, smartly dressed in a dark suit. He looked as if he was about forty years old, with the dark hair and complexion that characterized many Italians. His features were regular, unmemorable, almost pleasant, but his eyes were cold and dispassionate as he approached her.

She looked up at him, fixing her attention on the man simply because he appeared to be the only one in the room who understood – or at least the only one who spoke – English.

'What island?' she asked.

'Its name isn't important. It's a private island in a secluded part – a very secluded part – of the *Laguna Veneta*.'

'What do you want with me?'

'Your help, at least to begin with.'

'What kind of help?' she asked.

'Professional, of course. You and your husband removed

a book that was not your property.' He held up the fragile leather-bound diary Angela had taken from the old tomb on the Isola di San Marco.

'I'm not sure it's anybody's property,' Angela said, more annoyed now than scared. 'The grave we found it in was about two hundred years old, which means anything in it cannot possibly belong to anyone living today.'

'I'm not going to discuss the legal status of the possessions of a corpse with you,' the man snapped. 'We have spent a considerable amount of time and money trying to find this book, only to have you walk off with it.'

Angela struggled to sit up, then realized it was impossible. The man issued a brief instruction, and two of his companions removed her bonds and helped her to lean against the back of the sofa.

'Why was it so important to you?' Angela asked. 'And who are you anyway?'

'You don't need to know that.'

Suddenly, Angela realized she had no idea where Chris was or what had happened to him on the street.

'Where's Chris?' she asked, the pitch of her voice rising as anxiety swept through her. 'The man I was with. I'm not going to do what you want until you tell me what happened to him.'

The man smiled then, but it wasn't an expression of reassurance, rather a look of mild and disinterested amusement, the kind of look an indulgent parent might bestow on a wayward child.

'I've no idea where that man is right now,' he said. 'I don't even know whether he's alive or dead. When my men left him, he was unconscious – taken a nasty blow to the head. That might have been enough to kill him, or caused brain damage, or perhaps only given him a really bad headache. Frankly, I neither know nor care. It simply doesn't matter.'

'It matters to me,' Angela snapped.

'Well, it won't for much longer. We know that you work for the British Museum in London and—'

'How do you know that? How do you know that I work for the museum?'

'We have our sources. And that's the only reason you're here. You must have looked at the book you took from the tomb. If you did, you'll know why it's important. Now you'll supply us with a translation of what it says.'

Angela shook her head. 'I'm not a linguist,' she said. 'I work with ceramics. And in any case, that book is just a diary.'

'How do you know that,' the man asked mildly, 'if you can't read Latin?'

'OK, I'm fairly familiar with Latin, and I did translate some of it. But what I said is true: it's just a diary.'

The man shook his head. 'That book is far more than just a diary. The first section is a chronicle of events, yes, but that isn't the part we're interested in. It's the last dozen or so pages – what's written there is very different.'

'I didn't do more than just look at that section,' Angela pointed out.

'Well, now you're going to translate all of it.'

'Why? What could possibly be so important in a two-hundred-year-old diary? Important enough to justify all this?' Angela made a sweeping gesture to encompass the entire house and whatever lay outside the building.

'We're looking for something.'

'I guessed that. What?'

'A source document. A document that's older, hundreds of years older, than this diary. Twelfth century, in fact.'

Despite her situation, and her worries about Bronson, Angela felt her pulse quicken. Once history grabbed you, it never let go, and ancient texts had always held a special fascination for her.

'What document?' she asked.

An expression that could have been a smile flickered across the man's face. 'We don't know what it's called, but we do know that it exists. Or at least that it existed.'

'How do you know?'

'Because we've seen copies of copies of different parts of it – many of them to some extent contradictory. We believe that this diary might tell us exactly where to look for the original.'

Angela frowned. 'I don't understand. This diary – or whatever you want to call it – was written by a woman almost two centuries ago, and has been locked up inside her tomb since she died. How can you possibly know it contains information about this other document?'

'We've always known about the diary. We just didn't know where it was. The Paganinis were somewhat notorious in Venice, and we've studied the family archives. Carmelita Paganini's tomb was the next place we wanted to search, but we didn't know where it was.'

'It looked to me as if somebody had erased her name from the slab covering the grave,' Angela said.

'Exactly. Carmelita was an embarrassment while she was alive, and even more so when she was dead, at least to some members of the Paganini dynasty.'

'The brick in the mouth? They thought she was a vampire?'

'A primitive attempt to destroy her, but completely pointless. Carmelita Paganini wasn't a vampire – she just thought she was. She spent her life trying to achieve that nobility, but it's clear she never managed it. The crumbling bones in her grave are proof enough of that.'

'*Nobility?*' Angela asked.

The man smiled again. 'That seems to us to be an entirely appropriate term to use when referring to a higher form of life, to something superhuman.'

Angela opened her mouth to deliver a sharp retort, but then she glanced around at the other men and thought better of it.

'So this source document,' she asked instead. 'What do you know about it?'

'We don't know its name, so we just call it "The Source".

It was written in the early twelfth century, apparently by a lapsed monk who lived in part of the country that's now called Hungary.'

'It was called Hungary then as well,' Angela pointed out. 'It's one of the oldest countries in Europe.'

The man shrugged. 'Whatever. We've found several references to it in various archives, and some of them talked about a book written by Carmelita Paganini. According to one contemporary account, she'd not only seen the original text, the source document itself, and incorporated some of the passages into her diary, but also knew where it was hidden. That's why we've been so keen to find it, and why you'll now assist us by translating Carmelita's diary.'

'And why should I help you?' Angela said. 'You've attacked me on the street and kidnapped me. What makes you think that I'll do anything to help you?'

'I'm sure we can persuade you. I think you're right-handed,' the man replied, 'so we'll start with your left hand.'

Angela stared up at him, her blood turning to ice. 'What do you mean?' she demanded.

'Let me show you,' the man replied. He turned to one of the other men and issued a crisp instruction in Italian.

After a few moments the second man returned, carrying a jar perhaps six inches high and three or four in diameter, fitted with an airtight lid. It looked to Angela like a small version of one of the old Kilner jars her mother had used years ago for bottling fruit. Inside it was an almost colourless liquid in which several small pale objects were submerged.

'What's that?' Angela demanded.

'I suppose you could call them souvenirs,' the man said, moving the jar closer to Angela's face. 'You're not the first person we've needed to – what shall we say? – *motivate* – to assist us with the translations and other matters.'

For a few moments Angela stared at the objects inside the jar uncomprehendingly, then she recoiled with a gasp of disgust. What she had first assumed were some kind of vegetables – carrots, perhaps, or parsnips – were actually the severed joints of human fingers.

'Every time you refuse to do what we ask, we'll remove a part of one of the fingers on your left hand,' the man continued. 'You won't bleed to death, because we will cauterize the wound with a soldering iron. One of my men particularly enjoys doing the amputations. He uses a pair of bolt croppers if he's in a good mood. But if you annoy him, he'll do it by clamping your finger between a couple of pieces of wood and using a hacksaw. That takes longer, and there's a lot more blood, but he doesn't seem to mind that.'

Angela tore her horrified gaze from the revolting contents of the jar and looked up into the man's face. 'You utter bastard,' she muttered.

The man shook his head. 'Abuse won't help you,' he said. 'In fact, nothing can help you now. You've seen our faces, and we simply can't afford to let you tell anybody else what you've seen.'

For a few seconds Angela just sat there, numbly digesting the explicit threat. Because this was the point. She *had* seen their faces, and she knew with a terrifying sense of certainty that she would never be allowed to leave the island alive.

The man – whoever he was – had just casually delivered her death sentence.

30

The cellar door rumbled open, the light snapped off and the door closed sharply. Benedetta gave a little cry of shock and surprise.

Marietta shrank back on to the bed. It was the first time the light had been switched off since the morning after her arrival and the action alarmed her.

For a few seconds the only sound in the cellar was the breathing of the two girls, then Benedetta gave a low moan. 'What's going to happen to us?' she murmured, her words barely audible. 'I'm so frightened. Why has the light gone off?'

'I don't know,' Marietta replied, a tremor in her own voice.

A few minutes later they heard the familiar rumbling sound as the stone door at the top of the spiral staircase was opened again.

'Somebody's coming,' Marietta said. 'They'll put the light on before they come down.'

But she was wrong. They heard the sound of footsteps, several footsteps, descending the stairs, and saw a flickering glow that grew brighter with each passing moment. Then a figure walked into the cellar.

He was clad in a very dark robe, tied at the waist with a cord, a hood covering his head. It was a foul parody of a monk's habit, but Marietta had no doubt his thoughts were anything but godly. The man held a lighted candle in his right hand, and the flickering flame cast a fitful light over his features. Staring at him in horrified silence, Marietta made out a large, bulbous nose, a heavy jaw and dark, sunken eyes.

Then she looked behind the man and saw that he was simply the first in a procession of figures, perhaps a dozen in total, all dressed in the same dark hooded robes, and each carrying a large candle. The tiny, dancing yellow flames – the only illumination in the room – cast an eerie glow over that end of the cellar. The third man in the line was also carrying an ornamented wooden box, about the size of two shoeboxes, and apparently not very heavy.

From her door-less cell, Marietta had a good view of what they were doing. The line of men – and she was sure that they were all men – filed slowly from the staircase entrance over to one end of the cellar, where they formed a circle around the stone table positioned there. For a few seconds nothing happened, then the figure holding the box took a pace forwards, lowered it carefully on to the table and stepped back again. The other figures stood in silence, waiting expectantly.

A familiar rumble echoed through the cellar. The door at the top of the stairs was closing. Then Marietta heard another sound, and literally shook with terror. The slithering noise coming from the spiral staircase could only mean one thing: the man who had so frightened both her and Benedetta was coming back into the chamber. Moments later, he appeared in the cellar, and a pungent odour suddenly filled the confined space.

The figure paused, looked over towards the cells where the two girls were imprisoned, then made his way towards the hooded men, who each bowed low as he passed.

The man took up his position at one end of the circle, looked around at his companions, then raised his left hand in a casual gesture towards the man who'd been carrying the small box. He, in turn, bowed low again, stepped forward to the table, and carefully lifted off the box's lid.

That action seemed to act as a catalyst for another of the men who left the circle and walked behind his companions, lighting another half-dozen or so large candles mounted in freestanding candlesticks, each about five feet tall, illuminating the table, and allowing Marietta to see more clearly. His task completed, the figure returned to his place in the circle. Then four of the other figures moved, each removing what looked like a length of rope from their robes, and stepped forward to thread it through one of the holes driven through the four corners of the table. Then they too moved back into position.

Marietta found the silence that had accompanied these actions unnerving. Clearly, the men were following a well-rehearsed and predetermined sequence of actions. No orders or instructions needed to be given, because every man knew his place and what his function was.

The man who had carried the box down the stairs now reached into it and extracted what looked almost like a deep soup bowl, which he placed on the table in front of him. He then took out a short object with a rounded end and placed that inside the bowl. As he did so, Marietta heard the characteristic sound of stone striking stone and, rather to her surprise, realized that what she was looking at was a mortar and pestle.

The figure closest to the box raised both his arms high above his head, and Marietta could sense the anticipation from the other men around the table.

Slowly, he lowered his hands, put them inside the box, and took out a small, round object, brownish in colour. This he lifted high above his head, holding it aloft for a few seconds, then replaced it on the table directly in front of him.

Suddenly Marietta saw exactly what it was. The vacant pits of the eye sockets, the twin vertical lines marking the position of the nose, and the white line of the teeth were unmistakable. The object they appeared to be worshipping was a human skull.

196

What happened next was even stranger. The man holding the skull took a pair of pliers from the pocket of his robe and used them to snap off a small piece of bone, which he lifted up and showed to the assembled group. Then he placed it in the mortar and began to grind it up, the noise of the operation echoing around the room.

After a few minutes he removed the pestle and handed it and the pliers to the man standing beside him. Then he picked up the mortar with both hands and lifted it high above his head, and as he did so the other men around the table bowed their heads. Next, he walked round the circle to the man who'd been the last to arrive, the apparent leader, bowed low and showed him the mortar. The man looked closely at its contents and inclined his head, whereupon the man holding the mortar bowed again, walked slowly back to his original position and placed the object on the small stone table behind him, a table which Marietta had noticed when she'd first entered the cellar.

Now, the atmosphere changed, and an almost palpable thrill of excitement, of anticipation, seemed to emanate from the silent figures. The hooded ringleader bowed his head briefly and stepped back from his position. All of the other men bowed in their turn, and stepped back, away from the table. Then the hooded man hissed a single instruction, which Marietta heard clearly: 'Bring the first girl.'

Two of the men bowed, left the group and walked towards the cells where Marietta and Benedetta were being held. Marietta retreated as far as she could and gripped the wooden head of the bed firmly with both hands, determined not to give up too easily. But the men ignored her and entered Benedetta's cell.

The other girl howled in fear, her scream echoing around the cellar. Marietta half expected to hear the crackle of the taser, but the two men simply manhandled the girl out of her cell. As they dragged her, wriggling and screaming, past the open entrance of Marietta's cell, Benedetta stared with terrified eyes at her fellow captive, begging her to come to her rescue. But Marietta could do nothing for her.

The two men stopped at the table, holding Benedetta firmly by her wrists and upper arms. Two other men stepped forward, one in front of the girl and the other behind her, and seized hold of the white robe she was wearing. Simultaneously, each man tugged the material, and the two halves of the garment parted, leaving Benedetta completely naked.

There was a sudden collective intake of breath from the men surrounding the table as they saw Benedetta's naked body for the first time. She was, Marietta saw immediately, very beautiful.

Trembling, Marietta felt the seams of the robe she was wearing. They were thick and bulky, and when she pulled at one, it emitted a characteristic ripping sound. She realized that the seams were made from Velcro, precisely so that the robe could be torn apart in this fashion.

Marietta looked back at the scene in front of her. Benedetta was screaming even louder now, the sudden shock of being stripped naked adding immeasurably to her terror. But the other participants in the ritual were proceeding in silence, their movements measured and organized, despite the girl's yells and struggles. Benedetta was forced forward until she was standing at the end of the table. Then the men turned her round until her buttocks were pressing against the stone. Two other men stepped forward and grabbed her ankles, and then she was lifted bodily and deposited in the centre of the table and held there, squirming helplessly.

Then the reason for the ropes on the table – which Marietta could now see were actually leather belts – became obvious. Working with practised ease, the men holding Benedetta in place swiftly lashed the belts around her ankles and wrists. In seconds, the girl was strapped down on the table, spreadeagled across it, as helplessly as a butterfly pinned to a display board. But still she writhed and screamed, tugging helplessly at her bonds.

The dark-robed figures standing around the table gave no sign that they could even hear her. They just looked down at her struggling naked body, the flickering light from the candles which they still held giving their features a demonic cast.

Another two men stepped forward and stopped one on either side of Benedetta's head, which Marietta suddenly realized was resting on the small stone extension, the extension that she'd noticed when she'd first seen the table. And suddenly the purpose of the table was all too clear. One of the men held Benedetta's head still while the other strapped a leather belt around both her forehead and the stone, and then cinched it tight to prevent her from moving.

Yet another man approached the table, a funnel and a small bottle held in his hands. He walked across to Benedetta's head, placed one hand on her chin to force her mouth open, and pushed the funnel between her teeth. Then he removed the stopper from the bottle and poured a white liquid into the funnel.

Benedetta coughed and choked, but only when the bottle was empty did the man remove the funnel and step back.

Immediately, the girl started to scream again, spitting out some of the white liquid. But then the man who'd tightened the belt around her head produced a pad of white material, positioned it over her mouth and secured it in place with adhesive tape.

Terrified and nauseous, Marietta simply couldn't take her eyes off the scene in front of her, at the wriggling helpless figure of a girl she barely knew, and the cold and haughty appearance of the men – and she'd now counted thirteen of them – who surrounded her. Men who were about to do something unspeakable to their innocent victim, and Marietta feared that she, too, would have to endure the same fate within minutes.

With Benedetta's cries now reduced to little more than

a whimper, the silent figures drew closer, so close that any of them could have reached out and touched her body. But clearly rape was not their objective, Marietta thought. That, at least, was a small mercy. Then even that assumption was shattered when the hooded man issued another quiet instruction to the man on his right, and he, in turn, pointed at two of the silent, robed men.

One of them bowed in response, handed his candle to the man next to him, then stepped out of the circle and pulled his robe over his head. Underneath it, he was naked apart from his sandals, and Marietta could see immediately that he was completely prepared for the act he was about to perform. He folded his robe to form a pad, placed it between Benedetta's legs as a cushion for his own knees, pulled on a condom, climbed on to the stone table, lay on top of the girl and thrust himself into her.

Then the second man removed his robe as well, opened a small packet and took out a condom, clearly waiting for his turn on the table with the girl.

Marietta could hear Benedetta's muffled howl even through the gag, but then her attention switched to the hooded man, who had moved for the first time since he'd joined the others at the table, and watched him walk over to the girl's head. Behind him, another man followed, carrying what looked like a large white ceramic bowl. Marietta noticed that the attention of all the men around the table was not on the girl, but instead on what their leader was about to do.

She strained to see what was happening, but the old man bent down and his body completely blocked her view. What he did next provoked another agonized moan from Benedetta.

There was almost complete silence in the cellar, just the rhythmic pounding of the naked man riding Benedetta on the stone table, and her muffled cries of pain. Then Marietta heard a new sound, a kind of sucking noise.

And then, as the hooded man moved to one side and half-turned towards Marietta, she recoiled in shock. Even in the gloom of the cellar, illuminated only by the flickering light of the candle flames, she could clearly see the long pointed canine teeth gleaming white in his open mouth. They had to be false, inserted in his mouth for the ceremony, they just had to be. Marietta's brain wouldn't accept any other explanation.

For an instant she thought he had a beard, and then realized, with a further jolt of terror, that the dark, almost black, discoloration covering his chin and the sides of his mouth was fresh blood.

At last Marietta saw the appalling fate that awaited her. On the right-hand side of the other girl's neck was a round wound, and her blood was flowing freely from it into the bowl beneath.

Marietta couldn't help herself. She threw back her head and let loose a scream that was deafening in its intensity, a howl of absolute terror and utter dismay. The men turned as one to look at her, even the one lying on top of Benedetta, and their leader responded with an angry gesture.

One of the group walked swiftly over to Marietta, grabbed the front of her robe at the neck and ripped it forwards and down, the seams parting instantly to reveal her naked torso. He pulled out a taser from his pocket, held her around the throat so she couldn't wriggle free, placed the electrodes of the device between her breasts and pulled the trigger.

A surge of current ripped through her body, sending her limbs into spasm, and a moment later she slumped backwards and fell to the ground unconscious.

✝

31

Bronson had barely slept a wink. Every time he'd closed his eyes, a horrific full-colour image of Angela, blood streaming from a ragged wound in her neck, had flooded his consciousness. Just after six in the morning he gave up, climbed out of bed and got ready for whatever the day might bring.

He was keenly aware that there was nothing useful he could do. Angela's fate was completely in the hands of the *carabinieri*, and what really bothered Bronson was that he was certain somebody in the police force was leaking information to whoever had taken her. But there was nothing he could do about that, either, because in Italy he had no official standing, and he was familiar enough with the labyrinthine ways of Italian bureaucracy to know that registering a complaint would achieve absolutely nothing, except to make any further cooperation with the *carabinieri* almost impossible to achieve.

As far as Bronson could see, the only thing he could do was again study the book Angela had retrieved from the tomb on the Isola di San Michele, and hope he could identify something in it, some clue, that would help him find her. He didn't know much Latin, although he recognized that the Italian language he loved so much had been derived from it. But Angela had downloaded a Latin–English dictionary from somewhere on the web, and he supposed he'd be able to use that to translate some of the entries in the diary.

He switched on Angela's laptop, checked the signal strength on his mobile phone, and left his room, locking the door behind him.

He was the first guest to step into the dining room for breakfast. He wasn't hungry – he rarely had much of an appetite in the morning – but he knew he ought to eat something. He poured himself a cup of coffee and picked up a couple of croissants from the buffet, then carried them over to their usual table, and ate them while he stared through the window at the early morning bustle. Then he drank a second cup of coffee before returning to their room.

The first thing he did was to read all the notes and translations that Angela had already prepared. He'd done the same thing the previous day, but nothing of importance had struck him. Then he started looking at some of the Latin sentences on later pages in the book. As Angela had said, most of the text seemed to consist of diary entries, but towards the back of the book he found a separate section that looked rather different. There were no dates or times or places listed, only paragraphs of closely written Latin text.

Bronson looked at these paragraphs for a few minutes, picking out the odd Latin word that he recognized, then decided it probably was worth trying to make a reasonable translation of the text. But he'd barely even begun when his mobile phone rang.

For an instant his heart pounded with anticipation. Could it be Angela, calling him to let him know she'd been released by her captors?

'Chris Bronson,' he said.

There was a pause and then a heavily accented voice spoke to him in English. 'Signor Bronson. My name is Filippo Bianchi, and I'm a senior Venetian police officer. I may have some bad news for you.'

'Tell me,' Bronson replied in Italian, sitting down heavily on the bed.

'I'm sorry to have to tell you this, but a body has just been found,' Bianchi replied, switching to his native language, 'and it matches the description you gave of your former wife. We would like you to come to the police station in San Marco, which is near the mortuary, to identify the corpse.'

Time suddenly seemed to stop, and Bronson had the bizarre sensation of the room closing in around him, constricting his chest and driving the breath from his body.

For a few moments his mouth opened and closed, but no sound emerged. A loud and continuous beep sounded in his ear.

Then he regained control and took a deep breath. He realized he was clutching the phone so tightly that his fingers were pressing down on some of the keys. He released his grip slightly, and the beeping sound ceased. He gazed at the wall opposite, a tumble of emotions coursing through him.

'Give me the address,' he said, and noted down what Bianchi told him. Then he ended the call.

For a few seconds, Bronson sat motionless on the bed, his mobile phone still in his hand. This really couldn't be happening, he told himself. Angela simply could not be dead. Their week's holiday in Venice – a simple break from the routine of England – had turned into a nightmare that seemed as though it would never end.

Then he roused himself. He didn't want to go to the police station or the mortuary, but he knew he had no choice. Opening his map of Venice, he quickly found the location of the police station. He slipped the map into his jacket pocket and headed back down to reception.

Ten minutes later, Bronson stepped into the red-painted powerboat the hotel receptionist had arranged for him, started the engine, put it into gear and steered it away from the side of the canal.

It was still fairly early in the morning, and the water traffic was light, though as usual the streets around the canals were crowded with pedestrians, many of them obvious tourists. Less than a quarter of an hour after he'd set off from the hotel, he moored the boat in a canal about a hundred yards from the police station and walked slowly over to the building, subconsciously delaying the moment of his arrival there, as if that could possibly make the slightest difference to the outcome.

The mortuary was in an adjacent building, and Bronson was led there by Bianchi himself, who'd been waiting for him near the reception desk in the station. Bianchi was a bulky, heavily built man in his mid-fifties, and Bronson recognized him at once – he'd been the senior investigating officer who'd appeared on the Isola di San Michele to investigate the three dead bodies that he and Angela had found in the tomb there.

It wasn't the first time Bronson had visited a mortuary, though he'd never before been in the position he was in now. Normally, he was the presiding police officer, waiting for an anxious relative to confirm the identification of the body lying under a white sheet. He saw immediately that the Italians did things in much the same way as the British.

The viewing room was cold, much colder than the air-conditioned chill he'd experienced when they'd walked through the doors and into the mortuary, but it wasn't just the chill in the air that made Bronson shiver. It was a small oblong space, three walls painted white and the fourth entirely invisible behind a deep purple curtain, behind which he knew would be the fridges that held the bodies. A large but simple crucifix adorned the wall beside the door, and a row of half a dozen uncomfortable-looking metal and plastic chairs lined the adjacent wall.

He registered all that as soon as he walked in, but what gripped and held his attention was the sheeted corpse lying on a trolley directly in front of him, in the middle of the room.

Bianchi strode across to one end of the body and positioned himself there, a mortuary attendant beside him. Bronson stepped closer to the trolley.

'Are you prepared, Signor Bronson?' Bianchi asked.

Bronson took a deep breath and nodded.

The police officer gestured to the attendant, who released a safety pin from the sheet covering the body, and gently pulled back the material that covered the face of the corpse.

Bronson noticed the hair first. Blonde and about shoulder-length, the way Angela normally wore it. Then his gaze moved slowly down her face, noticing the closed eyes, small nose and wide, generous mouth. He took a step closer to the trolley, to the midpoint of the dead body, and for a long moment stared down at the woman's pale face, her skin white and waxy.

'Signor Bronson, can you confirm whether or not this young woman is your wife?' Bianchi asked quietly.

Bronson looked up at the police officer and the silent, unsmiling mortuary attendant standing next to him.

'Yes,' he said. 'I can.'

✝

32

Marietta awoke slowly in the darkness of the cellar. For a few seconds she had no recollection of where she was, but then she moved her left arm and the rattle of the chain and handcuff brought the hideous knowledge flooding back.

Instinctively she glanced down at her wrist, but her watch had been taken, so she had no idea what time of day or night it was. The last thing she recalled was the surge of current from the taser, a bolt of electricity so powerful that she'd lost consciousness. But she also knew, because of her previous experiences with the weapon, that she recovered quite quickly from it. So something else must have happened to her afterwards, because the cellar was now still and quiet and absolutely dark, and she couldn't see any sign of the silent and malevolent figures who'd so terrified her.

And what of Benedetta? The last image, burned indelibly into her brain, was of the girl strapped down on the table, one man violently raping her while another collected the blood pouring from the wound on her neck. Had she survived? Or was she lying dead, her body even then growing cold on the stone table, or on the rough wooden bed in the adjacent cell?

'Benedetta?' Marietta whispered. There was no response. She repeated the name, raising her voice. Still there was no reply. As the echoes of her calls died away, a deep silence fell once again. It sounded as if Marietta was entirely alone.

Tears filled her eyes, and panic gripped her as she remembered the way Benedetta had suffered at the hands of their captors. And with that memory came a sense of confusion. Because they'd both been prepared for the 'ceremony', Marietta had assumed that, once the men had finished with Benedetta, she would have suffered the same fate.

She reached up and felt her neck, her sensitive fingertips tracing the skin on both sides. It felt bruised. This didn't surprise her – the memory of the man with the taser grabbing her throat was still very vivid – but she could feel no evidence of a wound or any other damage. And she knew that she hadn't been violated. So when they'd finished with Benedetta, they hadn't come for her. Why not? And why had she remained unconscious for so long?

With her right hand, Marietta gently explored her body. She was naked – the white robe must have been ripped off after the taser hit her – and somebody had then dumped her on the bed and tossed the rough blanket over her body. She felt her left arm. Where the veins ran close to the surface of the skin, in the crook of her elbow, it was sore, and she guessed that she'd been given an injection to knock her out.

But this didn't explain why she, too, hadn't been raped and her lifeblood drained. Had the men been interrupted? But that was pretty unlikely, because they were on a remote island in the Venetian lagoon, where the only access was by boat or possibly helicopter. There was almost no chance, she knew, of anyone appearing there unexpectedly.

In fact, she could only think of one reason why she was still in the cellar and still alive: the hooded men must have got enough blood from Benedetta to satisfy their repulsive desires and hadn't needed hers as well. In which case, Benedetta must surely be dead.

Marietta shuddered. She'd been granted a temporary reprieve, but her prolonged and violent death would surely follow, as inevitably as night follows day. In fact, she guessed she had less than twenty-four hours to live.

The realization hit her hard. Ever since she'd been abducted, she'd been clinging to the hope that somehow she'd be able to escape. But what she'd witnessed just hours before had finally extinguished even this faint comfort.

Shaking with fear, Marietta curled up into a ball underneath her coarse, damp blanket and squeezed her eyes tight shut, sobs racking her body as she gave way to the utter despair that overwhelmed her.

33

In the mortuary, the three men stood in a rough circle around the trolley, staring down at the violated body lying on it, but their thoughts and feelings very were different. Bianchi was professionally distant and reserved, concerned only with the proper identification of the young woman whose death he would now have to investigate. The attendant was bored, if anything. But Bronson was trembling with emotion, so much so that he barely heard Bianchi's next words, and the inspector had to repeat himself.

'So you can confirm that this is the body of your wife, Angela Lewis?' he again asked softly.

'No,' Bronson said, a lot more firmly than he felt. 'I can confirm that I've never seen this woman before in my life. This is definitely not my wife.'

'But I thought . . . I mean, your description? Her hair, eyes, skin colour?'

'It's a good match, but this is definitely not Angela.'

Again Bronson looked down at the body lying in front of him, then he reached forward, towards the neck of the corpse, around which a padded bandage had been placed, and tugged down on the material. Immediately, the mortuary attendant pushed him back and started smoothing the bandage back into position, but by then Bronson had seen enough.

The girl's neck bore a large oval wound, the flesh cut and bruised around it, the blood faded to a dull red-brown colour.

'Signor Bronson,' Bianchi snapped, 'kindly remember where you are. Do not try to touch the corpse.'

Bronson looked at him levelly. 'Her skin's very pale,' he said. 'Was she killed like the others? Her blood drained from that wound in the side of her throat? Is that why you've put that dressing there?' He pointed at the bandage the attendant was still repositioning around her neck.

Bianchi stared at him in a hostile manner. 'What are you talking about?'

'I was the man who found the three bodies dumped together in the tomb on the Isola di San Michele, the corpses you were sent out there to investigate,' Bronson replied. 'I'm a policeman, and when I smelt rotting flesh, I took a photograph through the hole in the slab covering the tomb. When I looked at the picture afterwards, I could clearly see a mark just like that' – he pointed down at the sheeted corpse – 'on the neck of each of those girls. And

I saw the same thing on the body of the other girl your men found out on San Michele. I didn't find her, but I was out there, watching, when her body was removed from the scene.'

Bronson paused, looked again at the corpse on the trolley, then back to Bianchi.

'What you've got going on here, right now, in Venice, is the work of a serial killer.' Then he shook his head. 'No, in fact it's much more complicated than that. I think there's a gang of people who are snatching girls off the streets, sucking the blood from their necks, and then dumping the bodies.'

By now Bianchi had recovered his composure. 'What you just said is a complete fantasy, a fabrication, Signor Bronson. We have had some missing girls, it's true, and we have unfortunately discovered some bodies, but all this stuff about blood-sucking is complete nonsense.'

The mortuary attendant reached out and started to pull the sheet over the dead girl's face once more, but again Bronson stopped him.

'Then take off that bandage so we can all see this girl's neck,' he snapped. 'If I'm making all this up, then you'll be able to tell me exactly what she died from, and you'll be able to show me that her neck is unmarked.'

'I don't have to show you anything, Signor Bronson,' Bianchi responded sharply. 'I asked you here because I thought this body might be that of your missing partner. I'm relieved for you that it's not her, obviously, but I still have to try to identify this young woman and break the news to her family. I'm certainly not prepared to discuss how she died with you or with any other civilian. And here in Venice, that's what you are, Signor Bronson, just a civilian, a tourist. I suggest you remember that.'

'I know exactly what my status is in Italy,' Bronson said. 'But I also know that if this poor girl hadn't got a gaping wound on her neck, you'd be only too pleased to show me, just to prove me wrong.' He pointed at the sheeted figure. 'I saw her wound; I know that she died at the hands of these lunatics. And that makes at least five victims who have all been killed in the same way: massive blood loss from some sort of incisions made in the side of their necks, just like the sort of wounds supposedly inflicted by the vampires of fiction.'

Bianchi raised a warning finger. 'Signor Bronson, I suggest you refrain from repeating anything you've said here to anyone in Venice. If the newspapers start printing lurid stories, I'll know exactly where they got the information from, and I'll take great pleasure in arresting you.'

'On what charge?' Bronson asked mildly.

'I'll think of something. Now I suggest you get out of here, before you say anything else you might regret.'

An hour later, Bronson was back in his hotel room. The diary Angela had taken was the key to her abduction, he was certain, and he was keen to get back to it. Locking the door firmly behind him, he switched on Angela's computer again, and opened up the scanned image of the final section of the book, the part which obviously hadn't been written in diary format. Then he opened Angela's translation of the first part of the text, and read it again. He remembered that one word seemed to be repeated over and over again, a word which Angela had rendered as the 'answer'. That seemed to sit rather oddly in some of the sentences that she'd already translated into English.

But she'd obviously done more work on the book the previous evening, and had transcribed more of the Latin text, although none of this seemed particularly helpful. She'd also revised the translations that mentioned the 'twin angels' tomb, and had clearly decided that a more accurate meaning of the 'answer' would be the 'source'.

Bronson again read the passages Angela had translated. The text was specific about only one thing: that the tomb of the twin angels, the grave they thought they might have located in the cemetery on the Isola di San Michele, held the 'answer' or the 'source' or whatever the Latin word actually meant to the woman who'd written the diary.

It was odd, Bronson thought, the way the Island of the Dead seemed so intimately connected with the events they'd become involved with in Venice. The shattered tomb and the mutilated corpse had started the puzzle, and the cemetery had also been chosen as a dumping ground for the bodies of the girls once the group of killers had finished with them. And, of course, the vampire's diary itself had come from the first tomb, and contained references to at least one other burial on San Michele.

One way or another, the island and its ancient graveyard were inextricably linked to the events of the present day. Maybe, Bronson thought, he should go back there, take another look at that tomb of the twin angels, and see if he could work out anything useful from the inscriptions on the old stone. It wasn't much of a plan, and he wasn't sure it was even worth doing, but it was, he reflected, probably better than sitting in the hotel room trying to translate an old Latin text.

He shut down the computer, checked he had his camera and his binoculars, took his leather jacket out of the wardrobe, and walked down to the reception desk.

Half an hour later he was again sitting at the controls of his small red boat, and steering the small vessel north-east across the choppy waters of the Venetian lagoon.

34

Apart from a few visits to the loo, each time accompanied by one of her silent and unsmiling guards to the door of a ground-floor lavatory – which had a barred window and no internal lock or bolt – Angela hadn't left the elegant room in the house since she'd arrived. Early in the evening, a tray of food had been put in front of her, and around midnight she'd eventually tried to get some sleep on the wide sofa in front of the fireplace.

But she hadn't been idle that evening. The suave but indescribably menacing man had seen to that. He had finally introduced himself as 'Marco', but she had no idea if that was what he was actually called or just a convenient name he'd pulled out of the air.

As soon as he'd shown her the appalling collection of 'souvenirs', Angela had realized that cooperation with her captors was hardly a choice: it was an absolute necessity if she was to avoid the agonizing mutilation that the group was so obviously capable of inflicting. So when Marco had asked if she was prepared to complete the translations, she'd simply nodded her agreement.

She'd been led across to a large oak desk set in one corner, and been told to sit on a leather swivel chair right in front of it, an incongruously modern piece of furniture in the elegant and old-fashioned room. Even those few steps across the polished wooden floor left her feeling as weak as a kitten: presumably she'd been pumped full of a cocktail of drugs to keep her quiet while they transported her to the house – wherever it was – and her body was still feeling the after effects. She knew that trying to fight her captors or run out of the room would be completely futile. Before she could do anything to try to escape, she would have to wait until she'd regained her strength. And she also needed to find out a lot more about the house in which she was being held prisoner, and its location. And especially what lay outside the windows.

On the desk was a selection of reference books of various types, the majority clearly written in English, about half a dozen pencils, roughly half a ream of white paper, the battered leather-bound diary itself, and two separate piles of pages which she saw immediately were photocopies of the diary entries.

Marco had pointed to those two sets of pages. 'Ignore the one on the left,' he said. 'Those are just records of Carmelita's life: interesting but not important for us. The other section is the one we're interested in. You can start translating that right now.'

Angela shook her head. 'I'll need a Latin dictionary,' she said. 'I don't have the vocabulary to translate this. Can you find one on the Internet for me?'

Marco laughed shortly. 'We're not going to let you anywhere near a computer,' he said. Then he searched quickly through the pile of books at the back of the desk and selected a Latin–Italian dictionary.

Angela opened her mouth to point out that she didn't speak Italian, but before she could say anything, he had found another dictionary, this time a Latin–English version, and the words of protest died in her throat.

'And when I've finished?' Angela had asked. 'What then? You'll shoot me? Is that it?'

Marco had shaken his head. 'I think we can find a more interesting way to usher you into the next life,' he'd said. 'But I do have some good news for you.'

'What?'

'If you do a good job, you'll still be alive tomorrow. But after that, I can't promise you anything. And before you start work, let me point out that we've already translated some of the text ourselves, so we'll know if your version is accurate.'

'If you've done that, then why do you need me at all?' Angela had asked.

'You English have an expression about a gift horse. If we don't need you to do the translation, then we don't need you at all, so just be grateful. But it's not just translating the Latin. There are some unusual aspects of the text that we haven't been able to make sense of. That's the real reason why we want you to work on it.'

Without another word Angela had pulled the dictionary across in front of her, picked up a pencil and looked at the first sentence.

35

Sometime that morning – Marietta had no idea exactly when – the upper door to the cellar rumbled open and the light snapped on.

A few moments later, the guard appeared in the room, carrying a tray of food exactly as he'd done on previous occasions, and a plastic bag that contained her clothes. He walked across to Marietta, tossed the bag on to the mattress, placed the tray on the floor in front of her, and turned to leave.

'Please,' Marietta pleaded with him. 'Please leave the lights on. And what happened to Benedetta? Where is she? And who was that man – the one with those horrible teeth?'

'So many questions,' the guard said mockingly. 'But you needn't worry about Benedetta. We got what we wanted from her.'

'So where is she now? Did you let her go?'

'In a manner of speaking, I suppose we did. We sent her to San Michele,' he added.

For a moment, Marietta didn't understand the expression. Then it dawned on her that he meant the 'Island of the Dead', and the confirmation of what she'd feared hit her hard.

'You killed her,' she said flatly. 'That foul ritual last night. You raped her and bled her to death. You bastards.'

'You catch on quick,' the guard said. 'But at least she died for a good reason. There was a point to her death, just as there'll be a point to yours.'

'What point could there possibly be in snatching girls like me off the streets of Venice and then killing us?'

The guard looked at her carefully for a few moments. 'You're not just any girl,' he said. 'You and Benedetta were both special. That's why you were chosen. We've traced your bloodline.'

'My bloodline?'

'You and Benedetta are descended from someone who is vitally important to our society.'

'And you're going to kill me because of one of my ancestors? That makes no sense at all.'

'It does to us,' the guard said simply. 'You'll have company soon.'

'Who?' Marietta asked, though she dreaded hearing the answer.

'Another girl. We've got her in the house at the moment, but she'll be brought down here soon enough. But she won't be able to talk to you. No girly chatter with that one.'

'Why?' Marietta demanded. 'What have you done to her?'

The guard smiled slightly. 'Nothing at all,' he said. 'It's just that she doesn't speak a word of Italian. But don't worry. You won't be on your own for too long. Soon you'll be reunited with your friend.'

For a moment Marietta sat in silence, eyes downcast, guessing what he meant but hardly daring to ask the question that would confirm her fears. Then she looked at him directly.

'What do you mean?' she asked.

'You'll be back with Benedetta,' the guard replied. 'It's your turn on the table tonight.'

36

Bronson manoeuvred the boat through the water along the north-west side of the Isola di San Michele, past a tall greenish sculpture, probably made of copper, which depicted two figures standing on a small boat that rose from the waters a short distance from the Cimitero *vaporetto* stop. That side of the island was delineated by impressive walls formed from white stone and brown brick, with a large gateway in the centre and smaller towers spaced at intervals on either side of it.

He continued around the northern edge of the island to where his map showed a small inlet, lined with jetties.

He'd hardly even been aware of how the boat handled on his short trip to and from the police station in the San Marco district, but he'd got the feel of the craft on the journey out to the Isola di San Michele, and it had proved quite easy to control. Not quite as simple as driving a car, but not that difficult either. As he entered the inlet he pulled the throttle back, slowing the boat to little more than walking pace.

There were perhaps a dozen similar boats already moored at various points on the jetties, but there was still plenty of space left for him to use. He swung the boat in a half circle, so that the bow pointed back out towards the lagoon, then eased it in to a stop beside the jetty. He stopped the engine, climbed out of the vessel and secured both the bow and the stern mooring lines. A few moments later, he was making his way towards the centre of the old graveyard.

As he walked, Bronson tried to recall exactly where they'd found the tomb that Angela had believed was the one mentioned in the vampire's diary. The problem was that many of the sections of the cemetery looked fairly similar, and he was also approaching the area from a different direction, which meant it was difficult to get his bearings.

The good thing was that today the place wasn't crowded with tourists and locals, although on the far side of the graveyard he could see three separate funerals taking place. That morning the weather was clear, with unsullied blue skies, and the brilliant sunshine imparted a warm glow to the memorial stones, and even seemed to have breathed fresh life into the bouquets of cut flowers that decorated most of the graves. For the first time, the Isola di San Michele seemed a friendly, almost welcoming, place to walk and explore.

Bronson remembered that the tomb he was looking for lay in one of the older sections of the graveyard, so he made his way to the spot where he thought the grave should lie, then stopped short as he reached the end of a line of trees and looked over to his right. He had reached a section of the graveyard with numerous ancient tombs of the type he was seeking, but what had caused him to stop was the sight of two men standing beside a familiar-looking carved statue.

Bronson eased back into the shadows cast by the trees, took his compact binoculars from his pocket, and stared through the instrument at the intruders. He adjusted the focus, and immediately confirmed one thing: the men were right next to the tomb of the twin angels.

For a few seconds, Bronson studied the two figures, noting what he could of their physical appearance. Both were wearing casual clothes, jeans and white shirts, but each also wore a windcheater, one blue and the other dark grey, which suggested to Bronson that they'd most probably arrived on the island by boat. Driving a powerboat at speed over the water could be quite chilly, and he'd been glad of his leather jacket on his own journey. Not that that deduction actually helped him in any way. The two men could easily be workers sent out to San Michele to do maintenance jobs, or even a couple of bureaucrats counting the graves or something equally mundane.

Bronson moved the binoculars slightly so that he could see the tomb itself. From the angle he was looking at it, he could see one side of the structure, while the two men were on the far side, both of them looking down at the ancient stone. Then one of the men bent down beside the grave, and was lost to sight.

Bronson wondered if he should simply stroll through that part of the cemetery towards the grave he was interested in, playing the part of an innocent tourist, because he was still unsure about who the two men were. If they were just workers, he would be able to examine the grave without any problems, and if they were in some way connected with Angela's abduction, he might see them clearly enough to provide a photofit for the *carabinieri*. Or perhaps he could even follow them when they left the island. Either way, getting closer to the tomb seemed like a good idea.

He slipped the binoculars back into his pocket, stepped out from behind the tree, and started making his way across the grass that carpeted the area between the graves. He'd only gone half a dozen steps when he heard a sudden noise from behind him, and glanced back to see another man walking swiftly towards him through the graves. Instinctively, Bronson stepped to one side to allow the man to hurry past.

The new arrival nodded his thanks and stepped past Bronson. And as he did so, he abruptly turned and swung his right arm towards Bronson's head. But something in the way the man moved must have triggered some subliminal warning, because as he did so Bronson realized two things simultaneously: first, that the figure beside him was one of the men who'd attacked him in the street when Angela was abducted, and, second, that he was trying precisely the same technique again, swinging a heavy blackjack with the intention of smashing it into the back of Bronson's skull.

37

Angela had woken stiff and aching from her fitful sleep on the sofa, and had been allowed to wash in a bathroom adjacent to the lavatory she'd used the previous day. Her breakfast had consisted of a plate of pastries and coffee, and as soon as she'd finished it, Marco had told her to carry on working on the translation.

She had acquired her knowledge of Latin over the years that she'd worked at the British Museum, building on the lessons in the dead language she'd enjoyed at school, more years ago than she could now contemplate with any degree of comfort. But try as she might to concentrate on the words in front of her, her thoughts kept returning to the awful reality of her situation and, inescapably, to Chris. She had no idea whether he was alive or dead. If he was alive, if he'd survived the attack on the street, she knew he'd be trying to find her, and would be frantic with worry. But how on earth would he be able to track her down?

She had no idea how long she'd spent in a drug-induced state of unconsciousness, but it must have been several hours, perhaps even days, and it was entirely possible that she was no longer in Venice at all. Her only reassurance was that her captors spoke together in Italian, which presumably meant that she was still in Italy. But even that, she had to acknowledge, was actually pure conjecture. It was just as possible that she'd been snatched by a gang of Italians, and then taken to some other country entirely.

And she'd found the coolly dispassionate attitude of her captors enormously alarming. She really believed that any one of them could kill her with as little compunction or concern as he would exhibit if he swatted a fly. As far as she could see, the only reason she was still alive at that moment was because they needed her translation skills, and Marco – or whatever his real name was – had implied that they only wanted to see her version of the ancient text to check that whoever else they had employed to decipher it had got it right.

That meant they already had a good idea of what the Latin text said, which in turn meant that she had to do a reasonably good job herself. But not a perfect job, she decided. Perhaps she would make a handful of trifling errors in the translation – errors that she could explain away because of her unfamiliarity with Latin, and which might mean they would keep her alive for a bit longer while they ensured that she'd done the best job she could, and that the text she'd produced was accurate. That was the only thing she could think of doing to make her abductors think twice before killing her. And the longer she stayed alive, Angela knew, the better the chances of her finding some way of getting out of the house – wherever it was – and escaping. And maybe somebody, Chris or the police or even the occupants of a neighbouring property, if there was one, might discover where she was being held prisoner. It was a cliché, obviously, but it was just as obviously true: while there was life, there really was hope.

Angela dabbed her eyes angrily with a tissue, cleared her mind of all extraneous thoughts, and again focused on the task at hand.

Quite a lot of the Latin words were familiar to her. One of the advantages of learning Latin was that it had an essentially finite vocabulary, unlike English and other modern languages in common usage, which acquire new words, new meanings and new variants of existing words on an almost daily basis. Once you knew the meaning of a Latin word, you knew it for ever, because it would never change.

She remembered most of the declensions and many of the conjugations of verbs, and she was able to jot down the general sense of several of the sentences quite quickly, just leaving a handful of blanks for the words that she was either unfamiliar with or unsure of. Then she'd open the dictionary and flick through the pages until she found the first word she needed to check. Then she'd fill in the meaning, and move on to the next word. When she'd finished each sentence she paused for a moment to read it in its entirety, to make sure that it made sense, then re-wrote it in modern English.

The translation itself had proved to be relatively straight-forward, but she soon realized what Marco had meant when he referred to 'unusual aspects' in the text. Although the references to the tomb of the twin angels still seemed fairly clear, other passages in the Latin were ambiguous at best, and she was increasingly unsure whether or not she was getting it right. In some passages, Carmelita had referred to the Isola di San Michele as the *insula silenti*, the phrase translating as the 'island of the dead', but there were several occurrences of an entirely different phrase – *insula vetus mortuus* – which puzzled her.

Her literal translation rendered this as the island of the 'ancient dead' or 'old dead', which she really didn't under-stand. It wasn't clear to her whether Carmelita was using the expression as a synonym for San Michele, or if she meant somewhere completely different, possibly a more ancient graveyard located elsewhere in Venice.

And there was another phrase which sent a chill through her. The pages referred to *planctus mortuus*, which translated as the 'wailing dead' or the 'screaming dead'. 'Dead', as far as she was concerned, meant exactly that: death, the cessation of life. The dead could neither scream nor wail. But the same expression appeared in several places in the text, and the context suggested that

Carmelita was referring to a specific place where the dead had screamed.

Angela shook her head and continued working through the text.

38

When anybody asked him if he knew any of the martial arts, Bronson normally told them he had a black belt in origami – it amused him to see the conflicting emotions this statement usually produced. In fact, he'd trained to an intermediate level in aikido.

Perhaps the most unusual, and certainly the least known, of the oriental fighting techniques, aikido is purely defensive. No master of aikido could attack anyone using the art, because no offensive moves exist. But once an aikido practitioner is attacked, his or her response to that attack can easily prove fatal to the assailant. It relies heavily on unbalancing the opponent, essentially using the attacker's own weight and speed and aggression against him.

Bronson's tutor, a Japanese man barely five feet five inches tall and aged sixty-three, had told him years before that an aikido master could take on as many as three masters in any of the other martial arts, at the same time, and still expect to be standing when the dust settled.

Bronson frankly hadn't believed him, but one evening when the two of them had left the dojo and were walking over to where Bronson had parked his car, a gang of six scarf-wearing football supporters, high on drink or drugs, had streamed out of an alleyway directly in front of them, looking for trouble, and ideally searching for a soft target.

Bronson had stepped forward to face them, but with a courteous bow the old Japanese man had motioned him back, taken two paces forward and just stood waiting. His harmless appearance and placid stance had seemed to enrage the youths, and they'd spent ten seconds shouting abuse before launching themselves at him.

What happened then had had all the appearance to Bronson of magic. It was as if each youth encountered something akin to a catapult: the faster they slammed into the old man, the faster they were tossed aside. In a little under twenty seconds the six youths were lying broken and bleeding on the ground, and throughout the entire time the old man barely seemed to have moved, and when he stepped over the legs of the nearest youth to rejoin Bronson, he hadn't even been breathing hard.

'Now do you believe me, Mr Bronson?' he had asked, and all Bronson had been able to do was nod.

And now that training was going to save his life. Bronson swayed backwards, and the blackjack whistled viciously through the air a bare inch in front of his face. Then he stepped towards his attacker, turning as he did so, and seized the man's right arm. He pulled him forward so that he was off balance, and continued to turn his body so that his back was towards his assailant. Then he bent forward, still pulling on the man's right arm, and his attacker flew over his back to land – hard – on the ground directly in front of him.

Bronson hadn't practised Aikido for some time but, much like riding a bike, his brain still retained the moves and his body responded with the actions he'd practised so many times in the past. The throw he'd just completed was one of the first and most basic of the moves he'd learned, and he finished it off in exactly the way he'd been taught, by tugging on the man's arm at the instant before he landed, dislocating his shoulder.

The man screamed in pain as the bone was wrenched from its socket, the blackjack tumbling from his hand on to the ground. He was hurt, but Bronson knew he wasn't immobilized, not yet, and this was something he needed to attend to. He snatched up the blackjack, and swung it as hard as he could against the man's skull. His attacker flinched and raised his left arm in a futile defence, but there was no way he could avoid the blow. The impact jarred Bronson's arm, but had the desired effect on his target. The man slumped backwards, instantly knocked unconscious.

Bronson was certain he'd recognized his assailant – and

this meant that the two men by the tomb, only some twenty yards away, were surely part of the same gang.

Standing up, he turned towards the tomb of the twin angels and took a couple of steps forward. Then he dropped down, because one of the men had just swung round to face him, and was brandishing a semi-automatic pistol in his hand.

The sound of the shot was shockingly loud amid the tranquillity of the ancient cemetery, echoing off the walls of the church and the tombs all around him. The bullet just missed Bronson as he dived for cover, smashing into a tall stone cross behind him and sending stone chips flying in all directions.

The pistol added a whole new dimension to the situation. Bronson would have had no qualms about tackling the two men. As he'd just demonstrated, he was proficient in unarmed combat, and his whole body burned with fury against the men who'd snatched Angela. Taking on two Italian thugs and beating them to a pulp might well have helped him find her, but no level of anger or competence in hand-to-hand combat would help against a man carrying a gun. This radically altered the dynamics of the situation.

For perhaps a second, he remained crouched down behind another of the tombs, weighing his options and figuring the angles. He couldn't run, not even if he'd dodged and weaved from side to side, because nobody can out run a bullet. And he couldn't hide, either, because the other men knew where he was.

He had exactly one chance, and it all depended on the unconscious man lying on the ground a few feet behind him. Keeping as low as he could, he scuttled over to the unmoving figure, and crouched down beside him. He pulled open the man's jacket, searching desperately for a shoulder holster and a weapon he could use to save his life. But there was nothing, no sign of a pistol under either arm.

Bronson looked over to the tomb of the twin angels. The two men seemed to have separated: one had ducked back behind the tomb, and was keeping low, but Bronson couldn't see the second man, the one who'd fired the pistol.

Then another shot cracked out, the bullet again missing Bronson, but only barely. The second man had moved around to the east, to get a better shot at him, and was standing only about fifteen yards away in the classic target-shooting stance: feet apart, the pistol held in his right hand, and his left hand supporting his right wrist.

The next shot, Bronson knew, would probably be the last thing he would know in this world, because from that range the man couldn't possibly miss him.

✝

39

Almost despite herself, Angela was finding the task she'd been given quite fascinating. The dictionary was very comprehensive, and she had no difficulty in rendering the Latin expressions and sentences into modern English, albeit sometimes lengthy and rather convoluted modern English.

She knew that the grave on the Isola di San Michele dated from the early nineteenth century, and she still believed that the diary had been written by the woman who was buried there, and that the book had been interred with her by her family as a mark of respect. Indeed, the sections of the diary that she'd already translated back in the hotel room showed the unmistakable cadences of the kind of Latin she would expect to have been written by a well-educated person – male or female – of that period.

But the section at the back of the book, the text she

was now being forced to translate, was very different. Although Angela was fairly sure that it had been written by the same person who had authored the diary sections – the handwriting was quite distinctive – apart from the first few sentences, which seemed to act as a kind of introduction, the remainder of the text shared none of the characteristics of the earlier pages.

The more she read and worked on, the more sure she was that this Latin had been copied from a much older source, which would confirm what Marco had told her – most of it was a copy of a far more ancient document, interspersed with comments and additional material presumably supplied by Carmelita. Some of the language was mediaeval, she thought, maybe even older than that. She could find no explanation anywhere in the text to suggest what exactly the source book had been, but there was something faintly familiar to her about some of the phrases and expressions the unknown author had used, and Angela began to wonder if what she was looking at was a passage taken from a mediaeval grimoire. That might actually tie up with Marco's apparent belief that the source document dated from the twelfth century.

Whatever the source, the Latin text made for grim but fascinating reading. The passage began with a long paragraph, almost messianic in its fervour, which baldly asserted that vampires were a reality, and that they had existed since the dawn of time. These creatures were older than the rocks and the stones that formed the continents.

They had, the text claimed, been known to all the great writers of antiquity; and it even listed the names of a handful of ancient Greek philosophers who had explicitly mentioned them.

Angela had snorted under her breath when she translated that particular section. She was reasonably familiar with the works of two of the philosophers named in the book, and couldn't recall either of them ever mentioning anything quite as bizarre as vampires. And, she noticed, the author of the text had conspicuously failed to mention where these explicit references might be found, which was a sure sign that the references were simply a product of the writer's imagination.

Having established, to the author's satisfaction at least, that vampires existed, the text continued with the unsurprising claim that these creatures were not human in the usual sense of the word. They looked human, the writer stated, and were extremely difficult to identify, but they were actually superhuman because of their immortality, great physical beauty, and the enormous depth of knowledge gleaned over the ages that they had walked the earth.

Angela could see that, if this belief had become accepted by the general population in the days when it had been written, almost any reasonably attractive and well-educated man or woman could have been suspected of being a vampire. And, at the height of the various anti-vampire crazes that had swept Europe at intervals during the late Middle Ages, it was likely that many people would have suffered the consequences.

In the final section of what Angela was mentally calling 'the introduction', the writer set out the ultimate purpose of the treatise. In the following paragraphs, it was stated, fully detailed instructions would be provided so that mere mortals, *if seized with a true and honest wish and desire to achieve a state of sublime perfection*, might be elevated to a higher plane and actually join the legions of the undead.

She'd been right: what she was translating was a do-it-yourself vampire kit. Angela finished the introduction, read the Latin text and her English translation once more, then placed the page on one side of the desk.

Marco, who'd been sitting in a chair a few feet away from Angela while she worked on the text, stood up and walked over to the desk. He picked up the English translation she'd prepared, and nodded to her to continue working.

The next section of the text provided a stark reminder of the life of Carmelita Paganini, and of what she had tried to achieve. One sentence in particular served as a hideous confirmation of her apparent attempts to join the ranks of the undead, and even offered other people the opportunity of trying to join her. It also served as a further confirmation of Marco's contention that there was, indeed, an older source document that Carmelita must have seen.

This sentence read: *I now know the truth of the deeper realities that have governed the actions and conduct of my ancestors, and of the gift of eternal life that only the most dedicated adepts can enjoy, and I have had sight of the rules governing the conduct of those sacred rituals and measures which will enable seekers after this most exquisite of gifts to benefit to the fullest possible extent, to achieve immortality through the mingling of new blood with sacred relics, to become a sister of the night, a member of the holy brotherhood and sisterhood of blood, as I have done.*

Angela read the sentence again a couple of times, changed a few of the phrases to make it read better, and then put the page aside. The meaning seemed absolutely clear to her. Clear, but senseless. The woman who'd kept the journal and written those words had believed that she'd found the secret of eternal life, by becoming a vampire. Granted, the actual word 'vampire' didn't appear in the sentence, but the last few phrases seemed to be clear enough. Carmelita Paganini had believed she was going to live for ever, by feasting on a diet of blood and sacred relics – whatever they were.

There were only two problems with her belief, as far as Angela could see. First, vampires don't exist. They are a myth, a pre-mediaeval legend, with no basis in reality whatsoever. Second, Angela had found the woman's diary in a grave on the Isola di San Michele, lying underneath what was left of a wooden coffin, which contained the bones of the woman herself, the presumed author of the book, and she'd looked pretty dead to her.

Belief was one thing, reality quite another.

Angela turned round in her seat and looked across the room at where Marco was sitting in a comfortable easy chair. She knew what she was reading was rubbish and then she made the mistake of telling Marco precisely what she thought.

'I know exactly what this is,' Angela said. 'This book is some kind of do-it-yourself vampire kit. It's bullshit.'

The slight smile left the Italian's face and he stared at her in a hostile manner. 'I'm not interested in your opinion,' he snapped, 'only in your skill as a translator.'

Angela tried again. 'Look,' she said, 'the bones of the woman who wrote this are lying in a two-hundred-year-old tomb on the Isola di San Michele, crumbling away to dust. I think that's a fairly compelling argument to suggest that she didn't live for ever.'

'How do you know she wrote it?'

The possibility that the book had actually been authored by somebody other than the occupant of the old grave hadn't occurred to Angela. But it didn't change anything.

'I don't, but it was a reasonable assumption. But whether she did or not, I know – and I hope you do too – that vampires don't exist. They're a myth, nothing more.'

Marco didn't respond for a moment, then he shook his head. 'I already told you,' he said coldly, 'I'm not interested in your opinion, ill informed though it obviously is. Just get on with that translation.'

He stood up and walked across to where Angela was sitting. 'Have you found any references to the source yet?' he asked.

Angela nodded and pointed at the last sentence she'd translated. 'This says that she'd seen some other document, but I haven't found any mention of when she saw it or whereabouts it was.'

Marco scanned her translation swiftly and nodded. 'Good. Keep going. Let me know as soon as you find a mention of where the source might be hidden.'

In fact, the very next section of the Latin text seemed to provide a clue. An obscure clue, granted, but the first indication she had seen of where the other document, the mysterious 'source', might be concealed.

Carmelita had again referred to the ancient dead and the screaming dead, neither of which made very much sense to Angela, but the next sentence did provide what looked like a location. Once she'd translated it and rendered the words into readable English, it read: *Our revered guide and master has graced us with his sacred presence, and has instructed us in the ancient procedures and rituals, these being recorded by him for all time and for all acolytes in the Scroll of Amadeus, and then secreted beside the guardian in the new place where the legions of the dead reign supreme.*

She didn't like that last expression, though it could

obviously just refer to a graveyard somewhere; and the idea of a 'guardian' really troubled her. But, despite her unshakeable conviction that vampires were nothing more than a pre-mediaeval myth, it was the first part of that sentence that sent a chill down Angela's back.

It suggested that Carmelita had actually met, or at least seen, the person – Amadeus? – who had authored the source document. But that made no sense. Carmelita had died in the third decade of the nineteenth century. Whoever had written the source document must have died some seven hundred years earlier. Maybe she meant that there had been a succession of 'masters' through the ages, each acting as the head of the 'Vampire Society' or whatever name had been given to the group that Carmelita had been a member of.

But that wasn't what the Latin said. And Latin was a peculiarly precise language.

40

Behind the tomb on the island of San Michele, Bronson spotted a glint of metal from one side of the unconscious man's belt. Risking a closer look, he saw a dull black shape: the lower end of the magazine for a semi-automatic pistol, tucked into a quick-release leather pouch. There was no reason why a man would carry a magazine unless he also had a pistol, which meant he must be wearing a belt holster, not a shoulder rig.

Bronson looked up again at the man with the pistol. He was taking a couple of steps closer to him – shortening the range to ensure that his next shot would be the last he would have to fire.

The unconscious man was lying face-up, which meant the weapon had to be tucked into the small of his back, otherwise Bronson would already have seen it. Jerking him over on to his side, he rammed his other hand behind the man's back, inside the windcheater he was wearing.

His fingers closed around a familiar shape and, as the approaching man stopped and took aim, Bronson rolled sideways behind a vertical gravestone. As he moved, he racked back the slide of the automatic pistol with his left hand to chamber a round.

His movement took him just beyond the gravestone and, as he emerged from that fragile shelter, he aimed the pistol straight at the approaching figure, who swung his pistol towards him and fired two rapid shots.

Bronson flinched as a copper-jacketed nine-millimetre bullet slammed into the gravestone right beside him, but he held his aim and squeezed the trigger.

During his short career as an army officer, Bronson had become quite proficient with the Browning Hi-Power semi-automatic pistol, then the standard officer's sidearm, but he also knew how inaccurate such weapons were at anything other than very close range. So he wasn't surprised when his shot went wide.

But his target was clearly shocked to be under attack himself. He turned and ran, dodging around the gravestones as he fled.

Bronson rose cautiously to his feet, the pistol he'd grabbed – which he now saw actually was a nine-millimetre Browning, the weapon he'd got so used to firing in the Army – still pointing towards the fleeing figure. The second man had also taken to his heels, and was a few yards ahead of his accomplice, a bulky bag clutched in his left hand.

Bronson glanced down at the man lying on the ground. He was obviously unconscious, and no doubt would remain that way for some time. The noise of the shots had echoed around the island, and Bronson knew that people would start heading towards the area very soon, which would add to the confusion. He looked over at the tomb, at the two fleeing men, and made a decision.

What he should do was call the police, hand over the thug he'd knocked out and explain that he was one of the men who'd attacked him and Angela the previous evening. The problem was that he had absolutely no proof. And he knew only too well how the corporate police mind works: the most likely result of such actions would be that he – Bronson – would face a charge of assault or the Italian equivalent of grievous bodily harm.

No, that was never going to work. Even if by some miracle Bronson managed to avoid being arrested, it would be hours before his assailant would be in a fit state to answer questions himself. The best chance of finding Angela lay with the two men who were now about seventy yards away from him and running hard.

Bending over the unconscious man, Bronson unsnapped both the belt holster and the leather pouch containing the two spare magazines for the Browning, and put them in his pocket.

Then he sprinted after his quarry.

✝

41

Angela shook her head, and moved on. A second, much shorter, sentence followed, but two of the words in it were not listed in the Latin dictionary she was using. The translated sentence read: *There the open graves yawn ready where the fires burned in ages past, in the place where a little man once strutted and postured, and where a little* veglia funebre *once held sway.*

For a few moments, she stared at what she'd written. It sounded like directions to a specific place, and she had a vague idea what at least one of the two non-Latin words might mean, because it wasn't that different to a familiar English word. She looked at the desk in front of her, and at the other books and dictionaries stacked on it. One of them was a pocket-sized Italian–English dictionary. She picked it up, flicked through the pages until she reached the letter 'v', and read the entry for *veglia*. She didn't need to look up *funebre*, because the combination of the two words was listed in that entry.

A *veglia funebre* was a wake, or a vigil for the dead. Angela had guessed at the possible meaning of *funebre* because it looked so similar to the English 'funeral', or at least it probably had the same root.

Something else puzzled her about the way the sentence had been constructed. From what she knew of Italians, she doubted that any vigil for the dead could be described as 'little', and the repetition of the same phrase, the three Latin words which translated as 'little' – *parvus minor minimus* – so close together in the same sentence seemed to provide an unusual degree of emphasis, as if the writer was trying to convey some additional information.

Then there was the 'little man'. Angela didn't know a huge amount about Italian, and especially Venetian, history, but she did know that Napoleon had conquered Venice in the last decade of the eighteenth century, ending eleven hundred years of independence. His troops had sacked and virtually bankrupted the city; they had seized many of its most valuable treasures, shipping them off to Paris, where many remain to this day. He'd even stolen the Triumphal Quadriga – or Horses of St Mark – the famous bronze statues which for some time had graced the top of a triumphal arch in the French capital before the Venetians managed to have them returned.

When anybody spoke about Napoleon, the expressions 'petty tyrant' and 'little man' were often used as pejorative terms, though in reality the Emperor was of about average height for the time. The Venetians loathed him, for perfectly obvious and understandable reasons, and the expression Carmelita had used – *where a little man once strutted and postured* – could well refer to somewhere in Venice where Napoleon had spent some time – a district in the city, perhaps, or one of the islands. She couldn't think of any other historical figure who was likely to have been referred to as the 'little man'.

Then she had another thought, picked up the Italian–English dictionary again, and turned the pages until she reached the English word 'little'. The Italian equivalent was *po*, *poco*, *pochi* and other forms, depending on the noun being qualified, with *poco* probably the commonest. Angela wrote down all the variants at the bottom of the page she was working on, and added the two Italian words – *veglia funebre* – as well. Maybe there was a district of Venice called *Poca Veglia* or something similar.

There was a tourist map of the Venetian lagoon in the pile of books in front of her. She unfolded it and checked the names of the six districts, or *sestieri*, of the city, but none was even slightly similar to what she was looking for. Then she expanded her search to the islands of the lagoon, moving outwards from Venice itself. Even then, she nearly missed it, because she was expecting to see something like 'Isola di Poca Veglia', and she was already checking the names in the southern end of the lagoon, near Chioggia, when her subconscious mind raised a flag. Her glance snapped back to the area between Venice and the Lido and there, due south of Venice itself, well away from any other islands and fairly close to the Lido, she saw it: Poveglia.

In fact, it wasn't an island: it was three islands, shaped like an inverted triangle, with the point to the south. There was a small, regularly shaped, possibly even octagonal, island to the south, with two much larger landmasses, separated by a narrow canal that cut the island in two, directly to the north of it.

Angela looked back at the text she'd translated, and then again at the map of the *Laguna Veneta*. That had to be it. 'Po' and 'veglia' combined in a single word. That must be the place that Carmelita was referring to in her very simple and basic textual code.

But what about Napoleon? Was there any connection between the Emperor and the small island in the lagoon? One of the books stacked on the desk in front of her was an English-language guide to the history of Venice. She pulled it out of the pile, checked the index and then opened it to a section about midway through.

'Yes,' she breathed as she read the entry. During the Napoleonic Wars, the Emperor had used Poveglia as a storehouse for weapons, and there had been several vicious battles fought on and around the island. Napoleon definitely had a connection to the place, and might well have 'strutted and postured' there.

Angela was sure she'd identified the right island. But there had to be more to it than that. Just stating that the long-lost document was secreted on Poveglia was not enough: for a search to succeed, much more information was needed. Although the island looked reasonably small, she guessed it would still take a large team of people several days to search it.

She continued with her translation. The next line contained the word *specula*, which Angela had to look up. The dictionary suggested a number of translations, but a 'tower' or 'watchtower' seemed the most likely, and the Latin word *campana* or 'bell' seemed to confirm it. On the map of the lagoon it looked as if there was a tower of some sort at the southern end of the largest of the three islands.

She felt her excitement growing as she realized she might be close to identifying the exact place where the ancient document was hidden, but then her thoughts tumbled back down to earth with a bump when the further realization struck her. Marco would only keep her alive as long as she was useful to him, and the moment she had identified the hiding place and the old documents had been recovered, she didn't think he would have any further use for her.

Could she delay completing the translation? Or would Marco guess what she was trying to do and impose a brutal punishment in retribution? Angela shuddered as she remembered the jar and its collection of hideous relics, and bent forward again over the pages.

She heard a soft footfall on the wooden floor behind her

and glanced round to see Marco looking over her shoulder at the work she was doing.

'You've found something,' he said, more a statement than a question.

Angela nodded. 'I think so, yes.'

'Show me.'

She pointed to the last sentence she'd translated. 'The author of this section of the text employed a fairly simple word code, but it looks to me as if she was referring to an island called Poveglia. Have you heard of it?'

Marco nodded, almost sadly. 'Every Venetian knows about Poveglia,' he said quietly.

42

When the guard arrived with her midday meal, Marietta stared at him listlessly. She absolutely believed what he'd said to her that morning, and she'd resigned herself to the fact that she was going to die, painfully and unpleasantly, in that damp cellar within a matter of hours. There was no point in even attempting to establish a rapport with the man, of asking for mercy or anything else. His callous attitude towards her, and towards Benedetta, had become obvious. As far as the guard and the other men were concerned, Marietta and all of the other nameless victims of the bizarre cult were simply animals who would be slaughtered when their time came.

The guard followed his usual routine and placed the tray on the floor close to the wooden bed, then picked up the other tray he'd brought down that morning. Despite the terror that bubbled inside her, Marietta had eventually eaten all the food he'd supplied, just as she expected she would finally eat whatever meal she had now been provided with.

'This is your last meal,' the guard said, glancing at her, 'so you might as well make the most of it. I'll bring warm water and a towel for you to wash yourself later this afternoon, ready for the ceremony tonight.'

'And if I refuse? If I simply tell you and your revolting friends to go to hell, what then?'

The guard shrugged. 'That's your choice,' he said, 'but if you don't do what we want, you'll taste the taser again. And if you still don't cooperate, I'll ask a couple of the men to come down here and have a bit of fun with you before the ceremony. They'll enjoy it, but I don't suppose you will. It's up to you, really.'

Marietta held herself together until the man had walked out of the cellar, then she dissolved into tears.

43

Bronson sprinted across the graveyard after the fleeing men. He paused for a few seconds beside the tomb of the twin angels, staring at it with a sense of déjà vu. The stone side of the grave had been smashed open – a hammer and chisel were lying on the ground beside the shattered stone – and what was left of the ancient coffin was scattered about. The grave itself was obviously very old, and most of the wood had long since disintegrated to reveal the skeletal remains of the tomb's occupant. This corpse had also been decapitated, but this time the head was nowhere in sight. Could that explain what was in the bag that one of the men had been carrying?

Bronson shook his head and set off in pursuit of the two men. He wasn't concerned about them getting too far ahead of him, because they must have used a boat to get to the island. From the direction they were running, this boat was moored in the inlet at the northern end of the island, where Bronson's own vessel was tied up.

The last thing he wanted to do was storm on to the jetty and start a firefight. He needed the two men to make their getaway, so that he could go after them.

Instead of following right behind the two men, he angled over to one side and did his best to increase speed, though having to dodge around gravestones and tree trunks hampered his progress somewhat. The sound of a powerboat engine starting close to him – just a few yards away – indicated that he must be right by the jetty. He stopped and made his way cautiously in the direction from which the sound had come.

In a couple of seconds he reached the edge of the jetty, but remained out of sight as he surveyed the scene in front of him. A blue powerboat was already about ten yards out from the water's edge, and gathering speed. The man who'd shot at him was sitting in the bow staring back towards the island, his pistol held low in his right hand, clearly waiting for Bronson to show himself, while the other man concentrated on getting the boat away from the jetty as quickly as possible.

Bronson memorized what the men were wearing and the colour and type of the boat, and waited until they turned right out of the inlet, and the craft was lost to view. Then he stepped on to the jetty, ran down to where his own boat was moored, released the line and climbed aboard, starting the engine as he sat down on the padded seat.

He opened the throttle and the boat surged forwards. He pulled it round in a tight circle and headed for the entrance to the inlet, then swung the wheel to the right, to follow the other craft.

As he emerged into the open waters of the Venetian lagoon, he looked ahead. The blue boat was already perhaps a hundred yards in front of him, heading more or less east. But, as he turned in the same direction, the man in the bow pointed urgently back towards him. The other man glanced behind as well, and immediately turned the boat to the right.

Bronson knew he'd been spotted, and cursed. Wherever the two men had been heading, they were obviously not going that way any longer. They had turned south-west, towards Venice, and Bronson guessed their intentions. If they'd stayed out in the open waters, he'd have been able to follow them even at a distance. No doubt they were now heading into the city so that they could try to lose him in the notorious maze of Venice's canals and waterways.

†

44

Angela looked up at Marco. He seemed strangely subdued by her mention of the island.

'What is it about Poveglia?' she asked.

He stared at her for a moment, then shook his head. 'You really don't know?' he replied. 'Your ignorance staggers me.'

He reached forward, plucked a book out of the pile on the desk and slammed it down in front of her. 'It's all in here,' he snapped. 'Read it and educate yourself.'

Pulling a mobile phone from his pocket, Marco stalked across to the other side of the drawing-room and held a brief conversation with someone. It sounded as if he was issuing orders.

Angela glanced after him, then down at the book. It looked like a fairly typical multi-language tourist guide to Venice, but the title promised that it would reveal the hidden stories of the Venetian lagoon: 'the Venice that tourists never see', as the author claimed. The introduction pointed out that the city hosted around three million tourists every year, although most of them never got beyond Venice itself and the islands of Murano and Burano. There was a short chapter that dealt only with Poveglia, and by the time she'd finished reading it, Angela knew exactly why Carmelita had talked about the 'ancient dead' and the 'screaming dead'.

The dead on Poveglia greatly outnumbered the living in Venice. The island was covered in plague pits, a legacy of one of the most terrible periods in Venetian history. In the outbreak of 1576 alone, it was estimated that fifty thousand people had died from bubonic plague. Fifty thousand was only about ten thousand less than the total population of the old city today. And there had been at least twenty-two attacks of the plague before that one. According to some calculations, the bones of over one hundred and sixty thousand people lay in shallow graves on Poveglia.

The island had been used as a *lazaretto*, a quarantine station, in the fifteenth and sixteenth centuries, in an attempt to prevent the spread of infectious diseases to Venice. The city was a maritime republic, almost entirely dependent upon trade for its survival, and visiting traders who wished to step ashore in Venice would first be required to undergo a lengthy period of isolation. In fact, it was the Venetians who invented the concept of quarantine, the word deriving from the Italian *quaranta giorni*, or 'forty days'.

JAMES BECKER

But even this procedure clearly hadn't protected the city from the ravages of the Black Death, as the sheer number of deaths throughout that period bore witness. The city authorities had been ruthless in their attempts to keep Venice clear of the plague. Anyone displaying the slightest signs of infection would be shipped out immediately to Poveglia or one of the other *lazarettos* in the lagoon. One island was actually named after this function: Lazzaretto Nuovo.

According to the author of the book, it was popularly believed that weak but still-living victims of the plague were either tossed on the burning funeral pyres or thrown into the plague pits amongst the decomposing bodies, and then buried alive. Angela thought that the expression 'screaming dead' barely even hinted at the horrific events that must have taken place on Poveglia some half a millennium earlier.

And the horrors apparently hadn't stopped there. Much later, in the early twentieth century, a mental hospital had been built on the island. Some of the inmates had reportedly been subjected to inhuman tortures, mutilated and then butchered by a notoriously sadistic doctor. This man had apparently then gone mad himself, and had climbed to the top of the old bell tower and jumped to his death.

It was no wonder that the island was hardly ever mentioned in the guidebooks, and was almost never visited. In fact, the book stated that Poveglia was officially off-limits to everyone, locals and visitors. Angela couldn't think of a single reason why anyone could possibly want to go there. And that, of course, meant that it would provide an excellent hiding place for the ancient document Marco was seeking.

She put the book to one side and turned back to her translation, but the text didn't seem to provide any further details of where the source document might be hidden. Angela looked at the detailed map that was included in the chapter on Poveglia, jotted down a few notes, principally dates and events, and then sat back.

She didn't think it would have been buried in the ground somewhere, not least because of the plague pits that were the dominant feature of the island's soil, so that left one of the ruined buildings on Poveglia. The document couldn't possibly be hidden in the lunatic asylum – part of which had apparently also been used as a retirement home for senior citizens, a thought which made Angela shudder again – because the building hadn't been erected until 1922. Several of the other structures were also comparatively recent, certainly built after Carmelita's death.

The oldest structure on the island was the bell tower, the only surviving remnant of the twelfth-century church of San Vitale, which had been abandoned and then destroyed hundreds of years earlier. The translation Angela had completed was quite specific. It stated that after the source document had been prepared it had then been *secreted beside the guardian in the new place where the legions of the dead reign supreme.* Apart from the reference to the 'guardian', which still bothered her because she didn't fully understand it, the meaning was perfectly clear. The document had originally been hidden somewhere else but, after Carmelita had seen it, for some reason it had then been concealed in a different hiding place.

If her reading of the Latin was correct, and assuming the document still existed, that meant there was only one place it could possibly have been hidden on Poveglia: it had to be somewhere in the bell tower.

✝

45

Marietta lay on her back on the thin and uncomfortable mattress, eyes wide open and staring at the cracked and discoloured plaster on the ceiling above her. The food tray sat untouched on the floor beside the bed.

When the guard had casually, callously, confirmed her worst fears, when she had finally realized that there really was no hope, it had driven all other thoughts from her mind. The idea of eating or drinking didn't even occur to her. Her mind was filled with vivid images of the horrendous events of the previous evening – of Benedetta strapped on the stone table, struggling futilely against her bonds, her screams reduced to muffled grunts and moans as she was violently raped and her blood drained from the wound on her neck.

Now, Marietta knew what fate awaited her, knew that sometime – sometime soon – the guards would appear in the cellar and instruct her to wash her body. Would she resist? And, if so, how? There were no weapons she could use against her captors, no arguments or persuasion that would do anything to alter the events she knew would take place in the next few hours.

The choice was stark. Marietta was a fighter. But she was also a realist. If she refused to obey orders she knew the guards would simply rape her or beat her into submission, or just strip her naked and then hose her down. Her best, and in fact her only, choice was to do it the easy way: do her best to detach her mind from the awful reality of what was going to happen to her and hope it would all be over quickly.

She thought again of her family, of her father and mother, and of the mental anguish she knew they would be feeling after her disappearance. When they'd read reports in the newspapers, or seen television programmes about the other girls who had vanished from the streets of Venice, her mother had always said that the worst part was the uncertainty. For a mother, not knowing if her daughter was alive or dead was a burden not many could bear. At least if a body was found, the grieving process could start: the news would be devastating, in the proper sense of that word, but the family would be able to make their farewells, and then try their best to move on.

But when a person vanished, leaving no trace behind, every waking moment would be a torture. That could be the day where two grim-faced police officers would knock at the door to bring the final, dreadful news. Or – and this was the hope that Marietta was sure every mother would cling to – perhaps that would be the day when her daughter would at last walk back through the door.

Marietta closed her eyes again, but still the tears came, coursing down her cheeks, because she knew, beyond all reasonable doubt, that her own mother would never, ever, find out what had happened to her. And she felt her heart breaking as she realized this.

She took a deep breath and tried to get herself back under control. She knew she was going to die, but she was determined to do her best to die with dignity, not to scream, not to shout. And, above all, not to cry. She rubbed angrily at her cheeks with her free hand. She would show them.

She was a Venetian, after all, descended – so she'd been told – from important, perhaps even noble, blood. No matter what they did to her, she would cling to what shreds of dignity she could during her ordeal.

46

Angela was so engrossed in what she was doing that she didn't see or hear the drawing-room door swing open. She was just suddenly aware of a pungent and acrid smell, and of Marco jumping to his feet.

She turned round in her chair to look behind her and saw a figure clad in an all-enveloping black cloak, the hood covering his face, moving silently across the wooden floor towards her. She started to rise, but immediately Marco shouted out to her, 'Sit down and face the wall.'

The smell grew stronger as the figure approached, and Angela was seized by an overwhelming feeling of horror and dread, made worse by the uncanny silence with which the man moved. Even though she couldn't see him, because she was obeying Marco's commands to the letter and staring fixedly at the wall behind the desk, she knew that the man had stopped directly behind her.

Marco strode across towards her as well, and stood beside her.

'We may have it, Master,' he said, pointing down at Angela's translations of the Latin text.

'Where?' The voice was little more than a whisper, a sibilant hiss.

'Poveglia,' Marco said.

There was a short silence as the new arrival apparently digested this information, and then Angela heard his quiet voice again. 'Get the boat ready,' he said, 'and bring her as well.'

✝

47

Bronson pushed the throttle all the way forward to the stop, and the bow of the speedboat lifted in response to the increased revolutions of the outboard engine's propeller.

Ahead of him, the blue powerboat had also increased speed, and was now clearly heading directly towards the square inlet on the northern side of Venice that was known as the Sacca della Misericordia. There were two canals that opened off the inlet, and any number of smaller canals that connected with those two. Bronson knew that once they got into the canal system, he would have his work cut out trying to keep track of them, so he kept up his speed, heedless of the increasing number of boats manoeuvring in the water around him.

The blue powerboat swung left into the Sacca della Misericordia, weaving around *vaporettos* and gondolas and launches and various other types of craft, the driver pushing the boat much too quickly in the congested waters.

Behind him, Bronson was starting to close the gap, simply because he wasn't yet in the thick of the water traffic. But as he, too, entered the inlet, he was forced to reduce speed considerably. A *vaporetto* was heading straight for him, probably aiming for the Fondamente Nuove *vaporetto* stop down to the south-east, and Bronson was forced to turn the boat hard to the right to avoid a collision. He straightened up and steered around the passenger craft, the driver shaking his fist angrily at Bronson and mouthing expletives as he, too, took evasive action. Bronson ignored him, his attention still fixed on his quarry as he instinctively manoeuvred the boat around all the other vessels in the congested area.

The blue powerboat steered to the left of the Sacca della Misericordia and, still travelling quickly, started heading down the Rio di Noale canal, which would lead them directly to the Grand Canal and its myriad tributaries. Bronson knew that if his quarry managed to reach there, they could vanish into any one of the smaller canals, and he would probably never see them again. At all costs, he had to keep them in sight.

He increased speed as much as he dared – smashing the boat into the side wall of the canal or into another vessel would absolutely ensure that his pursuit would end prematurely – and powered into the canal after them.

A short distance down the canal the waterway split in a Y-junction, the wider Rio di Noale veering to the right, while a slightly narrower canal, the Rio di San Felice, lay straight ahead. That was the quickest route straight through to the Grand Canal, Bronson guessed, as the blue boat kept to the left of the stone breakwater that marked the junction.

Then he saw something that made him smile. At the end of the canal, where it narrowed still further, was a veritable logjam of gondolas, all manoeuvring either in or out of the Grand Canal at the junction ahead. The blue powerboat would have to slow down to a crawl to get through the mêlée. Either that, or they'd have to take a different route.

In fact, the blue boat did both: it slowed and turned. Bronson saw the wake diminish markedly as the driver pulled back the throttle, slowing down, and then accelerated again as he steered the boat into the entrance to another canal on the left-hand side.

Bronson eased back the throttle, ensuring that he was travelling slowly enough to make the turn, then accelerated again once he was inside the other canal. The sound of the two fast revving engines on the boats echoed off the walls of the surrounding buildings, and the waves from their wakes slapped hard against the stones that lined the canal.

The waterway ran straight for a short distance, but at the end it swung through about ninety degrees to the left. There were also two other canals that had junctions with the one they were in, both on the left-hand side and leading away from the Grand Canal. Bronson had managed to keep up with the other boat so far, and he knew that he could go on chasing the two men through the canals of Venice until he ran out of fuel or miscalculated some corner and smashed up the boat, but this wouldn't help him to find Angela. Instead, what he needed to do was convince the men he was chasing that he'd given up. He knew they wouldn't head for home until they were sure he was no longer on their tail.

But how could he convince the two men that he was a spent force? At that moment he could think of only one way to do this. It was a risky manoeuvre, and if it went wrong, he'd be dead in minutes. It all depended on timing, and the inherent inaccuracy of semi-automatic pistols, especially when such pistols were being fired from an unstable platform, like a boat travelling at speed.

The driver of the blue boat turned the wheel hard to the left, steered the vessel into the first of the subsidiary canals and increased speed again. This canal was slightly narrower than the one they'd just left, and there were only a few other boats in it, mainly moored at various landing stages and jetties along the sides. There were no gondolas in sight. It was as good a place as any.

Bronson pulled the Browning semi-automatic pistol from his pocket, pointed it in the general direction of the boat in front of him, and pulled the trigger twice. The shots boomed out, deafeningly loud in the narrow canal. As far as he could see, neither bullet went anywhere near its target, but that wasn't his intention. He wanted a reaction. A reaction he could use to his own advantage.

The driver of the blue boat obliged him.

He was just coming up to the entrance to another canal on the right, and swung the boat into it. As he did so, the man in the bow of the boat raised his own pistol and fired off a shot towards Bronson.

That was what he'd been waiting for. Pulling back on the throttle, Bronson spun the wheel hard to the right, to make sure that the boat would circle in more or less the same place. Then, rising in his seat, he clutched at his chest and slumped down out of sight, the Browning still in his hand, just in case the two men decided to come alongside his boat for a closer look.

From his position on the floor of the powerboat, Bronson could see nothing except the sky and the tops of the buildings that lined the canal, so he was relying entirely on his ears to deduce what was happening. He heard the sound of the engine of the other boat fade away sharply, which meant the driver had chopped back the throttle. Then the engine noise – and Bronson was sure it was the same engine – increased again, and appeared to be getting closer, though it was difficult to be certain of this because of the way the noise echoed from both sides of the man-made canyon. It certainly sounded as though the two men were approaching to make sure he was dead.

Bronson checked the Browning was ready to fire, and waited as the sound of the other boat's engine grew louder.

48

About an hour later, Angela was taken out of the main door of the house into the pale watery light of a cloudy afternoon in the Venetian lagoon.

After the hooded man had left the drawing-room, Marco had instructed her to make a complete translation of the rest of that section of the diary as quickly as possible, obviously hoping that the remainder of the Latin text would provide details of the precise location of the source document. It didn't. The only reference Angela found was to the 'campanile of light', which just served to confirm her assumption that the document must be somewhere in the ancient bell tower. From her reading of the chapter dealing with the history of Poveglia, she knew that the bell tower had for a time been converted into a lighthouse. But she still had no idea exactly where to start looking.

Marco and another of his men hustled her down the path towards the jetty at the end of the island, where two men were already waiting, standing in the stern of a powerboat, the rumble of the engine clearly audible.

'Why do you want me to go with you?' Angela asked, as Marco pushed her inside the small cabin.

'You've read and translated the Latin,' he replied. 'We don't know what we'll find when we get there, but there might be something, some clue, that you'll see and understand but we won't. That's why you're here.'

'What happens if you don't find what you're looking for?'

'You'd better pray that we do. Finding the source document is the only thing that's keeping you alive right now. If it isn't there, then we have no further use for you.'

The casual, almost conversational, tone of his voice scared Angela even more than the words he'd used, and she sat in silence as Marco handcuffed her wrists together, looping the link between the cuffs behind a hand rail, immobilizing her. Then he left the cabin.

A few moments later the door opened again and the hooded man entered, the now familiar stench preceding him. Angela shrank back in her seat as the figure passed right beside her, and then took a seat at the opposite end of the cabin.

Moments later, she felt the boat start to move, and soon the bow was cutting through the choppy waters of the lagoon, the waves thumping rhythmically against the hull.

She had no idea how long the journey would take,

because she didn't know where she'd been imprisoned, and the view through the side windows of the boat was so restricted that she could see almost nothing of her surroundings. And in truth, her thoughts were dominated by the hooded man she was sharing the cabin with. He had said nothing to her, and gave no sign that he was even aware of her presence, but the all-pervasive smell of rotting meat seemed to fill the air, and she was simply terrified in case he came close or, worse, touched her.

A few minutes later, Marco returned to the cabin and sat down opposite Angela, which actually made her feel safer and slightly more comfortable. At least the menace Marco represented was clear and tangible. The hooded man inspired only feelings of horror and revulsion, which were far worse than any physical threat.

'Who is that man?' she asked quietly, nodding towards the silent figure. 'He terrifies me.'

Marco smiled bleakly. 'He should.'

49

Bronson tensed as the sound of the boat drew closer, and a moment later he felt a slight bump as some part of the other craft touched his boat. He kept his eyes half-open, and lay as still as possible, the Browning held loosely by his side but ready to fire.

He could hear the two men talking as they manoeuvred their boat alongside his, their efforts hampered by the fact that the engine of Bronson's craft was still running, and the boat was describing a small circle at the junction of the two canals.

'I can see him,' one of the men said. 'He's not moving.'

'He must be dead then,' the other replied, 'or at least he's badly wounded. Let's get out of here before a police launch comes along.'

Bronson heard the noise of another boat's engine approaching, he thought from the opposite direction, though it was difficult to tell. But what he was quite certain about was that the blue boat was moving away. That sound was unmistakable.

For about thirty seconds he did nothing, then he eased himself up cautiously, and risked a quick glance over the side of the vessel. There was a slight bend in the canal to the east and, as he looked in that direction, he saw the blue powerboat disappear around it. The moment it was out of sight, he sat up, centred the steering wheel to stop the circular motion of the boat, grabbed his map of the Venetian waterways, and quickly worked out where he was.

He'd ended up in a canal called the Rio della Racchetta, and the men he'd been chasing would have to continue down the adjoining waterway until they reached the larger Rio del Gesuiti, because they'd already passed the only other canal entrance. What he didn't know was which way they'd turn when they reached it. Left would take them the shorter distance, out into the Canale delle Fondamente Nuove, the open water that lay on the north-east side of Venice. If they swung right, they'd have a longer run down the canal until they reached the *Canal Grande* – the Grand Canal – itself.

A wooden launch – its engine had been what Bronson had heard – swept down one side of the powerboat, the driver staring at him with some curiosity as he passed. He had obviously seen the pirouettes that Bronson's craft had been describing in the water, and probably thought he was drunk.

Bronson ignored him. His only concern was to try to second-guess the men he was following. The trouble was, he had very little to go on. When the blue powerboat had pulled away from the Island of the Dead, the driver had headed south-east. If his destination had been one of the islands at the north-eastern end of the *Laguna Veneta*, somewhere near Burano, for example, Bronson would have expected them to head in that direction. The fact that they'd continued along the north side of Venice suggested that they were going to sail around the eastern end of the island, and perhaps then turn south-west, towards the other end of the lagoon, where he knew there was a scattering of small islands.

It was a long shot, though, and for perhaps half a minute, Bronson sat at the wheel of the boat, his mind racked by indecision. He had just one chance. If he guessed wrong, he'd never see the blue boat again, which would mean he'd lose Angela. He had to get it right.

His mind made up, he spun the wheel and opened the throttle, sending the boat speeding south down the Rio della Racchetta, retracing the course he'd followed just minutes earlier. At the end of the canal, he turned the boat right and almost immediately left, back into the Rio di San Felice, where he'd seen the jam caused by the gondolas. As he made the turn, he prayed that this time the waterway would be clear.

It wasn't, but there were far fewer boats in the way. Bronson kept the speed up as much as he dared, then pulled the throttle back as he reached the nearest gondola. He started to weave his way through the jostling boats, his passage attracting a torrent of abuse in high-speed Italian, all of which he ignored.

A couple of minutes later he was through, and swung the boat to the left, into the *Canal Grande* itself. As he did so, he glanced to his left and saw a long wooden-hulled launch bearing down on him, just yards away. Bronson knew immediately that if he continued turning towards the boat, he'd never miss it. He reacted instantly, spinning the steering wheel to the right and pushed the throttle forward, sending his boat straight across the bow of the oncoming vessel.

There was a bang from the rear of Bronson's boat, as the bow of the much larger launch hit the left-hand rear of his powerboat, cracking the fibreglass and scattering paint flakes across the water. But the outboard motor was undamaged, and he was certain that the impact had been well above the waterline, so there was no danger of him taking in water. And in fact fibreglass boats of the type he was in were so full of air pockets that they were virtually unsinkable.

The driver of the launch immediately reduced speed, obviously intending to do the Italian marine equivalent of exchanging names and addresses. But Bronson had not the slightest intention of stopping or even slowing down. His boat's throttle was still wide open and the outboard engine roaring, so he twitched the steering wheel to the left and sped away, heedless of the angry shouts echoing from behind him.

The Grand Canal in Venice follows an S-shaped course from the Stazione Ferrovie dello Stato Santa Lucia, the railway station, to its southern end near the Piazza San Marco, where it opens out into the Bacino di San Marco and the much wider *canale* of the same name. Bronson had joined the canal about a third of the way along, so he knew he would have to contend with the fairly heavy water traffic for some time before he could get into the clearer and more open waters to the south of the city. And then, of course, he would have the even more difficult task of spotting the blue powerboat carrying the two men, amongst the hundreds of similar craft that plied the waters in and around Venice. And that assumed that he'd been right in his guess that the boat would be heading into the waters of the lagoon somewhere to the south of the city.

He also knew that although the men he'd been following now believed that he was dead or badly wounded, they would still be keeping their own eyes peeled for any sign of pursuit, and paying particular attention to anybody who looked like him. There was nothing he could do about the design and colour of his boat, but Bronson realized that there were things – three things, in fact – that he could do to try to change his own appearance.

He was wearing his black leather jacket, so he took this off and dropped it on the floor of the boat beside him. Underneath, he had on a plain white shirt, which would give him an entirely different appearance to anyone viewing him from a distance. And in his shirt pocket he had a baseball cap and a pair of large sunglasses with impenetrable mirrored black lenses. He took out the sunglasses and slipped them on as he powered the boat down the Grand Canal towards the open water at its end, then settled the cap on his head, ensuring that it completely covered the dressing over the wound on his scalp.

Unless he got so close to the other boat that the men in it could actually see his features, Bronson guessed that he now looked quite different. Rolling his shoulders to ease away some of his tension, and trying hard not to think about what could be happening to Angela, he focused on the task in hand: spotting the other vessel, a challenge that made finding a needle in a haystack seem easy by comparison.

50

Marco released Angela's handcuffs, and led her out of the cabin. The boat was already moored, a bow and stern line attached, and it was easy enough to step from the side of the vessel onto the landing stage. She looked around. The boat was positioned a short distance down the channel between the small octagonal island that lay at the southern tip of Poveglia and the middle island. In the distance, looking south, she could make out buildings on the Lido.

The octagonal island looked like a flat-topped fort, the inward-sloping sides made of stone, and mooring alongside that would have been difficult. But that wasn't their objective. A short distance along the level stone landing stage that marked the southern end of the larger island was an impressive-looking building. It reminded Angela of a typical Venetian *palazzo*, and must, she thought, have been part of the retirement home on the island, before being abandoned in the 1960s. The façade was covered with a web-like exoskeleton of rusting scaffolding. That, Angela knew from her research, was not part of some renovation project, but had been erected almost a quarter of a century earlier simply to stop the buildings from falling down.

She looked over to the north-east, and there, beyond the trees, rose the imposing stone bell tower, looking something like a church steeple, its tall red-tiled roof supporting a large metal crucifix at the very top. All the openings in the tower appeared to have been bricked up, possibly when the scaffolding was put in place. A chill wind blew in suddenly from the waters of the lagoon, bringing with it a swirl of mist, and from somewhere nearby Angela heard the faint sound of a bell ringing.

She glanced at Marco. 'Did you hear that bell?' she asked, and pointed towards the tower. 'I thought it came from over there.'

He looked at her dismissively. 'Impossible,' he said. 'The bell was removed in nineteen thirteen.'

'I know what I heard,' Angela insisted, but her voice lacked conviction. She'd read in the guidebook that the sound of a bell was still sometimes heard on the island.

The hooded man emerged from the cabin of the boat and began moving silently – his feet never seemed to make a sound – towards the derelict building that lay closest to the tower.

Marco checked that Angela's handcuffs were still secured, and then pushed her in the same direction, two of his men following behind.

The short procession entered the building through an opening that had obviously once been a doorway, but which now gaped open to the elements. Inside, it was a scene of almost total devastation. Rubbish and debris lay strewn across the floor. Plaster had fallen off the walls and ceiling, and in several places the floor timbers of the storey above had broken, and pointed downwards into the ground-floor room like long, blackened and jagged teeth. On many of the pieces of surviving plaster, graffiti had been scrawled. Cast-iron radiators stood forlornly against the walls, rust covering the areas where the paint had flaked off. In one corner, two windows had disappeared, and a heavy growth of vegetation had forced its way inside and was beginning the long slow process of reclaiming the building.

Angela was not of a nervous disposition, but she knew absolutely that if she had had any choice in the matter, she would have walked out, climbed back on to the boat and never, ever returned to Poveglia.

The very fabric of the building seemed to echo with the cries of the dying, and the knowledge that the thin soil on the island covered the bones of tens of thousands of plague victims weighed heavily upon her. If there was any place on the face of the earth where the dead could speak, this, this island of Poveglia, was probably it. She could so easily imagine the giant fires consuming piles of smouldering bodies, and the shallow graves tended by workers who were themselves diseased. Through it all would stalk the bizarre and otherworldly figures of the doctors, trying vainly to fight a contagion that they didn't understand and could not cure, their only protection against the disease being the hook-nosed masks they wore, filled with peppers and spices which they believed might filter out the infective elements. These men must have looked like massive predatory birds as they tried in vain to bring some relief to the sufferers.

Suddenly, a movement caught her eye and Angela gave a little cry of alarm. A shadow played across the wall as a beam of sunlight entered the building, and she could almost swear that she saw the shape of a man wearing a beak-like mask somewhere outside the building. Then the wind blew again and the shape dissolved and reformed, as the branches of the tree shifted.

'Come on,' Marco ordered, tugging at Angela's arm.

Following the hooded man, they stepped over and around the debris to the far end of the room and made their way carefully over to the bell tower.

Inside, little light penetrated because the windows and other openings had been bricked up. The tower extended above their heads, a vertical well of darkness. In the gloom, they saw the first few steps of a rusting spiral staircase which ran around the walls of the tower.

'So where is it?' Marco demanded.

For an instant, Angela didn't realize that he was talking to her, then she pulled herself together.

'The text doesn't say,' she replied. 'It just seems to

suggest that it's hidden somewhere here, in this place. There's nothing else I can tell you, and I did translate all the rest of the Latin.'

Marco looked at her for a long moment, then switched his glance to the stairs before turning to one of his men and issuing a crisp order in Italian. The man turned and strode swiftly out of the tower.

'We need torches,' he said. 'I don't think the document is hidden anywhere down here. People still come to this island – you can tell that from the graffiti they've scrawled on the walls – and if it had been found already, we would have known about it. So it's probably hidden somewhere that people wouldn't normally visit or explore.' He looked again at Angela. 'I hope you're not afraid of heights,' he said, 'because my guess is that Carmelita, or whoever hid it, probably put it right at the top of the bell tower. You're going up there to find it for us.'

When the man he'd sent back to the boat returned, half a dozen torches of different sizes in his hands, Marco stepped across to Angela and unlocked her handcuffs. Then he picked up the biggest torch, a squat, grey and clearly heavy instrument with a rechargeable battery, and shone a powerful beam directly upwards, tracing the course that the spiral staircase followed until it reached a level platform.

'That can't be the top of the tower,' Marco said. 'It's not high enough. There must be another staircase above that.'

'I don't want to do this,' Angela murmured. 'I really don't want to go up there.'

Marco shrugged. 'You've got two choices. Do this and you'll live, at least for a little while longer. Refuse, and I'll have one of my men strangle you right now and dump your body here. It's up to you.'

For a few seconds Angela stared at him, but she knew she had no option. She was quite certain that Marco would order her death with as little compunction as he would order a cup of coffee. She grimaced, reached down and picked up two of the smaller torches, then she strode across to the foot of the spiral staircase.

She switched on one of the torches and shone the beam at the metal treads in front of her. There was little dust or debris visible on them, and even the banister appeared to be intact and in reasonably good condition. She guessed that some of the infrequent and illegal visitors to the island probably climbed at least some distance up into the tower out of idle curiosity, if nothing else. That was good news, because it meant that the staircase should support her weight. Cautiously, she rested her left foot on the lowest tread, then began to climb.

Behind her, she heard the sound of footsteps and glanced back: Marco was following, torch in hand.

'Keep going,' he snapped. 'I'm just here to make sure you do what you're told.'

The staircase wound up the inside of the tower. For the first few steps, it felt extremely solid, but the higher she climbed the more unhappy Angela felt, realizing she was relying on bolts and fittings that had been in place for a very long time, without the benefit of any kind of maintenance or repair. She moved as close as she could to the wall, where she hoped the old metal might be stronger, and tested each step before she put her full weight on it.

The climb seemed endless, but eventually she stepped on to a platform that she guessed was virtually at the top of the main part of the tower, and looked around. Again, there was graffiti on the walls, which meant that other people had made the same climb fairly recently. There was no obvious hiding place at that level.

Marco appeared beside her within seconds. 'I told you the bell had been removed,' he said, pointing at a substantial beam that ran from one wall of the tower to the opposite side, and which had clearly been designed to support some heavy object.

'I did hear something,' Angela insisted.

She looked at the walls of the bell chamber, and at the bricked-up openings in the side walls, and shivered.

'I suppose this was where he jumped from?' she said quietly.

'Who?' Marco asked.

'The mad doctor. If the story about him in that book was true, I mean.'

'Nobody knows, and I don't care.' Marco looked all around them, quickly reaching the same conclusion as

Angela. 'There's nothing here,' he said. 'We need to get to the very top.'

Another short flight of stairs brought them to a second level, above the old bell chamber. And the stairs stopped there. Attached to one wall was a steel ladder, around which metal hoops had been bolted to prevent anyone climbing it from falling off. Like the spiral staircase, the metal looked old and rusty, and none too safe.

'Keep going,' Marco ordered again.

Angela swallowed hard. Heights didn't particularly bother her, but she had a horror of falling, and even the metal hoops around the ladder weren't much of a safeguard against that happening. But she knew she had no option. She tucked both the torches into the waistband of her trousers, because she'd definitely need both hands free to make the climb, then reached up and began the ascent.

It wasn't a long climb, perhaps twenty steps in all, and at the top she was faced with a wooden trapdoor set into the underside of a narrow platform. There was no bolt or catch, and the trapdoor swung open fairly easily as she pushed up on it. As it swung back against the wall with a dull thud, she took out one of the torches and shone the beam into the void above. Apart from an old broom, it appeared to be completely empty.

She reached up and placed both torches on the floor of the small platform, then heaved herself through the hole and stood up.

Angela could see that Marco was just beginning to make

the same climb, and for a fleeting instant she debated dropping some heavy object down on to the top of his head, but then dismissed the thought. Even if she succeeded in hitting him, she would still have to contend with the men waiting on the ground floor down below, and if Marco didn't reappear, she guessed that she wouldn't leave the tower alive.

The platform was about eight feet long and three feet wide, and the walls appeared to be just as solid and featureless as those on the two platforms below her. As far she could see, there was nowhere here where anything of any size could be concealed.

Marco pulled himself through the trapdoor and stood next to her. 'What now?' he demanded. 'Where is it?'

Angela shook her head in despair. 'I have no idea,' she said. 'I can only tell you what I translated from the Latin text. That didn't give any indication of where the document might be hidden, apart from mentioning this tower, and even that was far from explicit.' She looked around at the featureless walls of the platform. 'If it was ever here, maybe somebody found it and removed it, years ago.'

'I've already told you: if it had been found, we would know about it. It must be here somewhere.'

'But there's no possible hiding place here.'

Then a thought struck her and she walked back to the trapdoor and peered down the square-sided shaft up which they had both climbed. She turned back to Marco.

'How high do you think we've climbed?' she asked.

'Why?'

'Because the walls are square,' she replied. 'At the top of this tower is a tall steeple. If we'd climbed to the very top of the tower, the walls would meet at a point above our heads. There must still be a space somewhere above us.'

Marco glanced down through the trapdoor, then looked around and nodded. 'So where's the access?' he asked.

The ceiling of the space they were standing in was only about seven feet above their heads. Angela didn't reply, but simply picked up the broom and began gently tapping its handle against the ceiling. It didn't take long to cover the small space, and in one corner this technique generated a hollow-sounding thud.

'Here,' she said, and shone the torch beam at the ceiling. Almost invisible in the grubby whitewash that covered the ceiling was the outline of an oblong shape. If they hadn't been looking for it, there was no way they would ever have seen it. At one end of it was a small hole, inside which a few strands of frayed material could be seen poking out.

'What's that?'

'I think it's the end of a length of rope, probably used to pull the trapdoor closed from here. And then they cut the rest off to hide the fact there was an opening in the ceiling. Just hold this,' Angela snapped, the spirit of the quest taking over, despite the circumstances. She passed the torch to Marco, who looked surprised, but did as she had told him and aimed the beam where she indicated.

She pressed her hands firmly against one end of the

oblong mark and pushed upwards. There was a creaking and tearing sound, the noise of old dry wood moving against a solid object, and the section of ceiling lifted a fraction of an inch. She changed position, and pushed again, but the panel wouldn't budge.

'You hold the torch and I'll lift it,' Marco told her.

Angela took a few paces backwards and aimed the beam of her torch at the ceiling. Marco raised his arms and shoved against the wood. Nothing happened, so he stepped back a few inches and tried again, his face contorted from the effort. With a final snapping sound, the panel suddenly gave way and flew upwards.

A cloud of dust and small pieces of wood cascaded down over his head. Angela looked on in horror as a skeletal arm, held together within a carapace of leathery skin, swung down, the bony hand seeming almost to grab for Marco. Above his head, framed in the dark opening, she found herself staring into the sightless eye sockets of a partially fleshed human skull.

51

Bronson steered the powerboat out of the end of the Grand Canal and swung the bow around to the south. Directly in front of him, on the opposite side of the Canale della Giudecca, lay the long and narrow, almost banana-shaped, island of Giudecca, with the much smaller triangular island of San Giorgio Maggiore to the left.

If he *was* right, and the men were heading for the southern part of the lagoon, a good place to wait for them to pass would be near the end of Giudecca. He stopped his turn and aimed for the Canale della Grazia which separated the two islands in front of him. Once he'd motored through the gap, he steered the boat over to the right, stopping alongside the southern coast of the island just below Campiello Campalto.

Like almost everywhere else in Venice, the island of Giudecca was bordered not by a wall but by a level walkway perched only two or three feet above the surface of the virtually tide-less Adriatic. The edge of the walkway was interrupted by sets of shallow steps to allow people to disembark from boats, and by substantial lengths of timber driven vertically down into the seabed to act as mooring posts. A line of old-fashioned metal streetlamps marked the seaward side of the walkway, and on the opposite side of it were the front walls and doors of the houses and shops.

Several powerboats and launches were already secured alongside the walkway, but Bronson had no trouble finding a vacant mooring post. He looped the bow line of the boat around it and secured it with a quick-release knot, so that he would be ready to leave at a moment's notice. He shut down the outboard motor to conserve fuel, and checked to see how much he had left. It looked like about half a tank, which he hoped would be enough.

Then he pulled his binoculars out of his jacket pocket and climbed up on to the walkway using the nearest set of steps. He sat down, dangling his legs over the edge of the walkway. He could have begun his surveillance of the water traffic around the island from his boat, but the boat was bouncing and rolling in the waves that continuously washed against the shore of the island, and in the wake of every passing vessel; focusing on anything through the binoculars would have proved difficult. It made much better sense to use his binoculars from the stable platform that the walkway offered.

He had carried out numerous surveillance operations

in his short career as an Army officer, and later in the police force, but in those tasks he had been part of a large team, both static and mobile, and the target had usually been a particular individual to be followed and watched. If he'd been covering a building, it had generally been a single dwelling with only one or two entrances, and one team would be assigned to cover each. The emphasis had always been on team operations – a large number of people blanketing a small target – never would one man cover even a single location with any degree of success.

But out here, in the choppy waters of the Venetian lagoon, Bronson was going to try to do exactly this. He intended to look at every boat heading south that passed on either side of his position. If he'd been right in his guess, and his attackers had originally intended to sail around the eastern end of Venice, and they'd left the canal system on the north side of the city after their confrontation with him, then they would have to pass fairly close to him now to reach the same area. But he was also keenly aware that if the blue powerboat had managed to reach the Grand Canal before him, his attackers could already be well beyond his reach.

He started by checking all the small boats he could see out in the lagoon, and which were already a good distance away from him.

As he'd expected, there was a huge number of boats and launches in a variety of shapes and sizes and types and colours. Blue seemed to be quite popular, and twice he saw vessels that looked remarkably like the one he was searching for, but in both cases he was able to reject the sightings. One of the boats had three people in it and the other one at least four, possibly five, and he was fairly certain that the men he was chasing wouldn't have stopped to pick up passengers. What's more, these two boats were a long way to the south of where he was sitting, and whatever route the two men had taken, he doubted if they could possibly have got that far ahead of him.

Although he was concentrating on checking the vessels at the far end of the lagoon, Bronson was also watching those passing much closer to him. He knew that if he was to stand any chance at all of spotting the boat, he would have to establish a pattern for his surveillance, and not get fixated on watching just a single part of the lagoon. In fact, he knew he ought to use the binoculars as sparingly as possible, because it would be a fairly unusual thing for someone to be doing on the island, and he definitely didn't want to draw attention to himself. If this was going to work, he had to look pretty much like any of the other people going about their business on Giudecca.

So Bronson relied largely on his eyes, and quickly worked out a kind of pattern search that he thought would give him the best chance of spotting the boat and its occupants before they saw him. The most likely area for them to enter the southern half of the lagoon was, he believed, over to the east, so he concentrated most of his attention there. He looked that way for about thirty seconds, then looked down to the south of the lagoon for fifteen seconds, and finished his one-minute scan by looking over to the west, then back to the east again. It was boring and repetitive, but Bronson didn't care. It offered the best chance he was going to get to find Angela, and for that he could endure almost anything.

So he sat on the walkway, beside his powerboat, and watched, and kept watching, never letting his concentration flag for an instant, as the hull of his vessel rose and fell gently beneath him. Fifteen minutes passed. Then twenty, and then twenty-five. After half an hour, Bronson began to feel desperate. Either his guess about the destination of the two men was completely wrong or they had slipped past him somehow. Or maybe they'd just been much faster than he'd expected. In any case, he'd blown it.

Bronson sat there, following the pattern search that he was now convinced was a waste of time, and wondering what the hell he could do next. He toyed with the idea of simply getting back into the boat and motoring around the islands scattered about the lagoon in the hope that he might catch a glimpse of the blue powerboat that way. But even as he considered this course of action, he realized it would be a complete waste of time. There were over one hundred islands out there, and almost every one would have a powerboat secured to its jetty, and there was a fair chance that quite a lot of them would be blue.

He picked up the binoculars to check out another flash of blue he'd spotted some way down to the south, then muttered in irritation. That particular boat was blue and white, a completely different colour scheme. He lowered the binoculars again and for a few seconds just sat staring vacantly across the glistening blue waters of the *Laguna Veneta*, trying to work out his next move.

And then, almost without him being aware of it, he found himself looking directly at the blue boat with the two men on board. It had just emerged from around the east end of the main island of Venice, as part of a group of perhaps half a dozen other small boats and one larger launch, all of whose courses then began to diverge as they headed for their individual destinations.

Bronson didn't react in any way at all. He just sat on the walkway, looking back towards Venice while his eyes, invisible behind his mirrored shades under the peak of his baseball cap, remained locked on the vessel. The men in the boat appeared to be looking around casually as they headed south, but gave no sign that they were in any way suspicious of the man wearing sunglasses sitting by himself on the south-east side of the island of Giudecca.

Bronson waited until the boat was a couple of hundred yards distant. Then he climbed casually down the steps into his craft and started the outboard engine, which immediately rumbled into life. He released the bow line, and swung the boat around to follow the other vessel, keeping his speed well down, to ensure that he wouldn't get close enough to attract attention.

Then, as if linked by an invisible tether, the two powerboats, now almost three hundred yards apart, headed south across the *Laguna Veneta*, away from the city and towards the scatter of outlying islands.

52

Angela couldn't help it. She squealed in fright and stepped backwards, away from the horrendous apparition that had just appeared. But in seconds she'd recovered her composure. She was no stranger to old bones, and ancient corpses interested, rather than frightened, her. It was just the shock, and the unexpected appearance of the old body.

Marco had jumped back with a yell of fear, lashing out with his torch at the dangling corpse.

For a few seconds, neither of them moved, the beams of their torches shining across the open space towards the trapdoor, and illuminating the grisly body that had partially fallen through it.

'I didn't expect that,' Marco said, brushing dust from his clothes.

'Nor did I.'

Angela moved forward and shone her torch upwards. The skeleton – or what she could see of it – appeared to be largely articulated, skin and desiccated muscle still clinging to the bones. It looked old.

'There's a story,' Marco said, 'that the mad doctor from the lunatic asylum didn't jump from the tower, but was actually walled up here. Could that be him?'

Angela shook her head. 'I don't think so, because that was a hundred years later. The Latin text referred to a "guardian" for the source document. I think this body was placed up here to act as a kind of warning to anyone who wanted to get into the space above us. I think this is what Carmelita meant.'

'You mean this corpse was once a member of her group?'

'Not necessarily. From what I've read, finding a dead body on this island wouldn't be difficult. I think they just dug one up and positioned the corpse above the trapdoor before they closed it.'

It took a moment for the implication to hit them both.

'A plague victim?' Marco asked, his voice hushed as realization dawned.

'It's possible,' Angela said. 'We both know this island is covered in plague pits. But that doesn't mean that the corpse is still infectious. I'm not a doctor. I don't know how long the bacteria can survive once the host is dead.'

'But it could still be carrying the disease?'

Angela shrugged. 'I don't know. Maybe. But these days there are treatments available for the plague,' she added reassuringly.

She was silent for a moment before she voiced the logical conclusion. 'If I'm right – and the corpse was positioned there as a form of protection for the source document – my guess is that the people responsible probably thought the body was infected. That's why Carmelita referred to a "guardian".'

'So you think the document might be up there?' Marco asked, pointing upwards.

'That would seem likely, and I really hope so.'

'Well, we'll soon find out. Or you will, to be exact.'

There was an old broom, almost all the bristles long vanished, standing in one corner of the space. Marco picked it up, placed the head under the skull of the corpse and pushed upwards. The skeleton vanished from sight, the dangling arm disappearing as quickly as it had materialized.

Angela shone her torch through the trapdoor. In the void above her, it was surprisingly light, the daylight spearing in through gaps between the tiles, and she could clearly see the pointed shape of the top of the tower.

She turned to Marco. 'If you want me to climb up there,' she said, 'you're going to have to give me a hand.'

He nodded, put his torch down on the floor so that it illuminated that end of the platform, then walked across to Angela. Unceremoniously, he wrapped his arms around her waist and lifted her straight up through the open trapdoor.

Angela used her arms to lever herself completely through the opening, and shone the torch around her. The skeletonized remains of the body lay just a couple of feet away, but she ignored it completely. She wasn't entirely sure what she was looking for but, if her deductions had been correct, the lost source document that Marco and his cronies were seeking had to be somewhere nearby.

The sides of the steeple sloped gently towards each other, to meet at a point perhaps twenty feet above her head: it was difficult to estimate the distance exactly. She doubted if the hiding place would be that inaccessible. It was more likely to be within reach of her at that moment, somewhere on the floor or the walls nearby, simply because of the difficulty of getting to the top of the steeple. Even manoeuvring a ladder into the void would have been a virtual impossibility, and the sloping walls were unclimbable.

If the document – this scroll or codex or whatever it was – had survived, and was still hidden somewhere in the old bell tower, it had to be close by.

Angela moved the beam of the torch slowly around her in a complete circle. She was standing on what appeared to be a solid stone floor, pierced only by the open trapdoor. It seemed unlikely that there could be a cavity anywhere within it. She shifted her glance to the walls. Formed from solid timbers, with horizontal braces every few feet, they didn't look too hopeful either. She ran the torchlight over the walls from floor level up to about eight feet, the maximum height that most men could reach, but saw nothing that looked like a box or other kind of container.

Then she stopped. Among the pinpricks of light filtering through the gaps between the tiles, she thought she'd spotted something else. A glint. Something shiny. Without altering her position, she moved the torch back in the opposite direction, the beam of light illuminating the opposite wall. As it passed over one of the vertical timbers, she spotted something reflective.

She strode over to the upright, her sense of excitement mounting. The glint she'd seen was slightly to the right of the old timber, on one of the horizontal braces about five feet off the ground. The odd thing was that there seemed to be nothing on the wood that could have reflected the torchlight. Then she saw a long split that ran along the length of the brace. She bent slightly forward to peer into the crack, and discovered that the object that had attracted her attention was actually inside the timber. That really didn't make sense.

Angela looked at the top of the brace, and noticed two deep cuts running across it. Immediately she saw those, she guessed the reason for the wide longitudinal crack: over the years, the wood must have dried out and warped slightly. Somebody had fashioned a kind of box out of the timber, cutting off the top section and cutting out a hollow underneath it.

She took hold of the top of the brace and lifted the wood, which came away quite easily. Lying in a shallow depression underneath was something metallic. It was that which had reflected the torchlight, the metal glinting in the darkness.

Angela reached up and lifted it down. It was a metal

cylinder about ten inches long and three inches in diameter, one end sealed by a cap. Originally it had been painted dark brown, presumably to match the colour of the wood, but much of the paint had flaked off.

The cylinder was too small to contain a codex or a book, but it was easily big enough for a scroll or a rolled length of parchment.

'What is it?' Marco asked. He had levered himself up so that his head and shoulders were inside the void, and he was watching her closely.

'A steel cylinder,' Angela replied. 'Do you want me to open it?'

'No. Give it to me.'

She walked across the floor to the trapdoor and looked down at Marco. He'd dropped back to the floor below, his hand raised up ready to receive the object. Angela passed him the metal cylinder and then lowered herself back down through the trapdoor. By the time she'd dropped the last couple of feet, Marco had already twisted off the steel cap and was examining a length of parchment, a cruel smile on his face.

'Is that it?'

Marco nodded. 'Yes. We'll need your translation skills again,' he added as he carefully rolled up the parchment and replaced it in the cylinder. 'Get back down the stairs. You've just bought yourself another few hours.'

53

The trick with shadowing a car was for the driver of the pursuing vehicle to remain far enough away that the man under surveillance didn't realize anyone was following him, while at the same time keeping so close to him that he couldn't – deliberately or accidentally – get lost in traffic. This was why surveillance operations normally used a minimum of four vehicles, including at least one powerful motorcycle able to keep up with any car, and whose rider could cut through even the heaviest traffic. And all these vehicles would swap positions at frequent and irregular intervals so that the target would never be able to see one particular vehicle in his mirrors for long enough to register it.

Bronson, of course, was by himself, but the good news was that all he now had to do was keep his target in sight and avoid being spotted himself, a comparatively easy task in the open waters of the *Laguna Veneta*. There wasn't enough boat traffic for him to lose sight of the vessel, and Bronson knew that if it vanished behind an island and didn't reappear, it would have reached its destination. And that was what he was interested in, nothing else. Following the boat was simply a means to an end.

Once they'd cleared the quite heavy water traffic to the south of the island of Giudecca, the two men in the blue powerboat appeared to focus on the water ahead of them. But still Bronson was cautious and, once he'd established the direction the other boat seemed to be heading, he changed his own course slightly so that he was following a parallel course and heading more towards the centre of the Venetian lagoon.

Under other circumstances it would have been very pleasant, sitting in the powerboat in the bright sunshine, steering the vessel across the blue waters of the lagoon, the area dotted by picturesque islands, some of which had tall and elegant houses standing on them, others with low buildings, some quite dilapidated, while still other islands appeared deserted. Behind him, the bulk of the city dominated the northern end of the lagoon. In the clear afternoon light, over to the north-west, due to one of those freak atmospheric conditions that occasionally occur, he could quite clearly see the impressive snow-capped Dolomite mountains, looking as if they were only about ten miles away, though in fact they were actually about a hundred miles distant.

But Bronson was in no mood to appreciate the aesthetics

of the situation. All his attention was focused on the blue powerboat that was still heading south-west, towards the islands that lay near the Italian mainland. The number of other boats heading in the same direction had diminished considerably the further away they'd travelled from Venice, and now there were perhaps only a dozen or so craft within about half a mile of Bronson's boat.

As the other vessels moved away, he began to worry that the men he was following would become suspicious of him. He couldn't afford to let this happen, so when another three boats swung west and out of his sight, he realized he was going have to do something.

Easing back the throttle slightly, he picked up the chart of the *Laguna Veneta* and studied it for a few moments. He was getting close to the southern end of the lagoon, and he knew that the men he was pursuing couldn't go very much further. He looked ahead at the blue boat, which now seemed to be heading towards a loose group of small islands, quite well separated from each other.

Over to his right was a very small island, only about fifty yards across, which appeared to be uninhabited – or at least, he could see no sign of any buildings or other structures on it – but which looked as if it could provide a reasonable view of the island group towards which the other boat was heading. Making a decision, he eased back still further on the throttle and turned the wheel to the right. The boat heeled over as it changed direction, and Bronson aimed it towards a gently sloping muddy mound, fringed with bushes and a handful of trees, where it looked as if he could beach the boat safely.

A few moments later, he felt the fibreglass hull make contact with the seabed in the shallow water. Immediately, he switched off the outboard motor and pulled his leather jacket back on. He wanted to avoid the white of his shirt being seen on the island, which might alert his quarry that they were being observed.

He clambered forward to the bow of the powerboat, seized the line and vaulted over the side of the vessel, to land with a splash, up to his calves in water. He jogged a few feet up the muddy beach, took a firm hold on the bow line and heaved the boat a few feet further up the beach, then threw the rope around the stem of a large bush and tied it securely: the one thing he couldn't afford to do was lose the boat.

He checked that the binoculars were still around his neck, then ran a few dozen yards until he reached the southern side of the tiny island, found a vantage point where he could see across the water that lay beyond, and dropped flat on his stomach. In seconds he had located his target.

The two men were looking around, apparently checking out the handful of boats nearby, and Bronson congratulated himself on having hidden his boat from view. As he watched, the boat altered course slightly and headed directly towards one of the islands. Adjusting the focus of his binoculars, he switched his attention to their destination. Another small island, though probably at least ten times bigger than the islet he was lying on, it was dominated by a large, grey stone house.

As he watched, the boat decreased speed slightly and moved around the back of the island and out of sight. Bronson remained motionless for a few minutes and continued studying the scene. But the boat didn't reappear, although several other powerboats passed to and fro. Finally, he stood upright again and jogged through the undergrowth back to his own boat. There, he picked up the chart of the lagoon, identified the islet he was standing on, and the island behind which the boat had vanished, and marked them both on it.

Now he had something he could take to the Italian police, because he knew there was no way he could tackle the people on the island by himself. Even armed with the pistol, which was still a heavy and comforting weight in the pocket of his leather jacket, he would be outnumbered and outgunned if he tried any kind of a solo attack. What he needed to do was to get a bunch of heavily armed *carabinieri* out to the island as quickly as possible.

Bronson released the rope, gave the bow of the boat a hefty shove to refloat it, then splashed through the shallows and climbed aboard. As the boat drifted backwards, he started the engine, and swung the wheel to aim the vessel back towards the city of Venice. If this was the island where Angela was being held, he needed to get help. Fast.

54

The descent of the bell tower was noticeably quicker than the climb up, because Marco was clearly in a hurry, eager to show what they'd found to the hooded man who seemed to inspire such fear in everyone, not just in Angela.

On the ground floor Angela was again handcuffed by one of the men while Marco unrolled the parchment so that he and the others could examine it more closely. It was obviously old, stained by the passage of years, the edges frayed and torn, but the men handled it as if it was pure gold. Then Marco carefully slid it back into the steel cylinder and secured the end cap.

Within minutes, Angela was back in the cabin of the powerboat, her wrists again secured to a handrail as the boat picked up speed across the waters of the Venetian lagoon.

This time, the hooded man didn't share the cabin with her, instead he remained at the rear of the boat with

Marco and the others, and Angela was able to stare out of the window, back towards Venice. The afternoon was bright, but patches of mist drifted across the water, giving the lagoon a ghostly and ethereal appearance. Her view was partially blocked by the island of Giudecca, lying just to the south of Venice, but what she could see of the eastern end of the old city seemed almost to float, the mist obscuring much of the lower levels of the buildings. But even over the bulk of Giudecca, she could still make out the top of one of the most enduring images of Venice: the Campanile di Marco, the huge bell tower in the Piazza San Marco.

She remembered when she and Chris had joined the thousands of other tourists and walked around the square, looking up at the huge brick structure. The original, she remembered, had been built in the sixteenth century, but then collapsed unexpectedly in 1902. The people of Venice had rejected every new design produced by hopeful architects, and simply had the tower rebuilt to exactly the same plan as the original.

They'd been happy, that afternoon, despite the crowds milling around them, and had even thrown caution to the wind and ordered a coffee in one of the cafés that lined the piazza, wincing at the price but revelling in the atmosphere. Now, Angela pondered, as she stared back through the small cabin window towards Venice, she had no idea where Chris was, what had happened to him, or even whether he was alive or dead. And Marco had made it perfectly clear that her own lifespan was now measured in hours rather than years. She had no future, but without Chris beside her she realized she wasn't actually sure she wanted one.

For a moment, she felt like giving way, letting the tears flow, tears of utter and complete despair, but she steeled herself. If Chris was alive, she knew that he'd be tearing Venice apart looking for her, and she owed it to him, as well as to herself, not to give in without a fight.

There was nothing she could do in the bouncing speedboat, no way to attract attention, but once they got back to the island, maybe she could escape from the men, perhaps even try to swim to another island. She shivered at this prospect, not from fear, but at the simple realization that if that really was her last, desperate resort, then she'd be far more likely to die from hypothermia in the cold waters of the lagoon.

But even that might be better than whatever fate Marco had planned for her.

55

Bronson made good time getting back to Venice. Water traffic in the lagoon had thinned out considerably, and he was able to hold the boat at more or less top speed for most of the way. And time, he knew, really was of the essence.

He moored the powerboat as close as he could to the police station in San Marco, remembering his meeting with Bianchi there and the body of the young woman he'd been asked to identify. As his thoughts returned to that scene, Bronson once again gave somewhat guilty thanks that the pale and lifeless body had been that of someone he'd never seen before, and not Angela. If it had been, Bronson knew he would never have been able to forgive himself.

But now, finally, he thought he knew where she might be. And even if she wasn't on that particular island, he was quite convinced that the people there would know something about her, and might have been involved in her abduction. All he had to do was to convince the police to take action.

At the desk inside the station he asked to speak directly to Bianchi, but was told that the senior inspector was unavailable, which Bronson knew could mean almost anything. But he needed action quickly, and he certainly wasn't prepared to be fobbed off by the Italian equivalent of a truculent desk sergeant.

'That's a shame,' he said in Italian, 'because I think I know the whereabouts of the men who've been killing all these girls in Venice.'

The sergeant told him to wait, picked up the internal phone and held a very brief conversation. Less than two minutes later, Bianchi strode into the station's reception area.

'Oh,' he said, his step faltering as he recognized Bronson, 'it's you again. You have some information for us, I believe?'

'Yes,' Bronson said, and he began to explain how he'd seen two men vandalizing a grave on the Island of San Michele, and how, when he'd approached them, they'd shot at him.

Before Bronson got even halfway through his highly edited account of what had taken place on the Isola di San Michele, Bianchi began looking at him in what could only be described as a suspicious manner. But he waited until Bronson had finished – describing how he'd followed the men to an island out in the lagoon – before he responded.

'And I suppose you know nothing about a man we found out on San Michele?' Bianchi said. 'He's now in hospital, suffering from severe concussion, because somebody smashed him over the head with a lead-filled cosh.'

'I only saw the two men I've told you about, nobody else.' Bronson held Bianchi's unblinking stare until the policeman looked down at the notes he'd made.

'Very well,' he said at last. 'And are you sure you can identify this island again?'

Bronson nodded and showed Bianchi the chart of the lagoon he'd brought from the powerboat, on which he'd drawn a distinct circle around one of the islands at the southern end of the lagoon. He'd wisely left the pistol and the spare magazines locked up on the boat, having concluded that walking into a police station carrying an unlicensed semi-automatic pistol probably wasn't the sharpest of ideas. But he definitely wanted to hang on to the weapon in case he did have to take matters into his own hands in order to rescue Angela.

And Bianchi's immediate reaction when he looked at the chart suggested that this might be a possibility.

'I know this island,' he said. 'Are you absolutely sure this is where the two men went?'

'Yes,' Bronson replied. 'I didn't actually see them moor their boat or get out of it, because they went around to the opposite side of the island, behind the house.'

'You're mistaken,' Bianchi said flatly. 'That's a private island owned by a senior Italian politician. It's inconceivable that a man of his stature and standing in the community could possibly be involved in anything like this. And,' he went on remorselessly, 'I still do not see any evidence of the link you're suggesting between the men you followed out to the island and the abduction of your wife or, for that matter, the deaths of young women in this city. What, exactly, would be the connection between a vandalized grave on San Michele and either of these two crimes?'

Bronson just looked at him. 'We've been through all this, Inspector. Even if you won't admit it publicly, you know perfectly well that there's a gang of people operating in Venice who've been snatching girls off the street and bleeding them to death. The men I saw earlier today were vandalizing tombs on the Isola di San Michele which contain the bodies of people who they believe were once vampires. Those are the facts as I see them, and that is your link.'

'And your wife? Why was she had abducted? Does she think she's a vampire as well?'

Bianchi's face wore a slight smile as he asked the question, and Bronson resisted the temptation to plant his fist firmly on the man's jaw.

'No, Inspector. Like me, and I hope like you, she knows vampires don't exist.'

'Then why was she abducted?'

'Because when we examined the first grave on San Michele, she spotted an old book at the bottom of the tomb, underneath the remains of the body, which she removed. That's why our hotel room was burgled, and that's why Angela was abducted.'

'Why didn't you mention this before?' Bianchi snapped.

Bronson shrugged. 'It didn't honestly seem that important at the time. Now, I wish we'd just walked away from that first broken tomb and never spoken to a soul.'

'Yes,' Bianchi murmured, 'hindsight is a wonderful tool.'

'So this island . . .' Bronson continued. 'Are you going to send somebody to check it out?'

Bianchi nodded, somewhat reluctantly. 'You've made a report, and I am duty-bound to respond to it, no matter how unbelievable your statement is, and despite my personal misgivings. I will order one of our police patrol boats to go out there now and make inquiries.'

This wasn't quite the response that Bronson had been hoping for, but it was better than nothing.

'Can I go with them?' he asked. 'That way I can make sure they go to the right place.'

'Certainly not,' Bianchi said. 'If they find anything – which I doubt very much – I will call you at your hotel. You will be there, won't you?'

The inference was obvious. 'I might be out and about,' Bronson said, lightly, 'so it would probably be best if you called me on my mobile instead.'

Bianchi looked at him in silence for a few moments, and then nodded. 'Very well, Signor Bronson. Just ensure that you stay out of trouble. I wouldn't want our patrol officers to visit that island and find that you were already there. Do you understand what I mean?'

'Of course,' Bronson said. 'I can promise you that they won't see me anywhere near the island.' Which wasn't quite the same as saying he wouldn't go there, of course, but it seemed to satisfy Bianchi.

Ten minutes later, Bronson was walking quickly back through the crowded streets to where he'd moored the powerboat. He started the engine, cast off the line, and motored slowly away, deep in thought.

The first thing he was going to have to do, he knew, was top-up the boat's fuel tank, to ensure that he had enough petrol for whatever the night might bring.

He was also worried about Bianchi's apparent reluctance to take his claim seriously. The island might be the property of an Italian politician, but Bronson couldn't think of a single country anywhere in the world that didn't have a large and successful crop of corrupt politicians – and in Italy being corrupt seemed to be a part of the job description for a career in government.

His second worry was that Bianchi was only apparently going to send a single patrol boat over to the island, where the officers would presumably ask politely if anybody in the house knew anything about the bunch of murdered girls. He could guess the probable answer. And that was assuming that Bianchi actually sent anyone at all.

Bronson had seen the fast, blue-and-white patrol boats

in the Venetian lagoon – normally crewed by about three or four officers apparently only armed with pistols, though it was possible, Bronson guessed, that they might have heavier weapons inside the vessels. Even so, they were obviously more concerned with minor crimes, essentially traffic offences, committed on the waters of the lagoon rather than anything more serious.

But the thing that concerned him most wasn't anything Bianchi had said. It was actually something the inspector *hadn't* said. Specifically, it was a question the man hadn't asked. It was, of course, possible that Bianchi had simply missed it, in which case it just meant he wasn't a particularly good policeman, but Bronson doubted this. In his short acquaintance with Bianchi, the inspector had never struck Bronson as a particularly likeable character, but he had always seemed competent.

The other explanation was that Bianchi hadn't needed to ask the question because he already knew the answer, and this was a real worry.

326

56

Angela heard the engine note of the powerboat die away to nothing a few seconds after it reached the jetty. Moments later, Marco opened the door to the cabin and stepped inside.

Angela tensed, wondering if she dare try to escape right then but, even before he unlocked the handcuff, she realized any attempt was doomed to failure: another one of the men stood waiting by the cabin door, clearly ready for trouble. She doubted she could tackle Marco with any degree of success, and she certainly couldn't cope with the two of them. So she meekly allowed her wrists to be handcuffed in front of her, and was led along the path from the jetty and back towards the house.

She was almost at the door when an unearthly howling noise echoed from somewhere nearby. Angela froze in mid-stride, her eyes wide as she stared around her. She couldn't pinpoint the location of the sound, but she was certain it was very close.

'What on earth was that?' she asked.

Marco didn't bother to reply, just led her through the front door of the house and into the drawing-room. Only when she was standing beside the desk were the handcuffs finally removed.

'So what now?' Angela asked.

'I would have thought that was obvious. One of my men is making a photocopy of the scroll. As soon as he's done that, you can start translating it. And then we'll find the answer.'

'The answer to what?'

But before Marco could reply there was a double knock on the door and one of his men appeared carrying half a dozen sheets of paper. Marco took them, glanced at each in turn, and then placed them on the desk in front of Angela.

'Right,' he said. 'Get started.'

Angela knew she had no choice. She picked up the first sheet and looked at it. She'd already seen that the writing on the scroll was indistinct, the ink a faded grey against the brown of the parchment, but the photocopies were actually fairly clear. She nodded and reached for the Latin–English dictionary she'd been using previously.

Within minutes it was clear that what she was looking at was not a piece of text like those she'd worked on before. The first two pages appeared simply to contain a list of names, divided up into groups and interspersed by a number of Latin words that she had not encountered before. Words like *agnatus*, *abdormitus* and *cognationis* appeared frequently, and it was only when she translated these expressions that she realized what she was looking at. *Agnatus* meant a 'blood relative in the male line'; *abdormitus* translated as 'died', and *cognationis* referred to a 'blood relationship', a meaning that she'd guessed even before the dictionary confirmed it. The list was simply a genealogy, one section of a family tree.

The first name on the list was familiar to her, because she'd seen it somewhere in the very recent past, though it still took her a few seconds to place it. The genealogy that she was transcribing traced the blood relationship of a number of Italian families back to a single royal source: the Princess Eleonora Elisabeth Amalia Magdalena of Lobkowicz, Princess of Schwarzenberg, the woman who was also known as the Vampire Princess.

Angela sat back from the desk and stared across at Marco, who was sitting in his easy chair on the opposite side of the room. He was looking in her general direction, and when she met his glance, he nodded.

'Do you know what this is?' Angela asked.

'Yes. But you don't have to list all the members of the family. We're only interested in the names of the people who died here in Venice in the late eighteenth century. In fact, it's only one of those names that we need you to check, just to confirm his link to the princess.'

'Which is?'

'Nicodema Diluca.'

The name meant nothing immediately to Angela, though again the surname had a slightly familiar ring to it. She turned back to the photocopied sheets, quickly found what she was looking for and painstakingly traced the names of Diluca's forebears back to the Princess of Schwarzenberg. If the names and relationships listed were correct, then Diluca was undeniably one of her blood descendants.

'He's a descendant, yes, according to this,' she reported to Marco. 'Why is it important?'

He looked at her for a moment, then shook his head. 'You really don't understand, do you? It's all in the blood. There's nothing quite so important as the bloodline. That's why you won't find the name Carmelita Paganini listed anywhere on those pages. She wasn't part of the sacred family, though she obviously wished she had been. But she did do one thing useful. She – or rather her diary – pointed us towards the correct grave on San Michele.'

Then the penny dropped. 'The tomb of the twin angels?' Angela said. 'We found it, but I thought the name inscribed on it was Delaca.'

'You were nearly right. I have men out on the island now, recovering what we need.'

Angela didn't know what he meant by that remark, unless there was some other document or relic they needed hidden in that tomb as well.

Then there was an urgent double knock on the door.

Before Marco could even get out of his seat, the door swung open and a man Angela hadn't seen before stepped into the room. Obviously agitated, he strode over to Marco and held a brief but animated conversation with him. Partway through, they both paused to stare across at Angela for a few seconds. Then Marco smiled. The other man pointed back towards the door, and then left the room.

'What?' Angela demanded, conscious that Marco was staring at her again.

'I have good news and bad news for you, I suppose,' he said. 'The good news is that your ex-husband wasn't killed when my men attacked him on the street, because he's just been spotted chasing around the lagoon in a powerboat. The bad news is that he encountered two of my men in one of the canals in Venice and they shot him.'

Angela's face displayed the turmoil of emotions flooding through her body as she absorbed Marco's matter-of-fact statements, and for several seconds she found she couldn't speak.

'Is he . . . ?' she finally managed.

'Dead?' Marco supplied for her. 'I've no idea. Probably. But whether he's alive or dead makes no difference to you, here and now. The important thing is that he's no longer of any concern to us. We now have both of the things that we needed, the scroll and the relic, and that's all that matters. And we'll be keeping you alive for a little while longer.'

Angela was starting to recover her composure. She knew Chris, and knew he had a habit of bouncing back.

Just because he'd been shot at didn't mean he was dead. At least, that's what she would cling to. She turned slightly to face Marco.

'You're letting me live?' she asked.

Marco nodded. 'At least until you've finished the translation,' he said, and walked across to her. 'This scroll,' he continued, pointing at the photocopied sheets on the desk in front of her, 'is the most important document you'll ever see. This is the source, the sacred record. This is what we've been seeking all these years. Forget Carmelita Paganini's diary: this scroll contains the answers to every question we've ever wanted to ask. Translating it will keep you alive, at least for a few more hours.'

He paused and smiled. 'In fact, if everything works out as we hope, whether you live or die might not matter one way or the other.'

57

Despite the veiled threat Bianchi had made for Bronson to stay away from the investigation, he had absolutely no intention of sitting around in his hotel room waiting for the phone to ring. Angela had to be on that island, and he was determined – after all he'd been through – to stay close to her.

This time he knew exactly where he was going, and steered a direct course from the mouth of the *Canal Grande* across the waterway and through the gap between the islands of Giudecca and San Giorgio Maggiore. Once he was clear of the water traffic around the islands, he opened the throttle and accelerated towards his destination. He kept his eyes open, looking for any sign of the police launch that Bianchi had said he'd be sending to the island to investigate. He saw several of the distinctive blue-and-white craft in the lagoon, but none appeared to be heading in the direction he was going.

After several minutes of travelling at almost full speed, Bronson reached the small islet where he'd beached the boat previously. He throttled back, bringing the powerboat to an almost complete stop about fifty yards away from the shore of the islet, and for a few moments considered his next course of action. The problem he'd had previously was that the bulk of the house on the larger island to the south of him obscured his view of the jetty where the two men must have landed. It would obviously be far better for him to find a position from which he could see this part of the island, if only to observe the arrival of the police launch – assuming, of course, that one was going to turn up.

Finally he made a plan. He would head south, towards the end of the lagoon, just like any other tourist exploring this part of Venice, then turn round and come back. That way he would achieve two things: he'd get a far better look at the island itself, and, with any luck, he'd find another island from which he'd be able to watch. At all costs he had to avoid alerting anybody on the island of his interest in them. In other words, he had to play the tourist card.

Steering the boat around the islet, he meandered south, sitting on the plastic seat in the powerboat and looking all around him, exactly as an innocent tourist would do. But behind his mirrored sunglasses, he was focusing on the island to his right.

As he'd observed earlier, the island was a reasonable size – big enough for the house to look comfortable in its setting – and as he steered the boat further south, a small inlet came into view. Within it, he could see a wooden jetty and beside it a launch, quite a bit larger than the powerboat Bronson had hired. The inlet wasn't very big and as far as he could see, there wasn't much room for any other vessels if the launch was moored there.

Then he noticed something else. Behind the house, and about midway between the property and the inlet, was an area of level ground that appeared to have been tarmacked, and on it he could just about make out something painted in white. Playing the tourist again, Bronson looked casually around him, then turned back to look once more towards the island. And now, from his slightly altered perspective, he could see exactly what was on the tarmac.

It was a large white circle, inside which was painted a letter 'H': a helicopter landing-pad, which made perfect sense. Bianchi had told him that the island was owned by a senior Italian politician, so travelling to the island by boat would probably be a last resort. It would be so much more impressive, and cater to the politician's inevitable sense of his own importance, to arrive there by helicopter.

Bronson continued ambling gently south, past the island and towards a handful of others in the same loose group, most of which had houses built on them. Again, he tried to look like a tourist as he steered the craft around and past these islands.

About two hundred yards from the politician's island was another very small island, upon which was a simple structure that looked something like a car port – just a flat roof resting on four vertical supports with a rough wooden table underneath it. Bronson guessed that was probably a picnic spot, the roof providing some shade from the heat of the midday sun. He looked closely at the island, trying to see if there was anyone ashore there. He glanced at his watch. It was now late afternoon in November, and unlikely to be in use. Certainly, it appeared to be deserted.

Bronson spotted a narrow bay where he thought he could easily beach his craft. He took a quick look around, but there were no other boats near him, and less than ten minutes later, he was hauling on the bow line to pull the powerboat a few feet further up the muddy beach. He turned off the outboard motor, tied the rope around the trunk of a small tree that was growing near the beach, checked he had his binoculars and the pistol – just in case – and made his way quickly across the small island until he could see his target.

He had quite a good view of the front of the house, and of the small inlet with its wooden jetty, and the launch moored against it. He lay down, resting on his elbows, and peered through the binoculars. There was no sign of life around the house so he switched his attention to the lagoon that lay beyond the island.

And then, perhaps a quarter of a mile away, he saw an approaching police launch, its distinctive colour scheme making it quite unmistakable. It looked as if Bianchi had done what he had promised, and had despatched a police patrol to check out the island. Bronson was glad that both he and his powerboat were well out of sight.

He moved the binoculars again, and looked back at the house. It was, like many of the other properties he'd seen on the outlying islands, built of a kind of grey stone, the windows fitted with wooden shutters and the roof covered in terracotta tiles. But as he looked at it again, he was struck by something else. All the shutters on the windows were firmly closed, and the house seemed to exude an indefinable sense of desolation, of emptiness. If he hadn't known better – if he hadn't seen the two men in the powerboat arrive with his own eyes – he would have assumed that it was deserted.

But then, bearing in mind the activities of the group that had snatched Angela, they would hardly be likely to advertise their presence.

The police launch was now much closer. It had slowed down, and the bow wave was about half the size it had been previously. As Bronson watched, the boat swung around the end of the island and slowed even more, finally coming to a halt beside the entrance to the inlet, where the driver of the vessel reversed the direction of the propeller in a short burst to bring the boat to a stop. He didn't steer the boat into the inlet, which puzzled Bronson for a moment until he focused the binoculars more carefully and saw a substantial chain locked across the seaward end of the inlet, preventing the launch from entering.

Two police officers leapt nimbly on to the jetty from

the cockpit of the launch and walked unhurriedly along a gravel path towards the house. At the front door they paused and then one of them pressed the bell push. But the door remained firmly closed and there was no sign of life whatsoever from the house. Eventually, the officers stepped back from the door and looked up at the house. Even from the distance he was watching, Bronson saw one of them give an expressive shrug of his shoulders, then they walked back to the police launch and got back on board. The driver gunned the engine, turned sharply in a sudden spray of white water and accelerated away from the island.

For a few seconds, Bronson just lay there staring through the binoculars at the departing vessel. As searches went, the most accurate description of what he'd just witnessed would be 'pathetic'. The officers had made no attempt to look around the island, to try opening the main door, or even to try the other entrance to the house – there would certainly be a second and maybe even a third door into the property.

He sighed. If the Italian police weren't prepared to search the place, he would just have to do it himself.

With a deep sense of foreboding, he stood up, took a final look towards the house on the island, and strode back to the small bay where he'd left his boat.

✝

58

Angela sat at the desk and stared down at the text she was translating. In her work at the British Museum, she had quite often had to translate passages of Latin, usually sections of very old documents or inscriptions that dated back almost two millennia to the height of the Roman Empire, and she'd become familiar with the syntax and sentence construction of writings from that period.

But she'd also worked on documents that were much more recent, everything from documents produced at the height of the Byzantine Empire at the end of the First Millennium through mediaeval texts and all the way to passages that were only a couple of hundred years old. It had always fascinated her the way that Latin, though essentially 'dead' and unchanging, had been adapted by its users to the changing patterns of speech and writing over the centuries. It was sometimes possible to estimate the age of a piece of text simply from the way the Latin had been written, by the words that were used.

And what she was working on now was clearly much more ancient than the bulk of the diary that she'd seen before. The syntax suggested it was probably late mediaeval, dating from between the tenth and fourteenth centuries, hundreds of years before Carmelita Paganini had started keeping her journal. That suggested that Marco had been right in the date he'd ascribed to the scroll.

On one level, Angela was quite enjoying what she was doing, working out the meaning of the Latin sentences and transcribing them into clear and understandable English. But even as she worked, a growing sense of foreboding was creeping over her, a foreboding that gave way to a kind of numb resignation as she understood the full implications of the information contained in the scroll. Even the title of the text was disturbing, though not entirely a surprise: *The Noble Vampyr.*

Once she'd completed what Marco had told her to do with the genealogy, just confirming the link, the bloodline, which existed between Nicodema Diluca and the so-called Vampire Princess, she'd started working on the next page. But she hadn't needed to translate the initial section, because within a few minutes she'd realized that it was almost exactly the same as the Latin she'd already seen in the leather-bound diary, and had presumably been copied from the same source. This part of the scroll appeared to be essentially an introduction to the topic and included the attempt to justify the ridiculous claims that the author had made and which Angela had already translated.

But the second section of the manuscript was highly specific about vampires. It explained at some length about the way vampires were supposed to live and, according to the unidentified author, the reality was a far cry from the romantic images of suave, well-dressed vampires of the twentieth century drinking the blood of their willing victims. Clearly, none of the more contemporary writers had referred to this text or to any other ancient source documents that might have contained similar descriptions.

According to this treatise, vampires were both cannibalistic – which was hardly a surprise, given that their favourite diet was supposed to be blood drunk from the necks of nubile young girls – and scavengers. In fact, according to the translated text, the favourite hunting grounds of vampires were graveyards, where they would break into the tombs of recent burials and feast on the decaying flesh of the bodies they found there. The only inviolate rule was that the bodies of former vampires – the discarded hosts, as it were – were considered to be noble, and were never to be consumed.

The most reliable way to identify a vampire, the author of the text asserted, was by the smell of rotting meat which they invariably exuded, and which normally caused them to be shunned by mere mortals. But this, the author then explained, was a small price for the vampire to pay in exchange for the priceless gift of eternal life.

As she finished translating this particular sentence, Angela shuddered at her recollection of the hooded man and the appalling smell that seemed to surround him like a miasma. Whoever he was, he was clearly the leader of this group of deranged men, and had presumably decided to make himself seem as much like an authentic vampire as he could. She guessed that somewhere under his black robe he was carrying a piece of decaying meat to produce the odour she had smelt.

She shook her head and returned to the translation.

The next few sentences dealt with the misguided and usually futile attempts to kill vampires, attempts that the text stated were frequently mounted by people who simply failed to appreciate the inherent nobility of the vampire. Then the only guaranteed ways by which the death of a vampire might be achieved were specified in some detail. The most effective method was for the heart of the creature to be removed from the body and buried separately – as far away from the vampire as possible.

Decapitation also worked, but driving a wooden stake through the heart was, in the opinion of the author, useless because the heart remained in place, and the heart of a vampire was so powerful that nothing short of its removal from the body would guarantee death. Similar derision was reserved for the idea of placing some object – a brick or a length of timber – in the mouth of the vampire, and the author cited two cases that he had known of personally where a body had been buried with a brick driven into the jaw, and where the vampire had risen effortlessly from the grave after biting through the offending object. Again, he failed to be specific about where and when these alleged events were supposed to have occurred.

What bothered Angela the most about the text was the author's matter-of-fact acceptance of the existence of vampires. From the tone of his descriptions, he could have been talking about any natural phenomenon with which he would have expected most of his readers to be familiar. It was as if, at the time the author was writing, vampires were regular and accepted members of society who simply lived very different lives to most of the people around them.

Angela found such an attitude impossible to accept, and she repeatedly checked the text for any sign that the author was being less than completely serious. But there was no indication that this was the case. Whoever had created the original text was apparently absolutely factual in what he was describing – or, at least, he appeared to believe he was being absolutely factual. He was certainly convinced of the reality of the vampire as a living and breathing – albeit undead – member of the society in which he lived.

Again, Angela wished she had some idea who the author had been, and where and in which period he'd lived. She was still certain, from the Latin syntax, that the time period was roughly mediaeval, but beyond that she hadn't been able to pin it down.

She read the English translation she had prepared for a second time, then held it up to Marco, who walked over to the desk and took it from her with a nod.

Then she sighed deeply, and read the first sentence of the Latin text that formed the third part of the treatise written on the scroll: the section of the document which she now understood contained detailed instructions on how anyone who wished to do so could become a vampire themselves.

✝

59

Bronson cut the motor as he approached the entrance to the inlet. There was, he realized, no point in trying to sneak ashore. The island was too open to make any sort of covert approach feasible, so he allowed the boat to coast gently forward until it just nudged the end of the jetty, then stepped ashore, tying the rope around the heavy chain that barred the entrance to the inlet. As he did so, he noted that the chain itself was rusty, as was the padlock that secured it, and for the first time since he'd followed the two men, a scintilla of doubt entered his mind. It didn't look to him as if anyone had unlocked the padlock or moved the chain for quite a long time, otherwise at least some of the rust would have flaked off.

He looked at the launch that was secured to the jetty. The water was quite clear and he could see the curve of the hull where it vanished beneath the surface. The dark paintwork was liberally covered in marine growth, which suggested that the boat had been sitting there for some time – boats that were used regularly tended to have much cleaner hulls.

But that, of course, might also mean that the owner tended to commute by helicopter. It was an alternative explanation, but didn't do much to quell the doubts that were now nagging at him. The island really did look deserted.

He took out the Browning semi-automatic, removed the magazine and checked it, then replaced it in the pistol, pulled back the slide to chamber a round and cock the hammer, and set the safety catch. Then he walked slowly along the gravel path that led from the jetty and past the helicopter landing-pad to the house, looking all around him all the time as he did so.

He didn't ring the bell, just pressed his ear to the wooden front door and listened. There was absolutely no sound from inside the property. With the pistol held ready in his right hand, he walked all the way around the house, checking each window as he went, and listening at both of the other doors. Finally he accepted the sickening truth: he'd got the wrong island.

He couldn't understand it. This was definitely the place where he'd seen the two men in the blue boat disappear; although the restricted size of the inlet and the state of the chain that barred it suggested that the boat couldn't have been tied up at the jetty.

At that moment, his mobile phone rang. It was an Italian number, and when he pressed the key to answer it, he wasn't entirely surprised to hear the cool and indifferent voice of Inspector Bianchi in his ear.

'I did as you requested, Signor Bronson,' he said. 'I sent a launch to the island where you think your wife is being held, and the officers found absolutely nothing. There was nobody on the island, and the house is shuttered and barred. All you've achieved is to waste valuable police time, which is an offence in Italy just as, I believe, it is an offence in Britain.'

'I'm sorry,' Bronson said. There really wasn't anything else he could say. 'I was certain that you would find her there.'

'Well, we didn't, and I suggest that now you stop interfering and leave the business of investigating this crime to the professionals.'

And with this, the phone went dead. Bronson looked at it for a moment, then slipped it back into his pocket. The one thing he wasn't going to do was stop looking for Angela.

He replayed the sequence of events in his mind. He visualized the pursuit across the lagoon, and his decision to watch from the smaller island. He'd seen the blue boat slow down and then disappear from view. Then he remembered something else: there had been several other craft in the area, buzzing around the islands. Perhaps the men he'd been following, who'd clearly been checking around them as they approached the island – he remembered seeing them do this – had simply stopped the boat beside the chained-off inlet and waited there for a few minutes until the other tourist boats had cleared the area. And then they would have continued their journey, careful not to let anybody see their final destination.

Bronson groaned as the realization struck home. If these men were part of the gang responsible for the deaths of half a dozen young women in Venice, their caution was merited. The only encouraging fact was that there were so few islands any further south: their hideaway had to be somewhere nearby.

All he had to do now was find it.

✝

60

Angela had thought that the second section of the Latin treatise was bizarre enough, but the contents of the third and final part of the text were shockingly brutal.

It began simply enough with a declaration that it was possible for anyone who so wished to join the ranks of the 'favoured immortals', as it described vampires. But, the author cautioned, the process was lengthy and required the utmost dedication and commitment. As she translated the next few lines, Angela realized that dedication and commitment were only a part of it. The aspiring vampire also had to be prepared to become a genealogist, a grave robber and, finally and most shockingly of all, a rapist and murderer.

First, she read, it was essential to identify one of the most important of the vampire families. That concept seemed bizarre enough on its own. It suggested that vampires could breed just like normal people, and sparked a whole new line of thought for Angela. Would it be enough, she wondered, if just one parent was a vampire? Would that be sufficient to convey immortality and unpleasant dietary requirements on the children? Or did it have to be both parents? She shook her head. She'd become so immersed in this ridiculous piece of mediaeval fantasy that she wasn't thinking straight.

The reason for identifying a vampire family was then explained. Vampires, the author went on, had the ability to discard the body they were inhabiting and take over another one, when the first body became infirm or so well-known that continuing to live the lifestyle of a vampire became impossible.

When she'd translated that, she sat in thought for another minute or two. What could it mean exactly? And then it dawned on her. This was the crux of the matter. This was the explanation – both the reason and the justification. This was how people who believed in the reality of vampires were able to reconcile the claim of immortality with the fact that alleged vampires did actually grow old and die. It wasn't that they died, in the usual sense of the word. Rather, the author was suggesting, their essential life force was able to move from one body to another, and they simply discarded their previous body when it was convenient for them to do so.

Quite how you reconciled the completely different personality of the new host for the vampire's spirit with that of the previous person, Angela didn't quite understand, though perhaps the explanation was a lot simpler than that. Maybe people just looked for similarities in behaviour or appearance or anything else, and made the assumption that the vampire's spirit now inhabited a new host. And, as proving a negative is always virtually impossible, any protestations of innocence made by the new alleged vampire would be dismissed.

The important thing, the author then explained, was that once a human body had been inhabited by the immortal spirit of a vampire, a part of the vampire's essence would be retained in the flesh and bones, and especially in the skull.

There were two reasons for identifying the family of a vampire, he went on. The first was so that the corpse of a former vampire could be located and part of the skeleton, ideally the skull, obtained for the ritual. That was the first mention of any ritual or ceremony, but Angela was quite sure it wouldn't be the last.

So the first thing the aspiring vampire had to do was find the tomb belonging to a person who had been a vampire, break into it and remove the head. That was distasteful enough, but it was only the beginning.

A section of the skull then had to be removed and ground up into a powder, as finely as possible, so that the essence of the vampire's spirit could be released from the bone. But this operation would only be carried out once the other essential component of the formula had been identified and obtained.

This was the other reason for identifying the vampire family, because in order for the essence of the vampire's spirit to be released from the bone and then recaptured, the ground-up skull had to be mixed with the fresh blood of a female descendant of that same family.

The author digressed slightly at this point to explain, using quasi-scientific reasoning, how the female line retained the spirit of the vampire more strongly than the male line. The explanation frankly made no sense – like almost everything else Angela had translated – but it seemed to involve a woman's periods, when she, *voided her excess of blood to summon a noble vampyr and signify her willingness to be taken*. The blood of a female child was of no use, *for the essence is not yet sufficient strong in her*, and nor was the blood of a woman past childbearing age, or even that of a woman who had given birth. *She should bleed but be without child*, as the author succinctly put it.

The unknown author then moved on to the details of the ritual itself. First, a section of the skull was to be *ground exceeding fine* and placed in a suitable container. Only then was the girl introduced to the proceedings. Her body was to be washed thoroughly and she was to be immobilized in a *position convenient for all*. At least two people had to take part in the next phase of the ritual, for one would have to rape the girl, *to ensure her blood would flow sufficient free*, while the other person would bite into her neck to open the veins and allow the bleeding to start.

The text recommended allowing the blood to flow until *the heart could pump no more* – which would obviously mean that the girl would die as part of the ceremony – *for her sublime ecstasy in surrendering her soul and spirit* would help guarantee the success of the proceedings.

The blood was to be collected in a suitable receptacle and mixed with the powdered bone of the skull, and the mixture then drunk by the participants. The author cautioned that it might be necessary to repeat the process several times before success would finally be achieved.

At this point, Angela put down her pencil and sat for a few moments just staring at the Latin text. The document, ludicrous though its suggestions undeniably were, was essentially a recipe and, to a certain extent, a justification for repeated rape and murder, enshrouded in a quasi-religious ritual.

Then she started translating the final section dealing with the ritual, and found herself totally engrossed in the text. There was, the author asserted, a further refinement that was essential if success was to be achieved. As well as the ground-up bones of a long-dead vampire and the fresh blood of one of the creature's lineal descendants, the mixture also required the addition of blood taken from another woman, from someone who had never had any connection with any of the vampire families, but who otherwise met the same criteria. This infusion of blood, the author said, would give added strength to the mixture, and was to be extracted from the subject in the same way, by multiple rape and severing the blood vessels in the neck.

When Angela read that, she closed her eyes and shook her head, wondering how she could subtly alter the translation to avoid the inevitable conclusion from being drawn.

But as she reached for her pencil, she realized that Marco was standing directly behind her, and had already read exactly what she'd written.

'I knew that we'd find a more entertaining way to kill you than just a bullet,' he said. 'You'll be able to take your turn on the table tonight.'

61

Bronson tucked the Browning pistol into the waistband of his trousers and stared out across the still waters of the Venetian lagoon. Afternoon was steadily turning into evening, and the grey light of early dusk was deepening the aquamarine of the waters around the island.

There were two islands directly in front of him, both about the same size as the one he was standing on, and both inhabited. He could see lights shining through the windows of the small properties that had been erected on them. They looked homely, welcoming, and were also quite close together. That juxtaposition argued against either of them being the location of any kind of illegal activity, simply because anything that happened on one of the islands would be clearly visible to the people who lived on the other. The only way that either could be the place he was looking for was if the residents on both were involved in some kind of joint conspiracy. And that was a stretch.

Bronson scanned the islands through the binoculars, but saw nothing out of the ordinary. Then he looked over to the left, where another small island was visible in the fading light. But as far as he could see, there were no buildings of any sort on that one. It was a similar story when he searched the lagoon further to the west: just a couple of small islets without any sign of habitation. So where, exactly, had the two men vanished to earlier that afternoon?

He lowered the binoculars and stared out across the lagoon, despair clutching at his heart. He'd been so convinced that he'd found where Angela was being held, so sure that he'd be able to rescue her. But the cold hard reality was that he was no further forward than he'd been the previous day. All he could think of doing was climbing back into his boat and carrying out a visual search of all the islands in the vicinity, and just hoping that he spotted the blue powerboat – the right blue powerboat.

He was about to reach down to release the bow line when a tiny gleam of light attracted his attention. It was coming from the area between, and obviously behind, the two inhabited islands he'd already looked at. At first, it looked as if the light might actually be on the mainland, but when he brought the binoculars up to his eyes he could see that there was another island in the lagoon, quite some distance to the south, which he'd never noticed. He'd been so fixated on the island owned by the Italian politician that he hadn't thought to check any further south.

He studied it carefully through the binoculars, and noticed straight away that it was reasonably isolated. The only thing anywhere near it was a tiny patch of reeds and scrubby vegetation about a hundred yards away from its western shore. Bronson wasn't even sure that he'd find any solid ground there, but it was absolutely the only possible vantage point from which he could see what was happening on the island.

There was another grey stone house there, and some kind of outbuilding nearby. The light he'd seen was coming from a downstairs window, and was a mere sliver escaping through the gap between two shutters. Other than that, he could see no sign of life.

Bronson took a final look at both the island, where the thin vertical line of light still marked the position of the house, and the tiny clump of reeds, fixing their relative positions in his mind. Then he unhitched the rope, climbed down into his boat, started the engine and moved slowly away. At least the gathering darkness might help conceal him from anyone who might be watching from the island.

He steered the boat well out to the west, then turned the bow so that it pointed directly towards the reeds, closed the throttle still further and approached at little more than walking pace. He kept as low as he could in the vessel, knowing that the silhouette of a man sitting in a boat was very distinctive, and that by lying almost flat, his craft would hopefully just look like another shadow on the water in the gloom.

He turned off the engine when he was still a few feet clear of the reeds, and allowed the boat to drift into them. At the very least, they would hold the boat reasonably steady while he looked at the island through his binoculars.

But in fact, a few moments later the hull grounded, probably on mud, and the boat shuddered to a stop. That was better than he had hoped. Bronson climbed out of the vessel and pulled it further into the reed bed. The ground, such as it was, was soft and spongy underfoot, and several times his feet plunged into holes several inches deep, soaking his shoes and trouser legs. But he didn't care. His search for Angela was back on course.

Making certain that the boat was wedged tightly in place, Bronson stepped back on board and resumed his scrutiny of the island through his binoculars.

62

Marco hadn't finished with her. Despite his bleak statement to her that she would be dead – dying screaming in agony – within hours, there was still the final section of the text to be translated. And Angela knew she had no option but to comply.

Tears clouding her eyes, she again bent forward over the photocopied pages.

After describing in graphic detail the appalling ceremony designed to turn a human being into a vampire, and which would, almost incidentally, necessitate the rape and murder of not one but two young women, the author of the work had concluded by describing how an initiate would know if the process had been successful.

This section of the text was perhaps the least detailed of the entire corpus of work. The author admitted that there was no definitive proof, but suggested that an increasing dislike of consuming the meat of animals, of the beasts of the fields, and an aversion to daylight, were positive indicators. And if the initiate eventually found that he could only be sustained by the flesh of the recently dead, then it was certain that he would live for ever.

And now she even knew the name of the lapsed monk, as Marco had described him, and where he'd lived, because the very last section of the Latin text contained a single sentence that identified him, clearly written by the member of the society who'd copied down the words of the author. The translation read: *Inscribed by my hand this fourteenth day of the month of August in the year eleven hundred and twenty-six, from the sacred words of our most sacred and illustrious Master, the noble and revered Father Amadeus of Györ, Transdanubia.*

Angela had actually heard of Györ – it was one of the counties of what became known in the eighteenth century as the Districtus Trans-Danubianus, that part of Hungary which lay to the south and west of the River Danube. It was one of the twelve counties of Transdanubia whose boundaries had been established by Stephen I of Hungary, and which remained unchanged until 1920.

But if ever a monk – lapsed or otherwise – had been misnamed, it was Amadeus of Györ. His name meant 'lover of God', and what Angela had read had convinced her that she'd rarely read anything more evil, more contrary to the essential goodness preached by most religions and especially by Christianity, than the treatise in front of her.

She shuddered slightly, and handed the page to Marco, who retreated to his chair, where he read slowly through the rest of what she had transcribed.

'So what happens now?' Angela asked nervously.

Marco smiled coldly at her. 'The good news,' he said, 'is that you get to keep all your fingers. But you already know the bad news. You'll take part – in fact, you'll have a starring role – in the ceremony tonight.'

The slight smile left his face, and he nodded at her, his eyes travelling up and down her body appreciatively.

'It would have been helpful if you'd had your passport in your handbag,' he continued. 'But even so, we've managed to initiate some enquiries in Britain, and on the Internet, into your family history, and as far as we can tell there's no evidence that your bloodline – any of your ancestors, I mean – have ever been linked to one of the noble families of the immortals. So you're an ideal candidate for the ceremony. You're here on the island, and we need to dispose of you anyway, simply because you've seen our faces and you know too much about us. And, to look on the bright side, having you here means we don't have to snatch another girl off the streets of Venice. So your death will actually save the life of a stranger.'

Angela felt a chill of pure terror sweep over her. She opened her mouth to speak, then closed it again. Nothing she could say would make the slightest difference to her fate. She had fallen in with a group of people for whom the sanctity of human life meant absolutely nothing, and who would kill her without the faintest flicker of remorse or regret. The only thing that would concern them was whether or not her death could assist them in their pointless and horrendous activities.

Tears filled her eyes, and she dropped her head into her hands. That something like this could happen to her – to anyone – in a civilized country like Italy, in the twenty-first century, was simply appalling. She wondered where Chris was, whether he was even still alive, or if he was now lying on a slab in some mortuary in Venice. It had been a disaster and it was all her fault, she thought bitterly and inconsequentially. The holiday to Italy had been her idea. Everything had been her idea, even the visit to the Isola di San Michele, which had started everything.

'Let's go,' Marco said. The door of the drawing-room now stood open and two burly figures were waiting in the hall outside.

'Where to?' Angela managed, her voice barely audible.

'We have a convenient cellar. It's where we hold our ceremonies, in fact. And until tonight you'll have a bit of company, because the other girl is already waiting down there. But there's no point in you trying to get friendly with her,' he added. 'You'll both be dead before midnight.'

Angela snapped. She grabbed one of the pencils – the only thing she could see that even slightly resembled a weapon – and swung it as hard and as fast as she could towards Marco's face, aiming for his eyes.

But it was as if he'd been expecting it, and he effortlessly blocked the blow with his left arm, simultaneously swinging his right hand towards her, catching her a stinging blow with his hand against her cheek.

'You've got some spirit, I'll give you that,' he said. 'It's a shame you have to die tonight. If we'd had you here a little longer we could have had some fun with you. Taught you a little humility, perhaps. Take her away.'

63

Bronson had studied the island closely, trying to glean as much detail as he could in the fading light about the terrain and the buildings. It appeared to be quite large, the landscape dominated by another big house built of light-coloured stone, while behind that was what looked like a ruined outhouse of some sort. Most of the walls were still standing, but the roof had vanished. And a little way behind that was another much smaller building, apparently made of wood. At the front of the house, just about visible from where Bronson sat, binoculars glued to his eyes, was quite a large inlet with ample mooring spaces. He could see at least two boats there, both with dark paintwork, but the light had now faded to the point where he could no longer make out colours.

He completed his visual survey of the island and then sat back in the seat in his boat. Then he looked away, because a distant sound was becoming steadily more audible. A powerboat was approaching the area, and Bronson swung round in his seat to try to spot the vessel as it drew near. He assumed it was simply a tourist enjoying an early-evening boat ride, or possibly a police launch sailing through the area as part of its normal patrol route.

In fact, the boat was actually a reasonable-sized launch, and within seconds of spotting it, Bronson realized that it was heading directly for the island in front of him. The obvious conclusion was that the owners of the property – perhaps an Italian family – were returning home after a day out in Venice. And if this was the case, then Bronson knew he'd got it wrong yet again.

He focused his binoculars on the vessel as it approached. There were clearly several people on board the launch, their bulky shapes just visible in the twilight, although it was now too dark for him to be able to see their faces. He watched as the vessel slowed down, and then nosed gently into the inlet. In a few seconds, the sound of the engine died away to nothing, and Bronson watched expectantly for the passengers to alight from the craft.

But before this happened, the main door of the house swung open and two men and a woman stepped out, their figures briefly illuminated by the light streaming out of the property. Could it be Angela? His heart thumping, Bronson ignored the figures who were now walking from the jetty towards the house, and concentrated on trying to see the other three people more clearly.

He couldn't. The light was very poor, patches of mist

were drifting across the water in front of him, and their faces were invisible because they were walking away from him. Even through the binoculars all he could really be sure of was that there were two dark-haired men flanking a blonde woman. Bronson tensed. Angela was blonde, but so were a lot of other women in Venice. The reality was that they could have been anybody, but he kept watching all the same.

They were walking along a path that ran down the side of the house towards the back of the property. It looked as if the woman was having trouble walking – the men seemed to be supporting her on both sides. Perhaps, he wondered, she was physically disabled in some way, or possibly even drunk. The idea of a party going on in the house hadn't occurred to him until that moment, but it was a possible, perhaps even a probable, explanation for what he was seeing.

The three figures now seemed less important to Bronson than the new arrivals, and he switched his attention back to the area that lay between the jetty and the house itself, and concentrated on the people who were walking towards the front door of the property. And his idea about a party seemed to be supported by what he saw. In the light that streamed out of the front door, he could see that the new arrivals were all men, and all appeared to be dressed elegantly, white shirts and ties in evidence underneath the coats they were wearing against the chilly crossing of the lagoon.

It looked to Bronson as if he was watching a group of early arrivals turning up for a dinner party, out to enjoy an entirely innocent evening. He knew he had to be in the wrong place – again. He lowered the binoculars and stood up. He'd head back to Venice, grab something to eat and get an early night, and then start his search again in the morning.

He was actually standing in ankle-deep water beside the bow of the boat, ready to push it back, when a scream rang out across the lagoon.

64

Angela struggled as the two men hustled her out of the house and along the path that led to the ruined church, but she was as helpless as a child between the two heavily built men and her frantic attempts to escape achieved nothing. Out of sheer desperation, she released a single scream, a howl of terror that echoed off the building beside her.

One of the men raised his hand to strike her, but the other one stopped him.

'Don't do that,' he said. 'We don't want her bleeding everywhere. I'll give her a jolt instead.'

He pulled a taser from his pocket, held it in front of Angela's face, and then pressed it against her blouse.

Angela hadn't understood what the man had said, but she knew what a gun looked like.

'No, please, no. Please don't.'

Her voice rose to a crescendo, but was then abruptly cut short as the Italian squeezed the trigger. The current that slammed into her was like being hit by a truck, and she jolted backwards and then tumbled unconscious to the ground.

'Now we'll have to carry her,' the man with the taser said.

They each took one of her arms and looped it over their shoulders, and continued their short journey into the ruined church.

65

The scream galvanized Bronson. It was almost feral in its intensity, a primeval howl of anguish and fear, the sound of a woman pushed to her breaking point. And somehow, he simply knew it was Angela. He hadn't been able to recognize her through the binoculars, but the instant he heard the piercing scream he knew exactly where she was.

If he'd needed any confirmation, what happened next supplied it. There was a confused babble of voices, too far away for him even to tell what language they were speaking, and then he saw a faint but distinct blue flash, and the woman just seemed to collapse on to the path.

Bronson knew immediately what had happened to her: they'd used a taser. Then he looked on in horror as they unceremoniously dragged her into the ruined building behind the house.

For a few moments, he considered his options, limited

though they were. He didn't know how many people were on the island, but he'd already seen the two men with the woman he was sure was Angela, and at least four men had arrived in the launch, so he was severely outnumbered. He remembered the old Clint Eastwood line: 'the three of us – that's me, Smith and Wesson'; but even with the Browning Hi-Power as a force multiplier, he was still unsure if he could take on that many people, some of whom must be armed.

He definitely needed back-up. He took out his mobile phone and dialled the number Bianchi had given him at the police station in San Marco. His call was answered in a few seconds, but not by the inspector, who was now off duty. For a moment, Bronson considered trying to persuade the duty-sergeant to send a couple of boatloads of armed police out to the island, but after the fiasco of the earlier 'investigation', he doubted if he would be taken seriously. He really needed to speak to Bianchi himself.

'I've found my wife,' Bronson said, 'and I need urgent help to rescue her. It's essential that I speak with Inspector Bianchi as soon as possible. Can you please give me his mobile number?'

Bronson could almost hear the thought processes of the sergeant at the other end of the line, as he weighed up the possible consequences of giving a civilian – Bronson – Inspector Bianchi's mobile number, with the even more dire consequences of *not* giving him the number if it turned out that Bronson really had located the kidnappers and the woman then died.

'Very well,' the sergeant said. 'But if anyone asks, you got his number from the phone book, not from me. You understand?'

'Whatever you want,' Bronson agreed, and wrote down the number in his notebook, using the light from the mobile phone's screen to see what he was doing.

Still worried sick about Angela, he scanned the island again through the binoculars: the two men were walking back from the ruins. Then he heard the sound of another boat approaching, and looked over to his left. He could just about make out a launch – it looked slightly smaller than the other boat – heading for the island, and a couple of minutes later that boat, too, edged its way slowly into the inlet and stopped beside the jetty. Even more people were arriving, increasing the odds against Bronson still further.

He dialled the number he'd written down, pressed the button to complete the call and lifted the phone to his ear. He heard the ringing tone, and simultaneously the shrill sound of a mobile phone rang out over the lagoon. Bronson couldn't believe what he saw next: one of the figures walking from the jetty towards the house stopped and pulled a phone from his pocket. Bianchi was himself a member of the group that had abducted Angela.

66

'Yes, Signor Bronson?' Bianchi asked, his tone resigned. 'What do you want now?'

Obviously the inspector had recognized Bronson's mobile number or had stored it in his contacts list.

The one thing that Bronson wasn't going to do, now that he knew of Bianchi's involvement with the gang, was to reveal anything of what he knew. If the inspector realized that Bronson was only about a hundred yards away, he was sure that he'd be dead within minutes. They'd send out half a dozen men in a couple of boats, and they'd run him down in the dark and shoot him.

'I hope I haven't caught you at a bad moment, Inspector,' Bronson asked.

'Not really,' Bianchi replied smoothly. 'I'm just about to sit down to dinner with my family.'

A blatant lie, obviously, as Bronson could see the man

through his binoculars, standing on the path right in front of him.

'I just wondered if you had any more news.'

'No, I'm afraid not. Let me assure you again that the moment I learn anything I will tell you. Now, good evening, Signor Bronson.'

Bronson kept his eyes fixed on the distant figure, and saw the man snap his phone closed. That was the final confirmation – if any was needed – that it really was Bianchi who was standing on the island in front of him.

Bronson nodded to himself. That also explained something else. When he'd told the inspector about the book Angela had recovered from the desecrated tomb on the Island of the Dead, and described the subsequent burglary at their hotel, Bianchi hadn't asked how the burglars had known where to look for the diary. The only people who knew that Bronson and Angela had been in the graveyard that night, and who also knew where they were staying in Venice, were the two *carabinieri* officers. Bianchi had not asked the obvious question, because he'd already known the answer. Somebody in the Venetian police force – most likely Bianchi himself – must have given the information to the men on the island.

Bronson knew then that he was entirely on his own.

Pulling the Browning from his waistband, he removed the magazine and, working by feel, ejected all the cartridges from it. He repeated the process with the spare magazines he'd taken from the man in the graveyard on

374

the Island of San Michele, and then carefully reloaded each magazine again. It was a technique he'd learned in the Army. Stoppages – the pistol jamming – were far more likely if the magazine had been left loaded for some time. Emptying it and then refilling it helped avoid the problem. And the one thing he could not afford was the possibility that the weapon would jam.

Until that point, Bronson had been keeping the pistol purely for his own protection. But venturing on to that island meant he was taking the fight directly into the enemy's camp, and for that he needed all the help he could get. That included carrying the pistol in its holster instead of simply stuffed into his waistband, where it might snag on his belt or shirt.

Bronson clipped on both the holster and the magazine pouch, on the right- and left-hand sides respectively of his belt, and then did it up again. The pouch held the two magazines slightly separated so that each of them could be grasped easily. He inserted the magazines so that they faced in the same direction, with the forward lip pointing behind him, so that when he pulled out one of the magazines to reload the weapon, it would be the right way round to slide into the butt of the Browning. A fast and fumble-free magazine change could make the difference between life and death in a close-combat situation.

He loaded the last magazine into the Browning, pulled back the slide to chamber the first cartridge and ensured that the safety catch was on. Cocking any semi-automatic pistol makes a very distinctive sound, and he didn't want to risk doing it on the island – anybody hearing it would know immediately what it was. He slid the Browning into the holster, and ensured it was held firmly. Then he switched off his mobile phone and slid it into his pocket.

His preparations complete, Bronson climbed over the side of the boat on to the swampy vegetation, and pushed the vessel back into the water so that it floated free, then he stepped back on board.

✝

67

Angela's eyes flickered open and she looked around her. Or rather, she tried to, because wherever she looked she could see absolutely nothing. Impenetrable, Stygian blackness surrounded her. For a moment, she wondered if she was actually blindfolded, if somebody had put something over her head or her eyes to block out the light. She lifted her right hand to her face and felt her cheeks and eyelids and mouth, and realized that wasn't the case.

She sucked in a deep breath through her mouth. She knew she was in a very, very dark room, and for several seconds the confusion in her mind almost overwhelmed her, and she had no idea where she was or what had happened to her, or what had caused the dull ache she could feel in the centre of her chest between and below her breasts. Her nerves seemed to be screaming at the after effects of some trauma and her whole body was trembling in shock.

And then she remembered Marco's instruction to the

two men, to put her in the cellar. And with a sudden rush she also remembered fighting them every inch of the way, outside the house and along a gravel path, until one of the men had pulled out some kind of a gun and shot her. Instantly, her hand flew to her torso, her fingers probing for the bullet hole that she fully expected to find there. But that made no sense. If she'd been shot in the chest, she'd be dead, wouldn't she?

'What happened to me?' she muttered. She lifted her hands to her face, and only then heard the clanking of a chain next to her and felt the pressure of the handcuff which had been secured around her left wrist.

Then, from somewhere quite close by she heard a voice and realized she wasn't alone.

'Hello? Who's there?' Angela called out.

'I speak only a little English. My name is Marietta. They probably used a taser on you. They had to carry you down the stairs. You'll be sore all over, but it will pass.'

That helped a little. At least Angela now knew why she felt the way she did. And not being alone in the dark was a huge comfort.

'My name is Angela, and I don't speak any Italian. What are you doing here?' she asked.

The only response was a snuffling sound, as if the girl was crying. And then Angela realized that that was exactly what she was doing. Marietta – whoever she was – was sobbing her heart out, and for a few minutes she didn't say another word. Then the girl seemed to pull herself together and spoke a single sentence that chilled Angela to the bone.

'I've been brought here to be killed,' she said quietly.

There really was no adequate answer to that statement and for a few seconds Angela just lay on the bed, stunned into silence. Then she spoke again.

'You can't be sure of that. You can—'

'I'm very sure,' Marietta interrupted. 'Last night I watched them do it.'

Angela wasn't quite certain what the girl meant. She was obviously alive so she had to be talking about someone else, unless Angela had completely misunderstood what she was saying.

'What do you mean?'

'There was another girl down here. Her name was Benedetta.' Marietta's voice was fracturing under the emotional strain she was feeling, the words indistinct.

'Just tell me, Marietta. Take your time.'

'There's a ceremony. They made me wash and put on a robe. But they took Benedetta first and I watched.' Marietta's voice broke again, and for several minutes she sobbed uncontrollably before she regained some semblance of composure.

In a shaking voice, she hesitantly described the rest of the ceremony she'd witnessed. As she did so, Angela's terror increased. What the other girl was describing was an almost exact match for the ritual that had been described in the scroll – the *Noble Vampyr* document.

Until that moment, Angela had harboured the faint and completely irrational belief that what she was experiencing was somehow unreal, an elaborate charade or something of that sort. But Marietta's words, as she described the brutal rape and murder of another girl in that very room the previous day, completely destroyed even that tiny hope.

She shuddered when she heard Marietta's description of the ritual rape, but it was the very last part of the ceremony, the last acts that Marietta had witnessed, which frightened her the most.

'Please tell me that again,' Angela asked.

'The man who killed her, the man who bit into her neck, he was a vampire.'

Before she'd arrived in Venice, Angela would have unhesitatingly countered such a claim with a calm and reasoned statement of her own. Vampires, she would have said, do not exist and have never existed. Belief in such creatures is a pre-mediaeval legend with no basis whatsoever in reality.

She was tempted to say something like that to Marietta, but for a moment she didn't. Because, whatever the truth or otherwise of the vampire legend, she knew beyond any doubt that the group of people who were holding them believed absolutely in the reality of the undead. For them, vampires were undeniably real.

And, though she wouldn't even admit it to himself, the hooded man, the apparent leader of the group, bothered her more than she could say. His ability to move in complete silence, the fact that she'd never seen his face because it was kept permanently in shadow under his hood, and above all the stench of rotting flesh that clung to him all seemed so totally non-human that she was beginning to doubt her own mind. Her rational brain still rejected utterly the concept of the existence of vampires, but at that moment, in those circumstances and in that place, she was no longer certain that she was right.

But she tried to persuade the girl anyway. 'Vampires are not real, Marietta,' she said soothingly. 'You must have seen something else.'

'You didn't see him. He had huge teeth, long and point-ed, and he drank the blood from her neck.'

Angela let it go. 'So what happened then?' she asked.

'I don't know. I screamed and one of the men hit me with the taser and knocked me out. When I came round, the cellar was empty and Benedetta was gone. One of the men told me they'd taken her to San Michele, so I know she was dead.'

For a few moments, Angela sat in silence, wondering if she should share what she knew about the group, about the lapsed Hungarian monk Amadeus, about Nicodema Diluca, the Venetian who had claimed descent from the Princess Eleonora Amalia von Schwarzenberg, and who both Marietta and the dead girl had unfortunately been related to. But she knew that wouldn't help, wouldn't help either of them, and so she held her tongue.

There was just one last question she needed to ask, though she already knew the answer: 'But how do you know they're going to kill you as well?'

Marietta sobbed out her reply. 'Because they told me it's my turn on the table tonight,' she said.

68

The last group of men who had arrived by launch – including Inspector Bianchi – had now disappeared inside the house, and there was no sign of anyone moving about on the island. But that didn't mean that nobody was watching, so Bronson wasn't going to drive his boat into the inlet and moor it there. Instead, he decided that his best option was to steer a course that would take him well away from the island and allow him to approach it from the southern end, the shore opposite the jetty and furthest away from the house.

Bronson started the engine of his boat and immediately closed the throttle almost fully, muting the outboard's exhaust note as much as he could. Then he steered away from the island, out to the west, before starting a gentle turn that would take him on a semicircular course around to the south of his objective. The boat was moving at little more than walking pace, but that suited him fine. He knew that silence and stealth were both far more important than speed.

Keeping the boat moving slowly until he estimated that he was directly behind the grey stone house on the island, he turned the wheel to point the bow of the craft towards his objective. When he estimated that he was probably about fifty yards from the shore, he cut the engine completely and let the boat drift on in silence. A lot of the water in the Venetian lagoon was very shallow, and he guessed he might well be able to wade ashore, pulling the boat behind him. He should have checked the chart before the light faded, he realized, but it was too late to try to do so now. At worst, once the boat stopped moving forwards, he might have to swim ashore and pull it.

In fact, he wouldn't have to do either, because the shore of the island was looming up in front of him out of the murk, and the boat still had enough forward speed to reach it without any difficulty. The bow of the power-boat ran through a clump of reeds, and then grounded on something solid. Immediately Bronson stepped over the side, trying to be as quiet as he could, strode forward and tied the bow line around a projecting tree stump. With the boat secured, he crouched down to avoid being seen in silhouette, and studied the ground around him.

Over to his left was an old jetty, much smaller than the large landing stage he'd seen at the front of the house, and tied up to it was a small powerboat.

As he'd already established from his survey of the

island before night fell, the land was reasonably flat, and projected only a matter of a few feet above the water level in the lagoon. There were no fences or barriers that he could see, and the most distinctive feature was the bulk of the house that stood at the northern end of the island and was blotting out the night sky directly in front of him, a massive, featureless grey monolith, its shape relieved only by the lighter grey outlines of the shuttered windows.

Between Bronson and the house were the walls of the ruined building, which he now thought might be the remains of another house, or possibly a chapel or small church. The light wasn't good enough for him to tell for sure. And a short distance over to his left was the other structure, which looked like a wooden stable or a farm outhouse.

Bronson sniffed the air. He'd never thought he had a particularly sensitive nose, but he'd detected an unusual smell. He sniffed again. Whatever it was, it seemed to be emanating from the wooden structure.

He checked around him, then ran across to it. There was a single door on one side, and a window to the right, through which he looked cautiously. The interior was completely dark, but he had the strange sense that there was something, something large, moving around inside. He pressed his ear against the wooden wall, and quite clearly detected a rubbing, scuffing sound from the interior. The door was secured by a large new padlock and a substantial hasp, and he knew he wouldn't be able to unlock it or force it without tools. He could probably shoot off the padlock with the Browning, but that was hardly an option.

For a few moments, he wondered if Angela might be held captive inside the building, and if he should tap on the glass or the door, to attract her attention. But something stopped him – some visceral feeling that told him whatever was imprisoned in the shed was not human. His heart thumping, he stepped backwards, away from the door.

Instead, he switched his attention to the grey stone house and the ruins behind it. Choosing his path carefully, every sense attuned to any signs of life, he walked as quietly as he could towards the stone wall that marked the end of the tumbledown building.

As he approached, he realized that his earlier guess had been correct. It was a small church. A few of the roof trusses were still in place, but the battens, tiles and joists had long since vanished. What was left were the four stone walls, a couple of windows and the original door. The windows were above his eye-line, and the door closed, so he was unable to see what was inside.

Bronson did a full circuit of the building before pausing beside the door, the only entrance to the ruined interior. He checked all around him, looking and listening, but the night was dark and silent, the only sound the distant lapping of waves against the shore. Lights twinkled all around, principally from the city of Venice itself in the north-east, and from the mainland, which extended in an arc around to the north, but none of the other islands at this end of the lagoon appeared to be inhabited.

He made a final check, then took hold of the ring that formed the handle of the old church door and very slowly turned it. There was a faint squeak as the old metal moved, and then he felt the door give slightly. He pushed gently against it, and the door swung inwards almost silently. Looking round again, he stepped through the opening into the ancient building.

Dotted here and there across the old stone floor were piles of stones and lumps of wood. Grass and other plants were starting to grow in the cracks between the paving slabs that composed the floor. There had clearly been no attempt made to restore the building. Whoever owned the island was apparently quite happy to let the place fall apart, and for nature to reclaim the site. And yet Bronson felt uneasy. Why had the entrance door opened so easily? It was almost as though the hinges were kept lubricated, and that the door itself was well used.

Then he heard a door opening and closing somewhere beyond the ruined building. Footsteps, of at least two people, sounded from outside, heading towards him, and Bronson knew that he didn't have time to get out of the church.

He was trapped inside the building.

✟

69

Before Angela could reply, the cellar lights clicked on and she was able to look at her prison for the first time. Seconds later, a guard strode down the stairs and walked across the stone floor to Marietta's cell. He was carrying towels, two buckets of warm water and a pair of white robes.

'It's time,' he ordered. 'Get ready; and be quick about it. The first members have already arrived, and we don't want to keep them waiting.'

He tossed a towel and a robe on to the bed, gave Marietta a malicious grin, and left her to wash. Next, he stood at the entrance to Angela's cell. Stepping forward, he threw the robe and towel on to her bed, said something to her in Italian, then turned and left the cellar.

'What did he say to me?' Angela asked, once the cellar door had rumbled closed.

For a few moments, Marietta didn't respond. Then she gave a heavy sigh. 'He told you that the show was about to start,' she replied, 'and we'd both have starring roles. I think they're going to kill us both.'

The girl's voice sounded flat and resigned, as if she'd somehow managed to come to terms with the inevitability of her fate.

'I know,' Angela replied, her voice choked with emotion. 'They told me we'd die together tonight.'

For a minute or so there was silence in the cellar, then Angela spoke again.

'What are you going to do?' she asked. 'Will you co-operate with them?'

Marietta's voice broke into sobs. 'I'm going to do exactly what they tell me,' she said finally, and Angela could hear her starting to wash in the adjacent cell. 'What else can I do? If I don't obey their instructions, that bastard guard will send a couple of his men down here to rape or beat me. If I do as I'm told, I'll only get raped during the ceremony itself. And I've seen what happens down here, so I suggest you cooperate as well. In the end, it'll make it easier for you.'

'Dear God,' Angela murmured, as the appalling in-evitability of their situation hit home.

✝

70

Bronson knew that if he tried to leave, they would certainly see him. He had to stay where he was.

He ran towards the door, his trainers making almost no sound on the stone floor, and flattened himself against the wall beside it. Pulling the Browning pistol out of the belt holster, he held it in a two-handed grip, the muzzle pointing down towards the floor. He clicked off the safety catch, and waited.

But the footsteps didn't stop at the door. Instead, Bronson heard the two men – and he guessed from the snatches of conversation that there were only two of them – walk past the church and on – or so he guessed – to the wooden stable.

Easing the door open a crack, he peered out and crept forward to the corner of the wall where he could see the stable. Two shadowy figures were standing beside the door, both apparently looking down. One held a torch, the beam shining downwards to illuminate the padlock while the other man unlocked it. There was a faint metallic clicking, then they opened the door and stepped inside.

For a few moments, Bronson didn't move. If Angela was in the stable, he would be able to tackle the two men with his Browning, get her into the boat, and return to Venice before anybody could stop him. But this seemed way too easy. No, wherever Angela was, she'd be in a much less accessible location.

On the other hand, whatever was in the shed was clearly of some importance, otherwise why would the door be kept locked?

He turned back, intending to walk around the opposite side of the ruins of the church, where he would be invisible to the men in the stable, but he'd only taken three or four paces when an unearthly howl tore through the night.

He froze instantly. It sounded like a huge dog, and for a brief, terrifying moment, Bronson thought that the island might be protected by attack dogs. If it was, the dogs would pick up his scent wherever he went and whatever he did. The Browning would dispose of them – he wasn't worried about that – but the men in the house would know immediately that they had an intruder, and he would stand no chance against half a dozen armed men. He'd be lucky to get off the island alive, and there'd be no chance of finding and rescuing Angela.

Then he relaxed slightly. Guard dogs, or those trained to attack intruders, either worked silently or would bark or growl. The sound he had just heard was neither. It had been more like an animal in pain, and it had sounded close by. Bronson's thoughts spun back to the wooden stable. There had definitely been something alive inside it.

And that was where the two men had gone.

Bronson ran swiftly around the old stone walls of the church, a moving shadow in the deeper blackness of the night. Before he'd covered more than a few feet, he heard the howl again, echoing from the stones around him, and filling the air with a sense of mournful and impending doom. He reached the end of the ruined building and crouched down beside a bush. The door of the stable was open and a dim glow came from the window that he'd tried to look through before.

Keeping well to one side of the building, Bronson made his way stealthily back towards where he'd left the boat, then circled around to approach the stable from behind. As he did so, the animal howled again, the sound dying away to a threatening growl. Then there was silence broken only by a faint whimpering noise. Bronson edged his way along the rear wall of the stable, turned the corner and stopped beside the window. For a few seconds he just listened, relying on his ears to warn him of the approach of anyone through the darkness. But apart from the noises emanating from the shed, the night was silent.

Slowly, carefully, Bronson looked through the small window. Inside, the walls were unadorned, just plain wood. The men were still out of sight, somewhere over to his left, but beside the door, which was wide open, he saw a long wooden table, a number of tins and packets placed on it, together with several metal bowls, a handful of forks and spoons, and a couple of metal jugs that possibly contained water. It was fairly obvious what he was looking at: the table was where they prepared food for the dog.

Bronson moved slowly, infinitesimally slowly, to the right, steadily bringing more and more of the interior of the stable into view. until at last he could see the whole building. Breathing in sharply in shock, he stepped back. The occupant of the stable was not the dog he'd expected. And what the men were doing to the animal made no sense at all.

71

Bronson shrank back into the undergrowth beside the old church and waited. About fifteen minutes had passed, and the men had just left the stable and were walking back towards the ruins. For an instant, he thought they might have seen him, but their posture was wrong: they were too relaxed, too casual.

They were still talking together as they passed him, and then, stepping slightly in front of the other, one of the men seized the ring handle on the church door and pushed it open. They both stepped through into the ruins and disappeared, leaving the door wide open behind them.

Bronson stood up slowly. For a few seconds there was total silence, and then he heard a distant rumbling that seemed to come from somewhere close by. It sounded like one heavy stone being moved across another.

Bronson reached the open door, looked inside – and shook his head in astonishment. The two men had simply disappeared. He'd walked around the entire interior of the building, just half an hour before, checking for any other way out, and had found nothing. But now, as he stared across the weed-strewn interior, piles of stone and wood faintly illuminated in the moonlight, he realized that there had to be a hidden door, or trapdoor, or something, somewhere in the building, and he had obviously missed it.

And wherever that door was, and whatever space it gave access to, it had to be the most likely place for Angela to be imprisoned.

If he'd seen where the two men had gone, he would have been able to wait outside and tackle them. One man armed with a semi-automatic pistol facing two unarmed men was no contest. He'd missed that chance but, he rationalized, sooner or later they would have to come out. And when they did, he'd be ready.

It was a simple enough plan, and almost immediately it started going wrong.

Marietta looked up when she heard the cellar door swinging open. 'Not so soon, please, no,' she whispered.

Shaking with fear, she looked with terrified eyes towards the stairs, and almost wept with relief when she realized that she still had a little time left. The two men were dressed in normal street clothes, not the hooded robes they would wear for the ceremony itself. One of them was carrying a small metal jug, which he placed on a ledge on the wall behind the stone table. Then they walked across the stone floor and peered at both Marietta and Angela, presumably making sure that they had obeyed their instructions and were wearing their robes in preparation for the ritual.

One of the men nodded towards Marietta and smiled, then they both turned and walked back to the spiral staircase.

Bronson stepped silently into the ruined church. Most of the debris littering the floor comprised individual lumps of stone and lengths of wood or small piles of rubbish, far too small for him to use for concealment. The only option he could see was about halfway down the wall to his left, where somebody had made an effort to clear some of the timber and building materials. The result was a heap of debris about two feet high and eight feet long, positioned quite close to the wall. It was just about big enough for him to hide behind, at least lying down, and would keep him invisible to anyone entering through the church door, though if somebody stepped across to the side wall of the building, they would see him immediately. It was a chance he was going to have to take.

The Browning in his hand, he crouched down behind the collection of old timbers. The only sound he could hear was the wind sighing through the branches of the handful of trees on the island, the branches creaking and groaning faintly as they moved. Even the animal imprisoned in the shed seemed to have fallen silent.

Then there was a click and a faint rumble, and a black

oblong shape appeared at the far end of the church. Beyond it he could see electric lights illuminating the top of a staircase that was set into the wall. It was obviously a door which led down to a cellar.

Two figures – the men he'd seen in the stable – stepped out and into the church. Bronson tensed, as he prepared to run towards the hidden door and down the steps. But then he relaxed again. The men had left the cellar door wide open, which meant that they could be going back down again. It would be better to wait until they'd left the church completely, and then make his entrance.

But then he realized there was another possibility. They could have left the door open to allow other people to enter the cellar, and this changed the odds once again.

As the two men reached the main entrance to the church, Bronson heard another noise. From over to his right, from the house itself, he heard the sound of shoes on gravel. It was clear that several people were now approaching the old church.

By now, the two men were still clearly visible at the church doorway, presumably waiting for the arrival of the approaching people. Bronson glanced over at the secret door, but knew that if he left his hiding place, he'd be seen well before he reached it. He would have to wait, and pick his moment.

There was a brief instant of silence, and then the first of the new arrivals stepped into the church. Bronson stared across at the figure, disbelief clouding his mind.

The man – and Bronson knew the figure was male simply by the way he walked – was clad in a dark, possibly black, hooded robe, his face completely hidden. He looked like a caricature of a monk, though without any doubt Christian thoughts and prayers were a long way from his mind. Bronson had guessed from the few clues he had been able to find that the deaths of the girls might well have involved some kind of ritual. What he hadn't anticipated was that the ritual might involve a quasi-religious ceremony. But this was what seemed to be about to take place, because the hooded man was followed by others, all clad in the same all-enveloping robes.

The figures made their way in single file across the old stone floor, the hems of their robes just brushing the ground. Bronson counted eleven, plus the first man who appeared to be the leader of the group. He seemed to remember that thirteen was supposed to be the number of witches in a coven, and wondered if that was significant, if there was another man already waiting down in the cellar.

Then he heard a faint click, and saw that the lights on the stone staircase had been extinguished. A new light, faint and flickering, had sprung to life just inside the hidden doorway. Obviously the leader of the group had lit a candle.

As the man started to walk slowly down the staircase, Bronson heard something else: a single scream of anguish from deep within the chamber below. Could it have been Angela? One way or another, he was going to find out.

Bronson knew he was heavily outnumbered, and he had no idea if any of the group were carrying weapons under their robes, or if there were firearms stored in the cellar. Whatever the case, he had to get down to that cellar.

And suddenly he saw a way of achieving just that. The men filing down the stairs were walking slowly, but they were too close together for him to tackle one without the person in front seeing what was happening. Each man paused inside the secret doorway to light a candle before descending out of sight, which meant several of them were now clustered outside the doorway, waiting their turn. But then the last man in the group stopped and turned back to the church entrance. One of the two men outside the ruined building had said something – Bronson didn't catch what – and had attracted his attention.

The man walked swiftly back to the church entrance, muttered something to the men outside, and closed the door. Then he turned and walked back towards the hidden doorway, through which the last of his companions had just disappeared. At that moment Bronson holstered the Browning and made his move.

He ran across the debris-strewn stone floor after his target. The moment he did so, the hooded man turned towards him, obviously having seen some movement in his peripheral vision. When he saw Bronson, a sudden expression of panic clouded his features, and he opened his mouth to shout.

But Bronson didn't give him the chance, as he dived

forward and slammed his left shoulder into the man's chest. The impact drove every vestige of breath from his target's body, and he fell backwards, gasping for air.

The two men tumbled to the ground together, Bronson cushioned by the body that had fallen beneath him. The other man caught his breath and started to rise, but Bronson had anticipated his movement. He punched him – hard – in his solar plexus, and followed it up with a vicious short-arm jab to the chin. The man's head snapped backwards, the rear of his skull crunching on to one of the flagstones. His eyes rolled backwards and his body went limp.

Bronson stood up and looked all round him. He knew he had only seconds to act before somebody in the group noticed that the last man hadn't appeared.

He seized the man's right arm and pulled him into a sitting position, then wrapped his arms around his chest and lifted him upright across his body, like a bulky sack. Moving awkwardly across the ground to the pile of debris behind which he'd hidden before, he simply let go. The man's limp body crashed to the ground, his head again cracking on to the old stones. At best, Bronson guessed that he would have a concussion and a blinding headache for a few days. At worst, he might already be dying from cranial bleeding. Either way, he didn't care.

With some difficulty, he removed the man's robe. Underneath it, he was naked apart from a pair of sandals, confirmation, if it was needed, of the sort of ritual that was about to take place. Bronson didn't bother about the sandals, but swiftly pulled on the robe over his street clothes and then ran across to the door in the church wall.

Pulling the hood down over his features to conceal his face as much as he could, he picked up one of the large yellow candles lying on a shelf just inside the doorway, lit it from the box of matches that was also on the shelf, and began to make his way slowly down the stone spiral staircase.

72

The moment the light went out, Marietta gave a shriek of terror. She knew what the sudden darkness meant. For them, there was no more time. The ceremony was about to start, and within minutes she and Angela would be dying in agony.

She screamed again as the first hooded figure appeared at the base of the stone staircase, his features fitfully illuminated by the flickering light of his candle.

In almost complete silence, the remainder of the group appeared one by one at the bottom of the staircase and stepped into the cellar, the only noise the faint slapping of their leather sandals against the stone floor. As before, they moved slowly around the stone table, taking up their pre-arranged positions in what looked like a ghastly parody of a religious service.

Angela watched with mounting horror as the figures, all dressed in identical black robes, strode silently and menacingly across the cellar. Marietta had explained what had happened the night Benedetta had died, and it was obvious that the ritual tonight was going to be almost identical.

For a few moments, the men stood in unmoving silence around the stone table, apparently waiting for something. A couple of them turned slightly and looked back towards the entrance to the staircase. Then everyone in the cellar clearly heard the sound of another set of footsteps descending towards them, and seconds later a twelfth hooded man stepped into the room. There was only one space in the circle of figures, and the man stepped confidently forward and took his place within it.

The leader nodded his satisfaction. The circle was complete and, once the Master made his appearance, the ceremony could begin.

Bronson stood near the foot of the stone table, his head bowed respectfully, trying his best to emulate the stance of the other men in the cellar. Like them, he held the candle in his left hand but, unlike the others, his right hand was hovering close to the vertical seam that joined the two halves of his robe together at the front.

The garment had only one small pocket, nowhere near big enough to conceal the Browning pistol, and he'd had to leave it tucked into the belt holster. With the heavy robe over the top, the weapon was fairly inaccessible, and he knew that if – or rather when – he had to draw it, he'd have to be quick and get the robe open as fast as possible.

But his prospects were bleak. He knew that when he pulled the weapon, he might be able to shoot down two or three of the men, but in this confined space he would soon be overpowered. He would have to wait, and choose his moment carefully.

He was aware that there were other people in the cellar, besides the dozen men near him. He could hear faint movements, and the sound of sobbing, coming from somewhere in the darkness over to his left. Convinced it was Angela, he resisted the temptation to rush to her aid.

The scene Bronson was witnessing was bizarre in the extreme. Above ground, and away from the isolated island, life in the twenty-first century continued unabated, but what he saw in front of him was mediaeval both in its appearance and, he was sure, in its objective. In that cellar, at that time, the modern world had simply ceased to exist, and the ritual about to take place was designed to produce a result that wasn't even mediaeval in scope. It was far older, and far more evil, than that.

Suddenly he detected a change in the atmosphere. A sense of anticipation, of barely controlled excitement, filled the air.

And then he heard something: a soft, sibilant sound, coming from the stone staircase behind him. The noise could only be caused by the hem of one of the robes rubbing on the stone steps as someone else descended into the cellar. All the other hooded men who were now surrounding the stone table were wearing sandals, and he'd clearly heard their footsteps as they crossed the floor of the ruined church. Perhaps the new arrival was barefoot?

He detected a new and unpleasant odour, and then the thirteenth man entered the cellar. He moved silently to the opposite side of the stone table, his hands and face invisible in the folds of his black robe, and all the other men, including Bronson, bowed low in supplication.

For a few seconds, nothing happened, then the new arrival – the person Bronson now assumed was their leader – gestured to the man on his left, who bowed in acknowledgement and produced a small box which he raised above his head while the other men looked on with reverence. Bronson tried to keep his face in shadow as much as he could, but he knew he had to act just like one of the other acolytes in order to remain safely anonymous. So he moved the candle slightly to one side, so that its light no longer fell directly on his face, and looked up.

The man lowered the box, opened it and removed a skull, the bone dark brown and cracked with age, the lower jaw and parts of the cranium missing. There was a soft collective intake of breath at the sight of the relic.

'Behold the skull of Nicodema Diluca himself,' the man said, 'the legitimate descendant of the Princess Eleonora Amalia, the relic for which we have searched for so long.'

What happened next made no sense to Bronson. He

watched in fascination as the man used a pair of modern pliers to snap off a section of the cranium, and then proceeded to grind it up using a pestle and mortar, his movements slow and deliberate, almost ceremonial.

The operation took several minutes, because the man clearly wanted to reduce the fragment of bone to dust, but eventually he appeared to be satisfied and placed the pestle to one side. He lifted the mortar above his head, and again this action seemed to inspire a kind of rapture in the group around the table, the dozen men raising their heads to stare reverently at the stone container.

Finally, the man lowered the mortar and walked slowly around the table to show the contents to the leader, then he returned to his place in the circle and put the mortar to one side, on another, very much smaller, stone table behind him.

For a few seconds, nobody moved. Then the leader made another gesture, this time to the man on his right, who nodded and pointed towards the two men who were standing on Bronson's left. They both bowed slightly, then stepped away from the stone table and walked slowly away into the darkness that shrouded the other part of the underground room.

As they did so, a scream ripped through the oppressive silence, and Bronson could sense an almost palpable ripple of excitement coursing through the men around him. Working by feel with his right hand, through the thick material of the robe, he checked the Browning, trying to make sure that the hammer was cocked and the weapon ready to fire.

Then he heard another voice from the darkness, laced with fury and yelling in English, which he recognized immediately. Angela was somewhere in the room, together with at least one other young woman.

The leader of the group turned his head slightly to look towards the sound of her voice, as did several other men around the table. Bronson stared in that direction as well, trying to build up a picture of the layout of the room, so that when he moved, he wouldn't slam into a wall or trip over anything. As far as he could tell, in the fitful illumination provided by the candles, it had a low ceiling and no doors apart from the one leading to the spiral staircase. Along one side of the room were short dividing walls which formed small, door-less, internal rooms. Possibly they'd once been storerooms but now, even in poor candlelight, he could see that they were being used as cells.

He could just about see Angela, who was still shouting her defiance at the men. Bronson tensed, ready for action. And then he heard a sudden sharp crack and a brief flare of light from the darkness, and she fell silent. He didn't know for sure, but it looked as if one of the men had used a taser on her. He would pay for that, Bronson vowed, his hands clenched, blood pounding in his temples.

The leader of the group held up his hand, and immediately the attention of all the men around the table snapped back to him. He whispered something to the man on his right, who'd been acting as his assistant during the first part of the ceremony. This man nodded and then he, too, lifted his hand.

'Our master has made a decision,' the man said, his Italian smooth and educated. 'We have two subjects available to us tonight. As you know, one of these shares the holy bloodline of Nicodema Diluca, and she will enjoy the rapture of giving her lifeblood freely while two or three of our number offer their unworthy seed to her sacred womb.'

For a moment, Bronson didn't understand what the man meant. Then it dawned on him: despite the almost literary expression he had used, what he was actually talking about was multiple rape. Bronson felt his whole body tense with loathing and disgust.

'Our second subject,' he continued, 'has no direct connection with us, but has accidentally proved to be of enormous value to our quest. She was responsible for removing the diary of Carmelita Paganini from its resting place in her tomb. She has provided a translation of a part of that book, and this information in turn led us to the island of Poveglia, where we recovered the Source Document, the "Noble Vampyr" treatise written by our ancient and revered master, Amadeus. This holy text has confirmed the validity of our quest and the accuracy of our rituals, except in one important respect.'

There was a sudden silence in the chamber, and Bronson

could tell that every man there was totally attentive, waiting for the explanation.

'What we did not know until now was that, for the ritual to be successful, we needed to combine the blood of the descendant of Nicodema Diluca with that of a woman without connection to any of the sacred families. Our leader has decided that this Englishwoman, whose usefulness to us is now at an end and whose spirit must be released to the void for our own security, will fill that role. So this evening we will celebrate the passing of both spirits.'

The chill Bronson felt as he heard those words and understood what the man meant had nothing to do with the cool and clammy air of the cellar. Angela, it was clear, was also destined for multiple rape, and was then to be murdered. As if that wasn't horrific enough, the man's next statement showed the hideous depths of the cult's brutality.

'Afterwards, in accordance with the tenets of our quest and our sacred knowledge, we will then enjoy her directly, consuming her blood and her still-warm and ripe flesh in the manner prescribed by our sacred guide and master in spirit, the venerable and inspiring Amadeus.'

Several of the men appeared to nod, though the voluminous hoods that covered their heads and faces largely concealed any movement, and Bronson heard a faint murmur of approval.

'Now let us begin. Bring forward the first subject.'

There was a howl of outrage and anguish, and then the two men walked back towards the circle and the stone altar, each gripping the arm of a dark-haired girl in her early twenties who was struggling violently, trying desperately to get away. They stopped a short distance away from the stone table and held her as still as possible.

Two other men then left their places in the circle and stepped over to her, one in front and the other behind her.

His features invisible beneath the hood covering his head, Bronson glanced towards the girl, stark terror written all over her face, and then at the silent figures of the men surrounding the stone table. He knew he would have to make his move soon – he would not permit the men around him to do harm to this girl or to Angela. Or he would die trying.

73

But right then wasn't the correct moment. When the bullets started flying, Bronson wanted the innocent parties – the girl standing a dozen feet from him and awaiting her fate and, of course, Angela – to be as far away from the firing line as possible. It looked to him as if the ceremony would require the girl to be tied down on the table, and that would probably be as safe a place as anywhere in the cellar. So his best option was to wait until she was immobilized, because then she wouldn't panic and run into a stray bullet. And she would also be the focus of everybody in the room. That might give him time to step back to a suitable vantage point and cover the dozen men with his pistol. Quite how the scenario would pan out after that, Bronson didn't know. He would just have to think on his feet, and play the cards he'd been dealt.

He switched his attention to the four men who now surrounded the dark-haired girl. The two who had dragged her from the cell by the wall were still holding her bare upper arms, keeping her in position. Bronson couldn't see what the other two men were supposed to be doing. Then he found out.

Simultaneously, they both reached out, seized the material of her white robe and pulled violently on it. The Velcro seams ripped apart, the robe separating into two halves, front and back, which the men casually tossed aside before stepping backwards a couple of paces.

The girl emitted an even louder squeal of terror as her nakedness was revealed to all, and redoubled her struggles to get free. But it was an unequal contest, and the two men had no difficulty in keeping her still. They looked towards the leader of the group, and when he beckoned them, they strode forward, forcing the naked girl towards the end of the table almost directly in front of Bronson.

They turned her round so that her buttocks were resting against the old stone, then simply pushed her off her feet. The two men who'd removed her robe stepped forward and seized her legs, lifting her up and placing her writhing body flat on the table. In moments, the men had buckled the leather straps around her wrists and ankles, while another man tied a strap around her head as well.

He knew that it was time to stop this, before anything else could happen to the girl.

The men who'd been lashing the girl's body to the table

stepped back and resumed their places in the circle, and waited expectantly. Bronson knew without a shadow of doubt what the next act in these bizarrely mediaeval and simply monstrous proceedings was going to be. Somebody, one of the men around the table, was going to climb up on to the table, force himself on to the girl's body and rape her. And he knew absolutely that he wasn't going to stand by and let that happen.

Surreptitiously, he took a couple of steps backwards, moving slightly out of the circle, and took a firm hold of the Velcro seam of his robe, preparing to act.

Then the leader of the group spoke again to his assistant, and Bronson caught the faint sound of his voice, though not the words he spoke. The voice was weak and rasping, as if he hadn't used it for a long time or was simply unused to talking. The assistant nodded, then looked up and extended his hand, pointing directly at Bronson. And suddenly, every man in the room was looking at him.

As he stared across the table at the figures opposite, Bronson could just make out the glint of the leader's eyes under the hood, and below that the shine of his teeth, a faint horizontal bar of white in the gloom. But there was something else, something that sent a chill through Bronson's soul and literally raised the hairs on the back of his neck. It looked as if the canine teeth in the man's upper jaw were at least twice as long as they should have been, the ends sharply pointed.

But before he could react to the sight, the leader's assistant spoke directly to him.

'You go first,' he murmured. 'Give her something to scream about.'

✝

74

Bronson knew that he was the focus of everyone's attention. He assumed that there was some kind of sick prestige in being the first one chosen to violate the girl strapped down on the stone table, the girl whose desperate screams and moans were still echoing around the underground room. He had hoped that as soon as this part of the ritual began, he would be able to step further back, away from the group, and use the nine-millimetre persuasion afforded by the Browning to stop the action even before it started.

Clearly, that wasn't going to work. He had to act immediately.

He had just started to pull apart the seam of his robe when the man who had been assisting the leader raised his hand and spoke to him.

'Wait,' he said. 'You are eager enough, brother, but don't forget there is one more step we have to complete.'

Bronson relaxed a little and eased his grip on the material.

The assistant gestured behind him, and two of the men left the circle and stepped across to the end wall of the cellar, returning in moments with a small jug and a funnel. As soon as he saw these two utensils, Bronson guessed what they were going to do, and knew he had a few more minutes.

The two black-clad figures walked across to the girl. One of them pulled down on her chin to force her mouth open, then pushed the end of the funnel between her teeth. He held it in position and nodded to his companion, who began dribbling a white fluid into the top of the funnel, forcing the girl to swallow it. She choked and coughed, but to no avail; the two men continued with their actions until the jug was empty.

As soon as Bronson could see that they'd finished force-feeding her the milk, he stepped slightly away from the circle, as if he was preparing to remove his robe and carry out the rape as he'd been instructed by the leader of the group.

The assistant saw that he was moving out of the circle, and called across the table to him: 'Now we can begin. Prepare yourself, brother, for your appointed task, so that we may release the lifeblood from this willing subject – the blood that will allow us to fulfil our destiny.'

Bronson nodded, the movement barely perceptible because of his all-enveloping hood, and turned away from the table. Out of the corner of his eye, he could just make out the shadowy form of Angela climbing slowly to her feet as she recovered from the assault by the taser.

His plan was simple enough. He had to get out of the robe, because the garment was heavy and would restrict his movements, just as the robes would hamper the other men in the cellar. Being told to rape the girl actually provided him with an opportunity to dump the robe without arousing the suspicions of the rest of the group. Once he'd done that, he had the Browning and the spare magazines to control and, if it came to it, shoot down, the other men.

75

But before he could remove the robe, there was a sudden bang from somewhere behind him, and a hoarse shout echoed down the stone spiral staircase, followed immediately by the staircase lights coming on and the sound of somebody pounding down the steps. Then the single electric bulb over the stone table snapped on, flooding that end of the room with light. Seconds later, one of the two men Bronson had seen outside the church ran into the cellar, his face flushed and his breath coming in short gasps.

He blurted out something that Bronson didn't catch, though he did make the words 'naked' and 'robe', and in that instant he knew they'd found the man he'd attacked in the church.

Immediately, all the men standing around the stone table looked at Bronson, identifying him as the impostor.

In a single movement, Bronson pulled open the front of

his robe, pushed the hood back off his head and grabbed for his Browning.

In that instant, Angela called out his name, a single shrill syllable that echoed around the room. But two of the hooded men were already reaching for their own weapons, and Bronson knew he'd be out-gunned in seconds.

There was only one thing he could do to save the situation and buy himself some time. Taking rapid aim, he pulled the trigger. But his target wasn't one of the menacing hooded men advancing towards him. Despite the circumstances, Bronson still wasn't prepared to shoot down a man in cold blood – at least, not until he had absolutely no alternative. Instead, he raised the pistol higher, aiming it towards the ceiling, and the single lamp dangling there, and squeezed the trigger.

The sound of the nine-millimetre cartridge firing in the confined space of the cellar was deafening, the noise of the explosion echoing from the walls. The copper-jacketed bullet missed the light bulb, smashed into the concrete ceiling and ricocheted on to the back wall. Still carrying a lot of kinetic energy, it then bounced off the stone and hit one of the robed figures. Bronson heard a man call out in pain and fall to the ground.

He fired again, and again, the crashing blast of each shot deafeningly loud, the bullets ricocheting off the walls and ceiling, fragments of stone and red-hot copper from the bullet flying everywhere.

The last bullet hit either the light bulb itself or, more

likely, the lamp holder, because as well as extinguishing the single light in the cellar, there was a sudden flash and the staircase lights went out. Bronson guessed that the bullet's impact had blown a fuse somewhere.

Instantly, the cellar was plunged into darkness, the only illumination being the candles held by the hooded figures, several of which had already been blown out.

But there was still enough light to see the men around the stone table, and two of them were already aiming pistols directly at Bronson. He shifted his aim, bringing down his weapon until the sights lined up with one of the two men. As he squeezed the trigger, the other man fired, and Bronson felt a tug on the left-hand side of the heavy robe he was wearing as the bullet ploughed through the material.

The shot may have missed him, but Bronson had taken an extra half-second to make sure he didn't miss his target. The man gave a shriek of pain and fell backwards, clutching at his shoulder while his weapon cartwheeled uselessly from his hand to clatter on to the stone floor.

One down, but eleven men were still facing him in the room. The second man fired, but Bronson was already moving. He ducked down and took a few steps over to his right, moving deeper into the shadows that danced around the far end of the cellar. He heard the impact of the bullet somewhere in the darkness behind him, took rapid aim at the armed man and squeezed the trigger.

His shot missed, and his target dived off to one side,

finding cover behind the stone wall that marked the end of one of the cells built along the side of the cellar.

Then Bronson heard a sharp command, and almost immediately all the candles were extinguished.

For a few moments, the only sound in the room was the moaning of the man Bronson had shot. Angela, after her one yell of recognition, had said nothing else, and even the girl on the stone table had fallen silent.

The blackness was Stygian, impenetrable. Bronson took two silent steps to one side, so that he was no longer in the same spot where he'd been standing when the candles were put out. He slid out of the heavy robe and tossed it to one side, a few feet away from him, the garment landing with a muffled sound on the stone floor. Instantly, another shot crashed out, the bullet slamming into the rear wall of the cellar several feet away from him.

OK, Bronson thought. His assailants would fire at any sound they heard because he was a single vulnerable target: if he made a noise, he would die. The only advantage he had was that the men were probably still clustered near the stone table, so at least he knew where they were. But he couldn't fire at them, not in the darkness without any point of reference – the risk of hitting the girl on the table was too high.

For the moment, it was a stalemate.

Making no sound at all, Bronson stood up and started to ease his way along the wall beside him, touching it with his left hand – he needed to feel the old stones to ensure that he was going in the right direction. All he hoped to do was put a little more distance between himself and the other men. And if he could get as far as the back wall of the room, he could try to work his way across to the cell where Angela was being held and try to free her.

There was another sharp command from the other end of the room. The voice was quiet and he couldn't make out the words, but the effect was immediate. Bronson heard the sound of movement – someone was cautiously crossing the floor towards him, their robes rustling and their leather sandals slapping faintly on the old stones. He guessed that two of the men, both no doubt armed with pistols, had been ordered to move apart so that they could catch him in the crossfire.

Still he daren't fire blind. He might hit the girl. He could even hit Angela. And if he did shoot, the muzzle flash from his pistol would instantly give away his position, and he knew exactly what would happen if he did that.

He moved infinitely slowly, backing away from the sound of movement. Then he stopped and crouched down with his back to the wall, making himself as small a target as possible. He held the Browning ready in his right hand, his left pressed against the wall behind him, prepared to move or to shoot as events dictated, listening hard and desperately trying to make sense of what he was hearing.

Then, through the darkness, he heard another muttered command, and almost immediately two shots blasted out from opposite sides of the cellar, the bullets smashing into the wall where he'd been standing just moments earlier, then ricocheting away. The muzzle flashes illuminated the shooters for a split second, just long enough for Bronson to see where they were.

He fired once, at the figure on his right, then dived sideways, changing his own position.

Two more shots deafened him, and he knew immediately that his own bullet had missed.

Then the man spoke again, and this time he was close enough for Bronson to hear exactly what he said.

'Stop. That's far enough,' he said in Italian.

Then another man spoke from the opposite end of the cellar.

'Drop your weapon, Bronson.' The voice was familiar, and Bronson immediately recognized the hostile tones of Inspector Bianchi. 'You have no chance. Give up, and we'll kill you quickly. But if you don't surrender, I can promise that you'll take a very long time to die, though probably not as long as your interfering wife. We'll make sure she dies first, and we'll make you watch.'

Bronson didn't move or respond, figuring the angles. It's a basic rule of close combat that you never, ever, surrender your weapon. He knew that as well as anyone who'd ever served in the military of any nation, and he also knew that if he spoke, if he responded in any way at all, the men in front of him would open fire immediately.

But there was one thing he could do. He pressed the button on the left side of the Browning and slid out the magazine. Then he extracted a full one from the carrier on his belt and slid it into place in the weapon, the faintest of clicks confirming it was locked home. He replaced the half-empty magazine in the carrier.

'Very well, Bronson. It is your choice,' Bianchi said.

Then the sound of loud, angry shouts filled the air, followed by the clattering of shoes on the stones of the spiral staircase. Dancing torch beams illuminated that end of the cellar.

At the moment, Bronson knew he'd reached the end of his rope. Reinforcements had obviously been summoned from the house; they would pick him out in an instant with their torches and, no matter what he did then, he would die. The best he could hope to do was take a few of them with him.

Then, from somewhere over to his left, he heard a sudden movement. There was a faint snap, like the sound of a distant whip-crack, and a flare of dim blue light so transient Bronson wasn't sure he'd actually seen it. It was followed, an instant later, by a dull sound, like something heavy dropping on to the floor, from that side of the cellar. And then someone started to scream.

76

Reacting instinctively to the screams, Bronson took a couple of steps to his left. Then he stopped. The danger was right in front of him, the men still coming down the stone staircase. He stood up, raised the pistol in his right hand and braced his wrist with his left, waiting until he could identify a target. He would make every shot count. That was all he could do.

But something was wrong. The men in the cellar weren't reacting the way they should be, the way he expected.

In the flickering torchlight he could see that the men around him were moving quickly back towards the stone table and the foot of the staircase, the only exit from the room. And then he finally understood what the people coming down the stairs were shouting.

A dark figure appeared in the opening to the staircase, a powerful torch attached to his weapon illuminating the scene in front of him. But the moment he stepped into the cellar, a shot rang out, and he fell backwards out of sight. A second man took his place, and immediately opened fire, a burst of three shots from his sub-machine gun taking out two of the hooded figures, who tumbled to the ground screaming.

But another shot from one of the men in the cellar threw the man to the ground before he could fire again.

Another figure appeared, clad in dark combat clothing like the first two, and Bronson realized that – somehow – the Italian police were here. What he was witnessing was an assault by the Italian equivalent of a SWAT team.

The problem the police had was getting into the cellar. Normally, an assault would be mounted through multiple entrances and using the maximum possible number of officers. But the only way into this room was down the staircase, which put the assault team at a tremendous disadvantage. And the men in the cellar obviously had nothing to lose.

The third police officer had clearly seen what had happened to his two companions and tried a different tack: he aimed his sub-machine gun around the end of the wall, the beam of the attached torch seeking a target. But the hooded figures had scattered, some taking refuge behind the stone table, others in the cell nearest the staircase.

Bronson ran over to the wall on his right, getting as far away as possible from both the police and their targets. No bullets followed him as he moved.

The girl lashed down on the table screamed in terror.

Bronson stared through the gloom, and what he saw spurred him into immediate action.

One of the hooded men down at that end of the stone table had reached up, a blade in his hand, feeling for her neck, presumably so that he could permanently remove one witness to their activities. Bronson took a couple of steps forward to shorten the range, raised his pistol and aimed at the centre of the dark shape, squeezing the trigger as he did so. The Browning kicked in his hand, and the man tumbled sideways, his knife clattering to the floor.

Then more shots crashed out as the armed men in the cellar fired at the police officer. He replied with two short bursts from his weapon, the bullets striking stone. One hit the ancient skull sitting on the small stone table, sending shards of old bone flying as it disintegrated.

The cellar filled with the smell of cordite, and the stabbing beams of the torches attached to the sub-machine guns of the two men sheltering in the stairwell – another officer had just appeared there – erratically illuminated different parts of the room as the officers looked for targets.

Bronson shrank down, trying to make himself as small and insignificant as possible. He knew there was only one way this was going to end, because the hooded men were ludicrously outgunned, but the fight wasn't over yet. And he really didn't want to get taken out by a bullet from either side.

Suddenly, in the flickering light from the torches, he saw a round object hit the floor just to one side of the stone table, and knew exactly what it was. Immediately, he placed the Browning on the ground, shut his eyes and pressed his hands over his ears as hard as he could.

Half a second later, the stun grenade exploded, the blast obscenely loud in the confined space. Bronson opened his eyes; then closed them again as another stun grenade rolled across the floor. Once again, the cellar rocked with the massive blast. And then there seemed to be torches everywhere, as the rest of the assault team ran into the chamber.

Most of the hooded men were still in a state of shock after the two blasts, and offered no resistance. One of them, who'd been carrying a pistol but had dropped it on the floor, made a grab for it. But one of the assault team reached him before he could pick it up and smashed the butt of his sub-machine gun into the side of his head, instantly knocking him unconscious.

Bronson stood up, leaned back against the wall and raised both his hands high in the air. Frantically, he looked about him. Where was Angela? He guessed she'd dived for cover at the back of her cell as soon as the bullets started flying, and if she hadn't covered her ears when the stun grenades went off, she was probably still disoriented. She had to be somewhere near, but right then he couldn't see her.

Two members of the assault team walked over to him, their weapons pointing steadily at his stomach.

'Are you Bronson?' one of them asked him in Italian.

That was pretty much the last thing he expected them to say. Once he'd realized the men coming down the stairs were police officers, Bronson had presumed that he would be arrested with all the other people in the building and taken back to Venice.

He nodded. 'Yes. How did you—'

'Passport,' the second officer snapped. 'Now.'

Bronson reached around with his left hand, pulled the document from the hip pocket of his jeans and passed it over. One of the Italian policemen flicked it open, looked at the photograph inside it, then raised his weapon so that the beam from the attached torch shone straight into Bronson's face. He nodded, handed back the document and lowered his sub-machine gun.

Bronson tried again. 'How did you know who I was?'

Another figure, still wearing his black robe, strode over to the three men and pushed back his hood.

'They knew,' Inspector Bianchi said, 'because I told them.'

'But I thought—'

'I know exactly what you thought. You almost managed to wreck our operation. It's taken me nearly six months to get close enough to this group so that they would trust me. I only found out tonight, when they brought me here, to this island, where they were based.'

'So how did the assault team know where to come?'

'There's a tracking chip in my mobile phone. As back-up, I had six police boats out in the lagoon watching where

I was taken. If you'd just done what I told you, and left this operation to us, we might have managed to take them all alive. As it is, now I've got corpses to identify as well.'

'I saw two of your men shot when they tried to get in here. Are they OK?'

'Yes. They're just bruised. They both took chest shots, but they were wearing Kevlar jackets.' Bianchi smiled for the first time since he'd walked across to Bronson. 'Now, I have to get this situation tidied up. Don't leave the island until you've made a full written statement, and keep your diary clear. We'll probably want you to come back out here as a witness when these bastards go on trial.'

Sighing with relief, Bronson picked up the Browning pistol, clicked the safety catch on, and slid it into his belt holster. Nobody had asked him to hand it over, so he thought he might as well hang on to it. Then he walked across to the cell where Angela had been imprisoned.

She was nowhere to be seen. Bronson rubbed his eyes as he took in the roughly fashioned bed and mattress, and the chain and handcuff that had secured her to the wall. The handcuff was open, so he knew somebody – one of the policemen, perhaps – must have freed her. He stepped back into the middle of the cellar and looked round.

The injured members of the cult were sitting with their backs to the wall opposite the cells, their wrists handcuffed behind them. Some were receiving basic medical treatment, but there was little the assault team members could do for them. Bronson assumed that an ambulance boat was on its way. The dead men were still lying where they'd fallen, waiting for the arrival of a forensics team.

The girl who'd been strapped down on the stone table had been released. She was wrapped in a blanket and was clinging to one of the Italian police officers as if she never wanted to let him go. Bronson could only imagine the turmoil of emotions that were coursing through her body.

But he still couldn't see Angela. Perhaps she'd already been taken up to ground level. Perhaps. But a knot of anxiety was forming in Bronson's chest. He strode across the room to where Bianchi stood, issuing orders and directing his men.

'Where's Angela?' he demanded. 'Where's my wife?'

Bianchi pointed back towards the other end of the cellar. 'She's in the last cell.'

Bronson shook his head. 'No, she isn't. Are you sure none of your men took her upstairs?'

'Nobody has left here apart from some of my officers. She must be here.'

Then Bronson noticed something else. 'One of them is missing,' he said, pointing to the robed men.

'Who?' Bianchi demanded.

The cult members had had the hoods pulled clear of their faces. And as Bronson stared at each one in turn, he realized that the man who'd been directing operations wasn't there.

'The leader,' he said. 'Where is he?'

Bianchi snapped an order and two of his men immediately started to search the cellar.

Bronson stood there, thinking furiously. If Bianchi was right, and nobody had left the cellar up the spiral staircase, then there had to be another way out.

Somehow, the leader had managed to slip past everyone in the confusion of the police assault, and had grabbed Angela as he left.

Bronson groaned. He'd been so close, so sure that he'd managed to save her. But again she'd disappeared. And this time he had only the haziest idea where to start looking for her.

77

Bronson leaned against the wall of the cellar as he replayed the events that had just taken place. He'd seen Angela, seen exactly where she was, standing at the opening of the end cell. He'd heard her calling out his name.

Nobody had gone anywhere near her from that moment on. The attention of the hooded men had been entirely concentrated on the girl who'd been lashed down on the stone table. Then the shooting had started, and people had been moving all around the cellar, trying to take cover from the bullets, or firing themselves.

As Bronson recalled each of these events, he remembered something else: just before the screaming started, there'd been a noise like something heavy falling to the ground. But could it have been something else? Could it have been the sound of a stone door closing?

'I think there's another way out of here,' Bronson said to Bianchi.

Bianchi looked doubtful. 'An underground chamber is rare enough in the *Laguna Veneta*, and this is quite a big room on a small island. It's very unlikely there are any other spaces down here.'

Bronson reached out and grabbed a torch from the assault vest of a police officer who was standing next to Bianchi. The officer tried to take it back, but the inspector stopped him.

'Very well,' he said, sighing. 'But if you find a door, call me, and then we'll assess the situation.'

Bronson ran over to the cell where Angela had been imprisoned. That was the obvious – in fact the only – starting point. But all that was there was the crudely made wooden bed, a thin mattress and a single pillow. Under the bed was a rusty metal bucket and a partially used roll of toilet paper. The only other object he could see was the steel chain lying across the mattress, one end attached to a large eyebolt screwed into the stone wall, the other end dangling down, the open handcuff resting on the floor.

Bronson turned to his right, towards the opposite end of the cellar from the stone table. If there was a hidden door – and this was the only explanation that made sense – it had to be somewhere beyond the line of cells.

He gave the outside wall of the cell a cursory glance, then directed the beam of the torch at the solid wall of the cellar as he walked across to it. The old stones looked damp and cold; and none showed the slightest sign of movement when he pressed against them. Bronson used both hands, pushing his palms firmly against each stone at about chest level as he worked his way slowly towards the back wall of the cellar. He reached the corner of the wall, glanced back briefly and then resumed his steady and methodical progress. Using the same technique, he crossed the back wall of the cellar with exactly the same lack of result. Every stone he'd pushed had seemed absolutely solid.

But Angela had been in the cellar, and now she wasn't. She hadn't gone up the spiral staircase, so there definitely had to be another exit. He'd tried the walls without result. Now he had to look at the floor.

Bronson directed the torch beam downwards and stared at the old flagstones, worn down by countless feet over the years. It didn't look as if any of them had been moved in decades, possibly for centuries. He studied them anyway, looking for any sign of movement, of suspiciously clean edges or anything of that sort. Nothing.

He had to have missed something, some clue that would show him where the hidden entrance was located. Then he slowly became aware of something gnawing away at his subconscious. He'd seen something, or felt something – something that wasn't quite right, something out of place. Bronson jogged back to the side wall of the cellar, and started walking slowly along the wall, staring at the stones and touching each one that he pressed against before. He reached the end, then started on the back wall. And then it struck him.

The stones on the side wall had looked and felt damp,

as had those on the back wall, all except three of them in a horizontal line, about five feet from the junction of the two walls. Those stones were solid and cold, but not quite as cold as the stones on either side of them, and his fingers could detect no trace of damp.

He felt the stones above and below the three he'd detected, and they all showed the same characteristics: they were solid and cold but not damp. He'd found the hidden door. All he had to do now was work out how to open it.

Bronson shone the torch at the stones. Now that he'd identified the door, its shape was fairly obvious. He looked closely at the spaces between the stones. In an almost vertical line, from floor level up to about five feet above the ground, there was a straight edge where no mortar was visible.

But what he still couldn't see was how to get it open. He ran his fingers up and down the vertical edge, feeling for a catch or lever. He pushed against each of the stones in turn, in case one of them would work a hidden catch, but again without result.

There had to be a way of getting the door open. Almost in desperation, he pressed his left shoulder against the stones, braced his feet on the floor and started to push. His right foot started to slide, and he changed position. As he again put his weight on his right foot, he felt rather than heard a click under the sole of his shoe, and the stone door swung silently outwards.

Caught completely unawares, Bronson tumbled through the opening, and crashed to the ground on the other side. Immediately, powerful springs swung the door closed again, the solid structure clicking back into place with a muted thump, the same sound he had heard minutes earlier.

He scrambled to his feet, reached down and drew the Browning from his holster. Then he replaced the weapon. It was pitch black in the chamber, and if he couldn't see, he couldn't shoot. He needed light.

The torch had fallen from his hand as he'd tumbled through the doorway, and he crouched down and felt around on the floor, searching for it. His probing fingers touched something shrivelled and furry, and he recoiled. A dead rat, probably. In a few seconds, his hand closed around a cool metal tube, and he gave a sigh of relief.

But that feeling didn't last long. When he pressed the switch on the end of the torch, nothing happened. He shook it, and could hear a faint rattling sound inside it. The bulb or something had obviously broken when he fell.

He would have to find his way around by feel. Having made sure his pistol was properly seated in the holster, because if he dropped it he might not be able to find it again, Bronson extended both arms in front of him and started walking forwards.

Then he stopped dead. Somewhere in the darkness ahead of him, he could hear the faint sound of movement.

*   *   *

'What happened?' Inspector Bianchi demanded.

The black-clad police officer shook his head. 'I don't really know, sir. One minute the Englishman was standing close to the back wall of the cellar, then I looked away for a few seconds. I heard a noise and—'

'What kind of a noise?'

The police officer shook his head again. 'A kind of thump, I suppose. And when I looked back to that end of the room, he'd disappeared.'

'Right.' Bianchi called out to a pair of police officers who were manhandling a battery-powered floodlight into the cellar. 'Get that light on, and aim it at the back wall. We need to find where Bronson has gone – right now.'

78

Bronson was desperate for even the faintest scintilla of illumination that might allow him to see his surroundings. But there was nothing, no light at all. All he had to go on was what his ears could hear, or his probing hands could touch. The only possible good news was that if he couldn't see anything, then neither could anyone else.

What he could hear sounded like something moving cautiously over a stone floor, a kind of swishing, pattering noise that didn't seem to be very close. He swung his left arm around in a semicircle in front of him, then did the same with his right, and took a cautious step forward. Then he repeated the sequence of movements, making very slow, and very cautious, progress.

He estimated he'd covered about fifteen feet in total darkness before the faint noises he was hearing stopped altogether. Whoever – or whatever – was ahead of him was no longer moving.

*   *   *

Inspector Bianchi strode across the flagstone floor to the back wall of the cellar. The two officers had already positioned the battery-powered floodlight a few feet away and, as Bianchi approached, they switched it on. Instantly, that corner of the chamber was brightly illuminated, the white light bouncing off the old stones.

For a few moments, the handful of police officers stared at the wall. Then Bianchi turned to his companion. 'Tell me again what you saw,' he instructed.

Once more the officer explained the sequence of events.

'And he couldn't have left this room by the staircase?'

The officer shook his head.

'OK, you two, examine this corner of the cellar. Don't stop till you find the doorway.'

Then he went over to the group of handcuffed figures still sitting with their backs to the wall at the other end of the chamber. He looked at each in turn until he found the man who he'd cultivated in order to join the group.

'Stefano,' he said, crouching down in front of him. 'You're going to jail, probably for a very long time. I'm not going to offer you a deal, but if you answer my next question correctly, then I will at least tell the judge at your trial that you tried to help us when you were arrested. Now, we know that there's a hidden door at the other end of this room. How do we open it?'

The man named Stefano spat. 'Judas,' he snapped. 'I should have guessed you were too good to be true. A senior policeman wanting to learn our secrets and share in our triumph? A man who could misdirect any inquiries and provide us with some protection from the law? We should never have even talked to you.'

'I'll take that as a "no" then, shall I, you contemptible piece of shit?'

Bianchi motioned to two of his officers. 'As soon as you've got the wounded men out of here,' he said, 'get this lot upstairs. Before you do that, separate them and ask them individually about a hidden door and a secret chamber. They probably won't talk to you, but I suppose it's worth a try.'

Then he walked back to the other end of the cellar, where his men were still examining the wall. 'Have you found anything?' he asked.

One of the officers turned round to face him. 'We think we've spotted a doorway, sir. There's a vertical line, here, between the stones, which could be the edge of a door, but we've still no idea how to get it open.'

'There should be some tools in one of the boats. One of you, go out and see if you can find a hammer and chisel or a crowbar. If we can't work out how to open it, maybe we can break it down.'

Bronson took a deep breath and then held it to minimize the sound of his own breathing, the better to hear what was happening.

There was a scuffling sound from his left, a noise that

rose and fell erratically. He heard an angry squeal from the same direction, and guessed he was probably hearing a family of rats moving about. Then there was another noise, from somewhere to his front. Not loud, but unmistakable. He could hear the sound of beating wings, and then his ears, the only sense organs that were of any use to him at that moment and in that place, detected several faint squeaks.

Bronson relaxed slightly. As well as the rats, it sounded to him as if he was sharing the space with bats. And that was actually good news, because it meant there had to be a way out of the cellar to the open air, though how the hell he was going to find it in the pitch darkness was another matter.

And then he heard a noise that electrified him. A yell of pain, suddenly cut short, sounded through the cellar, not close but very clear. In that instant Bronson knew that Angela was somewhere in the darkness ahead of him.

His every instinct told him to run, to find her as quickly as possible, but instead he stayed where he was, trying to pinpoint the exact direction from which the sound had come. Then he started moving, just as slowly and carefully as he'd done previously, because in the blackness that was the only way to ensure that he didn't run headlong into a wall or trip over something.

Bronson stopped again. He'd sensed movement, somewhere near him. It wasn't something he'd heard so much as a subtle change in the air, a faint waft across his face. And then he smelt something rancid and deeply unpleasant that appalled him. It took him a moment to place it amid the other smells of damp and decay that filled the air. Rotting meat. The smell of decomposing flesh. He was sharing this chamber with a dead body.

But what he didn't understand was why the smell was getting stronger. He'd stopped moving, so the foul odour should have stayed more or less constant. But it wasn't. It was definitely increasing, which only made sense if he was getting closer to the corpse.

A horrifying thought struck him. Bronson took a couple of steps backwards, but still the stench grew stronger. Something – something foul – was near him, and getting closer.

He could still see nothing, but the feeling of revulsion was growing stronger by the second, and he knew he had to do something.

Almost without thinking, Bronson drew the Browning from his holster, aimed the pistol towards the roof of the chamber, and pulled the trigger. The noise of the shot was deafening, and the bullet ricocheted off the concrete ceiling and smashed into the floor a few feet away from him.

Bronson flinched, but his reaction had nothing to do with the firing of his weapon. What stunned him was the sight that had been illuminated for the barest fraction of a second by the muzzle flash of his pistol. Less than six feet in front of him, he'd seen the appalling spectre of the leader of the group who had abducted Angela, his arms outstretched and his hands formed into clutching claws as he felt around for his prey. The hood of his robe was thrown back to reveal his totally bald head, black eyes deep sunk into their sockets, and his mouth open to reveal a row of pointed teeth, the two canines so long they extended beneath his lower lip.

It was an image that burned itself into Bronson's brain.

He lowered the pistol, aimed it where he thought the figure should be, and pulled the trigger.

On the other side of the stone wall, Inspector Bianchi and his men clearly heard the shot. He now had four men inspecting the wall, probing for a catch, and pressing on the old stones, all without result.

'Find that bloody lever,' Bianchi shouted, 'and quickly. If Bronson could find it by himself in the dark, I can't think of any good reason why the four of you can't do the same thing. At least you can see what you're doing.'

This time the muzzle flash of the Browning revealed nothing apart from the darkness of the cellar. Bronson stepped backwards, turned to his right and fired the pistol again, with exactly the same result. The nightmare figure had vanished. And the stench, the rotting corpse smell, was now little more than a disgusting memory in his nostrils.

There was a sudden creaking sound from somewhere ahead, and almost immediately a faint light illuminated the oblong shape of a doorway perhaps thirty feet in front of him. A door to the outside had obviously been opened. And almost simultaneously, Bronson heard a dull thud from behind him as one of the Italian police officers finally stood on exactly the right stone in the cellar. Instantly, light from the battery-powered floodlight poured in, and for the first time he could see his surroundings.

He was standing in a chamber about half the size of the one used for the ceremonies, but this one was devoid of all structures and furnishings. Rats, frightened away by the sound of the shots, were now reappearing, scuttling around the perimeter of the chamber, and a handful of small bats wheeled and banked near the ceiling.

Now Bronson could see what he was doing, he ran forward, straight towards the doorway in the opposite wall. He could hear Inspector Bianchi calling out for him to stop, but that wasn't an option.

Bronson slammed to a halt beside the doorway. Ahead of him was a short, empty passage, two doors opening off it on the left-hand side, and a heavy wooden door, half open, at the end. He guessed that the leader had probably gone through that door to the outside of the building. With Angela.

He wrenched open the outside door. In front of him, the waters of the Venetian lagoon, black in the moonlight, lapped at a small muddy beach. He glanced quickly in all directions, but there was nobody in sight. A path, little more than flattened grass and compressed earth, led away to his right. On his left, an almost vertical bank rose, blocking his way.

Bronson turned right, the only way out, and ran up the path. The moonlight cast a pale white glow over his surroundings, and was sufficiently bright for him to see exactly where he was. The house was over to his right, and the ruined church almost directly in front of him. Near the house he could see several figures, clad in dark clothes and carrying weapons: obviously other Italian police officers, so he knew that his quarry wouldn't have gone to the main landing stage in front of the house. In fact, the only place the leader could possibly have gone was to the old jetty, at the other end of the island, where Bronson had seen the small speedboat. It was his only viable avenue of escape.

Turning away from the house, Bronson started to run, but after only a few seconds he saw a dark shape lying to one side of the path.

Bronson stopped in his tracks and aimed the pistol directly at it. He took a couple of tentative steps forward, then muttered an oath. The police officer had obviously had time to draw his weapon, because Bronson could see a Beretta nine-millimetre pistol lying on the ground beside him. But the weapon had clearly done him no good at all, because he was dead, his throat ripped apart, his head resting in a huge pool of blood.

Fearing for Angela, his blood pounding in his ears, Bronson ran on, checking left and right as he did so, and occasionally glancing behind him, just in case his quarry had decided to double back. He heard a commotion some way back, and guessed that Bianchi and his officers had followed him out of the chamber, and had just found the dead policeman.

Then, perhaps fifty yards ahead, he saw a figure, a blacker shape against the darkness of the sky. He caught a sudden whiff of decaying flesh, and knew he'd guessed right. The man was making for the jetty and the speed boat.

Bronson stepped off the path and on to the grass at the side. The man was still much too far away for him to use his pistol, and he couldn't see whether or not he had Angela with him.

Making maximum use of the moonlight to pick his route over the tussocky grass, Bronson ran on, closing the distance as quickly as he could. Then he saw a tumble of blonde hair on the right-hand side of the dark robe the figure was wearing, and knew the man was carrying Angela. She seemed to be unconscious or at least, as far as Bronson could see, her head appeared to be hanging limply.

He'd got within about twenty yards of them when the man clearly sensed his presence and glanced back at him. Bronson saw his face, saw the blood staining his mouth and chin. He brought the Browning up to the aim, wondering if he dared risk a shot. The moon disappeared suddenly, almost instantly it seemed, behind a thick cloud, and the figure vanished. The path in front of him appeared completely empty.

Bronson shook his head in disbelief, then carried on. He saw nothing for another hundred yards or so and then, as he approached the inlet that contained the old jetty, he heard the rumble of an engine and saw the man again. He was already standing in the bow of the powerboat and releasing the painter. Angela was lying in the centre of the boat, her body draped over one of the seats.

Bronson stopped, took careful aim at the standing figure and squeezed the trigger.

79

The Browning recoiled in his hand, but it was too late. The man had ducked down, stepped to the stern of the boat and opened the throttle. Bronson didn't dare fire again, because the man was now too close to Angela. He holstered the weapon and ran for his own boat, beached only about fifteen yards away.

Bronson pushed on the bow of his craft, but for several agonizing seconds it remained immobile. Then he changed his grip, lifted the bow slightly and pushed again, and this time the boat moved. He scrambled on board and, gasping for breath, started the engine and swung the craft around in a tight circle and set off in pursuit of the other boat.

Inspector Bianchi had just ordered his men to begin a line search of the whole island when he heard the rising scream of a boat engine fairly close by. He looked in the direction of the sound and saw two powerboats carving white wakes through the dark waters of the Venetian lagoon. As far as he could see, each boat contained a single figure, and it was immediately obvious to him what had happened.

'You four,' he ordered, 'take a police launch and catch those two boats. You three, come with me. We'll use the other boat.'

A couple of minutes later, the deep rumble of the marine diesel engines of the launches echoed around the landing stage, as the two boats set off in pursuit.

Bronson had pushed the throttle as far forward as it would go, and as he swung around the end of the island, he saw the other boat about seventy yards ahead of him. From over to his right, he heard the sound of another engine starting, and guessed that at least one of the police launches was following him.

Within moments he knew that his craft was faster than the one he was chasing. Only a little faster, but enough. Inexorably the distance between them closed: fifty yards, forty, thirty . . .

Then a police launch powered across the water directly in front of him, the driver obviously intent on reaching the fleeing craft first.

Bronson cursed and swung around the stern of the launch, then turned the vessel back in pursuit. He'd lost some ground, but he was still gaining on the other boat. The police launch was almost matching speed with him, and running parallel.

Bronson took one hand off the steering wheel, pulled the Browning out of the holster and aimed it at the boat in front of him, waiting for a clear shot.

Twenty yards . . . ten. The leader obviously knew that Bronson and the police launch were behind him, but there was nothing he could do to get away from the faster boats.

As Bronson's boat closed to a matter of a few feet, the leader swung his wheel hard over to the right, diving straight across his bow. Bronson reacted instantly, mirroring the man's actions, so that his vessel turned just as sharply. But it was too late – there was a screech of tearing fibreglass as the two boats collided, the port side of Bronson's boat smashing into the starboard side of the other vessel.

The two boats jammed together, the gunwale of Bronson's slightly smaller craft riding up over the side of the larger vessel. Instinctively, he reached out and pulled back the throttle. As he did so, he lost his grip on the Browning, which fell from his hand and clattered to the floor.

Just feet away, the hooded man stared at him, his face white in the moonlight, the streaks of blood down his chin clearly visible. He obviously saw that Bronson didn't have a weapon in his hand, and rose up from the boat, his arms outstretched as he reached for his next victim.

And at that moment Angela recovered consciousness, and screamed.

Bronson looked in sheer terror at the appalling spectre looming over him, then bent down, both hands scrabbling desperately to try to find the pistol. The stench of decomposition rolled over him in a nauseous wave as his hand closed around cold metal. He snapped off the safety catch on the Browning, pointed it straight in the centre of the dark shape in front of him, and squeezed the trigger.

Once, twice, three times, he fired, the sound of the shots rolling across the dark waters. As he fired, Bronson knew that the nine-millimetre copper-jacketed bullets couldn't possibly have missed the target. Not at less than six-feet range.

But still the figure came on, his black robe blotting out the moon, as he reached for Bronson.

80

Bronson was never quite sure what happened next. He fired again as he was enveloped by the dark shape, then tumbled backwards, the back of his head cracking sharply against the seat as he fell.

When he came to, Angela was beside him, cradling his head in her hands in the stern of the boat.

'Wake up, Chris, damn you. Wake up,' she muttered. Then, as his eyes flicked open, she bent down and kissed him on the lips. 'Thank God,' she said simply.

In the distance, Bronson heard the rumble of another boat's engine. A police launch was just drawing alongside, Inspector Bianchi standing in the stern and staring at the two boats, still locked together and rocking in the chop disturbing the surface of the lagoon.

'Where is he?' Bianchi called over to them.

Bronson looked up at Angela. 'Where did he go?'

'I don't know,' she replied. 'I saw him jump at you after

the boats collided, and then you shot at him. He seemed to fall right on top of you, but when I reached the end of the boat he'd gone, and all I could see was his robe. There was no body, and no blood. I didn't hear him fall into the water, but he must have done.'

Bronson sat up, ran his palm over the tender bruise on the back of his head – it was already noticeably swollen and bleeding – and looked across at the inspector.

'I don't know,' Bronson explained in Italian. 'I banged my head when he leapt on to the boat so I didn't see. Angela says he must have jumped into the water and got away.'

'Right,' Bianchi snapped, and turned to the police officer driving the boat. 'Tell the other crew to start quartering the area. We're probably looking for a body, but it's possible the man is still alive. Either way, I want him found.'

With a throaty roar from its turbo-charged diesel engine, the second police boat swung away, two searchlights snapping into life as the crew started their search.

'You shot him,' Bianchi said, a statement rather than a question.

'I shot *at* him, Inspector,' Bronson replied, 'and that's not quite the same thing. He dropped his robe,' he added, passing it over to the police officer.

'You'd better get back to Venice, Signor Bronson. That looks like a nasty wound on your head, and you need to get it checked. We'll stay out here until we find the body, and I'll send somebody round to your hotel to take a statement in the morning. It's been a long night for all of us. Oh, before you go, you'd better give me that pistol, unless you've managed to acquire a licence for it in the last twelve hours. And any ammunition you might have picked up as well.'

Bronson handed over the pistol, holster and spare magazines, then spent a couple of minutes separating his powerboat from the one the cult leader had been driving. Once he'd freed the gunwale, he waved a hand at Bianchi, started the boat's engine again and motored away.

As they headed back towards the lights of Venice, Bronson slipped his arm around Angela's shoulders and she nestled her head against him.

'How's your head?' she asked.

'I'll live,' Bronson said. 'It feels like a bad bruise, but I don't think it needs stitches. All I really want to do is get back to the hotel and lock the door against the world. It's been a hell of a night for us all, and especially for you.'

Angela shivered. 'Thank God it's all over. I really thought I was going to die in that bloody cellar. I couldn't believe it when I saw you there – and carrying a gun.'

'Well, we're safe now. Just don't think about what happened tonight.'

Angela was silent for a few moments, then looked up at Bronson again. 'Are you sure he's dead? That foul creature?'

Bronson nodded. 'At that range, I couldn't possibly have

missed. I fired four or five shots into him at a range of about six feet. If that didn't kill him outright, he'd bleed to death in minutes. He's dead, that's for sure. Tomorrow, Bianchi will tell us he's recovered the body, and that'll be the end of it.'

81

Bronson and Angela walked into the hotel dining room the next morning only a few minutes before breakfast stopped being served. Angela had bathed and dressed the wound on his head as soon as they got back to the hotel the previous night and then they'd fallen into bed. They'd talked for a few minutes about the traumatic events of the previous few days, and especially the last frantic hours out in the lagoon, then exhaustion had overtaken them both and they'd quickly fallen asleep.

Bronson collected a coffee pot, a couple of cups and the last remaining basket of bread and croissants from the serving table and took everything over to the table by the window where Angela was sitting. She fell on the food as if she was starving.

'God, I'm famished,' she said, between mouthfuls of croissant.

'I'm not surprised.' Bronson poured her a cup of coffee, then sat back in his chair and looked at her.

'What?' she said, smiling.

'I just like looking at you, that's all,' Bronson replied, 'and for a while there I really didn't think that was something I was ever going to be able to do again.'

Angela shuddered. 'Don't remind me,' she said. 'I never thought I was going to get out alive. You know, I still can't believe you managed to find me.'

Bronson had explained about his visit to the Isola di San Michele and the events that had followed it the previous evening.

'I don't think I could have lived with myself if I'd lost you a second time,' he said, taking her hand. 'You know, I was certain that Inspector Bianchi was one of the bad guys, but now I'm really glad I was wrong, because if he had been, my guess is we'd both be dead now.'

Angela nodded, and in a halting voice described in more detail the code-breaking she'd been forced to do.

'It was appalling stuff,' she finished. 'That scroll I found in the bell tower on Poveglia – which is a severely creepy place, by the way – was neither more nor less than an authorization to go out and commit multiple rape and mass murder. But what really bothered me about it was the whole tone of the text. It was so matter-of-fact about vampires, as if they were simply another sector of society that everyone would have known about. Oh, and by implication everyone could become one if they really wanted to, and were prepared to follow the rituals.'

'I had a question about that,' Bronson said. 'They had a female wolf chained up in a stable, and before the ceremony started I saw two men go into the building and milk her. And then they forced the milk down poor Marietta's throat. What the hell has that got to do with becoming a vampire?'

Angela's face was pale and strained as she remembered what she'd been through. 'That was something they got completely wrong. My guess is that the members of the vampire group had studied all the ancient literature. They would certainly have read about the eighteenth-century Vampire Princess of the Schwarzenbergs – Eleonora Amalia. Almost every contemporary source agreed that she was a vampire, and her body was autopsied after her death, something that was only very rarely done in those days, and almost never on a member of the aristocracy. It's now thought that the procedure was performed not to find out why she died, but simply so her heart could legitimately be removed from her body. Because she was of royal blood, they couldn't decapitate her or burn her corpse. Wrenching out a vampire's heart was supposed to make sure they stayed dead.

'But one of the other odd things about Eleonora Amalia was that she drank the milk of wolves, and my guess is that the members of the group discovered that and thought it was just something else they – or rather their victims

– should do. But, according to other sources, Eleonora Amalia didn't think she was a vampire, and she drank the milk for an entirely different reason, though it was based on another old legend – Romulus and Remus. She was trying to increase her fertility.'

Angela stopped talking and looked across at Bronson. Then she voiced the unspoken question that was upper-most in both their minds.

'Last night . . . the leader of that group . . . was he really a man, do you think?'

Bronson shook his head helplessly. 'I don't know,' he muttered. 'What I do know is that he was the most terrify-ing thing I've ever seen.'

'When I came round after that taser hit me, he was carrying me, and I'll tell you this: he was incredibly strong. For part of the time he literally held me in one arm. You're strong, Chris, and I'm sure you could pick me up fairly easily, but I very much doubt if you could carry me very far, especially not over such rough ground.' Angela paused, and Bronson noticed her hand was shaking. 'There's something else about it that bothers me. I know it's not definite proof either way, but there is one consistent factor that seems to crop up in all the records about—'

She broke off as the door to the dining room opened and Inspector Bianchi walked in. He crossed over to their table, pulled up a third chair and sat down.

'Good morning, Inspector,' Bronson greeted him in

Italian. 'Would you like a coffee?' Without waiting for an answer, he picked up an unused cup from the next table, poured coffee into it and slid it over.

'Good morning. I think we've wrapped up almost everything on the island,' Bianchi said, sticking to English so that Angela could understand what he was saying. 'The forensic people are still out there, and will be for a while, but I'm pretty certain we've got all the evidence we need, including the pistol that was used to kill my superior officer here in the city. I hope this means an end to these disappearances and murders.' He paused for a moment to taste his drink. 'But I'm afraid we've still not found a body in the lagoon.'

Bianchi glanced at Angela, then continued. 'But it's only a matter of time. The currents in the lagoon can be fierce. We think that man's corpse probably sank below the surface soon after he fell into the water, and simply drifted away. Trying to spot a body in the water at night is very difficult.'

'But you are *sure* he's dead?' Angela asked.

Bianchi nodded. 'We would certainly have spotted that man if he'd been swimming away from the scene. And there are bullet holes in his robe, in both the front and the back, so clearly your shots must have badly wounded him, at least. If his corpse doesn't turn up over the next couple of days, it will probably have washed out into the Adriatic, and we'll never find it.'

Bronson opened his mouth to object, but Bianchi held

up his hand to forestall him. 'No doubt you have your own views about this, Signor Bronson, but what I've just described seems to us to make logical sense, and will be what our final report into this matter will say. We already have his accomplices in custody, and the circumstances of their arrest mean that their trial should be almost a formality.'

Bronson nodded slowly. 'Perhaps you're right,' he said. 'That's probably the best way to handle this. Stick to the facts, produce the bodies, line up the suspects and then let justice take its course.'

'And Marietta?' Angela asked. 'How is she?'

Bianchi finished the last of his coffee and smiled. 'She's fine. Well, she's obviously still very traumatized by her experience, as I'm sure you are, too, but she's back with her family, and her boyfriend.'

'Send her my love,' Angela said, a tremor in her voice. 'She was so brave in that cellar.'

'I will.' Bianchi stood up. 'Make sure you come to the police station in San Marco before you leave Venice, please,' he said. 'You are both material witnesses in this case, and the prosecution may well decide that we need you here when the trial finally takes place, so it's essential that we have your full contact details. Other than that, enjoy the rest of your holiday in Venice. And if I might make a suggestion, please try to avoid going near any other graveyards or churches while you're here.'

Bianchi extended his hand and Bronson shook it. Then

he kissed Angela on both cheeks, turned and left the room.

Bronson sat down again and looked across at Angela. 'So they've got the killers,' he said, 'and they'll prosecute them for the multiple murders. They might need us as witnesses, but we'll have to wait and see. That means we might just get another trip out here to Venice, all expenses paid.'

Angela looked at him for a moment. 'You were going to say something to the inspector? Something about the body?'

Bronson nodded. 'Two things, in fact. I know it was dark last night, but I took a quick look at that robe when I handed it to Bianchi. He was right about the bullet holes, but I didn't see any blood. And dead bodies don't sink – they float.'

'So what are you saying? That he's still alive?'

'No. He can't be. That's simply impossible. It's just a bit odd, the way it all happened at the end. And you were about to say something when Bianchi arrived?'

'Oh yes,' Angela remembered. 'It's only a small thing. If you look back through all the accounts of vampires, from every country that has a tradition relating to the undead, you'll find a mass of contradictions. Some say you can only kill them by beheading them, others that they're terrified of a crucifix, or held at bay by garlic. In some countries, sunlight kills them. As far as I know, there are only two things that seem to be consistent everywhere. First, and most obviously, vampires live on human blood.'

She paused for a second, and glanced at Bronson. 'And the second thing is that vampires have a very distinctive smell. They reek of decay, of decomposing flesh.'

Bronson caught his breath as he remembered his experience in the secret chamber, and what he'd smelt in those moments when the leader of the group attacked him. 'I'm not sure I'm hearing you right,' he said, trying to smile. 'Is this really my precious, logical, scientific Angela? Are you saying that you think we really did meet a vampire out on that island?'

Angela shook her head slowly. 'Vampires don't exist,' she said. 'Everybody knows that. But we have been in contact with a very strange person, someone I never, ever want to see again.' She got up and stretched. 'We've got one more day left in Venice. I'm not visiting any of the islands, and definitely no churches, but do you think we'd be safe if we did some shopping? I've always fancied some handmade gloves.'

Bronson stood up too, and put his arms around her. 'After what happened yesterday,' he said, 'I'll happily buy you ten pairs.'

Epilogue

Venice is a maze of narrow streets and canals, lined with old buildings. Because of the continuing problems with flooding and subsidence, many of the older properties and especially a number of the early palaces, the *palazzi*, have been abandoned because water damage to their lower floors has fatally weakened the entire structure. Sad, crumbling and in some cases too dangerous to enter, these ancient buildings endure mainly because they are supported by adjacent properties. Without this, most of them would have collapsed decades or even centuries ago.

Beside one small canal at the southern end of the Cannaregio district stands a tall and narrow building that dates almost as far back as the founding of the city. Last inhabited in the early nineteenth century, both its doors – the canal and the street entrances – are locked and barred and the windows shuttered, as they have been for decades. It is beyond repair, the foundations slowly crumbling away into the waters below. Occasionally, the occupants of properties nearby can hear the rumble and splash as yet another piece of masonry falls away and tumbles down the interior of the building.

They have grown accustomed to these sounds, and rarely even remark on them. But these are not the only sounds that have recently been echoing through the old building.

Sometimes, late at night, the family who live next door can hear a faint slithering and swishing sound from one of the rooms on the very top floor of the doomed building, a room that they know has not been occupied for many years. Sometimes, the noises are loud enough to wake their children. And neither of their cats will even enter the rooms on the side of their house that abuts the deserted property.

They don't know exactly what is making the noises, but they have their suspicions, because of the smell. Faint, but all-pervasive, the ruined house is beginning to smell distinctly of rotting flesh. Obviously something has got in there and died, they tell each other. And maybe the other noises are rats feeding on the remains.

Recently, the noises have started getting louder, and the smell stronger.

Author's Note
THE REAL VAMPIRE CHRONICLES

Vampires in history

Many people think that belief in vampires is a comparatively recent phenomenon, but in fact the myth of a bloodsucking creature of the night can trace its roots back for thousands of years, and there is one school of thought that suggests that perhaps the most famous murder of all time was the result of an attack by a vampire.

The Bible is strangely silent about the weapon used by Cain to kill his brother. In Genesis, it only says that 'Cain rose up against Abel his brother, and slew him'. Over time, numerous objects were suggested as the likely murder weapons, typically rocks or lengths of wood of some kind, though another theory stated that it was the jawbone of an animal, the teeth specially sharpened. Shakespeare made reference to this as the weapon in *Hamlet*.

But the Zohar, the group of books that provide the foundation of the Jewish Kabbalah, offers another suggestion entirely. In that work, there is no doubt whatsoever about the circumstances of Abel's death – it states explicitly that Cain bit his brother on the throat. So it could be argued that the world's first known vampire was actually the biblical Cain.

Unlike most other monsters and demons, where belief is often restricted to a particular geographical area or linguistic group, the vampire legend appears to have roots in nearly every country of the world. In Iran – ancient Persia – a vase was found that depicted a man being attacked by a huge creature apparently trying to suck his blood. The mythical Babylonian deity named Lilith, possibly the woman who was supposed to be the first wife of Adam, was reputed to drink the blood of babies. Some sixth-century Chinese texts refer to so-called 'revenants' or the living dead. Other cultures around the world, from the Aztecs to the Eskimos, and from India to Polynesia, have legends that refer to creatures that are remarkably consistent, and eerily similar to the vampires of European fiction.

Blood, and especially the blood of virgins, became an important cure for ailments in the eleventh century, being prescribed by both witches and doctors, and even the Catholic Church recognized and latched on to the symbolic importance of this belief, offering wine as the 'blood of Christ' as a part of Holy Communion.

Belief in vampires gained ground during the Renaissance, but reached almost epidemic proportions in central Europe in the fourteenth century. The Black Death, the plague that decimated the population of Europe, was popularly believed to be caused by vampires. According to one theory, in their haste to dispose of corpses, it is quite possible that many people were buried in plague pits whilst they were still alive. Their frantic efforts to free themselves from the earth above them could have fuelled stories about the vampire myth, as the dead would literally seem to be rising from their graves. And there were documented cases of suspected vampires being symbolically killed before being buried, often by beheading.

Then there were the real-life vampires. Or people who just about qualified for the title. In the mid-fifteenth century, a man named Gilles de Rais, a respected French military officer, began torturing and killing children to use their blood in various experiments. He was believed to have killed between two hundred and three hundred children before he was caught and brought to trial.

Further to the east, Vlad Tepes Dracula – the 'Tepes' meant 'impaler' and 'Dracula' the 'son of Dracul', while 'Dracul' itself meant 'devil' or 'dragon' – the Prince of Wallachia, now a part of Romania, was also bathed in blood, though by an entirely different mechanism. As the name 'Tepes' suggests, his particular speciality was impaling, and he killed literally thousands of his own people as well as every enemy of his country that he could get his hands on. His particular speciality was eating meals outdoors surrounded by newly impaled victims, who might last for hours on the stakes before finally expiring. And he was, of course, at least in name, the inspiration for the villain of Bram Stoker's novel.

Still in Eastern Europe, the sixteenth/seventeenth-century Countess Elizabeth Báthory von Ecsed (later known as the 'Blood Countess' or 'Blood Queen') is said to have become obsessed with preserving her youth and looks and, according to some sources, resorted to a study of alchemy and the occult to determine a method that would work. Once again, the answer was 'blood', and she began the systematic kidnapping and killing of young girls – the 'virgin' concept again – allegedly to obtain their blood, which she would then either drink or bathe in.

As time went on, the social status of her chosen victims began to rise, because the countess apparently believed that the blood of the nobility would be more pure and effective than the blood of the simple peasant girls who were her first victims. Suspicion eventually fell on her because of the sheer number of unexplained deaths of young girls in the area, but she was spared trial and execution because of her status. In 1610 she was sealed up in a windowless tower room in her home – Cseite Castle, then in Hungary, now part of Slovakia and today known as Čachtice – for the rest of her life. Her four accomplices, the servants she had employed to select, kidnap and torture her victims, were all swiftly tried and three of them executed. According to some reports, the countess and her servants were responsible for some 650 deaths altogether, though they were convicted of only eighty.

The stories about her bathing in blood first surfaced considerably later, in the eighteenth century, and it's now believed that, although the countess and her cohorts were certainly responsible for a large number of killings, her motive may have been simple sadism, as many of the bodies of their victims bore the unmistakable signs of torture, including beating, mutilation and burning.

Superstitions about both vampires and werewolves began to gain ground in Eastern Europe around this time. There was a persistent belief that *vrykolakas* (the Slavic word for 'werewolves') would become vampires when they died, which linked the two legends firmly together. And the wolves – the ordinary kind – that roamed the forests of Europe at the time also became associated with the vampire legend.

Among the largely illiterate population of Europe, the vampire was more than a legend. For many people, the creature of the night was as real as anything else in their lives, a monster to be feared and killed whenever possible. And the results of that fear, and of the steps taken to prevent a vampire from ever rising from its grave, can still sometimes be seen today.

Excavations that took place during 2000, in one of the older cemeteries of Český Krumlov in Bohemia, uncovered an eighteenth-century graveyard containing eleven bodies, three of which had been buried in an unusual fashion. Bodies are normally laid to rest east–west, but these were lying north–south. One skeleton had been decapitated and its skull placed between its legs, and also had a stone forced between its jaws. It was believed that moving the head well away from the neck would prevent the vampire replacing the head on its shoulders, and the stone would stop the jaws from being able to chew, an essential first step in turning a dead body into a vampire. All three of these skeletons had been pinned down with flat, heavy stones, to immobilize the bodies.

The remains were taken to Prague for anthropological examination, where it was ascertained that all three were male, and nitrogen analysis confirmed that the skeletons dated from between 1700 and 1750, the height of the anti-vampire craze in central Europe. The sternum of one body revealed a hole consistent with the left side of the chest, above the heart, having been impaled with a sharp object.

The identity of the three corpses has not been ascertained, and almost certainly never will be because of the paucity of records. But other 'vampires' were much better known, even notorious.

Princess Eleonora Amalia

The prologue of this novel describes the burial of Princess Eleonora Amalia of the Schwarzenberg dynasty, and is factually accurate in almost all respects. Eleonora became sick in about 1740, and her health declined rapidly. In those days, about the only known treatment for any serious illness was blood-letting, which was believed to flush out evil spirits. She was moved from Krumlov to Vienna to get better medical treatment, but she died at about six in the morning on 5 May 1741 at the Schwarzenberg Palace in the city.

The empire's leading physicians assembled for a post mortem, an unusual step as such examinations weren't usually performed on aristocrats. She apparently had a large tumour in her lower abdomen which had metastasized, invading her lungs – cancer, in short – but the outward signs were as if her body was being drained of blood from day to day, not helped by the blood-letting, obviously. Her preferred physician was Dr Franz von Gerschstov, who also headed various commissions charged with investigating vampires, and who believed that vampirism was contagious. The probability is that the post mortem – which was extremely expensive – was actually an intervention, intended to stop the vampire rising from her grave. That allowed the heart to be legitimately removed from the body to avoid the indignity of impaling or decapitation.

But if the princess was a vampire, that meant there must be another, very powerful, one in the area, who had infected her. Anti-vampire fever swept the land, with the corpses of suspected vampires being dug up and burned, decapitated or impaled. The Schwarzenbergs were traditionally buried in the family tomb in St Augustine's Church in Vienna, but the princess's body was returned to Bohemia the same night she died for burial, apparently by her own wish in an addition to her will made a few days before her death. This may have been a forgery, and an attempt to avoid Vienna having a potential vampire buried in the heart of the city.

At the castle in Krumlov, one life-size portrait of her has revealed under X-ray examination that the princess's head had been removed and a new section of canvas sewn in its place – a symbolic beheading, perhaps?

The milk of wolves

Eleonora had found it difficult to conceive after producing her first child, Maria Anna, in 1706, and had finally resorted to an old remedy to enhance her fertility – she drank the milk of wolves. Their milk was believed to strengthen the female reproductive system and encourage the birth of male babies, and was based on the legend of the twins Romulus and Remus. She had cages built at the castle in which captured wolves were bred, and where the females were milked – a difficult task, and one that caused the animals to howl, an eerie and penetrating sound that could be heard for miles around. At that time, wolves were greatly feared and reputed to be both in league with the devil and friends to vampires.

In 1722, aged forty-one, Eleonora finally gave birth to a son. In 1732, the same year that the word 'vampire' first appeared in the German language, her husband was shot dead in a hunt near Prague, accidentally killed by a bullet fired by the Emperor, Charles VI. Her son was taken from her to live in the Emperor's court near Vienna, while she spent her remaining days roaming the corridors of Krumlov Zamek, the family castle.

Contemporary vampires

After the superstitions and legends that characterized the Medieval and Renaissance periods, the Age of Enlightenment followed in the eighteenth century. Various attempts were made by scholars, priests and others to debunk the vampire myth, as well as other superstitions that were prevalent at the time. But the legend of the vampire proved to be almost as immortal as the creatures it described, and the stories and beliefs persisted.

Vampires started to migrate from the graveyards and forests of Eastern Europe to the pages of Gothic novels and the verses of Romantic poets. *The Vampyre* by John William Polidori is mentioned in this novel, and that was followed in 1847 by *Varney the Vampyre*, the longest novel ever written on the subject to that date. To some extent, the popularity of vampires in fiction then declined somewhat, but enjoyed a sudden revival when Bram Stoker's *Dracula* was published. Since that time vampires, in one form or another, have always been with us.

Nosferatu in the printed word and on the silver screen

The origin of the word 'nosferatu' is obscure. The first recorded reference in print was in a magazine article of 1885, and three years later in a travelogue entitled *The Land Beyond the Forest*, both written by the British author Emily Gerard. The travelogue described the country of Transylvania (its Latin name translates as 'the land beyond the forest'). In both she stated that 'nosferatu' was the Romanian word for 'vampire', but there is no known and identifiable corresponding word in any form of the Romanian language, ancient or modern. The closest are *necuratul* ('the devil') and *nesuferitul* ('the insufferable one').

An alternative explanation, which has been accepted by many writers, is that 'nosferatu' is derived from an old Slavonic word *nesufur-atu*, which was apparently itself derived from the Greek *nosophoros* (νοσοφόρος), meaning 'plague-carrier' or 'disease-bearing'. The obvious objection to this etymology is that Romanian and other Slavonic languages are Romance in origin and contain very few words of Greek. It's also significant that, though the word *nosophoros* is a valid compound word in the Greek language – meaning that the two parts of the compound word are individually valid and are correctly combined – there's no evidence that the word ever existed in any phase of the Greek language. So this suggested etymology relies on an unknown Greek word that somehow gave rise to an unknown Romanian word, which seems fairly unlikely.

It has also been suggested that *nesufur-atu/nosferatu* was a technical term in Old Slavonic that had migrated into common usage, but never appeared in a Romanian dictionary. That is a somewhat difficult argument to sustain, given that the sole purpose of a dictionary is to record words in common usage, and it would be reasonable to expect that it would have been recorded somewhere.

So we'll probably never know exactly where 'nosferatu' originated, but the balance of probability is that Emily Gerard either misheard a Romanian word or was misinformed.

Bram Stoker, of course, used the word in his novel *Dracula*, but his usage suggests that he probably believed it meant 'not dead' or 'undead' in Romanian, not 'vampire', and he used it as a calque or loaned word.

The silver screen showed the world the face of the vampire for the first time, with the 1922 film *Nosferatu: Eine Symphonie des Grauens* (*Nosferatu: A Symphony of Horrors*), starring Max Schreck as the vampire, his appearance taken straight from the descriptions in folklore: bat-like ears, hairy palms and sharp pointed teeth. In 2010 the film was ranked number 21 in *Empire* magazine's list of the 100 best films of world cinema, and was basically an unauthorized movie version of Bram Stoker's *Dracula*. The word 'nosferatu' was popularized by it because the studio hadn't obtained the rights to the novel, and so several changes had to be made. 'Count Dracula' became 'Count Orlok', and they used the word 'nosferatu' as a synonym for 'vampire', and this has essentially remained its meaning until today.

Bela Lugosi then took over the vampire role as Hollywood latched on to the character, while in England a few years later, Christopher Lee strutted his stuff as the suave, handsome, almost romantic, antihero. Since then, vampires seem to have appeared almost everywhere, and in a bewildering variety of forms, from the leather-jacketed stars of *The Lost Boys* through the almost tragic hero of the Anne Rice novels, to the extreme violence of *From Dusk Till Dawn* and the sexy light-hearted exploits of *Buffy the Vampire Slayer*.

At least in one sense, then, the vampire does seem to be truly immortal.

Why Venice?

Venice is a beautiful, romantic and mysterious city, with a fascinating and extremely colourful history. And vampires – in both fiction and reality – feature in that history. The 1988 film *Vampire in Venice* starred Klaus Kinski in the title role, and more recently *The Vampires of Venice* was an episode in the *Doctor Who* television series.

That's the fiction, but this is reality.

This picture shows the skull of a sixteenth-century supposed female vampire which was discovered in a mass grave – a plague pit – in Venice in March 2009. The brick jammed into her jaw was intended to stop her feeding on the other plague victims buried with her.

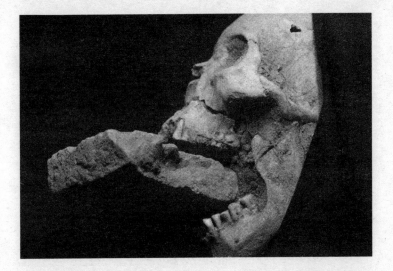

So Venice seemed an ideal location for this novel. There are over one hundred islands scattered around the Venetian lagoon, some with busy, populous settlements, others far too small to live on, and still others on which ancient ruined houses stand as stark reminders of the difficulties of establishing a viable habitation in the salty, marshy waters.

Venice itself can be spooky enough on a fine day. When the mist rolls in from the Adriatic, even small figures can cast giant shadows in the narrow streets and across the canals. Out in the lagoon, the islands become isolated worlds of their own where, in my imagination, almost anything could – and in this novel did – happen.

James Becker
Principality of Andorra, 2011

THE MESSIAH SECRET
James Becker

**The world's most dangerous mystery is
about to be revealed . . .**

AD 72: A band of warriors march across a mountainous
wasteland. Only they know what they carry.
And once they've reached their destination,
they will all die to protect it.

AD 20: In a crumbling mansion deep in the English
countryside a piece of ancient parchment has been
found. Written in arcane code is the answer to
a mystery that has explosive implications.

Enter **Chris Bronson**. Determined to solve the mystery
that has puzzled scholars and thinkers for nearly two
millennia, he embarks on a journey to one of the
most remote and hostile parts of the world.

But someone is following him.

Someone desperate to protect the centuries-old
secret. And who is far more dangerous than
he could ever have imagined.

9780553825046

Sam Christer lives in London.
The Stonehenge Legacy is his first novel.

THE
STONEHENGE
LEGACY

SAM CHRISTER

sphere

SPHERE

First published in Great Britain as a paperback original in 2011 by Sphere

A CIP catalogue record for this book
is available from the British Library.

ISBN 978-0-7515-4518-0

Typeset in Bembo by M Rules
Printed and bound in Great Britain by
Clays Ltd, St Ives plc

Papers used by Sphere are natural, renewable and
recyclable products sourced from well-managed forests and certified
in accordance with the rules of the Forest Stewardship Council.

Mixed Sources

Product group from well-managed
forests and other controlled sources
www.fsc.org Cert no. SGS-COC-004081
© 1996 Forest Stewardship Council

Sphere
An imprint of
Little, Brown Book Group
100 Victoria Embankment
London EC4Y 0DY

An Hachette UK Company
www.hachette.co.uk

www.littlebrown.co.uk

To my son Elliott in his last year of sixth form – I couldn't be prouder of everything you've done or how you've done it.

PART ONE

The stones are great
And magic power they have
Men that are sick
Fare to that stone
And they wash that stone
And with that water bathe away their sickness

Laghamon

1

Mist rolls like vaporous tumbleweed in the dead of the Wiltshire night. Out in the flat, sprawling fields hooded Lookers tilt their heads skywards to witness the first sliver of silver. The moon is new, showing only a faint flash of virginal white beneath a voluminous wrap of black-velvet haute couture.

On the horizon, a pale face turns in its cowl. A fiery torch is raised in an old hand. Hushed but urgent words pass from Looker to Looker. The sacrifice is ready. He has been brought from his fast. Seven days without food. No light, nor sound, nor touch, nor smell. His body has been cleansed of the impurities he has ingested. His senses sharpened. His mind focused on his fate.

The Lookers are robed in hand-woven sackcloth, belted with string plaited from plants, their feet shod in rough animal skins. It is the way of the ancients, the creators of the Craft.

3

The Cleansers remove the man's grimy clothes. He will leave this world with no more than he entered it. They pull a ring from his finger. A watch from his wrist. And from around his neck, a crude gold chain dangling a symbol of some false god.

They carry him, fighting, to the river and immerse him. Cold water fills his mouth and gurgles and froths in his corrupted lungs. He struggles like a startled fish, seeking a safe current to escape the hands of his captors.

It is not to be.

Once purified, he is dragged spluttering to the shore. The Bearers fall upon him and bind him with strips of bark to a litter made from pine, the noble tree that stepped with them from the age of ice. They hoist him high on to their shoulders. Carry him like proud and loving men bearing the coffin of a beloved brother. He is precious to them.

Their walk is long – more than two miles. South from the ancient encampment of Durrington. On to the great avenue, down to where the bluestones and the forty-ton sarsens are sited.

The Bearers make no complaints. They know the pain their forefathers suffered moving the mighty stones hundreds of miles. The astroarchitects trekked through hills and valleys, crossed stormy seas. With antlers of red deer and shoulder-blades of cattle, they dug the pits where the circle now stands. Behind the Bearers come the Followers. All male. All dressed identically in hooded, coarse brown robes. They have come from across Britain, Europe and all corners of the

4

globe. For tonight is the new Henge Master's first sacrifice. An overdue offering to the gods. One that will rejuvenate the spiritual strength of the stones.

The Bearers pause at the Heel Stone, the massive chunk of leaning sandstone that is home to the Sky God. It dwarfs all around it, except the gigantic sarsens standing eighty yards away.

In the centre of the megalithic portal a bonfire flickers in the darkness, its smoking fingers grasping at the moon, illuminating the Henge Master as he raises his hands. He pauses then sweeps them in a slow arc, pressing back the wall of energy surging between him and the horseshoe of towering trilithons.

'Great gods, I feel your eternal presence. Earth Mother most eternal, Sky Father most supreme, we gather in your adoration and dutifully kneel in your presence.'

The secret congregation of hooded figures sinks silently to the soil. 'We, your obedient children, the Followers of the Sacreds, are gathered here on the bones of our ancestors to honour you and to show you our devotion and loyalty.'

The Master claps his hands and leaves them joined above his head, fingers pointing in prayer to the heavens. The Bearers rise from their knees. Once more they lift upon their shoulders the naked young man tethered to the rough litter.

'We thank you, all you great gods who look over us and who bless us. In respect to you and the ways of the ancients, we dedicate this sacrifice.'

The Bearers begin their final journey, out through the

giant stone archways towards the sacrificial point that lies on the line of the solstice.

The Slaughter Stone.

They lay the young man upon the long grey slab. The Henge Master looks down and lowers his joined hands to touch the forehead of the sacrifice. He is not afraid to look into the terrorised blue eyes beneath him. He has prepared himself to banish all feelings of compassion. Just as a king would exile a traitor.

He slowly circles his joined hands around the man's face as he continues the words of the ritual. 'In the names of our fathers, our mothers, our protectors and our mentors, we absolve you from your earthly sins and through your mortal sacrifice we purify your spirit and speed you on your journey to eternal life in paradise.'

Only now does the Henge Master separate his palms. He spreads them wide. Half of him is lit bone-white by the moon, half blood-red by the fire. His body is in balance with the lunar phase. His silhouette against the great stones is that of a cruciform.

Into each outstretched hand the Bearers place the sacred tools. The Henge Master grips them, his fingers folding around smooth, wooden shafts carved centuries ago.

The first flint axe strikes the head of the sacrifice.

Then the second.

Now the first again.

Blows rain down until bone and skin collapse like an eggshell. With the death of the sacrifice comes a roar from

6

the crowd. A triumphant cheer as the Master moves back, his arms spread wide for them to see the sacrificial blood spattered on his robes and flesh.

'Just as you shed blood and broke bones to assemble this godly portal to protect us, so too do we shed our blood and break our bones for you.'

One by one the Followers come forward. They dip their fingers in the blood of the sacrifice, mark their foreheads. Then walk back into the main circle and kiss the trilithons.

Blessed and blooded, they bow before silently disappearing into the dark Wiltshire fields.

2

LATER THAT MORNING
TOLLARD ROYAL, CRANBORNE CHASE, SALISBURY

Professor Nathaniel Chase sits at a desk in the oak-walled study of his seventeenth-century country mansion and through the leaded windows watches morning twilight yield to a summer sunrise. It's a daily battle that he never misses.

A colourful male pheasant struts the lawn, cued by the first light on the dew-soaked grass. Dull females follow in the bird's wake, then feign disinterest and peck at fat-filled coconut shells strung out by Chase's gardener.

The male proudly spreads his wings to form a cape of iridescent copper. His head, ears and neck are tropical green and his throat and cheeks an exotic glossed purple. A distinctive white band around his neck gives him a priestly stature while his face and wattle are a deep red. The bird is melanistic – some kind of mutation of the common pheasant. As the professor looks closer, he suspects that a few generations back there must also have been some crossing with a rare green pheasant or two.

Chase is a successful man. More than most ever dream of being. Academically brilliant, he has been hailed as one of Cambridge's finest brains. His books on art and archaeology have sold globally and built a following beyond those bound to buy them for study. But his vast fortune and luxuriously refined lifestyle don't come from his learned ways. He left Cambridge many years back and turned his talents to sourcing, identifying, buying and selling some of the rarest artefacts in the world. It was a practice that earned him a regular place in the rich list and a whispered reputation as something of a grave-robber.

The sixty-year-old takes off his brown-framed reading glasses and places them on the antique desk. The matter in hand is pressing but it can wait until the floor show outside is done.

The pheasant's humble harem break from their feeding to pay the cock the attention he craves. He stomps out a short, jerky dance and leads the buff-brown females towards a stretch of manicured privets. Chase picks up a pair of small binoculars that he keeps by the window. At first he sees nothing except grey-blue sky. He tilts the glasses down and the blurred birds fill the frame. He fiddles with the focus wheel until everything becomes as sharp and crisp as this chilly summer morning. The male is surrounded now and warbling short bursts of song to mark his pleasure. Off to the right lies a shallow nest at the foot of the hedge.

Chase is feeling sensitive, emotional. The display outside his window touches him almost to the point of tears. The male with its many admirers, at the peak of life, vibrant in colour and potency preparing to raise a family. He remembers those days. That feeling. That warmness.

All gone.

Inside the grand house there are no pictures of his dead wife, Marie. Nor any of his estranged son, Gideon. The place is empty. The professor's days of plumage-spreading are done.

He puts the binoculars down beside the fine casement window and returns to the important paperwork. He picks up a vintage fountain pen, a limited-edition Pelikan Caelum, and savours its weight and balance. One of only five hundred and eighty ever made, a homage to Mercury's fifty-eight-million-kilometre orbit of the sun. Astronomy has played a vital role in the life of Nathaniel Chase. Too vital, he reflects.

He dips the nib into a solid brass antique inkwell, lets the Pelikan drink its fill and resumes his chore.

It takes Nathaniel an hour to finish writing on the fine cotton-blend paper that bears his own personalised watermark. He meticulously reviews every finished line and contemplates the impact the letter will have on its reader. He blots it, folds it precisely into three, places it into an envelope and seals it with old-fashione d wax and a per-sonalised stamp. Ceremony is important. Especially today.

He places the letter in the middle of the grand desk and sits back, both saddened and relieved to have completed the text.

The sun is now rising above the orchard at the far side of the garden. On another day, he'd walk the grounds, perhaps take lunch in the summerhouse, watch the wildlife in the garden, and then enjoy a mid-afternoon snooze. Another day.

He opens the bottom drawer of the desk and pauses as his gaze falls on what lies in there. In one determined move, he takes out the First World War revolver, puts it to his temple and pulls the trigger.

Outside the blood-spattered window, pheasants squawk and scatter into the grey sky.

3

THE FOLLOWING DAY
CAMBRIDGE UNIVERSITY

Gideon Chase quietly puts the phone down and stares blankly at the walls of his office where he's been reviewing the findings of a dig at a Megalithic temple in Malta.

The policewoman had been clear enough. 'Your father is dead. He shot himself.' Looking back, it's hard to see how she could have been any clearer. No wasted words. No hyperbole. Just a verbal slap to the guts that sucked his breath away. Sure, she'd thrown in a 'sorry' somewhere, murmured her condolences, but by then the twenty-eight-year-old's brilliant professor-in-waiting brain had shut down.

Father. Dead. Shot.

Three small words that painted the biggest imaginable picture. But all he could manage in reply was 'Oh.' He asked her to repeat what she'd said to make sure he'd understood. Not that he hadn't. It was just that he was so embarrassed that he couldn't say anything other than 'Oh.'

It has been years since father and son last spoke. One of their bitterest rows. Gideon had stormed out and vowed never to talk to the old goat again and it hadn't been difficult to keep to his word.

Suicide.

What a shock. The great man had wittered on all his life about being bold, daring and positive. What could be more cowardly than blowing your brains out? Gideon flinches. God, it must have been ugly.

He moves around his small office in a daze. The police want him to travel over to Wiltshire to answer a few questions. Help fill in some blanks. But he's not sure he can find his way out of the door, let alone to Devizes.

Childhood memories tumble on him like a row of falling

dominoes. A big Christmas tree. A melting snowman on the front patch of lawn. A pre-school Gideon coming downstairs in pyjamas to open presents. His father playing with him while his mother cooked enough food to feed a village. He remembers them kissing under the mistletoe while he hugged their legs until they had to pick him up and include him. Then comes the thump. As a six-year-old, enduring the pain of his mother's death. The silence of the graveyard. The emptiness of their home. The change in his father. The loneliness of boarding school.

He has much to think about on the journey south to Wiltshire, the county where his mother had been born, the place she'd always lovingly called 'Thomas Hardy Land'.

4

WILTSHIRE

Few know of its existence. A secret vault of cold stone, scaled to epic proportions by prehistoric architects. A place unvisited by the uninitiated.

The Sanctuary of the Followers is an unseen wonder. It is the size of a cathedral and yet a mere bump in the turf on the fields above, almost invisible to the human eye. Below ground, it's the jewel of an ancient civilisation, the product of a people whose brilliance still baffles the greatest brains of modern times.

Fashioned three thousand years before Christ, the place is an anachronism, a vast temple as out-of-time, breathtaking and impossible as the Great Pyramid of Giza.

Buried in its subterranean tombs are the architects of both Stonehenge and the Sanctuary. Their bones rest in the midst of more than two million blocks of stone, quarried from the same sources. Just as the Giza monument was a near-perfect pyramid, the Sanctuary is a near-perfect semi-sphere, a dome arcing over a circular floor, a cold moon sliced in half.

Now footsteps resound through the Descending Passage as though rain is falling into the cavernous chambers. In the candlelight of the Lesser Hall, the Inner Circle gathers. There are five of them, representatives of the giant trilithons sited inside the circle of Stonehenge. All are cloaked and hooded: a sign of respect for generations past, those who gave their lives to create this sacred place.

Upon initiation, Followers become known by the name of a constellation that shares the initial letter of their own first name. This shroud of secrecy is another age-old tradition, an echo of an epoch when the whole world was guided by stars.

Draco is tall and broad and exudes power. He is the most senior, the Keeper of the Inner Circle. His name comes from the Latin for 'dragon' and the constellation that almost three thousand years ago cradled the northern world's all-important pole star.

'What is being said?' He gives a flash of perfect teeth beneath his hood. 'What are they doing?'

The 'they' in question are the police, the Wiltshire constabulary, the oldest county police force in the country.

Grus, a thickset man in his early fifties, pounces. 'He shot himself.'

Musca paces thoughtfully, candles casting spectral shadows on the stone walls behind. Although the youngest of them all, his large physical presence dominates the chamber. 'I never expected him to do this. He was as devoted as any of us.'

'He was a coward,' snaps Draco. 'He knew what we expected of him.'

Grus ignores the outburst. 'It presents us with *certain* problems.'

Draco steps closer to him. 'I read the signs as well as you. We have time enough to ride this storm before the holy nexus.'

'There was a letter,' adds Grus. 'Aquila knows someone working on the investigation and a suicide note was left for his son.'

'Son?' Draco casts his mind back and a vague memory surfaces. Nathaniel with a child, a skinny youth with a mop of black hair. 'I forgot he had a son. Became a teacher at Oxford?'

'Cambridge. Now he'll be coming home.' Grus lays out the implication. 'Back to his *father's* home. And who knows what he might find in there.'

Draco creases his brow and looks fixedly to Musca. 'Do what must be done. We all thought well of our brother. In life he was our greatest of allies. We must ensure that in death he does not turn out to be our worst of enemies.'

5

STONEHENGE

An evening mist swirls around the base of the stones, a meteorological sleight of hand creating an archipelago in a sea of clouds. To motorists zipping past on the nearby trunk roads it's a scenic bonus but to the Followers it is much more.

This is twilight. *L'heure bleue*. A precious, twice-a-day time between dawn and sunrise, sunset and dusk. When light and dark are in balance and the spirits of the hidden worlds find a fragile harmony.

The Henge Master understands. He knows that nautical twilight comes first, as the sun sinks between six and twelve degrees below the horizon and gives sailors the first reliable readings of the stars. Astronomical twilight follows, as the sun slides from twelve to eighteen degrees below the horizon.

Degrees. Geometry. The position of the sun. A sacred triangle mastered by men like him from century to century. Stonehenge wouldn't be here without them. Its location is not accidental. Divined by the greatest of ancient augers and archaeoastronomers, its siting was planned by the most advanced of minds. Such was the precision of its build, the circle took more than half a millennium to complete.

And now, more than four millennia later, the Followers lavish upon the stones a similar rapt attention to detail.

The Henge Master assumes his position at exactly the moment that nautical twilight enters astronomical twilight. He stands as still as the bluestone soldiers circled around him, guarding, protecting.

He is alone.

Like an ancient haruspex, he waits patiently for the gods.

And soon, in a soft rustle of voices, they speak. He absorbs their wisdom and knows now what to do. He will worry less about the professor's suicide and more about the son. He will check that the sacrifice was given a proper burial – it would be disastrous if the remains were to be unearthed. Above all, he will ensure that the second stage of the renewal is completed.

The ceremony must be finished.

The milky vapour rises around his legs. In the wondrous half-light the sarsens come alive. A trick of the eye? A *trompe l'œil*? He doesn't think so. The new moon is barely visible to the uneducated but to an archaeoastronomer like him it is a beacon in the cosmos. Across the vaults of heaven, orbital maps arrange themselves, celestial cycles spring into being and with every atom of his body he senses completion of the sun's shift from Beltane to the solstice.

Seven days to *solstitium* – the moment the sun stands still. And all attention will be on the dawn. When it really should be on the dusk that will follow.

Five full days will pass after midnight on the solstice, then in the fertile evening twilight of that mystical evening will come the first full moon following *solstitium*. The time of renewal. When he must return to the Sacreds and complete what he has begun.

The sky has darkened now. The Master looks for Polaris, the North Star, the Lodestar, the brightest light of *Ursae Minoris*. The closest blink of godliness to the celestial pole. His eyes fall down the black curtain of the sky to the prehistoric earth, to the Slaughter Stone, and he shudders as he hears the command of the Sacreds.

The gods will not tolerate failure.

6

WILTSHIRE POLICE HQ, DEVIZES

DI Megan Baker wants to forget this particular day. And it's still a long way from over. The stick-thin thirty-one-year-old has a sick child at home, no husband to help since she kicked him out, and an arsy DCI who has landed her with a messy suicide. Now she must stay late to see the grieving son, face to face. That, and the combination of unpaid bills cluttering her handbag, is enough to start her smoking again. But she doesn't.

Her parents have said they'll have Sammy again, they always do – and it's 'never a problem', unless you count the patronising lecture and the scalding looks when she collects her poorly four-year-old daughter several hours later than promised.

But she won't give up. Being police is what she always wanted. What – despite a failed marriage – she still wants.

A shot of coffee and several sticks of gum take away the craving for nicotine. Her mobile rings and she looks at the caller display. CB – short for *Cheating Bastard*. She couldn't bring herself to enter her ex-husband's real name. *Cheating Bastard* seemed more appropriate. He is a uniformed inspector in another local division but their paths still cross. Too often. At work and during painful access visits.

CB doesn't want agreed visits. Oh no. That would cramp his shag-everything-with-a-pulse lifestyle. He expects to turn up whenever he wants to see Sammy. And that's just not fair. To her daughter or to her.

The urge to throw the ringing mobile at the wall is almost irresistible. She snatches it off her desk a beat before it trips to voicemail. 'Yes?' she snaps.

CB also has no time for pleasantries. 'Why didn't you tell me Sammy is sick?'

'She's got a fever, that's all. She'll be fine.'

'You a doctor now?'

'You a parent now?'

18

He emits a laboured sigh. 'Meg, I'm concerned about my daughter. You'd shout at me if I didn't ring, now you're shouting because I have.'

She counts to ten and spits out his name, 'Adam, Sammy's fine. Kids pick up bugs at playschool all the time. Her temperature's high, she was a little sick last night, that's all.'

'It's not measles or one of those things?'

'No.' Megan suddenly doubts herself. 'I don't think so. Mum's with her, there is nothing to worry about.'

'*You* should be with her. When she's sick a little girl wants her mum not her grandma.'

'Go to hell, Adam.' She hangs up and feels her heart pounding. He always does that to her. Winds her up. Brings her to snapping point.

The desk phone jangles and she nearly jumps out of her skin. It's reception. Gideon Chase is downstairs. She tells them she is on her way and takes a final slug of the now-cold coffee. Talking to the family of the deceased is never easy.

Reception is empty except for a tall, dark-haired man with shock etched on his pale face. She takes a long breath as she approaches. 'I'm Detective Inspector Baker. Megan Baker.' She offers a hand and instantly notices the well-worn blue plaster on her index finger is in danger of coming off.

'Gideon Chase,' he murmurs, careful not to dislodge the dubious Band-Aid. 'Sorry I'm late. The traffic.'

She smiles sympathetically. 'It's always bad. Thanks for coming so quickly. I know this must be difficult.' She opens a door with her swipe card. 'Let's go through to the back. We can find somewhere quiet to talk.'

7

To an archaeologist like Gideon Chase, locations and first impressions are of particular importance. A stretch of scorched red Egyptian sand or a dark-green field of English countryside say much about the possible discoveries that lie ahead. The cheap, windowless, wooden door that DI Baker opens and ushers him through does the same.

It's a dull box, floored in black carpet tiles and walled in shades of scuffed grey. Decor as welcoming as a grave. The only bright thing in the room is the woman DI. Reddish-brown hair, sharply dressed in a russet jersey top and flared black trousers. Gideon perches on an uncomfortable moulded chair and out of curiosity nudges the edge of the table in front of him. It's bolted to the floor.

Megan Baker is big on first appearances too. With a background in psychology and criminal profiling, she is already appraising the man with dark, Hugh Grant-style hair. He has brown eyes, a full mouth and good cheekbones. His fingernails show no trace of nicotine and have been cut not chewed short. No wedding ring. Many married men don't wear them but those with strong values do, and he radiates traditionalism. They are epitomised in his blue wool blazer with its leather-patched elbows, an item of dress cultivated in college cloisters rather than council estates. And it doesn't go with the black cashmere pullover or floppy green shirt. Any woman in his life could have told him that.

She slides an opened envelope over the table. 'This is the note your father left.'

Gideon looks at it but doesn't move. It's spattered with dark marks.

She realises what has caught his attention. 'I'm sorry. Putting it in a different envelope didn't seem the right thing to do.'

The right thing to do.

So much of his upbringing has been about the right thing to do. All of it inadequate preparation for the moment you get handed an envelope spattered with the blood of your dead father.

'Are you all right?'

He fingers a flop of hair from his face and looks up at her. 'I'm fine.'

They both know he isn't.

He glances down at the envelope and his own name staring up at him in his father's copperplate capitals.

21

For the first time in his life, he is pleased that his father preserved his own eccentric style and used a fountain pen instead of a Biro or felt tip, like the rest of the world seems to do.

Gideon catches himself thinking fondly of the old man and wonders if it's just a passing moment, if one effect of death is that you suddenly find respect for the things you used to despise. Does it somehow wipe the slate clean and compel you to think only good of those you thought badly of?

He touches the corners of the envelope. Lifts it a little but doesn't turn it over.

Not yet.

His heart is thumping, like it used to when he and his father argued. He can feel the old man in the letter. He can feel the presence through the parchment. He flips the envelope and pulls it open. As he unfolds the letter, he feels annoyed that the police have read it before him. He understands why: they needed to read it. But they shouldn't have. It was addressed to him. It was private.

Dearest Gideon,
I hope in death the distance between us is less than in life.

You will find out many things about me now that I am gone. Not all are good and not all are bad. One thing you may not discover is how much I loved you. Every moment of my life I loved you and I was proud of you.

My dearest son, forgive me for how I pushed you away. Looking at you every day was like looking at your mother. You have her eyes. Her smile. Her gentleness and her sweetness. My darling, it was too painful for me to see her in your every breath. I know that is selfish. I know I was wrong to banish you to that school and ignore your pleas to come back home, but please believe me, I feared I would have fallen apart if I had acted otherwise.

My sweet, wonderful child, I am so proud of what you have become and what you have achieved.

Do not compare us. You are a far better man than I ever managed to be and I hope one day you'll make a far better father too.

You may wonder why I have taken my life. The answer is not a simple one. In life you make choices. In death you are eternally judged on them. Not all judges are good ones. I hope you judge me well and judge me kindly.

Believe me, my death was a noble one and not as pointless and cowardly as it may seem. You have a right to understand of what I speak and a right not to care a jot and to live your life without giving me a second thought.

I hope you choose the latter.

My solicitor will be in touch and you will find that all I have amassed is now yours. Do with it as you will, but I beseech you not to be *too* charitable.

Gideon, as a child we played games – do you remember? I would devise treasure hunts and you would follow clues I left. In death I leave you clues as well and the answer to a mystery. The greatest treasure of all is to love and be loved – I hope beyond hope that you find it.

It is best that you don't search for the answers to other mysteries, but I understand you may wish to, and if you do, then you do so with my blessing and my warning to be careful. Trust no one but yourself.

Dearest son, you are a child of the equinox. See beyond the sun of the solstice and focus on the rise of the new moon.

Things that you first think are bad will prove good. Things you think good will be bad. Life is about balance and judgement.

Forgive me for not being there for you, for not telling you and showing you that I loved you and your mother more than anything in my life.

Your humble, penitent and loving father,
Nathaniel

It's too much to take in. Too much to understand all at once.

He runs his fingertips gently over the letter. Feels the words 'Dearest Gideon'. Lets the fingers of both hands rest on the line 'My sweet, wonderful child, I am so proud of what you have become . . .' Finally, almost as though he's reading Braille, his fingers find the words that moved him the most: 'Forgive me for not being there for you, for not telling you and showing you that I loved you and your mother more than anything in my life.'

Tears well in his eyes. He feels, impossibly, like his father is reaching out to him. The sensation is that of a prisoner and visitor divided by glass, putting their hands together to say goodbye, touching each other emotionally but not physically. Invisibly divided by life and death. The letter has become a wall of glass, the way his father has chosen to say goodbye.

Megan watches without interrupting and with only occasional glances at her wristwatch to quell the rising guilt about keeping her sickly four-year-old waiting at Grandma's. She can see the suicide letter is tearing Gideon apart.

'Would you like some time alone?'

He doesn't react. Grief is packing his head like cotton wool.

She clears her throat. 'Mr Chase, it's getting very late now. Would it be possible to make an appointment to see you tomorrow?'

He climbs out of the numbness. 'What?'

She smiles understandingly. 'Tomorrow.' She nods to the letter. 'There are some things we would like to ask you about. And I suspect you'll have questions of your own.'

He has a lot of questions and now they start to spill out. 'How did my father die?' He looks pained. 'I know you said he'd shot himself, but what happened exactly? Where was he? What time . . .' His voice breaks with emotion. 'When did he do it?'

Megan doesn't flinch. 'He shot himself with a small hand gun.' She can't help but add the details: 'A Webley Mark IV, a First World War pistol.'

'I didn't know he even owned a gun.'

'It was registered in his name. He'd fired it several times at a local range.'

His shock deepens.

She moves on to the more difficult bit. 'You can see him, if you like. We've had official identification from his cleaner, the lady who discovered him, so there's no need, but if you want to, I can fix it.'

He's not sure what to say. He certainly does not want to see what remains of his father after he put a bullet through his head. But he feels obliged to. Wouldn't it be wrong not to? Isn't it *expected*?

The DI pushes her chair back and stands. If she doesn't take the initiative, the dead guy's son will still have her sitting here at midnight. 'I'm sorry, we really have to wind this up now.'

'Forgive me. I know it's late.' He picks up the letter, folds it and slides it back into the spattered envelope. 'Is it all right to take this?'

'Yes. Yes, of course.'

He places it gently inside his jacket. 'Thank y
thank you for staying so late.'

'No problem.' Megan produces a card with her deta
it. 'Call me in the morning. We can fix a time then.'

He takes it and follows her out of the room. She guides
him through the security-locked doors and out into the dark
cold of the night and now-empty streets.

As the door clacks shut behind them, Gideon feels numb.

He unlocks the old Audi and sits frozen in the driver's
seat, keys shaking in his hand.

8

TOLLARD ROYAL, CRANBORNE CHASE,
SALISBURY

The estate is set in a singularly beautiful, historic chalk
plateau straddling Dorset, Hampshire and Wiltshire – not far
from the palatial retreat that Guy Ritchie and Madonna once
shared.

Gideon has never been here before and trying to find it in
the dark has taken more than an hour and proved exhaustingly
difficult. He wishes he'd thought things through a little more –
booked into a hotel or asked the police to find him somewhere. Now he's faced with nowhere to sleep unless he breaks
into the house.

The fruits of his dead parent's dubious labour are impressive. The mansion must be worth ten million pounds, maybe more. Perhaps his father's 'trade' – grave-robbing, as Gideon had often called it – was one of the reasons why he had taken his life.

Gideon drives through tall metal gates into a darkened garden as foreboding as a cemetery. The driveway winds on for nearly half a mile before it sweeps around a marble centrepiece with an elaborate fountain that's lit but not working. Soft, yellow garden lights cast a jaundiced glow through the leaves of ancient trees. He kills the engine and sits for a minute looking at the old house. It's a shell – empty of life.

He gets out and walks a flagged path around the east wing. While he has no keys, he reasons that he's unlikely to get into trouble for breaking into a property that's just been left to him.

He trips another set of security lights and the intense burst of white forces him to blink. There's a scurry of activity in hedges and undergrowth not far from the house – foxes or rabbits, he guesses.

A security box on a far off wall catches his eye. It probably isn't primed. If you commit suicide, you don't set the alarm. And given that the police were sloppy enough not to padlock the front gates, it's unlikely that they've already phoned the company for the key code and appointed someone custodian.

He peers through the panes of a quaint orangery attached

to the side of the building and can't quite bring himself to break in. A little further down he looks inside a laundry-cum-storage room. The door is modern. Less expensive to replace than anything else he's seen so far.

A good whack with the heel of his boot should do it. A solid boot somewhere around the lock. He takes a closer look. Best to get things right before you go hoofing away.

The door jamb around the handle looks already splintered.

He gives it a push and it opens.

'Damn.' Gideon curses the police. Unlocked gates and now a damaged door that should have been secured.

The air inside the house is stale and dry. Was this how the police entered? A crazy kick and rush by local plods after a call from a hysterical housekeeper?

He switches the light on and realises his last thought didn't make sense. The cleaner who found his father most probably had a key. There would have been no reason for them to break in.

The place must have been burgled.

Or worse still – is in the process of being burgled.

9

Musca has found nothing.

He has ransacked the lounge, searched all eight bedrooms, several bathrooms and two reception rooms and so far he's found nothing of any value to him. Sure, the old guy's house is stacked full of fabulously expensive stuff. No doubt a regular burglar would be swinging a full swag bag over his shoulder and whistling a merry little tune as he strolled down the plush halls, but luxury goods are not what Musca came for.

Books, diaries, documentation, photographs, computer files and any form of tape recordings are what he's hunting in the treasure hunter's lair.

He's already wrecked the library. Yanked down, opened up and shaken loose hundreds upon hundreds of old books. Now he's heading into the study – the place he's told the professor killed himself.

He walks over to the casement window and closes the thick red curtain. He shines his torch on to the desk, finds an antique brass lamp and flicks it on. In the mellow light, his eyes fall first on the revolving walnut chair, then the Victorian desk and the large dark-red map of blood spread across the cream blotter.

He shivers. The darkness of the house seems to close in on him. Tower above him.

Click.

Musca whirls towards the door. *Just natural noises of an old building?*

Crack.

He lunges for the lamp switch. Eases away from the desk and slides back towards the door. Leaning against the wall, he wills his heart to slow down.

All is silent.

Then again the soft creak of wood.

He knows now exactly where the sound is coming from. The rear of the house is full of old wooden floorboards, many warped and loose. As he discovered when he came in. He slips his kit bag off his shoulder and dips a hand inside. His fingers close around a small iron crowbar. Perfect for busting open a flimsy back door or a skull.

A moment passes.

Then another.

And another.

He starts to wonder if he's alone or not. Whether someone's come in and spotted him. Maybe even called the cops. Musca can't stand the waiting any longer. He rummages in his trouser pockets and finds his cigarette lighter. If he can't find anything incriminating, then the least he can do is ensure no one else does.

He pads back to the desk, gingerly slides open a drawer and finds a pack of A4 printer paper. Perfect. He tears open the cover wrapping and holds the flame to a wad of paper until it starts to smoke and catches ablaze. He carries the burning bundle to the curtains, flames flailing into the darkness, and holds the blaze beside the long cloths until they ignite.

The curtains create a roaring column of fire, a furious wash of orange and black. Musca retreats two steps. A tide of smoke rises around him.

As he turns, he sees a tall figure in the doorway.

There's a small burst of light, like a switch being turned quickly on and off, and then the ghostly silhouette suddenly pulls the door shut. Musca drops the flaming paper and rushes to the thick mahogany door. A key in the lock clicks twice.

He's trapped.

10

Gideon is no hero.

The first and last time he had a fight was at school – and even then it wasn't much of a brawl. He took several punches in the face from the year bully and was left with a bloody nose and no money for tuck shop.

He's filled out a lot since then. Grown bigger and broader. The former is down to genes and the latter to years of rowing at Cambridge. But ever since that harrowing moment he's developed an acute instinct for danger and an understanding that a quick brain is almost always better than a bully's quick hands.

Gideon's already called 999. Now he's picking his way as

silently as possible through the place just to make sure he hasn't made a silly mistake.

The door to the study yawns open and the light from the hall shows the big, chunky key in the lock. When he sees the figure torching the curtains he makes up his mind to lock the door and keep him there until the cops come.

But now he's thinking it over.

He's trapped someone in a burning room and if he doesn't let them out, they're going to die. So what? A bit of him really asks that. *So what* if he dies? Will the world actually miss the kind of low-life that breaks into a dead man's house and steals from him before he is even laid to rest?

Gideon opens the door.

There's a roar of flames as the draught blows in. He steps back, arms up to his scorched face. Through a molten wall of orange, a black shape hurtles at him. He is slammed against the wall. His body shudders with the impact. A fist smashes into his left cheekbone. A knee thuds into his crotch. He doubles over in pain. Takes a boot full in the face.

Flat out on the floor, his breath shallow and his lips leaking blood, the last thing Gideon sees before dizziness swallows him is the giant wave of flames and smoke rolling his way.

11

Musca charges across the sprawling lawns behind the manor house, his heart flinging itself against his chest. Above the fizz of the flames he hears the siren – just one car by the sound of it. It's way past midnight and he knows the police won't be coming mob-handed. At best, they'll have despatched that single squad car, with probably a couple of PCs in it.

Still, it was wise to have parked in a lane far behind the estate. The lawns are clear and open and he's soon able to escape the glare of the lights. Problem is, the darkness is virtually total and he can't find the exact place in the wall he climbed over – the point that will guide him back to the car.

He stumbles through a clump of thick rose branches and is almost sent sprawling by a molehill so large its owner could probably run for the governorship of California. Finally, he finds the landmark he'd made a mental note of: a greenhouse, the lower half built out of brick and the top of hard wood and double-glazed glass. He counts thirteen paces along the wall and finds the spot he has to climb.

There's a snag.

When he'd entered the grounds, he'd climbed a small tree on the other side. Dropping ten feet hadn't been difficult. He's just over six foot tall, so he'd been able to sling his bag over, dangle from his fingertips and then drop the rest of the way.

Now he can't get back.

No matter how high he jumps, or even *runs* and jumps, he can't get close to the top of the wall. Musca puts the kit bag down and frantically searches for something to stand on. An old compost bin, maybe a spade or garden fork to lean against, or if he's really lucky a ladder.

There's nothing.

He glances across the dark lawns. Flames spilling out of the side of the house. The cops have their hands full. He calms down. There's time enough to do this without making mistakes.

The greenhouse.

He rattles the door. Locked. Through the window he sees wooden racks full of plants. One of those would do just fine. He rushes back to his bag and realises he's left the crowbar in the old man's study. Never mind. Brute force will do.

Musca steps back and hammers a heel through the glass and hardwood frame. He jerks the doors open and slips inside.

He's right, the wooden tables are perfect. He pulls one free from the soil that it's sunk in, sending dozens of tomato plants spilling as he pulls it outside. He looks again towards the house.

Suspended in the blackness is what appears to be a bouncing ball of light. Torchlight. A cop with a flashlight is checking the grounds – moving quickly towards him.

Musca has killed and is ready to kill again if necessary. He peels away to the left of the light and heaves a heavy stone into the side of the greenhouse.

'Stop, police!'

He smiles as the torchlight rushes towards the noise. A second later he's behind the beam and the policeman is slumping unconscious to the ground.

Musca returns to the planting table and jams it against the garden wall.

Twenty seconds later, he's gone.

12

Megan is listening to her four-year-old's snuffling and laboured breathing. Every half-hour she wakes and passes a hand over the child's head. Sammy's on fire. For the eighth time that night she wets a flannel and gently lays it on her daughter's forehead.

Her mobile rings. It jerks her out of a tense state of half-sleep and she grabs it before it wakes Sammy.

'DI Baker.'

'Inspector, it's Jack Bentley from the control room.'

'Hang on,' she whispers as she climbs out of bed. 'Give me a second.' She works her way on to the landing. 'Okay, go ahead.'

'We just had an incident in Tollard Royal, the beat officer asked me to call.'

'Bit off my patch, Jack.' She glances down the corridor. Her mother is stood at her bedroom door, scowling.

'I know that, ma'am. There's been a fire in one of the big houses out there. A burglary too, according to the report. A police officer was assaulted by the offender as he fled the scene.'

'You need to call me about this?'

'They've taken a civilian to hospital. They found your business card on him.'

Megan turns away from her mother's accusatory gaze. 'Do you have a name? What did he look like?'

'I don't have a physical, but we ran a trace on a car parked there, an old Audi A4. It's registered to a Gideon Chase from Cambridge.'

She thinks she knows the answer but still asks the question, 'Who's the house owned by?'

Bentley taps up the info on his computer. 'Property is in the name of a Nathaniel Chase. He's listed on the electoral roll as the only resident.'

'He *was*. The man they've taken to hospital is his son. I saw him a few hours ago. He only drove down here because I had to ring him and tell him his father had died.'

'Poor bugger. Not his night, eh?' The penny drops with Bentley. 'Was that the professor chap who shot himself?'

'The same.'

'At any rate, two officers turned out, PCs Robin Featherby and Alan Jones. Jones is getting treated for neck injuries and Featherby asked me to call and let you know. Said to say sorry for ringing late but figured best to tell you now than get shouted at tomorrow.'

37

'He figured right. Thanks Jack. Have a good night.'

She turns her phone off just as her mother slips into the bedroom to check on Sammy. They're going to have a row. She just knows they are. Rather than do that, she slopes off downstairs to make a cup of tea.

As the kettle boils, Megan recalls her brief meeting with Gideon and the strangely disturbing letter from his father. There's no way this incident at Tollard Royal is just a burglary gone wrong.

No way on earth.

13

TUESDAY 15 JUNE
SALISBURY

When Gideon opens his eyes it's morning and he thinks he's back at home in his own bed. In a blink he realises how wrong he is. He's in hospital. There'd been a fire and a burglary at his dead father's house and the doctors at Salisbury District had insisted he'd stayed the night, 'for observation'.

He's straining to sit up when the matronly form of ward sister Suzie Willoughby appears. 'You're awake, then. How are you feeling?'

He touches his head, now throbbing in protest. 'Sore.'

She lifts a chart off the bottom rail of the bed, glances at it and inspects him more closely. 'You got a bump on the head, a split lip and a nasty cut to your left cheek, but the X-rays say nothing's broken.'

'I should be thankful for small mercies.'

'Something like that.' She looks at his cut face. 'It's less angry than it was, but maybe we should put a couple of stitches in there.'

'It'll be okay, I'm a quick healer.'

She can see he's squeamish. 'They don't hurt. Not like they used to. Have you had a recent tetanus injection?'

'Not since I was a kid.'

'We'll give you one then and just check your blood for infection, better safe than sorry. How's your throat?'

He feels as though he's back in boarding school, being checked over by Sister to see if he's trying to skive lessons. 'It's a bit rough, but I'm okay. Actually, I think I'm fine to go home, if that's all right.'

She gives him a look that says it isn't. 'Doctor will be around in about twenty minutes. He'll give you the once-over and if everything's fine, then we'll discharge you.' She fusses with the thin blankets. 'I'll get you something for the headache and some water for the throat. Best you drink *lots* of water. Flush the system. The fire you got caught in gave off a lot of smoke and you sucked it down into your lungs. You'll probably be very sore and coughy for a few days.'

He nods gratefully. 'Thanks.'

As she waddles off, he thinks about what she said. *The fire*. He remembers everything now: the intruder in his father's study, the blazing curtains, the fight in the hallway.

The nurse returns with a plastic cup of water and a couple of small tubs of pills. 'Do you have allergy reactions to paracetamol or ibuprofen?'

'No.'

She shakes out two paracetamol pills. 'Take these and if they don't work, the doctor will give you something stronger.'

He has to drink all the water to swallow them. Vicky – his ex – used to be able to pop pills, *any* kind, without even a sip of water, but he has to empty half the Thames down his neck to swallow just one. Funny he's thinking about her today. It must be the whack to the head. It's more than a year since they broke up. Queen Vic went back to Edinburgh after completing her doctorate, as she'd always threatened to do, and the separation made them both realise that it was the right time to move on. *Shame*, Gideon thinks, there are times when he still misses her. Like now.

Sister Willoughby is hovering.

'Do you think you're up to visitors?' She sounds almost apologetic.

Gideon's not sure how to answer. 'What kind?'

'The police. There's a lady Detective Inspector just arrived in reception.' A hint of mischief twinkles in her eyes. 'You don't have to see her if you don't feel up to it. I can have her sent away.'

'It's fine. I'll see her. Thanks.' His head throbs out a protest. Megan Baker is emphatically not the kind of company he wants right now.

14

The Inner Circle assembles in one of the outer chambers of the Sanctuary. A waist-high ring of purest beeswax candles casts a spectral glow over the emergency gathering convened by the Keeper.

Musca stands in the centre, disgrace hanging like a stone around his neck.

'You have failed.' Draco's voice cannons off the cavernous stone walls. 'Failed your brothers, failed our Craft and endangered all we stand for.'

Musca knows better than to protest.

Draco's voice grows cruel. 'For the sake of us all, summarise the list of "gifts" you left for the police.'

Musca recites them blankly. 'A tool bag. There was a crowbar, screwdriver, hammer, duct tape, wire cutters—'

Draco interrupts: 'And enough DNA to convict you for burglary, arson and perhaps attempted murder.'

'It's not traceable to me.'

'As yet.'

'I have no criminal record,' protests Musca. 'My fingerprints or genetic fingerprints are not on file anywhere.'

Draco slaps him across the face. 'Don't add insolence to incompetence. Afford me the respect I deserve as Keeper of the Inner Circle.'

Musca puts a hand to his stinging cheek. 'I apologise.'

Draco looks across the darkened room. 'Grus, can we make this evidence go away?'

'Have it lost?'

Draco nods.

'Not yet. There is the small matter of the policeman he assaulted as well. But later, yes. I'm confident that can be done.'

'Good.' He turns back to Musca. 'Did anyone see your face?'

'Not the policeman, it was dark. But the son. I am certain he saw me.'

Draco bounces a question across the chamber: 'Do we know *how* he is, *where* he is?'

The smallest among them, a red-haired brother known as Fornax, answers. 'He's in hospital in Salisbury, detained overnight, no serious injuries. He'll be discharged tomorrow, perhaps even later today.'

Grus speaks out, his voice calm and mature: 'The Lookers will keep tabs on him as he leaves.'

'Good.' Draco has another question for Musca. 'To be clear, you found nothing inside the house that would alert the world to us?'

'Nothing. I searched all the rooms. Upstairs and down-stairs. There were hundreds – perhaps thousands – of books, but no records, no documentation and no letters that in any way mentioned the Sacreds or our Craft.'

Grus speaks again. 'Perhaps he remained loyal until the end.'

Draco doesn't think so. 'We know of your affection for our lost brother, but it is misplaced. His suicide is more than untimely; it's selfish and potentially disastrous. He knew what was planned and what was expected of him.'

The Keeper switches his attention back to Musca. 'You are absolutely certain that there was nothing in that house that referred to us and our Craft?'

'If there was, there isn't now. I'm sure the fire destroyed the entire contents of the study.'

Draco's anger and anxiety subside. Perhaps the mistake with the forgotten bag is the price that has to be paid for a cleansing fire that safeguards the secrecy of the Craft. But a bigger problem remains. Nathaniel Chase had a vital role to play in the Craft's destiny. A key position in the second phase of the ceremony.

Now he's gone, that role has to be filled.

And quickly.

15

Megan Baker smoothes out her charcoal-grey mid-length suit skirt and sits on the hard chair next to Gideon's bed. 'So, what on earth happened to you?'

'I'm afraid I don't remember much.'

She glances to the nurse now at her side. 'Is there some-where more private than this? A place he and I can talk?'

The nurse has to think for a second. 'There's an exami-nation room down the corridor.' She points. 'Use that. Flip the sign on the door so you don't get disturbed.'

Megan looks back towards Gideon. 'Are you good to walk?'

'Sure. I'm fine.' He slowly swings his legs out of bed, taking care the ill-fitting pyjamas don't reveal more of him than is acceptable. 'Forgive my appearance.' He gestures to the striped and faded flannels that finish way above his ankles.

They enter the room and the nurse leaves them.

Megan flips the sign to 'Engaged', shuts the door and pulls out two chairs, one from behind a desk. 'So what happened after you left the police station?'

He feels stupid. 'I hadn't really thought things through. After I left you, I realised I didn't have anywhere to stay. It seemed like a good idea to go to my father's and sleep there. I suppose deep down I felt drawn to it.'

'That's natural enough.'

'Maybe. Anyway, the back door had been broken open so I called 999 and went to have a look around.'

She laces one leg over the other. 'You should have waited until the patrol car arrived. Didn't they tell you to wait?'

He can't remember if they did, but he doesn't want to get

44

anyone in trouble. 'I suspect so. I just wanted to have a look inside and make sure I hadn't raised a false alarm.'

'Which you clearly hadn't.'

'No. I hadn't. I saw this man in my father's study. He was setting it on fire.'

'How? What exactly was he doing?'

The image is clear in the archaeologist's head. 'He had one hand – his left – full of papers and he lit them with a cigarette lighter, one of those cheap little ones.'

'Disposable. A BIC?'

'Something like that. He lit the papers, then set the curtains on fire and was about to do the same with my father's desk.'

'When you confronted him?'

'No, not exactly. At first I just pulled the door shut and locked him in. Then I realised I had to let him out, otherwise he'd have probably died.'

'Some people might have been tempted to leave him in there.'

'I was.'

'Good job you didn't. I'd be charging you with a criminal offence this morning if you had done.'

'I know.'

She studies him. He's an academic, not a fighter. One of those men who looks tall enough and fit enough to handle himself but evidently never learned how.

'So you opened the door and he just starts laying into you?'

'Virtually. He pushed me out of the way and I grabbed him around the waist, rugby-style. Only I didn't take him down and he started punching and kicking me.'

She looks at the bruising. It's unusual. 'He cut your cheek quite badly. From the mark, I'd say he was wearing some jewellery on his right hand, maybe a signet ring.'

'I didn't notice. Just the pain.'

'I imagine.' She lifts her handbag from the floor. 'You mind if I take a shot of this, the outline is really clear?'

'I suppose not.'

She slides back the cover on the tiny Cyber-shot that she carries, then virtually blinds him with a camera flash. 'Sorry,' she says from behind the lens, 'just one more.'

Another flash and she clicks it closed. 'We may want SOCO to look at that.' She drops the camera back in her bag. 'If we can catch the guy that laid that ring on you, he should go down for assault, burglary and arson. A nice trio, he could get a good stretch for that.'

'Could?'

'Afraid so. The English judiciary will listen to any sob stories about him wetting the bed as a child, his father being an alcoholic or such like. They call it mitigating circum-stances. Did you get a good look at him?'

Disappointment shows on Gideon's face. 'No, I'm afraid not. It all happened so quickly and it was really dark.'

Megan has a degree in psychology and spent two years working on secondment to one of Britain's top profilers. She can see a lie coming before it's even crossed a guy's lips. She frowns and tries to look confused. 'I don't quite get it. You clearly noticed the lighter in his hand – the BIC. But you didn't see his face.'

Gideon feels uncomfortable. 'I don't know. I guess my eyes were drawn to the flame.'

'I can understand that. But despite all the light from the fire – from the papers in his hand and from the blazing curtains – you didn't get at least enough of a look at him to give a rough description?'

He shrugs. 'Sorry.'

'Mr Chase, I want to help you. But you're going to have to trust me.'

He looks surprised. 'I do. Why wouldn't I?'

She ignores the question. 'Are you sure you can't tell us anything about the man. His size? Weight? Hair colour? Clothing? Anything?'

He can feel her eyes boring through him but he's staying silent. He has a photograph of the man, snapped on his mobile phone, just before he'd shut the door. The burglar must have been there in connection with his father's secrets, and he intends to discover precisely what they are long before the police do.

Megan is still waiting for an answer.

He shakes his head. 'I'm sorry. I just can't help you.'

She flashes him a smile so bright he nearly flinches. 'You will,' she says with an icy coldness. 'Believe me, you will.'

16

Protecting the precious stones principally means stopping people from climbing on them or defacing them. To that end, English Heritage has erected fences, traffic barriers and ropes, and only allows people into the roped-off relics on special occasions or with written permission.

The government-funded body is good at its job but has no idea just how devoted some of its subcontracted security staff are. The likes of Sean Grabb are devout members of the Followers of the Sacreds. Long after their paid shifts have finished, they still watch the precious site.

Thirty-five-year-old Grabb is one of those sleeves-rolled-up, slightly overweight guys who always gets a job done and is never short of a good word for those who work for him. He heads up a team of Lookers who keep Stonehenge under constant vigil. Three hundred and sixty degrees. Twenty-four hours a day. Seven days a week. Three hundred and sixty-five days a year.

He and his Lookers never stop looking. Some of it is done openly during the Heritage-paid shifts, some covertly by tiny remote cameras strategically placed across the landscape.

Grabb has been a Looker for ten years. Known inside the Craft as Serpens, he is following in the deep footsteps of his father, grandfather and every other traceable male in the paternal line. With him today is twenty-five-year-old Lee Johns, a relatively new recruit, yet to be formally admitted into the Craft's hallowed ranks. He's tall and thin with pimply, undernourished skin and, outside of his work uniform, lives in unwashed denims and rock band T-shirts. He's not too bright and has weathered his share of problems, including drugs and homelessness. By his early twenties, society had written him off as an eco-hippie troublemaker. For a while he sought solace in the company of other protestors and agitators. He never totally fitted in.

His life started to have meaning only when he drifted down to Stonehenge en route to Glastonbury, where he'd hoped to score some cheap gear and maybe string together a bit of money from low-level dealing. But he never made it to the music gathering. The solstice was so breathtaking he felt unable to even move from the henge. He stayed, helping clear up and volunteering for any kind of work in relation to the magical stones.

He's been working with Sean for close on three years now and they have something of a master and apprentice relationship. Sean is his sponsor and dispenses wisdom as regularly as he does the sludgy brown tea from his trusty flask. Every watch he quizzes his protégé in the effort to ensure he's fit to be admitted into the closed circle of the Followers.

'Question one.' Grabb gives his pupil a pay-attention stare. 'What are the stones and what do they mean to those of us in the Craft?'

Johns grins – an easy one. 'The stones are our Sacreds. They are the source of all our earthly energy. They are our protectors, our guardians and our life force.'

Grabb splashes a reward of tea into Lee's brown-ringed mug. 'Good. And *why* do the Sacreds bestow such blessings on us?'

Johns cradles the dark elixir as they stand by the traffic barrier on the car park. 'We are the Followers of the Sacreds, descendants of those who placed the great ones here thousands of years ago. The bones and blood of our ancestors nourish the Sacreds in their resting places, just as one day our remains will follow them and complete the circle.'

Steam wafts from the top of Grabb's steel thermos cup. He sips the hot tea and asks, 'And *how* do the Sacreds bless us?'

'With their spiritual energy. They transfer it through the stones to us and their blessing protects us from the ravages of illness and the humiliation of poverty.'

Grabb is pleased. His pupil is learning his catechism well and that can only reflect kindly on him. He pours more tea into Lee's mug. 'And what do the Sacreds expect in return?'

'Respect.' He pronounces the word with sincerity. 'We must recognise them, respect them, have faith in them and follow their teachings through their appointed oracle, the Henge Master.'

'That's right, Lee. Remember those who would steal our heritage. Remember the Catholics and their commandments written in stone supposedly passed down from God. They cooked up that story two thousand years after the Sacreds had been established here in England.'

Lee nods. He understands. He must not be sidetracked or seduced by other religions, false-belief systems that have big gold glittering palaces for adoration, that collect money each week from congregations and create their own banks and states. 'Sean,' he starts, thirsty for reassurance. 'I know you can trace your bloodline all the way back to the greats who carried the bluestones and the sarsens. I understand why that makes you worthy for the blessing and protection of the Sacreds, but what about people like me? We're outsiders. We don't come from around here.'

Grabb recognises the insecurity; it's a regular thing with Lee. 'We are all from *around here*, my friend. Five thousand years ago the population of Britain was tiny. Way back then, you and I were probably brothers, or cousins at worst.'

Johns likes that idea. And it makes sense too. Even the Christians believe in Adam and Eve and how one moment of sex somehow spawned all of mankind. Or something like that, he can't quite remember. Brothers – him and Sean.

'You're doing real well, Lee.' Grabb puts a broad arm around the kid's near skeletal shoulders and shows him how proud he is.

But in reality he's worried – worried about how his protégé will face up to the horrors of the challenge that awaits.

17

After a tetanus shot and what he viewed as a completely unnecessary taking of blood, Gideon is discharged from hospital in the late afternoon. The only good thing is that the DI was able to get the keys to his father's house biked over before the discharge was completed.

Approaching the grand house in a taxi from the hospital, he can see that the damage is considerable. The lawns have been churned up by fire engines and the side of the building is shrouded in the remnants of black smoke. Windows are blown in and boarded up, brickwork cracked.

Right now he doesn't care. The place is still just bricks and mortar to him. Only when he lets himself in through the colossal front door does he feel any emotion.

When his mother died, Gideon was distraught. He went from being confident and extrovert, trusting in the world and his place in it, to being disturbingly introverted and wary of people. The death of his father is bringing on another change. He is uncertain of what but he feels it. Inside him is a volatile mix of anger, frustration, resentment and a residue of unfairness. A swirling blend of components that he knows is going to alter the DNA of his personality irrevocably.

He wanders the big empty house and feels acutely alone. He has no brothers or sisters, no grandparents. No children. He is the end of the Chase line. What he does with the remainder of his life will determine not only what the world thinks of him but the whole Chase lineage.

He drops his jacket in the hall. Climbs the grand staircase to a long open first-floor landing and searches for a place to wash and crash for a while.

The house is plainly not equipped for life four hundred years after it was built. The big rooms with their high ceilings must cost a fortune to heat. No wonder his father appears to have lived in only a couple. The windows are draughty and need replacing. Most of the walls are flaked with damp. Floors creak worse than the planks of an old sailing ship in a storm and it must be fifty years since the place saw a decent lick of paint.

His father's bedroom is the smallest of all and gives him the strangest of feelings. It's crammed with emptiness. The old man's things are everywhere but they have become depersonalised, as though blasted with some radioactivity that eradicated all trace of him.

A pile of books towers by the bed. Near them is a white mug, an inch of tea still in it, a crust of mould on the surface. He guesses it was the last morning cuppa or late-night drink his father tasted.

The quilt is pulled back on one side of the high, wooden-framed double bed. The indent in the old spring mattress, grey base sheet and crumpled feather pillow show exactly where Nathaniel slept. The other side of the bed is pristine. Gideon feels himself frown. For all Nathaniel's legendary brilliance and inarguable wealth, his father lived like a squatter and died lonely.

He casts a last look around the little bedroom and notices the remains of an old bell circuit above the door, a hangover from the time a nanny or butler slept here waiting to be called by the master of the house. He is reminded of a boyhood visit one wet weekend to a National Trust home and the single interesting comment from the tour guide: the property, he'd said, was veined with secret passages so servants could pass quickly and discreetly from upstairs to downstairs.

Gideon wonders if his father's place is the same. He steps out into the corridor, kicking up a swirl of dust motes. He ponders if there's another room behind Nathaniel's tiny bedroom.

There isn't.

The landing runs down to a casement window overlooking the garden. He walks down and to his right sees an odd join in the wallpaper. He taps the wall. It sounds like plasterboard. He knocks a metre to the left and then a metre to the right.

Stone.

He taps again on the board. All over and around it. The plasterboard area is big enough to be a door. There's no visible handle or hinges, but he's sure it is. He gets down on his knees and digs, just as he would in an archaeological trench. His fingers find the edge where the skirting board meets the landing floor. He tries to pull it open but it is jammed tight. Out of frustration he pushes rather than pulls.

It bursts open, belching out a breath of musty air.

Gideon bolts upright. A sliver of darkness is cut into the wall. He reaches inside and finds a light switch. He is astonished by what he sees: a narrow room like a very long cupboard. One wall is stacked floor to ceiling with books. Another contains old VHS tapes, some DVDs. Set into the far wall is an old pre-HD plasma TV.

His mind trips into overdrive. Why did his father have a hidden room? What's on the tapes – and why are they in this place? Why are dozens of books in here and not on show downstairs?

Why was his father so determined to keep all this secret?

PART TWO

18

Jake Timberland is thirty-one but tells anyone who doesn't know better that he's twenty-seven. There's something about thirty or over that he simply isn't ready to have pinned on him. In Jake's circle of friends, age is like the big birthday badge fastened on your chest when you are a kid, proclaiming 'I AM 5'. Only at thirty it might as well say 'I AM Slippers. Carpets. Dogs. Families. Volvos. I AM DULL.'

And dull sure ain't Jake. Especially on a night when he's done more chemicals than Pete Doherty and Amy Winehouse put together.

He's not rich. But his father is. Banker bonus rich. The kind that comes from so far back in the family tree that the damn thing must have been a sapling in the garden of Eden when Adam was still pawing around. One day Jake will cop for the lot, but until then he has to make do with a five-million-pound pied-à-terre in Marylebone and an allowance that's just enough to run the Aston, pay his club bills, make the occasional investment and enjoy the odd night on the town.

Jake is the only son and heir of Lord Joseph Timberland and he's been papped with some of society's hottest models, page-three girls and wild-child daughters of ageing rock stars. Sure it helps that your best buddy is a lensman at *Heat* magazine, but then what are friends for?

Tonight he is dressed to kill. A shimmering silk and cotton blue suit with a plain saturated-blue shirt and new black Italian leather shoes. He already has his sights set on a real hottie. A lithe piece who's breezed into the VIP area at Chinawhite's and is acting like she owns the place. Her perfect teeth say she's American long before you hear her laugh and chat over-loudly to her entourage. Soaring cheekbones, warm brown eyes, carefully scrunched long dark hair and fabulous legs that stretch from a retro dashiki-style miniskirt in green, hot pink and coral. She looks like a film star hippie.

Just watching her sends a rush of blood to his head.

Then she glances his way.

Oh, man. Jake thinks he's going to blow like an oil well. He floats across the floor, pulled by her sheer sexual gravity. The lithe one is surrounded by lots of pretty young things, boys and girls, but it seems she has eyes only for him.

'Whoa, fella. Hold up.'

The voice and a big black hand on his chest come out of nowhere.

60

'Excuse me.' Jake peers disdainfully at the big fingers spread like the jaw of a crocodile near his puny white neck. 'Do you mind?'

He's speaking polite and perfect English into the face of a man so large he can't see beyond his shoulder-span. 'You need to back up a little, sir. The lady over there is having a party and there are no strangers allowed.'

Jake gives in to a nervous laugh. 'A party without strangers? Just let me introduce myself to the young lady, I'm—'

The crocodile snaps. The finger-jaws grab Jake's throat and have him walking breathlessly backwards all the way to a seat in the far corner of the VIP lounge.

As he struggles for breath, an older man with short white hair squats on his heels and looks deep into Jake's eyes. 'Son, we're sorry to have had to do that. Now we're going to order you a complimentary bottle of whatever you like and you're going to stay right over here and drink it. Okay?'

'This is my club,' protests Jake, his voice raspy. He surprises himself by standing up. But once on his feet he has no real idea what he should do next. His way forward is blocked by crocodile man and another black-suited animal. He'd need ladders to climb over them.

Beyond the mountain range of their muscles, his eye again catches that of the beautiful young American. She murmurs to a blonde beside her – and, to Jake's amazement, starts to walk his way.

There is no mistaking her intention. Her eyes never lose

contact with his. Whoever she is, she's coming over to talk to him.

The mountains shift menacingly towards him but he doesn't care. They say love hurts. Jake guesses he's just about to find out precisely how much.

19

Gideon's mobile is chirping downstairs like a bird trapped in a flue.

He knows he won't get to it before it trips to his message service but hurries out of his father's hidden room and tries anyway.

He misses it by seconds.

The voicemail kicks in as he scours the worktops for pen and paper. He finds a rip-and-stick pad by the fridge. The front page bears a rough shopping list – cheese, biscuits, fruit, chocolate – the last supper his father never had.

He plays back the missed call, scribbles down the number and punches it in once the message has ended.

The voice at the other end is a woman's. 'CID. DI Baker.'

His hopes drop. 'This is Gideon Chase, you just called my mobile.'

'Mr Chase, thanks for ringing. I called to fix a time for you to see your father's body.'

The words stun him. He'd been fearing this. She'd even

asked him about it. But now it's come he feels totally unprepared. 'Right. Thank you.'

'The funeral director is Abrahams and Cunningham on Bleke Street in Shaftesbury. Do you know where I mean?'

'No. I'm not local, I don't know the area at all.'

'Well, it's easy to find. It's on the right, not far down from the Ivy Cross roundabout. They've suggested ten a.m. tomorrow. If that's not suitable, I can give you a number and you can make your own arrangements.'

There isn't a time on the clock face that seems *suitable* to see the semi-obliterated body of your father. In true English fashion, Gideon says the opposite of what he's thinking. 'Yes, that would be fine.'

'Good. I'll confirm with them.'

'Thanks.'

Megan senses his tension. 'If you'd like I could get an officer to accompany you. Would that help?'

'I'll be okay on my own.'

'I understand.' She sounds sympathetic. 'Call me if you change your mind.'

Gideon hangs up and heads back upstairs.

He re-enters the secret room with a degree of trepidation, worried that the tapes are going to turn out to be pornographic. He tells himself he can live with it. Because it may be worse. It may relate to Nathaniel's grave-robbing, his tomb-raiding, his highly questionable 'trade' in prized artefacts.

He stands for a moment and surveys the room. Years of training have taught him to take in the landscape before you start digging it up. The old saying about needing to know the lie of the land is true in archaeology – the terrain can lie like a faithless lover and lose you years of your life.

He knows that his father was the last person in here before him. The way it is, is how *he* left it. Generally tidy. Neat, except for a couple of open DVD cases. Orderly. There is a leather desk chair positioned in front of the wall-mounted TV and a low coffee table in the middle of the room. It's marked with shoe polish on the near side, from where his father must have put his feet while watching the screen. There's a crystal glass that smells of whisky, but no sign of a decanter or bottle. He suspects the liquor is stashed in one of the built-in cupboards at the bottom of the shelving that fills the room. There are boxes on the back shelves. He wonders how much his father was drinking at the end. Next to the glass is an ancient laptop computer – the type that still takes floppy disks – a notepad and a small and ugly clay pencil holder that he recognises instantly. He made it at school and brought it home for Father's Day.

He can tell that the room has been used for logging, reviewing and filing. But what? He finds the TV remote control within reaching distance of the chair and turns the set on. Built into the wall beneath it are three shelves, one holding a chunky, near-industrial VHS player, one for a DVD machine and a bottom one that looks like a place to throw junk – cables, open tape boxes and loose coins.

The TV throws up a haze of broken white and black fuzz as it stirs itself. The DVD whirrs into life and fights for channel supremacy. Up on to the screen comes an out-of-focus, grainy picture. It's a digital copy of old Super 16mm film by the look of it. It sharpens and shows his father reincarnated as a more youthful man, speaking confidently from the stage of a lecture theatre: 'Stonehenge is a miracle of the ancient world. To build it today, with all of our machinery and mathematical know-how would be impressive. To have begun building it five thousand years ago, without computers, CAD packages, cranes and trucks and barges to carry those monoliths is beyond wonder.'

Gideon is bored already. His childhood had been littered with nonsensical theories about Stonehenge being a temple, a burial place for ancient kings, the world's first astronomical observatory, a cosmic link to the pyramids in Egypt. And most ignorantly of all, the birthplace of the druids.

He turns off the film and fires up the old VHS machine. It clicks and clunks as the mechanical heads shuffle around and lock on a tape that has been left in there. A big close-up of a beautiful woman's face appears on screen. Beautiful enough to suck the air from his lungs.

It's his mother.

She is laughing. Holding her hand up to the camera and looking embarrassed that she's being filmed. He finds the volume. 'Turn it off, Nate. I hate that thing, *please* turn it off.'

Her voice makes him tremble. He can't help but step forward and put his fingers to the screen.

'Nate. Enough now!'

The shot pulls wider. Marie Chase sits on a gondola in Venice against a cornflower blue sky. She turns her head from the camera faking annoyance with her husband. Her hair is dark, long and thick – exactly the same texture as Gideon's – and it is being made to dance on her shoulders by a light summer's wind. In the background, St Mark's bobs away as a stripe-shirted boatman punts them across the lagoon. The shot is wide enough now for Gideon to tell that she's pregnant.

He stops the tape and looks away wet-eyed to the stacked shelves. They're not all full of home movies, of that he's sure. The last thing his father watched was his mother because he was reconnecting with happier times, probably the happiest of his life. It's the kind of thing people do when they're experiencing the worst of times, the worst of their lives.

Everything on the shelves was important to his father. Important enough to classify and to protect. But not as important as this precious memory of the only woman he really loved.

Gideon walks to the books. They are all red, leather-bound journals, the lineless type favoured by artists and writers. He tries to pull down a volume from the top left-hand corner but the covers are stuck together. He prises them apart.

He opens the book on the first page and reels from another emotional blow. It's dated the day of his father's eighteenth birthday.

The handwriting is the same but somehow hesitant:

My name is Nathaniel Chase and today is my eighteenth birthday, the day I come of age. I have made a promise to myself that from this instant onwards I will keep a meticulous record of what I hope will be a long, eventful, happy and successful life. I will record the good and the bad, the honourable and the dishonourable, the things that stir the soul and those that leave me indifferent. My tutors say that much can be learned from history, so perhaps as the years unfold I shall learn much about myself by keeping an honest record of the passing years. No doubt, if I am famous I will publish these small literary missives, and should I be a nonentity then at least in my winter years I shall gain some warmth from looking back and reflecting in the hot optimism of my youth. I am eighteen. A great adventure awaits me.

Gideon finds it too painful to read on. He glances along the rows. Is this stuff in all of them? Every event, emotion and detail of Nathaniel Chase's great adventure?

He runs a finger along the red spines and counts off the years: his father's twentieth birthday, his twenty-first, his twenty-sixth – the year he met his wife; his twenty-eighth – the same as Gideon is now; his thirtieth – the year Nathaniel Gregory Chase and Marie Isabel Pritchard married in Cambridge; and his thirty-second – when Gideon was born.

The fluttering fingers stop. He has entered his own space. His eyes drift down to the thirty-eighth year. The year Marie died.

His hands stretch to the slim volume and he begins to lever it out of the vice-like grip of those either side, but he cannot bring himself to remove it. Instead, he jumps on two years. To the fortieth of his father's life.

He withdraws the diary. Two years after his mother's death. He feels prepared for whatever the eighth year of his own life has to offer.

Only he isn't.

It's not written in English. It's not written in any recognisable language.

It's in code.

Gideon pulls out the following year's book.

Code.

And the year after.

Code.

He rushes to the end of the room and stoops for the final volume. Again he freezes – this book will bear the last entries of Nathaniel Chase's life.

His heart is like a raging bull butting his rib cage. He swallows hard, lifts the volume from its shelf and opens it.

20

She smells like cinnamon. And she's high as a kite.

Jake Timberland notes these things as the beautiful American kisses him goodbye on the pavement. She's maybe twenty-two at most. And it's not a peck on the cheek. It's a proper smacker. She holds his face between her manicured fingers and her lips gently touch his. But he lets her make the running.

And she does. A little brush of the tongue – just a glance against the underside of his upper lip. His eyes dance beneath closed lids. She moves back. 'Bye.' A smile and she steps away.

'Wait.'

She smiles again as she folds herself daintily into the back seat of the limo. The black guy with the crocodile hands slams the door shut and shoots him a look that's more than just a warning; it's a declaration of war.

Fuck it. Jake squares his shoulders and approaches the tinted rear window. For the second time that evening, a massive hand explodes like a grenade in the middle of his chest, sending him sprawling. The bodyguard slips into the passenger seat and the limo is gone before Jake's anywhere near getting to his feet. The most beautiful woman he's ever met has just watched him fall on his butt. Not a good way to end the evening.

He gets a few strange glances as several couples slalom past into the depths of Soho. The pavement is soaked from an earlier downpour and his clothes are now wet. He brushes himself down and digs in his pocket for a handkerchief to wipe the mud and grit from his hands.

Something flutters to the floor. He bends and picks it up. It's a bar mat, the advertising ripped off, and there's a message in pen on it: 'Call me tomorrow on number below x.' Next to the kiss is a small squiggle of a padlock.

Jake stares at the doodle. He knows it. *Jesus*. Now he understands what all the security was about.

21

Gideon holds the diary in shaking hands. He sits on the room's hard floor, rests his back against the shelving, afraid to read. He feels beaten – as though assaulted and battered by some invisible enemy. Floored by the ghost of his father.

He looks up at all the handwritten journals around him – a complete personal history of the father he never knew. And the man wrote more than twenty years of it in code.

Why?

He shakes his head and blinks. Darkness presses like shovelled earth against every pane of glass in the house. He feels entombed. Carefully, he opens the cover and on the right-hand inside page is the inscription: ΓΚΝΔΜΥ ΚΛΥ.

It makes him smile. He runs his fingers over the top of the page and feels himself slipping back to childhood. His father never kicked a football with him, never swung a cricket bat, never took him swimming. But he played mind games with him. Nathaniel spent hours devising puzzles, teasers, problems and games that imbued in him powers of logic and the roots of classical learning.

The letters ΓΚΝΔΜΥ ΚΛΥ are ancient Greek, which his father considered the first true alphabet, the source of European, Latin and Middle Eastern alphabets. And he recognised its importance in mathematics, physics and astronomy. His son was made to learn every letter. To test the boy, and to break the boredom, the professor devised a simple code. The twenty-four letters of the Greek alphabet assumed reverse values to their English equivalents, so Omega represented A and so on until Alpha represented X. The obsolete Greek letters Digamma and Qoppa represented the final English letters Y and Z. For years Nathaniel would leave his son coded notes around the house – until the relationship became too strained for any form of communication.

Gideon struggles to remember the code. It's been more than fifteen years. Then it comes to him. ΓΚΝΔΜΥ ΚΛΥ means VOLUME ONE. He glances up again at the dozens of books and wonders how many coded words have been written. It could take a lifetime to decipher them all.

A lifetime to translate a lifetime.

He turns another page, and feels queasy. The handwriting is a savage reminder of the suicide note. He tries to make sense of the first paragraph but he is too rusty to get further than a few words. From the low coffee table he picks up some paper and a couple of pens – black and red. He constructs a table, writing the Greek letters on the left and to the right, the English.

Ϙ	Qoppa	Z		Μ	Mu	M
Ϝ	Digamma	Y		Ν	Nu	L
Α	Alpha	X		Ξ	Xi	K
Β	Beta	W		Ο	Omicron	J
Γ	Gamma	V		Π	Pi	I
Δ	Delta	U		Ρ	Rho	H
Ε	Epsilon	T		Σ	Sigma	G
Ζ	Zeta	S		Τ	Tau	F
Η	Eta	R		Υ	Upsilon	E
Θ	Theta	Q		Φ	Phi	D
Ι	Iota	P		Χ	Chi	C
Κ	Kappa	O		Ψ	Psi	B
Λ	Lambda	N		Ω	Omega	A

Using the table, he scans the opening page and quickly translates ΛΩΕΡΩΛΠΥΝ into NATHANIEL and ΧΡΩΖΥ into CHASE. The journal is written in the first person and contains his father's day-to-day thoughts.

He flicks through a dozen or so more pages, not looking for anything in particular, fascinated that he can travel backwards or forwards through days, months or years of his father's life.

Halfway through the journal, the writing becomes bolder. The passages look as though they've been written with vigour and excitement. Years of speed-reading have trained Gideon's eyes to hop diagonally down a document in search of key words.

ΖΕΚΛΥΡΥΛΣΥ, ΨΝΚΚΦ and ΖΩΧΗΠΤΠΧΥ leap out at him.

He hopes he's made a mistake. Prays that tiredness has made him jump to the wrong conclusion. On its own, ΖΕΚΛΥΡΥΛΣΥ may be innocuous enough; he'd expect his father to mention it. It means STONEHENGE.

It's the other two words that are chilling his soul.

ΨΝΚΚΦ is BLOOD.

And ΖΩΧΗΠΤΠΧΥ is SACRIFICE.

22

MARYLEBONE, LONDON

Jake Timberland flings his suit in a corner and sits on the edge of his giant black leather bed with built-in fifty-inch plasma and room dimmers. He's too wired to get any sleep and strangely enough not in the mood to go hunting cute-ass-would-be-wags for the rest of the night. In any case, the date isn't over. Thanks to his mobile phone, it's about to go virtual. The beauty of technology.

In his left hand is his iPhone and in his right the piece of paper with the padlock doodle that the American lovely gave him. Caitlyn to be more precise. Caitlyn Lock.

Just being seen within touching distance of 'The Lock', as she's known, could make him an 'A-Lister'. He reckons that right now she'll be doing one of three things. She could still be partying, which he doubts because the gorillas probably wouldn't allow her that much freedom. She could be having a drink with some of the other clean-cut cuties she was hanging with. Possible. Or she could be a good little girl and already in bed. Probable. Whichever it is, she'll be thinking about him. You don't kiss someone like she did and then not think about it later.

What he has to do is tap into that. Tap in and stretch it while it's still fresh. Give himself something to build a little romance on. And the perfect tool to pull off that little trick is sexy texting. Nothing hard core. Just a couple of short notes to say that he can't stop thinking about her. Start off casual and polite then feel his way in, reveal a little more of his emotions. No point simply gushing it all out on the first message. If you do that, the girl won't reply, she'll just leave you hanging on until you try again.

Jake gets typing. *Hope you got home ok. It was great to meet you tonight. Jake.* No, that's not good. He rewrites: *Hope you got home ok. It was GREAT to meet you tonight. Jake.*

Still not right.

He remembers her age. Considerably younger than him. He adjusts again: *Hope u r ok. Gr8 2 meet u! Jake x.*

He allows himself a satisfied smile and hits send. Phones

are terrific. He watches the little virtual envelope on the screen fold itself up, develop wings and then fly off, straight to the heart of the woman he loves. Well yeah, maybe. For now it's lust, pure and simple. But let's face it, without that, love probably doesn't have a chance.

The phone beeps. Wow, she's replied quickly. Good sign.

U can ring if u want x.

Not what he expected. Not what he wanted either. A little text flirting before turning in for the night was a perfect idea, but a conversation right now could blow things. He thinks. When a girl says you can ring *if you want,* that's not a request, it's an instruction.

Jake pulls off his socks and shirt, grabs a glass of water from the bathroom and climbs in bed. He feels almost panicky as he calls her.

'It's Jake. Hi.'

'Hi there.' Her voice is soft and a little sleepy. 'I wondered if you'd ring or text.'

'Even after you saw me sit down in a puddle?'

She laughs a little. 'Especially after you dumped your ass in a puddle.'

'Actually, *I* didn't dump my ass – one of your apes did.'

'That would be Eric. He has a thing for me. I've seen him rough guys up much worse. Much, much worse than you got and I didn't even kiss them.'

'Remind me not to put Eric on my Christmas card list.'

'He's just protective.'

'So I noticed. Why did you do that?'

'Do what?'

'Kiss me.'

'Ah, that would be because I wanted to.' Her voice is almost sleepy. 'And let's face it, *you* wanted me to.'

'I did?'

'I've never seen a man aching so badly to be kissed.'

He laughs. 'You've *no idea* how much.'

'Oh, I've an idea all right. You were sticking it in my hip. Pretty big clue.'

He feigns shock. 'Oh my God, was I?'

'Yeah right, like you didn't know.'

'Let's change the subject before one of us gets embarrassed.'

'It won't be me.'

'I believe you. How do I get to see you again?'

'Good question.'

'And?'

'*And* you have to be patient. You can use this phone to call me, it's my own pay-as-you-go, but it may be a while before we can meet up.'

'What about my aching?'

'Be inventive. Goodnight.'

The phone goes dead.

He's left staring at it. Wondering how he's going to cope with his pounding heart and a hard-on so big he could spin a plate on it.

After yesterday's sleepless night, Megan is relieved to have her daughter tucked up and sound asleep in her own bed tonight. Loath him as she does, Adam had a point. She switches off the bedroom light, closes the door on her already snoring angel and the army of soft toys surrounding her. Sammy's temperature's down, she's less clammy and feverish. Come the morning her little angel may be back to her normal self.

Megan wanders into the open-plan kitchen-lounge of her small cottage and empties the last of a bottle of Chianti into a glass. Maybe she'll turn on the TV and watch something dull, clear her head of the worries about Sammy, money and the ever-present problem of balancing motherhood and her job.

But the Chase case is bugging her like a wasp. Suicides usually put a gun to their head and mess up the walls for one of three reasons: they can't live with the guilt and shame of something they've done, they're afraid of something they've done being exposed and their personal or private reputation ruined, or they're desperately ill, either physically or mentally.

Nathaniel Chase doesn't seem to fit any of those categories. She's pulled all the background intelligence she can. Bank records, mortgage accounts, stockbroker dealings, everything financial and personal on both father and son.

But there are no real clues. Fascinating family — and deceptively wealthy. Or at least now the son is. He's getting it all, the solicitors told her. From what she can see, that turns out to be more than £20m in property, cars, stocks and savings. As well as the estate and the two cars garaged in it — a seven-year-old Range Rover and a vintage Rolls valued at more than a million — there are paintings and antiques held in vaults, collectively worth in excess of five million. There is Nathaniel Chase's portfolio of personal investments and private banking matters, all routed through UBS in Switzerland. Another six million. Strangely, UBS didn't handle his company activities. He left that to Credit Suisse and this year's figures show a bottom-line profit of more than a million. The old professor owned land across the county too, no doubt of obscure archaeological worth.

Now it's all Gideon's.

She looks again at the money trail. If in doubt, follow the cash. If it's not about sex, it's about money. If there's no other explanation, then it's money. Always money.

Could the son have faked his father's suicide? He had so much to gain and she knows he's lying to her. Might explain why he didn't identify the man who attacked him in his father's study. Maybe the attacker was an accomplice. Perhaps Gideon Chase is really a murderer and a fraudster?

Then again she could just be very tired and not thinking straight. She gives in and switches on the TV. *The X Factor*. Fantastic. Utter drivel. Just what she needs to forget about work.

24

It's the middle of the night and Sean Grabb can't sleep.

He knows a good rest is a long way off. Years away. He pulls a fresh bottle of vodka from his fridge, unscrews the top and swallows almost a quarter without even getting a glass. He's not so dumb that he doesn't understand what's happening. If any sane man had done half the things he has, they'd be hitting the bottle as well.

That's how he rationalises it, as he finally gets a tumbler from the loose-hinged cupboard in the tatty kitchen of his terraced home. Some nights the memories are just too much to bear. They hit the back of his retinal screen like the flash frames of a horror film. Tonight is one of those nights. The image of the sacrifice's smashed skull won't go away. Nor that of his dull empty eyes or his moon-white, bled-out flesh.

Grabb downs another blast of vodka. It was done for the greater good. He gets that. But it doesn't stop the horror show rerunning in his head. One blink and he's back there dealing with the corpse. Dead meat, that's what Musca had called it. Told him to treat the kid that way. Imagine the body was a rack of lamb, a leg of pork.

They threw the mutilated corpse into the back of Musca's van and drove out to the abattoir, for which he had keys. The kid weighed a ton as they hoisted him up on to the processing line. Musca dangled him upside down, like a stunned cow, then he slit his throat and drained the last of the blood into a run-off grid.

Grabb can still hear the clank of the chains, the buzz of the electric motor and the ghostly echoes of equipment clunking into life and towing the dead body along the line. Then the monstrous mangling. The decapitation. The organ removal. The skin peeled off by hydraulic pullers. He almost threw up when Musca had to free flesh clogged from the claws of their automated accomplices.

He takes another hit of vodka. But the images stick. They're clogged in his memory. Stuck as doggedly as the awful clumps of flesh that jammed the process line. He tells himself that the visions will fade but deep down he knows they won't. They'll always be there. Now the soft, warm wave is coming. Not fast enough, but it's coming. He can feel it rolling in. But it won't wash away the guilt. Or the fear of being caught.

The line stripped the kid's bones clear of any shred of flesh or evidence that could be used against them or anyone. The advanced meat recovery system at the plant reduced it all to mechanically recovered meat – ready for human or animal consumption. It was so damned efficient it even produced neat packages of bone, lard and tallow. The blood and fecal matter just got dumped, washed away like sewage.

'No need to worry,' Musca kept saying. 'No need to fret.'

But he *was* worried. *Is* fretting. Not just about the nightmares. Or the guilt. But that it's all got to be done again.

Soon.

25

Caitlyn Lock squints through the morning's bitter yellow haze across the shimmering water of the Thames. She is lying in the warm soft bed at her father's apartment, just one of his many properties. There is a house in Rome. Another in Paris. And two or maybe three more in Spain and Switzerland. So many she can't remember. Then there are the places back home: LA, New York, Washington. Pop is famous and loaded. And Caitlyn is on track to become more famous and loaded than he is. Or her mom.

She will talk about her father at the drop of a hat, but not her mother. Oh, no. Mom is out of bounds. Kylie Lock is a minor Hollywood star who walked out on them to set up with her toy boy co-star. Caitlyn can barely give her the time of day, let alone free publicity. If she was honest, maybe she'd admit understanding what she sees in François, a dark-eyed Frenchman who tops six feet and looks like he could model swim shorts.

She gives up hugging the quilt and slips naked out of bed. Hands on hips, she admires herself in the long mirror next to the giant picture window overlooking the London Eye. She turns. Strikes a coy look over her shoulder and completes a three-sixty. Her mom would kill to have a body like this.

81

She turns sideward, studies the Union Jack tattoo on her behind. No one but her and the tattooist who put it there has seen it yet. She pads over the cream shag pile carpet to the low table with her cellphone on it. She laughs and picks it up. It's untraceable. Packed with pay-as-you-go credit that no one but she and her girlfriends know about. She turns it on and taps in the pin. While waiting for it to find a network, she looks at her ass again, thinking how hard her pop will kick it if he ever finds out what she's about to do.

The phone finds a signal and she thumbs her way through to the camera function. It takes a while for her to stop giggling and shoot some pictures. Most are hazy and badly framed – finally she takes one that will do just fine.

She sits on the edge of the bed, brings up Jake's number and adds a brief message. She hits *send* and collapses with laughter.

26

Chepstow, Chepstow and Hawks looks more like an antique auctioneers than a law office. A legal professor at Cambridge once told Gideon you can classify the client according to the lawyer he engages and Chepstow and Co. seems to prove his point. Traditional and reliable no doubt, but old-fashioned and dusty. The place fits Nathaniel to a T.

A grey-haired, bespectacled woman in her fifties tells him

politely that Mr Chepstow is ready to see him and leads the way to a mahogany-panelled door bearing its occupiers' brass nameplate. The man rises from behind a squat walnut pedestal desk in the corner, framed by a curtain-less sash window. 'Lucian Chepstow.' He thrusts a Rolex-wristed hand from the cuff of a blue pin-striped suit.

'Gideon Chase. Pleased to meet you.' He silently curses his automatic politeness.

'I'm very sorry about your father. Please take a seat.'

Gideon occupies one of two leather library chairs positioned on the near side of the grand desk, while the lawyer, a man in his early forties with grey-white hair, returns to his seat, smoothes down his jacket and sits.

'Have you been offered tea? Or water?'

'I'm fine, thanks.'

Chepstow places his hand on the desk phone. 'Are you sure?'

Gideon's irritated to be asked twice. He puts his uncharacteristic edginess down to unfamiliarity, the unpleasant circumstances. 'Thanks, but really I'm fine.'

The door opens. A worn old man lumbers in – shoulders slightly rounded. Unmistakably Lucian's father, the practice's founder. 'Cedric Chepstow,' he mumbles, almost as though answering a question. Without offering his hand, he takes the chair beside Gideon. 'I hope you don't mind my coming in. I want to offer my condolences. I knew your father very well. Splendid fellow. I've been his solicitor for twenty years.'

Gideon considers pointing out that Nathaniel never qualified for the title 'splendid' but lets it slide. 'No, not at all. Thank you.' He adds, almost surprising himself, '*How* well did you know him? What *exactly* did you do for him?'

The Chepstows exchange glances. The question has clearly thrown them, and that interests Gideon.

'More professional than personal,' concedes the old man. 'We handled all the legal paperwork connected with his businesses – deal memos, contracts, agreements, some import and export documentation, those kind of things. He was one of our major clients.'

'I'm sure he was.' It comes out with a little more acid than Gideon intended.

Lucian feels obliged to chip in. 'Your father was very driven. Very successful, Mr Chase. He was a pleasure to work with.'

Gideon stays focused on Chepstow senior. 'And personally?'

He purses his dry old lips. 'I'd like to think we were friends. We shared the same love of history, same respect of generations gone.'

Lucian withdraws an envelope from a drawer in the desk, keen to get on with the business side of the meeting. Gideon isn't. 'My father left me a letter.'

The old lawyer flinches.

'A suicide note. Do you know of anything that would make him take his own life?'

Cedric's eyes widen.

84

Gideon looks from one to the other. 'Can either of you tell me what he might have done, what he was ashamed of that made him feel so desperate and so depressed?'

Chepstow senior plays with a fold of wrinkled flab beneath his double chin. 'No, I don't think we can. There isn't anything. Certainly not legally. Nor could we share such information, even if we knew, because of client confidentiality.'

Now Gideon can't hide his annoyance. 'He's dead. So I presume such confidentiality doesn't apply.'

The old man shakes his head like a professor about to point out an elementary mistake. 'That's not how we work. We respect our bonds to our clients – for ever.' He looks Gideon up and down. 'Mr Chase, let me assure you, to the very best of my knowledge – personally and professionally – there is nothing your father should be ashamed of. No skeletons in his closet.'

'Skeletons?' Gideon laughs. 'My father was a grave-robber. He stripped tombs in Syria, Libya, Mexico and god knows where else. He sold historic and irreplaceable objects to foreign governments or private collectors who had no right to them. I'm sure he had a whole necropolis of skeletons to hide.'

Years of experience have taught Cedric Chepstow to know when arguments are winnable and when they are not. 'Lucian, please inform Mr Chase of his father's will and ensure he has a copy.' He creaks his way out of the chair. 'Good day to you, sir.'

Lucian Chepstow doesn't speak until his father has left and shut the door behind him. 'They were close,' he says. 'Your father was one of the few mine spent time with.'

Gideon's still annoyed. 'Seem like a good pair.'

The timid lawyer doesn't respond. He passes a sealed letter over the desk and pulls another copy across his red, leather-edged blotter. 'This is the Last Will and Testament of Nathaniel Chase. It's witnessed and fully in accordance with English law. Would you like me to talk you through it?'

Gideon takes the envelope in both hands. His mind still on Cedric Chepstow. The old man probably knew what his father was hiding. Why else react like that? Why the resort to 'confidentiality', covering himself with the pathetic 'to the best of my knowledge'?

'Mr Chase. Would you like me to talk you through the will?'

He looks up and nods.

'I should warn you that one of his requests is unusual. Your father made pre-death arrangements at the West Wiltshire Crematorium.'

Gideon frowns. 'That's unusual?'

'Not in itself. Many people prepay and prearrange their own funeral requirements. But after cremation at West Wiltshire he wished his ashes to be scattered at Stonehenge.'

27

Jake Timberland saw himself stepping out of the shower this morning and almost died. He dragged the scales from beneath the sink and stepped up to be judged. Fourteen stone. Holy fuck. He stepped off and back on again. It wasn't a malfunction. At five foot eleven he could carry thirteen but at fourteen, before you know it you look like a fat man's body double.

His misery morphed into determination. Fifty sit-ups later he could see his six-pack rising through the flab again and felt better.

Now he's sitting in a winged chair in his club downing the third cappuccino of a breakfast meeting. He's listening to his guest, Maxwell Dalton, talk about cash-flow problems, the downturn in the economy, a slide in ad revenue and how he needs investment or he could go out of business. Dalton is chubby with big glasses as black as his hair and baggy suit. He runs a website that showcases short films made by the kind of people who can't get proper jobs in TV.

'How much do you want and how much do I get in return?'

Dalton laughs nervously. 'A hundred thousand for 10 per cent?'

Jake's expression makes it clear that's not going to work. 'Twenty per cent?'

He says nothing. His attention is focused on the fried egg on Dalton's plate.

'Twenty-five?' Dalton pleads, then adds, 'At a push I could go to thirty.'

Jake quite likes the idea of saying he's in media. No doubt it would increase his pulling power. At a stretch, he could even describe himself as a film producer cum distributor. 'Maybe we can do a deal. But not at a hundred k and not for thirty per cent.'

Dalton looks disappointed.

A hundred thousand is nothing to Jake. He could even get his old man to stand the whole stash. If not, he could raise it if he cut down on the Cristal, skipped the winter skiing and tanked the overdraft. 'Listen, Max. I'll put fifty thousand into your company but for that I want fifty-one per cent of it.'

'Controlling interest?'

'Exactly.'

Finally, a glum Dalton spits out a reply, 'I'm sorry. Forty-nine is really all I'm prepared to go to in terms of equity and for that I'd want seventy-five thousand.'

Jake smiles. 'I want to help you not fuck you. But that slice is not worth seventy-five. I'll go to fifty k for forty-nine per cent. Final offer.'

Dalton is in a bad place. With the landlord banging on the door for the rent. 'All right.'

As Jake stands to shake on the deal, his iPhone buzzes. 'Excuse me.' It's Caitlyn – he instantly recognises her number. He opens the text and when he unzips the picture attachment his eyes nearly pop. Beneath the Union Jack tattoo is: *I have the flag. Do you have a pole big enough for it?* ☺ *Call me x.*

Jake smiles across the table at Dalton and offers a hand. Could be that he gets to screw two people in one day.

28

Sammy is well enough to go to nursery but Megan's mum Gloria insists on coming round to look after her grand-daughter. For once the DI gets away without a lecture. She's grateful. After the short drive to Devizes police station, she is at her desk sipping a cup of black tea in the open-plan CID room, reading the full statements of PCs Featherby and Jones.

Gideon Chase is lucky. Very lucky. If the two plods had been more than a village away when the 999 came in, they probably would have arrived too late. Featherby found him unconscious in the hall and managed to drag him outside, before calling the paramedics and fire brigade.

She studies the crime scene photographs, shots of flame-blackened brick walls and burned-out windows. The fire team's report seems consistent with Chase's account. No doubt the seat of the blaze was the curtain area of the down-stairs study on the west side of the house. No doubt at all. That room and most of the corridor and the adjoining reception area have been gutted. It'll cost a pretty penny to sort out.

The incident report in her hands says Chase slipped in and out of consciousness until the medics got him into the ambulance and cleared his lungs with pure oxygen. Seems to shoot down her theory that he might have been involved in his father's death and got an accomplice to fake the attack. Unless of course the accomplice got greedy. In that case, an attempt to kill him would make sense.

But it doesn't. None of it makes sense.

She puts down the papers and wonders again why Gideon lied to her. He seems decent enough. Intelligent, well turned-out, polite, maybe a bit quirky. But then academics are.

So why lie?

Does he know the man he surprised? Unlikely. Her info says Chase spent most of his childhood at boarding school and his father only moved to Tollard Royal in recent years. Until then they'd lived in more modest accommodation either in the east of Wiltshire or over in Cambridge where Nathaniel was a don.

So why? There are only a few other possibilities. Maybe he's afraid. Many victims of crime are frightened to identify attackers in case they come back. Or someone else comes back. Fear of being victimised. Makes some sense.

Chase certainly isn't fearless. Then again, he doesn't strike her as being particularly afraid either. Not what her mum used to call cowardly custard. There's another possibility.

Maybe he knew the old man was involved in something and it was connected to the intruder at the house. Perhaps Gideon arranged to meet him there, they'd argued, the man threatened or assaulted him, Chase called the police.

It doesn't fit. She glances down at the report again. There's no doubt that he was unconscious and left for dead. The man who made the emergency call was calm and composed – not groggy from an assault and with a chest full of smoke.

But she feels close to the truth. Nathaniel Chase was up to something bad. She's sure of it.

'Baker!'

Megan looks up from her desk and her heart sinks. DCI Jude Tompkins is heading her way. These days the forty-year-old blonde is certifiably insane. Jumpier than a box of frogs. Her upcoming marriage – her second – is the cause of the manic personality shift.

'Are you done with that suicide yet, Baker?' She settles her crash-dieting-behind on the edge of Megan's desk.

'No ma'am.' Megan fans out the PC statements. 'I'm just going through the reports. There was a fire at the dead man's house.'

'I heard. What are we talking, burglars? Squatters?'

The DI explains. 'The son went back there after we asked him in to talk to us. He found an intruder in the study about ready to torch the place.'

'What was he, some kind of a junkie?'

'We don't know. He knocked our man unconscious and

left him for dead. If a local patrol hadn't been around the corner, the Chase family line would have come to a complete end in just forty-eight hours.'

Tompkins takes it in. Unsolved burglary, arson and attempted murder are not what she wants on her crime sheets. The whole division is under pressure to improve the figures. 'I get that it's more complicated than I thought. Can you juggle another case as well as this one?'

It's not really a question. The DCI drops the file on Megan's desk. 'Sorry. It's a missing person. Give it a look over for me.'

She watches the DCI turn and leave. Delegation is a wonderful thing. You just shift your garbage to someone else's bin and leave them to jump on the lid until they get it to fit. 'Boss, any chance of an extra pair of hands?' she calls.

Tompkins stops and turns. A smile on her big round face.

Megan knows it's hard to turn down a plea for help in an open office. She gives the DCI a desperate look. 'Just for a day or two?'

Tompkins beams. 'Jimmy Dockery. You can have Sergeant Dockery for forty-eight hours, then he's back on vice.'

Megan shuts her eyes. Jimmy Dockery? She puts her hands over her ears, but it makes no difference. She can still hear the whole office laughing.

29

The Henge Master has been expecting the call.

It was simply a matter of when. He excuses himself and steps away from the highly distinguished company. He has two phones in his pocket. A BlackBerry that he uses publicly and a cheap Nokia that is a 'burner', a no-contract, non-traceable phone with credit he can purchase almost anywhere. He takes out the Nokia. It's Cetus.

'Can you speak?'

'Wait a moment.' The Master walks into an open court-yard. 'Go on.'

'The Chase boy has just come in for his father's will.'

The Master searches a jacket pocket for his cigarettes. 'And?'

'He was asking what Nathaniel might have been ashamed of.'

'He used that word, did he? Or is it your interpretation of what he said?'

'He used it. He told Lupus that he'd been left some kind of letter. Apparently, the police recovered it from the scene.'

The Master lights a Dunhill with a gold monogrammed lighter. 'What's in it? Some form of accusations or confession?'

Cetus tries to allay his fears. 'Nothing so drastic. If there had been anything explicit in there, no doubt the gentlemen of the constabulary would be camped in my office asking awkward questions.'

The Master blows out smoke and looks across the courtyard. 'But they have been in touch. You said so and Grus says some DI thinks she's got herself something of a case.'

'That's true but it's routine. They found invoices in Nathaniel's study and wanted to know if we still acted for him. And don't worry about the DI.'

'I shan't.' The Master paces a little. 'From what Nathaniel told me, they had a fractured relationship. Unfortunately, his son is unlikely to be our friend.'

'That would fit with his behaviour at my office.'

The Master thinks for a few moments. 'A shame. Given his father's contribution to the Craft, he'd have been an asset. Did the police ask about the will?'

'Of course.'

'And presumably he gets everything?'

'Everything.'

'You must have done well out of this fee-wise.'

Cetus is offended. 'I treated Nathaniel well. He was a friend, remember.'

The Master berates himself. A crass remark. 'Forgive me, I shouldn't have made light of the situation.' He looks to a junior colleague at the edge of the courtyard pointing to his watch. 'I'm going to have to go.'

'Are you thinking of postponing?'

'We can't.' The Master takes a final draw on the cigarette

before dropping it and grinding it into the gravel. 'The divination is clear. The completion must be at midpoint between evening twilight on *solstitium* and morning twilight of the day after, or it has no meaning.'

Cetus is quiet and the Master senses something. 'We will be ready with the second offering, won't we?'

'We will. All will go as planned. But what of Chase the Younger?'

The Master nods at the colleague hovering not far away. He silently mouths that he'll only be another minute. After the man is gone, he concludes the call: 'I will have the son taken care of. Just make sure the other arrangements go as planned.'

30

Caitlyn's instructions were clear. Rent a room. Chill a bottle of champagne. Put two tubs of Ben & Jerry's in the mini-bar – any flavour except Cake Batter. Run a bath – three quarters full. No smelly stuff – just water, hot water. Bring protection. Non-flavoured and ribbed. At least five. Make sure there's plenty of dope and ecstasy.

Caitlyn is plainly used to getting whatever she wants. Fine by him. At least there's no mistaking what this get-together is going to be about. No need for small talk, no painful progressing from kiss to fumble to hopefully much more. He has cancelled everything he had planned for the rest of the day. Which wasn't that much.

He has little problem getting the stuff. He already has a block of Lebanese Black and a few days' worth of Es and he picks up the ice cream and a couple of bottles of Louis Roederer Cristal in the Food Hall at Selfridge's. Then he drives over to Hyde Park and books a suite at Été, a discreet boutique hotel noted for its French cuisine. Even he considers arguing over the thousand-pound room tariff – then he remembers that he's now in the media and is about to bed a celebutante.

The suite turns out to be almost worth it: a king-size bed draped in a golden quilt, heavy matching window curtains lined in burnt orange and tied back to reveal a small terrace and some white metal seating. He draws the curtains and lights the Egyptian-style pot lamps either side of the bed.

He plugs his iPod into a docking station. What to put on? The sudden question scares him. You can tell a lot about a person from their choice of music. He wheels through some of his later downloads and settles on Plan B's *The Defamation of Strickland Banks*. 'Love Goes Down' is coming to an end when there's a rap on the door.

It's smack on two p.m. He was sure she was going to be late. He was wrong. He opens the door. She's carrying a light-cream coat over her arm and wearing a near-translucent gathered-sleeve tea dress. 'Don't just stare, let me in!'

He steps aside. 'Sorry, you just look so . . .' He realises she's worried about being seen and shuts the door quickly. '. . . beautiful.' As he turns she's right next to him. She drops the coat and a small matching handbag and kisses him. It's like being gently electrified. Flows all the way through him. This is already about more than the great sex he knows is going to follow.

Caitlyn breaks for air and smiles. 'I have an hour. That's all. Sixty minutes. Let's get started.'

31

DEVIZES

Detective Sergeant Jimmy Dockery is Wiltshire's Horatio Caine. Or so he thinks. He speaks slower than a dying man with asthma and even on the dullest days wears sunglasses. The kind that went out of fashion with *Top Gun*.

Bullied as a kid, the ginger whinger got his own back by becoming a cop. The only problem is, unlike the *CSI: Miami* lieutenant, he's not a hot shot. He's not even a luke-warm shot. But he is the Deputy Chief Constable's son and everything pales into a ginger fuzz after that single fact.

'I heard you need help, Detective Inspector.' He hovers over her shoulder, then slides into a seat alongside and flashes his best smile. 'Glad to be of service.'

Megan feels a shiver of revulsion. 'Thanks, Jimmy.' She

pulls over some stapled statements and a thick file. 'This is background on the Chase suicide. You know about that, don't you?'

He looks blank.

She resists screaming. 'Professor Nathaniel Chase, international author, archaeologist, antiquities trader, has a place out on Cranborne Chase, at Tollard Royal where the rich folk live.'

'Oh, yeah, I know who you mean.'

She knows he doesn't but ploughs on. 'Google him, and there's background on him in here, as well as the suicide.' She opens the file and points out a list of contact numbers. 'This is the mobile number of Gideon Chase, Nathaniel's son. He has asked to see the body. Would you mind making sure he's dealt with sympathetically?' She wonders if Jimmy's repertoire stretches that far.

'Consider it done.' He smiles broadly and widens his eyes. It's a little trick he's picked up. A dead certain way of letting her know that's he is more than just willing to do his duty at work.

She can't believe he's hitting on her. 'What are you waiting for, Jimmy?' She tilts her head. Much as she might study a strange insect that's appeared from beneath a rock. 'Apparently, I only have the pleasure of your company for two days, so now is a really good time to get started.'

He takes the hint, walks away with a backhanded wave. 'Later, boss.'

Megan unclenches her fists. She has to learn to relax. Not

suffering fools is one thing, wanting to crack them in the nose is another. She makes black tea in the small kitchen area off the main office and comes back to her desk just in time to catch the phone ringing. She spills some of the hot drink on the paperwork in the rush to grab it. 'DI Baker. Damn.'

There's a hesitation on the line before the caller answers. 'This is PC Rob Featherby from Shaftesbury. My sergeant said I should call.'

'Sorry, Rob, I just spilled something. Give me a sec.' She shifts the paperwork away from the spreading dark puddle and blots it with tissues from her bag. 'Back with you. Apologies again, what were you saying?'

'Myself and PC Jones turned out to that burglary over in Tollard. I had the control room call you – they did, didn't they?'

'They did. Many thanks. How's your colleague?'

'He's fine. Lost his voice for a bit. Which was no bad thing.'

She laughs. Like most coppers, black humour is what keeps her sane. 'I just read your report. Very thorough. If we ever get this on *Crimewatch*, they should book you.'

He's flattered. 'Thanks. I try to remember as much as possible.'

'How can I help?'

'Are you still interested in the case? The break-in I mean, I know you're investigating the suicide.'

'What have you got?'

'Well, the scenes of crimes mob lifted some good sets of

footprints from the lawn and soil beds this morning and they match prints inside the house.'

'Excellent.' Her optimism gets the better of her. 'Have you got a suspect?'

He laughs. 'We wish. It gets better though. The offender left behind a canvas bag, a sort of break-in kit. It's filled with tools.'

'Rob, I'm about forty miles from the Chase estate. Do you think you could meet me over there in, say, two hours' time? I'd really like you to walk me through where things were found, what you think happened.'

'I'll have to check with my sergeant but I don't see why not. If there's a problem, I'll call you back. Okay?'

'Fine. Thanks.' She hangs up. She's glad of the chance to see Gideon Chase again – the opportunity to find out why he's lying.

32

HYDE PARK, LONDON

The hour is up. Caitlyn is dressed and at the door ready to leave.

She got everything she wanted. The guy is cute. Obedient. A pretty good lay. Granted, he could learn to be a bit more patient but that's a lesson all men could do with attending a few boot camps on.

Jake hasn't bothered getting dressed. He's slung on a white towelling robe. He'll step in the shower when she's gone. Or maybe he'll keep the smell of her on him all day. He approaches her, his eyes still hungry. 'Do I get a kiss goodbye?' He pops an ecstasy tablet on to the tip of his tongue.

She steps forward and smooches it off him, a reward for his attentiveness. She swallows and steps back a pace. 'If only they made Es that tasted like Ben & Jerry's.'

'Everyone would be high all the time.'

'*Exactly*.'

'So you liked the Cherry—'

She interrupts. 'What wasn't there to like. You did well.'

He smiles. 'And when might I get the chance to do well again?'

'Don't get clingy. I can't do clingy.'

He looks taken aback.

'Same time, same place, next week. You book. Get everything the same again, only I'll pay. Okay?'

Now he feels cheap. 'That's not necessary. What about a more regular date? A movie, a club, dinner. You do that kind of shit, don't you?'

She breaks up laughing. 'Man, you've no idea the hell my father would put you through before you even got to buy me coffee.'

He goes silent on her.

She buttons her coat. 'Look, I have to go. Same time next week?'

He nods.

'For what it's worth, I like you. Let's see how next week goes. Then we can talk about whether we risk the wrath of Daddy for the sake of dinner or a cup of coffee.'

He has nice crinkly lines in the corner of his eyes and a really friendly smile. She gives in to a moment of softness and puts her hands around the back of his neck, kisses him in a way she hasn't kissed another man. Relaxed. Non-urgent, non-demanding. Intimate.

It shocks her. 'I have to go.'

Jake barely has time to open his eyes before she's clicked open the door and is down the corridor. 'Hey!'

She turns her head.

'I'm going to surprise you.' He makes a pretend phone out of his thumb and little finger and holds it to his right ear. 'Listen for your mobile. Be ready for my message.'

33

Megan draws her Ford alongside the patrol car parked outside the gates of the Chase estate and winds down the passenger window. 'I guess you're Rob Featherby?'

A good looking dark-haired man in his early twenties smiles across at her. 'I am. I just arrived myself. Shall we drive on up?'

She gestures towards the house. 'Lead the way.'

The PC gives her a playful look, starts the engine and heads off.

They park behind an Audi in the drive and step out into warm sunshine. Featherby brings a thick envelope with him packed with photographs of evidence recovered from the scene.

Megan presses the buzzer and raps the heavy door-knocker for good measure. After close to a minute, she looks towards the A4. 'He must be in, that's his vehicle.'

The PC gives the bell another long ring. As he takes his finger off the button, the door opens. Gideon Chase holds it and peers through a foot-wide gap. He looks pale, shaken.

'Sorry to have to trouble you,' Megan says. 'We need to ask a few more questions.'

Gideon can't face it. 'It's not convenient.' He starts to shut the door.

She puts her foot against it. 'This is PC Featherby. You have met, though you don't remember it. He dragged you out of the fire the other night.'

The revelation pulls Gideon up short. He marshals his manners and extends a hand. 'Thank you. I'm most grateful.' He glances at her and reluctantly opens the door wide. 'Best go right through to the back. The kitchen's the only place I've got to know so far.'

They head in as he closes the door. His head is screaming from decoding several diaries and he really doesn't want them here.

'Big kitchen!' Megan shouts, trying to alter the mood.

She runs a hand over an old Aga. The only thing missing is femininity. There are no curtains, vases, casserole pots or stacks of spices. It's been reduced to the worst thing she can think of – functional masculinity.

Gideon joins them. 'I'm a little embarrassed.' He looks towards Featherby. 'You should at least be able to offer the man who saved your life a cup of tea or coffee but I'm afraid there's no milk. I can do black, if that's any good?'

'I'm okay, thanks,' says the PC.

'I'm fine as well,' Megan adds.

Gideon folds his arms defensively. He leans against the cupboards and tries to look bright. 'So how can I help you?'

She notices his red eyes and presumes stress is starting to take its toll. 'Forensics from Rob's station found quite a bit of evidence in relation to the break-in. I've asked him to walk me through it, so I can best assemble a profile of the offender. Is it okay with you if we do that?'

He looks helpless. 'Of course. What do you want me to do?'

'Nothing.' She tries to be gentle. 'We just need access to the study, that side of the house and the gardens. Do we have your permission to do that?'

He'd rather they didn't but doesn't feel like he can object. 'Sure. I'm just sorting some of my father's things upstairs; please shout if you need me.'

She nods. 'Thanks. We will.'

He wanders off, feeling like he's being banished.

Featherby leads the way to the burned-out study. Megan

104

looks at the blackened walls, ceiling and floor. 'What a mess.' The place stinks of the fire. 'You say the source of the blaze was around the curtains and desk?'

He circles a hand around a coal-black spot on the floor. 'Right about here. That's what the chief fire investigator said.'

She makes mental notes. The offender did this in the study, not the lounge. It was premeditated. He was searching for something and either found it and burned it, or ran out of time. If the latter, he wanted to make sure no one else discovered what he couldn't. 'Any accelerant used? Any petrol or oil from the kitchen?'

Featherby shakes his head. 'Not that I was told of.'

She steps into the corridor and shouts up the stairs. 'Gideon! Do you have a minute?'

The archaeologist hangs his head over the banister.

'Was your father a smoker?'

He thinks for a second. 'No. I don't think so. From what I can remember he was strongly against.' He gives a resigned look. 'It's possible he started in the last few years, after I lost touch, but I think that's unlikely. Anything else?'

She smiles up at him. 'No, not for now.'

He disappears and she returns to the study. The constable looks at her for an explanation. She takes time out to educate him. 'The offender is a smoker. He used his own lighter, a disposable BIC. The son said he saw one in the intruder's hand before he accosted him in here. This person's not an arsonist, has never committed arson before. Had he been, he'd have used an accelerant. He's also unlikely to have a criminal record but given the way he disabled your partner, he may well be ex-services.'

Featherby is fascinated. 'How can you be sure?'

'I can't. That's why I said not likely. Use your common sense though. This is what in profiling is called a mixed scene – some of the job was highly professional and some total bungle. You go breaking the law and you need an element of luck to keep things as you planned, otherwise you're off script and then anything goes. This offender didn't get any good luck. The householder came back while he was torching the place, caught him unawares, called the cops and almost trapped him in a burning room. At that point the guy acted off script and was thinking only about survival and escape, hence why he disabled but didn't kill PC Jones and forgot the tool bag.'

Featherby's seen enough burglaries and car break-ins to know she's making sense.

Megan's not finished. 'Arson wasn't the original intention. It was an afterthought. He was looking for something, something that presumably he didn't find.'

'So why set the fire?'

She thinks. 'So no one else could find it. Meaning whatever it is, threatens him or whoever he's working with.'

Featherby nods towards the hall and staircase. 'Did he give you a description?'

She screws up her face. 'Don't even go there. He couldn't remember a thing about the way the man looked.'

'Pity.'

'Forget it for now. Concentrate on the offender. As well as not having a criminal record, he's not too bright. But he is bold. It takes balls to break into a house, especially one where someone's just died. So let's presume our individual is confident, strong and relatively mature. I guess he's thirty to forty-five years old, works doing some kind of physical labour. Given that only about six per cent of Wiltshire is ethnically diverse, we can assume he's white.'

The PC puts it together. 'White male, manual worker, thirty to forty-five, smoker, no criminal record. That's amazing, given that you're just looking at a burned-out room.'

She almost starts explaining that the room is the last thing she's looking at. What she's really studying is the invisible clues that all offenders leave about their behaviour.

'What do you think is the guy's connection to the deceased?'

She takes a beat. 'Smart question. And if we crack it, we solve all the mysteries of this case.'

'But there *is* a connection, right?'

'At least one. Probably several.'

He looks confused.

Megan explains. 'The intruder may have professional links to the deceased. He might be a gardener, window cleaner, car mechanic. He probably knew the professor because he regularly did jobs for him or delivered to his house. That would also make him more confident about coming up here and breaking in. But I think he may also have known Nathaniel Chase because he was mixed up in whatever the old man was.'

'I don't get it.'

She expands. 'Chase had a lot of money. Too much for a man like him. He was dirty, I'm sure of it. The only question is, what kind of dirt?'

Sitting at the top of the stairs, Gideon feels like someone's stabbed a pin in his heart. But deep down he knows she's right. His father was involved in something bad. Bad enough to keep secret.

34

Just before midnight they come for him.

They move quickly and don't speak. There's no going back now. Lee Johns will soon be known only as Lacerta. But the change of name is going to be painful. He's been blindfolded and driven for miles in preparation. He's about to be initiated.

He has earned the right to know of the Sanctuary's existence but it will be some time before he is entrusted with its location. The strong hands of unseen men lead him through the Descending Passage and into an antechamber. Still blindfolded, he is stripped and washed, led naked to the Great Room. It is vast. Cavernous. More than a hundred square metres. So high, the ceiling is invisible, a black shroud somewhere up above.

The smell of hundreds of burning candles fills the cool air. Fear and nakedness heighten his senses. The stone slabs beneath his feet feel as hard and cold as ice.

The Henge Master raises a hammer, a symbol of the craft of the ancients who created the resting place of the Sacreds and the Sanctuary. He looks across the congregation and lets it fall. A gigantic marble block is pushed across the single entrance and seals the chamber.

'Let the eyes of the child be opened.'

The blindfold is removed. The initiation has begun.

Lee's heart pounds. He is in an entirely circular room. Through blinking eyes he sees in front of him a life-size replica of Stonehenge. It is complete. As perfect as it was on the day it was finished. At the centre is a cloaked and hooded figure, his face covered in shade and unrecognisable.

The Henge Master speaks: 'Behold the embodiment of the Sacreds. The divinities rested here centuries ago, when our forefathers, the founding Followers, built this cosmic circle and this Sanctuary. In here, you are in their presence. Out of respect, once initiated, you will ensure your head is always covered and your eyes always lowered. Do you understand?'

He knows how to respond. 'Yes, Master.'

'You are brought before us because you are deemed fit by members of our Craft to become a lifelong Follower. Is that your will?'

'Yes, Master.'

'And are you ready to pledge your life, your soul and your loyalty to the Sacreds and to those who protect them?'

'Yes, Master.'

'The Sacreds renew us only as long as we renew them. We honour them with our flesh and blood and in return they protect and renew our flesh and blood. Do you pledge your flesh and blood to their immortal holiness?'

'Yes, Master.'

From behind him, incense begins to burn inside handheld copper thuribles swung on heavy chains. The air fills with the smells of sweet spices, onycha and galbanum. The Henge Master spreads his arms wide. 'Bring he who wishes to Follow to the Slaughter Stone.'

Lee Johns is led through the circle to the stone. He feels an urge to look at those around him. Sean warned that he must not do this, must not look into the face of any of those inside the Great Room, especially that of the Master.

A voice in his ear tells him to kneel. The floor is bone hard. Hands force him flat. Four Followers fasten his ankles and wrists, spread-eagling him across the mottled Slaughter Stone. The Henge Master moves close, followed by five incense swingers, all members of the Inner Circle. 'Do you believe in the power of the Sacreds and all who follow them?'

'Yes, Master.'

'Do you trust unquestionably and unhesitatingly in their power to protect, to sustain and to heal?'

'Yes, Master.'

'Do you dedicate your life to their service?'

'Yes, Master.'

'And do you swear upon your life and the lives of all members of your family and those you hold dear never to speak of the Craft outside of your brotherhood unless given permission to do so?'

'Yes, Master.'

The incense burners swing their thuribles in a series of circles over his tethered limbs and torso, then step away. The Henge Master holds a long dark blade fashioned from razor-sharp stone cut from the first trilithon of the henge. 'I draw this human blood, flesh and bone in the hope that you will accept him as one of your servants and will afford him your protection and blessings. Sacred Gods, I humbly beg you to find a space in your affections for our brother.' He moves to the Slaughter Stone and slashes cuts from wrist to shoulder, from ankle to top of the leg, and from neck to the base of the spine.

Lee tenses. The wave of shock hits him. He fights not to scream. A blast of adrenalin overwhelms the pain. He feels a hot scratch that becomes a burn, then an ache as the mutilation progresses across his body.

The bleeding lines of flesh create a star shape beneath the eyes of those looking on. They've endured the same ritual, the same naked humiliation. They know the pain that he is about to endure.

The Henge Master kneels. From beneath his cloak he recovers the ceremonial hammer. He puts the stone blade to the initiate's skull.

'With the blood we shed for you, we add the flesh and bone that proves our loyalty and devotion.'

The Henge Master swings the heavy hammer and sees it connect with the knife's butt. The blade slices free a piece of scalp and skull.

Now he screams.

Darkness grabs him and holds him tight.

By the time Lee Johns recovers consciousness, the Great Room is empty. He lies where he was, still tied, face down. The marble block has once more sealed the chamber. He knows his fate.

35

FRIDAY 18 JUNE

It's a cloudless morning, the start of what weathermen predict will be the warmest day of the year so far. Megan smothers Sammy in factor-thirty, puts the tube in her lunch bag, drives her to nursery.

She's keen to get to work and draw up an offender profile of the burglar at Tollard Royal. The trip there yesterday provided a rich source of psychological clues – most based on the physical evidence Rob Featherby and the Shaftesbury crime team had gathered from the scene.

The first thing she does when she reaches her desk is review the evidence list: (1) Bag of tools discovered near back wall of garden. (2) Blood found on broken glass of greenhouse. (3) Small piece of cloth found on wild rose bushes. (4) Disposable cigarette lighter recovered from ground near molehills. (5) Footprints taken from soil beds, lawn and house.

Megan takes it in reverse order. The footprints are a size-ten trainer, brand to be determined. That's a full size larger than the average UK male, giving an indication – though no *guarantee* – that the owner is above the average male height of five feet nine inches. She guesses he's around five-eleven. There's also the indentation in the soil beds. In several places he'd been on the flat of his feet, as well as on his heels. These were deep impressions, signs of slipping or being off balance. Likely he was having difficulty because of how dark it was. Or maybe he was carrying a little too much weight to make a perfectly agile burglar. At five-eleven the average male weighs about thirteen stone. She hedges her bets and puts the intruder at around thirteen and a half. That kind of weight and height mean he'll probably have a forty-two-inch chest and thirty-six or thirty-seven-inch waist. The size is impor-tant because he may well have thrown away the clothes or even given them to a charity shop as many offenders do.

Megan considers the disposable lighter. Highly likely it's the one the man had. She has got to trust Gideon Chase's vision on this point at least. No mileage in not doing so. It's a multi-coloured Christmas edition BIC. Given it's now June, it might indicate that the guy is only an occasional smoker. Or it could be that he bought it in a multipack, these things often come in threes. That would make him more regular. She hopes his fingerprints are on it. Even if he used gloves in the house, the wheel and other parts of it could produce latents.

Third on the list is a small piece of fabric recovered from the rose climber. It's 100 per cent black cotton but according to PC Featherby, forensics got excited because the colour is so strong. They believe it's new or at worst has been washed only a couple of times. Megan's more cautious. It could have been bought months ago and left in a drawer. Still, there was a good chance of tracing the owner if it had been bought new.

The blood on the greenhouse is being analysed, but already she knows from the lab that it's Rh (D) O+, the same as almost forty per cent of the country. Tox tests may provide clues to drug addiction or undue alcohol consumption.

She takes a hungry chew of an energy bar and wonders what it's supposed to taste of. She guesses chalk and soot. Amazingly the label purports it to be Chocolatey Bliss. She wolfs it and moves on to consider the most impressive of the physical finds. The bag of tools.

Megan has seen several burglary kits in her time. Usually they contain glass breakers, tape and lightweight blankets to help get through windows without too much noise or injury. Often there are extra sacks in which to stow stolen goods and spare surgical gloves to prevent fingerprints. Heavier mobs bring along bolt-cutters, lump hammers and steel chisels to get through safes. Some carry blow torches and even plastic explosives.

Not this guy. He brought a crowbar, screwdrivers, a lump

hammer, some kind of metal spike with a handle on it, duct tape and a lethal-looking axe. It confirms her suspicions that he's not a professional. It also tells her that he probably didn't have long to plan for the job, he just grabbed what he had in his tool shed or garage.

She wonders what the urgency was. Why move so quickly, so recklessly? Because someone had told him to? Forced him to? The absence of other bags indicates that he didn't go with the intention of stealing multiple items. He was after one or maybe two specific things.

She looks again at the photographs Rob Featherby gave her. The axe is the most interesting. It's not for chopping wood, that's for sure. It looks like an expensive piece of kitchen equipment. She can't tell without seeing it for real but it could be a boning cleaver. Maybe the guy works in a kitchen.

She turns her thoughts to how he escaped. Greenhouse racking was found up against a back wall that led to a scrub of public land and then a B-road. The thick overgrown grass had been trampled. Mud in the road showed several sets of tyre tracks. It all means he had good local knowledge. He knew where to park out of sight and was comfortable that the road didn't have a high volume of passing traffic.

Megan nails him down as ex-military, moderately intelligent, not university material. A mixed offender: one who showed signs of organisation and planning but also a serious lack of ability to carry them through. She summarises the profile:

- White male.
- 30–45.
- Manual worker – possibly in catering business, local pub, restaurant.
- Former armed services, probably army, lower rank.
- Lives locally.
- Drives car or van.
- 5 ft 11 inches.
- 13½–14 stone.
- 42-inch chest min.
- 36-inch waist min.
- No previous criminal record.

Megan hesitates before adding another line, a final word: 'Ruthless.'

She's sure the offender isn't a regular burglar or robber, but he didn't hesitate to choke a policeman unconscious and left Gideon Chase to die in a fire.

Whoever he is, he'll kill rather than be caught.

36

TOLLARD ROYAL

The screech of wild geese wakes Gideon.

He's groggy and his whole body aches as he makes his way

to the bathroom. Through a window he watches four of the birds fighting for territory around the garden's small lake. Flapping and flying at each other in full beak-to-beak combat. After an ear-piercing cry, the loser and its mate flutter away low over the surrounding fields.

He investigates the old showerhead over the rust-stained enamel bath. It is coked up with limescale, yet although the pipes cough and wheeze, it runs surprisingly fast. No shampoo, but there is a bar of soap on the sink. He takes it, climbs into the tub and pulls the flimsy plastic curtain around him to catch the erratic spray.

The hot water feels good. It eases some of the tension in his shoulders as he remembers what he'd discovered in the journals he'd read late last night.

Thirteen months after the death of his mother, his father joined the Followers of the Sacreds. At first Gideon thought this was some kind of local historic society. Only it wasn't. It turned out to be something very different. He reasoned his father took some desperate spiritual comfort from the stones, much in the way that many grieving people do from the church. Nathaniel called them 'Sacreds' and came to regard each rock as a touchstone, a source of help. His writings detailed how one stone could give spiritual renewal and banish depression, while another could provide physical strength and resilience. And there were others.

Gideon's amused at the thought of Stonehenge as some kind of magical aromatherapy circle. Who'd have thought that his much-published brilliant father would have believed such a thing? Marie's death must have driven him off the rails. That would explain things.

The hot water suddenly runs cold. He clambers out of the tub and grabs a hard grey towel. He dries and puts his old clothes back on. They smell of smoke from the fire but he can't bring himself to go through his dead father's wardrobes and drawers, not even for underwear.

Downstairs, he finds an opened box of Bran Flakes but no milk. He pours a handful into a cup and dry chews his way through them while looking out the kitchen window. Several pheasants strut by as though they own the place, glancing at him as they go about their business. He finishes the meagre breakfast, grabs a glass of tap water and takes it back upstairs.

Books are strewn all over the place but he's in no mood to tidy. All he wants to do is read. Devour the text until he can make some sense of it all. He picks up last night's final volume and follows the decoded notes he made in pencil above his father's writing:

The ways of the Craft are wonderfully simple. Divinely pure. Our ancestors were right. There is not one single god. There are many. No wonder the leaders and followers of every religion fervently believe that they alone have discovered the Messiah. They have merely discovered *one* Messiah. They have stumbled upon spiritual trace evidence of the Sacreds – of lives the Sacreds have touched – of gifts they have given.

It is a shame that these followers pray so indiscriminately to their particular gods. If only they knew their deity was capable of delivering a single specific blessing alone. Man's desire to monopolise religion has closed his mind to its multifarious benevolence.

Gideon tries to stay open-minded. Evidently, his father believed that the stones were vessels. Houses for the Gods. Was it so mad? Billions of people have believed similar things: that gods live in their places of worship, that they hover mysteriously in golden tabernacles on high altars, or that they can be conjured up by ritualised gestures or mass prayers. He guesses his father's beliefs are no more ridiculous.

He looks down at the book in his hands and the dark ink from his father's pen. The page has physically absorbed the man's inner thoughts. Even decades after they were written, the words convey something that he can't quite grasp – an emotional contact with his father. It's almost like he's touching him.

Gideon wonders if that's what happens when you touch the stones? Do you absorb thoughts and feelings, wisdom, from people who lived long before you – the wisest of the ancients – people so great that they were considered to be gods?

Only now when the notion of the Sacreds doesn't seem so insane, does he return to the words that troubled him.

ΨΝΚΚΦ.

Blood.

ΖΩΧΗΠΤΠΧΥ

Sacrifice.

Only now does he dare read the entry in full:

The Sacreds need renewal. It needs to be constant or else their decay and decline will be accelerated. The evidence is already there. How foolish it is to think that we may draw from them but not replenish them. The divinities are rooted in the blood and bone of our ancestors. They gave themselves for us. And we must give ourselves to them.

There must be sacrifice. There must be blood. Blood for the sake of future generations, for the sake of all, and especially that of my darling son.

Gideon's shocked to see himself mentioned. But not as shocked as when he reads on:

I will willingly give my own blood, my own life. I only hope it is worthy. Worthy enough to change things. To alter the fate that I know awaits my poor, motherless son.

37

'Have you found my missing person, yet?' DCI Jude Tompkins bowls the question down the corridor to Megan Baker, who is skittled while carrying a cup of tea from the pantry area back to her desk.

'No ma'am. Not yet.'

'But you're doing it, right? You've been through the file I gave you and you have some leads?' She gestures grandly in the air. 'And I'm absolutely sure that you've also already contacted his family and got your hands on at least one photograph.'

Megan ignores the sarcasm. 'Ma'am, I'm still working the Nathaniel Chase case.'

'I know. I'm not Alzheimic. I recall with total clarity that you're also working the missing person case I gave you – so work it.' She gives a caustic stare and veers off towards her own office.

Megan curses. She walks to her desk, slops hot tea from the flimsy plastic cup on to her fingers, and curses again. She wipes her hands on a tissue and flips open the MP file her boss dumped on her. She'd been hoping to *sub*-dump it on Jimmy Dockery but he's gone AWOL.

She reads through the summary: the twin sister of some twenty-five-year-old bum called Tony Naylor has reported him missing. Several times by the look of things. Naylor is unemployed, has an alcohol dependency problem and appears to make a bit of cash-in-hand labouring on building sites.

He's a typical drifter, the hand-to-mouth kind. No mum and dad. No fixed abode. Just wanders around drawing benefits and working on the quiet. A ghost in the machine. She reads on. The only regular contact he seems to have is with the sister, Nathalie. He calls her – reverse charge – once a week.

Megan looks for a number, dials it and lets it ring.

'Hello.' The voice is hesitant.

'Miss Naylor?'

'Who is it?'

'This is DI Baker from Wiltshire Police. I'm following up on reports you made about your missing brother.'

'Have you found him?'

'I'm afraid not. That's *not* why I'm calling. Do you have a few minutes to talk?'

The young woman lets out a frustrated sigh. 'I've already gone through everything. I've given all the details to the policemen at my local station. Why don't you talk to them?'

'I'm from CID, Miss Naylor, you spoke to uniformed officers.'

'Oh, I see.' She seems to understand the distinction. 'All right then. What do you want to know?'

'When did you last talk to him?'

'Three weeks ago.'

Megan checks her notes. 'I'm told he usually rings you every week.'

Nathalie corrects her. 'Not usually. *Always*. He never forgets to ring me.'

'Do you know where he was and what he was doing work-wise when he last called you?'

Nathalie hesitates. 'Listen, I don't want to get Tony in trouble. Can I tell you something without it affecting his benefits?'

Megan knows better than to make deals. 'Miss Naylor,

you called us because you were worried. I can't help find your brother unless you're honest with me.'

There's a pause, then Nathalie opens up: 'When I last spoke to him he said he'd been in Swindon. Helping out some Paddies, I think. Digging and cementing and such like. He said it was a job somewhere over near Stonehenge. He fancied going, he said, because he'd never seen the place.'

'And you've heard nothing since?'

'Nothing at all.'

'Any names for these Irish guys?'

'No. He talked about a Mick, but I'm not sure if he meant Mick as in Michael or as in the Micks, you know, the Irish.'

'And you don't have any contact numbers for him?'

'None other than his mobile and that's dead. Sorry.'

Megan moves on. 'The last time you spoke, did you and he argue about anything?'

'*No!*' She sounds almost offended.

'Miss Naylor, if there is any bad blood, recent or previous, between you and your brother, I need to know.'

The sister gives an ironic laugh. 'Tony and me are like chalk and cheese but we never fall out. We've never had a cross word in our lives.'

Megan sees no reason why she should lie. 'Okay. Does he have any other friends, particularly any *lady* friends that you know of?'

'No, no special ones. He's a bit of a lad, given the chance, but . . .' she dries up. 'Put it this way, Tony isn't the kind of guy that a woman wants to spend a lot of time with.'

123

'Why's that?'

She blows out a long breath. 'Where to start? He's not so hot on his hygiene. A shower once a week is more than enough for our Tony. And he's not romantic. Tony probably can't even spell romantic.'

Megan finishes writing. 'If I send a PC round, could you give him some photographs, recent ones of Tony?'

She thinks for a minute. 'Latest I've got is one of them passport ones, you know, the type you have done at the train station.'

'How old is it?'

'About five years. It wasn't even *for* a passport, we was just messing about after a few drinks. I made him have his picture taken with me.'

'Should be fine. You give it to the bobby I send round and I'll start chasing things up and we'll see if we can find him. All right?'

'Yeah. Thanks.'

Megan hangs up and finishes the last of her tea. She has a bad feeling about Tony Naylor. His sister was his only anchor and without a falling out, there's no reason why he'd set himself adrift. Which means he's going to be easy to find.

He's either in jail, or in the morgue.

38

It's a fifteen-minute drive from Tollard Royal to Shaftesbury. But Gideon Chase makes the journey last twice as long. He checks and rechecks the map and goes at a snail's pace in Ashmore and East Melbury.

In Cann Common he glides the old Audi off the road near Ash Tree Lane, bangs shut the door and just walks for five minutes. There's not much to see. Retirement bungalows. A whitewashed cottage. Black smoke billowing from a garden fire. Endless green fields.

Gideon doesn't really care what's around him. He's thinking about what he doesn't want to see. His father. Dead. Laid out in a funeral parlour only minutes away. Some mortician no doubt hoping his reconstruction disguises the fact that a bullet blew the man's brain away.

Gideon suddenly throws up. It splatters the pavement in the quiet cul-de-sac. He retches again and feels bad that he didn't make it to the verge or a drain. If anyone is watching, he knows what they'll think. He's a drunk with a monstrous hangover. Fat chance.

Embarrassingly, he doesn't even have a handkerchief to wipe his mouth. He uses a hand and then rubs it on the grass. Thank you Mother Nature. He turns and sees a sour-faced granny in a doorway glaring at him. There and then he decides on a course of action that will make him late. So be it.

He climbs back into the car with a sense of purpose and

drives quickly through Cann Common. He comes to a roundabout and spots a Tesco.

Inside, he feels like he is in *Supermarket Sweep*, rushing the trolley down the aisles, throwing in milk, bread, beans, pot noodles, orange juice, anything he can think of. Then, most importantly, toothpaste, shampoo, shaving foam, razor and blades. He grabs packs of underwear, socks, deodorant and even a hairbrush.

Straight after checkout, he rushes to the washroom to clean up. It's such a luxury to use his own toothbrush, not one left by some anonymous guest of his father. He remembers something and goes back into the store and picks up cheddar, a packet of biscuits, some chocolate and a selection of fruit – the items from his father's shopping list pinned to the fridge. The ones he never lived to buy.

On the way out Gideon casts a greedy eye at a small café. He's been dreaming of eating a full English breakfast. Maybe later. He asks an old guy walking a Labrador how to get to Bleke Street.

A couple of minutes later he's there – literally at Death's door.

Abrahams and Cunningham is to funeral directors what Chepstow, Chepstow and Hawks is to solicitors. Traditional. Old-fashioned. Grim. For a split second, he's taken in by the illusion that he's wandered into some old aunt's quaint hallway. The brushed-velvet striped wallpaper and thick dark-green carpets guide him into a dowdy reception area.

It's empty. A discreet sign is pinned to the wall: 'Please ring for attention', below it is a polished brass plate with a white marble button. He doesn't ring. Instead, he wanders. Down the corridor he goes. He doesn't really know why. It's a compulsion. He wants to see beyond the dull and easy façade. Understand a bit more before he steps into the black business of burials and cremations.

Behind the first door, the room is filled with caskets. A showroom. Where the gentle persuasion no doubt begins. Oak or cedar instead of cheaper pine or chipboard. Next-door is a staff room. A few chairs, a big table, microwave oven, sink and coffee machine. Life goes on, even around death.

The third room shocks him. First the smell. Embalming fluid. Then the metal. Too much of it. Steel sinks, trolleys, implements. A young man in a white coat looks up from a slab of grey flesh. 'Excuse me, you shouldn't be in here.' He hesitates, walks around the lifeless form laid out on its trolley. 'Are you a relative? Can I help you?' The man comes towards him, trying to block Gideon's view as he advances. 'If you go back to the reception area, I'll call through and have someone help you, Okay?'

Gideon nods. He notices the man has put his hands behind his back, hiding the red mess on his white rubber gloves.

'Sorry,' Gideon says as he exits and heads back to the bell. This time he pushes it. Within a minute, a stout man in his mid-forties with curly hair and brown rectangular glasses appears, straightening his dark suit jacket as he approaches. 'Craig Abrahams. Mr Chase?'

He extends a hand. 'Gideon Chase.'

'I'm very sorry for your loss, Mr Chase. Would you like to see your father straight away or would you like to sit down first and talk about the arrangements?'

'I'd just like to see him please.'

'As you wish. Please follow me.'

He trails the man down a river of old blue Axminster and through a door at the far end into another corridor, less well lit. Abrahams stops outside a room marked 'Chapel of Rest'. He coughs, covering his mouth respectfully. 'Before we go in, there are two things I'd like to mention. We took the liberty of dressing your father in clothes that the police gave to us. If they are not appropriate, we will of course be happy to change them for any that you prefer.'

'Thank you.'

He gives Gideon a serious look. 'Secondly, our cosmetic artist has done considerable work, but I'm afraid you may still be a little shocked when you see him.'

'I understand.'

'Many clients expect their loved ones to be exactly as they remembered them. I'm afraid that simply isn't possible. I just want to prepare you for this eventuality.'

Abrahams smiles sympathetically and opens the door. The smell of fresh flowers hits Gideon. The curtains are drawn and large candles flicker everywhere the eye falls. Nathaniel Chase is laid out in a mahogany coffin with a crêpe interior, the top of the casket hinged open so his head is visible. Gideon approaches the body and he can tell the artist has done a good job. At first glance there is nothing to suggest that his father put a gun to his temple and pulled the trigger.

Slowly he notices things. The skin is too orange. The hair combed in odd directions. His father's head is misshapen near the left ear – the point the bullet would have exited.

Abrahams touches his arm gently. 'Would you like me to leave you alone for a while?'

Gideon doesn't respond. He feels like his emotions are being fast-blended. Regret. Love. Anger. Churned up into a curdled and sickening shake. Fleetingly, he remembers his mother's funeral. The tears. The black clothes. The men with the long, strange car. Standing at the graveside gripping his father's hand so tightly because he felt like he was falling off the edge of the earth. It all comes back to him.

'I've seen enough, thanks.' He smiles at his father, kisses the tip of the fingers and places them on the misshapen head. The brief contact isn't enough. He can't just leave it at that. He leans over the casket and puts his lips to his father's head. Something he can't ever remember doing before now. Walls in his subconscious collapse. Tears flood his eyes. Gideon wraps his arms around the man who made him, and he sobs.

Craig Abrahams slips silently out of the room. Not out of discretion. He has a phone call to make. A very important one.

39

Nine days to go.

The Henge Master is reminded of the fact wherever he looks. It's staring at him right now from the calendar on his grand antique desk at work. On the front page of *The Times* folded neatly for him by one of his assistants. It is everywhere.

In just over a week he must complete the second part of the renewal ritual. He has to prepare the Followers for the nexus. And they are nowhere near ready. If only Chase hadn't ruined everything. Had he held his nerve and done what had been expected of him, all would have been well. But it isn't.

The Master's eyes stray to a gold frame and the gentle face of his wife. Today is their wedding anniversary. Their thirtieth. But it could have been so different, had she not defied the medics and their so-called expert opinions. Their high-tech 'no-mistake' diagnosis: PH. Two letters that twenty years ago meant nothing to either of them. They'd both stared at the consultant in disbelief as he said it. Only the twitch in his eye gave away the fact that it meant anything serious.

It was terminally serious.

PH.

Pulmonary Hypertension.

They'd put down the shortness of breath and dizziness to her being tired. Doing too much. Burning the candle at both ends. No proper job–life balance. A career in law versus raising a young family. It was bound to take its toll.

PH.

'Uncurable.'

He'd almost corrected the consultant, Mr Sanjay. He wasn't disputing what the earnest medic meant, just his poor English. He wanted to point out that it was 'incurable' not 'uncurable'. A man of Sanjay's standing, regardless of his origins, should have known that there was no such word. But suddenly there was. And his sweet, gorgeous wife kept repeating it to herself.

'Uncurable.'

PH.

Then he found the miracle. The Sacreds. Within weeks of embracing the Craft, 'uncurable' didn't exist any more. PH was gone. It vanished as quickly and mysteriously as it had materialised. The hospital ran three months of exhaustive diagnostics before they finally admitted it and almost grudgingly gave her a clean bill of health.

It had baffled them. They had come to hold their cold stethoscopes to her precious breasts, to inspect her blood and peer at charts and notes. They all agreed – there had been no misdiagnosis – and yet the PH had gone. She was cured.

The mobile phone lying on the leather blotter on his desk rings. He looks at it for a moment before answering. 'Yes.'

'It's Draco. The son is at the funeral parlour.'

'Anything unusual happen?'

131

'No. I'm told he became emotional when he saw his father.'

The Henge Master drums his fingers on the desk. 'Maybe time has healed whatever rift there was between them.'

'Maybe.'

'Go easy on him. Be open to all possibilities.'

'I always am.'

'And of the other matter?'

'Yes.'

'The Sacreds will decide.'

Draco is worried. 'Are you sure there is time?'

'The Sacreds are sure. Inform the Lookers.'

40

It's early afternoon when Gideon gets back to the house. He is emotionally drained but he knows it would be unnatural to feel any different. Not after seeing your dead father laid out in a coffin, cosmetics barely disguising his bullet-blasted head. But he won't wallow, it's not his nature. Life knocks you down, you get up and get on with things.

He realises he is repeating advice his father gave to him. For so long he has tried to deny the man. It comes as a shock. The old man had a much bigger impact than he appreciated. Gideon makes himself a cup of black coffee and sits in the lounge looking absent-mindedly out on to the tumbling lawns. He never had his father down as a gardener. Most probably their shape and maintenance has been done by hired help.

He is close to falling asleep when the front doorbell shocks him with its alien jangle. He goes to the door, opens it, the chain still on. A stocky bald man of around forty stands there in jeans and a blue T-shirt.

'Afternoon, I'm Dave Smithsen.' He nods to a big white box van parked by the Audi, his name proudly stencilled in black down the side. 'I own a building company. I heard from someone in town that you'd had a fire. Thought you might need some help.'

Gideon flips the chain. 'I do, but in all honesty, I'm not sure now is the right time. My father very recently died.'

Smithsen sticks a hand through the gap. 'I know, my condolences. I was due to do some work for him.' They shake and the builder pulls a wad of notes from his pocket. 'Mr Chase paid me to repair some old iron guttering around the back and fix a broken tile. You best have it back. I'm very sorry.'

Gideon takes the money. He looks at it, about two hundred pounds, and returns it. 'You keep it. Maybe you can fix the roof when you repair the fire damage?'

'Thanks.' The man pockets the cash and smiles sympathetically. 'Let me get you a card from the van. You can give me a ring when you feel like it. My old man died just over a year ago, I know what it's like. Parents are funny – they drive you mad while they're around, then when they're gone, you feel like your world exploded.'

Gideon starts to think that putting off the work isn't a good idea. Nothing to be gained from delaying. 'I'm sorry, I'm just being daft. If you'd like to take a look at the damage and give me an estimate, I'd be grateful to get the job done.'

Smithsen weighs him up. 'You sure? It's no trouble to come back.'

'No. Go ahead.' He steps outside. 'I'll let you in from the back. Do you want a drink? I've just put the kettle on.'

'That'd be great. Tea, two sugars, please.'

Gideon pads through the house. It feels strangely reassuring to have the mundane distraction of a workman around the place. Normality. An acceptance that life goes on. He unlocks the back door.

It doesn't take the builder long to size up the job. The walls are made from heavy stone, little real damage done. They'll need pressure washing inside and out and probably repointing in places. Gideon puts down a mug of tea for him. Smithsen thanks him and carries on making pencil notes on a sheet of folded paper.

The inside of the study is a big mess. The parquet flooring is ruined and will need to be relaid. The window will have to be replaced. The ceiling plaster has all cracked off and the beams and joists are exposed and blackened by smoke. He wanders through to the kitchen where Gideon is stood sorting through the morning's post. 'Sorry to interrupt.

Do you mind if I take a look upstairs, over the study? I think the floor may have been made unsafe because of the fire.'

'Sure, go ahead.'

'Thanks.'

Gideon wonders how many more letters are going to arrive in his father's name and how long he'll feel a stab of loss every time they do. Another thought hits him. One more disturbing. The door to the room is open. He drops the post and runs up the stairs.

The man is nowhere to be seen.

He rushes into the bedroom. Smithsen is not there.

Gideon dashes into the corridor and into the little room. The builder is on his knees in the corner. He looks up with half a smile on his face. 'There's a bit of a creak in the middle but it's probably all right. Is it okay to take this carpet up and do some proper stress checks?'

'No. No, it's not okay.' He can't help but look and sound flustered. 'Look, this is a mistake. I'm sorry. It's too soon. I'm going to have to ask you to leave.'

Smithsen stands up. 'I understand. No problem. But I wouldn't spend time in here until you've had the place checked out. The fire has probably damaged the beams and you might have a bad accident if the floor is unsafe.'

'Thanks. But right now I need you to go.'

The man gives him another sympathetic look. 'Sure. I'll put that card through your letterbox. Ring me when you're really sure that you're ready to have things done.'

Gideon follows him down and says goodbye at the back

door. His heart is hammering. Maybe he's paranoid. Spooked by nothing. The guy seemed honest enough, even nice. He was just trying to help out.

But something is nagging him. He watches the builder's van drive off and then he returns to the room.

His father's books have been moved.

41

Caitlyn Lock has a simple rule about men – one date, one goodbye. Simple as that.

Sitting in her father's apartment, she is reminding herself of all the reasons to stick to it. But there is something about Jake Timberland that makes her want to throw caution to the wind.

It's not just that he is good-looking. They always are. Or that he is wealthy. They all have to be. It's that he's . . . well . . . so . . . British. Which after all is why she is in the damned country in the first place. To get a slice of Britain. See something older than her grandmother's house. A culture that shaped the world, a people that dominated half the globe. Queen and Empire and all that weird stuff.

And deep down, yes, she had even thought about meeting a man like him. The kind who is exotically unusual and *deep*. Awkward even. She knows that there's more to Jake than meets the eye. Maybe even romance. Her parents' split had pretty much drop-kicked that thought out of her, but now it's back, prompted by the text he's just sent. A picture message of a beautiful sunrise. Below it the words, 'Sit with me through this. Drive with me through the night to a place full of ancient magic. Be with me through a cherry-coloured sunrise and laugh with me until sunset.'

The proposition is a delicious one. No nightclubs and paparazzi wolves. No prying eyes of her father's security team. Pure escapism. The message appeals to her spirit, one starved of the taste of freedom. She types in a simple reply: 'Yes!'

She doesn't know how she'll get past the men in suits who are always watching, with their radios and surveillance logs, but she will. Tonight she'll escape the golden cage and fly.

42

The builder's surprise visit and nosing around has made Gideon feel vulnerable. The big old house is isolated. He's been attacked once already and doesn't want it to happen again. He certainly doesn't want to lose the books and the secrets they contain about his father. He needs to take precautions. Lock the gates. Put the alarm on.

It takes several calls and more than an hour to convince the security company that he isn't a burglar. Finally they tell him how to reset the system and he's pleasantly shocked at how noisy it is. Not that it matters. You could let off a small nuclear explosion and it would probably go unnoticed around here.

Which is why he searches the place for things to defend himself with. He finds an axe in the shed and takes a large knife from a wooden block in the kitchen. The best he can muster. Makes him feel slightly deranged, carrying them around while making beans on toast for a late lunch but deranged is better than scared.

Afterwards, he finds a handheld controller to lock the garden gates. He activates them, then sets the alarm to cover the downstairs and retires to his father's hidden room with a cup of tea, bottle of water and his knife and axe. He knows life can't go on like this. But right now he needs to feel secure not scared rigid. He remembers the builder's comments about the floor being unsafe. What if he's right? What if the fire has burned the support timbers and any second now they give way. He'll fall through, break his back probably. Gideon feels like he's going mad. Fear is spreading through him like a virus. He's got to kill it off.

Methodically and unemotionally, he clears his head by deciphering the journals. By late evening finds he's able to translate automatically, rather than writing out the symbols first. He reads how Nathaniel believed followers of the Sacreds were saved from the outbreak of Asiatic Flu, Russian Flu, in 1889, when a million people were killed. Similarly, how they avoided the 1918 Spanish Flu outbreak – a virus that went on to claim the lives of almost fifty million people.

It was the same in 1957, when Asian Flu swept the world and wiped out almost two million people. And in 1968, when Hong Kong Flu killed a million and again in 2009, during the deadly outbreak of Swine Flu, the H1N1 virus. None of the Followers perished.

Gideon is sceptical but fascinated by the claims. He guesses it's possible. A psychosomatic reaction to the stones brought on by powerful beliefs. Lourdes springs to mind. From what he can recall, more than two hundred million people have made pilgrimages there. His atheist's mind equates the two. The healing powers of the stones versus those of the waters of a grotto in the foothills of the Pyrenees. Both as equally incredible as each other.

He looks at his watch. It's almost one a.m. He's hungry and exhausted. Too tired and anxious to go downstairs or make anything to eat. He vows to look over just one more page and then turn in for the night.

He wishes he hadn't. The passage he's focused on makes his blood run cold:

Gideon knows only that his mother had a fatal illness. The single good thing about the word 'cancer' is that it scares off further interrogation, especially in a child. I hope he goes through his entire life not knowing that it was CLL, never realising that it was hereditary. I put my trust in the Sacreds, in the bond I make with them, in the clear blood of mine that I pledge to purify that of my child.

139

He reads it again. His brain pounds as he tries to take it in. Only the key words – cancer, hereditary, CLL – stay sharp in his mind.

CLL.

What is it? Does he have it?

Will it kill him?

43

The Henge Master walks in the comforting dark circle of the Sacreds, his eyes turned to the pin-prick stars. The night sky is an avalanche of black soot, a limitless mystery, a dark hurricane hurtling towards the sleeping heads of the ignorant. It is his duty to look for them. To understand for them. To save them from their own folly.

In the unseen currents and dark streams above, he senses the shift, the wheeling constellations, the lethargy of the Lyrids, the impatience of the coming and deadly Delta Aquarids. He feels the pull of the tides, the shift of winds across oceans, the growing cracks in the core of the earth.

As always the innocent will come running to the summer solstice, their heads beaded, their hands clasped. Their vaunted hopes of wild lovemaking and drug-induced euphoria. They will choke on their own naivety. Every last one of them. Even those who think they are wise have no idea, no understanding that the important thing is not the solstice and the sun. It is the full moon that follows.

Balance. Always balance. So many only ever see the obvious. Just as the greatest magicians fool us by distraction, so do the gods. Only the chosen can see beyond the cosmic illusions. Let the blind prostrate themselves and pose in the dazzling show of light at the equinox. Redemption lies in the twilight. The moon is rising to its most powerful apex.

The Master knows the importance of the unseen. Farmers since time began have learned this primary lesson. The crop we see depends on what we cannot see. The darkness in the earth must be respected, it must be loved as much as the brightness in the sky. The ancients knew – and their children know – the earth's unseen powers of growth need to be nourished. They need blood meal, the richness of bone, the coolness of the grave. Scientists say blood on soil provides vital nitrogen, but it obliges with much more than just chemicals. Blood contains something else. Soul. And the more the soil has, the more it wants.

In forty-eight hours the summer solstice will bring tens of thousands to Stonehenge. The ignorant will jibber-jabber like baboons. They will clamber like cavemen on the stones. They will claim to be touched spiritually by an energy they have yearned to feel.

If only they knew the truth. The brutal truth. Because by then the circle will be empty. The Sacreds will be in the Sanctuary.

The Master smiles as he walks away. Tomorrow he will return and begin his pilgrimage. He will supplicate himself before each and every god and absorb their divine spirits. He will be their vessel, their portal through the black earth to the ancient temple below.

44

Eric Denver has been head of security for the Lock family for almost twenty years. Husband, wife and now daughter. Guardian angel to them all. Thom Lock is a self-made multi-millionaire. When he was made Vice President of the United States, he had no choice but to accept Secret Service protection for himself. But he put his foot down when it came to Caitlyn. He was determined that his only child would have something more personal and *private*. Hence Eric. Given her wild behaviour, it's a good job he signed him up. Tongues would certainly wag in Washington if the smile-less ones in the corridors of power knew half the things she gets up to under cover of completing her studies in the UK.

Eric gives the VP daily reports, but he leaves stuff out. The kid's got to have room to breathe. Even he can see that all the attention and private scrutiny suffocate her some-times. So occasionally, like now, he turns a blind eye when things get a bit loose.

Just before midnight, six of Caitlyn's girlfriends roll in

and all but fall down the corridor outside her apartment. They're clutching handbags and bottles of champagne. On their slim faked-tan arms are six muscled youths straight out of an army poster. Big, brawny heads, biceps like rugby balls, eyes glazed from booze and dope.

Eric and Leon, his number-two, step forward and block the march of the dirty drunken dozen. 'Homework club's cancelled, kids,' he says, recognising a couple of the girls' faces. 'You need to be getting off now.'

The tallest of the youths – blond-haired with the kind of physique few would want to test – swaggers forward. 'Hey, we don't want no trouble, brother. We just come to party with Caitlyn.'

Eric raises an eyebrow. 'Brother' is not a term he takes easily from a white kid. 'No partying tonight, my friend. Miss Lock already has an important date – with a cup of cocoa and a TV show.'

Blondie's about to push his luck when Caitlyn opens the front door. Four of the girls scream with drunken excitement and rush her. The guys start to follow but the two bodyguards block the door. Music explodes from a Bose system rigged into the walls. Black Eyed Peas' 'Rock that Body'.

The guys are having a stare-out when two of the women briefly reappear from the apartment. One of them jumps into Eric's arms and tries hard to kiss him. He pulls her away and puts her down. She smoothes out her sparkling blue cocktail dress. 'Please let us all in Eric, pleeeze. You can't keep Caitlyn cooped up like this. She needs some fun.'

The girl smells of booze and perfume, mouth-fresheners and spray-on deodorant. 'C'mon Janie, you and these friends of yours need to go home, you know the score. Caitlyn had her fun the other night.'

The situation changes in a second. One of the youths spins and shouts, 'Fuck him, Janie, we're outta here.' He and his friends tow a couple of the girls back to the lifts. 'C'mon, let's go to China's.' The call brings the others from the apartment. One of them giggles then stumbles and breaks a heel. Leon helps her up and she hobbles off holding the shoe in a hand.

As the apartment door bangs shut, Caitlyn's voice screams through the wood: 'Thanks a-friggin *lot*.'

Eric smiles and listens to the lift ding, then goes back to the apartment door and knocks lightly. 'Caitlyn, we're just looking out for you.'

'Screw you. I'm going to bed.' Another door slams deep inside the apartment. He looks at Leon. 'Could be worse.'

'How so?'

Eric grins again. 'We could have let them in. Then we really would have had trouble.'

45

They hail taxis in the road outside Caitlyn's apartment and head north of the river into the frothy wash of endless partyland. Eric and Leon make coffee in their adjoining apartment and watch a TV among a bank of monitors linked to security cameras on the landing, lifts, stairways and outside areas. They relax now that Caitlyn's sulking in her room and they're not traipsing around Soho or the West End watching her back. Neither really fancied another late night. Tomorrow they'll think differently. Tomorrow they will know that amid all the shouting, kissing, comings and goings, they both missed something. Something significant.

Caitlyn.

The angry voice from inside the apartment wasn't her voice. It was Abbie Richter's. The young American is now snuggled up in Caitlyn's king-size bed, ready for a good night's sleep and no doubt a tongue-lashing from Eric in the morning when he finds out they switched.

Caitlyn is in the front seat of the VW Campervan Jake Timberland has hired for this very special occasion. He looks across from the well-worn steering wheel. 'Vintage Type 2,' he brags, adding ironically, '*Whopping* 1.4-litre engine that will whisk you to your secret destination at a dizzying sixty miles an hour. Check out the rock 'n' roll rear seat.'

Like a small child, she scurries from the front to explore the back of the van. She finds cupboards stacked with snacks, a DVD player, flatscreen TV, fitted oven and fridge full of champagne, strawberries and three different types of ice cream. 'Yay!' she shouts as she inspects the flavours and eyes up a back seat that converts into a double bed.

Caitlyn returns to the front and pecks him on the cheek before sitting back down. 'I love it. Love it, *love* it.'

'Glad I could please.'

'I'm so sparked up! So, where are we going?'

'Somewhere you've never been. Where few have trod but many have dreamed.'

She play-punches him on the arm. 'Cut it out. Tell me.'

He laughs. 'No. It's a surprise.'

They cross the river and head west out to Hammersmith, past Brentford, north of Heathrow then south down a river of endless black tarmac. They stretch their legs at a service station near Fleet, then climb back in and Caitlyn soon falls asleep.

Jake drives for another hour, fighting off tiredness by listening to the radio and taking occasional glances at the sleeping beauty in the passenger seat. Sometimes he lifts her hand. Just to hold it. His mind running away with him. Imagining their relationship is already more than it actually is. Finally he sees the sign he's been looking for and pulls off the road. He parks up, kills the engine and retreats into the back to pull out the bed.

The sudden stillness causes Caitlyn to stir. He leans close and strokes her hair as he whispers, 'We're here.'

She murmurs. Her eyes flicker open but she's having trouble fighting the pull of sleep.

'Come and lie down in the back. You can sleep better for a while.'

She gets it together enough to stumble through to the bed

he's laid out. She curls up quickly and he lies next to her and pulls the quilt over them. Her eyes closed, she asks, 'Where are we?'

'Wait until sunrise,' he says, kissing her lightly.

46

Lee Johns has lost track of time. He doesn't know how long he's been slipping in and out of consciousness. It could be hours or days. He's only aware of those long moments when pain is clamping his limbs and screams are climbing his throat.

Left naked face-down on the floor of the Great Room, he's been close to death and has lost several pints of blood. The icy Slaughter Stone under him has chilled his body to hypothermic levels.

He wakes. Feels a deep, rhythmical bludgeoning in his head. But is glad to be alive. He can move a hand. The bindings have been cut. Two robed and hooded Helpers see him stirring and step forward. They carefully lift him from the floor and wrap blankets around him.

It's over.

Johns is stiff and barely able to walk. His senses are peculiarly heightened. He has no feeling in his feet but can hear loud echoes from his own footsteps like he's walking on the surface of a giant drum. The Helpers support him as he sways unsteadily down the cold, shadowy passageways. 'We are taking you to the cleansing area,' says a distant voice. 'You'll be washed and dressed, then instructed.'

The words seem to leave an imprint in the air, like a sound wave on a recording screen. Johns strains over his shoulder and sees the syllables trailing behind him like the fluttering tail of a multi-coloured kite.

They must have drugged him. He's hallucinating, that's all.

They take him to a deep stone trench being filled by a roaring waterfall. It's red. Blood red. And it's steaming on the floor like a pan of spilled tomato soup. Johns stands naked, terrified, frozen to the spot.

'It's all right, *trust* us.' A Helper holds his own hand under the cascading blood and as it touches his skin it becomes transparent. Crystal clear. As pure as a mountain stream.

Johns steps in and closes his eyes. The steam from the shower smells like rusty iron. It feels like a thousand needles are being jabbed into his scalp. His heart bucks hard as the hot spray spikes into his head like thorns.

Slowly his cold-numbed nerves come tingling to life beneath the warm downpour. Finally, he opens his eyes. He looks at his hands and body. The water is running clean. No blood. Everything's normal.

The Helpers stand at the edge of the trench, holding towels for him. He steps out, leaving wet footprints as he pads across the slate floor, mist drifting from the cleansing area. In front of him are his own clothes and a rough sack robe. It is his. He is a member of the Craft. He's been accepted.

There's a full-length mirror in the corner. He twists his body to see the extent of the wounds caused by the Master. *Strange.* He twists his right forearm and then his left arm to inspect the initiation cuts. He checks the mirror again.

'What's going on?'

Those around him say nothing.

'I was bleeding. But I can't see any scars.' He angles his body again in front of the mirror. 'There's nothing. Not a mark.'

A cloaked shape fills the doorway.

Johns looks across and recognises the rugged face beneath the hood. Sean Grabb, Serpens, his Craft brother.

Proud mentor smiles at protégé. 'Get dressed, Lacerta. There are important duties to be done.'

47

SATURDAY 19 JUNE

Just after four a.m. the sky begins to lighten. Jake gently wakes Caitlyn.

She is jelly-legged as he helps her from the Campervan and starts to shiver in the cool morning air. He rushes back for a couple of blankets and the bag of goodies he's packed up from the fridge.

'Where are we?' she mutters as he snuggles her beneath his arm and the warm wrap. 'I still can't see anything.'

'You will in a minute. It's a piece of old England. Tomorrow, it will be flooded with thousands of hippies like you, but this morning, right now, it's ours. Just yours and mine. I booked it.'

'Booked it?'

'Everything is buyable these days. Others had paid to tour the site but I paid them off. Bought them out. Just for you.'

She's too touched and tired to say anything.

They shuffle across the damp grass in the receding darkness and gradually she starts to see it. Something huge. Rising out of the rosy warmth of the breaking dawn. Her pupils pulse wide as she stares at the monumental shape. '*Jesus*, what is it? It's like some weird space ship.'

And it is. It's just like a massive stone UFO crashed into the ground. Jake throws open his arms in a grand gesture. 'Welcome to Stonehenge.'

'It's . . . awesome.' She skips and takes in the heady scene, then wanders back into his arms and kisses him deeply. They hold each other beneath the fading constellations and block out everything that exists except themselves.

'Come on.' He takes her by the hand. 'Let's go to the centre.'

They run together and she can't remember when she last felt like this. So free. So energised.

Jake stands back to take photographs. Snaps on an old pocket Nikon and knows he's going to keep the images for ever. One day when they're both old, he'll dig them out and they'll remember today. History in the making.

Caitlyn pauses, breathless, wraps her arms around one of the sarsens. She looks like a child clinging to the leg of a giant. She laughs and poses for him.

Click.

She scoops a hand behind her hair and pouts.

Click.

She kisses the stone and strokes it.

Click. Click. Click.

'One more!' he shouts and she obliges, leaning against the stone and blowing a kiss right down the lens.

Click.

He stops shooting and gives in to another urge to kiss her.

They lock together. Her back against the giant stone, him pressed hard against her soft warm body. Raw sexual energy rushes through them both.

She closes her eyes and goes with it. Rises like a bird on the hot thermals of his passion. She yields to the invasion of his hands beneath her clothes, the conquering of her flesh. The mystery and magic of his romantic surprise have overwhelmed her.

He spasms against her. It's not as passionate as she hoped. In fact it's off-putting and embarrassing. Less of an orgasmic peak, more a sudden and awkward crash of his forehead against hers. Caitlyn flinches and grabs her bruised head. Jake pulls away from her.

'Ow!' she exclaims, mad that the moment has been ruined.

A hand slaps across her mouth. A stranger's hand.

She manages a brief panicking glance at her unconscious

lover before a hood is pulled over her head and duct tape wrapped around her mouth.

Within sixty seconds the fields are empty and silent, save the first birdsong of a new day. The sun finishes its slow upward arc into the bruised sky above the henge.

48

Serpens drives the Campervan. On the floor in the back is the blindfolded and bound form of Jake Timberland. Lacerta follows in his friend's old Mitsubishi Warrior. Caitlyn Lock is tied up and tightly gagged in the rear.

The instructions to the Lookers had been clear. Keep surveillance on the site and wait until the Sacreds choose. Be patient. Like the last victim, it would be *their* will. And it was. The couple arrived in twilight. They invaded the circle. They touched the stone that the Master said would be touched. They had been drawn to it. Just as the Master said.

The Followers call that particular trilithon the Seeking Stone and there's no doubt in Serpens' mind these two lovers sought it. They chose their destiny. Draco will be pleased. All of the Inner Circle will be. He and Lacerta have done a good job.

Ordinarily, Serpens doesn't take them at the circle itself. Once chosen, they are followed. Sometimes for weeks. Sometimes months. Greater care is usually shown before any abduction is executed. But time is against them. The stars are shifting. There is only a week to go to the change of the moon phase. The renewal must be completed. There is barely time to cleanse the sacrifices, to make them pure.

The lad in the back has suddenly started banging his feet on the wooden floor like a toddler having a tantrum. He will learn to be quiet. He'll soon know to be silent. Serpens turns up the radio. Before long he takes the van off road, through land that the Craft own, through woods and vales once home to Mesolithic, Neolithic and Bronze Age tribes.

Serpens pulls over in a quiet place not far from the isolated track that leads to the hidden entrance of the Sanctuary.

Lacerta tucks the Warrior behind the Campervan and waits for his mentor to make the next move. All he knows is that they are going to leave the sacrifices there and drive the van to a barn, where it will be kept until dark. Later it'll no doubt be taken to a scrapyard and crushed.

Serpens kills the engine and climbs into the back. At least the guy's stopped kicking. Learned his lesson. Best not to fight it. Best not to resist what's going to happen next.

49

Lacerta wanders towards the parked Camper. He wonders why Serpens is still in there. Nothing is happening. Through the window he sees him crouched in the back. He opens the door and sticks his head in, 'Everything okay?'

'No, it's not.' Serpens turns. 'Everything's very much not okay.'

Lacerta climbs in and shuts the door. 'Why, what's wrong?'

Serpens moves back and reveals the body on the floor. 'He's dead.'

'*Dead?*'

It's one of those words that you just have to repeat. 'Dead.'

He emphasises the point by picking up Jake Timberland's arm and letting it fall.

'Fuck.'

'Fuck indeed.'

Lacerta is in shock. He steps closer and peers at the crumpled form on the floor. 'What's wrong with him?'

'You mean, apart from the fact his heart's stopped and he has no pulse?'

'I mean, what killed him?'

Serpens shakes his head. 'I don't know. Maybe I hit him too hard. Maybe you tied him up too tight and he suffocated.'

For almost a minute they both stare guiltily at the corpse and wonder which of them was responsible.

Both are aware of the fate that awaited the couple. Sacrifice. That would have been much worse for the guy. But it would have been done under the eyes of the Gods. Done with their blessing, in their honour and with their protection. Under controlled circumstances. Carefully planned procedures to protect everyone concerned. Nothing like this. This is a screw-up.

Lacerta breaks the silence. 'What are we going to do?'

The older man sits back and puts his head in his hands. 'I'm trying to think, trying to work something out.'

'We could just dump them both.' He nods towards the pick-up. 'No one knows about the girl or him. We could drive them somewhere away from here and just leave them.'

Serpens thinks about it. 'Did she see your face?'

'No. I don't reckon so.' He reconsiders. 'Maybe. But even if she did, it was only for half a second.'

Serpens grimaces. 'That's all it takes. You see a lot in half a second.' He has another thought. 'She'll know where she was, what time. It's too risky.'

'Then we kill her.' Lacerta shrugs. 'She was going to die anyway. We can make it look like the boyfriend got rough. He was almost humping her back there at the stones. I bet he's given her one earlier in the night. His DNA will be all over her. The police are bound to think he did it.'

His mentor shakes his head. 'She's been chosen. She touched the Sacreds and it's our duty to supply her to them.'

Lacerta is panicking: 'It's *our duty* to stay out of fucking prison.'

Serpens stays calm, gets his head together. 'We need to drive this Camper somewhere, get it out of sight. Then I'll call my contact in the Inner Circle. It's up to the Master to decide.'

'What about the girl?'

He nods. 'You stay here with *him*. I'll take her into the Sanctuary.'

Lacerta is not happy. Even in this remote location, far

from any road or house, he doesn't want to be left alone with a dead body. 'Hurry up.'

Serpens runs to the Warrior. The girl is red-faced and struggling in the back of the cab. At least she's alive.

Caitlyn sees the panic on his face. The fear is contagious. It makes her kick and thrash against the bonds.

Serpens considers taking the duct tape from around her mouth and trying to calm her down but decides against it. Best get her inside as quickly as possible. Get her locked up. Call Draco and tell him about the awful mess they're in.

50

Yesterday's personal discovery gave Gideon a restless night.

CLL.

It stands for chronic lymphocytic leukaemia and is a dreadful disease that occurs when the DNA of the lymphocyte cell mutates. As years pass, damaged cells multiply and the mutant army kills off normal cells in the lymph nodes and bone marrow. Blood-forming cells are eventually overwhelmed and the body's immune system surrenders – it no longer has the ability to fight off infection.

It is how his mother died.

He knows all this because he spent all night reading about it online. He also found out that the disease is hereditary. But not always. CLL inheritance is a game of medical roulette. Maybe he has it, maybe he hasn't. Only time will tell.

Deep in his memory something stirs. Rises from the sands of forgotten nightmares. He wasn't a healthy child – he was plagued by colds and hay fever, coughs and dizzy spells. One time he fell really sick. A raging fever and heavy sweats. It was so bad his father took him out of school. Had him hospitalised and seen by specialists. There were machines and monitors, needles in his arms, stern faces and long adult conversations just out of earshot. Then they let him go home. His father had red eyes, like he'd been crying.

And he remembers something else. For a second, he has to stop himself. Needs to make sure his mind isn't playing tricks. The diaries have churned him up, left him exhausted and emotional. He could be suffering from false memory syndrome, implanting things into the past that hadn't happened.

But he doesn't think so.

His father made him lie down in the cold metal bath in their old house. He remembers it distinctly because he was embarrassed. He was naked and the bath was empty. Then Nathaniel poured cold grey water all over him. Doused him from head to toe, told him to splash it over his face and in his hair. Urged him not to waste a drop.

He was shaking from cold and fear when he got out. His father wrapped him in a towel and held him tight, told him not to worry, said the water was special and would take the sickness away. And it had. Almost instantly. He went back to school days later and felt perfectly well.

Another piece of his childhood jigsaw falls into place. He's never been ill since that day. Not even a sniffle. Whenever he has cut himself, it has healed quickly.

Gideon walks to his father's old bedroom and looks in the mirror on the dressing table. The injuries he sustained in the fight with the intruder downstairs have gone. He puts a hand to his face. The skin is unblemished. There's no trace of the split lip or cut cheek. It's like it never happened.

51

Black carrion crows settle on the jagged ridge of an old barn that has seen little care in the last twenty years. Draco points at the avian army as he walks through the long grass with Musca.

He bangs on the dark twisted wood of the barn door and the birds scatter skyward, then swoop and settle into treetops edging the vast field.

From inside there comes the noise of urgency. Metal against metal. Things being moved. Serpens has already seen them through cracks in the barn boards and opens up. He looks embarrassed. 'Sorry about all this.'

Draco says nothing. He is sorry too. Sorry about the screw-up. Sorry he has to come and sort out the mess. The two men slide past Serpens. He locks the door again. Rolls a broken scarifier back behind it, positions the long metal arm that connects to a tractor so it jams against one of the door beams. 'Thanks for coming.'

Draco looks quickly around. 'Are we are alone?'

Serpens nods. 'I have sent Lacerta home.'

'Good,' says Musca. 'At least you've done one thing properly.'

Draco gets straight to the point. 'Where is the body?'

Sean points across the barn at the Campervan. 'He's in there.'

'And the woman?'

'Safe at the Sanctuary. In one of the meditation rooms.' It is a euphemism. They are merely spaces chiselled in the thick stone walls, no bigger than a broom cupboard. The supplicant can't kneel, let alone sit or lay down. Air dribbles through letterbox-sized slits by the feet and head. 'Did she say anything?'

'Nothing you could make any sense of. Just screamed.'

Musca smiles. 'She'll stop after an hour or two.'

Serpens slides open the Camper door and they climb in. Draco leans over the corpse. 'Have you searched him?'

Serpens shakes his head. Musca opens up the glovebox and pulls out hire documents, a driving licence and a bag of something. He holds it up to the windscreen. 'Ecstasy. A nice little stash.' He drops it on the driver's seat. 'There's a name here.' He flicks through the agreement. 'Edward Jacob Timberland, address New Cavendish Street, Marylebone.' He picks up the driving licence and looks at the photograph. 'Yep, that's our guy. Thirty-one years old.' He flips it over. 'And six points to his name.'

'He won't be worrying about those any more,' says Draco. He takes a deep breath. 'So he and his girlfriend hire the VW for a hippy trip to Stonehenge. That means they won't be missed for a day or two.' He gives them a smile. 'Not as bad as you thought. The Sacreds picked the perfect sacrifices, free souls who can take time off and play at being children of the sixties.'

Serpens looks relieved. 'So what do you want me to do with him?'

'Nothing. We'll keep the van here until after the ceremony and then we'll dispose of the bodies together. Go get yourself a decent breakfast. And relax. You can leave the girl to us now.'

52

DCI Jude Tompkins stomps into the CID office with a face like thunder. 'Baker, Dockery, conference room, five minutes. *Don't* be late.'

She's gone as quickly as she appeared. Jimmy looks across desks to Megan. 'What's all that about? I have to see an informant in ten minutes.'

'I think this is more important, Jim. You'd better ring your man and stand him down.'

'Shit.' He rips the desk phone from its cradle and punches in a number.

Megan calmly finishes reviewing the document she was working on, saves it and locks her computer. She grabs a plastic cup of water from a dispenser in the pantry and wanders down the corridor to the meeting room.

It's crowded. Full of bigwigs. She tries to put ranks and names to faces. There are five or six sergeants, at least three inspectors, two DCIs, the Detective Chief Super, John Rowlands, and there at the top of the table is Jimmy's old man, the Deputy Chief Constable, Greg Dockery. He's flanked by two smartly dressed civilians she doesn't recognise.

'What's the score?' asks Charlie Lanning, a uniform inspector, taking a seat next to her. 'Something to do with the solstice? Bloody hedgerows are already full of dopeheads. It's going to be worse than ever.'

'Your guess is as good as mine.' Megan gestures to the end of the conference table. 'The suits look too serious for solstice ops. Too official. Could be a Home Office review. Or maybe more cutbacks.'

'Nothing left to cut in my unit. We're not down to the bone, we're into it and almost out the other side.'

They don't have to wait long.

The Deputy Chief raises his voice. 'Your attention please.' He waits a beat for the noise to die down. 'You have been gathered for a matter of urgency. To my left is Drew Blake of the American Embassy and to my right Sebastian Ingram of the Home Office.' He picks up a large photograph that has been face-down on the table. 'This is Caitlyn Lock. She is twenty-two years old. She is an American citizen at university in London and she is missing.' He turns the photograph left and right for all the room to see. 'Some of you may recognise this young lady. Miss Lock is something of a celebrity. She won the US reality television show *Survivor* and is the daughter of Hollywood film star Kylie Lock and of course the Vice President of the United States, Thom Lock.' Most in the room are taking notes and Dockery pauses briefly before continuing: 'At this stage we have no reason to believe any harm has come to Caitlyn. There has been no ransom demand. She is known to be something of a free spirit, so this may simply be an innocent disappearance with a new boyfriend. However, she has not been seen since midnight last night so it is extremely important that we find her.' He scans the faces around the table, lets the point sink in, then gestures to his Detective Chief Superintendent.

John Rowlands stands. The head of CID is lean, a little over fifty and serious-looking. He's the only officer in the county who's also worked in the Met on homicide, abduction and terrorism cases. 'Just before midnight Caitlyn Lock tricked her private security team into believing she was in bed when in fact she had slipped out of her father's apartment in central London, just south of the river, to be with a man known to her friends only as Jake. She later telephoned one of these friends from a service station in Fleet, heading west, and said she didn't know where she was going – she was being treated to some kind of surprise. The friend said she sounded happy and excited and mentioned an old Campervan but gave no description, no make or colour.' He lets them process what he has given them. 'Given the solstice, the van and the timing, this young woman could well be on our patch. If she is, I want her found and returned to London before the maids have changed the sheets on her bed.' He turns to his left. 'I will head the inquiry, DCI Tompkins will be my number-two. She will give you the operational details and your duties straight after this meeting. Surrounding forces are setting up their own investigations and the national press is being informed of Caitlyn's disappearance.'

He hears groans around the room.

'Be smart, people. The public and the press have the power to find this girl much quicker than we can. They are our eyes and ears. Use them, don't abuse them. And don't be stupid. All press enquiries have to be channelled through the communications office. Now go and get something to eat. It will be your last opportunity for quite a while.'

53

Draco catches it on the radio. Not all of it but enough. Something about the daughter of a Hollywood actress and an American politician going missing with her boyfriend. In a Campervan. He pulls out his burner and calls Musca. 'Have you listened to the news in the last hour?'

'No. Not been near a TV or radio.'

Draco starts to think. 'Wait.' He opens the browser on his phone and pulls up the BBC News page. It's the lead story. Beneath a picture of the girl. 'Listen to this.' He reads aloud: 'US reality star Caitlyn Lock, daughter of Vice President Thom Lock and actress Kylie Lock has disappeared from her father's home in south London with an unnamed man. Miss Lock, twenty-two years old, is thought to be in the south-west of the country and police have issued an appeal for anyone who sees her to call them immediately on the number below. She is of athletic build, five feet nine inches tall, has dark shoulder-length hair, brown eyes.' He pockets the phone. 'You went to the Sanctuary after we split up this morning, does it sound like the girl?'

Musca can hardly answer. 'I think so.'

Draco winces. 'Why? Why do you think so?'

'She's American. There's no doubt about that. She looks athletic and young as well.'

Draco shuts his eyes and wishes it wasn't so. 'Get over there now. I'll call the Master.' He hangs up, unsure what to do. If the girl *is* the daughter of the US Vice President the Americans will be going crazy to get her back. They might be using spy technology for all he knows, listening in to phone calls from all over the world.

He glances up at the sky, almost expecting to see a drone hovering above him. If they can do that, he's said too much already. He calls the number. 'It's Draco. I have to see you. It's urgent.'

'I understand. I'll be there as soon as I can.'

They both know where for such an emergency. Draco has little time for courtesy: 'When you hang up, dump your burner somewhere public. We may be compromised.'

The line goes dead. He breaks open the back of his phone and pulls out the battery and the sim card in order to discard them and the hardware separately. Without wasting time, he gets in his car and drives quickly but within the speed limit to the Sanctuary. He takes three detours en route to dispose of the phone. Each time he looks up and wonders whether he is being watched.

54

The Henge Master comes and goes unseen through his own entrance to the Sanctuary, one that only he knows, one disclosed in the sacred books that he inherited.

He walks the unprotected passageway to his chamber and waits for Draco. Before long there's a knock on the heavy door and he shouts, 'Come.'

Draco enters hesitantly.

'Sit.' The Master's voice gives away his irritation at being summoned at such short notice. He gestures to the semicircle of stone benching opposite him.

Draco adjusts his cloak as he settles. His voice is low and apologetic. 'The girl chosen by the Sacreds turns out to be

165

the daughter of the American Vice President. It's on the news.'

Shock registers on the Master's face, then disappears. 'That may well be, but as you just said, she has been chosen.'

Fear glistens in Draco's eyes. 'Master, do we not need to distance ourselves from her? The US security services and every police officer in Britain are going to be searching for her.'

'And they are more important than those we follow?'

'No, Master.'

'I repeat – she has been chosen. Has she not?'

'Yes, Master, but—'

'Enough.' The Master's sharp tone cuts right through him. 'Our beliefs, our activities have gone uninterrupted by the police for centuries. Our existence has been kept secret for thousands of years. That is not due to luck. We are guided by the will of the Sacreds and that is a greater force than any police constabulary or government in existence.'

Draco understands. 'I am sorry. I believed caution would be prudent.'

The Master nods. 'You have done well to consider it and are right to alert me.' He looks over his steepled fingers. 'The girl is the one on the radio, Caitlyn Lock?'

'Yes.'

'And her boyfriend – what of him?'

Draco swallows. He fears the blunder could somehow be seen as his fault. 'The boyfriend is dead. He died when he and the girl were taken by the Lookers. It was an accident.'

The Master doesn't look concerned. 'Or it was the will of the Sacreds. Perhaps the male was not worthy. What of his body and the vehicle the press are speaking of?'

'In a barn not far from here on land we control.'

'Dispose of both, quickly.' The Master rises from the stone seat. 'We are done. I am expected back. Call the Inner Circle and inform them of our meeting and my wishes. The stars are aligning, the moon is changing. We go ahead as planned.'

55

Megan is assigned to run actions on the Campervan and report directly to Tompkins. In addition to Jimmy Dockery, she's been given two other detective sergeants – Tina Warren and Jack Jenkins. Warren is a waster. She can tell that already. Fit to make tea, run errands and put petrol in a car. Jenkins is more promising. Newly promoted, a little green but bright.

Megan divides the work. 'Jack, get a statement from this friend of Caitlyn's, the one she last spoke to. Ask her again about the vehicle. I know she didn't get a description but ask. She may remember something.

'Jim, take a team to the Fleet service station on the M3. We are looking for CCTV footage from the garage forecourt, also from the car park – it's likely they used the toilets as well. Ask in the shops and restaurants, hand out photographs, jog memories. They probably bought some-thing out there. Find out what – and who sold it to them. If we're lucky, they asked for a guide map or even direc-tions. Check with all the security. They may have images of the couple on a camera here or there. Tina, get inter-view teams at the services before and after Fleet. See if they stopped there.'

They all look at her for further instructions.

'*Now*, please. Treat this as though the girl's life depends upon it.'

Even before they've gone, Megan rings a friend in traffic and asks for a list of Campervans. While she waits, she goes online and sets up a vehicle search. There are dozens of campers: Fiat Cheyennes, Ducatos and Komets, Ford Transit Auto-Sleepers, Winnebagos, VW Transporters, Toyota Hiaces, Hymers, Bedfords, Mercs. Then she stops. Her profiling instincts kick in and she starts to think. Not about the vehicle. About the people in it. Impulsive people. Rich people. Caitlyn is hardly likely to move in the circle of paupers. Her lover will have money. He will want to impress her. Surprise her.

None of the vans on her screen do that. She types 'Celebrity Camper vans' and fifty-three thousand entries appear in a third of a second. Over fifty pages of results. The one topping her lists is the VW. She hits a link: 'VW Campervans for hire'.

It brings a smile to her face. It's the Mystery Machine. The van Scooby-Doo and Shaggy drove around in. She types in 'VW Camper vans to hire *in London*.' Her heart sinks. Half a million results. She browses and it turns out not to be as bad as she thought. The keyword search is too loose, it's inaccurate – she should have written 'Campervans' not 'Camper vans'. She finds a number for a VW Campervan Association and soon assembles a shortlist of dealers in the London area.

After a couple of hours the list is even shorter. Several people hired Campervans within the last twenty-four hours but only one stands out. He paid on an Amex Gold card and his name is Jake Timberland. Her heart jumps – the way it always does when she knows she's got her man. Before telling the DCI, she has one more call to make. One she's dreading. Sammy is going to need looking after again.

56

Caitlyn can't move. She can't see and can't breathe properly.

She feels like she's been buried, standing up. Entombed in stone. There's barely enough room to raise her hands to her face and feel the sweat of fear pouring off her.

'*Jake!*' She screams his name but knows he's not going to answer.

Emblazoned in her memory is an image of him slumped on the ground inside the strange stone circle. There was something about the way he didn't move that made her feel

169

sick. '*Jake!*' Somehow shouting his name keeps him alive. At least in her mind.

Her fingers feel the rough stone in front of her. They find a tiny slit and the thin stream of air that's keeping her alive. She just hopes whoever took her captive are professionals – seasoned kidnappers who know what they're doing and not weirdo rapists or serial killers. If it's a pro kidnap gang, they're after money and her life is not in danger. Well, not immediately. Soon they'll come and clean her up, feed her, make the film, a message to her parents most likely, and the game will start. She's been trained for this. Eric Denver has run her through it dozens of times and her father has run her through it. Even her damned mother has gone over the possibility with her that this might happen.

She sees now that she was crazy to go with Jake. To slip out of the safety of her own security net. A bad thought hits her. One that saps what little remains of her esteem. Maybe Jake helped set her up. Perhaps he'd been thinking about it right from the first moment he met her. The alternative is almost as bad. If he wasn't, then where is he? She knows kidnappers rarely take two hostages at a time. It's too complicated, too much of a struggle. She feels the sickness rise again.

'*Jake!*' Her scream tails off into a whimper. It's been hours since they locked her in, since anyone talked to her. Her spine is hurting. Her shoulders, the back of her head and her knees are raw from rubbing against the stone walls. And unless she's mistaken, and she's pretty certain she isn't, she's soiled herself.

Despite the pain, the cramp and the humiliation Caitlyn keeps falling asleep. Deprived of stimulation, her crazy over-active brain simply shuts down and she drifts off, drifts to some far away place that bears no resemblance to this dank dungeon. She is in one of those fitful dozes when the cell wall slides back and she slumps forward. Men in brown robes and balaclavas beneath their hoods catch her and lower her to the ground.

She comes round on her back. Dizzy and glassy-eyed, staring at a high black ceiling and a huge cast-iron chandelier ringed with thick burning candles.

Four hooded faces appear in Caitlyn's line of vision and a low rasping voice issues a chilling instruction. 'Strip and wash her. The ceremony goes ahead.'

57

For once, Megan's ex seems happy to have Sammy for the night. He even promises home-cooked food and not a Happy Meal. A weight off the working mum's mind.

She returns to the Campervan case filling her desk and the Facebook photographs of Jake Timberland she tracked down by following the lead the Amex bill gave her. Things happen quick when there's a break. Over in London a Met team has confirmed that the young Englishman isn't at home in Marylebone, another is showing his picture to Caitlyn's minders and a third is visiting Jake's parents, Lord and Lady Timberland. Meanwhile, itemised mobile and landline phone records are being studied along with Switch and credit card bills. The wheels of investigation are turning fast.

Megan places photos of Timberland and Lock side by side. They make a good couple. The press are going to go crazy on this one. There'll be enough pressure to squash a battleship. She looks at their faces and figures the romance – if that's what it is – must be recent. If they'd been an item for any length of time, they would already have been splashed across the gossip mags.

Then comes a moment of doubt. Perhaps she's got the wrong guy. Maybe there's no connection between Jake and Caitlyn. Could be that he just happened to take a three-day minimum hire on a cornflower blue Camper on the same day she did her vanishing trick. Perhaps she's up a hill in a Winnebago with someone else and doesn't even know Edward Jacob Timberland exists.

It could all be coincidence.

Megan hates coincidences. Coincidences are God's way of seeing if police officers can do their job. She hopes the motorway teams come back with video of the couple with the Camper that will prove there's a link between everything.

She looks again at Caitlyn's photograph and then checks the girl's Facebook page. Obviously handled by a publicist and vetted by her father. There is nothing too personal on there – just fashion, music and girly gossip. Bland stuff.

She tries Twitter. Even more disappointing. Then she checks Jake's Twitter account. Dating Caitlyn Lock would be the kind of thing any man would find difficult to keep quiet about. She draws a blank. There's nothing from the last day – no hint of the journey to Wiltshire. She scrolls back twenty-four hours and feels her heart leap. Her eyes hook on a coded piece of male bragging: 'I have a plan to win my new muse, to unlock her chains and make her mine.'

Encouraging. Even tantalising. But not quite enough. She trawls back further and finds another gem: 'I have met this American and I'm smitten. She is everything I dreamed of.'

The remarks all point to him running off to Stonehenge with Caitlyn for some quality time out of view of her security. Lust makes everyone go crazy – even sons of English lords and daughters of American film stars. Come to think of it, especially them. They must have run off together. Gone off radar. Maybe even eloped.

No. She's getting carried away. They certainly did not get married. The Camper was hired for three days only. Off radar is right though. They must have conspired to trick the girl's security and grab some time together.

But something doesn't make sense. Something she can't quite put her finger on. Then the penny drops. Caitlyn must have planned to call in to her minder *before* the alarm was raised and everyone went crazy. Why didn't she? It's the kind of protocol her father and everyone would have drummed into her. *Always call in, whatever you do, always call in.* And she would have. Of course she would.

But she hasn't. That means something is wrong. Terribly wrong.

58

Fear stabs Caitlyn like a hot spike in the heart. A group of hooded men have her pinned to the floor. She's going to be raped. She's sure of it. Well, she'll bite their throats out rather than let that happen.

One grabs her left wrist, another her right. She kicks out. Feels her foot connect with soft flesh. 'Leave me the fuck alone!' Deep down she knows shouting and fighting is pointless but she sure as hell isn't going to give in peacefully. 'Get the *fuck* off me!'

Unseen hands clasp her ankles. They pull open her blouse and tug down her jeans. They turn her over, unclip her bra and pull off her panties. She thrashes and screams until her throat burns and her energy is spent. She's done. She has no more resistance.

They're going to take it in turns to debase her – she just knows they are.

Someone pulls her hair and slides a hood over her head. They haul her to her feet and cuff her hands. She's unsure what's happening but is relieved she's not been molested.

Firm fingers grip her arms and shoulders. They push her in the back – force her to walk. Caitlyn's heart is beating so fast she feels like she is going to die. *Don't panic. Stay calm.* She mentally repeats the instructions Eric gave her. *Whatever happens, you deal with it. One second at a time you deal with it – or you die.*

They walk her down dark mazy passageways, then make her step into some kind of pit. They pull the hood from her head and from the blackness above a waterfall of steaming hot water is unleashed. The shock makes her gasp for breath. She's in some kind of step-down shower. Isn't she?

Then Caitlyn realises. It's not water. It's blood.

They're showering her in blood.

59

When Draco and Musca pull into the car park at Stonehenge, it's crowded with staff busying themselves for the solstice. People are everywhere. Extra toilets are being set up and bins slotted on poles, ready for the avalanche of litter that will inevitably come.

Serpens wanders away from the group he's been supervising and slips in the back door of the Merc. Draco doesn't even wait for him to settle. 'We have to get rid of the Camper and the body tonight.'

The Looker's instinct for survival kicks in. 'I'm not driving it. There are police on every major road.'

'What about your boy?' asks Musca. 'Would he do it?'

'Lacerta is young but not stupid. He'll get stopped. You know he will.'

'Sooner or later the police will find the vehicle,' says Draco. 'They are checking all roads, car parks, anywhere the dopeheads can hide. It is only a matter of time.'

'What if we use the Ecstasy we found in the glovebox?' says Musca. 'Make it look like he and his girl overdosed.'

Draco shakes his head. 'You can't just cram drugs down his throat. He won't be able to swallow and digest, none of the chemicals will be absorbed. The autopsy will show you did it after he'd died.'

'What if there's nothing of him to autopsy?' presses Musca. 'We torch the van and him in it, make it look like they had an accident.'

Draco's interest is awakened. 'How so?'

'Well, they were tired, pulled off the road, parked up in the field for the night.' Musca struggles to complete the picture, then adds: 'Maybe the guy was making a cup of tea and the stove blew. The cooking gas canister went up. You should get a good explosion from one that size.'

'Can you rig something like that?'

Serpens nods. 'It can be done. But they'll only find the man's body. They'll wonder what happened to the girl.'

Musca tries to fill in the gap. 'They had a row. She walked off. Hitched a ride. Got dropped at the train station and is now out of the area.' It's the best he can manage. 'If she's out of the county, she's someone else's missing person and the police will slacken off.'

'Can you deal with the body?' Draco looks deep into Serpens's eyes. 'We need you to do this.'

He feels like he doesn't have a choice. It was his blow that killed the guy. He wants a drink. Needs one badly. Finally he nods.

'I'll help you,' volunteers Musca. 'You don't have to do this alone.'

60

Caitlyn opens her eyes and gasps. Blackness. She's upright and back in the mind-numbing void that's become her personal prison. She has no recollection of them returning her to this hell hole. She must have passed out in the shower. The shower of blood.

Slivers of light are bleeding through what must be a panel right in front of her eyes. One that can be removed so they can see her. Feed her maybe. She realises now that it's not the same hole as she was in. It's slightly different. The space is bigger. Not much, but still bigger.

Gradually she notices other differences. The handcuffs are gone. She can lift her arms from her sides. She feels the walls that enclose her. Stone to the front, the sides and the back. She is certainly in another crevice, no change there. She stretches her arms as wide as she can. Probably less than a metre. She can't raise her hands beyond her elbows.

There's something touching the back of her legs, at knee-level. A ledge? She tries to sit and finds it takes her weight. It feels like a blessing. She's still barefoot but has been dressed in some sort of robe with a hood. She moves her head, shoulders and hips, lets the fabric rub against her. It's rough. Feels like sandpaper against her breasts.

She starts to piece together the missing parts of the night before. They stripped her of her clothes. Showered her in blood. Dressed her in their robes. Words come back too. There weren't many to analyse. But one was enough.

Ceremony.

That's what someone had said. '*The ceremony goes ahead.*'

But what kind of ceremony? And what in God's name are they going to do to her?

61

DCS John Rowlands already feels like he's gone a week without sleep. The clock is ticking fast and the leads are coming slower than he hoped. The pressure is relentless. The Chief Constable, the Home Office, the Deputy Chief Constable and the Vice President's private secretary are all on his back.

Teams of DCIs and DIs shuttle in and out of his office, tossing what bits of information they have on to his wrecked desk. Jude Tompkins and Megan Baker are the latest to take their turn. He greets them with what's left of his charm. 'Ladies, welcome to the pleasure dome. What have you got for me?'

'Some good news.' Tompkins clears a plate and a crust of pizza from a seat. 'DI Baker has a positive on the vehicle. And the boyfriend.'

His blue eyes widen. 'Tell me.'

Megan puts a ripped DVD on his desk. 'A compilation of CCTV footage, sir. The first clip is from the petrol pumps at Fleet. It's in colour and you can clearly see Lock and Jake Timberland, the man who paid for the Campervan rental.'

Rowlands doesn't need his notes. 'Son of Lord Joseph Timberland.'

'That's right.'

He picks up the disk and slides it into a player on a shelf beneath a TV behind him. Megan talks as he fiddles with a remote control to find the channel. 'The vehicle you are about to see, sir, is an imported right-hand-drive Type 2 Vintage in cornflower blue with chrome wheel hubs and refurbished interior.' A picture of the van comes up on screen. The Camper pulls up at the pump. Two figures get out. And then they become clear. Jake shows Caitlyn the pump and starts her off. Leaves her to fill up and walks towards the shop to pay.

'Freeze it please, sir.'

Rowlands stops the picture with the remote.

'Look in his right hand.' Megan smiles. 'A gold credit card. Amex. It's the one he used to pay for the rental.'

Rowlands nods and turns off the DVD and TV. 'Good enough for me. Jude, get someone to make copies of the footage for the investigation teams and the press. Talk to the communications office and call a conference for eight in the morning.' He turns to Megan. 'Well done. Make sure your team know we think they're doing a first-class job.'

'I will. Thank you, sir.' She gets up to leave but pauses.

Rowlands glances at her. 'Is there something else?'

'Sir, if there *is* a press conference in the morning, I'd like to be part of it. I'd like the experience, sir.'

He smiles and turns to the DCI. 'My, you have got an ambitious DI here.'

Tompkins nods. 'She's aching with it.'

He looks back to Megan. 'No, Detective Inspector, you may not.'

'Why not, sir?'

It's Tompkins' turn to smile now. 'Two reasons, Megan,' she says. 'Firstly, you're doing too good a job on the inquiry to be wasted posing about in front of cameras. Secondly, you're too inexperienced to be put in front of those dogs. Not enough gravitas for the press pack, do you see? It's late, so why don't you go home, get some well-earned rest and see your kid.'

Megan has to fight not to show her anger at the put-down. 'Thank you ma'am – for your kindness and concern –

180

but my daughter is being well looked after by her father, so if it's okay with you, I'll go back to my team and resume the job. The one the Detective Chief Super says I'm very good at.'

Point made, she wheels around and walks away before they can get in the final word.

62

Serpens checks his watch. Midnight. The time has come.

He stands and waits outside the old barn, his thoughts as black as the night sky. Psychologically things are piling up. Crushing him. Pressing him down. Not giving him a moment's relief.

The disposal of the sacrifice earlier in the month had got to him. He'd been involved in selections before but never afterwards. Never the bloody carnage of it all. And now he's crossed the line even further. He's taken someone's life.

The realisation that he'd killed the man in the Camper is eating him. He's a tough guy, been involved in plenty of fights in his time, even got a criminal record, but not for anything like murder.

Maybe if he went to the police he'd get away with a charge of 'accidental murder'. If he came clean now and told them everything he knew, there'd be some deal to be done. Possibly even immunity from prosecution. But the Craft would get to him. They'd find him and they'd kill him. He knows they would. They have brothers in the police – in the courts – in the prisons. They'd get to him all right.

Serpens hangs his head. It's a crisis of faith. That's all it is. Everyone has one. He's sure they do. Musca appears out of the clouded moonlight, a white plastic carrier bag in his right hand. 'All right?' he says and puts an arm around Serpens' shoulder as they head inside. 'Don't worry, all this will be over in half an hour. We'll go straight to Octans' afterwards. He'll alibi us. Say we've been there all night play-ing cards. Everything's going to be fine.'

Musca always says *everything will be fine*. Draco too. And for them it always is. Fine lives with fine consciences, not a guilty thought in their fine heads.

The barn is lit by a paraffin lamp on an overturned wooden crate a couple of metres from the Camper. It casts a yellow delta of light into the cobwebbed rafters. The two men disturb a colony of bats as they walk to the Camper. Musca laughs and points to the fluttering creatures. 'Creepy little fuckers. I wish I had something to shoot them with.'

Serpens pulls back the sliding door on the VW. A small interior light flickers on and reveals the fly-covered corpse. He steels himself for the task ahead. 'What do you want to do with him?'

'Wait. Put these on.' Musca hands him a pair of thin latex gloves. 'Better safe than sorry.'

Serpens stretches them and awkwardly squeezes his hands in. 'Okay, watch and learn,' says Musca. From the tiny kitchen he takes the complimentary food hamper left as a gift by the van hire company and smiles. 'Just what we need.' From cupboards he collects a plate, knife, fork, saucepan and toaster. He opens a can of beans from the hamper, tips them into the pan and places it on the cooking ring. He puts two slices of bread into the toaster and then produces a bottle of vodka from the carrier bag he brought with him. He unscrews it and pours some into a tumbler. 'Almost there, my friend. Almost there.'

Serpens watches in a trance as Musca opens the cupboard beneath the cooker and turns on the gas. He strikes a match, lights a ring on the small hob and then turns it off and smiles contentedly. 'So, that's all our preparation done.' He points to the corpse. 'The scene is set. We have our man left on his own in the Camper after a row with his girlfriend.' He points to the vodka. 'Man gets blind drunk – a reasonable reaction to being ditched part-way through a romantic break, right?' He points to the hamper. 'Then, because he's wasted he gets hungry and tries to make himself something to eat.' Musca picks up the vodka bottle and splashes it around. 'Unfortunately, because our heartbroken friend is on his way to being pissed he gets clumsy and spills his drink. On him-self. On the floor. On the cooker.' Musca raises his arms violently. '*Voom*! Suddenly he's a fireball. He panics. Falls over and knocks himself out. Within seconds the Camper is on fire, even the barn and he tragically burns to death.' Musca pulls down the corners of his lips to create a sad face. 'Sometimes unrequited love ends badly.'

Serpens is not in any state to fault the plan. 'So the fire destroys the evidence?'

'Right.' He wags a finger. 'But we should take care.' He points to the body. 'First off we pour half this bottle into Mr Heartbreak. Then we make it look like he fell. We crack his head on something – in the same place where you hit him. That way any autopsy will find the injury is what they term "consistent with the fall" and not with you whacking him.' He grins. 'Finally, we soak him in the last of the voddie, light our bonfire and run.'

Serpens looks disturbed but nods his agreement.

'Okay, let's get it done. Help me sit him upright.'

Timberland's body is heavy and cumbersome. It makes sickening cracking and gassy noises as they pull it into a sitting position. Musca tilts the head back, pulls the lips apart and pours vodka down the dead man's throat. Serpens wants to throw up.

'Best let some of that settle for a minute,' says Musca. 'Or else it'll just come straight back up.' He leaves Serpens holding the corpse while he turns on the gas, heats the beans and makes the toast. 'All done. Let's move him to the drawers there, in the wall opposite the cooker. Open the bottom one. We can make it look like he slipped and cracked his head.'

Serpens flips it open and takes a deep breath. The two men struggle again to lift the body. Timberland was smaller than both of them but he's like a rag doll and weighs a ton. Finally, Musca takes him under the arms, slides him backwards and drives the back of the skull down on to the bottom drawer.

He lets the body fall and stands back to admire his work.

A little vodka has spewed out of Timberland's mouth, on to his shirt front and on to the floor. Apart from that it's perfect.

'Finale time. You ready?'

'Guess so.'

Musca takes the open bottle of vodka and pours it over the head and chest. He lays the empty near the hands. He turns off the gas under the beans to extinguish the flames. When he's sure it's out he turns it on again and cranks it up high.

He gives Serpens a look, takes the carrier bag that he brought with him and unscrews the other bottle of spirits. He douses the corpse again and the cooker then points to the door. 'Best stand outside.'

They step out of the Camper into the cold barn and the yellow paraffin light. Serpens watches Musca pour the last of the vodka on to the floor of the van and return the empty to his carrier bag. 'Three, two, one.' He strikes the match. Lets it catch, then throws it on to the floor near the corpse.

'Run!'

They sprint like scared kids through the barn and out into the surrounding field. From the safety of the darkness, they see flames building. The old wood begins to crack in the rising fire. Suddenly, there is a guttural thud. The cylinder explodes.

The barn's rafters splinter and fall in. A scream of nesting bats scuttle skywards away from the spiralling orange flames.

63

Caitlyn knows about women who've been held captive for years. Imprisoned in cellars. Even locked in wooden crates. She knows of their horrors because Eric told her all about them. Said it would teach her to be careful – remind her to stay safe. The unlearned lesson chills her. Maybe others have suffered her fate, entombed in a thick stone wall, where you can scream your lungs out and never be heard.

Eric's warnings drift back to her. The horror stories he'd thought would keep her safe. Teenager Danielle Cramer from Connecticut, kept in a secret room under a staircase for a year. Nina von Gallwitz, held for 149 days until her parents paid out more than a million Deutschmarks to get her back. Fusako Sano from Japan, kept captive for ten years. An entire decade.

She can remember them all. All their faces. And they were the lucky ones. Eric showed her the long list of Dutch, American, English and Italian women who had not been so fortunate. Ones who had been taken, held and killed, even though ransoms had been paid.

His words come back and haunt her. 'They take you for sex, for money, for torture, even to get revenge on you or your parents. These are dangerous people, Caitlyn. Some of them are insane enough to take you just to become famous. Whatever you do, don't mess with our security.'

But she had done. She screwed up and she can't make it good. She wants to cry. Wants to sob her heart out. But she doesn't. She won't. She tells herself that she never cried during thirty-nine days of *Survivor* and she sure as hell isn't going to start now.

Caitlyn tries to think of something different. She recalls her time on the reality show. The welcome party, the first tasks, the guys who were hot for her. Thirty-nine days, twenty competitors, fifteen episodes that made her a household name. Once she swam naked during the live telecast. It gave the censors a fit. Damned nearly got the whole series scrapped. But it was a ratings blockbuster.

She'd do it again. Any time. Shock and glamour have become her middle names. It almost makes her smile. Even in this dusty crevice of a prison she can still taste the sweetness of her old life – the money, the fame, the controversy caused by her wild spirit. But for how long? she asks herself. How long before the whackballs holding her send her mad?

64

Gideon is down to the last two tapes.

He's watched close to forty and despite the thunderstorm raging in his head, he's determined to view the last of them before turning in.

He slides one into the player and watches his father appear on screen. The young professor doesn't look much older than Gideon is now. After a few seconds, Marie Chase can be heard behind the camera: 'I think it's working, Nate. Yes, yes, the red light is flashing. You can start when you want.'

Nathaniel takes a breath to compose himself and brushes a straggle of windblown hair from his face. He's wearing a thick blue fleece, dark pants and walking boots. There's snow on the ground and an all-too-familiar backdrop. Stonehenge. 'I take you back almost five thousand years,' he announces, sweeping his hand across the landscape. 'Back to the days when our ancestors dug this circular ditch, some three hundred feet in diameter, twenty feet wide and up to seven feet deep.' He squats on the ground and places his hands in a furrow where the ditch had been. 'Beneath this spot, archaeologists found the bones of animals that died two hundred years before this ditch was even dug. Why did our forefathers put them there? Why use a pile of old bones to line a new ditch? The answer of course is that these bones came from special sacrifices to the ancient gods.'

Gideon smiles. His father the self-publicist had been well known for spicing up dull university lectures with his own home movies. On the screen, the young professor leaves the ditch and as he walks the circumference of the stones expounds a now familiar theory about the discovery of more than two hundred human skeletons on the site. 'The seventeenth-century historian John Aubrey found these burned human bones in fifty-six different holes. Were they too offerings to the gods? Was Stonehenge both a crematorium and a temple, a ritual slaughterhouse for celestial gratification?'

Having just read the diaries from a decade later, Gideon finds it strange to watch his father pose the questions in such a sceptical tone. Stranger still to think of what might actually be true. The tape rolls on to the final stage of development: 'Some three thousand years ago, unknown hands moved these bluestones from the Preseli Mountains. We still do not know how they achieved such a feat. They were erected as a circular monument, the entrance aligned towards sunrise at the summer solstice.' Nathaniel walks to the bigger sandstones, his hand stretching to the skies. 'These giant sarsens, some more than three times my height and weighing as much as forty tons. Stood on their ends by incredibly talented ancient builders, they were capped with horizontal sarsens using sophisticated mortise and tenon joints, a technique that seems way before its time.' He walks deeper into the circle. 'Here in the heart of the henge, a horseshoe-shaped arrangement, five pairs of standing sarsens with giant horizontal caps – the trilithons.'

Gideon views the rest of the tape at double and even quadruple speed, making his father comically dash all over the site jerkily pointing out the Heel Stone, the Slaughter Stone and the north-eastern entrance.

He takes a short break, makes a mug of tea and returns to watch the last uncatalogued video. He pulls it from its cardboard sleeve and sees a label in the centre that hasn't been written in his father's faded hand. It reads: 'To Gideon, my loving son and pride and joy.'

He hasn't seen the handwriting in decades but recognises it instantly. It's his mother's.

65

Jimmy Dockery pulls on a Tyvek suit and curses the fact that he's the one who's been called out in the dead of night. It always seems to be him that cops for the worst of jobs, the graveyard shifts with their mundane crime scenes. Any bit of mess – get Jimmy to mop it up. First it was chasing missing persons, sweeping up after some old man's suicide, and now it's a burned-out barn. In his head he's a better investigator than that. If his father, the Deputy Chief, knew the kind of crap they sent him on, he'd sack them all.

Dockery flashes his ID and ducks the fluttering yellow tape. An exhausted-looking PC takes his name and he wanders into the blackened ribs of the barn. Soco arc lights illuminate the charred metal remains of the Campervan. A burned-out replica of the one he saw on the footage he recovered from the service station. The one half the police in the country are looking for. Jimmy picks his way over a non-contamination pathway to the vehicle. Inside, a man and a woman are on their knees inspecting the body.

'Is it the girl?' Jimmy asks. 'The one who's missing.'

The question bounces off the back of Home Office pathologist Lisa Hamilton.

She recognises his voice. 'No, it's a man – and *Sergeant* – just a word of warning, don't crowd me, don't press me, don't annoy me and don't *on any account* mess up my crime scene.'

'Understood.' It's water off a duck's back to Jimmy. Everyone is always giving him a list of don'ts. Besides, he has a soft spot for Lisa. Even at two in the morning, she triggers something primeval inside him.

From over her shoulder, he can see that the corpse looks like badly barbecued meat – a sickening mix of pinks and blacks. Tattered remnants of clothes are stuck to charred bone and tarry puddles of human fat are spread on what's left of the base board of the Camper. Jimmy notices part of the vehicle's metal frame is bent upwards 'There been some kind of explosion?'

'Gas canister by the looks of it,' says a young SOCO, a spotty-faced lad with spiky hair. 'From the blast pattern, it seems like it blew under the cooking ring.'

Jimmy moves around them and scans the rest of the

burned-out vehicle. 'So no sign of the girl?' he calls over his shoulder. 'You sure bits of her aren't in here?'

Lisa Hamilton cranes her neck upwards from her crouch. 'You seriously suggesting I might have missed a whole woman?'

He feels stupid. 'Of course not. It's just that we're all going crazy trying to find her.'

The pathologist continues scowling. 'This isn't about any missing woman. Right now my concern is this man, here. And I'm trying to afford him the dignity and respect he deserves by properly investigating his death.'

Jimmy gets the message and backs off. Other SOCOs are hard at work bagging and tagging whatever can be picked or scraped from the floor and walls. He sees a stack of paper bags containing a broken tumbler, burned saucepan, an empty vodka bottle and blackened cutlery and crockery.

A female SOCO appears at his shoulder with a plastic evidence bag. 'We discovered a driving licence and hire documents in the glove compartment. They're smoke-damaged but intact.'

Jimmy holds the bag up to a light so he can read through the covering. The writing is just about legible. 'Edward Jacob Timberland.' As he says it, he feels a wave of sadness. Putting a name to the body always alters things. He calls towards the pathologist. 'Prof, I'm going to go back to the station. When will your report be ready?'

She doesn't break from her examination. 'After breakfast.

I'll mail through an outline and be available mid-morning if you want me to run through it in person.'

'Thanks.' He'd like that. A nice chat over coffee. Who knows what might come up. Jimmy raises a hand as he leaves. 'Goodnight everyone.'

There are muffled replies as he heads out of the barn.

'Good *morning*,' shouts the professor playfully. 'Get your facts right, detective, it's already morning.'

66

Gideon can feel his heart thump as he slides the old VHS tape into the player.

The woman who comes on screen is barely recognisable as the mother he loved. He expected to see the beauty from the video in Venice. Laughing. Vivacious. Full of life. But it's not to be.

She sits in a sick bed, resting against a plump white mountain of pillows and from the angle of the camera it looks like she's filming herself. The skeleton-thin face, the prematurely white frizzy hair and bloodshot gaze are cameos of pain.

Marie Chase is close to death as she smiles at her son through the TV monitor and through the ages. 'Giddy, my darling. I'm going to miss you so much. I'm hoping that you will have a long and very happy life and know what a joy it is to be a parent. Once you were born, my life felt complete. I never wanted for anything more than you, me and your father to be happy together.' She fights back her emotions. 'Darling, that's not to be. I don't have much time now, but there's something I have to tell you so I leave you this message for when you're older, old enough to see me in this state and not be frightened.'

Gideon has to wipe tears from his face. He realises for the first time that he'd never been allowed to see his mother in her final days, in the period when she wasted away so painfully. Marie Chase is crying too as she reaches out to her only child. 'Giddy, no one but you *has* ever or *will* ever see this recording. Not your father. Not anyone. Just you. I have something I must tell you personally and your father respects that. He is a good man and he loves you more than you know. I hope you look after each other when I'm gone.' She reaches to the bedside cabinet and raises a glass of water to her parched lips, then forces another brave smile.

Gideon smiles back. He misses her. More than he has ever admitted to himself.

Marie Chase completes her message from beyond the grave, her final words to the son she never saw grow up. Then she tells him what she always told him at night as she switched his bedside light off and kissed his head: 'There's nothing to be afraid of, sweetheart. I love you and will always be there for you.'

The tape turns into a snowstorm of grey fuzz and spins

noisily into rewind. Gideon is left gazing at the blank screen, his mind still fizzing from the shock of the secret that she just shared with him.

67

It's three a.m. when Jimmy Dockery turns up at Megan Baker's desk clutching a chipped mug full of steaming coffee. 'You got a minute, boss?'

'Sure.' She waves to a seat. 'What's on your mind?'

He sits, looking exceptionally tired. 'This lad that died in the Camper.'

'Timberland.'

'Yeah.'

'Don't worry. I'm not going to ask you to talk to the parents. The Met can do it. They made contact after we pulled their son's Amex bills.'

'It's not that.'

'What, then?'

He blows out a long breath and takes a steadying sip of coffee. 'The fire scene was a mess. Parts missing from the body, probably blown off, skin melted. And his head was just a big black ball. It was all wrong.'

She understands. He's badly shaken and doesn't want to talk to male colleagues about how it's affected him. 'Do you want me to fix for you to see the psychiatrist?'

He looks aghast.

'Jimmy, when I was training, I saw a guy hit by a train. A suicide. I couldn't sleep for days. Eventually, I found talking to a shrink really helped me.'

'Thanks, but I didn't mean that. I meant *the scene* was wrong. Wrong for what was supposed to have gone on.'

She's intrigued. 'How so?'

He suddenly wonders if he's going to make a fool of himself. 'You'll see the prof's report in a few hours so maybe it's worth waiting until then.'

'No, go on, Jim. If you've got a theory, a gut feeling, I want to hear it.'

'All right.' He rests his elbows on her desk. 'Location, location, location. Right?'

She looks confused.

'That's what estate agents say is the single most important thing.'

She nods, still not sure where he's going.

He tries to explain. 'So you've got a Campervan, a rugged little home from home. You can go anywhere in it. It'll survive whatever the elements throw at it. But you choose to park up *inside* a barn. A building so far off the beaten track, I bet most locals don't even know it's there.'

She gets his drift. 'Strange, I grant you. A barn isn't the right location for a Camper.'

He relaxes a little. 'That's the first thing, okay. So this Timberland guy was a posh nob. A rich guy. Son of a lord, right?'

'Right.'

'So if a guy like that hires a vintage Camper to take his new girlfriend out, what else might he bring along for the trip?'

She thinks about it. 'Soft drinks for the journey. Maybe snacks, probably food. I imagine champagne, maybe a bottle of rosé or a chilled white, some decent glasses.' She gets into her stride. 'Picnic blankets, hamper, sunglasses, maybe a surprise present for her.'

Jimmy smiles. 'Fine. I didn't get as far as you did but look at the list of stuff forensics identified.' He slides a piece of newly printed A4 across her desk and watches as she reads it. 'What you'll see on there,' he adds, 'is a dented can with burned bits of beans inside, fragments of silver tin foil – probably from a chocolate bar – two empty vodka bottles and some staple foodstuffs like bread and butter. Nothing you wouldn't expect. He probably bought some of it, but most of it is likely to have been freebies from the gift hamper that comes with the rental.' He jabs a finger at the bottom of the sheet. 'The little fridge in there protected what was inside from the blast. So here we have some fancy ice cream and a full bottle of Bollinger champagne.'

'What are you getting at?'

'The vodka. Two bottles. To have got through that but not opened the champagne that's hard-core drinking. Surely if you buy the Bolly, that's what you're going to open first?'

Megan jumps to her own conclusion. 'It's hard to start a fire with champagne, but not with vodka. You think the spirits were used as an accelerant?'

He shrugs. 'I'm not even sure you can set fire to champagne, can you?'

'I don't know. She looks off into the distance, remembers another world, her wedding when she last drank champagne. I'm not going to waste any trying to find out though.' She thinks about his hunch. 'You're right, the vodka bottles and the champagne don't make sense. Nor does parking a van inside a barn. And the fact that the girl is still missing makes me even more suspicious.'

Jimmy swings a chair alongside Megan's desk. 'Do you think maybe the two of them had a fight over something and she cracked him one, a bit harder than she meant, then panicked?'

Megan shakes her head. 'Not her. Remember who she is. The daughter of the Vice President wouldn't behave like a halfwit and try to torch the scene, she'd have called Daddy for help.'

He sees her point. 'And I guess it doesn't explain the vodka bottles, either.'

'Quite. What I'm wondering though, is why she wasn't in the Camper with him.'

'They had a row and she stormed off?'

'Doesn't work for me. If she'd have done that, she'd have called home. This isn't a girl who's going to catch a train back to London.'

They sit in silence, both cycling the same thoughts. Jake Timberland is dead because someone killed him. Caitlyn Lock is missing because someone took her. Find Caitlyn and you catch the killer. Hopefully, before he kills again.

68

Serpens and Musca drive separately to Octans' place. They shower while Volans puts their clothes and shoes in two separate sacks, ready to be incinerated later that morning. They put on the fresh clothing and footwear that's been laid out for them.

Plates of cold pizza and cans of chilled beer mark their places at the card table. None of them speak about what has happened. They play poker, gin rummy and crib until streaks of daylight seep through the dusty window of the backroom. Four old mates on a boys' late night out.

Grabb hasn't touched a bite, though he's drinking like a Viking. Disposing of the body has cemented his guilt about the killing. He only cracked the lad with a small rock, no bigger than the palm of his hand. It shouldn't have killed him. The kid must have had some skull defect or something wrong with his brain.

But Serpens can't escape it. He's a killer and it doesn't sit easy. If he gets caught, it will be the end of his parents. They're in their eighties, barely mobile, living in sheltered accommodation. They stuck by him when he went to prison. His mother thinks he's stayed out of trouble since then. Gone straight. Grown up. Become someone they are proud of.

'Do you want another card or are you going to stick?'

Serpens looks at Musca and throws his hand in. 'I have to

go and get some rest.' He turns to the other two men. 'Thanks for this, for the food and everything.'

Musca gets up, follows him to the door. 'You okay to drive? Do you want me to take you home?'

He shakes his head. 'I'm fine.'

Something has broken between them. Musca feels it. 'Why don't you come back and stay with me for the rest of the day? It might help you.'

'I'm fine, I told you.' There's tension in his voice.

They briefly lock eyes, then Serpens opens the front door and walks out into the cool light of dawn.

Musca follows. 'Hang on.'

Serpens is past hanging on. He zaps open his Warrior.

Musca halts him with a firm hand on his shoulder. 'Wait a minute, we really need to—'

The punch Serpens throws is fast. It's one that's been in his mind for three months. Borne out of frustration, nurtured by resentment, unleashed with anger. It hits Musca smack in the mouth, sends him staggering backwards and falling on the pavement.

By the time Musca puts a hand to his lips and sees the blood, the Warrior has already spun rubber and gassed exhaust down the street.

Octans and Volans stand in the doorway looking worried. The noise, the altercation. The scene may well have been witnessed. But they're nowhere near as worried as Musca. He knows Serpens is going to be a problem. A *big* problem.

69

Chief Constable Alan Hunt likes his desk tidy. A tidy desk is a tidy mind. Always end the day with it clear, no business unsettled. John Rowlands, who is sat opposite him, would say it's because he came up the modern way. Masters degree in law. Fast-tracked through the ranks. Chairman of the Association of Chief Police Officers. Home Office golden boy with political nous and a financial expertise at stretching budgets.

Sat next to the Chief Super and across from Hunt is the crumpled shape of Deputy Chief Constable Greg Dockery. It's six a.m. and there is only one piece of outstanding business ruining the otherwise clear slab of beech between the three men: a large blow-up of Caitlyn Lock.

Hunt's small and tidy hands touch the photo. 'So where is she, John? Why haven't we heard anything from whoever has her?'

Rowlands scratches grey stubble peppering his chin. 'I expect the kidnappers to make contact later today. They seem to be professional. Happy enough to kill the boyfriend to take her. Now they have her, I'm sure they'll issue a ransom demand.'

'I agree,' says Dockery. 'I would take the silence to mean they've been busy. Probably monitoring the situation. Watching how we react to her disappearance. They may well have moved the girl by another vehicle to a safe location.'

Rowlands taps his watch ominously. 'The first forty-eight applies to kidnapping more than most.'

Dockery sees the Chief frown. The boss's fast-tracked ascendancy evidently excluded force jargon. 'John means the first forty-eight hours, sir. Statistically, our chances of solving a major crime – especially kidnapping or murder – are halved if we don't catch the offender in the first two days.'

Hunt smiles. 'I only believe in good statistics, Gregory, you should know that.' There's polite laughter around the table, then he adds, 'After I got your call about the Timberland boy, I rang Sebastian Ingram at the Home Office to update him. They're putting the SAS on standby and want the Yard to send over a team from its Specialist Crime Directorate.'

Dockery knows better than to doubt the wisdom of such a move. Rowlands is less diplomatic. 'Sir, this is *our* inquiry. We are more than capable of handling it. I've had direct experience of hostage negotiations.'

The Chief tries to placate him. 'It's not about ability, John; it's about political responsibilities and budgets. We are scratching for funds to keep traffic cars on the road. An investigation like this could bleed us dry for the rest of the financial year.'

Dockery tries to sweeten the pill. 'We'll make sure you stay involved. Whoever they dump on us. He's going to have to work every bit as long and hard as you and your team.'

The desk phone rings. They all know a call this early won't be good news. Hunt takes it and briefly talks to his secretary before being put through to someone important enough to make him sit up straight and grow tense.

After less than a minute, he replaces the phone on its cradle and coolly passes on his news. 'Gentlemen, Vice President Lock and his ex-wife have just boarded a private jet in New York and will be with us shortly.'

70

Stripped to the waist and barefoot in black tracksuit bottoms, Draco exercises in the purpose-built gym at his lavish country home. The long, mirrored-walls indulge a near-constant checking of the muscles he's painstakingly crafted. He looks ten, maybe twenty years younger than his actual fifty. Serpens is on his mind. A man he never liked. One he is sure is true to his star name – the snake.

A few metres away, his burner rings. The call he's been waiting for. The update. He abandons his sixth mile on the treadmill, guns down the music channel on a sixty-inch plasma and answers it. 'Everything go all right?'

'Not everything.' Musca sounds tense. 'We got the job done as planned but our man has fallen ill.'

Draco understands the code. 'Anything to seriously concern us?' He picks a white hand towel off a bench and mops sweat from his face.

'Possibly, yes.'

Draco drops the towel and reaches for a water bottle. 'Where is he now?'

'At home.'

'Check on him. See if he's feeling any better.'

Musca rubs his jaw, nursing the spot where Serpens punched him. 'I'll wait until lunchtime, let him sleep a little, then I'll go round and have a chat.'

'Don't leave it too long.' Draco thinks on it a second. 'Best not to take any unnecessary chances at the moment. If he's *really* sick, we need to find a cure. A permanent one.'

71

Gideon is almost too exhausted to leave his bed. His mother's video message and her goodbye secret were the final straw. Grief, insomnia and emotional turmoil are now all taking their toll. First there had been his father's revelations – the Sacreds, the Followers, the sacrifices. Then cancer. The CLL that killed his mother. Then her private words to him. Arrows in his heart.

He heads downstairs and triggers a nerve-jangling burst of bells. Still in shock, he turns off the alarm system that he'd forgotten he'd set the night before. Heart still pounding, he makes a mug of dark tea and sits by the kitchen window to watch the last of the sunrise.

Briefly, as golden light comes over the trees and flower

beds, he forgets the personal horrors in his life. Then, when the tea is gone and the distraction over, the worries come back. Are his genes ticking time-bombs, primed to explode like his mother's did? Or did the strange childhood baptism his father performed with water from the stones cure him? He remembers the words in the journals: 'I will willingly give my own blood, my own life. I only hope it is worthy. Worthy enough to change things. To alter the fate that I know awaits my poor, motherless son. I put my trust in the Sacreds, in the bond I make with them, in the clear blood of mine that I pledge to purify that of my child's.'

Gideon wearily trudges back upstairs to the diaries. They lie strewn where he left them, open at pages that seemed significant. So many refer to the stones. Stonehenge, a site his father published books on, its links to the vernal equinox, the earth's precessional cycle, its mystical connections with the celestial equator, Plato, the Great Sphinx.

Mumbo-jumbo. That's what he always felt it was. Yet some of the fragments he's discovered are coming together, forming a path like crazy paving that leads to the heart of his strange and troubled childhood. His father forced him to learn Greek, wrote codes in it and gave him the worst birthday gift a ten-year-old could ever get – a copy of Plato's *Republic*. Not the racing bike he'd lobbied for but instead a wedge of impenetrable philosophy about happiness, justice and the fitness of people to rule.

Looking at the diaries, he sees the old philosopher's shadows in his father's words. Passages emphasise the role of the Sacreds in celestial mechanics and the Platonic year – the time required for a single complete cycle of the precession of the equinoxes. In hard numbers, about 25,800 years. About the same amount of time Gideon thinks it will take him to fully decode and understand everything his father has written.

72

Chief Constable Alan Hunt heads up the eight a.m. press conference. News of Jake Timberland's death and the imminent arrival of the girl's parents have ratcheted up the pressure. He can't let this go wrong. Not when he's in the running for the Met Commissioner's job. He knows that how he handles this inquiry is going to determine whether or not he gets the job.

Reporters settle around a well-planted forest of TV cameras and radio microphones. Flanked by Dockery and Rowlands, he taps the desk microphone and hears thunder crackle across the hall. He learned long ago of the benefits of knowing the sound levels before you speak. 'Ladies and gentlemen, thank you for attending at such short notice. At two o'clock this morning, my officers discovered the body of a thirty-one-year-old male in a burned-out vehicle. A vehicle we had been seeking to locate in relation to the disappearance of Caitlyn Lock, who most of you know is the daughter of Kylie Lock and Vice President Thom Lock.'

The Chief pauses to give the print journalists a chance to get their notes up to speed. 'Given this development, I have asked that our force receive the assistance of expert officers from the Metropolitan Police.' He raises a cautionary hand. 'I need to stress to you that these are preventative and cautionary measures. At this moment we have no indication of Miss Lock's whereabouts and have received no communication from her or anyone else to suggest that her life is in danger. Operational command of the inquiry is currently in the hands of Chief Superintendent Rowlands, reporting directly to Deputy Chief Constable Dockery. They are ready – within reason – to answer your questions, but first they have a request for your assistance.'

DCS Rowlands clears his throat, picks up a press pack and holds it high so everyone can see the photograph of Caitlyn on its front. 'You are all going to receive one of these handouts. Inside is a DVD containing video footage and still photographs of Miss Lock, the man she travelled down from London with, Jacob Timberland, and the VW Campervan they were driving. We are interested in any sightings of this van or these people over the last twenty-four hours. No matter how trivial people think it is, we urge them to come forward and tell us exactly what they saw.'

A reporter jumps in. 'Can you confirm that the dead man is Jake Timberland, the son of Lord and Lady Timberland?'

Rowlands bats him off. 'The family of the deceased has not yet formally identified the body, so that is not something I am prepared to do.'

'Can you confirm that the dead man was murdered?'

Again he reacts cautiously. 'I am yet to receive the full report from the Home Office pathologist who carried out the post-mortem examination. I won't prejudge her findings.'

'Where was the dead man found?'

Rowlands hesitates. 'The exact location is something we are not currently prepared to disclose. I hope you understand there are aspects of this case that we need to hold back for operational reasons.'

An old hack with skin the colour of bacon sniffs an opening. 'Is that because you fear Caitlyn Lock has been abducted and only the kidnappers know the location of where they murdered her boyfriend?'

It's an astute question and too close to the truth for comfort. Greg Dockery steps in to field it. 'I have to emphasise what DCS Rowlands has said. The investigation is in its early stages and there is information that we need to hold back for operational reasons. We need you to respect that and help us find Caitlyn. You won't help her, us, or even yourselves with speculative journalism.'

Hunt senses that the reporters are going to keep on poking and prodding unless they get something juicier. 'Ladies and gentlemen, I can't overstate the importance of your role in this inquiry. Responsible reporting is essential. There may be an innocent reason behind Miss Lock's disappearance, there may not. If she is being detained against her will, those people will be reading everything you write and listening to everything you say. That is why we have to be circumspect. At this point that is all we have to say. Thank you for your attendance.' He allows a fractional pause for unrest to grow, then gives them what he knows will be their headline lead: 'Later this morning, I will be meeting in person with Vice President Lock and Kylie Lock, who are flying in from New York as we speak. I hope to have good news for them. I hope we will have knowledge of their daughter's whereabouts and if not, I hope to reassure them that the force and the people of Wiltshire, and the government and people of the United Kingdom, are doing everything within their powers to find her and bring her safely home. Thank you again for your attendance.' He stands, grabs his papers from the desk and walks slowly and confidently off the conference stage.

73

News that the Met has been drafted in doesn't go down well at the post-press conference team briefing.

Jude Tompkins pulls Megan aside at the end. 'The Chief Super has just talked to Barney Gibson from the Specialist Crime Directorate. He'll be here in an hour with a couple of others and they'll take over operational control. John will report to them and I will report to him. I need you to go to see the pathologist, get a briefing on Timberland's death. Once you've reported back, you're off the case.'

Megan is stunned. 'What?'

'Did you mean, *pardon, ma'am*?'

'I thought Rowlands said I was doing a good job.'

'You were. Right up until the point you wanted to dance in the spotlight. Now I need you to go and carry out my orders, not question them. Warren and Jenkins have already been reassigned.'

Megan manages a polite nod before turning away and mouthing a silent stream of obscenities that doesn't stop until she's back in CID.

Jimmy Dockery calls to her from his desk 'Boss—'

She doesn't let him finish. 'Get your coat, Jimmy, you've pulled.' She grabs her jacket off the back of a chair and her car keys off the desk.

74

Serpens is in meltdown.

The guilt is unbearable. Images flash relentlessly in his tortured mind. The young man dismembered and minced at the abattoir. The vodka-soaked body set ablaze in the Campervan in the barn. There is no escape from it all.

Despite this being the busiest time of the year for the security company where he works, he calls in sick. Head pounding, he guns up the old Mitsubishi and drives. He has to get away from it all. Find some peace.

An hour later he's in Bath. A well-scrubbed tourist city where he holidayed as a child. A place with happy memories. Maybe enough for him to come to peace with himself.

He parks at the Southgate Centre and buys a six pack of lager and half a litre of Scotch. Wise old locals glare soberly at him as he drinks while he wanders. By the time he's circled Grand Parade and Boat Stall Lane, the beer is finished. He takes a leak in bushes off Orange Grove and meanders east towards the banks of the river.

Resting in the cool shade, his back against a tree by the water, closes his tired eyes. A monstrous mosaic of sounds and sights forms in his head – the empty noise of the rolling bottle that Musca threw into the Camper, the rough scratch of a match, the dull boom that rocked his heart and the fireball that roared through the Camper, splitting the old barn's parched rafters.

Serpens unscrews the top of the Scotch and takes a swig as hot as the flames that haunt him. The more it burns the better. He swallows it down in painful gulps. He killed the guy. Cracked him with a rock and brought his life to an end. One minute the poor sap is on top of the world, making out with his girl, then thwack, he's dead and his corpse is about to be burned to cinders.

Serpens' phone rings. It's not a shock, it's been going all morning. He knows who it is and what they want. He pulls it from his pocket and hurls it into the river. *Plosh*. Makes him smile for the first time in days. He takes another jolt of booze and coughs. It must have gone down the wrong way.

Nearly drowned himself. Drowned in Scotch, now that would be a fitting way to end it all, wouldn't it?

Noisy children run past him. A red-faced young boy chases an older girl who's teasing him. Life in the making. He gets groggily to his feet, watches them spin around a tree, giggle and head back to a tartan picnic blanket, where a woman is laying out cling-filmed sandwiches and cans of pop. Happiness. An alien world to him.

Serpens gulps more of the whisky. Pours it down his throat until it kicks back like water in a blocked drain. He drops the bottle to the balding grass, spreads his arms wide and falls like a felled tree into the fast flow of the Avon.

75

Under the brutal glare of the autopsy lights, Jake Timberland's body looks even worse than Jimmy Dockery remembers it. What's left of the fire-blackened and blast-damaged corpse has been opened up and the internal organs extracted and weighed.

Professor Lisa Hamilton reads the minds of the two detectives opposite her. 'It wasn't the fire or the explosion that killed him. The blast blew out some of the blaze in the van interior so there was enough viable tissue, organs and fluid left to establish that he'd been lying dead on his left side for about ten hours before his body was burned.'

Megan double-checks the time. 'Ten hours?'

'About that.' Lisa explains her approximation. 'After death, gravity takes over. Blood stops pumping from the heart and as it settles it marks the tissue.' She gestures to the splayed corpse. 'He was moved a long time after his heart had stopped beating. We know this because of the extent and position that the blood stained the skin. Somebody moved him from the position he'd originally been left in after death and laid him out in the Camper to make it look like he'd had an accident. Unfortunately, they dropped him on the wrong side, his right, with his back slightly raised. Entirely inconsistent with the evidence provided by post-mortem staining.'

She moves around the autopsy table and glides a hand over Jake's grey torso. 'The cause of death is a massive heart attack, brought on by a heavy single blow to the back of his skull with some form of improvised weapon. I found particles of soil and some pretty dense rock embedded in the bone.'

Jimmy paints the scene. 'So, he's hit on the back of the head outside somewhere, then shifted back into his van and laid out on the floor by the cooker. The offender sets the Camper on fire to make it look like our friend here had been on the booze, fallen over and caused the blaze.'

Lisa nods. 'Almost. Remember, I said that there was post-mortem staining on his left side because that's how he'd been lying for ten hours.'

Megan understands her point. 'What you're saying is, whoever killed him spent those ten hours working out what to do. *Eventually*, they came up with the plan to put the

213

Camper in the barn, move him around to look like he'd fallen and then torch everything.'

'Exactly. Another thing: although forensics found two empty vodka bottles near the body, there were no traces of metabolised alcohol in his system. His blood showed only tiny amounts of ethanol but the liver was clean. This is entirely inconsistent with him consuming vast amounts of spirits.' Jimmy is about to ask a question, but Lisa doesn't let him. 'Examination of lung tissue showed no evidence of smoke inhalation. No particles, no tissue damage. Nothing. He'd clearly stopped breathing before the fire had started.'

'The whole scene was faked,' concludes Megan. 'Credit where it's due, Jimmy, it's exactly as you said it was.'

'Really?' says Lisa, expressing genuine shock.

'Really,' repeats Jimmy, proudly.

76

The Master keeps his phone call with Draco as short as possible. 'Have you solved our operational problem?'

'Unfortunately not. Our man wasn't available.'

'Uncontactable?'

'I am afraid so. He isn't on any of his numbers. I've left messages but he hasn't returned them. And he phoned in sick at work.'

'And do you think he is?'

'No. I've been to his house and he's not there. Nor is his vehicle.'

The Master tries to be positive. 'He has been under stress lately. It could be that he felt the need to get away, clear his head. Would that fit his character?'

Draco is not sure. 'It's possible. I have people asking his friends where he might have gone. We're also trying to get one of them to reach out to him. Perhaps he'll return their calls.'

'Good.'

Draco feels the need to reassure his leader. 'We'll find him.'

'I am banking on you doing exactly that. Hold for a moment.' He pauses while an assistant presents him with a file of documents for signature and in a hushed voice reminds him of his lunch appointment with a county judge. He waits until the assistant has left before picking up the conversation with Draco. 'And on the *other* matter, I have a plan to give us some breathing space. Can you meet me?'

'Of course. What time?'

The Master checks the calendar on his desk. 'Three p.m. I'll have about an hour. Don't be late.'

77

Megan and Jimmy park a mile from the burned-out barn. It's in the middle of the largest area of chalky grassland in north-west Europe. A bleak and isolated table of endless land.

Down in a dip dotted with wild flowers they finally see the charred hulk, an ugly black wound on Salisbury Plain's soft green skin. Megan points to tracks through the grass. Vehicle marks and footmarks heading to and from the barn. 'Have we got lifts of any tyre prints?'

'I think so.'

She scowls at him. 'You're a DS; you either *know so* or it *isn't so*. Make sure we have them.' They walk on a few steps and she sees he's hurt by her sudden frostiness. She stops. With time and patience she knows he could become a good copper. 'Look around Jimmy and you'll hear the grass tell you stories, tales of who's been coming and going.' She leans close, so that his eyes are guided along her pointing finger. 'Over there – those deep depressions are where the fire trucks came in.' She swings him round and points again. 'Over here – indentations from at least three different kinds of vehicles, much lighter ones than the first. I'd take a guess at some of these coming from our Camper and maybe two other vehicles.'

'Why two others?'

She wishes she had a tape measure to help explain. 'Look

at the depth and the width of each track. This gives you the thickness of the tyres and indicates the length of the wheel-bases. Do you see now that they're different?'

He does. 'So two cars. That would mean at least two people.'

'Good. Get traffic to carry out a thorough inspection. SOCOs will have looked at the marks already but traffic are best at this type of thing.' She squats down and gazes across the grooves in the long grass. 'Question: why would these people be travelling separately rather than together?'

He looks up and down the tracks, then hazards a guess. 'One guy stays in the barn minding the Camper and our deceased. The other one goes away to do something, maybe get the vodka, arrives later?'

'Good.' She gives him an impressed nod as she stands again. 'Let's go further. What does that tell you?'

He's confused. 'What do you mean?'

'What does that tell you about the *relationship* between the two men?'

Jimmy's lost. Behavioural science is foreign to him.

Megan helps out. 'One of them is a doer, the other is a teller. The guy who stays with the body is the doer. It's the worst and riskiest of jobs. He was told to do it by the teller. This is evidence of rank, a pecking order, a structure that those two parties accept.' Her eyes wander to the massive black wound in the earth and scabs of charred barn timbers. 'Of course, it might be *two* doers at the scene and *two* tellers arriving later.'

'Organised crime?'

She shrugs. 'Of sorts. Just how organised, we're still to find out.'

78

By mid-morning Gideon needs a break. He makes a short trip to the shops and returns with a newspaper, two-litre carton of milk and stack of ready-meals. He wolfs down a greasy, microwaved lasagne then resumes his decoding of the diaries.

Very quickly it becomes apparent that the more his father learned of the Followers the more he was drawn into their ways: 'I have dispensed with my watch, such a crude instrument. My world is to be governed by an older way, one calibrated to the spiritual: sidereal time, the rule of the great astronomers, the natural instrument that we use to track the stars that guided them and their learning. The real importance of the sidereal zodiac has become known to me, the significant alignments of the great signs with the galactic equator.'

The words are as difficult to digest as the lasagne. His mind drifts back to his childhood. His father had taken him into the garden late at night and pointed out the stars. He'd named various constellations and spoken of the orbits of the sun and the moon. Magical stuff.

Across the room, beneath a dust cover in the far corner, he spots his father's old telescope. How had he not seen it before? It's shrouded in a polythene cover yellowed with age. Gideon bends down and unwraps it like he's been given a surprise present.

The telescope is a Meade. So expensive, so prized, that his father never let him use it unless he was there right by him. It was an indulgence Marie would never have allowed. Thousands of pounds' worth of reflector optics, almost observatory standard, with zero image-shift microfocuser and special mounts for cameras.

As he stands again, he cracks the back of his head on the low roof above. He gives his skull a rub and glares accusingly at the ceiling panel. It looks odd. He presses hard on it and it pops loose at the bottom. As Gideon lets go, the panel swings down on a hinge and reveals a side-sliding window and beyond it a long, flat roof.

Gideon twists a key, slides the window back and climbs out into bright sun. The ledge is bitumen, flat and turns a corner. He walks it gingerly around the hidden room to a wide open space.

Right above the centre of the house, on an area between two red-tile apexes, is a small wooden shed about ten feet long by six feet wide and five feet high. It's so peculiar that he immediately recognises it. One of his father's handmade observatory boxes. A shelter from the wind and rain, equipped with hinged roof.

Inside he finds his father's things. They are spread

everywhere. An old camping kettle, cups, tea bags, pens, paper, astronomical charts, reference books and photographs. Lots of photographs. On the walls and on the floor.

It is easy to imagine the old man sitting here stargazing. Lost in his own world. Drawing up charts. Gideon unrolls one of them. It shows the sun aligning with the galactic equator at the time of the summer solstice. He finds another. A depiction of the position of key planets at the point of the winter solstice.

He looks at the photographs pinned to the walls. An exhibition that he's never seen by an artist he barely knew. There are dozens of Polaris, enough to trigger memories of his father explaining the role of the great North Star, how over the ages its position as the leading light for astronomers and sailors passed from one star to another.

He studies pictures of another star cluster: Pleiades. The Seven Sisters. A line from Byron comes to him: 'Many a night I saw Pleiads, rising thro' the mellow shade, Glitter like a swarm of fireflies tangled in a silver braid.'

In a nostalgic mood he sits on the floor and slowly sifts the photographs and charts. And then he sees it. A single image that shatters the pleasant moment. Stonehenge.

It's a high-angle, side-on shot that shows the circle, not as it is now, but as it must have been when the ancients first completed it. Gideon looks closer. Faint white lines run from the giant stones to pricks of white above them. Gradually he realises what he's looking at. Stars and constellations. The stones are aligned with planetary and stellar movements. Thin lines divide the chart into four. Tiny letters mark out north, south, east and west. Two more faded words – one at the top and one at the bottom – are barely visible. Earth. Heaven.

Gideon feels cool air prickle the back of his neck. The Followers evidently didn't just believe Stonehenge was central to all their lives. They believed it was much more.

The centre of the sidereal zodiac.

The centre of the entire universe.

79

By the time Megan and Jimmy leave the burned-out barn, the roads have started to jam with cars crawling towards Stonehenge. Megan curses the pre-solstice traffic. They get back to HQ an hour later than she hoped. She immediately calls her ex to check on Sammy.

'How's it going?' Adam sounds surprisingly chatty.

'Good.' She plays with the wire on the phone. 'Or at least I thought it was until a few hours ago. I'm off the inquiry.'

'Why?'

'Her Majesty Jude Tompkins, that's why.'

'Seriously?' He sounds sympathetic. 'What's going on? They scaling the case down?'

'No. Just the opposite. They're bringing in bigwigs from

the Met. No room for yours truly. Just as it was getting interesting.'

'You got a lead?'

'Not on the girl, but the boyfriend's death is now officially a murder. Pathologist confirmed it.'

Adam tries to be helpful. 'Look Meg, if you want me to have Sammy tonight, I don't mind. If you think some more time will get you back on the case, then I'm more than happy to have her.'

'You sure?'

'Totally. I love having her stay during the week.'

Adam has Sammy every other weekend. That's the agreement. The routine. She wonders if he's soft-soaping her for some ulterior motive. 'What's the catch? Because if you think I'm going to alter visiting and custody arrangements, I'm not.'

'Don't be cynical,' he snaps. 'I was just offering to help.'

She sees the door of opportunity closing. 'Then okay, thanks. Having her tonight would really be a big help.'

'Great. I'll take her to KFC.'

'Don't you dare.'

They both hang up smiling.

Jimmy puts a mug of black tea down in front of her. 'Don't know how you can drink this stuff without milk.'

'Like everything else, you get used to it.' She leans back in her chair and checks her computer for case updates. She clicks an icon and watches a message pop open.

'Yes! Yes! Yes! Thank you God.'

'What?' Jimmy leans in to read her screen.

'Records found a match for the fingerprints SOCOs lifted from the Camper.' She jabs at the monitor. 'Prints from the handle of the side door and from the interior side of a window belong to one Sean Elliott Grabb. He's got spent convictions for burglary and assault.'

'And a lot of explaining to do,' says Jimmy.

80

Megan feels like she's shaking hands with a giant. The grip crushing her fingers belongs to the new man in charge, Metropolitan Police Commander Barney Gibson, from the formed Specialist Crime Directorate.

'Take a seat,' he says with a deceptively gentle smile. 'And tell us about the autopsy.'

Megan sits at a table already supporting the elbows of Jude Tompkins, the Head of CID John Rowlands and Gibson's number two, Stewart Willis. She knows this is her last chance to get back on the case. 'Sir, the post-mortem examination was performed by Professor Lisa Hamilton. She puts the time of death at somewhere around ten hours *before* Jake Timberland's body was burned in the Camper. Her findings mean that the blaze was staged to make it look like he'd been killed in a drink-related accident. He hadn't.' She slides a full copy of the post-mortem examination across the table. 'This report clearly indicates that Timberland had been murdered.'

Gibson speed-reads the first page 'Cause of death?'

'It's on the next page, sir. Blunt trauma and heart attack. He was hit on the back of the head with something heavy like a rock.'

'*Not* a rock but something *like* a rock?' He glares at Megan.

'It *may* have been a rock, sir. It certainly wasn't a brick or a hammer but it could have been a boulder or stone.'

'I see.' He reads a little more of the report then looks up. 'The professor mentions soil and grit samples embedded in the skull. Do we have anything back from the lab to suggest where these might have come from?'

'No, sir. But I believe them to be from Stonehenge.'

Gibson seems surprised. 'Why?'

'The solstice, sir. I think it's reasonable to assume that Timberland hired the van to take Lock to see the sunrise there. They would have arrived in the early hours of the morning. Which is the time I think they encountered their attackers and the time Professor Hamilton cited as his TOD. It's possible that Timberland tried to stop Lock being abducted and in the struggle he was killed.'

'Many things are *possible*, Detective Inspector.' Gibson looks towards his DCS. 'Stewart?'

Willis weighs up Megan with his tiny brown eyes. 'Kidnapping someone like Caitlyn Lock takes careful planning, long-term surveillance and expert execution. We're

224

talking about the Vice President's daughter. The type of people involved in that kind of swoop and snatch operation come with full military training and automatic weapons. They don't come empty handed and hit people with "something like a rock".'

Gibson gives Megan a judgemental stare. 'Anything else, DI Baker?'

She feels humiliated and intimidated. She knows she has one last chance to change their minds about her. 'Yes, there is, sir. SOCOs found fingerprints on the door handle and a window of the Camper. They fit a local criminal.' She glances directly at Willis. 'A *petty* local criminal called Sean Grabb from Winterbourne Stoke. His home is not far from the henge.'

Gibson looks to Rowlands. 'Can you have someone check this man Grabb out? If he *is* as the DI suggests, he may simply have come across the Camper by mistake.' The commander looks back at Megan. 'It's possible your *petty* criminal was lifting tools from barns and sheds and he opened the Camper out of curiosity and got a nasty surprise.'

'Many things are possible,' says Rowlands, pointedly.

Megan sees an opening in the cross-fire. 'Sir, I'd be very happy to track down Grabb.'

Gibson slides the pathologist's report across to Tompkins. 'I'm told you and DS Dockery have other pressing duties.'

Megan fights the urge to storm out. 'Sir—'

'You can go, Baker,' the commander nods towards the door. 'We're grateful for your work.'

Megan doesn't breathe until she's outside. She walks into the ladies room, screams and slaps the wall. Those bastards are going to follow up on *her* leads.

81

Caitlyn senses something different about the hooded men moving her from her hell hole. They're on edge. More careful with her than usual. Much slower. Less relaxed. Her heart lifts. It must be because they've decided to let her go. Then her hopes fall again. More likely they're just moving her to another location. It's something kidnappers do. More useless wisdom from Eric.

No sooner has her sight adjusted to the light than a blindfold is slipped over her eyes. She reaches up to her face but hands grab her wrists. They cuff her. Cold metal jaws bite her flesh.

They walk her down a corridor. The loss of sight makes her sway like she's seasick. Unseen hands sail her round several corners and then halt her in a room where the temperature is at least ten degrees warmer.

'Sit her down.'

The voice is male. Educated. English. Authoritative.

She is positioned on a chair. It feels good. Wood and leather, not cold stone.

'Caitlyn.' The voice is calm and measured. 'We are

going to ask you some questions. Easy questions. It is very important that you answer us honestly. Do you understand?'

She reminds herself of what Eric said. Build contact – any form of contact – with your captors. It can be the difference between life and death. 'I understand.'

'Good.' The voice sounds pleased.

'Can I have something to drink? I'm very thirsty.'

'Certainly.' He waves to one of the Helpers.

'Not water,' she pleads. 'Anything but water. I've drunk enough to drown. Maybe coke or juice?'

'We only have water.'

Caitlyn feels a glass being pressed into her hands. She raises it, tips it a little too much and spills some while she drinks. Someone lifts the tumbler from her hands.

'What is your name?'

A different voice. Younger. Thinner. A slight accent. Not so educated.

'Caitlyn Lock.' She says it with pride.

'How old are you?'

'Twenty-two.'

'Where were you born?'

'Purchase, New York.'

'What is your happiest memory about your father?'

The question throws her. 'Say again?'

'Your father, what is your happiest memory of him?'

It hurts even to think about it. There's a long pause as Caitlyn decides what to say to them. 'My dad used to read to me. Every bedtime he'd sit beneath the quilt with me and read until I fell asleep.' She manages a pained laugh. 'He made up stories about a fairy princess called Kay and her adventures, and then . . .' She fights hard not to cry. 'Then I'd fall asleep holding my daddy's hand.'

'And your mother, what is your happiest memory about her?'

She is hurting. The image of her father is clear in her head. She misses him. Aches to slip her hand in his and feel safe again. 'I don't recall much about my mother.'

'Try.'

She takes a minute. She's thought badly of her for so long it takes an effort to remember the better times. 'I guess I remember her tying yellow bows in my hair for my first day at school. Cos I hated the blue uniform. I remember making waffles with her at grandma's house. Almost every time we went round. And she used to sit me up on a cushion in her make-up room on the lot and have her own personal artist pretty me up.'

Now she thinks of it, she has lots of good memories of her mom. If only the woman hadn't cheated on them, hadn't left them.

'Okay. That's enough.'

The voice is the older man again.

She hears a click and a dying buzz, like something electric was just turned off. Footsteps cross the floor to her.

'Why are you asking me these things?'

No one answers. Hands start to lift her from her seat.

'Jake, what happened to Jake?' There's desperation in her voice. 'Where is he? Can I talk to him?'

They're turning her around, forcing her to walk.

'Tell me! Tell me what happened to him.' She digs her heels in, leans backwards, makes it hard for them to push her. Strong hands sweep her off the floor.

'Motherfuckers!' She wriggles and kicks but at least four of them are holding her, carrying her. 'My father will kill you for this. My father's men will get you and kill every fucking one of you.'

82

The private Citation jet crosses the Atlantic at a cruising speed of almost a thousand kilometres an hour. The flight is less than six hours — almost two quicker than a regular transatlantic charter.

Vice President Lock and his estranged wife Kylie buckle their seat belts as the jet zips into UK airspace. They've barely spoken throughout the journey and the grief-laden silence continues as an armour-plated Mercedes and detail of Secret Service agents whisk them away from Heathrow.

Six police outriders, sirens wailing, accompany them on the last leg of their journey. In Wiltshire, they're held up by a straggling pilgrimage of cars and campers crawling through the country lanes towards Stonehenge. They pass them, corralled by the outriders, and finally arrive at police head-quarters in Devizes.

Thom and Kylie Lock are shown into Hunt's office and after a round of handshakes and hellos settle at the large conference table. Opposite them are Commander Barney Gibson and Home Office Minister Celia Ashbourne. The woman, a small but forceful northerner in her late-forties, starts the meeting. 'The Home Secretary sends his apologies. Unfortunately it was impossible for him to cut short his visit to Australia. I am here to assist you and to assure you that the British government and all its agencies are doing everything possible to find your daughter.'

'We are making good progress,' says Hunt. 'The vehicle Caitlyn travelled in has been found and although burned out, it is being thoroughly analysed by forensics.' His face saddens. 'As I think you know, we also recovered the body of the young man she'd been travelling with.'

Kylie Lock reaches in her handbag for a tissue.

Hunt continues: 'Did either of you have any knowledge at all of their relationship?'

She shakes her head.

'It must be new,' says Thom Lock. 'Believe me, the team I had guarding Caitlyn would have reported any meaningful relationship.' He senses his wife's growing distress and takes her hand. The first sign of affection between them. 'Have you had any contact from whoever has taken our daughter?'

'None at all.'

'Do your investigators have any intelligence on who her captors might be?'

'We have the most senior detectives from the Met's Specialist Crime Directorate working on that at the moment.'

'MI6?'

'The Special Intelligence Service has been informed,' Ashbourne cuts in. 'At the moment we don't think it would be advantageous to involve them actively. Should a clear foreign or terrorist dimension develop then we'll reconsider.'

The Vice President exhales. 'Mrs Ashbourne, my ex-wife and I appreciate your efforts and the hard work of the police service. But – and I hope you don't mind me saying this – we both would feel more comfortable if the operation were integrated with specific people I can send you. The FBI has noted specialisms in this field.'

Ashbourne smiles compassionately. 'I understand how you feel Mr Vice President, I have a daughter the same age. Rest assured we are more than willing to cooperate fully in terms of exchanging information with the FBI and appropriately apprising them – and you – of any progress that's being made. However, clear control of this investigation is of such paramount importance that operational integration really isn't advisable.'

The Vice President drops his wife's hand and leans forward. His eyes glint with steel forged in the white heat of campaign trails. 'Minister, Chief Constable, I spoke with the President of the United States before I got on the plane. It was very late but he was concerned and kind enough to call me to express his concern as a personal friend and as the ultimate guardian of all American citizens. We can move forward here in one of two ways. You can accommodate my request and secure the deep gratitude of Kylie, myself and the President. I recommend that you do that. Or in a few hours the President will personally call your Prime Minister and express his grave concerns over how this investigation is being run. He will then hold a press conference on the White House lawn to share those concerns with the American people.'

Hunt nods understandingly. 'Mr Vice President, we would welcome the assistance of the FBI. I will have my staff officer make arrangements with the Director General's office.'

Kylie Lock speaks for the first time. She wants to ask only one question and the nervous pitch in her voice betrays how frightened she is of what the answer may be. 'Please tell me, Mr Hunt, honestly, do you think my daughter is still alive?'

The Chief Constable answers without hesitation. 'I am sure she is. I feel confident that we'll soon find her.'

Kylie smiles, relieved.

Thom Lock's eyes tell a different story. He would have said exactly the same if he'd been in the chief's position. He knows the truth. It's unlikely his daughter will get out of this alive.

83

Megan can't face another minute at work. She shuts down her computer, grabs her stuff and slips out into the car park. The only consolation is that Sammy doesn't now have to stay at Adam's.

Lost in anger at being dropped from the big case, she almost misses Gideon Chase walking towards reception. His head is down and it's clear he's burdened with even darker thoughts than her own. 'Gideon,' she shouts.

He lifts his eyes, forces a weak smile and turns and heads towards her car. 'Inspector, I was just coming to see you.'

Megan glances at her watch. 'You should have called. I have to pick up my daughter. Is it something that can wait until the morning?'

He looks disappointed. 'Of course, not a problem.'

But she can tell that he doesn't mean it. 'What's wrong? Why did you drove out here to see me?'

He's been rehearsing things in his mind for the past hour but now he's really not sure where to begin. 'You were right. I haven't been telling you the truth about everything.'

'What do you mean?' For a second she can't remember what it was that she had been accusing him of lying about.

'I saw the man who broke into the house, my father's house.' He holds out his mobile. 'I got a picture of him.'

She takes the phone from his hand. The photograph is not good. Shaky. Burned out a little by the cheap flash. Badly framed. Everything you shouldn't do if you're trying to take a good picture. But there's enough to go on. A face to fit her profile.

Megan looks long and hard at the shot of the stocky man with rounded shoulders and short blond hair. He's just as she imagined. White male, mid-thirties, somewhere around fourteen stone, quite broad, forty-two- to forty-four-inch chest.

'I took it just before I shut the door on him,' Gideon explains. 'If you look closely, you can see the papers burning in his hand.'

She squints at the tiny screen and sees he's right. The photo is better than she first thought. It's evidential. 'Why didn't you want us to know about this?'

He shrugs. 'It's hard to explain. I guess I thought I could track him down before you did.'

'Why would you want to do that?'

'To ask him about my father. Find out what he'd been involved in. What it had all meant to him.'

She senses there's more to it than just a need for personal retribution. 'What do you mean, "*what* it had all meant to him"?'

Gideon freezes. He wants to tell her, have her help him make sense of things but he also doesn't want to seem crazy. 'My father kept diaries all of his life. Every year since he was eighteen.'

Megan doesn't remember any reports mentioning diaries found at the house. 'So?'

'I think they could be important.' He studies her, looking for a reaction. 'Do you know anything about the stones and the Followers of the Sacreds?'

'What stones?'

'Stonehenge.'

She laughs. 'Listen. I'm having a very bad day and I can't work out riddles. What is it? What are you talking about?'

'My father was a member of a secret organisation. It was . . .' he corrects himself, '. . . it *is* called "the Followers of the Sacreds".'

The DI gives him a cynical look. 'So what? Your father had a secret club. He wouldn't be the first. The police service is full of Freemasons and the like. I'm sorry, I really have got to go.'

'It wasn't like Freemasonry,' Gideon snaps. 'This group is dangerous. They're involved in all kinds of things, rituals, maybe sacrifices.'

Megan scans him. He's clearly exhausted. Depressed. Possibly even post-traumatically stressed. 'Gideon, have you had any decent sleep recently?'

He shakes his head. 'Not much.'

Now it all makes sense to her. His father's death and the burglary and attack on him must be taking their toll. 'Maybe it could be a good idea to see a doctor? They can give you something to help you rest. Get you through things for a few weeks.'

'I don't need drugs or advice, inspector. I need you to take me seriously. My father killed himself because of this group, the Followers of the Sacreds. I don't know exactly why. But I think it all has something to do with me.'

She looks from her car to the front door of the station. Only one will take her home to her daughter.

'This has to wait until tomorrow,' she says. She holds up his phone. 'I am keeping this until I can make a copy of the photograph that you showed me. I'll give it back when I see you.'

Gideon nods disappointedly. 'Please come to the house. I'll show you the diaries. Then you'll see things differently.'

Megan hesitates, her own personal safety is always at the back of her mind and Chase is showing signs of becoming unstable. 'My DS and I can come around at ten in the morning. Is that all right?'

'Ten is fine.'

They say goodnight and she walks to her car looking down at the mobile that he gave her and the face of the blond-haired man with a fistful of fire.

PART THREE

84

MONDAY 21 JUNE, SUMMER SOLSTICE
STONEHENGE

High on the hillsides surrounding the stones, Lookers watch the revellers gather like ants around the giant sarsens. The pilgrims hold hands, forming their own human circle against the Megalithic landscape. Throughout the dark hours of the night the men of the Craft have watched them come.

Thousands of strangers. People of multiple nationalities, ages and beliefs. Pagans, druids, Wiccans, heathens, Christians, Catholics and Jews. Some of them to worship. Others just to witness the spectacle. They have come. Just as they always do.

Out in the darkness, in the undulating Wiltshire fields, there are illegal camps and the crackle of small bonfires, lit as in ancient times to mark the passing of the solstice. The site itself has been flooded with a wave of pagan colour since access to the stones was opened in the night.

The mystique, the ancient customs and practice of the solstice come up against the machine of modern organisation. Crowd control, hygiene, traffic routing. And devotion to one of the oldest gods. Money. Even the samba bands are selling CDs of their own works, with souvenirs as plentiful as drugs and booze.

They have journeyed from across the world for this day and as they near the henge, they become aware that the intense police activity is not only for them. Word travels about the missing American girl and her dead lover and many kneel and pray out of respect and hope.

The drumming that has gone on all night picks up a heavier, more urgent rhythm. The air buzzes with excitement. White-robed druids rehearse their prayers. Bare-chested pagan men dance with pensioners in anoraks and hippy women with beads and flowers in their hair.

Primitive horns start to sound, the orchestra of the old infiltrated by new immigrant vuvuzelas. Waves of cheering, clapping and chanting ripple across the pond of people. Innocent eyes, some glazed with drugs, others bright with virgin anticipation, are now all trained on the pink sky, waiting for the magic, straining for the first flash of sunlight to pierce the most famous stone circle in the world.

The sun breaks and penetrates the ringed sarsens. A giant cheer erupts.

Aside from the Lookers, there are no Followers anywhere near the henge. They know better. Instead, they are gathered miles away in the Sanctuary. They kneel on the cold stone of the Great Room. The place where their gods are located.

85

When Gideon wakes he squints at his watch and knows instantly that he'd been right going back to the police. It's nearly ten in the morning of the longest day of the year and he's just had his first real sleep for almost a week. A weight has been lifted from his shoulders.

He showers, shaves and hurries downstairs. The security buzzer sounds just as he's filling the kettle. He presses the electromagnetic release and on the monitor watches Megan's car glide through the grand iron gates and up the gravelled driveway.

He opens the front door. 'Good morning,' he says brightly.

'Morning,' replies Megan, less enthusiastically. 'This is Detective Sergeant Dockery.'

The DS smiles from beneath his sunglasses and offers his hand.

'Pleased to meet you,' says Gideon shaking it vigorously. 'Come through to the back.'

The two officers trail him into the kitchen and settle around a rectangular pine table while he makes hot drinks and small talk. 'I guess you're busy with the solstice?'

'Very,' says Megan. 'The roads are crazy. I should do what my ex does, stay away from work at this time of the year. Drives me mad.'

'It alternates,' says Jimmy. 'One year the mob is well behaved and the next they let rip like wild animals.'

Gideon sorts out teas and coffees, milk and sugar and then joins them at the table. Megan sees this as her cue to gear-change the conversation. 'Last night you spoke about your father's diaries and implied that they might shed some light on his death. Can we see them?'

He puts his cup down and stands. 'Yes, yes you can. But you need to know something.'

'What?'

He walks to the foot of the stairs. 'They're not easy to follow. Wait, it's best I show you what I mean.'

He goes to the hidden room and selects one of the volumes that he has decoded. He returns slightly breathless and hands the diary to Megan.

'What is this language?' She holds the book at arm's length, as though it might somehow help.

'Code,' he explains. 'My father wrote all the diaries in code. He devised it when I was a kid, as a way to teach me Greek.'

She squints at the open pages. '*This* is Greek?'

'Not really. It is Greek but Greek backwards. The letters have reverse values to their English equivalents, so Omega represents A and so on.' He reaches for a pen and on the edge of an old newspaper writes out ΜΥΣΩΛ ΨΩΞΥΗ. He hands it to Megan. 'What do you think that says?'

'Megan Baker.'

He looks spooked. 'How do you know that? You barely looked at it.'

She smiles. 'What else would you write? You're trying to

interest me, have me take a personal stake in understanding the language. So it follows that you would write something personal, and the only personal thing you know about me is my name.' She turns the pages of the journal. 'Why did your father do this? Why did he feel the need to write in a code that only you and he understood?'

Gideon is not completely sure. 'So no one else could understand it?'

She weighs it up. 'You write a diary because one day you want someone else to read it. People think otherwise but it's true. If what your father has written is important, then he wanted you to read it and perhaps do something with it. Something he thought *only* you could do. Maybe he wanted you to translate and publish it?'

Gideon suspects publication is the last thing Nathaniel wanted. But her words have touched a nerve. 'You think he wants me to approve of all this? Be a part of it?'

'I don't know. What is the "*this*" that you're talking about? Why don't you tell us?'

Over the next couple of hours he tries to. He reads them some of the important extracts he's translated – about the Followers of the Sacreds, the powers of the stones, their roles as all-healing gods. He even discloses some details about his mother's death, her fatal disease and Nathaniel's fear that he may have inherited the condition.

Megan is not sure how to voice what's on her mind without offending him. In the end she just comes out with it. 'It is possible that your father was mentally ill.' She tries to soften the blow. 'He was a brilliant man. He could well have hidden something like that.'

'He wasn't mad,' insists Gideon. 'There's a lot of truth in what he wrote.'

'Provable truth?' queries Jimmy.

Gideon gets up from his seat and goes to the window. He looks out over the lawns that his father walked. He feels uncomfortable having the police in the house, about discussing his father and his private life, but their scepticism gives him no choice. 'When I was a kid, I was ill. *Very* ill. It was probably the start of the same disease that killed my mother.' He looks back from the garden to the officers. 'You know what my father did? He took me home from hospital and gave me a cold bath. A special bath that cured me. The water he sat and bathed me in was collected from Stonehenge. When I could walk again, he took me there and made me touch all of the stones, the giant sarsens and even the smaller bluestones. Since then I've had no trace of that disease. No illness. My health is remarkable. My skin and body recovers from cuts and bruises faster than anyone else's that I know.'

Jimmy gives Megan a discreet but telling glance.

Gideon sees it. 'I know you think I'm crazy, but I'm not.' He returns to the table, reaches across it and takes Megan's right hand. 'You cut yourself, right? How long have you had that blue plaster on your finger?'

She looks at the dirty wrap. 'I don't know. Maybe a week. It was quite a deep cut.'

244

'Look at my face.' Gideon angles his jaw towards her. 'You came to see me in hospital after I was assaulted. You saw the cuts and bruises. Do you see them now?'

She doesn't.

'What happened to the wound to my jaw that they wanted to put stitches in?' He sees a flash of doubt in her eyes and tilts his chin. 'And the split lip? Do you see any sign of it? Any trace at all?'

Megan's heart races. She doesn't. His skin is unmarked. Not even a scratch.

There's a flash of triumph in Gideon's eyes. 'You still have a plaster on a little cut. From a week ago. Now tell me that my father was mad. Tell me that there is no truth in any of his writings.'

86

The top brass had a sleepless night. A call in the early hours turned the investigators' lives upside down. A call from Caitlyn's kidnappers.

By the time the Chief Constable and his team assemble in his office the story is already out. A tip-off, no doubt from inside the force. The world's press is camped outside police HQ.

Commander Barney Gibson kicks off the emergency meeting. 'At two a.m. a call was put through to the incident room. As a matter of routine it was recorded. I will play it for you in a moment. The call has been traced to a public telephone box. No surprise in that. Except this call box was not in England – it was in France.' He waits for the significance to sink in. 'It was made from a public box off Rue La Fayette almost in the centre of Paris. French police are at the scene and are looking for camera footage, but I'll be very surprised if they find any. They'll go over it for fingerprints or any other trace evidence that might match against our fingerprint or DNA databases.'

Hunt is anxious to move things on. Thom Lock has been informed and is on his way from his hotel. 'Please play the tape, Barney.'

Gibson presses a digital recorder placed in the middle of the table. They hear a voice. Male. English. The sound quality is poor. 'You've been expecting this call, we know you have. We have Caitlyn Lock and shortly you will hear our demands.' A pause and a click. The girl's voice floats eerily into the room. It's low and sad. 'My dad used to read to me. Every bedtime he'd sit beneath the quilt with me and read until I fell asleep.' She laughs sadly. 'He made up stories about a fairy princess called Kay and her adventures, and then . . .' It's clear she's close to tears. 'Then I'd fall asleep holding my daddy's hand.'

Everyone around the conference table is a parent and the tape visibly distresses them. Caitlyn's voice strums their nerves. 'I don't recall much about my mother. I guess I remember her tying yellow bows in my hair for my first day

246

at school. Cos I hated the blue uniform. I remember making waffles with her at my grandma's house. Almost every time we went round. And she used to sit me up on a cushion in her make-up room on the lot and have her own personal artist pretty me up.'

Gibson clicks off the recording. 'Technicians are examining it and checking for authenticity. And Chief Constable, I believe you will be validating it with Vice President Lock this morning.'

'I will. Thank you, Barney.' Hunt turns to his press officer, Kate Mallory. 'How widespread is the leak, Kate?'

'Very, sir.' She's mid-thirties, balloon-faced with round glasses and straggly black hair. She slides copies of national newspapers across the conference table, her fingers black from print ink. 'All the majors have it.' The *Mirror*'s bold-print front-page headline screams: 'France Now Key In Lock Case.' The *Sun* leads with a giant screen-grab of Caitlyn in a bikini and just one word, *Survivor?*

Kate Mallory reads the first few lines of the *Mirror* article: 'The search for kidnapped American beauty Caitlyn Lock, daughter of US Vice President Thom, sensationally switched to Paris last night as top British cops rushed to investigate a cross-channel call from her captors. Kidnappers made contact via a special line set up by the police for public information. The gang is understood to have played an Al-Qaeda style recording of Caitlyn, in which she revealed intimate details about herself, her father and her mother.'

'Enough,' calls Hunt. 'For what it's worth, I've put a call in to the editor to complain.' He shrugs. 'I guess we have little choice but to hold a news conference and answer their damned questions.'

'You could consider a complete news blackout, sir,' suggests the press officer. 'It's defendable on the basis that the young woman's life is at risk.'

Hunt throws his copy of the paper down on the table. 'What's the point? The news is already out there!' He looks around the faces and then back to Mallory. 'Kate, we can't conduct an inquiry of this scale if the press know about it before our own operational staff. Do your best to find out who leaked. I want a full investigation into this sloppiness.'

The door to the conference room opens and the Chief Constable's PA leans in. 'Vice President Lock is here, sir. He has two men with him who say they are from the FBI.'

87

While Chief Constable Hunt briefs Vice President Lock another tense meeting is under way in an office just down the corridor. FBI agents Todd Burgess and Danny Alvez are face to face with John Rowlands and Barney Gibson.

'I'm really hoping we can help you guys,' says Senior Supervisory Agent Burgess. Tanned and toned, he looks half his forty-five years. 'Both Dan and I know Thom Lock and the President well and we can keep heat off your backs, pro-viding of course you're open and honest with us.'

Gibson understands classic Yankspeak when he hears it. Tell us everything and we'll tell you nothing. 'Who's top of your likely list when it comes to kidnap gangs? Thom Lock especially piss anyone off?'

Both Americans laugh.

'Thom has pissed everyone off,' says Burgess. 'New York organised crime families, Chicago animal liberation groups, west coast environmentalists, even the Russians over in Brooklyn.'

'Then there are the terror groups,' adds Alvez. 'He's a Republican who backs the War on Terror. A hawk in foreign-policy terms. Al-Qaeda, the Colombians, the FPM, PLF, ANO, they all stick pins in effigies of Thom Lock.' He switches the heat back to Gibson. 'What have you guys found so far?'

'Not much,' confesses the commander. 'We're working with intelligence services to grab everything we can. Data, email, voice messages. Anything that's out there about Caitlyn, we're on it.'

Danny Alvez is mid-thirties, Hispanic with dark eyes and short black hair. He's been waiting for his chance to ask the big question. 'What do you guys make of the tape?'

Rowlands gives him a straight reply: 'We haven't had feedback from the tech staff yet. To me it sounded genuine, though I'm suspicious of why they used audio tape and not video.'

'Agreed,' says Alvez. 'It's certainly Caitlyn though. We talked to Thom and Kylie and the information about the ribbon and book is accurate and to the best of their knowledge has never been made public.'

'We pinged the tape to Quantico via a secure upload,' adds Burgess. 'Our labs say it contains multiple edits, made on several digital sound layers. They think an initial taping was done with Caitlyn, then it was drop-edited on to another recording device and the completed message played down the line from Paris.'

'Why?' asks Gibson. 'Why would they do all that rather than just put her on the phone?'

'They're real pros,' says Burgess. 'They probably know all recording devices, even digital ones, leave a kind of sound DNA. By over-recording like this, you mix up the sample evidence. Machinery and source become much harder to detect.'

'I just wonder,' says Rowlands, 'if the explanation is simpler than that. If the recording was faked somehow. What if Caitlyn's voice was actually recorded here in England, sent to Paris and then played back down a French phone line?'

Alvez shakes his head. 'Our analysts say the call was definitely made in France. They lifted the background atmos and they're sure it was Paris.' Rowlands' theory grows on him a little. 'Suppose the background noise could have been mixed in from the French side, but it seems a stretch.'

Gibson isn't convinced. 'Come on, they could have gone through the tunnel and been in Paris within four hours of the abduction. Thousands of illegal aliens get across the channel every year, it would be nothing for a professional gang bold enough to target a politician's daughter.'

Burgess agrees. 'Or by private plane, coast to coast in half that time. That's the way I'd do it.'

Alvez nods. 'Me too.'

John Rowlands is outnumbered three to one, but he doesn't care. 'She's here. I'm sure she is. My gut tells me this tape is a wild goose chase. Caitlyn Lock is still within our reach.'

88

Publicly, Kylie Lock hasn't said anything about her daughter's disappearance. She let her husband fix everything with the British police, the Secret Service, the FBI and the President's office. He's good at all that. Despite all their differences, she knows he cares about Caitlyn's welfare every bit as much as she does. If anyone can get those people to find her, it's Thom. No doubt about it.

But sometimes he's wrong. Out of line. Not that he'll ever admit it. Oh no. Even now he won't accept that it was a stupid mistake to have Eric look after Caitlyn instead of a Secret Service detail. Everything always has to be done his way.

Well, today is going to be different. Today it's her turn to step up. And step up is what she is going to do. In a way only a mother can. From the heart. That's why she's called a press conference.

Kylie looks in the mirror a final time, hides her eyes behind her low-profile black Prada sunglasses. She is wearing a mid-length grey Givenchy dress, her blonde hair is swept and tied back. She's ready for anything the world can throw at her.

After taking a deep breath, she walks into the top-floor conference room at the Dorchester. Settles behind the long trestle table covered in an immaculate white cotton cloth. It's topped with a small angled sign bearing her name and she can see a cluster of microphones and Dictaphones. She looks up and the room seems to convulse. An explosion of shutter clicks and blinding white light. She can see the editorial heads of the BBC, ITN, Sky, AFP, Reuters, PA, CNN, Inter Press, Pressenza, EFE and UPI. And a million others. They have risen from their seats, out of respect for her, not as a famous actress but as a worried-sick mother.

She can feel the heat from the blisteringly hot TV lights strung on their steel poles. People everywhere. At the rear a long line of video cameras are sited on a raised platform. She is flanked by a giant suited bodyguard and a round-faced black woman in her early fifties. Charlene Elba, a rough-and-ready veteran of her Hollywood press campaigns. Elba taps the main desk mike, gets the ball rolling. 'Ladies and gentlemen, thank you for coming. All of you are aware of the great efforts being made by law enforcement agencies in many countries to find Caitlyn Lock. Both Kylie Lock and Vice President Thom

Lock are immensely grateful for the endeavours of those detectives and individuals. However, this morning we will not be addressing any issues relating to the inquiry.' There is a pause. 'Today Kylie would like to directly address whoever has her daughter. Afterwards, she will do interviews. The press session will last ninety minutes, after which Kylie has to leave for a personal meeting with the Chief Constable of Wiltshire and representatives from the British Home Office and the FBI. We thank you again for your attendance.'

Kylie takes a second to compose herself before attempting the task of making an impression on the audience. She can feel the cynicism. Hazard of the profession, she guesses. She takes off her sunglasses. Her eyes are bloodshot and it's apparent that she is not wearing more than a brush of powder. The features are familiar to all of them. 'Whoever you are, whatever you want, please don't hurt my baby.' There's a tremor in her voice. 'Think of your own mother, think of your own wife or your own sister. How would you feel if they were in Caitlyn's place? What would you say to whoever had them? You'd say this. Please, please don't hurt the person I love most in the whole world. Please let them go.' She has no notes in front of her, just a plain piece of paper and a pen. She looks down at them for what seems an over-long period of time.

Then she looks up. Her eyes fix on the cameras and the watching press pack and they are brimming with tears. 'My Caitlyn has a heart of gold. She is the most caring, loving, wonderful daughter that a mother could have. Her whole future is ahead of her. Half a century of life in front of her.

She has the right to meet the man of her dreams and fall in love, to raise her own family, to sit her own grandchildren on her lap and to know she has made the world a better place with her presence and her legacy. Please don't take that from her. Don't take away all that love that she can give, all her dreams, all her future.' She quickly blots a running tear from her cheek. 'I would gladly give everything that I have to get my daughter back. And that is what I am prepared to do.' She turns over the sheet of plain paper in front of her and holds it up to the cameras. 'This is my bank statement. I am lucky. I have ten million dollars to my name. I promise that I will give you that whoever you are. Everything I have, everything I can raise. In exchange for the safe return of my daughter.' Her eyes narrow and her face hardens. 'But be aware of this, I am also prepared to give that money to anyone who successfully leads the police or any other investigators to your door and who can recover Caitlyn safely and bring you and anyone involved in taking my daughter to justice.' She takes a long slow breath, seems to relax her shoulders a little. She gestures to the giant beside her. 'This man is Josh Goran.' She puts her trembling hand on his broad forearm. 'He is America's most successful private investigator and bounty hunter.' She takes strength from talking about him. 'He is a former major in America's Air Force Special Operations Command unit. For the foreseeable future, he will be working solely for me and will be completely dedicated to securing my daughter's safe return.'

Goran points a big finger straight down the eye of the nearest camera lens trained on him. 'For those who have Caitlyn, I have a message. Please take the lady's money now and give her up. It's an honest offer that Kylie Lock has made. She means it.' He looks around the room, up at the ceiling. 'Please take up that offer. You'll be sorry if you don't. Real sorry if I have to come and take her from you.'

89

Megan is trying to forget being dropped from the Lock case and concentrate on the silver dog tag Jimmy Dockery has placed in the palm of her hand. It's from around the neck of Tony Naylor, the missing bum case that Tompkins dumped on her desk just as everything else was getting more interesting.

The cheap tag had been handed in by a jogger out on Salisbury Plain and listed on a CID lost and found circular because of the inscription on the back: 'Happy Birthday T. Luv Nat x.' Jimmy had noticed the tag matched the one Tony wore in the train station picture taken with his sister. To round things off, Nathalie Naylor had just confirmed it as the one she'd bought for her brother.

What's interesting Megan is not that it was found but *where* it was found. A lay-by in the middle of nowhere. But not any old nowhere. A nowhere on the closest main road to the burned-out barn where Jake Timberland's body was discovered.

Jimmy is staring at her staring at the small silver block. 'You trying to contact the dead?'

She turns the tag over. 'I wish I could. I'd certainly ask Tony Naylor what he was doing out on that road. Not the kind of place you go for a walk. It's bleak, desolate, unattractive.' She hands the tag back to her DS. 'Naylor was a drifter, no money, no home, certainly no car. How did he get so many miles from a town or village with nothing around but unploughed fields and scrub?'

'Someone must have driven him out there or he hitched a lift.'

'Why?'

'Maybe he heard there was farm work?'

She looks at Tony Naylor's photograph in the file on her desk. The thin-faced twenty-five-year-old has been unemployed most of his life. When he has bothered to earn a living, it's never been far from a town centre and a pub. Back-breaking shifts as a crop-picker or farm labourer out in the middle of teetotal-nowhere-land are not his style.

Naylor is dead. She knows he is. She thinks it and she feels it. And she knows that very soon she'll be picking up the phone in front of her and breaking bad news to his twin sister.

'Jim, see if you can get operational support to divert some men from the barn and run radar over the field.'

'You think he's buried out there?'

Megan nods. 'I don't think it. I'm sure of it.'

90

There comes a point when you have to take the game to the opposition.

Change defensive into offensive.

Be proactive rather than reactive.

Gideon runs all the axioms through his mind as he stands nervously outside the office of D. Smithsen Building Contractors. It's an ugly collection of Portakabins on a run-down industrial estate. In the yard are old and dust-ridden flat-bed lorries. Pot-holed tarmac is covered in boils of spilled gravel and cement. Incongruously, there is also a pristine, personally plated black Bentley.

Gideon takes a deep breath and breezes into the latent hostility of a sour-smelling and grubby reception area.

'Good morning. I'm looking for Mr Smithsen. I have some work I need doing.'

The woman behind the cheap desk looks annoyed at the interruption. She puts her magazine down and gets to her feet. 'Take a seat, I'll see if he's busy.' She jerks open a sliding door, leans in and then turns back to Gideon. 'You can come through.' She drags the door wider and steps to one side.

David Smithsen rises from a torn leather chair to greet his visitor. 'Mr Chase, how are you?' He gestures to a seat.

'I'm okay, thanks.'

Smithsen sits back behind his desk 'You certainly look better than when I saw you last.'

'That wasn't a good moment.'

'I'm sure it wasn't. Now, how can I help you?'

'Thought it was about time to get that work done. You know, the repairs to the study, the damaged brickwork. And the roofing.'

'Roofing?'

'You mentioned you were going to do some for my father. He'd given you a deposit.'

Smithsen slaps his forehead with his palm and smiles. 'Of course. I'm sorry. I remember now. I thought you meant roofing over the study.'

Gideon smiles. It's time to stop the pretence. He has no intention of hiring the builder. It was simply an excuse to confront the man. 'When you came out to Tollard Royal, you went upstairs and snooped around, went through some of my father's private books.'

Smithsen looks horrified. 'I went to check out the safety of your ceiling, that's all.'

'No, you didn't.' Gideon's voice is calm but he feels increasingly nervous. 'Mr Smithsen, I knew exactly how and where I'd left those books and you'd moved them, tried to look for something and I think I know what.'

The builder stays silent.

'You were looking for the same thing as the man who broke into the house, the one who left me in the fire.'

Smithsen tries hard to look offended. 'Mr Chase, really I—'

Gideon cuts him off. 'Listen, I know what you are part of.

What you believe in. You think I want to expose you or stop you?' He shakes his head. 'The Craft is thousands of years old. I understand how important it is.' He leans forward across the builder's desk. 'I want to be part of it. Talk to the Henge Master. Talk to those in the Inner Circle who have to be spoken to.' He pushes the chair back and stands. 'Then come back to me, Mr Smithsen. You have my numbers.' He is halfway out the door when he stops and leans back inside. 'By the way, the books have been moved. And I've arranged for couriers to deliver very detailed extracts and a personal letter to the police in twenty-four hours, unless they hear directly from me.' He gives him a parting smile. 'The clock is ticking. Be sure to contact me *very* soon.'

91

At six o'clock, Megan shuts down her computer and leaves to pick up Sammy. Adam is looking after their daughter and wants to buy them all dinner. Play happy families again. Despite instincts to the contrary, she finds herself giving in.

The Harvest Inn is not far from his house, so they walk over and sit outside. Adam brings a pint of lager, a large glass of white and an apple juice to the weathered wooden table and benches. He takes Sammy to the small swings while Megan orders their food. She sits looking at the evening sun dip behind the play area and for a moment things seem like they used to be.

Sammy runs from the swings to a sandpit. Adam makes sure she's safe, then leaves her there to scrape up a mess and wanders back to the table. 'She's growing so quickly.' He sits down and raises his drink. 'Here's to the great job you're doing with her.'

'And to you.' She tilts her glass his way. 'You're a lousy husband but a good dad.'

'I know. I realise that now.' He looks towards Sammy, bent like a puppy scrabbling sand between her legs. 'She is part of you and part of me. There's nothing I wouldn't do for her and . . .' He seems to run out of courage, then adds, '. . . and nothing I wouldn't do to have you back.'

'Adam—'

'No, please. Let me finish. I messed up. I'm sorry. Really sorry. Can't we wipe the slate clean?'

Megan looks down at the table. 'Things like adultery can't just be wiped clean, Adam. It's not spilt milk.'

The food comes and saves further embarrassment. By the time they've finished, Sammy is asleep on her father's lap. They walk back to his house and Megan puts her to sleep in the spare room. Adam opens a bottle of brandy. The one they bought in France on their last holiday before Sammy was born. They end up talking. About work. About Sammy. About the reasons behind his affair. They talk until all the poison has seeped out and there's no more cleansing and talking to be done.

Megan feels wrung dry. She kisses Sammy's beautiful sleeping face and does what she knows she shouldn't do. She goes to bed with her cheating ex. There's no wild sex. No passionate bridge building. Just a truce, sealed by lying close together. Taking comfort in what they had. What they might be able to have again.

92

TUESDAY 22 JUNE

The morning sun spills through a split in Adam Stone's cheap bedroom curtains and glints off an old mirror on the dresser opposite. Megan has been awake for hours, lying next to the father of her child, watching the warm daylight slip into the room and slowly climb the walls.

She's about as confused as she can be. Her head full of regrets, hopes and warnings. Sammy comes running into the room and chases all her thoughts away. Her cheeks are red from sleep and her eyes are lit up like Christmas. She jumps on to the bed with a squeal and tries to scramble in with them.

Megan slows her down. 'Shush, baby, don't wake Daddy.'

Too late. Adam has been kneed into consciousness. He raises himself, bleary-eyed, into a sitting position, back against the padded headboard. 'Come here, baby girl, give me a big love.' She's in his arms in a second and Megan is left even more churned up than she was ten minutes ago.

The three breakfast together in Adam's small kitchen and he chats easily. Caringly. Just like he used to. 'You got a busy day ahead?'

She pours coffee for them both. 'Do they come any other way? Even off the Timberland murder I'm as busy as hell, and no doubt there's going to be some cleaning up to be done after the solstice.'

He chews on buttered toast as he talks. 'I checked last night with control. By that point, there'd been about ten public order arrests, half a dozen for possession and a couple for dealing drugs.'

Megan is relieved. 'Thank you God for small acts of mercy. Did they say if there was anything new on the Lock case?'

'The press are still feeding on the mother's press conference.' He licks butter from his fingers, hands her the TV remote and gestures to the small set tucked away across the room. 'Try Sky, they usually know what's happening before we do.'

She finds a news report on the film star's presser. It's made up of a soundbite from Josh Goran, a dull interview with a pale-looking Alan Hunt, several shots of men who could be FBI agents, a meaningless comment from someone at the Home Office, random shots of Paris and finally, footage of John Rowlands and Barney Gibson looking wiped out and pissed off as they leave police HQ in separate cars.

'So,' says Adam, finishing the coffee and looking for his jacket. 'What are you doing tonight?'

'Meaning?'

He smiles warmly. 'Meaning, are you coming back here?'

She's not sure. It seems too hard to simply forgive and forget. 'Let me think about it. Right now, I have to go home and change. There's something important that I have to do this morning. Can you drop Sammy at nursery for me?'

'Sure.' He tries his luck again. 'And tonight?'

'*May-be.*' Her face softens. 'Let's just see how the day plays out.'

93

Jimmy Dockery steps into the road and flags down the camouflaged Range Rover. The driver, a sixty-year-old man dressed like a farmer, pulls to a stop in the deserted lay-by, gets out and briskly walks around the back. Jimmy follows him to the rear of the 4×4 with more than a little trepidation.

'Morning, Detective,' says the driver in an upper-class English accent. 'Looks a nice day for it.'

Jimmy isn't so sure. 'Morning. Let's hope so. How are the crazy monsters today?' He peers through the glass of the tailgate at Tarquin de Wale's two Turkey vultures caged in the back.

'They're fine,' says de Wale. 'Did I tell you last night when you came round that I raised them from chicks?'

'You did.'

'They're of Canadian parentage, you know. Best you can get.' He starts to slide the giant cage out of the vehicle. 'Give me a hand.'

Jimmy has a moment of self-doubt. Maybe this is a crazy idea. The extra assistance that Megan told him to enlist from operational support hadn't been forthcoming. Not a sniffer dog for miles around. And the ground radar team is booked up until Christmas. Tarquin's vultures seemed an inspired way to search for dead flesh. Tommy Naylor's dead flesh to be precise.

'Can't wait to see if the chaps can pull this off,' says de Wale. Jimmy had read in the *Police* magazine about German detectives using buzzards to detect buried corpses and exotic animal breeder Tarquin de Wale had been quoted as saying he'd be willing to cooperate freely with any police force in England wanting to give it a try. Well, this is his chance.

According to reports, on every occasion the German birds had been tested they'd found the flesh. Buzzards are said to have an incredible sense of smell. From three hundred feet up, they can detect a tiny morsel of rotting meat. And unlike bloodhounds they don't tire quickly.

The detective slips on his shades and for once they are necessary, the midday sun is high and bright. 'Mr de Wale, if you make this work then we are both going to finish the day as heroes.'

'Of course it will work,' says de Wale, confidently. 'Have faith.'

Jimmy helps him lift the back of a wire cage big enough

to restrain two grown Alsatians. They put it on the ground. Wings extended, the birds' full span is over six feet. They grunt and hiss at the intrusion.

De Wale slips a customised muzzle on the birds' white beaks, then attaches GPS tracking bands to their legs so he can pinpoint the exact spot if they find anything. 'You said you had something belonging to the missing man?'

Jimmy hands over Tony Naylor's silver dog tag and de Wale holds it in front of the striking bald red heads of the two birds. 'If he is out there, even if he's buried, these two will find him. Even without this little trinket.' He hands it back.

The exotic animal breeder walks to the front of the Range Rover to set up the electronic equipment in the passenger seat of the vehicle. After a few moments, he returns with a wide smile and eyes full of childish excitement. 'Ready, old chap?'

Jimmy raises an eyebrow behind his shades. 'About as much as I will ever be.'

94

The hour-long journey feels the longest and loneliest drive of Gideon's life.

He spent most of last night lying awake, worrying about this day. And now it's here. He sits in the car with the engine turned off, staring out of the window, hoping to halt time.

West Wiltshire Crematorium is set in ten acres of tranquil Semington countryside. But none of the beauty of the landscaping distracts from the fact that they are about to burn his father's body. Incinerate it. Blast it in an oven until all that is left is a featureless grey powder. Ashes to ashes, dust to dust. He's heard the phrase a thousand times, but only now does he really understand what it means. From nothing to nothing.

Every emotional connection to his father will be gone. He will be left solely with memories. Mixed ones. Sure, there are Nathaniel's books and tapes, but they're purely factual artefacts. Archaeological reminders of the father he didn't know rather than the one he did.

The morning sun is hot on his face as he gets out of the car and walks along the immaculately clean path. Up ahead, he sees the crematorium, a distinguished and understated building that looks modern with lots of hardwood beams and doors, bright stained-glass windows and a smart red-tiled roof.

Gideon hears footsteps and turns to see Megan hurrying to catch him up. He hadn't expected her to come and is touched that she has. She's wearing a mid-length black dress and black flat shoes, with a black raincoat over her arm. 'Hello,' she manages, slightly out of breath, 'I hope you don't mind me coming?'

'Not at all. It's very kind of you to bother.'

She affectionately touches the sleeve of his new black suit as they walk towards the front doors. 'I guessed you wouldn't know many people down here and thought you might appreciate some moral support.'

He takes a deep breath. 'I do. Thanks.'

Megan misses out the fact that she's also interested to see who else might turn up. What their relationship to Nathaniel Chase might be and how Gideon behaves during what's bound to be a testing ordeal.

An usher shows them through to the chapel, where the coffin is already in place. He had declined the offer of following the hearse from Shaftesbury. Too slow. Too painful. And also rejected the idea of having any kind of eulogy.

Only Gideon and Megan are in the congregation as the casket slips out of public view. He bows his head and she squeezes his hand reassuringly. He tries not to think about his father's corpse slipping into the retort, the special area of the furnace, where it will be exposed to savage temperatures of more than a thousand degrees. His archaeological training means he knows that cremation vaporises soft tissues and organs. Only hard bones will be left behind. Staff will use some kind of cremulator to pulverise what's left, reduce it to dust, to powder.

Ashes to ashes.

He tries not to think of the man he has lost. The things he wishes he'd said. The words he regrets uttering.

Dust to dust.

He is here to get things done. That's all. To fulfil his father's request that he should be cremated and his ashes scattered at Stonehenge.

The service is over in less than fifteen minutes. No fanfare. No wailing. Nothing but silence and emptiness.

267

On the way out, a staff member tells him he can collect his father's remains in a couple of hours or in the morning if he prefers. He chooses to come back later. He wants to end the day knowing that it's over. That he never has to return here.

The two of them walk to their cars. Gideon stands at the door of his Audi looking lost.

'Pub,' she says, surprisingly. 'We can't go away from here without having a drink to give your dad a proper send-off.'

95

Caitlyn hears a terrible rumbling.

Cool air wafts into the fetid hole. Hands reach in through the wall and pull at her.

Her body is so stiff and heavy that she feels as though she's been nailed to the hard stone slab. They pull her urgently out of the cavity and stumble her down a narrow dark corridor into a circular room lit by candles. Caitlyn tries to shield her eyes. Rings of small flickering flames burn painfully bright. Behind closed lids, circles are seared into the chemical screens of her retinas. She panics for a second, struggles for breath.

Two men loop ropes around her wrists. They walk her like a seaside donkey. Drag her clockwise. Always clockwise. Twenty circuits of the cold and featureless stone room. Caitlyn is dizzy by the time they stop and let her drink tepid water. Her stomach rumbles. Hunger pains stab and cramp her.

When they are done exercising and watering her, they take off the donkey ropes and retreat to the outer circles of the wall.

Now she can do anything she wants. Only there isn't anything to do. There is nothing but space around her. Space in which she is trapped by the people on the outside of the space. She understands that this is some kind of mindfuck. First they brick her up in a wall so she can't move. Then they give her as much room as she wants. And she still can't move.

Free will. They are messing with her free will.

Caitlyn sits. Crosses her legs. Shuts her eyes and shuts out her world of horror. She tries to find herself. Tries to connect to some iron thread that can't be broken, some invincible strand that she can always hold on to.

Gradually, she forgets the people around her, the smell and light of the candles, the cold of the stone floor, the cramps in her stomach and the burn of the gastric juices in her windpipe. The space. More than anything she shuts out the space. She is nowhere. She is in the safe darkness of her dreams.

Caitlyn feels her legs aching. She is growing weak. She feels herself falling. Tumbling backwards. The hooded men snap at her like a pack of dogs. They pick her up and half-drag half-walk her to the cleansing area. They push her into the steaming water. Watch her wash and re-dress. Walk her back to her cell.

Back to the place with no space.

Back to her nightmare.

269

96

In a black fluttering flash the birds lever themselves into the pale sky above the empty fields. They're gone within seconds. Not even distant specks on the horizon. Tarquin de Wale looks at the sat-nav app on his laptop. He can see their flight lines tracking high into the wild-blue yonder. 'Jolly fast, eh?'

'What if they don't come back?' asks Jimmy. 'You could spend the rest of your life trying to catch them.'

'Vultures aren't built to fly far.' The old eccentric doesn't take his eyes from the computer screen. 'They're lazy scavengers. They ride the thermals mainly. Until they get a whiff of food, then *zoom.*' He smacks his hands together. 'Besides, Wiltshire is the only habitat they know. Their natural home now.'

'Lots of army activity around here,' warns Jimmy. 'I hope they don't get shot down.'

'No problem. Here they come,' says de Wale excitedly.

The vultures swoop down low over the Range Rover and settle in the field about a hundred metres in front of the two men. Instantly, they start to forage. Senses bristling, they flutter and land a few feet away and nudge the earth again. The smaller of the two skips to the side and hammers his beak into rutted tracks two hundred metres from the remains of the barn.

Jimmy watches with mixed emotions. He'd hoped for

more. Something spectacular like when sniffer dogs go crazy and start whimpering and digging as though they're trying to find a short cut to Australia. But the vultures don't provide any such show. They lazily forage for almost an hour and don't venture out of the field next to the torched barn. Jimmy is feeling pretty dejected. He checks his watch. 'Let's call it quits. It was worth a shot.'

'I'll get a treat and clap them in,' says de Wale.

'Okay.' Jimmy glances at the laptop screen while the buzzard master goes to get some dead mice out of a sealed sandwich box. The computer has been recording the birds' flight paths using the GPS. Plotting lines on a grid. But these lines go pretty much straight up and down the field, almost as though they'd been mowing a lawn or ploughing crops.

It is a thought that he can't shake. Strange creatures. Why would they do that? He goes back to his car. Roots in the boot until he finds some spare evidence bags and then climbs over the stile that leads to the field. Jimmy lines himself up with the pecking buzzards and starts to collect samples. Soil samples.

It is a long shot, but if he is right, the vultures have found what remains of Tony Naylor.

The missing man's body has somehow been pulped and spread like muck across the open field.

97

Megan puts two glasses of wine down on the pub table that separates her and Gideon. It's a schizophrenic kind of place. Half bistro, half old-fashioned boozer. Crab cakes and dominoes. Rocket salad and pork scratchings.

'Thanks.' He pulls the glass towards him but doesn't drink. He's got things on his mind. Things he wants to say. 'Do you remember when you came to my father's house, I told you that I thought he'd killed himself because of this secret society, the Followers of the Sacreds?'

She nods apprehensively, worrying about his mental health. 'Yes, I remember. This was the secret organisation you said he mentioned in his diaries.'

Gideon detects the scepticism. 'Do you think I'm crazy? All screwed up with grief and trauma?'

'No.' She tries to be sympathetic. 'You're certainly not crazy. But I do think you're very stressed out.' She leans forward and speaks quietly. 'Gideon, it might well be that your father was involved in some kind of secret organisation, but I doubt it had anything to do with his death.' She flinches at the thought of what she's about to say. 'I'm sorry, but in my experience people take their own lives for a lot of highly personal reasons, and it's never about membership of some private club or other.'

He shakes his head and shifts the glass nervously around the table. 'The man who broke into my father's house and set fire to the place belonged to this group.' He leans closer. 'And this isn't a scout group I'm talking about. This is something bad.'

Megan slips into her more official interview mode. 'You might believe that but you can't prove it, can you?'

'I *know* it,' says Gideon. He puts a fist to his heart. 'In here, I know it.'

'In law that's not enough.' Megan can see he's hurting but there's nothing to gain from letting him delude himself. 'Don't you think that if your father was in such a society, such a close brotherhood, then some of them would have turned up today to show their respects? There was no one there. No one but you and me.'

The comment stings. 'Maybe they didn't know about it. It wasn't in any newspapers.' He has another thought. 'Maybe they *chose* to stay away.' He looks at her icily. 'Perhaps they expected the police to be there.'

She sees what he's driving at. 'That's not only why I came.'

'No, of course not.' He realises it sounded bitter. 'Sorry.' He finally takes a drink of the wine. Sour apples. He has no taste or appreciation of anything at the moment. 'I had a builder round the other day, said he'd heard there'd been a fire and wanted to help fix the damage. He told me he'd done work for my father, so I ended up letting him in to do a valuation. Next thing I know he's upstairs poking around.'

She puts her glass down. 'Did he take anything?'

'Didn't have time but I found him in my father's private room trying to look through the diaries I showed you.'

She's not sure what he means. 'Your father's private room? You mean his bedroom?'

'No. The room next to it. He had built a secret area at the end of the landing. That's where he hid all his journals. If you didn't know it was there, you'd never spot it. But I'd left the door open.'

Megan wonders for a moment whether he'd accidentally let a con man or another burglar into the house, someone sizing the place up for antiques. 'This builder, did you get his name?'

'Smithsen, Dave Smithsen.'

She digs out a pen from her bag and writes the name on a beer mat. 'Do you want me to check that he really is a builder?'

'No need. I went to see him. I asked him outright if he was involved in the Followers with my father. He denied it.'

Megan takes a long look at the tired and grief-stricken man across the table. Hidden rooms. Secret sects. Builders that he mistakes for prowlers. The guy is sick. Paranoid. She wouldn't be surprised to learn he's suffering from some form of post-traumatic stress.

'Gideon, I think you're reading too much into all this. You're all churned up and need some time to get closure on your father's death, the break-in and the attack on you. You'll get respite when we lock someone up, and hopefully that will be soon. We're running face-analysis data on the

274

phone photo you gave us and we've got word out with our informants on the streets.'

He nods.

Megan sees it's not enough. 'We're taking all this seriously. I promise you.'

'No, you're not,' he snaps. 'My father took his life because of something that this group was doing. Something awful. And you're not taking it seriously at all. You're just concerned with the damned break-in and no doubt your crime figures.' He slugs down the rest of his wine and stands. 'Thanks for the drink and coming out here. I'm going to go. Need to get some fresh air. Be on my own.'

98

Megan thinks about everything Gideon said as she drives back to Devizes. She's sure his fears and paranoia are unfounded. He's just mixed up and stressed out. By the time she's back at her desk, she has a simple plan to banish any nagging doubts and prove there's nothing in any of his accusations.

She hits the phone and uses her network of contacts to get the direct line of Professor Lillian Cooper, Head of Haematology at Salisbury District Hospital. The professor is a close friend of someone she knows. Megan dials the medic's number and manages to coax out of her the result of the blood tests Gideon had taken when he was kept overnight following the fire.

'The test results are negative. No disorders of any kind. Your man is the picture of perfect health.' Professor Cooper sounds bored as she flicks through his file. 'In fact, looking at his notes there's been nothing wrong with Gideon Chase since he was a kid.' There's a long pause. The plastic tap-tap-tap of computer keys clacks down the line. 'Well, I'm really not sure about the accuracy of what I'm reading.' There's surprise in her voice. 'It seems he was misdiagnosed when he was young. There's a record here of him having CLL, chronic lymphocytic leukaemia.'

'What is that exactly?'

'CLL is an awful disease. Doesn't usually show in people under forty. Must be in the family. It manifests when the production of blood cells malfunctions and the process gets out of control. The lymphocytes multiply too quickly, live too long. You end up with too many of them in the blood, then they fatally overwhelm the normal white cells, red cells and platelets in the bone marrow.'

Megan wants to make sure she fully understands. 'But he doesn't have this – he was misdiagnosed?'

'Yes, that's right. Hang on.' There's another pause while she scans the notes again. 'I'm sure he was misdiagnosed but no one seems to have admitted that they did it. Most peculiar. It says he exhibited an advanced stage of the disease and needed preliminary treatment. Then months later his blood tested clear, just as it did when we screened him.' She sounds exasperated. 'It just doesn't fit. Simply doesn't fit at all. CLL is an incurable condition, it never just vanishes.'

'And professor, you're sure he *is* clear of it now?'

'I have to be cautious. You can never say anything terminal has gone for ever, but looking at the file in front of me, I'd have to conclude that he no longer has the disease that he was previously diagnosed as being fatally ill with.'

Megan thanks her and hangs up. It's not what she expected to find. Not at all. The medical records support Gideon's unbelievable story about being cured because he was washed in water from the stones at the henge.

The next call that the DI makes secures the business trading records of David E. Smithsen. She follows with requests for his work and home telephone records and his credit card bills and bank account details.

From the deluge of documents that electronically floods in, Smithsen appears to be a successful, respectable builder and professional landscape gardener. Megan uses Google Maps to look at aerial and 3D images of his business premises and his house. The home is lavish, detached, probably an old farm that has been converted. At least five, maybe six bedrooms. Several extensions. She zooms in. A swimming pool cum gym by the look of it. Big fences all around. Electric gates and cameras. Somewhere in the region of five to six acres. She values the spread at around three million pounds. Minimum. Megan taps her computer keys. And it doesn't look like he has any mortgage. In fact, no debts of any kind. A DVLC search shows he has a soft-top Porsche, presumably for his wife and a Bentley bearing his personal plate. Another click of the computer keys and she finds he has a cool million in the bank.

Smithsen's business accounts look in order. He and his wife are directors of a limited company with an audited annual turnover of eleven million pounds and a profit of one and a half million. The income seems consistent with his lifestyle. She runs a criminal records check and it comes back squeaky clean. Not so much as a parking fine.

Everything is completely above board, but it doesn't *feel* right. She must have missed something. Megan looks more closely at the mobile phone records. He has the latest 4G iPhone but hardly uses it. She goes line by line down the itemised call list and sees he has rung home on it, booked the same restaurant a few times and downloaded a couple of emails. A guy as successful and busy as he is should be showing high call usage. She goes back to his landline records and scrutinises them. They show a similar pattern of low activity. Either he is terrific at delegating and has everyone running around making calls and money for him. Or he has another phone. One that isn't billed to his work or home addresses.

Megan is sure he's running an off-the-shelf, pre-paid phone. No contract and no trace of owner. A 'burner', as street kids call it.

Why would a millionaire businessman do that when he's already got a state-of-the-art iPhone? She leans back at her desk and smiles.

He's keeping something secret. That's why.

99

As he walks in the dying evening light towards the stones, Gideon tries to remember exactly when he came here last. Probably twenty years ago just after he'd fallen sick.

He is carrying his father's ashes in a scatter tube chosen for the purpose and he feels sad and nostalgic. He looks out across the field and gathering mist and remembers how his father had held his hand and led him across the misty fields towards the towering stones.

Two decades on he experiences an echo of that fear. A reverberation of the anxiety he had felt when he was eight years old and he'd been left for a few moments in the midst of the giants. It had felt like eternity. The shadowy ghosts, as big as trees, closed in on him. Crowded him. Reached jagged hands out for him.

Gideon recalls it all. His father had spoken strangely that day. Talked about how there were things in life that he wouldn't be able to fully understand but should respect. Like the moon. A goddess watching over him. A powerful force linked to his unconscious powers and the cyclic rhythms of life – human fertility, crop growth, the changing of the seasons. He was too young back then to understand it.

Gideon looks across the great sarsens and bluestones. He sees his father putting a hand on one in the middle of the circle and reaching out to him. Telling him that the soul of the universe was buried deep in this rock, protected and preserved for ever.

He hadn't wanted to take his father's hand but he did. It was frightening. Like a charge of electricity surging through two points. A crackling, blistering energy that bound them together. Then his father took him around the circle. Made him touch all the other stones. Pressed him against them and held him there as the current pulsed back and forth between stone and flesh.

'Good evening.'

The voice startles him. Comes out of nowhere. He turns quickly.

It is his father.

For a split second that's what he thinks. His heart is beating crazily. He gasps for breath. The man in front of him is of the same size and shape as his father. Probably a similar age. In the gathering mist the resemblance is unnerving.

The old man smiles. 'I didn't mean to startle you. I'm sorry.'

'It's okay. I was miles away.'

The stranger steps nearer. He is now taller and broader than Gideon first thought and has short grey-white hair. His eyes are piercingly dark. 'You shouldn't be in here, you know. Access is by appointment only. You have to book in advance.'

'I'm sorry.' Gideon looks off towards the car park.

'It's all right. I don't mind. What do you have there?' The stranger nods towards the tube.

'My father's ashes. He wanted to be scattered here among the stones.'

The man gestures to the henge. 'I imagine then, that this place meant a great deal to him?'

'It did.' Gideon glances at the nondescript tube. 'He was an archaeologist and studied them in great detail. He thought the stones were magical. Maybe even sacred.'

The stranger smiles. 'Many people do. That's why they come. I'm very sorry to have heard about your loss.' He tilts his head respectfully. 'I'll leave you now to fulfil your father's wishes. Good night.' He turns and walks away.

Gideon stands for a second and looks around. It is now getting really dark and the mist is rolling in like a slow tide. He feels a chill, knows that if he leaves things much longer, he won't be able to fulfil his father's strange request.

The lid to the tube is tight but he carefully levers it free. He doesn't know where to begin and where to end. Should he just shake the tube and walk away, grey powder streaming like a dud flare? Or should he try to distribute the remains as evenly as possible?

He remembers reading in the diaries how human remains were found all around Stonehenge. Hundreds more were buried in nearby fields, ancient camps where the stone workers had lived.

Gideon looks into the end of the tube and walks to the first stone in the opening opposite the Heel Stone. He heads clockwise, shaking the ashes out around the small circle of sarsens and bluestones. The container is empty before he reaches the end but he completes the ritual, shaking it until the circle is closed.

Then he finds himself strangely drawn to the middle and compelled to kneel. He mouths the words he couldn't say when he saw the body at the crematorium. In the darkness he whispers, 'I'm sorry, Dad. Sorry that we didn't know each other better. Sorry that I didn't tell you I loved you. That we didn't find a way to overcome our differences and share our dreams. I miss you. I'll always miss you.'

Black clouds creep across the pale rising moon. Before Gideon can get to his feet a hood is pulled tight over his head.

Four Lookers drag him to the ground.

100

Megan is about to switch off her computer for the night when it pings with a message. Tired, she opens it. It's an alert from the force's facial recognition unit. They've found a street camera match to the fuzzy camera-phone shot Gideon had taken of the burglar.

She reads the text: 'An individual male matching the facial biometrics of your target has been identified by camera XR7 in Tidworth. Click on the icon below to view more stills and to contact coordinating officer.'

She shifts the cursor to a little picture of a camera and clicks it. Her heart jumps. The shots are fantastic. Close to a dozen of them. In several the suspect is stood outside a shop, locking and unlocking the premises. It is a butcher's shop. Damn. She'd thought about a chef or catering worker, not a butcher.

The psychological profile she'd drawn up comes rushing back to her: white male, thirty to forty-five, manual worker, possibly in catering business, local pubs, restaurants. He fits it to a T.

Megan is so elated she doesn't notice her ex and her daughter in the CID office until Sammy shouts.

'Mummy! Mummy!' The four-year-old comes running between the desks.

Megan opens her arms and gathers her up.

'Got a lost child here,' Adam says. 'Told me her mother was a famous detective. So I thought I'd return her in person.'

She kisses Sammy and rearranges her on her knee. 'What are you doing here?'

He gives her a cheeky look. 'I was working a tip-off that you might come out with us.'

Megan thinks about telling him to back off, take things more slowly. But he and Sammy look so happy together.

Adam sits down at her desk, just at the exact moment Jimmy Dockery walks into the room. The two men catch each other's eyes. There's a crackle of curiosity in the air. The kind that makes a cat's tail stand up and fluff out.

Jimmy had come with news for Megan. Good news. Important news. But now he doesn't want to give it to her. Not with her husband sat there. It'll have to wait until the morning. He waves and wanders out of view.

Adam watches him go and allows himself a smug smile.

101

Gideon is trying to make sense of what's happened. He remembers his head being covered, strong hands holding him, a sharp spike of pain in his leg. They must have drugged him and taken him somewhere to sleep it off.

The hood is off and he's sat in the dark on a cold stone floor. Candles flicker in all four corners. It's small. Small and has no door.

He's in a cell.

Maybe it isn't a cell. Maybe it's a tomb.

Half-drugged, he struggles to his feet and sways unsteadily. He paws at the walls. There's no way out. His father had written about people being buried inside a Sanctuary. This could be it. He has been walled up in the Sanctuary and left to die.

He feels anxiety climb his chest. There can't be much air in this place. It can't last long. He picks up a candle and extinguishes the others. No point burning precious oxygen. Standing with the single light burning out, he reasons that they're not going to leave him here to die. He told Smithsen that he'd taken precautions, a planned delivery to the police of damning documents, unless he was free to call it off.

The candle burns out.

His heartbeat rises and his hopes fade. Surely they're going to have to come to him, find out what he knows, how much he can hurt them.

There is a guttural rumbling of stone. Narrow slits of light appear in the middle of two opposite walls. Hooded, robed figures flood the small room. Gideon doesn't fight as they overwhelm him, cuff his wrists and drag him through an exit. No hood or blindfold this time. Something has changed.

The corridor they're leading him down is long and winding. Gradually the lighting on the walls becomes more ornate. It even starts to feel warmer. He's flanked by two men. The one on his right pulls an iron ring sunk into a wall. Hidden pulleys go to work. A section of stone slides noisily back. They push him into a chamber.

The stranger he saw in the mist at Stonehenge sits in a hooded brown robe behind a circular table made of honey-coloured stone. 'Sit down, Gideon.' He waves a hand to the seating opposite him.

Gideon lowers himself on to a crescent of cold stone. His eyes never leave the robed figure in front of him.

'You don't recognise me, do you?'

'I saw you at the henge.'

The Master smiles. 'I met you several times before, when you were a child. Your father and I were friends.'

Gideon is surprised. 'Then you know what he went through. What happened to my mother and what he had to do to save me.'

'Indeed, I do.' He studies Gideon. 'You have clearly learned much, presumably from your father's journals. But do you actually understand what you have been reading?'

'I think so.'

'So tell me.'

'You are the Henge Master, the spiritual leader of the Followers of the Sacreds. My father was a senior and trusted member of your Inner Circle. You, he and many others give your lives to the protection of the Sacreds and the renewal of their energy.'

The Master cracks a thin smile. 'Not quite right. But close.' He's keen to learn how much more Nathaniel's boy knows. 'Do you have any idea how the spiritual energy of the Sacreds is sustained?'

'Human sacrifice. Offerings made before and after both the summer and winter solstice. At specific moon phases. My father described them as necessary for the restoration of celestial and earthly balance.'

The Master looks impressed. 'You are a good scholar. But there is a big difference between theory and practice.' He folds his robed arms. 'You sought us out, Gideon. What is it that you want?'

'Acceptance. My mother and father are dead. You are my family. I am already a child of the Sacreds, you know how my father baptised me as a child.'

The Master nods. 'Indeed. He bathed you in waters from the Sacreds and asked them to protect you from the disease that had killed your mother. He promised them his own life if they afforded you a long and healthy one.'

Gideon's eyes well up. Once more Nathaniel's words come back to him: '*I will willingly give my own blood, my own life. I only hope it is worthy. Worthy enough to change things. To alter the fate that I know awaits my poor, motherless son.*

The Master rises from behind the table and walks the chamber. 'The Sacreds are not monsters. They do not demand arbitrary human sacrifice. It is a fundamental matter of give and take, part of the cycle of life and death. In return for protecting your life, Nathaniel promised them his own. He undertook to become a sacrifice.'

Gideon's mind goes blank. 'The suicide?'

'No. That wasn't an offering. That was a selfish act of desperation. He wanted to stop the Inner Circle following a course that he didn't agree with.'

'What course?'

The Master exhales wearily. 'Your father made great studies and believed that the unalterable doctrine of the Craft was that those who received the gifts of the Sacreds were the chosen ones, the ones who should be sacrificed. He contested that anyone who had drawn from the divine well and prospered should in their later years pay the divine price. The Inner Circle disagreed. They believed that this ancient practice needed to evolve. That the Sacreds should pick their own sacrifices.'

'How so?'

'Easily.' The Master opens his arms in a relaxed gesture. 'People are drawn to them. The Lookers – the men who took you from the henge – they wait and watch. When someone is compelled to touch a specific Sacred, one that is in ascendancy in the sidereal zodiac, then they identify themselves as the correct human sacrifice.'

The Master sits on the stone bench next to Gideon. What

he wants to say next will unnerve the boy, possibly shake him to his core. 'The Craft is a democratic body. We follow rules laid down centuries ago. However, the interpretation of those rules is the right and duty of each successive Master and his Inner Circle. When your father took his decision to oppose the Circle's views on sacrifices, he as good as sealed his own fate.'

Gideon looks lost. 'I don't understand. Why was my father's opinion so important compared with everyone else's?'

The Master sees that Nathaniel hadn't told the boy everything. 'Because, Gideon, when the matter was put to the vote, I wasn't the Henge Master. He was.'

102

Caitlyn's screams pierce the foot-thick stone like a high-speed drill. She can't take any more. The blackness, the stillness, it's driving her insane. She hammers her fists, knees and head against the rough walls of the vertical tomb.

The two Lookers guarding her rush to the detention crevice. They can't let her harm herself. She mustn't die before the chosen time. They trigger the release locks and Caitlyn tumbles out and crashes painfully on to her knees. Her body is a patchwork of cuts and her long black hair is matted with sweat and blood. She snarls and kicks out at them. 'Get off me. You fucking bastards, let me *go*.'

The Lookers pin her down on her back. Her face is covered in blood and her manicured hands are cut to ribbons. Her forehead shows several deep gashes where she has crashed her skull against the stones. The men exchange glances. She has gone berserk in there. Thrashed around in some kind of deranged fit and tried to kill herself.

Caitlyn wants to end this nightmare now. Even if it means dying, she wants it to stop. But gradually she calms down. Her mind takes control again and the wild animal inside her is quieted. The men keep pressing her down on the cold stone floor. One is astride her, kneeling on her arms, pinning her wrists. The other is knelt across her ankles. Only now as the bloodrush subsides does it hit her.

They are amateurs.

She has seen Eric and his team carry out restraint techniques. They never do it like this. A twist of a wrist is enough to incapacitate anyone, if you know how. A finger dug into a nerve point can stop a heavyweight boxer, if you know how. These guys don't. They are completely without 'know how'. They're making it up as they go along.

Caitlyn stares into the eyes of the hooded man pressing down on her. 'Okay. I'm okay now.'

He eases himself off her arms. Stands over her. Wary and ready to pin her down again. 'We need to take a look at her head wound,' he says to the younger man.

They help her to her feet and are about to cuff her wrists

when Caitlyn pulls her hands away. She drives a knee hard into the groin of the man in front of her. The second Looker grabs her from behind. She leans into him. Uses her body weight to knock him off balance then runs him into the wall behind them. As he hits the stone, she crashes her head up, making sure the back of her skull does maximum damage to his face. It's a sickening blow. He loses hold and slumps down behind her. His nose is broken.

Caitlyn stands unrestrained in the torch-lit corridor of the Sanctuary.

103

Gideon is filled with a dizzying emptiness. The revelation that his father was once the Henge Master leaves him drained. This is not what he expected to discover. He'd sought the truth. Needed a reason for his father's suicide. Someone to blame. He hadn't been prepared for this.

The Henge Master is not concerned with Gideon's feelings. He merely wants to learn how much Gideon knows, how dangerous a threat he represents. 'Do you have any idea what this place is? Where we are?'

'The Sanctuary.' His voice is flat. His thoughts elsewhere.

'And do you know its location?'

It's a tougher question. One that drags Gideon out of his state of shock. 'My father wrote only about the nature of the

Sanctuary, not its location. That said, I haven't decoded all of his journals. I am sure there will be passages where he gets more specific.'

The Master tries to read the boy's eyes. It is possible that Nathaniel kept the location secret. It is also believable that his son knows it and understands that to reveal it would be dangerous. 'You are well informed for an outsider. For a non-initiate.' He clasps his hands. 'And that presents us with a problem. What are we to do with you?'

Gideon moves closer to him. 'Let me be part of things. Let me join you. I don't know what else I am to do. Given the loss of my father. His vow. I am to be irrevocably linked with the Sacreds whatever happens.'

'Should we even want to admit you to the Craft, I'm not sure you are ready. Initiation is a searching ceremony. It involves total trust between the Henge Master and the initiate. Trust is all the supplicant has to hold on to as his blood is shed. The pain is excruciating, unimaginable.'

Gideon hangs his head. 'It is what I want.'

The Master puts a hand beneath Gideon's chin, raises his face and looks into his eyes. 'Who is to say you wouldn't continue your father's opposition from within our ranks?'

Gideon becomes animated. 'I don't wish you or the Followers harm. I want to be welcomed into the fold. Just as my father *once* was. I want my life to be lived to the full, under the blessing of the Sacreds. I don't want it to be cursed with sickness. And I certainly don't want to spend the rest of my years fearful that I may be attacked or have my home set ablaze.'

The Master can see there is good reason why Gideon should be motivated to embrace the Craft. And killing him poses the risk of their existence being made public. The Craft would be exposed and the ritual of renewal interrupted. He paces. 'There is a way for you to demonstrate your loyalty, your commitment. If you were to fulfil it, I would personally vouch for your trustworthiness And the initiation would begin tonight.'

'What is it?'

'Your father's books. Deliver them to us and you may become one of us.'

Gideon shakes his head. 'I know what the initiation involves. I am willing to let you put a knife to my flesh and a hammer to my bones. Isn't that enough?'

'No. The books are the knife you hold to *our* flesh and your threats the hammer you raise above *our* bones.'

Gideon thinks of a way to break the stalemate. 'I will give you a quarter of the books before my initiation and I will make the phone call that will ensure nothing is delivered to the police. After my initiation, I will give you another quarter of them. A year from now I will surrender another 25 per cent.'

'That is only 75 per cent. When will we receive the final instalment?'

'Perhaps never.' Gideon smiles. 'Or when I have learned enough of the Craft to please you. When you are ready for *me* to take over as Master.'

104

Caitlyn runs for her life. Sprints as fast as her bare feet can manage. She reaches the end of a short, dark passageway. It goes left and right. She chooses right. Barrels down the corridor, thankful for the looseness of the rough gown she's wearing.

She's fast. Gym sessions every day. Five kilometres on the treadmill. Five on the elliptical trainer. Now she is glad of every workout. They injured her, starved her and scared her, but she's still strong and fit.

The passage curves and disappears into a dark haze. With any luck she's following an outer wall. Outer walls mean exit doors. She glances over her shoulder. No sign of the men. The place is bigger than she imagined. Much bigger. The stones beneath her flying feet are inscribed with something. It looks like someone chiselled writing on to them. Gravestones. Caitlyn realises she's running on graves. Her heartbeat kicks up another notch. She looks up and realises something else. The passage is circular.

Dead ahead are the two hooded men she fought off.

Only now there are more of them. Many more. All waiting for her.

PART FOUR

105

The only investigator not at the Chief Constable's early morning all-agency briefing is Josh Goran. Not that he minds. He's already made sure he's never out of the information loop. His team have a range of journalists, police officers and civil servants on their payroll. The ten thousand bucks he pressed into the palm of field agent Alvez made sure he's bang up to date on everything and anything of note.

Inside the overwarm conference room, Alan Hunt's deputy, Greg Dockery, makes a plea to the seven men sat with him. 'We need a full and confidential exchange of key intelligence. We have to bury our differences and work together. That's why we're here. Later today Chief Constable Hunt will personally reassure Vice President Lock of the resources that are being deployed to recover his daughter. Commander Gibson, please give us your update.'

Barney Gibson looks across the table and already sees operational fault lines. The two FBI agents have taken up one side, the Wiltshire officers the other and his own Met colleague is sat apart from either camp. Cultural schisms, unbridgeable divides during the course of only one operation. 'In the early hours of this morning we received further communication from the group we believe are holding Caitlyn. The call was traced to France, but this time not Paris. It came from a public box in Cannes, in the south of the country.'

John Rowlands throws up his hands in despair. 'I'm sorry, I just don't buy it. They are no more in the south of France than we are.'

The Chief shoots his Head of CID a blistering look. 'John, forget your own pet theories for a moment, we can speculate all we like afterwards. Let's listen to the tape first.' He takes a beat then readdresses the whole group. 'From the timing and nature of the recording you'll see that they've responded directly to Kylie Lock's press conference.'

Barney Gibson presses play on the small digital recorder in the centre of the conference table. The room's expectant silence is broken by a distorted male voice. 'The price for the safe return of Caitlyn Lock is twenty million dollars. Her mother has promised ten, we expect her father to do the same. The conditions are as follows: the FBI, the British police and that bounty hunter will all state publicly that no surveillance will be mounted on an agreed exchange. And no attempt will be made to arrest any people involved in the exchange. Only when we have this guarantee of safe passage will we give further details of our conditions. Please understand this: we have the resources to hold Caitlyn Lock for as long as we wish. Years if necessary. Sooner or later our demands *will* be met.' Caitlyn's voice suddenly fills the room. She sounds calm but weak. 'Mom, I'm in Cannes near the Carlton Hotel where I stayed with you and François before the film festival at the Palais des Festivals. It's raining today on La Croisette and the Palais is hosting a video gaming conference. Pop, I'm being well looked after. No one has hurt me. *Please* do what they say.' The distorted male voice returns. 'Let me be clear, unless we see the televised guarantees, this will be our last communication with you.'

The tape hisses to a stop. The investigators sit in shocked silence. Barney Gibson knows they're all imagining how Caitlyn's parents are going to react when they hear it. He rises above the emotion and ploughs on. 'The details given in the tape are correct. The weather in Cannes yesterday was as described and the exhibition mentioned is indeed taking place. Technicians both sides of the Atlantic have confirmed the call was made in Cannes and the background sounds are consistent with those of this particular spot on the Côte d'Azur. Todd, do you want to say something about it?'

'It is a bitch of a recording,' says the FBI man. 'Our techies stripped it down while your guys were sleeping and they confirm that, like the first one, it was assembled on several different levels. The two voices were recorded separately. They spliced them together, then added a third track, a continuous background noise. We analysed the woman's voice and we are certain it's Caitlyn. The distorted male

299

voice, we think is English, the same that we heard on the first tape.'

'First Paris, now Cannes,' observes the Deputy Chief. 'They keep shifting her. Are probably moving again as we speak.'

'It would explain why they are using phone boxes,' says Gibson. 'They don't mind being traced because by the time we have a fix on it, they're no longer there.'

'Or they never were,' says John Rowlands, still unconvinced that Caitlyn has crossed the Channel. 'It could just be one guy on a motorcycle travelling around Europe sending these clips down the wire. I don't necessarily buy that she is even out of the UK.'

'We have to plan for either eventuality,' says Hunt, ending the speculation. 'Greg, keep me informed of how resources and emphasis is split on this one.'

The deputy nods. 'Sir.'

'What about their demands, their conditions?' asks John Rowlands.

Hunt raises an eyebrow. 'The British Government, police and people do not negotiate with kidnappers. It's policy. We never have and never will.'

Danny Alvez nods in agreement. 'Vice President Lock has said the same kind of thing. It may be different because this is his own daughter, but I doubt it.'

'No way,' says Burgess. 'Thom is hard line. He ain't gonna blink on this one. These sons of bitches can wait as many years as they want, he still ain't going to negotiate with them.'

106

Any moment now the target will appear.

He will be white, thirty to forty-five, and will perfectly fit Megan's psychological profile. She just knows he will.

The DI is parked across the street from a big-windowed shop in Tidworth, her eyes never leaving the area beneath a sign boldly proclaiming: 'Matt Utley. Master Butcher.' Once she's got a good ID on him, she'll get a search warrant and turn his house over. See if there's any clothing to match the snagged samples found at the Chase estate in Tollard Royal. Or maybe tools that serial-match those recovered from the kit bag he left behind.

It's eight-thirty and she's been sitting patiently for an hour. Her mind wanders for a moment, back to her renewed relationship with her ex-husband. Everything seems to be going well. Adam spent last night at her house – *their* old house – and this morning Sammy skipped in with a smile as big as a slice of melon.

At eight-forty a man jogs across the road right in front of her, opens the shop door and turns on all the lights. She watches him pull on a red-and-white-striped apron and busy himself behind worktops and freezer counters. He's in his early twenties, she guesses. Not her target. Just after nine he flips a sign in the door window to declare the place open. She waits a while longer. At nine-thirty, Megan gets out of the car, pulls out her pocket book and wanders in.

A brass bell dings as she opens and shuts the door. She doesn't wait for a greeting. 'I'm Eileen Baxendale. Council rates review unit.' She puts pen to paper. 'What's your name?'

'Carl, Carl Pringle.' He seems totally flummoxed. 'I don't know nothing about the rates.'

'You don't? Well, who does?' She looks around pointedly.

'You need to speak to Matt. Mr Utley. The owner. I just work for him.'

'And when can I do that?'

'He isn't coming in today. Said I was in charge.'

'He's sick?'

'Didn't say. Just said I was to run the place and he'd call me later.'

She has enough information to find Utley. He will be on the electoral role, registered with the tax and health authorities. There is little point grilling the kid for any other scraps. 'Okay, I'll come back later in the week.' The bell dings again as she leaves.

On the journey back to HQ, she phones in her requests for background checks on her missing butcher. With any luck they'll be on her computer by the time she gets in.

When she walks into the CID room, Jimmy Dockery greets her with a sheet of paper and a smile. 'I've been to the labs. Look at this.'

He slaps the forensic report down on her desk, points at a crucial part and summarises: 'The field near the burned-out barn was covered in minute particles of human debris.'

302

Her eyes widen. 'You got the dogs out there?'

He laughs. 'No, not dogs. Something even better. This is going to sound insane but I read about German detectives using buzzards to search for corpses. So when I couldn't get ground radar or sniffer dogs, I contacted an exotic bird expert and he had two Turkey vultures fly the field we visited.' He proudly taps the report again. 'This is what he came up with.'

Megan is impressed. She reads from the microbiologist's paper: 'Samples of soil were tested and contained human traces. All identified DNA was that of a single individual.'

'You said Tony Naylor was in that field, boss. You were right.'

She forces herself to be cautious. 'Let's make sure it is Naylor before we tell anyone. Try to get a familial DNA match via blood from his sister or parents. Check the national database to see if we ever tested him in connection with an offence.' She thinks of something else. 'Oh, and get the landowner interviewed, I sure as hell want to know how he came to be crop spraying with human remains.'

107

Gideon leaves the Sanctuary in the same way he entered it. Hooded, cuffed and driven in the back of a plain looking builder's van.

After twenty minutes the vehicle lurches off-road and stops. Its back doors creak open and he hears birdsong spill in from outside. It's still early morning. Pre-rush hour. The floor beneath him dips as someone climbs in, swings his feet around and pulls him by the ankles across the van floor. They dangle his feet outside the vehicle, sit him upright and pull the cloth sack from his head.

It's not Dave Smithsen staring into his face. It's the man who almost killed him. The one who left him for dead in his father's burning study. Gideon's eyes drift down to the man's hands. There, on a small finger, is the distinctive signet ring that opened up the wound on his face. Behind the man is what looks like deserted woodland. The perfect place for a grave to be dug and a body to be hidden.

Smithsen walks into view and is smiling. 'This is Musca and from now on you will know me only as Draco. You will treat us both like long lost brothers. Either that or we'll kill you. It's your choice.'

Musca pulls a gun from the seat of his trousers, presses the barrel hard into Gideon's forehead. 'I don't mind which.'

Draco sits casually on the back ledge of the van and puts an arm around Gideon in a gesture of mock chumminess. 'One of our rules is secrecy. Enforced secrecy, if you get my meaning. And the Master relies on Musca and me to enforce it.' He squeezes Gideon. 'If you live, then you live by the rules. On no account do you speak about the Craft, the Followers or the Sacreds to any non-members. Ever. You don't telephone us. You don't turn up at our houses or our businesses. You never contact us. We contact you. If we call you on the phone, you don't mention your name or our names. You use the name that you will be given, should you be initiated. You use that name at all times. Don't forget these things. If they slip your mind, my friend's finger might slip too.'

Musca's eyes dance and he pushes the gun harder against Gideon's skull. 'Boom.'

Draco gets to his feet. 'Put him in the front, then you can go.'

Musca guides Gideon around to the passenger's door, helps him into the cab, slams the door and heads to a Mercedes parked nearby. The indicators flash orange as he zaps the central locking.

Draco talks as he starts up the van and drives. 'Here's how it goes. I take you home and stay with you while you collect these books that your father has written. You hand them over to me and I return you to the Master. It is that simple.'

'Then you should be able to manage it, shouldn't you?'

Draco laughs. 'You and I need to get some things straight. The Inner Circle voted a few hours ago on your initiation. The Master's vote carried it. One vote. That's all. So listen rather than talk. All right?' His eyes flash menace. 'For the next twenty-four hours you are *my* responsibility. I will deliver you to the Master's knife and hammer. If you survive the initiation, mine will be the first face that you will see. From that point on, I own your loyalty. You do what I say, when I say, how I say. Do you understand?'

Gideon can see he's riled. 'Clear as day. You're acting tough but really you're just the Master's messenger boy. You don't do anything unless he tells you.'

Draco hits the brakes. The van skids to a halt and the engine stalls. He throws a meaty right-hander into Gideon's face, cannoning his head into the side window. Gideon tries to fend him off with an arm but Draco is already out of his seat, raining blows down on his head and face.

The beating lasts less than ten seconds. Draco holds him by the neck in iron-like fingers and delivers one final blow. The most painful one of all. 'Remember this, Mr Smartmouth, when we're alone, *I* am your master. I own you. I was ready to kill your father and I'm more than ready to kill you.'

108

The rest of the journey to the Chase estate takes place in a painful silence. Particularly so for Gideon. His lip is busted and a tooth feels loose.

Draco frogmarches him through the front door and straight upstairs to the hidden room.

'Neat job,' he says as Gideon reveals the panel in the land-ing wall. He taps it with his big perma-grazed builder's knuckles. 'Not bad at all. If I hadn't already been in the room behind here, I would never have guessed one existed.'

Gideon ignores him and steps into the long narrow space.

Draco can't hide his shock when he sees the shelves are empty. Just dust and faded paintwork marking where the diaries had been.

Gideon blots his bleeding lip. 'What did you expect?'

'Watch your mouth.' He smiles at his own joke and walks the room. Knocks on walls. Thumps his heels in a few places. 'Are there any more secret places in here?' He bangs his foot down again on the flooring.

'Aren't you worried about my damaged rafters?' says Gideon sarcastically.

'They're *oak*,' chides Draco. 'It would take the Great Fire of London to burn them down.'

He bangs his way along a line of ceiling panels. Gideon's eyes focus at the far end, the one above his father's telescope.

Draco stops just inches short of it. 'So where are they? Where have your old man's books gone?'

The sound of electric chimes pre-empts a reply. The gate bell. Draco looks edgy. 'You expecting anyone?'

Gideon shrugs. 'No. There's a security monitor in the kitchen. We can see who it is.'

They go downstairs. The small wall-mounted screen shows a woman waiting in a car idling outside the gates to the house.

'I know her,' says Gideon. 'It's the detective heading the investigation into my father's death. She'll be able to see my car and your van on the drive.'

'Let her in but get rid of her quickly.' He heads towards

the fire-damaged study. 'Looks like I've got some work to do after all.'

Gideon buzzes Megan in, opens the front door and walks outside to greet her as she parks. He blots his lip once more on the back of his hand.

'Good morning, Inspector. I didn't expect to see you today.'

She grabs her handbag as she climbs out and shuts the door. 'I wanted to see how you are.' She notices the swollen and bloodied mouth. 'Which doesn't look very good. What happened?'

Gideon touches his mouth again. 'I took a fall while trying to fix up the study. It's not as bad as it looks.'

Her eyes drift past him as Draco comes walking out towards his van. 'You having some work done?'

Gideon glances towards him. 'Yes, Mr Smithsen did some jobs for my father and he kindly came by when he learned of the fire.'

'That's neighbourly.' She remembers their conversation in the pub near the crematorium, what Gideon had told her about the builder's previous visit and how he suspected he was linked to his father's death.

'Can't believe Mr Chase's bad luck,' says Draco loudly, as he steps closer to them. 'What's the world coming to? You lose your father, then the scum of the earth break in and nearly burn you out of house and home. Terrible affair.' He heads back to the van, rattles a large bag full of tools.

Megan knows they're being watched, given no real chance to talk. 'I came by to ask you a few more questions about your father – is this a bad time?'

'It is,' answers Gideon. 'Do you mind if I call you? I can come into the station, if that makes it easier for you.'

'That would be fine.' Out of the corner of her eye, she sees the builder watching them. 'Before I go, can I use your loo? It's quite a drive back.'

'Of course. Let me show you where it is.'

They peel away from Draco and once through the door she leans close and asks. 'Are you all right?'

'Not really. I have to go with him when you leave. They want my father's books.' He flicks a light on in the corridor and glances back towards the open front door. Draco slams shut the van door and is heading their way. 'I can't talk now.'

Megan has no choice but to slip into the downstairs toilet as Draco strides through the front door and pulls Gideon towards him. 'I saw you both talking. What did she just say to you?'

Gideon tries not to panic. 'Take your hands off me. It was my father's funeral yesterday. She was just being sympathetic.'

He unclenches his fists and lets go of Gideon's shirt. 'Get her out of here. Quickly. Or you'll be going to another funeral.'

109

Gideon walks Megan to her car and holds the door for her. He knows he only has a few seconds.

'I was threatened this morning at gunpoint.' He nods to the house. 'By Smithsen and another man. The burglar who attacked me. They're working together.'

Matt Utley's photo flashes in her mind. She wants to tell him about her trip to the butcher's shop but there's no time. 'Get in the car. We can sort all this out down at the station.'

He glances nervously to the front door. 'I can't do that. I *have* to go with him.'

'Why?'

'My father killed himself rather than condone what they're doing.'

'What *are* they doing?' She looks at him quizzically, remembering again his fragile mental state.

Gideon sees doubt rising in her eyes. 'I told you before. *Sacrifices.* I think they're about to make another one.'

Megan wants to challenge him but spots Smithsen by the side of the house. He's carrying a length of burned timber, trying to look busy. Now is the wrong time. She starts the engine and slips off the handbrake. 'I'll call you later.'

Gideon steps away as she drives off. Smithsen walks towards him, his eyes tracking the car to the electronic metal gates and out on to the country lane.

'What was that all about?'

'Money,' says Gideon. 'My father traded artefacts. Made millions from them. Probably some tomb-robbing in his time. The force's art and fraud people want to interview me about his last set of accounts.'

'She ask about your face?'

'I told her I'd had an accident.'

'Good.' He turns and starts back to the house. 'Come on, we're wasting time. Let's get those books and get out of here.'

'Wait,' says Gideon. 'You think I'm stupid enough to leave them in the house?'

Smithsen's face sets like concrete. Gideon digs his car keys from his pocket and opens the boot of the Audi. The builder peers inside and sees a thick blanket-wrapped bundle. He leans in and tugs off the outer layers. Inside are four A4 diaries, two from each decade of Nathaniel Chase's time in the Craft.

'Is this all?'

'All for now.'

Smithsen opens one up and stares at the coded text. 'How do we even know this is what you say it is?'

Gideon takes the book from him. 'Only my father and I understood this code and that's a good thing. Good for me and good for you. Most people would just throw these things away if they came across them, but they would be wrong to do that. Very wrong.' He closes the journal, rewraps it in the blanket and hands the bundle over. 'That's my side of the bargain. Now complete yours.'

110

By the time you reach the rank of DI, you've usually suffered a few professional wounds. And if you are a woman, you've certainly set some personal rules along the way. From leaving early at end-of-case parties to never marrying another copper, you've laid down the markers. Megan has broken both of those little beauties. But there is one guideline she always follows.

Look at the bigger picture. Don't make knee-jerk decisions. Stand back and weigh everything up. Big. Small. Important. Mundane. Take every factor into consideration.

Which is why she doesn't beat down her boss's door and ask for an arrest warrant and a tactical firearm unit to take in Dave Smithsen. Instead, she talks it through with Jimmy and tries to make sense of it all. 'I saw Gideon Chase this morning. He looked like he had been roughed up. Said he'd been threatened at gunpoint by two men. A builder called Smithsen and the man who broke into his father's house last week.'

Jimmy's surprised. 'I thought you said Chase hadn't seen the burglar?'

'I did. It turns out he had.'

'So why did he lie about it?'

'Long story. Says he felt he had a personal duty to find out what his father was mixed up in.'

'So where did he get threatened and why?'

She shakes her head. 'I don't know all the details. I didn't have the chance to ask him. Smithsen was there with him at the house, fixing the fire damage.'

Jimmy adds it all up. 'So this builder and his burglar mate threaten Chase and then a few hours later he comes round to his house to fix it up? Sounds strange.'

'You're right. It *is* strange. But it got me wondering whether the suicide of Nathaniel Chase isn't somehow connected to the ransom demand for the kidnapped American girl.'

Jimmy's eyes widen. 'Why? How on earth can you connect the two?'

'Cast your mind back to when you saw Jake Timberland's body in the barn. You said you had a gut feeling that the crime scene had been staged. Can you remember what you put that down to?'

'Sure. Location, location, location.'

'That's right. Well, location is the factor that's been bugging me. Both cases share the same focal point. Stonehenge. It's where Lock and Timberland were probably heading for a romantic sunrise before the kidnap and murder. And it's the place Nathaniel Chase wrote books about and where he wanted his ashes scattered. Come to think of it, it's also where his son claims he was cured of hereditary cancer when he was a child and where he believes a prehistoric cult makes human sacrifices so they can benefit from its powers.'

Jimmy screws up his face. 'You don't really go for all that mumbo-jumbo, do you?'

'Just playing devil's advocate for a minute. Why not? People have been digging up the bones of thousands of human sacrifices for centuries. The practice has been recorded in the Bible and dozens of other historic documents.'

'I get the history, but even if such a cult still existed, why would it want to sacrifice an American politician's daughter and the son of an English Lord? And how do you explain the ransom demand?'

Jimmy's logic pulls her up short. The cult is a stupid idea but one she's not yet ready to completely write off. 'Cults pick victims for a whole range of reasons. Just like rapists and murderers, they have their own secret criteria. It could be sexual, racial, gender-oriented. Maybe it fits or offends their belief systems. Perhaps Caitlyn fitted one of those categories.'

'And Timberland?'

'It could be that he didn't fit the criteria, that's why he got killed. He was just defending Caitlyn. Being gallant.'

Jimmy shows his ace card again: 'And the ransom?'

She taps her fingers on the desk. Her nails sound like a hungry woodpecker. 'Forget the ransom for a minute. I'm not done with the locational aspect.'

Jimmy thinks that argument is just as flawed. 'Stonehenge. Okay. So how could a cult carry out a ritualistic killing there? The place is slap bang in the middle of two busy roads. Always crawling with tourists. Twenty-four-hour security.'

Megan's eyes light up. 'What if the security team at Stonehenge is involved?'

Jimmy thinks for a second. It would certainly change things. 'Sean Grabb worked security there. I heard he's been missing since the abduction and murder.'

'You sure?'

'Overheard it in the canteen. And remember this guy has previous for burglary and assault.'

Megan looks energised. 'So if Grabb and others working security were part of the cult, they could fix access to the site at any time they wanted.'

'It's possible. I'll check with English Heritage and the security company they use. See what Grabb's attendance record is like. Could be that he pulls sickies all the time and often goes missing. Or maybe this is the only day he's had off for years.'

Megan is only half-listening. 'Good. Good idea. Give it a shot.'

Jimmy has implanted another idea in her head. One more unorthodox than any she's considered in her career. One that could solve the case. Or get her sacked.

111

Cuffed and hooded in the back of Draco's van, Gideon tries to work out the route they are taking back to the Sanctuary. He's sure from the turn out of his gate that they're heading west from Tollard Royal along the B3081 past the King John Inn.

He wriggles into a seated position behind the driver's wall at the front of the van and navigates according to which direction he gets thrown. A jerk to the left tells him Draco has turned right and is driving north. Gideon tries to judge the passing minutes and comes to the conclusion that they've reached Shaftesbury and are now headed in the direction of Gillingham and Warminster.

The last part of the journey is the quietest. Few cars can be heard. From the reduced speed and increasingly bumpy ride, it seems they've gone off road. Gideon is thrown around for several minutes before the vehicle stops and its back doors clunk open.

Three, maybe four men pull him out and manhandle him over hard ground. They walk him into a chilly, enclosed space where footsteps create echoes. Some kind of door is being unlocked in front of him. There's a lot of noise now. Sounds of people grunting. Things shifting. Something heavy sliding.

'Quickly,' someone shouts.

A hand goes around the back of his head, pushes him down, urges him forward. Makes sure he doesn't crack his head on something. He hears rumbling, grunting again behind him. No one says anything for maybe a minute. His mind goes into overdrive. The silence around him feels toxic.

Finally Draco speaks. 'You're going down some steps. Watch you don't fall.' There's sarcasm in his voice.

Gideon hears the slap and echo of footsteps in front and

316

behind as he descends. The steps are solid. Thick stone in a large space, nothing to soak up the sound. Exactly twenty of them.

The descent stops and two sets of hands grab his arms and walk him briskly for almost thirty seconds.

'More steps,' comes the sarcastic voice.

Another twenty.

He recognises the smell of being deep underground. He knows the odours of the earth – peat, chalk, running damp, sandstone, flint, wet iron, rich moulds. They all zing like sharp perfume notes to his trained archaeological senses.

Guiding hands halt him. The hood is plucked from his broiled face. Torchlight. He is deep inside the Sanctuary. A part he has never seen. Those around him are robed and hooded. That's what the delay must have been for, before they started the downward climb.

'Get him stripped and prepared,' says Draco, his voice tough now, as hard as the stone. Gideon tries not to think about what's happening to him. He concentrates instead on forming a mental picture of where he is. A large underground space in open fields at the end of an hour-long drive. He guesses he's thirty miles from Tollard Royal. Thirty miles probably north, perhaps a little west.

Draco interrupts his calculations, leans in close, his warm, sour breath in Gideon's face. 'Listen to me. I am going to teach you how to respond to the Master during the initiation ritual. Don't shame yourself or me by getting any of it wrong. And remember, many agonies will visit your mind and body. If you are truly devoted to the Sacreds, then you will survive.' He smiles. 'If not, you will perish.'

112

Lillian Cooper's pager bleeps on her hip. The haematology consultant unhooks it and curses the message from her secretary: 'DI BAKER HERE TO SEE YOU.'

A long day just got longer. The bath and the glass of chilled white will have to wait. She starts the walk along a zig-zag of hospital corridors back to her office and thinks. Detectives don't turn up announced. Not unless there's trouble. And trouble is what might well be there. She's already behaved unethically, breached internal guidelines and contravened countless clauses of the Data Protection Act by giving the DI confidential information.

'Megan Baker. Apologies for coming over unannounced,' The police woman rises brightly from a chair outside the small office and proffers a hand.

'Not a problem,' says Cooper. 'Please come in. What can I do for you?' She can feel her heart drumming.

Megan takes one side of a desk and opens a cappuccino leather Padovano handbag that Adam bought her in Italy three years back. 'It's about when we last spoke. About Gideon Chase.'

She produces a small sheet of paper and passes it over.

Cooper picks it up and looks at it. 'I don't understand. Who are these people?'

Megan produces her friendliest smile. 'I need your help. Just once more. I want you to access the health records of all the people on that list and tell me what you find. Their hospital and GP surgery records.'

The professor is aghast. She leans away from the paper as though it's white hot. 'Inspector, I shouldn't have helped you the first time. I'm certainly not going to repeat the mistake another half a dozen times.'

'It's not half a dozen.' Megan is steely-eyed. 'It's four people. And it would be a bigger mistake not to help.' She sits forward on the edge of her chair. 'The first name on that list, Nathaniel Chase, is the father of the man you looked at for me. We have reason to believe Sean Grabb, David Smithsen and Matt Utley may be connected to Nathaniel's death and to another matter we are investigating. Grabb is currently missing from work and a warrant for his arrest has been issued. All I need to know about him, and about the others, is whether they have, or have had in the past, a major medical problem. That's all.'

'Inspector, I really—'

Megan can see she's softening. 'Just tell me if they have ever been signed off work by their doctors. And if so what for.' She opens her hands in a gesture of simplicity and finality. 'It's not much to ask.'

Cooper looks worried. She shakes her head. 'It would be

traceable. Any search I do like that is electronically logged. It comes back to the computer. Even if I use a different workstation, I still have to log in. I could lose my job just for getting you the information.'

Megan scratches her head. She'd been expecting this. It wasn't how she wanted the conversation to go, but it was what she anticipated. 'Doctor, you know from our mutual friend what kind of person I am. Any assistance you give me is solely for the public good. I assure you of that.'

'That's not the point. It's just not right.'

Megan is going to have to play dirty. 'Lillian, you are married and you are having a long-term affair with a married police officer. How right is that?'

The woman gasps. 'I can't believe that you bring my private life up like this.'

'Believe it.' Her face hardens. A look toughened in the tempering heat of countless interview rooms. 'Please don't preach to me about right and wrong and don't judge me. I'm trying to solve a serious crime and save people's lives. I am prepared to do almost anything I have to in order to do that, and right now I need your cooperation.' She grabs the list of names from the desk and holds it up in front of the medic. 'Now Professor, will you please help me? Or do I have to call my friend at the *Gazette and Herald*?'

113

The main passageway of the Sanctuary is lit only by the smoky, orange flames of an endless line of wall-mounted torches. Long black scorch marks taper up the stone walls like vaporised ghosts.

The passage curves relentlessly downwards and inwards. It's just like his father described. St Paul's beneath the earth. A vast cathedral-like area with magnificent chambers and crypts. Gideon is trying to blot out what's happening to him – what is *about* to happen to him. Under different circumstances, he'd be overjoyed to be here, professionally elated at the prospect of opening up the tombs beneath his feet, carbon dating and forensically piecing together the lives of the people buried beneath him.

Four hooded Bearers guide him into an opening so narrow he barely sees it. The top of his head brushes the underside of the thick lintel as he passes through. Another twenty steps and they take a similar squeezed turning into a smaller chamber. A moon face with sagging jowls rises and speaks from beneath a sackcloth hood. 'You must disrobe and shower. Then we will dress you for the initiation.'

They guide him into a separate area where he hands over his clothes and steps into a dark stone trench. There is nothing to wash himself with. No shampoo. No soap. He stands naked and alone. A torrent of water bursts out of the blackness above him. Hits him so hard it whiplashes his neck and drops him to his knees. Gideon shuts his eyes and covers his face with his hands. The flow last minutes and then stops as unexpectedly as it started. He is given a towel and led naked down the corridors to the Great Room.

The sight of the chamber takes his breath away. A life-size replica of Stonehenge fills it. As complete as the first moment it had been finished. His father had declared this to be the true tabernacle of the ancient gods. Their original resting place, while the monument in the fields near Amesbury was built.

A loud guttural rumbling turns Gideon's head. The Great Room is being sealed. A sinister brown tide of hooded devotees swells around him. A surge of bearers edge him to the circumference of a fiery ring of tall, thick candles. Beyond the flames stands the Henge Master, in his hands the ceremonial hammer and chisel. Instruments that may take Gideon's life. Fear wakes inside him. He feels it coursing through his body like a poison.

The initiation has begun.

'Behold the embodiment of the Sacreds.' The Master raises his hands and turns slowly. 'The divinities rested here centuries ago, when our forefathers built this cosmic circle and this Sanctuary. In here, you are in their presence. Out of respect, once initiated, you will ensure your head is always covered and your eyes always lowered. Do you understand?'

Gideon responds as Draco instructed him. 'Yes, Master.'

'You are brought before us because you are deemed fit by

322

members of our Craft to become a lifelong Follower. Is that your will?'

'Yes, Master.'

'Are you ready to pledge your life, your soul and your loyalty to the Sacreds and to those who protect them?'

'Yes, Master.'

'The Sacreds renew us only as long as we renew them. We honour them with our flesh and blood and in return they protect and renew our flesh and blood. Do you pledge *your* flesh and blood to their immortal holiness?'

'Yes, Master.'

Thuribles of incense swing behind him, slowly releasing their sweet and spicy aromas. The Henge Master spreads his arms again. 'Bring him who wishes to Follow to the Slaughter Stone.'

Gideon is led through the ring of candles into the circle. He remembers Draco's warning to keep his eyes averted from the Master. Before him is the terrifying slab they call the Slaughter Stone. He freezes. Unseen hands push him to his knees and then to the floor, securing his wrists and ankles. Fear runs wild inside him.

'Do you believe in the power of the Sacreds and all who follow them?'

Gideon thinks of his father lying in this exact spot. Chained as he is now. About to have *his* blood spilled so his son might escape the agonising death suffered by his wife.

The Master raises his voice, repeats the question. '*Do you* believe in the power of the Sacreds and all who follow them?'

'Yes, Master.'

'Do you trust unquestionably and unhesitatingly in their power to protect, to sustain and to heal?'

'Yes, Master.'

'Do you dedicate your life to their service?'

'Yes, Master.'

'And do you swear upon your life and the lives of all members of your family and those you hold dear never to speak of the Craft outside of your brotherhood unless given permission to do so?'

'Yes, Master.'

Members of the Inner Circle swing their thuribles over him and then step away. The Henge Master produces the stone blade that was fashioned from the first trilithon. 'I draw the human blood, flesh and bone in the hope that you will accept him as one of your servants and will afford him your protection and blessings. Sacred Gods, I humbly beg you to find a space in your affections for our brother.'

He slashes a deep cut from each of Gideon's wrists up to his shoulders, from each ankle to the top of each leg. Finally, from the neck to the base of the spine. Gideon chokes back a scream. He sees his mother before him, memories of her putting him to bed, kissing him goodnight, smiling at him. Then comes a flash-frame of her in Venice on the film his father made. Then the message she taped for him. The awful secret she revealed to him.

He feels a violent blow to his head. Knows what it is. The brutality of the hammer and the chisel. He hears the Henge Master's voice far away. Blackness steamrollers him. The only words left ringing in his head are those his mother spoke to him from beyond the grave.

114

Megan uses her hands-free device to call Jimmy from her car as she returns to Devizes. 'Are you alone?'

'Give me a sec.' He steps away from his desk and into the corridor outside CID. 'I am now.'

'How did you get on with the check on Sean Grabb?'

'Good. Security firm were very cooperative. They knew about his previous criminal record, he'd told them. They gave him a chance. Say he's turned out to be a model employee. Always punctual and to the best of their recollection, he's never had a day off unless for a holiday.'

'That's because he's never had a day's illness in his life,' says Megan. 'Neither has his father or his grandfather, who lived to be almost a hundred.'

'Good genes by the sound of it.'

'It's more than that.' She glances at her handbag on the passenger seat. In it are the notes she made when Lillian Cooper finally cracked. 'Dave Smithsen, our builder friend, has also never been sick. Not so much as a day off school. And it's the same with Matt Utley, the butcher cum burglar at the Chase estate.'

'They're healthy people. What does that prove?'

'Gideon Chase said the stones had healing powers. Claimed they'd cured him of his childhood cancer and protected people in his father's cult. Remember how quickly his face healed after the fight with the intruder?'

'Boss, you're not from round here but believe me, Wiltshire's a very healthy place to live,' says Jimmy, not sure of what she's driving at. 'Good healthy stock – no big city pollution, not many fast-food restaurants, lots of country walks and healthy living from when you're a kid.'

'Jimmy,' she interjects. '*Everyone* gets sick sometimes. Food poisoning, hay fever, genetic disorders, whatever. Country air and a walk down a farm lane don't stop you getting ill or injured. But these people had none of it.'

'That doesn't prove anything. My father is strong as a bull and has never been injured or ill to my knowledge. Neither has my mum or me for that matter.'

They both fall silent as they realise the implication of what he's just said.

115

Megan lets herself into her house, heads straight to the fridge and a half-finished bottle of Sauvignon Blanc. She kicks off her shoes and flops on the sofa, brimming glass in hand. She and Adam are supposed to be having a romantic night. Her parents have taken Sammy so they can go out for dinner and be alone. If ever she wasn't in the mood for pressured sex, it is now.

She has done a lot of hard thinking on the drive home. About Gideon. About Jimmy. About Jimmy's father – her Deputy Chief Constable. *Jesus.*

She hears a key in the door and shivers.

Adam calls her name from the hallway. 'Meg, you upstairs?'

'In the lounge, getting pissed.'

He appears in the doorway and smiles. 'Are you all right?'

She nods, then says, 'No. Not really.'

He goes to her. She's clearly tense and he thinks he knows why. She's worrying. Stressing unnecessarily. 'Sweetheart, don't get worked up about tonight. I'm fine if you just want to stay in and watch a movie. We can curl up on the couch, like we used to when Sam was a baby.'

Tears brim in her eyes and now she feels embarrassed. Awkward but grateful.

Adam goes back to the fridge and finds another bottle of wine to top up her glass. He grabs himself a beer as well and goes to sit with her. Sit where he used to sit. The way things used to be.

Megan puts her head on his chest, closes her eyes and starts to cry.

116

Gideon can't tell if he is regaining consciousness or is still in the middle of a nightmare. Waves of trauma crash in his head. So much pain. So much shock. Torrid images sweep him back and forth like a child in a rolling sea. An underground Stonehenge. Black eyes beneath sackcloth hoods. A giant ring of burning candles. His mother's face. An ancient stone blade and ceremonial hammer. His father's diaries. The Henge Master's raised hands. His naked body chained to the Slaughter Stone. The burning stab of the knife in his wrists and legs and back. The taste of his own blood as it runs into his mouth.

Now he sees a boy. An eight-year-old with dark hair and big hopeful eyes. He is holding the hand of his father and they are standing in a swirling mist in an open field. Stonehenge. Only it isn't. They are inside a circle of tall, spectral figures. The vaporous shapes keep shifting, becoming wider then stretching thin like smoke rising from lamps in the ground, then gushing higher like black jets of oil, burning red like the fires of hell, turning gold like the strings of some massive harp.

Now Gideon sees only a waterfall of stars. Galaxies of stars pouring into the centre of the henge, swirling in a vast, bottomless cosmic pool. The stars begin to fade. Rocks are falling behind him. Rumbling like an earthquake. The Stone Gods on the edge of the pool are moving, crossing the darkness of his mind. Closing in on him. One grasps his ankle chains. Another lifts the metal restraints around his wrists and then drops his limb like the arm of a rag doll. His heart hammers in his cold, naked body. The giant Gods lean over him. Then they shift. Drift away. Vanish like the mist he remembers around Stonehenge.

The only light in the Great Room, the pale flickering glow from the ring of candles, goes out. Gideon is alone in the stony darkness.

117

Adam gets up long before Megan to make breakfast. Just as he used to. Everything is going to be just like it was.

He hears her come out of the shower. Ushers her back into their sex-wrecked bed. Hurries downstairs and returns with a tray of toast, orange juice, fruit and a flower from the small cottage garden.

She smiles. 'It's been a while since you treated me like this.'

'It's been a while since you let me.'

They kiss and almost simultaneously glance at the bedside clock. 7.10 a.m. No time for anything except food. She bites hungrily into the hot buttered toast.

'I'll take Sammy to nursery,' he says perching on the edge of the bed. There's something on his mind. 'What you said last night, about crazy cults and Stonehenge. Do you really believe it? Or was it just the messed up day and bottle and a half of wine talking?'

'Bit of both, I suppose.' She hadn't told him everything. Only some of her speculation about Lock and Timberland. Why they'd been drawn to the site, the lure of the solstice and its sacred connotations. She's interested in his professional opinion. 'You think it's daft to consider a cult rather than a kidnap gang?'

He shrugs. 'Aside from the odd one or two, the Charles Mansons of this world, I don't believe cults are anything more than a few nutty fanatics who like a strange dance and the odd prayer or two before a bit of dressing up and frantic sex.'

She laughs.

'Listen, Stonehenge is commercially marketed as being magic, mystical and all that stuff. The security staff over there actually tell you it's a sacred site, they warn you that you mustn't on any account even touch the stones. They are paid to say that, to perpetuate the myths. It's a pagan place of worship. Go there any day of the week and you'll see nut-jobs from all over the world kneeling and praying before those rocks. You're bound to come across stories about cults and all their oddities.'

She's missed being able to talk to him like this. Confide in him. Bounce work off him. 'So you don't buy it? It's all just legend and folk tales. Like turning water into wine and feeding thousands with a loaf of bread and a couple of fishes?'

'You know, Meg, Wiltshire is full of ghosts and myths. St George is supposed to have slain a dragon over at Uffington. Merlin is supposed to have been at Stonehenge.' He laughs as he stands up. 'Don't get too hung up on it all and I wouldn't go mentioning it to anyone at work who is brighter than Jimmy.'

He bends down and kisses her. 'Got to go.'

'Thanks. Tell Mum I'll call her later.'

She hears his feet thunder down the stairs and the front door slam.

Adam starts up his old BMW, a four-year-old three series he bought cheap at auction. He backs off the drive and calls the station to see if anything urgent is happening. He's struck lucky. Sounds like a nice quiet shift ahead.

Next he swaps phones and makes a private call. The kind he doesn't want Megan knowing about. 'It's Aquila,' he says. 'I'm not entirely sure, but I think we might have a problem.'

118

The Henge Master sits in the flickering candlelight of his chamber and muses on the tricky issue of timing. Three days until the first twilight of the first full moon after the summer solstice. The time the ritual must begin. He must be precise.

The sacrificial offering has to start in astronomical twilight on the evening of this coming Sunday and be completed by the start of nautical twilight on Monday morning.

There is much to plan. Bearers to be chosen. Lookers to be detailed. Trusted Followers will soon start arriving from across the world. They will be ensconced as guests in the homes of their British counterparts.

The police activity has lessened but it is still considerable. Too intense to take chances. The newspapers write of little else but the young woman held captive just metres from him. She is less troublesome now. Six days without food has taken the fight out of her. After the pointless escape attempt she has become more placid. He thanks the gods for small blessings.

Then there is Gideon. Spread out in his chamber are the coded diaries Chase brought with him. The Master can't make sense of what they say. The boy has probably made copies of them. He's not stupid. Seems every bit as smart as Nathaniel was. Every bit his equal. Should he survive the effects of the initiation, he may prove an asset rather than a liability.

The door to the chamber opens and the hooded form of Draco enters.

'What is it?' The Master's clipped tone betrays a building tension.

'Thank you for seeing me at short notice. I was contacted this morning by our brother Aquila. His wife, a detective inspector working from headquarters, is starting to make the kind of connections we don't find helpful.'

'In what way?'

'About the American girl and her English boyfriend. She has been speculating that they had been drawn to Stonehenge because of the solstice. That the American had been kidnapped close by.'

The Master is unconcerned. 'I've read as much in the tabloid press. The police won't make it their focus. 'They know the media make up a new line every hour.'

'But this woman is also investigating the Nathaniel Chase suicide,' says Draco. 'And a missing person. The young man chosen as our last sacrifice.'

The Master nods. 'Now I understand. It is good that you raise this. And good that Aquila reported his concerns with us. I will have the detective taken care of.'

119

Jimmy Dockery is missing.

He hasn't turned in to work. No one has seen him. The computer on his desk is off. There's no response on his radio. He hasn't phoned in sick and from the checks Megan has done he's not at home. No car on the drive. No sign of life.

There could be a perfectly reasonable explanation. But that's not what she's thinking. She's imagining the worst. And with good reason. Gideon Chase is also missing. He doesn't answer his landline or his mobile. He's not at home either. She just drove back from Tollard Royal and there's no trace of him.

Could Jimmy be with Gideon? It's the obvious connection. But why? Was Jimmy following up on things they'd discussed? She censors more sinister thoughts. Megan would like a face-to-face with Dockery Senior. She'd love to look the Deputy Chief in the eyes and see if he knows anything about his missing son. She can't believe she's thinking like this. She remembers what Adam had said. That it would be professional suicide to start talking to other people at work about what is going on in her head. She shakes off the dark ruminations and determines to busy herself. Wait for either Jimmy or Gideon to turn up.

Master butcher Matt Utley is top of her to-do list. She heads to the property office to take another look at the evidence recovered from the burglary. She now feels sure that the axe she noticed in the recovered bag will turn out to be some kind of butcher's cleaver.

Megan briefly passes the time of day with Louise, the recently widowed property officer, and tells her what she needs. They carry on chatting as the fifty-two-year-old disappears in the back and shouts above the noise of rooting through paper bags and boxes on metal shelves. 'You sure about the dates and case number, Megan?'

'Sure I'm sure.'

Louise reappears. 'Let me check again.' She types in the reference in her computer. 'Sorry, I don't have any entry record.' She looks puzzled. 'There's no trace of anything at all being logged. These numbers you gave me, they don't match anything in the back.'

Megan is thrown. 'Then *where* is it? I saw this evidence personally. I went over it with the PC who recovered it and my own DS said he was—' She runs out of words.

Jimmy told her he'd log the evidence in. She clearly remembers him picking it up off her desk. Her blood runs cold.

Another thought hits her.

She thanks Louise and rushes back to her desk. Opens her computer mailbox. Frantically scrolls down the messages. Panic makes her heart race. She types quickly into the search box.

Nothing.

Types again. This time slower. Scrolls manually through the messages. Still nothing. Flushed with shock, she checks her recent documents tags and deleted files section.

Blank.

They've all been permanently erased. 'Oh God.' She covers her face with her hands. The automated mail that alerted her to the face-recognition match with Matt Utley has vanished.

She has nothing on him.

Every shred of evidence has disappeared.

120

'You don't look so arrogant and full of yourself now,' says Draco, leaning over Gideon and looking into his bloodless face. The Keeper of the Inner Circle knows what he's been through. Hell. He's been there himself.

Draco picks up a wrist manacle, puts a key in it. The chain is dangling to the screwed hook in the stone floor. 'Before I let you out, I need to know if I can trust you.'

Gideon is weak, traumatised. 'You can.' His voice is slow and hoarse.

Draco unlocks the manacles. Two men materialise out of the shadows and lift Gideon to his feet. He is a dead weight and has trouble standing. Blood rushes painfully to his head. He feels incredibly weak, hungry.

He drifts light-footedly across the Great Room, disorientated, as though in the middle of an out-of-body experience. The hooded men around him seem to be shimmering, surrounded by golden auras that expand and shrink as they breathe in and out. When Draco speaks, clouds of white waft from his mouth. Like breath on a cold winter's day.

He knows they are moving him down passageways but he can't feel his feet. Can't feel anything. Yet his sight and hearing are highly sensitised not dulled. He can hear the moisture shrivelling up in the hewn sandstones around him. He can see the entire corridor reflected in the dark eye of an ant in the mortar where the wall meets the floor.

They stop in a panic. Their halos mingle and seem to catch fire. Their voices overlap, spill on to each other, their words are green, red, brown. Gideon laughs. They spin him round. He senses uncertainty. There are other men across from him. Men and a woman.

A beautiful woman. Young, dark haired and gorgeous.

His mother.

Gideon knows it is her. She is alive. They pull him away from her. But she sees him. For a split second, he is sure his mother's eyes catch his.

He is wrestled away. He cranes his neck and looks for her over his shoulder. But she is gone.

121

Megan knocks lightly on the door of Jude Tompkins' office and peers in. The DCI is a long way from being a friend, but seems to be the only person she can turn to now.

'Ma'am, I'm very sorry to disturb you. I need to talk in confidence about an important development.'

The office is dark. Tompkins frowns through the puddle of yellow light spilled from a desk lamp. 'What is it, Baker?'

'Ma'am, Jimmy and I have been following up on the Naylor case.'

The DCI looks up, casts her mind back and remembers the file. 'Tony Naylor?'

'Yes, ma'am, that's right.'

She downs her pen and sits back. 'Okay, come in. Tell me quickly. Gibson and Rowlands have got me chasing my own tail.' She gestures to a seat.

'Thank you, ma'am.' Megan shuts the door and sits. 'To cut a long story short, Naylor is dead.'

Some of the tension on the DCI's face eases. In terms of time, money and resources, a dead missing person is usually better than a live one. 'You've got a body?'

'Sort of, ma'am. Naylor's body was reduced to fertiliser and spread across a field.'

The DCI puts her head into her hands. Wearily. A dead murdered person is a whole other matter. The last thing she wants right now. She scrubs at her mat of lacquered hair, tries to get the blood flowing. 'You have forensic evidence, Baker?'

'We got a sample from his parents, ma'am. The match is perfect.'

Tompkins widens her tired eyes, sits more upright and stares across the desk. 'Have you told them any details?'

'Not yet.'

'You said he was *fertiliser*?'

'Maybe a wrong description, ma'am. Somebody, some *thing*, pulverised his body then spread it across what used to be a crop field near Imber.'

She pulls a sour face. 'So how did you find it?'

'We got a lead from a dog tag found by a jogger. Naylor's sister identified it, from the inscription on the back, as one she'd bought for him.' Megan can see by the exhausted look on her boss's face that now is not the time to mention the rather unorthodox deployment of Turkey vultures. 'DS Dockery organised a search, brought back soil samples. The lab ran quick PCR tests on them and found scraps of human flesh in the earth. These samples were taken from a huge field, from right across it. And all of them contained the same DNA. Labs then matched those to the familial DNA we took.'

Tompkins is impressed. 'Well done. Another time, this would be our major case of the year.' She glances down at the files on her desk, a mass of papers, the photographs of Jake Timberland and Caitlyn Lock. 'Was that what you wanted to discuss confidentially, or is there something else?'

'There's more.' Megan gestures to a giant map of Wiltshire on the wall of the office. 'It's where we found Naylor's remains that disturbs me, ma'am.' She gets to her feet, walks over to the map. 'Here.' She lands a finger out in the desolate woods and fields of Salisbury Plain. 'It's barely a mile from where Jake Timberland's body was found.'

Tompkins gets up to join her at the map. She peers at the bleak spot. 'So who owns this section of land?'

'That's what's interesting, ma'am. If you look at the Land Registry, it says the Ministry of Defence owns everything out there. But that's not quite true. I dug around a bit and it transpires they own 99.9 per cent. The 0.1 per cent they don't own is this section. The bit with our field and our barn in it. The place where we've discovered the remains of two bodies within a matter of days.'

'So whose is it?'

'It's owned by Nathaniel Chase. Or at least it was, until he killed himself. Now it belongs to his son. Gideon.'

122

The rule of three. It was one of the first things that producers taught Caitlyn when she went on *Survivor*.

Rule one: humans can't survive more than three hours exposed to extremely high or low temperatures unless they are wearing proper clothing. Rule two: humans can't survive more than three days without water. Rule three: humans can't survive more than three weeks without food.

Caitlyn thinks they should have added a fourth: humans can't survive when they're imprisoned in a block of stone and mind-fucked by whack-jobs in dressing gowns.

The cramped conditions are physically gruelling. The lack of fresh air is an agony. She is permanently shivering with cold. But what's really killing her is the boredom. She's being crushed to death by her own fears and imaginings.

Her teeth chatter. She knows her body temperature is falling critically but there isn't enough room to do any form of exercise vigorous enough to generate heat. They are giving her water but she's dehydrating. The persistent migraines are so bad she feels like she's going to black out. Hunger pains are constant and it's so long ago since she ate she can't remember. In the Camper with Jake. That must have been it. A lifetime ago.

Another stomach cramp chews through her abdomen and Caitlyn doubles up in pain. She knows exactly what's happening to her body. Wishes she didn't. It's eating itself. Chewing through her reserves of fat and muscle. Laying to waste all the years of good nutrition and hard work in the gym. Already she can feel her well-toned biceps and quads softening, shrinking.

After her appearance on *Survivor*, Caitlyn was signed up as an ambassador by GCAP, the Global Call to Action against Poverty. So she knows every dirty detail about starvation. On average, it's how one person dies every second. Four thousand an hour. A hundred thousand a day. Thirty-six million a year. She doesn't want to be one of them. Not another awful statistic.

Dizziness washes over her again. She slides to the floor so she doesn't fall and crack her head. A sickening blackness engulfs her. She's uncertain now whether she's awake or hallucinating. Men are lifting her out of her cell and walking her to the showers. Her vision is blurred and she feels faint, struggling to breathe.

Out of the corner of her eye she sees a dark huddle. People moving towards her. Hooded captors, holding someone.

Jake.

He's alive.

She struggles to focus. Sees him surrounded by other men, robed and mean-eyed. Like the monsters who have been guarding her. He looks naked. His chin is sagging on his chest as they lead him by the arms. She wants to say something but her mouth won't work. Wants to run to him but can barely stand. Blood rushes through her like a queasy tingling virus and she collapses in the smothering dark.

123

Megan and her boss are still staring at the map. They've come to the same conclusion.

Two dead bodies found in such a small area, both discovered within days of each other, and on land owned by a rich and powerful man who unexpectedly killed himself. It's a combination of factors that can't be ignored.

'Pull Gideon Chase in and give him the third degree,' says Tompkins. 'Rattle his cage and see if he's a grieving son as white as pure driven snow or whether there's something else to him.'

'Ma'am, I've been trying to get in touch with him all day, without any luck.' She hesitates before adding, 'I've also been unable to contact DS Dockery. He seems to have gone off radar.'

Tompkins fears this is a classic case of the left hand not knowing what the right is doing. 'Is he already with Chase,

Baker?' The thought amuses her. 'Is your DS already a step ahead of you?'

Megan doesn't rise to the bait. 'Perhaps, ma'am. But that doesn't explain why I can't contact either of them. Chase's landline is tripping to answerphone and I've tried both their mobiles and left messages.'

'Then perhaps Jimmy's dragged him out to the middle of the Plain. Reception out there can be bad.' The thought jolts her into a more strategic worry. 'Actually, we need to get operational support to cordon off the scene where you found Naylor's remains and find a forensic archaeologist to search the area.'

'I've already had the scene secured, ma'am. I took the liberty as soon as the results came in. You were unavailable at that time, otherwise I'd have updated you earlier.'

The DCI's door opens and her secretary leans in. 'The Chief and the Deputy would like to see DI Baker, ma'am.'

Tompkins looks surprised. 'Why?'

'I'm afraid I don't know. The Chief's PA didn't give a reason, just said I was to find her urgently.'

In Megan's experience, 'urgently' isn't a good word. Never has been. Never will be.

'I'll come with you.' Tompkins pulls her handbag off the corner of the desk chair. 'If it's urgent for you, it's urgent for me as well.'

124

The Henge Master rises and embraces the new initiate. 'My son, it is so good that you are now with us.' He holds Gideon's head to his face. Hugs him like a father embracing a lost child. 'Sit. You must rest.' He turns to Draco. 'Leave us. I will call for you when we are done.'

The Master smiles as he sits alone with Gideon at the circular stone table. 'The ceremony is draining. You will feel weak and tired for some hours, but your body will heal, regenerate quickly.'

On the table in front of him are wooden platters and jugs of water and juice. The boards are piled with chopped raw fruit.

'The food here is perfect for your purified body. Blueberries, cranberries, figs, bananas. Power foods. Please eat. You need to build your strength.'

Gideon picks a little. He has no appetite. He glances around. The dark stone walls seem to suck all of the light from the room.

'Such a famous fruit and such a powerful symbol, don't you think?' The Master holds an apple in the palm of his hand.

'You mean Adam and Eve?'

'No, no, I don't. I was thinking of something Greek.'

Gideon knows he is being tested. His brain slowly moves up a gear. 'Ah, the Twelve Labours. Heracles had to steal golden apples from the garden of the Hesperides.'

The Master smiles then bites the apple. 'You *are* indeed your father's son.' He nods towards the coded diaries spread at the end of the table. 'When we are finished, I want you to read to me. Explain the code.'

Gideon pulls the stalk from a rich red cherry. 'I have some questions.'

'Ask. This is your time. I am here to help you learn to become a valued member of our Craft.'

'I am curious about the Sanctuary. How and when it was built, where exactly it is.'

The Master smiles. 'You will learn the location of the Sanctuary in good time and when you are fit enough I will personally guide you through its magnificent chambers.'

Gideon looks offended. 'I am still not to be trusted?'

The Henge Master sighs. 'The initiation begins your journey of faith, it does not complete it. I think you know that we are approaching an important time in our calendar. One that no one can jeopardise. After that, we will revisit this issue.'

'The ritual of renewal. I presume that is what you mean.'

'I do. In three days it will be completed and then we will allow you to leave.' He smiles. 'On stepping outside you will know the location of the Sanctuary.' He laughs. 'You will know it instantly.'

'And until then I am to stay here? As what? A prisoner?'

'Of course not. As a scholar. We shall talk every day. You will educate me about Nathaniel's writings.' He picks up a diary from beside him. 'And I will educate you about your duties as a Follower of the Sacreds. It will be time well spent.'

125

The two policewomen don't say much as they walk the short distance to the Chief's office suite. They're asked to wait outside for a moment, then his PA ushers them through.

Alan Hunt and Greg Dockery sit at a conference table not far from the door. Neither seems to notice that Tompkins has tagged along.

'You asked to see me, sir,' says Megan, trying to hide her nerves.

'I did, Detective Inspector.' The Chief flashes a politician's smile and nods to a chair. 'Please sit down.' He looks to Tompkins. 'This is nothing to worry about, Jude.'

'Relieved to hear it, sir. With your office saying it was urgent, I thought you'd appreciate me being here.' She helps herself to a seat alongside Megan.

Hunt ignores the comment and turns to his deputy. Greg Dockery fixes his eyes on Megan. 'We have just been informed that the Home Office are about to publish their annual review.' His tone is almost funereal. 'And it will be highly critical of the Wiltshire Constabulary. Particularly, about our attention – or what they see as our lack of attention – to long-term unsolved cases. With that in mind, we need to be proactive and head off any rebukes.' He musters a smile. 'This is good news for you, Baker. As of this minute, you are the acting head of our new taskforce, Operation Cold Case. If you make sufficient progress, if this appointment heads off the criticism, then you can expect accelerated promotion to the rank of DCI. Congratulations.' He stands up and leans across the desk to shake her hand.

Megan is surprised and confused. 'Thank you, sir.' She rises to grip the extended palm.

'Starting when?' asks Tompkins coldly. 'With respect, we're badly stretched, sir. As well as the Lock case, DI Baker has a very full workload, including a new murder. The timing really isn't good.'

'Starting right now,' says Hunt acidly. 'Timing is never good, Jude. There's always a reason to put off change. We'll assign someone else to clear the DI's workload.'

His deputy picks up the impetus: 'This is a major opportunity for you, Megan. It'll be good for you. The posting is in Swindon. You will need to clear your desk today. You start in the morning.'

She swallows. 'Sir, I have a young daughter who goes to nursery in Hartmoor. I need a little more time.'

Hunt cuts her off. 'You don't have time, Detective Inspector.' He glances at his watch. 'Nor do we. You are very lucky. You've landed a hell of a job. Now go and make the most of it.'

'Yes sir.' Megan leaves in a dignified silence, followed by Jude Tompkins. Once outside the door, the DCI takes her by the arm. 'Come back to my office. We need to talk. You're bright, Baker, but not that bright. Jobs like this don't just fall like rain out of the sky. I would have known if a job as strategic as this was in the offing.'

347

The DCI doesn't say any more until they're back in the privacy of her own room. She shuts the door and shoots Megan an accusatory stare. 'You are being bumped out of here. Shifted doubly quick. What have you been doing? Is it Jimmy? Have you been bedding that ginger toe-rag?'

Megan is horrified. 'I certainly have not.'

'Good. I credited you with more sense than that. So what is it?'

'This has nothing to do with my private life. And, not that it is any of your business, I'm actually back with my husband.'

'So illuminate me. What the hell is all this to do with, then?'

Megan tries to figure it out. Her boss is right. The new job isn't a bump up, it's a bump out. She's not being promoted. She's being shut down.

Tompkins can't sit. She paces and glares with anger. 'Things have never been busier. We've got a suicide, two murders – Naylor and Timberland – and a VIP kidnapping. And the top brass want to ship out my DI in the middle of it all.' She moves closer to Megan. 'Think, Baker. Think hard about anything unusual you have found or that has happened to you. Tell me about it. Is there anything at all in any of the cases that you have been holding back? Doing a bit more work on. I need to know it all. Now.'

126

A night spent on a bed of straw in a stone cell has left Gideon aching from head to toe. The Master can call him a scholar all he likes but he knows exactly what he is. He's a prisoner. No less captive than the pale young woman he saw as they led him from the Great Room. The one in his delusional post-initiation state he thought was his mother. It was the girl off the news. He realises now. Caitlyn Lock. The daughter of the US Vice President. That was the woman he'd seen. From what he can remember she had a lover, an Englishman. He supposes he is also being held somewhere, probably in a cell like his own.

Then he remembers. Remembers his father's book. Immurement. Ancient Britons adopted the practice of the Greco-Romans. They walled-up errant citizens, confined them in tiny spaces until they starved to death. The Followers employed the same practice to purify the body of the sacrifice and rid the mind of any form of visual or audible stimulus.

Gideon pities her. She must be going insane. Pressed up against dark dusty stone with no way to move and nothing to do. A living hell. He stands and walks his small cell. Seven strides long by three wide. Luxurious compared with how they'll be keeping Caitlyn.

He sits on the straw bed and falls deep in thought. The

349

Sanctuary is a circular structure. He can picture the Descending Passage. The corridor of the Outer Circle. The Great Room. The cleansing area. The Master's chamber. Some outer chambers. The cell that he is in right now. From this first-hand knowledge and the descriptions in his father's diaries, he believes he has a good mental map of the entire place. Including where they must be holding Caitlyn.

There is only one gap in his knowledge.

The exit.

127

Megan has spent another night at her parents' house with Sammy. After news of her so-called 'promotion' and the doubts that Tompkins raised, the last thing she could face was an evening with Adam and his bullet-train desires to resume normal family life as though nothing had ever happened.

She steps in the shower and tries to clear her head. All of yesterday's worries are still there. Gideon is missing. Jimmy is missing. She is going to have to uproot Sammy and move to Swindon.

She towels dry and dresses. Tompkins promised she'd put the skids under the whole change of jobs thing. Slow it down. Make it manageable. But Megan doubts even the DCI will be able to get the Chief and the Deputy to change their minds.

Her parents have fed and dressed Sammy and Megan thanks them and drives to nursery, her mind on autopilot. Yesterday's twist in events has brought her and Tompkins closer together. Closer than they'd ever been. She'd even felt confident enough to confide in her. The DCI had typically demanded every last detail and Megan had given it to her. Everything. Gideon Chase's theories about cults. The disappearing evidence that linked butcher Matt Utley with the break-in at the Chase estate. Everything. She was surprised – and somewhat relieved – she hadn't been laughed out of the station.

Having dropped Sammy and kissed her goodbye, she uses her mobile to phone HR and tell them she's going to the doctors' and can't come in today. Maybe not tomorrow either. She looks at the keypad and then tries the numbers she has for Gideon and Jimmy. Another blank. Gideon's absence can only be bad news. She turns the car around and heads out to Tollard Royal.

It's a sunny, clear day and the hour-long trip is almost therapeutic. It's a tiny village on the southernmost boundary with Dorset. Not much there of tourist interest. A thirteenth-century church and a Quaker burial ground. Only Ashcombe House, home to Cecil Beaton, Guy Ritchie and Madonna, is worthy of note.

At the Chase estate the gates are locked. She presses the buzzer repeatedly and calls his phone lines again. Nothing.

Megan gets out of the car and walks the tall brick walls of the perimeter until she's out of sight of any passing traffic. If Utley found a weak spot in the home's defences, she can.

351

And she does. After a little tree-climbing and a jump that Sammy would have applauded, she makes it on to the top of the wall. She goes down on her knees, grips the brick edge, hangs low and drops into the garden. She emerges from the soil and shade on to the long back lawn.

'Gideon!' she shouts up towards the house. Doesn't want to spook him, have him mistake her for another intruder.

It takes several minutes to negotiate the lake and the back of the house. There's no one here. His Audi is parked on the gravel out front and judging from the glistening spider webs spun across the wing mirrors, it hasn't been moved for a while.

Megan rings the bell. Bangs with her fist and shouts his name again, even through the letterbox. Nothing. She scribbles a note for him to call her and pushes it through the metal flap. She withdraws her hand and stands frozen in thought.

The last time she saw Gideon was with Smithsen, right here. And he looked scared. At the time she wrote it off as a psychological reaction to his father's death. Now she knows that she was wrong. Maybe he's even lying dead on the floor inside.

She tries to rationalise. Smithsen wouldn't really kill him, would he? Not after seeing her at the house, not after talking to her, a detective, on the driveway. He'd be mad to. The logic is enough to stop her breaking in. At least until she has spoken to Jude Tompkins.

Megan retraces her steps, climbs back over the wall and heads to her car. As she starts up the engine, she sees a flash of something in her rearview mirror. A man in a green jacket moves quickly out of her line of sight.

She is being watched.

They are following her.

128

Once past the King John Inn, Megan pushes hard on the Ford Focus's accelerator as she heads into the open countryside around Ashmore. Sixty, seventy, eighty. Easy for the little car. If they are tailing her, then they are going to have to show themselves.

Just before a tightish left-hander, she catches a glimpse of another car, way back. It's moving fast. Every bit as fast as she is. It could be the lure of the open road that has tempted the driver to put his foot down. She has to find out.

Megan knows that until they get to the aptly named Zig Zag Hill, the B road offers nothing more testing than gentle bends. The Focus is soon doing way over a hundred. She has opened up at least four hundred metres between her and the following car. As she hits the vicious right-hander at the foot of the hill, she pumps the brakes and the Ford deftly keeps its balance going into the left switchback that instantly follows. Her heart kicks like a mule. She works the brakes again, slowing as quickly as she can without smearing telltale rubber.

Megan glides the car off road into the copse of trees on the right. She stops as deep in the clearing as she can manage. Within seconds, the car behind her zips past. It's a Mercedes. Cream-coloured. That's all she can make out.

Now comes the real test. If Merc man is just driving for fun, he'll work the hill and put his foot down as soon as he is clear of the bends. She won't see him again. But if he *is* following her, within the next minute or so, then he's going to be wondering where the hell she is. He'll probably swing it around, check he hasn't missed a turning, maybe even double back.

Megan reverses carefully out of the copse and cautiously resumes her journey to HQ at a more sedate pace.

She sees the Merc just past Cann Common. Pulled up. Brake lights on. Two people in the front. A cheap personalised plate ending: 57MU.

Matt Utley.

She remembers Gideon saying he saw Utley with a gun. The brake lights on the Merc go off and it noses out of the lay-by in front of her. She hits the accelerator and burns through the gears, as though she's going to ram the car. She doesn't. At the last moment she pulls right into a small access road to half a dozen houses set back from the road. It runs parallel to the main road and she uses it like a pit lane on a race track. Only Megan isn't stopping.

The back end of the car drifts as it floats over the grass and tarmac. Somehow she keeps control. Swerves out of the close back on to the B road. Heading right past the Merc.

For a second her eyes catch those of the driver. It is Utley all right. She has seen his photograph often enough and long enough not to be mistaken. She thinks she recognised his passenger too. She only got a brief glance of the thick-set man in a white shirt, but there was something about his outline, the curve of his shoulders and the shape of his head that was familiar.

She accelerates hard along Higher Blandford Road and doesn't let up until she's crossed Christy's Lane and made it on to the much busier A350.

Megan keeps one eye on her mirror all the way back to Devizes. Her brain is reeling from what she's just been through. What she saw.

The man in the front seat of the car with Utley was her husband. It was Adam.

129

They only let him out to go to the toilet.

The rest of the time, Gideon spends locked in the solitary confinement of the stone cell. They bring him meagre food and each passing hour makes him feel more like a prisoner.

He realises there are only two days to go before the Followers complete the ritual of renewal and offer up the life of the woman he saw. They can't take risks. And he could well be a risk. They know his father tried to stop anyone outside the Craft being sacrificed, so there's a chance he might try to do the same.

The bolts on the door are drawn back. It creaks open. Two robed men walk in, say barely anything, except that he is to be taken to the Master.

He walks the corridor his father walked and imagines the secret life of the man he never really knew. How had *he* felt after *his* initiation? What were *his* thoughts after he'd just been initiated into one of the oldest and most secret brotherhoods in the world?

The Lookers leave Gideon inside their leader's chamber. The Master shows him to the stone table, where Nathaniel's diaries are stacked. His voice is business-like. 'Time for you to read to me. Illuminate me. Then I will enlighten you.'

Gideon opens one of the last of his father's journals. He knows exactly the passage that he's looking for. He clears his throat and begins: 'If this diary is being read, I pray to the Sacreds that it is *you* Gideon who is doing the reading. You were always the most methodical of children, so I presume you will have started from the beginning and this will be one of the last entries you will read. Now you will know of my differences with the Inner Circle, of their desire to force me to accept their will. I cannot bend to their ways. I must not and I shall not. If you take, so shall you give. *You* personally. Not you by proxy or by threat. It is entirely wrong that if you take, you force someone else to give. This is not the way holy people repay their debts. It is the way of the selfish, the untrustworthy, the dishonourable. The way of a man I deemed a friend. A person I allowed into my own house and trusted like a brother. A man who tainted everything in life that I respected.'

Gideon stops reading, turns the diary round. 'Here.' He places a fingertip besides the inscription 'ΟΩΜΥΖ ΙΥΛΦΗΩΣΚΛ'. 'Do you recognise this name?'

The Master cannot read the code but he knows he is looking at his own name. It is hardly surprising to him to see it written disparagingly in Nathaniel's diary. It proves something to him. The books are truly as dangerous as he feared they would be. 'Your father and I didn't always see eye to eye. Nor was he right about everything. He was a brilliant man, this you know. But it made him difficult. He couldn't be reasoned with.' He stands, moves away from the table and paces slowly. 'Tell me, do you share his views?'

'On what?'

'On me. On the fellowship. He probably wrote in detail about it. Our differences of opinion, especially as far as the rituals are concerned.'

Gideon responds without hesitation. 'He did. I know better than anyone that my father wasn't always right. For years we barely spoke. Now he is gone.' Gideon pauses reflectively, then looks straight into the Master's eyes. 'My wish is only to experience a long and healthy life. To show my loyalty to the Sacreds and if you help me do this, then of course my unquestioning loyalty to you.'

The Master embraces him. It is the best answer he could

357

have hoped for. Gideon returns the gesture, though he would rather drive a knife through the man's heart.

The Master pulls back and holds him proudly by the arms. 'Now it is time for me to illuminate you, to reveal to you secrets that will leave you breathless.'

130

Megan sits in her car in the supermarket car park and waits.

She can't go home and she can't go to work. All she can do is dwell on the awful, fleeting image of Adam in the Mercedes with Utley. It was as bad as catching him in bed with another woman. Yet one more rotten, stinking example of his cheating, lying and betrayal.

She thinks of Sammy and wonders how he can have had the gall to come home to them and play the perfect father and husband while keeping all his secrets. Secrets of belonging to other women, other men, anyone except her and their daughter. Now the sadness turns to anger. Her skin flushes and prickles with the rising rage.

It's late afternoon when an old Jag stops alongside her Focus. The window slides down and the driver breaks Megan's festering mood by shouting, 'Get in.'

The waiting is over.

DCI Jude Tompkins listens patiently as Megan tells her about being followed by Utley and her husband Adam. She calls for a vehicle check and confirms the Mercedes is registered to Matthew Stephen Utley of Tidworth. 'I could check on your husband's movements over the last couple of hours but not without people asking me why I want to know.'

'Don't bother,' says Megan. 'I know it was him.' She chews at a blooded nail. 'I feel so stupid. I thought he came back because he wanted to be with me and Sammy.'

'You'll have time to beat yourself up about that later,' says her boss. 'Right now we have to work out what to do about your daughter. Who we can turn to without raising suspicions.'

'Mum has Sammy,' says Megan. 'I called her and said Adam has been aggressive with me. She won't let him in the house or near Sam. My dad is at home too, so everything will be okay.'

'Good. I did some checking this morning. Double-checking, if you like, to make sure we weren't jumping to the wrong conclusions.'

'And?'

Tompkins slides a mugshot out of her handbag. 'Sean Elliott Grabb.'

'Suspect with his prints on the VW Campervan.' Megan takes the picture. 'Worked security at Stonehenge.'

'Right. He's dead. Turned up in Bath. Fished out of the Avon.'

'Murdered?'

'Too early to tell,' says Tompkins. 'Grabb and Stonehenge.

That's yet another connection to the Timberland, Lock and Chase cases. There are far too many coincidences for my liking.'

'So what do we do, ma'am? Where do we take this?'

'That's what I'm worried about.' Tompkins gives her a studied look. 'The Chief and Deputy want you out of Devizes, right? They're packing you off to Swindon. So I don't think we can trust either of them.'

'What about Jimmy Dockery? Any sign of him?'

'He's done a Lord Lucan. Completely vanished.' She scratches the back of her head. 'I'm thinking of taking all this out of force, going to Barney Gibson, the Met Commander.'

Megan is surprised. 'He's going to think you're mad.'

Tompkins smiles. 'I know. That's why you are going to tell him, not me.'

131

The Henge Master guides Gideon through the mazy inner sanctums of the Sanctuary. He raises his hands towards the chiselled walls and ceilings. 'The ancients quarried far and near for this stone. It was hand-picked and dressed by initiated builders. The precision was incredible. Each piece sanctified by the Sacreds. Two million individual blocks interlocked. The entire structure erected without mortar.'

Gideon rubs a hand along the smooth walls as they walk.

The twisting corridors become narrower and the ceiling height falls as they descend into the heart of the temple. 'Why has this place never been discovered?'

The Master smiles. 'Because there is no reason to look for it. No one knows of its existence and all archaeological digs are focused around Stonehenge. Occasionally there are finds – a wooden henge in line with the Sacreds, a crematorium, the bones of dead soldiers, ancient axes and tools. This is enough to satisfy academic appetitites.'

'But there is more?'

'*Much* more,' says the Master. 'Not only the Sanctuary but other sacred places that are all aligned and linked, blessed and protected. And not just here. Across the world.'

Gideon is dazzled by the extent of the unknown. He has a thousand questions.

'Come,' urges the Master walking again. 'In all, it took more than a hundred thousand people over two centuries to complete the Sanctuary and Stonehenge.' The Master leads him through a spiralling labyrinth of tunnels. 'They quarried without machines, used rough wooden sleds and their hands to haul titanic weights hundreds of miles, sometimes across deep stretches of water. They built scaffolding from felled trees, ropes and pulleys from grasses, tree bark and vines. They dug a fully functional and entirely original sewerage system. It still works perfectly. Channelled through the plain to the Sanctuary to fall into deep chalk pits fed by underground streams.' He stretches upwards and touches an open hole in the sandstone blocks. 'Ancient air ducts ensure a steady flow of oxygen. These vertical tunnels are also star shafts. They point to specific stars, certain constellations. The Sanctuary is a precessional clock that also allows us to keep our charts and calendars, just as our forefathers did.'

The Master leads them through a narrow arch into a passageway running directly below the Great Room. 'While the Sanctuary's initial purpose was to be a temple for the Sacreds, it was also a Neolithic teaching hospital, a form of university cum town hall where science, health and administration were practised.'

'Their society was that advanced?' asks Gideon.

'Every era has its outstanding leaders, even the Neolithic one.' The Master walks on through the passageway and produces a large iron key hung on brown string around his neck. 'Let me illustrate the point.' He unlocks a narrow oak door and they slide through into the pitch black.

The air is even cooler and their footsteps echo even louder. The Master lights a wall torch and several large, floor-level candles. As their eyes adjust, they see a large and perfectly circular chamber dominated by a dark block in the middle. The vast walls are hewn from blood-red granite, reminiscent of Egyptian tombs. On the walls to the left and the right as far as Gideon can see are dozens and dozens of open coffins all angled so the skulls of the dead have a perfect view of the large Pantheon-like single star shaft in the centre of the room.

'A crypt,' observes Gideon. 'Who were these people and why the special treatment?'

'These are the ancients. Our predecessors. The brilliant men who designed and built the Sanctuary, Stonehenge and all the henges, barrows, burial mounds and avenues linked to them.' The Master moves slowly around the room lighting more torches and candles. 'But this is more than a sacred resting place, Gideon.'

The giant stone block in the middle becomes increasingly visible. Fashioned out of polished sandstone, it is at least five metres high and three metres wide. On two sides are shelves filled with maps and scrolls. The other two are divided into what look like dozens of small ovens filled with rubble.

Gideon is amazed. He approaches it like a cat stalking a bird.

The young archaeologist is almost too afraid to touch any-thing. It is a library. A museum. A time capsule filled with ancient scripts, artefacts, carvings and tools.

'How far back does this go?' he asks.

'Right to the beginning.' The Master points to the top of the cube. 'Up there you will find original carvings. The first plans for the Sanctuary and Stonehenge. Over there in the largest coffins you see the remains of the first sacrifices, those who completed the Sanctuary and the henge.'

'The builders were sacrificed?'

'It was their will. They knew that in offering themselves to the Sacreds, they ensured blessings for their children and the generations to follow.'

Gideon stands in awe. Around him is an archaeologist's dream. An Aladdin's Cave of ancient history and civilisation. The discovery of a lifetime. His pulse races. 'I never read anything about any of this. In all the diaries I found, there was no mention of this place or anything in it.'

'Nor should there have been. Speaking of it, or writing about it, is forbidden.' The Master moves closer to him, smiles again. 'Nathaniel knew of this chamber. He did much work in here. Among the parchments and documents in the archive, you will find his own labours, contributions to the star maps and charts that all Masters are obliged to complete.'

So much history in one space. So much knowledge. So many secrets. The Master breaks the spell by motioning to the door. 'We must go. I have more to show you and very little time in which to do it.'

Reluctantly, Gideon leaves the chamber and the Master extinguishes all the lights, relocks the door. They walk to the end of the passage and begin a steep and precarious climb up a seemingly endless flight of open-sided stone steps. They cling like ivy to the outer wall of the Sanctuary. No safety panels or guard rails. A sheer brutal drop beside them.

'Take care,' says the Master. 'You may still be a little weak from the initiation.'

It's good advice. After more than a hundred steps, Gideon finds himself sweating and struggling for breath. The man in front pushes on like a mountain goat, taking each stone slab with a powerful and confident stride.

Gideon keeps one palm on the wall. He notices the intricate carvings in the stone. Ancient art depicting farmers working fields, women carrying babies, herds of cattle gathering by streams. Across the walls he sees other scenes.

Workers raising giant blocks of stone, the first outlines of the henge being formed. People at burial mounds, their heads hung low. Scenes showing the orbit of the sun, the constellations of the stars and the phases of the moon. Up above, there is a more frightening depiction.

Men in robes are gathered around a bound figure over the Slaughter Stone, the hammer of the Master is raised. It reminds him that the young American woman, the one from the news, is immured somewhere below them.

He sways on the steps.

A hand grabs a clump of his robing. The Henge Master pulls him tight to the wall. 'Be careful.'

He steadies himself and breathes slowly. 'I'm okay.'

'Good. Then we go on.'

Within a few steps, they reach the top. Gideon sees now that there is another set of stone stairs descending on the other side, running straight down towards the chambers and the Great Room.

The Master again uses the key from around his neck.

The area that Gideon steps into is a world removed from the archive chamber and in its own way even more surprising.

The first thing that strikes him is the light. The bright white fuzz of fluorescent tubes, flickering and buzzing like trapped and angry ghosts. The floor and the walls are grey. But not stone. Concrete. Plaster. It is as though he has walked into a giant modern warehouse or garage.

In front of him is what he guesses is an acre of sealed concrete. Hundreds of metres of plastered walls. The Master walks forwards on to a slatted steel gantry some ten metres above the floor. Gideon follows. There are vehicles parked at the far end. Chunky 4×4s and something distinctly familiar. Draco's white builder's van.

The place is more than a garage. He can feel it in his gut, long before his eye roams over the vast greyness. The space is divided into other distinct areas. There are dozens of metal lockers; clusters of changing benches, tables and chairs. A kitchen section with rows of sinks; endless worktops to cut and prepare food on; lines of tall refrigerators and freezers; microwaves, stoves, ovens and pans.

Enough room and equipment in here to feed an army.

'It's our operational centre,' says the Master casually. 'Below ground we respect our traditions in the way our ancestors did. Above the surface, we are an elite force. Tomorrow you will come here and work. You will play your part in the preparations for the great day.'

132

SATURDAY 26 JUNE, ONE DAY
TO THE NEW FULL MOON

Dawn sleepily pulls at the dark curtains of the sky like a red-faced toddler tugging blankets at the foot of its parents' bed. Lookers surround the dew-soaked fields of Stonehenge.

They stand in the empty car park. No tourists have been allowed to book any early visits to the site.

The Henge Master walks the public footpath trodden by millions, steps across the newly cut grass. Enters the iconic circle. Today will last sixteen hours, thirty-seven minutes and five seconds. The altitude of the sun is 61.9 degrees.

Tomorrow it will make its first major shift for ten days and drop to 61.8. He looks to the ever-changing sky as he enters the horseshoe of trilithons.

Moonset was more than an hour ago. There is no sign of the lady in white. She dances in the unseen darkness almost a quarter of a million miles away. At nine tonight she will return and she will appear in 98 per cent of her full virgin glory.

Almost ready.

A gentle wind blows across the open fields. The Master stretches out his arms to feel the energy of the Sacreds. Everything that happens from now on is about precision. Precision, alignment and the final will of the gods.

133

Caitlyn has never prayed. Her father comes from lapsed Jewish stock and her mother from a brand of Protestantism so casual she might as well have been an atheist.

The only things her family have ever believed in are fairness, goodness and kindness. Do unto others as you'd have them do unto you. Not the kind of upbringing that prepares you for being held hostage, immured in stone and starved to death. That's where she has been since she injured herself and they moved her. In a tiny immurement cavity stuffed with memory foam. She can feel it against most of her front and back. Like being sandwiched between mattresses.

Caitlyn closes her eyes and tries to pray. Her mind is such a spiky jumble of fear that she can't even focus a single silent plea to any or all spiritual saviours. For the first time since they locked her up, she starts to cry.

134

It is exactly eight a.m. when Megan follows her DCI into Barney Gibson's makeshift office. She last saw him and his operational sidekick Stewart Willis six days ago, but the two men look ten years older. Endless shifts, sleepless nights and the stress of the inquiry are breaking their health.

Tompkins lays it out for them. 'Almost a week ago, DI Baker sat in this same room and told you that she believed Caitlyn Lock and Jake Timberland had been on their way to Stonehenge when he was killed and she was abducted. We have information that now seems to confirm that. And we think we know who is responsible. Incredible as it seems, there is good reason to believe that an ancient pagan cult may be behind the abduction.'

'Unlikely,' says Willis. 'We have reliable intelligence that an international crime syndicate has Lock. Ransom demands have already been made.'

Tompkins holds her ground. 'I'd ask you to stay open-minded, sir. What DI Baker is about to tell you is going to sound fanciful but I assure you that there is strong circumstantial evidence to support it.'

Gibson is starting to think it was a mistake to consent to this confidential meeting. 'Jude, why didn't you take this to John Rowlands or your own Chief?'

She knows she's on thin ice. 'Sir, there is a possibility that my own force may be implicated. Physical and electronic evidence has already been tampered with. The inquiry could be compromised from within.'

'Those are very serious allegations. You put me in a difficult position.'

'I do, sir. And I apologise. But given the circumstances, I believe it is entirely appropriate that we seek your guidance as senior external officers heading this major investigation.'

'Point made.' He turns to Megan. 'So, Detective Inspector, what's the story?'

Megan knows she's only got one shot at maintaining her credibility. 'While investigating the suicide of Professor Nathaniel Chase, a published archaeologist and world-renowned expert on Stonehenge, his son Gideon made me aware of diaries written by the professor about a secret cult dedicated to the stones of the henge.'

'Druids?' interjects Willis.

'No, sir. This society predates any druid movement. If you need a comparison, think of the Freemasons. I believe we are talking about an ancient craft-based order that has matured over centuries and wields considerable power and influence.' No sooner have the words crossed her lips than she regrets them. If either Willis or Gibson is a Freemason, her case is dead in the water. 'Sir, coded diaries discovered by Gideon Chase suggest that the cult derives some form of blessings and protection from Stonehenge providing human sacrifices are periodically made to their gods.'

The two men are looking at each other, thin smiles on their lips. 'I find this very hard to believe. Human sacrifice is unknown in modern day Europe,' says Gibson. 'Even in America, where they have more than their share of extremists, there are only a few documented cases over the past hundreds of years. I'm really struggling to buy into this theory of yours.'

'I was too, sir,' says Megan. 'But certain events have changed my mind.'

Willis glances impatiently at his watch. 'And they are?'

'It all seems to come back to Stonehenge. It is at the centre of all our recent major cases. Nathaniel Chase, an expert on the henge, commits suicide. Lock and Timberland are attacked while visiting the stones. Sean Grabb, one of the men we wanted to interview about those attacks, is found dead in Bath. He was working security at Stonehenge. And all of this happens around the summer solstice.'

Gibson seems interested. Or maybe amused. It's hard for

Megan to tell. 'Sir, I've checked the medical records of Gideon Chase. He told me he had cancer as a child and the stones cured him. According to the records, his claim seems to be true.'

Willis frowns. For him, it's just not credible. 'Are you telling me that his medical records say he was cured of cancer by a ring of stones?'

'No, sir. They say he had an incurable form of cancer and was cured. They give no explanation, simply because they couldn't find one.'

Gibson lets out a sigh of exasperation. 'DCI Tompkins said evidence had been tampered with. What evidence and what tampering?'

Megan realises his patience is wearing thin. She summarises as tightly as possible. 'Someone broke into and set fire to the home of Nathaniel Chase. But not before trying to recover or destroy something of value. We think the intruder was after the secret diaries we now know the professor had written about Stonehenge and the cult connected to it. His son Gideon managed to take a camera-phone snap of the burglar. Our facial recognition software produced a match with a local man. And we also recovered physical evidence from the break-in. Tools in a kit bag that had been left behind. When I last checked, sir, all that evidence was missing from the property store. All trace of it had been wiped from the computer log. As had the electronic bulletin sent to my mailbox about the facial match. Everything had been erased from my files.'

Gibson makes notes then looks up at Tompkins. 'We need to talk separately about this and how we handle it.'

She nods.

The Met Commander sits back and weighs up Megan. As crazy as everything sounds, she seems a first-class officer and not the type to get carried away on flights of fancy. He is also aware that she is supposed to be in Swindon setting up a new cold case unit. What she shouldn't be doing is speaking confidentially to him behind her chief's back.

He leans forward and clasps his hands on the desk. 'You're an experienced officer, Megan, so I'm sure you're aware that our investigation is on a knife edge. We have the FBI, Interpol, private investigators and most British police forces all chasing leads. The strongest of inter-agency evidence demonstrates that an international crime syndicate has taken Caitlyn and is extorting money from her parents. The asking price is currently twenty million dollars. I respect the manner in which you came to us, but at the moment I cannot risk deploying resources to investigate your claims, I—'

'But sir—'

He stops her. 'Let me finish.' A stern pause. 'I need proof. I need to see the coded diaries you mentioned. I need evidence that there have been human sacrifices in the past. I need something forensic before I even think about switching precious time and people away from where I have directed them. Bring me that and you'll get a different response.'

Tompkins pushes her chair back. 'Thank you, Commander.' She nods to Willis. 'Chief Superintendent. I'd like the assurance that this conversation remains confidential for the moment. For obvious reasons.'

'You have it,' says Gibson. 'But only for the moment.'

135

The day before the ritual is the start of a holy period. A time of reverence. The Master, the Inner Circle and all Followers begin a devout fast. They do it out of respect for the sacrifice. They drink only water. They abstain from any sexual acts of any kind, either practised or witnessed, until the first evening twilight after the completion of the ceremony.

The Henge Master explains the pursuit of purity to Gideon as they sit in his chamber. 'The ritual of renewal is sacred to us. But that does not mean we are barbarians. No. The most important person among us right now is the one who will be sacrificed.' He rests his left hand on the four diaries. 'I believe that through your father you may well have learned more about the sanctity of life and its meaning in death than most.'

Gideon is unsure where this is leading. 'All I know is, he was willing to give his life to save mine. To give me the chance to raise children of my own.'

'Exactly. A single sacrifice for the greater good of the

many.' The Master studies the young man opposite him. 'It is our practice that one of our Followers, usually a member of the Inner Circle, spends the last stressful hours in the company of the sacrifice. To give moral and spiritual support until the very last moment. And to ensure that nothing can happen to them before the ritual begins. This is a role, Gideon, that I would like you to perform for us.'

He can't hide his shock. 'I don't understand. Why me?'

The Master smiles. 'I think you do, Gideon. I think you know why I have shown you mercy and favour. Why I have invested my personal trust and faith in you, despite those close to me doubting the wisdom of letting you live.'

Gideon feels a chill creep through him.

'It is important to me that I go into the ritual with a clear mind and an open spirit. Tell me, Gideon. Is there something your father told you that you haven't shared with me?'

Gideon shakes his head. His denial is true. But he knows what the Master is driving at. He sees his mother again. The frail old woman whom he barely recognises sits up once more in her deathbed. She speaks the words that turn his life upside down.

Nathaniel is not your father, Gideon.

The Henge Master reads it in his eyes. 'Then your mother told you. *I* am your father, not Nathaniel Chase.'

136

Megan pulls the car into the kerb a street away from her house and walks the rest of the way. She's trying to cool down. The meeting with Gibson and Willis had been a waste of time. Made her and Tompkins look foolish. The DCI said as much. The two Met men hadn't believed a word that had been said. They wanted facts. Wouldn't listen to anything else.

Megan feels alone. Vulnerable. Edgy. She's not just walking to cool down, she's also taking precautions. Adam might be at the house. Adam, the husband she thought she was falling in love with again. Adam, the man she saw sitting alongside burglar and police attacker, Matt Utley. She can't see any strange cars near her home. She loiters in the quiet cul-de-sac for almost five minutes before she feels safe enough to go inside.

The house is empty. But he's been here. She knows he has because there's a note propped up on the dining table, bearing his writing. She snatches it away from the vase of flowers.

'Meg. Gone back to mine. Call me when you've got your head together.

A x.

P.S. – we need to talk about me seeing Sammy.'

She screws it up, drops it in a full pedal bin. Her heart is racing. She gathers swimming clothes and thick towels for her and her daughter, takes a quick look around and then steps out on to the drive and locks the door.

There's a man there. A man who has been watching her home and waiting for her.

137

Father and son look at each other across the ancient stone table.

'When did you find out?' asks Gideon.

The Master bows his head. 'Not until Marie was dying.' He looks up, his eyes glassy. 'Nathaniel sent for me when she was in the hospice. She told me just hours before she passed. There was nothing I could do. It was too late to seek intervention.'

Gideon is surprised to feel anger rising. 'And what was she to you?'

The Master scowls. 'What *was* she? She was everything. Everything and nothing. She was the woman I couldn't have but would have married. The person I would have spent my life with had we not argued and drifted apart. If she hadn't met Nathaniel.'

'What do you mean?'

'We were childhood sweethearts. After our relationship broke up, she moved away, to Cambridge. It was there that she met Nathaniel, and married him. I didn't see her until a year after the wedding when she moved back to Wiltshire.'

Gideon does the maths. His sainted mother had apparently broken her marriage vows with the monster sat opposite him only a year after pledging her eternal love to the man he thought was his father. 'How could you?' He stands, face flushed with anger. 'She'd only just got married and you seduced her.'

'It wasn't anything like that,' says the Master, undisturbed by Gideon's rage. 'It just happened. You'd have to understand how intensely I loved your mother to begin to realise how that one moment of weakness surprised us both.'

'One moment?' Gideon doubts it. 'I was the result of one moment of weakness?'

The Henge Master gets to his feet and comes round the stone table. 'I had no idea until your mother passed. How could I then approach Nathaniel? What could I have said to him about you?'

'Did you know the cancer was genetic?'

He nods.

'And you persuaded my father to join the Craft to protect your own son, to protect me?'

'Yes. It is what a father should do. I needed to protect you.'

The Master embraces him. Holds him tight. As tight as a father would hold his long lost child.

138

Jimmy Dockery steps down the driveway towards Megan. He can see she is scared. 'Don't be frightened, boss.'

But she is. She backs off, retreats towards her own front door.

'I need to talk to you.' He takes another slow step her way.

She drops her handbag, turns the keys in her clenched right fist into a spiked knuckleduster.

He glances at the makeshift weapon, a dismissive look on his face. 'You want to fight me?'

'Come any closer, Jimmy, and I'll kill you.'

He can tell she means it. He doesn't have much time. He lurches forward and makes a pretend grab with his left hand. Megan falls for it. She throws a spiky cross with her right. He steps inside and blocks hard with his left forearm, knocking the keys from her fingers. He could pick her off now with one knockout blow to the jaw. Instead, he snatches her left wrist and whips it up behind her back. Slaps his other hand across her mouth.

Before she knows it, he's bundled her around the side of the house. She tries to kick out but Jimmy is wise to it. He spreads his legs and holds her like an adult would a kicking toddler in a tantrum.

'I'm not going to hurt you.'

Megan carries on kicking.

'Boss, stop it. You were right, okay? I've been following Smithsen and you're right.'

She's not sure that she heard him properly. But she caught enough to stop thrashing and fighting.

Jimmy takes his hands off her.

She turns to face him. 'What did you say?'

'I know where they go. Where Smithsen and the others meet.'

139

The Henge Master opens the diary and points to his own name. ΟΩΜΥΖ ΙΥΛΦΗΩΣΚΛ. 'James Pendragon,' he says aloud. He puts a fist to his heart in a gesture of pride. 'It's a name to be proud of. A family line that stretches back through Celtic times. Back to the most famous king of Briton. Back into the mists of mythology and beyond. We are the stuff of history you and I.'

Gideon is familiar with both fact and the fiction. 'King Arthur is more fairy tale than reality,' he says.

The rebuke does nothing to cool the Master's familial passion. 'Really? Arthur Pendragon, the great Briton King? Or Riothamus the King, or the Cumbrian King, Pennine King, King of Elmet, Scottish King, Powysian King or even the Roman King? You think all these are kings of fantasy? You are a learned man. These legends are rooted in more than mere myth. They have endured.'

'And you?' asks Gideon, a hint of bitterness in his voice. 'What of you is fact and fiction?'

The Master shrugs. 'I am certainly no king, but I do serve and lead our people, the Followers. I am the only child of Steven George and Alice Elizabeth Pendragon. I have never married, and apart from you I have no children.'

'Are they still alive? Your parents, I mean.'

'Very much so. Your grandfather is ninety and your grandmother eighty this year. Both are in excellent health.'

Gideon's emotions are in turmoil. Despite her deathbed confession, he still yearns for his mother, and still feels guilty about what happened between him and Nathaniel. Now he is face-to-face with his birth father and a family tree of mythical dimensions that overwhelms him.

The Henge Master senses the dilemma. 'You will need time to come to terms with things.' He grips his arm. 'Thankfully, we will have it. Once the ritual is over, we can get to know each other. Find ways to bridge the years.'

Gideon still has dozens of unanswered questions but not now. Now is a time of silence. Inner thought.

'So,' says the Master. 'Will you accept the task that I asked of you? Can I rely on you to be the last companion for the girl, the chosen one?'

Gideon nods.

'Good. Very good.' The Master embraces him again.

As they come apart, they lock eyes. 'You are no longer Gideon. You are Phoenix. Your given name is Phoenix.'

He is confused. 'I understood Followers adopted star signs that began with the initial letter of their first name.'

'They do,' says Pendragon, his face suddenly stern again. 'The name I always wanted for my son was Philip. It is what I always called you when I thought of you. From now on, you will be known as Phoenix.'

It feels like a crude trick, a psychological blow to undermine him. This disownment of his name hurts him. Strips him of his identity.

'Our family motto is a simple one,' says Pendragon. '*Temet Nosce*. Thine own self thou must know.'

140

'You nearly broke my damned arm, Jimmy.' Megan nurses her bruised limb.

'Sorry,' he says. 'I tried to stop you without hurting you. I could have been much rougher.'

She straightens out her clothes. 'Bully for you. Where the hell did you learn that physical stuff?'

'Got picked on a lot at school. Ginger hair, makes you a target. My old man took me to taekwondo lessons.'

'Tompkins is going to kick your arse. You've been off radar so long.' She stretches her arm several times.

'You told her?'

'Had to tell someone.'

Jimmy realises he's at the point where he has to explain things. 'You didn't trust me, I could tell, so I went off to find something that would prove to you that I wasn't part of this crazy cult tied to the dead professor and Stonehenge.'

She looks at him suspiciously. 'And did you?'

'I followed Utley and Smithsen. They certainly know each other. Caught Utley at home and followed his Merc. He met up with Smithsen in a lay-by on the A360. They got into the back of Smithsen's van, maybe he took something out. Then went their separate ways.'

'Which ways?'

'Utley back east towards Tidworth and Smithsen headed west.'

She maps it out in her head. 'There isn't much out there, not until you loop north to Devizes.'

'It's all military. Part of the MOD buy-up.'

'Did you stay on Utley? Or follow Smithsen?'

'Decided to go after Smithsen. As far as I could.'

'And?'

'He went north past Westdown Camp and Tilshead. After a couple of miles, he forked sharp left. Towards Imber.'

'Imber?'

'It's a ghost town. Way into restricted access. No one has lived there for more than sixty years. It's just empty houses. Buildings remain standing but no one is home. The church still holds the odd service every year.'

Megan remembers the map on Tompkins' office wall and her records search. 'It's where Nathaniel Chase owns a strip of land. One of the few bits that the War Office couldn't buy up.'

'Can't think why anyone would want to own it. From what I know, soldiers just shoot the shit out of the place. Then drive over it in tanks and even bomb the land around it.'

'A lot of work for a builder?' ventures Megan.

'Doubt it. The army would just fix it up themselves. They'd use squaddies to do basic bricklaying and bang up some boards on doors and windows.'

She weighs things up. If Gideon Chase is still missing, it's possible he is being held somewhere in Imber. They could be holding Lock there as well. 'I don't know what to do, Jimmy. I can't go to Tompkins with this and your old man and the Chief want me transferred to Swindon.'

'What?'

'I'm being bumped. Shifted sideways. It's a long story. How do we get to look around Imber without anyone at work finding out?'

'I know exactly how.' He gives her a confident smile. 'In fact, I've already got someone who can help us. He's waiting in my car.'

141

The chamber they've moved Gideon to is much bigger than the last one. About six metres long by four metres wide, he'd say. A penthouse compared with the matchbox they've been keeping him in. But it is still a cell.

The door is open, flanked by two Lookers, one of whom Gideon has seen before with Draco. Inside, high on all four walls are burning torches. On the hard stone ground are two makeshift wooden bunks filled with straw. In the corner of the room, two narrow stone troughs filled with water.

If he's right, the chamber is no more than a twisting fifty metres of corridor from the steep stairwell that leads to the warehouse. It doesn't take him long to work out why that is. They bring the girl here so it's easy to move her into a waiting vehicle.

Gideon hears footsteps outside. A mix of men's voices, shadows across the gated doorway and then four Lookers lumber into the cell. At first he doesn't see the woman between them. Two of the men lift her under her arms while others grab her feet. They swing her on to a bunk.

One of the men is Draco. He hangs back while the first two Lookers leave. 'She is weak, hasn't eaten anything for almost seven days.' He puts his arm around the well-built Looker next to him. 'This is Volans. He's going to be right outside the chamber. He has instructions to fetch a doctor if you think her condition is deteriorating. Do you understand?'

Gideon nods.

'Good, because this woman must not die. Her health is our single priority. For the next day at least.' He gives Gideon a soldierly slap and steps out of the cell with Volans, shutting the iron door behind them.

Gideon wonders if the Master has told Draco about him. About their relationship. It would be the clever thing to do if he was worried about the support of the Inner Circle. It's what he would have done in his position.

He takes his first look at the sacrifice. Easy to imagine that not so long ago she was very pretty. Even without make-up and her thick black hair matted, he can tell she is naturally attractive. Her short hooded robe has ridden up and he can see a flash of a Union Jack tattoo, a sign of another time, a symbol of flirtatious rebellion and youthful defiance. Gideon bends over her and pulls it down to preserve her modesty.

She slaps his hand away. 'Leave me alone.'

He is startled and steps back.

The woman sits up defensively in the bunk. Disorientated. Fear ingrained in her eyes. 'Keep away. Keep away from me!'

'I'm not going to hurt you. Honestly, I'm not.'

She looks around. Her prayers haven't been fully answered but at least she's no longer in that claustrophobic hell hole. She can breathe and stretch. And lie down. She looks at the stranger near her, her eyes almost black.

'Who are you? Why are you in here with me?'

142

A mountain of man gets out of Jimmy's black Golf GTI. 'Josh Goran, ma'am. Pleased to meet you.'

He towers over Megan as they shake hands. He has short dark hair, blue eyes, looks like he has been hewn from granite. Then it comes to her. He's the guy from the TV news appeals. From Kylie Lock's press conference. She guesses Jimmy has already told him about her. 'You'd better come inside. We can talk better there.' They follow into the cottage. And once the door is closed, Jimmy fills in some of the gaps. 'Josh has been retained by Caitlyn's mother to find her.'

'And return her safely,' adds Goran.

'I know,' Megan says. 'You're some kind of bounty hunter cum private eye, right?'

'Rescue and return operative,' he says. 'I have two decades' experience in what is the US equivalent of your SAS. Only better.' He cracks a Hollywood grin. 'Ma'am, I think we're kindred spirits. Seems you and I are both being kept out of the loop. It's why Jimmy here came to me.'

'I don't know anything about that,' she confesses.

'With due respect, ma'am, I think you probably know more than most.'

'Meaning?'

'From the intelligence that I've gathered – and believe me, I've gathered a lot – your local police, the FBI guys, I think they're giving too much credence to this theory that

Caitlyn's been kidnapped by an organised gang and is being held in France somewhere.' He nods towards Jimmy. 'I think you and Jim are much more likely to be on the right trail, ma'am.'

She can't help but interrupt. 'Josh, you're going to drive me crazy calling me ma'am. Megan will do.'

'Megan,' he says, through a whiter-than-white smile. 'In my experience if you kidnap someone and take them abroad, you leave traces. Driving's the easiest option. But you do that and you have to dodge a whole lot of surveillance cameras. You got to buy ferry or train tickets, without being seen or recognised. These days that's impossible. You flee the country, you leave signs. But in this case the Feds, your British police and my operatives, they've come up with zip. You know why? Because the perps never left the country. They're still here. Still local.'

Megan agrees. But there are still loose ends. 'What about the recordings of Caitlyn?'

He shrugs. 'Not necessarily what they seem. Be easy enough to have made the recordings of Caitlyn here and then had a guy catch the Eurostar from London and play an edited tape down a French phone line. Point of contact proves nothing.'

'Except that the kidnappers are well organised,' adds Jimmy.

'You can bet on that,' says Goran. 'These guys are very well organised. Part of the reason I think they've set up camp right in the middle of that military no-go zone.'

'Imber is owned and patrolled by UK forces,' says Megan. 'It's impossible for anyone to go in and out of there without clearance.'

Goran grins. 'Not at all. You have working farms nearby and there's a public footpath thirty miles long that runs around the firing ranges. Besides, the military have the dumbest guards alive. Believe me, I've worked with them most of my life.'

Megan smiles. 'So do you think you could work out a way to get in?'

'I'm ahead of you. I'm taking a surveillance team out there tonight. Zero one hundred hours to be precise. You want in?'

PART FIVE

Little Imber on the Downe,
Seven miles from any Towne,
Sheep bleats the unly sound,
Life twer sweet with ne'er a vrown,
Oh let us bide on Imber Downe.'

– Anon.

143

The black Ford Transit that rolls south from Devizes down the deserted A360 bears the green letters 'ATE' and a fluttering red flag. Beneath the official logo of the Army Training Estate are the words 'Specialist Scientific Research Unit'.

The van's six occupants wear high-visibility rainproof jackets emblazoned with the same crest. They carry in their pockets laminated ID cards and official authorisation to conduct a nocturnal wildlife survey in and around the IRPP, the Imber Range Perimeter Path, that skirts the live-firing area.

Megan looks around at the team and can't help but be impressed. 'It's amazing what you can pull together when you are chasing a potential pay cheque of ten million dollars.'

'Indeed it is,' says Josh Goran, sat in the back on a flipdown seat opposite her. 'Take a bow, Troy my boy.'

Troy Lynton looks up from the submarine glow of his laptop screen and gives a modest smile.

'Troy's our cyber king,' explains Goran. 'The world's best hacker, forger and fixer. Give him a little time and there's nowhere in the virtual world he can't access and nothing he can't steal or alter.'

Megan and Jimmy are crammed in the back with the two Americans. The driver is a man called Jay, who appears to be English. The front passenger is Luc, a former Dutch soldier who has been working with the crew for the past two years.

'Right now there are no major military manoeuvres planned at Imber, so troop numbers are minimal,' says Goran. 'Most guys will be lying back at barracks or bedding locals. We should be able to move around without restriction.'

Half an hour later, the van's headlights illuminate a warning sign: LIVE FIRING RANGE CLOSED TO THE PUBLIC: KEEP OUT.

The Transit trundles slowly on, then pulls over in front of a deserted farmhouse. Jay guides the vehicle up behind it, out of sight of the main road.

'Okay,' says Goran. 'Let's move.'

They grab backpacks and quickly spread in different directions. Goran has equipped them all with two-way radios, compasses, night-vision goggles, flashlights and, for the sake of the cover story, cameras and clipboards. Lynton has also briefed them on Imber's stone curlews, roe deer and badgers.

They move silently past shells of buildings, windowless and doorless brick hulks more reminiscent of Kosovo than Wiltshire. Once-beautiful thatched roofs have been replaced with rusted corrugated iron. Wildflower gardens have become mud pits, churned by the caterpillar tracks of tanks. Sprouting in the darkness, they see a red-and-yellow sign declaring, DANGER: UNEXPLODED MILITARY DEBRIS.

Jimmy and Megan stick to the instructions Goran has given them and methodically work their way through the ruins of Imber. English Jay does the same along a northern stretch towards Littleton Down, while Goran scouts the outer parts of West Lavington Down and Lynton works east through Summer Down.

They search for three hours. And find nothing.

As they regroup, Goran lays out a map on the bonnet of the van and jabs a finger south of Imber. 'This here is the very heart of the firing range. The military call it the danger zone. We've barely been in it. So far, we've just skirted the outer areas.'

Jay glances at the topography. He's still catching his breath. 'It would take all day to drive around that amount of land, let alone walk it and search it.'

No one argues with him.

'So now we have to make a decision,' says Goran. 'It'll be sunrise any minute. If we carry on, there's a high risk of being stopped and no longer any documented excuse for us being here.'

'We need another cover,' says Lynton. 'We simply swap the nocturnal survey for a daytime one. It's Sunday. No one is likely to call ATE and check. But I have to get near a computer and printer to change our papers and pin down some details.'

Goran looks at his watch. 'Zero four hundred hours. I say we pull out of here before we're seen. We grab a few hours' sleep while Troy creates the new documents. Regroup at midday, return and work until nightfall.'

Megan agrees along with the rest but suffers a pang of motherly guilt at the prospect of leaving Sammy with her parents again.

They're in the process of packing the rucksacks in the van when Goran quickly raises an arm. They freeze. From way off in the distance blink the headlights of an approaching vehicle. They take cover behind derelict buildings and the car zips past on the road heading out of the village.

'White builder's van,' says Goran, getting to his feet. 'It had a name like Smith and Son on the side. The back light over the number plate was out, so I don't have a registration.' He looks to Jimmy and Megan. 'Did either of you recognise it? Did it mean anything to you?'

'Yes,' says Megan. 'It meant a lot to us.'

144

The Henge Master sits alone in the darkness of the eastern chamber. He is waiting. Passing time. As he did yesterday morning. And the morning before.

It has always been the chore of Masters to plot the sunrise and sunset over the Sanctuary and Stonehenge. It is the Followers' own geocentric model. Like the Greek philosophers, like Aristotle and Ptolemy, they follow a belief that a fixed point of the earth is the centre of the universe.

All things revolve around them. Only the Followers are wiser. It is not the orbit of planetary motions alone that they focus on. It is also their effect that is important. The resultant swirl of spiritual forces. The realignment of souls and energy. The gravitational drift of eternal power and essence.

The knowledge of the Followers predates all others. Theirs is the science that gave birth to astronomy, astrology, geography, meteorology and all others. The wisdom of the ancients.

Through the eastern star shaft, the Master sees the first trace of sunrise. Not dawn. This is different. More precise. The exact time the upper edge of the great orb appears above the horizon. The moment that the balance of power shifts. The split second the rule of night is over.

The first gasping breath of a newborn day.

Eyes fixed on the rising red and orange disc in the

morning sky, the Master wonders for a moment about his new recruit. Phoenix. His son. His own flesh and blood. Today will be a telling one for him. For both of them. Blood is said to be thicker than water. Sunset will put that theory to the test. When the ball of fire dips in the west and the last of its trailing edge sinks below the horizon. The answer will be known.

Then history will be written.

145

Caitlyn wakes screaming.

The cell is compost black, wall torches long since burned out. Gideon heaves himself from the straw bunk beside her.

'Eric! *Eric*, help me!'

He follows the nightmare voice, feels his way in the utter blackness. The red glow of torches held by Lookers spills through the iron doors of the cell and he catches a glimpse of her. Knees tucked high against her chest, eyes glazed with terror.

'What's happening in there?' calls a Looker.

'Help! *Someone*, help me!'

Gideon tries to calm her. 'It's okay. You're all right.'

'*Help!*' The screams are louder.

He sits on the edge of the wooden bunk and tries to steady her. 'Caitlyn, you're dreaming. Wake up.'

Two Lookers step quickly into the cell, torches grotesquely illuminating their faces.

'It's okay,' says Gideon, half-turning to them. 'Light the wall torches and she'll calm down. She's just frightened.'

He puts his arms around her and holds her. 'Don't worry. No one is going to hurt you.' The words stick in his throat. Liar.

Light gradually crawls across the walls as the lit torches burn. Caitlyn wakes from the horror of her dreams to face the stone-hard reality of her fate. She holds Gideon for protection. Her voice is rough and raw. 'I need some water.'

The two Lookers wait for Phoenix to give his consent.

'Get her some, please.'

The taller of the two, the man previously introduced as Volans, moves to the back of the cell and fills a pot beaker with water from one of the stone troughs. He hands it to her and she drinks.

Gideon looks again at the two robed men. There is something different about them. The way they are holding themselves, the way they stand. He looks into their faces. Reads their concern, their intensity of focus. Then he notices their robes.

They are armed. Both are carrying guns.

146

Megan wants to chase after him. Wants to get up behind Smithsen's van and put him in a ditch. Find out what the hell he's doing on MOD land at four in the morning.

Goran unclips the radio from his belt. 'Command to Echo Leader. We've eyeballed a white van heading east out of Imber. Name on the side is Smithsen – Sierra Mike India Tango Hotel Sierra Echo November. Recon and report until otherwise instructed. Over.'

There is a hiss and then a crackly reply, 'Copy that, Command. Over.'

Megan looks irritated. 'Who was that?'

Goran looks smug. 'I have surveillance units pegged to all corners of the compass,' he says. 'They'll be effective for a while yet, until the roads fill up. After that, it's going to become more difficult. Echo Team is on the van and will report back.'

'I wish you'd told me you had those kind of resources. How can I help if I don't know what you're running with?'

The American grins widely. 'Sorry, lady. I'm afraid you only get to learn about my resources on a need-to-know basis.' He can see she's about to give him a mouthful. 'We don't have time to argue. We've got to get out of here before it's fully light.'

Megan glares at him. 'Wouldn't you like to know exactly

where that vehicle came from?' She looks into the twilight, in the direction of the MOD danger zone and the route Smithsen took.

As he is about to reply, Goran's radio spurts to life again. 'Echo to Team Leader. We've got a problem. I think the target just made us.'

147

Caitlyn's unsure of the man she's sharing a cell with. He introduced himself yesterday as Gideon but she was too sick to do anything but just stare warily at him. Why is he in here with her? What does he want? He's dressed like all the others but behaves differently. Not as mean. She looks across to him.

He acts friendly. Like he's on her side. But he *is* one of them. She knows he is. The other guards listen to him. He told them to light the torches on the wall and they did it. They did as he said. No hesitation. He has influence over them. So why is he in the cell?

She feels weak and nauseous as she creaks her way out of her bunk and tries to take a step or two. He sees the tension on her face. 'Are you okay?'

'Why do you care?' She glares at him like a frightened animal.

'I'm not here to hurt you.'

Her heart jumps. A sudden rush of hope. 'Have my parents paid the ransom? Am I going home?' She forgets her caution and goes over to his bunk. 'That's it, isn't it? It's why I'm in here instead of that goddamned hole in the wall. It's why you're being nice to me. You're preparing me for my release. Acclimatising me.'

Gideon stands and steadies her. 'No, Caitlyn. That's not it.' He glances towards the iron bars. 'For all I know, your parents haven't even been asked for a ransom. The people who abducted you are not after any money. I'm sorry.'

She doesn't understand. If they don't want her money, then what do they want? The fear returns to her face. 'So what's going on, then?' She gestures to the room. 'Why this?'

'Sit down. I'll try to explain.'

She sits, nervous as a kitten.

Gideon feels her panic infecting him. What he says next could unhinge her. But he has to let her know, she must understand what is going to happen. She has to realise that these are her last hours alive.

148

Draco's eyes are fixed in his rearview mirror, his hands locked on top of the van's steering wheel. About five miles back he caught a glimpse of something behind them. A dark blur way back. Maybe five hundred metres. Tiny but enough. The road out of Imber is always deserted. Always. But not today. The blur is still there.

'Can you make out what's behind us?' he says to Musca, beside him. 'What kind of vehicle?'

The big butcher swivels in the passenger's seat. He struggles with the shape. Not a van. Not an estate. 'Too far back to see properly. A hatchback maybe. A Focus or a Golf, that kind of thing.'

'Did you see where it came from?'

He turns back round. 'Not a clue. Why?'

'The army doesn't let anyone park down here. So where the hell did it come from and what's it doing out at this time?'

Musca leans forward so he can see it more magnified in the wing mirror. 'Maybe they're lost.'

'Maybe.' Draco takes his foot off the gas and slows the van down to thirty. Another glance in the rearview. A blood-red rising sun and the small black car. It's closing the gap. The builder slows to twenty-five.

'I'm going to brake and pull over without indicating. Get yourself ready.'

Musca eases a subcompact Glock 26 from his waistband and cradles it on his lap.

Draco hits the brakes. The car slides into a gravel run-off.

The hatchback swerves, its horn blaring. But it doesn't stop. A window rolls down and the driver shakes a meaty fist.

Neither Draco nor Musca speak. Their eyes stay fixed on

the tail-light of the car as it carries on down the dusty road. They watch until it completely disappears.

'Pissheads,' guesses Musca. 'I'll bet they've been on an all-nighter and are heading off to work.

Draco restarts the stalled engine. It makes sense. They might be going over to Tilshead or Westdown Camp. 'Let's hope so,' he says. 'Today is not the day we want anyone on our tail.'

149

'You must be fucking *crazy*,' Caitlyn says, backing away from Gideon. 'Cults and and sacrifices? This is not for real.' She paces nervously around the cell.

Gideon glances to the door. The Lookers are out there. Volans and the others. They are waiting. They will hear.

'And this place?' She raises her arms. 'What is it? The room next to the fucking *death* chamber? Are you and your whack-job buddies going to take me somewhere and roast me over a fire?' Her mind can't cope with the madness of what he's been trying to tell her.

He lets her vent. Pace. Blow off steam. Then he completes the picture. 'Just before twilight you will be moved from here. You will be washed and changed into ceremonial robes and taken to the Great Room inside the Sanctuary. There the Master will perform a pre-sacrificial ritual.'

Her eyes widen. He's deranged. Insane. Isn't he?

Gideon tries to reassure her. 'It is not sexual, but it is painful. Your body will be cut with the marks of the Sacreds. One incision for each of the trilithons. This is down your arms, your legs and your spine. Your wounds will be anointed with water of the Sacreds and you will be left for five hours.'

'And then what?'

'The Bearers will take you to the river. You will be immersed in the waters that the ancients crossed to erect the temple that you are in and Stonehenge.'

As she hears the word, she thinks of Jake. The last intimate moments they spent together.

'The henge is where the final part of the ceremony will take place. The offering.'

She stares in utter disbelief. His words are from a lexicon of lunacy. Offering, sacrifice, Bearers, Sacreds. 'How?' The question jumps from her of its own accord. 'How will it be done?'

'It will be quick. Merciful.'

'Merciful? What kind of word is that?' She looks down. Her hands are trembling. It's all so crazy she can't believe any of this is going to happen. 'Where's Jake? Is he . . .' Even saying his name distresses her. 'Is he going to go through all this as well?'

'No.' Gideon tries to be gentle. 'Your boyfriend is dead. The police found his body a few days ago. In a Campervan.'

Caitlyn loses her breath. It's what she feared. Locked in

that hole, she's thought as much a hundred times, but the news still breaks her.

Gideon wraps his arms around her and feels her sob against his shoulder. Her whole body shakes as the tears come.

Over her shoulder, he sees a face at the bars of the cell. The face of his father.

150

Sammy is already awake and causing mayhem by the time Megan gets back to her parents' place. She has make-up plastered across her face and over half the bedroom furniture.

'Making myself pretty, Mummy.' She smiles proudly and puckers her newly lipsticked lips.

'Come on, let's get you cleaned up.' Megan sets the shower running and tries to wipe up some of the mess.

Her daughter walks to the low cabinet beneath the sink and collects her own bottle of shampoo. 'I'm a big girl now, I can wash myself, Mummy.'

It makes Megan smile. Her daughter is growing up. Another few months and she'll start big school. It doesn't seem five minutes since Sammy was a babe in arms. Time is going so fast.

The water is fine and she helps Sammy over the edge of

the cubicle, careful she doesn't catch her toes, then closes the door. 'You okay in there?' She presses her face to the already steamed-up glass. Sammy slaps the other side, giggles.

Megan holds her head and pretends to be hit, puts her face back to the glass.

Sammy slaps it again and giggles even louder.

This kind of clowning could go on all day.

'Very funny,' says a deep voice behind her.

Megan spins round.

'Adam.' Her head fills with panic. 'How did you get in?'

He smiles thinly. 'Back door. Your mum left it open. I must have told her a dozen times to lock it. She just doesn't listen, does she?'

Her heart is thumping. 'What do you want, Adam? What are you doing in here?'

He shuts the bathroom door behind him. Traps them both in the bathroom. 'Where were you last night, Meg?'

'*What?*' She tries to sound indignant.

'You were out all night. And not in your car. You left it on the drive, and you weren't working. So *where* were you? Who were you with?'

'I think you should leave, Adam.' She tries to step around him but he blocks her.

She stares him down. 'Where I go and what I do is my business. Nothing to do with you. Now get out.'

His face colours. A vein in his neck twitches.

Megan tries for the door.

Again he blocks her. Slips his left hand the other side of her so she's trapped between his outstretched arms.

'Let me out.' Megan doesn't shout. She has one eye on Sammy. Her baby girl is sat squeezing shampoo down the shower drain.

'When I'm ready, Meg. Now tell me where you were.'

He is so much bigger than she is. She knows she'll lose any fight between them. But it doesn't stop her trying. She drives a knee hard between his legs. He catches it with one hand. His fingers lock like a grip wrench. He squeezes until he sees pain on her face. With his other hand, he grabs her throat and pushes her hard against the bathroom door. 'I hear you've been offered a job in Swindon. Promotion. Good for you. Best you take it.' He glances towards his daughter. 'Best for everyone. That way you keep your nose out of my life and out of everything else around here. Do I make myself clear?'

'Daddy!'

The voice shocks them both. A soaking wet Sammy is out of the shower.

'Princess!' He grabs a towel, wraps it around her and scoops her into his arms. 'Let me take a look at you.' He pulls open the bathroom door. 'Do us a favour, Meg, and make a cup of tea while I get my daughter dry.'

151

The Henge Master sits poring over ancient maps and astronomical charts spread on the stone table. The day's celestial movements are critical. The time is coming.

'Father.'

Both the voice and the word surprise him. Father. How he has longed to hear it. 'Phoenix. Come in. I had forgotten that I'd sent for you.'

Phoenix. The name pricks Gideon like a thorn in his flesh.

'Sit down.' The Master gestures to the stone bench by the table. 'How is the girl? She looked distressed when I saw you.'

'Understandably so.'

'What did you tell her?'

'Her destiny. What will happen to her today. It's right that she be given an opportunity to come to terms with this, make peace with her own god.'

'And perhaps be accepted by ours.'

'Indeed. I would like to stay with her, if that's possible. Right until the very end. I think she needs me to give her strength.'

'The very end. Do you think you are ready for that?'

'I'm sure I am.' Gideon pauses, as if weighing their words. 'Father, we have no more secrets. You think you hold something over me but you don't. I know where we are. I know it from your name, *my* family name, my heritage. I know it from the great forces that you can muster, from the architecture and archaeology of this Sanctuary, from the position of the star shafts and the alignment with the henge. I know it, Father.'

James Pendragon's eyes are glittering in the dark. He walks closer to his son. 'You are right. The time has come when we need to trust each other more. But know this: the ceremony has a certain vividness. It can be shocking. Are you sure you wish to be that close to the woman?'

'I am sure.'

'Very well. You may stay with her until the ritual of renewal has been completed, the Sacreds honoured and our debt repaid.'

'And then?'

'Then we reap the benefits. The autumn equinox is but twelve weeks away. This is the time the Sacreds will bless us.'

Gideon's eyes fall on the scrolls of paper on the Master's desk. They look identical to those he found in Nathaniel's observatory.

The Master follows his eyes. 'Do you know anything about archaeoastronomy or ethnoastronomy?'

'Not much,' he confesses. 'The former is the study of how ancient people understood the movement of planets and stars and how they shaped their cultures around those movements. The latter is more the anthropological study of sky watching in contemporary societies.'

The Master looks pleased. 'That's right. Our Craft

combines the two. We use historical records, such as those you have seen in our archive, and we keep looking, checking constellations and planetary movements. The alignments with the henge and the Sanctuary are critical to our beliefs.'

'I know.'

'Of course you do. You are one of the few who understands that nothing here is accidental. The position of every building block and star shaft, the physical alignments with sunrise in the east and sunset in the west, the architectural homage to magnetic north, the tilt of the Descending Passages to mirror the inclination of the earth, it all has sacred meaning.' The Master grows thoughtful. 'I must leave shortly. There are things I need to attend to outside of the Sanctuary. We had a problem earlier today. Nothing to worry about but I have to go.'

'Anything I can assist with?'

'No, no. Not at all. It would help if you could keep the girl calm. She will grow more anxious by the hour.' He picks up a long slate knife from among the maps.

The ceremonial blade.

He holds up his right hand and cuts into the palm. Blood trickles in a crimson snake down his wrist. 'Give me your hand.'

Gideon tentatively stretches his hand out and the Master draws the blade across his palm. Pendragon looks into his son's unblinking eyes and takes the blooded hand in his own. 'Blood on blood. Father and son. We are as one.' He holds up their entwined fingers and draws Gideon tight to him.

'When I next see you, it will be after the ritual has begun.' He grips his son's hand tighter. 'Swear to me now, as my blood runs in yours and yours in mine, that our souls and our truths are aligned, that I can lay all my trust in you and in this bond between us.'

'I swear it, Father.'

Gideon watches the crimson drops drip from his elbow and knows it won't be the last blood shed today.

152

Josh Goran flips his mobile shut, amazed at what Jimmy has told him. He and his boss are no-shows. The woman says she's staying with her kid and Jimmy's apparently busy chasing another lead. He can't believe it. The cops here are worse than the FBI. Hundred per cent amateurs.

Goran gets his men moving. Things are already running behind schedule and Echo Team has been compromised. Forced to abandon the surveillance on the builder's van. But he isn't worried. If there is anything to find out on the training range, he'll find it.

They get back to Imber by early afternoon. The road into the range is as deserted as it was in the early hours of the morning. But as they cruise past the restricted signs, the empty buildings and devastated gardens, they see ripples of mud on the road.

'Fresh tank tracks,' says Luc from the front passenger seat. 'Not even wet yet.'

'Challenger, most probably,' observes Goran. 'Piece of shit. I saw them in Kosovo. Brits would have been better sticking to the old Chieftains.'

'Or Rotem K2's,' says Luc. 'Korean Black Panthers. They've got fire-and-forget technology and full nuclear, biological and chemical armour protection.'

'K2's are an army equivalent of a Kia,' shouts Lynton from the back. 'Who'd go to war in a Kia?'

They all laugh.

Goran takes the Transit off road down a dirt track, west towards Warminster. It bumps around for about a mile and a half then they park up and drag out rucksacks filled with cameras, clipboards, fake documentation and specimen bags. Their cover this time is as members of the International Entomological and Natural History Society. Insect hunters. Lynton has mocked up IENHS access documentation to the Imber range and even filled their bags with research papers on bees, bugs and all manner of weird creatures.

Luc and Jay drop ramps from the back of the van and unload four Yamaha YZ125 trail bikes.

'Echo, November, Sierra and Whiskey Teams, this is Command,' Goran barks into the radio. 'We are go. Repeat, we are go. Command out.'

The four bikes start their outward sweep, while Echo, November, Sierra and Whiskey recon teams begin to walk inwards from the circumference of the range.

411

153

Warminster is eight point two miles west of Imber.

It takes the Henge Master twenty-five minutes to make the journey. On any day other than Sunday he would have done it in only nineteen. But Sunday is a day for church-goers and tourists, and the old Saxon town has eight major places of worship and the kind of surroundings people don't want to hurry past.

His vehicle rumbles through the main gates of Battlesbury Barracks and halts behind the parade ground. As he makes his way to his office, each soldier he passes stands to atten-tion and salutes their commanding officer, Lieutenant Colonel Sir James Pendragon. Routine and ritual is as important in his public life as it is in his secret one.

Settled behind his desk, he instructs his staff officer to send his guest through. The man he's travelled here to meet. Wiltshire's Deputy Chief Constable, Gregory Dockery, is in plain clothes – a grey wool suit with white cotton shirt and grey tie. In his sacred robes he would be known only as Grus.

'How are you?' Pendragon shakes his hand and gestures to a pair of brown leather Chesterfields.

'I will be glad when tomorrow has come.'

'As will we all.' Pendragon smiles as he sits. 'How are you managing your interested parties, the FBI, Interpol, Home Office? Tell me.'

'Vice President Lock is back in the US. He rings the Chief five times a day. His wife is drunk or drugged all the time that she's not on TV crying or pleading. The Home Office people are bored. They seem resigned to dealing with the fallout when the girl's body turns up. As for Interpol, well, you know how useless Interpol is. Might as well ask the post office to find her.'

'So all is good?'

'Not quite.' Dockery grows fidgety. 'I think we may have a potential problem with the lone American wolf.'

Pendragon nods. 'Major Joshua Goran, former Special Ops Command. I wondered how long it would be before he started causing trouble.'

'Goran has a couple of my men on his payroll. They're only feeding him what we want, but I got word that dogs in his pack are sniffing around Imber.'

'Makes sense. Draco said he saw people out there this morning. They tailed him and Musca for a little while but pulled out when they realised they'd been seen.'

'Any harm done?'

'I don't think so.' Pendragon muses for a moment on the incident. 'Most of our resources are stretched in preparation for tonight and tomorrow morning. But I will increase surveillance at the Sanctuary. I'll make sure Goran is not a problem.'

'Good.' Dockery creaks forward on the leather, places his hands on his knees. 'I also have some difficulties within the force, but I'm hoping they're being dealt with.'

'You mean Aquila's woman?'

'Yes. She's off the case. Hunt was confused of course, but bought the reason for the transfer in the end. She starts a new cold case unit in Swindon tomorrow and we've destroyed any physical or electronic evidence she had put together. I also had Aquila pay her a visit this morning. I'm told it had the desired effect.'

'Let's hope so. And your son, what about him and the woman?'

Dockery flinches. 'He remains a worry. Seems he has a lot of faith in the DI.'

'Son or no son, you can't allow him to become a problem, Gregory.'

'I am aware of that. And your own child?'

'Touché. I don't think I have any worries there though. He passed the initiation of course, and he is more than aware that he already owes his life to our cause.' Pendragon's face hardens. 'So why the visit? What is on your mind?'

Dockery creeps to the edge of his seat. 'I have a suggestion. An unorthodox one. However, one I think you can sanction. If you agree, I'm certain our plans will go ahead tonight without any fear of interruption.'

154

The Apache helicopter swoops across Salisbury Plain at more than a hundred and fifty miles an hour. It banks high into the bright blue sky before looping back over the sun-parched Imber range.

The gunship is fitted with an M230 chain gun, synched to the helmet sights of the pilot and gunner. Even more deadly are its semi-active laser-guided Hellfire II missiles, capable of destroying tanks, buildings and bunkers. It's a flying arsenal.

But this flight is non-aggressive. An impromptu run-out. The pilot Tommy Milner and his two-man crew sweep the plain to find a group of trespassers reported within the restricted area. A welcome break from the boredom of sitting around.

Milner calls in a result after only a few minutes.

'Targets spotted. Twelve in total. Spread twelve o'clock, three o'clock, six o'clock and nine o'clock. Do you want exact verbal positioning or will you take refs off our data screen. Over?'

'We got the data,' says the base's air controller. 'Processing now. Can you describe movements?'

'Charlie will give you details. I'm just going to hover so we can fix the cameras for you.'

Co-pilot Charlie Golding takes his cue. 'Two distinct groupings. Four on motorcycles moving outwards towards

Imber circular footpath as just described. Eight more in splits of two, on foot, moving inwards.'

Milner hits the zoom on one of the high-powered video surveillance cameras.

A soldierly form, dressed in some type of black uniform, fills the screen. 'I have one of the trespassers full frame,' says the pilot. 'As you can see he is on some form of non-military motorcycle, travelling at slow speed.'

'Thank you, Apache One. We have the imaging. Standby for further instructions. Over.'

The controller turns to Lieutenant Colonel James Pendragon. 'What do you want us to do, sir?'

The Master rises from the seat he'd taken near the monitors. 'Send a ground patrol to clear the range. Lock these fools up until the morning. Then let them go.'

155

Megan has spent most of the day in shock. Adam's surprise visit scared her. She knows exactly what he was doing. He was showing that he could find her, get to her or Sammy, any time he wanted. Well, it had worked. She's still shaking long after he's left.

Adam is still on her mind as Jimmy drives her out to West Lavington to meet a contact of his. A man who sounds almost as frightened as she is.

'He's terrified,' says Jimmy. 'Wouldn't agree to speak to you unless it was way out in the country, somewhere he felt safe.'

Megan glances out of the window at an endless green blur. 'Well, this is certainly way out in the country.'

They pull into the grounds of Dauntsey's, a five-hundred-year-old red-brick boarding school set in a hundred acres of secluded countryside on the northern edge of Salisbury Plain.

'His name is Lee Johns,' explains Jimmy, parking in a line of parents' vehicles near a stretch of sports fields. 'He worked security at Stonehenge with Sean Grabb, the guy who turned up dead in Bath.'

'And what, he just came forward today?'

'No, I only found him this morning. I've been working my way through the security firm's roster and finally caught him at home.'

A few minutes later an old Honda pulls in and parks up.

'This is our boy,' says Jimmy. 'Best you get the rest of the tale from him.' He slides out of his seat and heads across the car park.

Megan watches from the passenger seat and weighs Johns up as he approaches. Spotty-faced, mid-twenties, tall and thin but doesn't walk proud. He's a stooper. Self-conscious. Doesn't look the kind that makes friends easily. Probably a loner. Lives by himself, doesn't eat well and doesn't have a girlfriend.

Jimmy opens a back door for Johns, returns to the driver's

seat and makes the introductions. 'Lee, this is my boss, DI Baker. Tell her what you told me and don't mess about.'

He looks at her like she's about to eat him.

'Go on. I won't bite,' she says.

'You're going to think I'm crazy.'

'Try me.'

'I work – *worked* – a lot with Sean Grabb. He was a good bloke. He sort of took me under his wing when I came up here. Sorted me out like. He got me a job, helped me get my head together and encouraged me to get off the gear I was on. You know about Sean, right?'

Megan nods.

Johns lowers his head. 'He was a good bloke. A mate.'

Jimmy pushes him. 'Tell the DI what you said about the cult and Stonehenge.'

He looks up. 'It's not a cult. It's a religion. A proper religion. Goes back before Christ and everything. Sean was really into it. He believed the henge was some kind of sacred thing that was the home for ancient gods. He would go on and on about it, the power it had. He said the people who worshipped there were good people, doctors, lawyers and stuff, even coppers.' He looks towards Jimmy. 'No offence, like.'

'Go on.'

'Well, I got interested more because Sean was a mate and I wanted to stay tight with him. They took me somewhere weird and held this kind of mass and blessing.'

'Where?' asks Megan.

418

He shakes his head. 'I don't know. They put a hood over my head. I couldn't see. They drove me somewhere. I remember the inside though. It was like a big old church, a cathedral kind of thing.'

'Warminster?' suggests Jimmy.

'Might have been. I don't know. I've not been in any churches anywhere since I were a kid. Anyways, I didn't get to see it going in or coming out. Sean said it would be some time before I would be told where the meeting place was.'

Megan is anxious not to let him wander too far off track. 'Lee, do you know about Caitlyn Lock, the American who was kidnapped at Stonehenge?'

'Only what I saw on the news.'

'This group and their secret place, do you think they have her there?'

He looks shocked. 'The American? No, I don't see them doing anything like that. No way.'

She can tell he's scared. What interests her is *why*. 'Jimmy says you know about something that's supposed to be happening today?'

He looks uncertain.

'Tell her, Lee.' The DS glares at him.

'All right. Look, it might be nothing. I mean, I'm not that involved with these people, right? I just work security at the henge and went along to the ceremony with Sean.'

'We've heard all that,' Megan snaps. 'What is it, Lee?'

He takes a deep breath. 'There is something big going down at the henge. Extra security has been put on. Dozens and dozens of extra uniforms. I'm on a detail that starts at six and stops anyone getting within a mile of the place.'

'Aren't there prayers, masses and ceremonies happening there all the time?'

'Yeah, there are, but security is usually low level for that sort of stuff. A couple of guards to make sure no one messes with the Sacreds. Tonight is different. The area is completely shut to the public. No bookings from this afternoon until tomorrow.' He turns to Jimmy. 'Look at their records. You'll find it's for maintenance of the stones, but what happens out there tonight is nothing to do with maintenance. At least not the kind most people would expect.'

156

Luc van Daele is the first to run into an army ground patrol. He sees the Saxon armoured personnel carrier kicking up dust and spitting out fumes straight ahead. It's not a surprise that they've turned up. In fact, he expected them much earlier than this.

He gears the dusty trail bike down to an unhurried halt and steps off. The engine dies as he turns away from the vehicle and speaks quickly and quietly into his radio. 'I've got visitors. A personnel carrier with four-up. They're just coming over for a chat. I'll keep this channel open as long as possible. Over.'

The big, camouflaged Saxon grinds to a noisy halt and several soldiers spill out. Time to put Lynton's cover story to the test. Van Daele wriggles free of his rucksack and digs out his false papers. 'Hi there,' he shouts with a friendly smile. 'You guys work on a Sunday as well, eh?'

A clean-cut soldier in his late twenties is first to speak. He's kitted out in standard green and brown field gear. The tactical recognition flash on his arm puts him at captain-level with the Yorkshire, one of the British army's largest infantry regiments. 'You're trespassing here, sir. This is a restricted area. I need you to step away from the motorcycle and come with us.'

'I think you're mistaken.' Van Daele holds out a plastic file filled with paperwork. 'I'm with the International Entomological and Natural History Society. My colleagues and I have permission from the ATE to carry out a survey on rare myriapods and isopods.' He can see the soldier doesn't have a clue what he's talking about. 'Centipedes, lice, pill bugs, stuff like that.'

The captain takes the documentation but doesn't look at it. 'I'm sorry, sir. It doesn't really matter what this says or what you're doing, I'm under instructions to remove you from here.'

Luc knows better than to argue. 'Okay. No problem.' He waves a hand resignedly. 'I can easily put up with going home early to my wife and children.' He takes back the papers, shoves them in his rucksack and goes to start the bike.

The young captain steps in his path. 'I'm afraid you can't do that. You have to travel in the carrier with us, back to our barracks. One of my men will take care of your vehicle.'

'Hey, come on now.' Van Daele pushes the officer's arm away. 'I'm happy to ride this off your range, that should be enough for you.'

The captain calls to his men. 'Welsby, Simmonds, Richards.'

Three squaddies quickly crowd van Daele and move him away from the bike. Two of them are no more than kids. He could crack their heads easily enough. Leave them flat on their backs shouting for Mummy. But not without looking anything but like an insect collector.

157

Megan and Jimmy let Johns go and drive towards Stonehenge. She has mixed feelings about what she just heard.

'How much do you believe him, Jimmy?'

He drives with one hand on the wheel. 'Lee is an ex-junkie. Hard for these people to get out of bed without lying. What's on your mind?'

'He used the word "Sacreds". He didn't call them stones.

He called them Sacreds. The same word that Gideon Chase used.'

'Sounds like he didn't make it up then, not if Chase used the same word.'

Megan is still chewing things over. 'He's not telling us everything. He's either more involved than he says he is, or less. Either way, he's holding back for some reason.'

Jimmy puts his foot down as they clear Shrewton and join the last stretch of road to Amesbury. A brown sign for Stonehenge comes up on their right. 'You want me to pull into the car park?'

'No, not for a minute. Just drive around the place.'

He slows to a crawl as they pass the monument, then turns right off the A344 and heads past it on the other side down the A303. In the grounds around the henge they see more than two dozen black-suited security guards being organised into groups.

'Well, it looks like he was telling the truth about some of it,' says Jimmy.

'Take another right,' says Megan. 'The lane, there. Park up and we'll walk.'

Jimmy indicates and starts to manoeuvre. As he turns he's confronted by a 'Road Closed' sign weighed down with sandbags in the middle of the lane.

'I'll stop further down and turn around,' he says. 'Otherwise we'll have to go all the way to Winterbourne Stoke and back through Shrewton.'

He pulls out and starts a three-point turn. Megan glances

across the open countryside. 'I'm puzzled about something else that Johns said back there.'

'What's that?' he spins the wheel and straightens up.

'He mentioned that he thought people like doctors and police were members of this religion. When he said it, he looked towards you and said, "No offence". Why did he do that?'

Jimmy knows what she's getting at. 'I told him I knew all about the movement. That my father has always been a member but that I never wanted to be. I said my old man was in the force, the Deputy Chief Constable, and he could check on that easily enough if he wanted. That's how I got him to open up and tell us about tonight.'

'Is that true, Jimmy? That your father is a member of the Followers? Is that why I'm being shipped out to Swindon?'

'It's just something I said to Johns to get him to talk.'

Megan looks into his eyes and sees he's masking his emotions. 'You think he is, don't you?'

Jimmy looks away. He's riddled with doubts. His father has been his lifelong hero, the reason he joined the force, the one man in the world who has always been there for him. He can't accept he's mixed up in something as awful as all this. Won't accept it. Not yet. Not until there's overwhelming proof.

158

Caitlyn starts to dry retch. There's nothing she can do about it. She sits on the edge of her bunk, then drops to her knees. The intense heaving comes in painful spasms.

Gideon looks on feeling helpless. He puts an arm around her, gives her a drink, holds the clay cup to her lips. But he can see that he's of no real comfort. Her condition is deteriorating fast.

She sits with her back against the wall and places her hands on her tummy. 'My stomach feels like I've filled it with battery acid.'

'That's pretty much what it is. Gastric acid, secreted by the lining of your gut. Can you remember when you were taken? When you last ate anything?'

'I don't know. I've completely lost sense of time, of day and night.' She thinks. Grasps at the last few days. 'Wait. It was Saturday, the early hours of the morning. The day before the solstice. The nineteenth.'

'Today is the twenty-seventh. Sunday, the twenty-seventh.'

'Oh God.'

'They've done this to purify you. The ritual demands that at least seven days pass without food passing your lips.'

His eyes are on the bars and the two Lookers stood outside. 'Caitlyn, they're going to come for you soon. When they do, they are going to start the ritual and part of it will involve taking you outside. I'm going to be with you.

425

Security will be tight. Even tighter than it is now. But this is the only chance we will have.'

'Chance?' Her spirits lift a little. 'What chance? What are you going to do?'

His eyes hold hers. 'Everything I can.'

159

High in the clouds, the hovering Apache is the first to realise what is happening. The three motorbikes are making a run for it. Dust kicks up from the terrain and the trail bikes are suddenly screaming across the plain in opposite directions.

'Trespassers dispersing. Are you catching this, control?' Milner widens the camera focus to show as much of the ground below as possible.

'Copy. We've got it, Apache. Ground patrols are ready to engage.'

Milner spots the big fat Saxon lumbering across the range, then the trails of two small, faster Land Rover Snatch 2's crossing from the west.

'Don't often see bikers out here,' remarks Golding off-mike. 'Especially ones behaving like those guys.'

'Never mind, good to give the old bird a spin, better than sitting around.'

Golding is as relaxed as the pilot. 'No point having big equipment if you don't use it, I guess.'

They both laugh as they watch the onboard monitor and the run the bikes are giving the army vehicles for their money.

'Could be an op,' says Golding. 'Maybe 76th Foot or the 19th are playing the part of the trespassers?'

'Might even be outsiders,' says Milner. 'You sometimes get the SAS or Marines coming down here for a workout before going out to the Middle East.'

One of the bikes pulls a sharp turn, leaves a Land Rover for dead and then blazes off in an entirely new direction.

'They're going to lose these guys.' Milner points to the monitor. 'Look what they're doing. They've spread themselves so wide, so quickly. The patrols aren't going to catch them.'

'Someone's going to get it tonight.' Golding clicks on his radio. 'We've got one trespasser heading south into the cover of trees near Heytesbury. Do you want us to reposition or stay as we are, covering the others?'

'Keep your position, Apache One.'

Five minutes later it's all over. The bikes have outmanoeuvred the ground patrols and disappeared. Only four more of the trespassers, all of whom were on foot, have been captured. Apache One wheels around and heads back to base.

160

STONEHENGE IS CLOSED.

From what Megan and Jimmy can make out, similar CLOSED signs have been posted on all approaches to the historic site. The public car park is shut and all non-public roads have been closed.

The two police officers walk along the tiny grass verge of the A344 and past the ugly stretch of fenced-off tarmac where coaches and cars normally pull in. They cross the road and peer through another stretch of fencing towards the most complete part of the henge.

'What's going on, Jimmy?' She is staring at the dozens of uniformed security staff. They are all over the site.

'No idea.'

They stand and watch. Groups of guards begin fixing massive sheets of black plastic to the wire mesh fencing. Blocking out any views from the nearby highways. Megan scurries towards the nearest team. 'Hi there. What are you guys up to?'

They ignore her and carry on stretching out a vast swathe of black plastic.

'What are you doing?' shouts Jimmy.

'Minding our own business.' The reply comes from an older, unshaven man wearing a black T-shirt and cargo pants.

Megan slaps her police ID against the wires. 'I'm a police officer. I just made it my business.'

The man gets up off his knees. Stanley knife in hand, he walks her way. 'Carry on,' he calls to the others. He pins a smile against the wires, right next to her ID. 'It's a private party. Booked by a VIP for tonight. Now tell me exactly why any of that can be your business?'

Megan ignores the aggressive tone. He's probably an ex-cop in a dead-end security job who wants to make out to his cronies that he's more important than he is. 'And the sheeting.' She gestures to the river of black now rolling across the field. 'What's that for?'

He looks at her like she's dumb. 'Privacy. Private land. Private party. Get it? If you pay out big money for your own personal pleasure, you don't want nosy parkers at the fences troubling you all night. Understand what I mean? Now if you want to know more, you can ring my office. Maybe they'll tell you who made the booking. Maybe they won't. Now excuse me, I've got a job to do.'

He turns his back and walks away.

Bastard, she thinks.

'I've got the number for the security company,' says Jimmy. 'I'll call them from the car.'

Megan slaps a hand against the wire as she walks away. 'Looks like your informant was right. They're preparing for something big tonight. Something they apparently want to keep very, very private.'

161

The cell door creaks open and the draught causes the torch lighting on the wall to flicker.

'Phoenix.' Musca beckons him away from the sacrifice.

Gideon leaves Caitlyn on her bunk, lying on her side, her eyes glued to the hooded and robed figure filling the door frame.

Musca is wearing white cotton gloves and holding another pair. 'Put these on.'

'Why?'

The big butcher looks at him as though he's stupid. 'Fingerprints. We don't want any prints on what I'm about to give you.' He leans closer. 'We will come for her in an hour. You need to tell her. So she has this final time for herself. For her to prepare for her death.'

It's more than just a ritual to Musca, Gideon can tell. It's sadism. The thrill of watching someone suffer. The man is enjoying it.

The big butcher steps outside the cell and takes a sheaf of plain A4 paper and a cheap pen from one of the Lookers. 'Give her this. Tell her she's allowed to write a final letter to anyone she likes. You can assure her they'll get it.'

'And will they?'

'Providing she doesn't do anything stupid like try to describe any of us or where she is, then yes, they will.'

'I understand. Anything else?'

'No. Sixty minutes, that's all she has. Not a minute longer. Make sure she's ready.'

The cell door clanks closed.

Caitlyn is sat up, anxiously watching him as he returns.

He hands the pen and paper to her. 'They have given you this. To leave a message.'

'For my parents?'

He can see that she's got the wrong idea. 'It's not for ransom. I told you, there isn't going to be any ransom demand. These people have no plans to release you.' He sits alongside her and tries to help her through. 'This is it. They are getting ready to start the ritual. You have an hour, that's all. Then it will begin.'

162

Caitlyn writes two letters. One to her mother, one to her father. She wishes it could be just one. But it can't. This is the way that she has to do it. Her parents' divorce is screwing up her death almost as much as it did her life.

Words don't come easy. At first, they don't even come at all. Longhand is an alien lifeform to her. And letters like this, well, nothing prepares you for drafting letters like this. They should be the sole preserve of old people or people with awful diseases.

In the end she just writes down what she's thinking.

431

Thank you for bringing me into this world, for giving me your beauty and your love of fun. Momma, I'm sorry we argued so much about Daddy and François. Love whoever you want to love. Love them both if they'll let you! I wish we'd had a chance to kiss and make up.

Be happy Mom.

Love Caitlyn xxx

Her note to her father is touchingly different.

I'm sorry, Daddy. I know I should have done what you said. Please don't blame Eric. I tricked him, that's all. I love you Daddy and will miss you. If there is a heaven, I'll have coffee and pie waiting for you, thick cappuccino like we had in Italy together and a Mississippi mud like the one we made a mess of in the Hard Rock in London. Big kisses from your little girl, I'll always love you, Daddy xxx

Gideon doesn't look at the letters when she's finished. He just takes them off her and folds them in three. 'Are you okay?'

'Not really.'

She looks drained. Like the life has already gone from her. She pours herself some water.

'Damn it!' She hurls the pot to the floor and starts to sob. 'I don't want to die. Oh, please God, don't let them do this to me!'

163

The security firm's number goes straight to answerphone. A recorded message. No one available until tomorrow.

'Have you got the owner's home number?' asks Megan.

'Yeah, John Doran-Smith. I've got a mobile.' Jimmy thumbs through his notebook again and punches in the digits.

No answer.

Jimmy leaves a message, makes it sound serious, official police business, the man has to call him urgently.

Something's happening. Megan knows now. She switches her thoughts back to Lee Johns. What is he not telling them? There are three main reasons why people like him start becoming helpful to the police. They're afraid of going to prison. They need money for something, probably drugs. Or they're into something they simply don't know how to get out of it.

She turns to Jimmy. 'Did Johns ask you for any money?'

'Not a penny.'

'He talked to you solely because his mate Grabb disappeared?'

'Right.'

'We should sack ourselves.' Her face colours. 'How could I be so stupid? He must have been with Grabb when they murdered Timberland and took Lock.'

Jimmy quickly dials Lee Johns' mobile number. They

should never have let him go, she knows that now. Half her mind was still on Sammy at the time.

'No answer, boss.' Jimmy holds up the phone as though to prove the point.

'You know where he lives?'

The DS doesn't need any bigger hint. He starts up the car.

'Pray he's there, Jimmy.'

164

The visit of the Master to the henge is unexpected.

Trusted members of the Inner Circle speed up the positioning of the black sheeting. The site is completely cleared. Only when veteran Lookers are in position outside the makeshift privacy curtain does the Master pass through the passageway under the road to the sacred site.

The day is finishing in cloud, the sun sinking mournfully low in the west. Time is of the essence. He walks the edge of the field. As always, he will enter the linked arms of the giant sarsens on a sun-line from the Heel Stone to Altar Stone. He stops at the horseshoe of five great trilithons and kneels.

'Sacred rulers of our universe, I supplicate myself before you, seeking your guidance and wisdom. I do so in all my mortal frailty and loyalty. I dedicated myself to the ritual of renewal and have ensured all preparations to honour you are in place. The one you chose is ready. A small repayment of the vast debts we owe you.'

He glances up, sees a further ominous dimming of the daylight. An unexpected storm may be brewing. A force of nature augmented by the Sacreds.

'Lords, our enemies are gathering. They close on us just as clouds surround the sun and moon. I know this to be a trial, a test of our faith and our resolution as Followers, but I cannot undertake it without your guidance. Without your consent.'

He feels his arms growing heavy. They drop by his side as though exhausted from holding a great burden. There is no need to talk now. The Sacreds know everything.

They are in his mind. In his doubts. They race through every atom of his existence. When they are done they leave him prostrate and gasping for air. But the Master has his answer.

He knows what he must do.

165

Kylie Lock slams the phone down on her husband.

The cheapskate son of a bitch still won't agree to match the money. Okay, she gets that publicly he can't do it. Vice Presidents don't negotiate with terrorists, that she understands. But he could still put his hand in his damned pocket. Do it privately. She could tell the police and the press she raised the extra bucks herself.

But he won't even do that. Can't compromise his precious principles. Oh no, that would bring his *integrity* into question. Would cost him votes is what he means. Thom 'Iron Man' Lock can't be seen to parley with the bad guys. Not even for his family. Certainly not in election year.

She stomps around her suite at the Dorchester. Rage building. Can't even take it out on Charlene. The press aide has gone sick with food poisoning. On this day of all days. Kylie goes to the minibar, looks at the vodka. God she needs it. But she won't. She takes a bar of chocolate instead. Sits chewing on the bed, watching TV and listening to the radio at the same time. She needs some valium. Or amphetamine. She snatches up the TV remote, switches to Sky News. Praying for another fix of news about her baby.

Kylie fires up the iPad and browses the internet, searching for snippets of information about her daughter. She shouldn't. The web gossip is bitter. Twisted. Cruel. There is already a virtual tombstone, spray-painted with messages from fans. Mostly boys.

But she has to read it. All of it. She has to tune in to everything and anything to do with Caitlyn. Because deep down, deep inside her, she feels something she can't explain.

Something instinctual. Maternal. Her nerves are jangling. Something bad is happening to her baby. She just knows it.

166

The sound is the one Caitlyn has been dreading.

Metal on metal.

A worn key turning in an old lock. The cell door is opening. They have come for her. The ritual is about to begin. She is going to die.

Gideon puts his arms around her. 'Be ready,' he whispers. 'Whatever I do, whenever I do it, be ready to fight for your life.'

He can feel her heart hammering against his chest. She is trembling from head to toe.

'It is time,' says an impatient voice by the door.

Caitlyn clings to Gideon.

'Be brave. Be strong.' He peels her off him, holds her hand. 'I'll be with you.'

She takes a deep breath, tells herself to keep her wits about her. Don't fall apart now. It would be the worst thing to do. The fight isn't over until all hope is gone.

From somewhere deep inside, she finds courage, pulls her hand free from Gideon's and walks towards the two robed men waiting by the cell door.

Draco nods to Gideon, gestures to the letters on the girl's bunk. Gideon understands and rushes to collect them.

They walk the corridor of death, flames crackling from burning torches fixed to the walls and reach the cleansing area.

Caitlyn is pulled from Gideon, undressed and manhandled into the deep stone trench. Clear, cold mineral water powers down on her from the channelled inlets set in the rock ceiling. She shivers, fighting for breath.

Gideon turns away as the Cleansers pull her from the water, dry her and dress her in the long sacrificial robe. One of the Lookers walks over and talks quietly to him. 'Come with me, Phoenix. You must stand for her in the Great Room. The circles of light are lit. They await her there.'

Gideon doesn't want to leave her side. He feels a tug on his elbow and looks back at Caitlyn as they walk. He can't see her face, he wants to see her face, make some human connection with her. But he can't. Too many people around her.

In the Great Room, he looks helplessly around the chamber, smells the newly warmed wax of the candles. He looks up and sees that the star shafts are open. The sunless sky is grey and edging towards twilight.

Time is running out.

His eyes fall to the Slaughter Stone, the spot where Caitlyn will be strapped down and the marks of the trilithons opened up on her legs, arms and spine. There is a noise outside. Footsteps. They are bringing her in. The ritual is about to begin.

Draco's hooded head appears in the doorway. His dark eyes fix on Gideon. 'Come with me, now! The Great Room must be cleared. There's a change of plan.'

167

'Is there no other way round, Jimmy?'

The DS shakes his head. 'Bulford's a horror. You've got half the bloody army out here: 3rd Mechanised, the Rifles, Royal Logistics, even the RMP.'

Finally, they edge past the slow-moving convoy of squaddies and Jimmy works the car hard down Marlborough Road, takes a right into Hubert Hamilton Road, then a left into Harrington. At last they're in the road where Lee Johns lives.

They slew to a halt, get out and sprint through a communal garden, up white concrete steps to a run-down flat. Megan keeps her finger pressed on the button while Jimmy shuffles along the small balcony to bang on the lounge window.

There's no answer.

She crouches and shouts through the letterbox. 'Lee, it's DI Baker and DS Dockery. We need to talk to you. *Urgently.*'

Still nothing.

'Put the door in.'

Jimmy hesitates.

'Put it in, Jimmy, or I'll do it.'

He steps back, plants a kick below the handle. His foot bounces off the lock but the door doesn't break. He steps back again and delivers a firmer thump with his heel. This time it swings open and they pile in.

Jimmy runs through the lounge into the small kitchen.

Megan takes the bedroom. Then the bathroom. Nothing. He isn't here. She goes back into the bedroom. Opens the wardrobe and the chest of drawers. Full of clothes. Into the bathroom again. She finds his toothbrush. No sign of a hurried exit.

They wander outside, thinking about where next to hunt. Forty metres down the street Megan notices a thin man holding a newspaper in one hand and a sandwich in the other.

It's him.

Johns sees them on the stairs. And starts to run.

He's quick too. Much faster than Megan expected an ex-junkie to be. He makes a break for the fields behind Harrington Road. She barrels after him. Jimmy jogs back for the car, hopes to head him off as he comes out on Marlborough Road.

Megan is catching him.

Johns glances over his shoulder and sees her gaining. He also notices Jimmy is not there. It doesn't take a lot of working out to figure he is following in the motor.

Johns peels away from Marlborough Road. He's not going for the open fields. He's not that stupid. Instead he goes north towards a dense copse. With any luck, he'll lose her in there.

But he doesn't make it.

Megan finds an extra burst of energy just as his tank runs empty. She takes him down metres from the edge of the woodland.

They are both breathing heavily but the DI is fitter and

stronger. She grabs his wrist and twists his arm hard up his back.

He kicks a little but his lungs are on fire.

'Don't even think about it, Lee.'

168

Six Followers, led by Draco and Musca, briskly escort Caitlyn and Gideon back to their cell.

She is terrified by the men's haste, their infectious nervous energy.

'What's going on?' Gideon asks Draco.

'Wait a minute.'

The Lookers push the sacrifice inside and Draco pulls him away from the bars. 'The Master has changed the plans for the ritual. He has been to the henge and he has himself become a vessel for the Sacreds. The gods are within him. He is in the Great Room right now, allowing them to take their places in the Sanctuary.'

'He is *switching* the location for the ritual?'

'That's right. He believes it safer to take place here, than out in the open.'

'And that accords with tradition?'

'It does. The henge in the Great Room comes from the same tabernacle stone as those on public display. In many ways it is a holier site.'

Gideon realises the implications of the switch. They're not going to take her outside. He will have no chance to help her escape. He looks through the cell bars. She will be put to death just a short walk from where she is now.

'I have to see my father. I must speak with him.' He tries to push past him.

Draco blocks his way. 'That's not possible.'

'I must.'

'I said it is *not* possible.' His eyes narrow. 'The Master has left instructions that he must not be interrupted. Twilight is upon us. The ritual has begun.'

Gideon is returned to the cell and the door locked. Caitlyn sits on her bunk, her hair still wet, awkwardly holding the ceremonial gown about herself. It is split up the back so the knife of stone may be used on the naked flesh displayed beneath it.

Gideon slips off the rope from around his waist. 'Here, use this. It will help you fasten the gown.'

She takes it and chokes back a sob. 'It's stupid, isn't it? I'm about to be killed and here I am worrying about showing my ass.'

He understands her need to maintain some self-respect, some dignity. 'It's not stupid. It's dignified.'

Caitlyn looks to the door. She's almost too scared to talk. 'What's happening out there?'

'They're going to complete the ritual here, not at the henge.' He wishes he had better news to break.

Her face is heavy with sadness. She looks completely lost.

'Can you just hold me for a moment? I feel like I'm going to fall apart.'

Gideon moves closer. She wraps her hands around his waist and rests her head on his shoulder. It feels good to be comforted. To cling on to someone who doesn't want to hurt her.

'Hey!' One of the Lookers rattles the cell door. 'None of that. Back away from her.'

Gideon gives the man a withering glance. Does the idiot think he's planning to have sex with her? How stupid. He knows as well as anyone that a defiled sacrifice wouldn't be any use to anyone.

No use to anyone.

How could he not have seen it.

He might still be able to save her life.

169

The Henge Master stands clad in a hooded ceremonial sackcloth robe bleached red using an ancient mixture of beets, madder and chokecherries. Beneath his hood there is a moon-like crescent, the outline of his shock of grey-white hair.

The Sacreds have been positioned in their tabernacles. Special sanctuary lights, multicoloured glass tubes filled with virgin candles, have been positioned and lit at equidistant spaces around the henge.

Through the star shafts he sees the colour of the sky.

Twilight is but a blink away.

The Master is close to exhaustion. The strain of transporting the Sacreds to the Sanctuary has wearied him. But he will not fail.

He raises a ceremonial stone sprinkler, filled with water washed from the Sacreds and creates a divine line from the Altar Stone inside the horseshoe of trilithons, out through the eastern arches of the sarsens, across the Slaughter Stone to the Heel Stone.

From a pocket in his gown, he draws the ceremonial stone knife and gazes upon the slab where the sacrifice will be cut. Five cuts. One for each of the mighty trilithons where the Chief Sacreds reside, the gods of the sun, moon, stars, earth and afterlife.

She will be left for five hours. One hour for each god. Afterwards, she will be untethered and washed again in blessed waters. Then she will be offered.

The Master's hand falls to his other deep pocket. He feels that they are there. The sacrificial hammers. He turns his attention to the two Bearers watching and waiting from the other side of the opening to the Great Room. In their grasp is the rough litter made of pine, ready to convey the sacrifice on her fatal journey.

He is ready.

He nods. The Bearers move instantly away.

170

'What were you running for, Lee?' Megan twists his arm even further up his back as she stands over him. 'I don't have time to mess around and neither do you.'

'All right. *All right*, I'll tell you.'

She sees Jimmy crossing the field and lets go of Johns. The kid struggles to his knees. Cradles his twisted and aching arm. 'I got scared. I saw you at my place and just freaked.'

She pulls him to his feet. 'You and Sean Grabb killed Jake Timberland and you helped him kidnap Caitlyn Lock. In policing terms, you are screwed, my strange young friend.' She jabs a finger in his bony chest. 'We already have the forensics to link Grabb with the killing and the abduction. And I'm sure that once we go hunting for your DNA, we'll find it. Juries love DNA. Three letters that they'll believe more than anything an ex-junkie like you could dream up.'

Johns has been jailed before. He doesn't want to go back. He looks beyond them, down the road to the big open world. Balancing his options. Finally he speaks: 'I want immunity, right? A guarantee I ain't going to get charged with nothing.'

'Dream on,' says Jimmy. 'We're past immunity. It's down to damage limitation now. Hurry up. What have you got before we throw the charge sheet at you?'

He nurses his arm again. 'Not much. It's not like you think.'

She glares at him. 'Don't piss about, Lee. We need everything. No lies. No leaving bits out. Everything.'

He puts his hand to his head. Images are swimming back to him. The man lying dead in the van. The pretty woman screaming and kicking. Him in the Camper suggesting they kill her rather than get caught. 'It was an accident. Nobody meant anyone to die or anything.' He sees their unbelieving looks. 'I mean it. We were after them because the girl touched one of the Sacreds. Things got out of hand. Sean hit the bloke and when we drove him away he died. It freaked us out. We didn't plan it like that.'

'I said don't leave things out.' Megan jabs him again. 'Why were you at the henge? Who wanted them and for what?'

He swallows. 'A stranger has to be picked for the ritual. Sean said it had been decided that it would be whoever touched one of the Sacreds. It didn't have to be that girl or the bloke with her, it could have been anyone, you know? They just got themselves in the wrong place at the wrong time.'

'So where is she?' asks Jimmy.

'She's at the Sanctuary, the place I told you about. But like I said, I don't know where it is.' He can see their anger. 'Really. I've never seen it from the outside. Out along the A360. Out near Imber, that's all I know. We stopped on a road just before the village, near the range. Sean went on

446

from there with the girl in his Warrior and I waited in the Camper with the stiff.'

Megan wants to crack him. 'You're talking about a young man whose life you stole. Show some respect.'

'Go on,' says Jimmy.

'Sean came back and said he'd phoned someone. A member of the Inner Circle. He looked relieved. He thought it was all going to be all right.'

'So what was all that earlier today?' Megan asks. 'That story about something happening at Stonehenge?'

He colours up.

She reads his face. 'If this girl dies, you're getting charged with murder.'

He understands. 'A man called Matt Utley, we just call him Musca, came to me.' He looks towards Jimmy. 'He knew you were trying to get hold of me, to talk to me about Sean. He says that I'm to contact you, tell you that something's going off tonight at the henge.' Johns glances back to Megan. 'I was confused like, because something was supposed to be going off there tonight. It's the start of the ritual.' He dries up.

'Go on, Lee.' Jimmy's voice is firm.

'Tonight is when the girl should be, you know, sacrificed. And it should be at Stonehenge.'

'Should be?'

'That's the point,' he explains, looking from one to the other. 'They know you're on to them. They know everything. Musca wanted me to say this to you. So you'd go to the stones.'

She lets out a long sigh. 'So where would be the right place?'

'The Sanctuary, I guess.' He puts his wrists together and offers them out to Jimmy. 'You've got to lock me up. Put me in protective custody somewhere. Musca said he'd kill me if I fucked this up. Said I'd go the same way as Sean if I didn't do what he wanted.'

'Get him locked up,' she says. 'DCI Tompkins can deal with him.'

171

The crazy son of a bitch is at it again. Phoenix has his shirt off and his hands up the back of the sacrifice's robe. The bastard is feeling her behind. Volans presses his face to the bars of the cell, he can't believe what he is seeing.

'Hey!' He rattles the cell door. 'Leave her alone, you dog. I told you once.'

The two of them are in the corner trying to hide but he can still see them. Musca appears in the passageway. 'What's going on?'

'That idiot is trying it on with the girl.'

'What? Stop them. Open the damned door.'

Volans fumbles with the keys. Musca catches a glimpse of them kissing. 'Quickly. Come on.'

The two Followers stride into the cell and catch Gideon and Caitlyn locked in a passionate embrace, oblivious to the noise around them.

'Stupid fool!' Musca grabs him by the hair, pulls him away from her.

Caitlyn steps back. Face full of desperation.

Musca spins Gideon around and crashes a fist into his face. But he doesn't go down, he bear hugs him and holds on for dear life. Caitlyn lunges forward. A jagged shard of broken pot plunges into the side of Musca's neck. She feels the warm spurt of blood on her face and knows she's hit a main vein.

Musca shudders. Gideon lets him slip to the cold floor, then pulls a gun from his waistband. Volans is frozen. Stuck between helping his dying brother or securing the sacrifice.

'Get the fuck away from her,' Gideon says. 'I won't hesitate to kill you.'

172

'Caitlyn, take his gun.'

Shaking with adrenalin, she draws the weapon from Volans' waistband and pulls the bunch of keys from his hand.

'Kneel down. Face the wall!'

As Volans moves, Gideon glances at the gun in his hand.

He's never held a firearm before, has no idea how to use it. No clue where the safety guard is or whether it's even loaded.

'Let's go!' He pushes Caitlyn out of the cell and closes the iron door behind him. He grabs her by the sleeve and they sprint down the passageway. Behind them come Volans' cries for help.

In Gideon's mind is a mental map. One he knows is incomplete. But it's all they've got. He figures the most direct escape to be past the Great Room, on to the curving passageway of the the Outer Circle, then past the Master's chamber. It would lead them to the stone staircase and the warehouse exit.

But that's not where he's heading. He's following a hunch. One that will get them free. Or get them killed.

173

The Master steps hesitantly from the Great Room and looks around. The sacrifice should be here by now.

He hears noises spilling down the corridor, turns and walks back towards the cell. Four Bearers are running towards him. Without the litter.

'She's gone,' shouts one. 'The girl is out of her cell.'

'My son, where is he?'

'Also gone.' The voice is that of Draco, hurrying up to

the Master, blood on his hands. 'They've killed Musca and taken Volans' gun.'

'Block the main exit,' says the Master. 'They will head for the stone steps into the anteroom.' He feels ashamed that he trusted his child, personally guided him around the Sanctuary.

Draco despatches the Bearers. 'And the avenue, what about the passageway from your chamber?'

The Master shakes his head. 'He doesn't know of it, but secure it anyway.'

'I'll go myself.' Draco takes two men, instructs the rest to search the Sanctuary.

The Master looks into the emptiness of the Great Room. He can sense the displeasure of the Sacreds. But he is calm. The place is a fortress. There is plenty of time to recapture the girl and to complete the ceremony before first light.

He walks towards the Great Room, then thinks better of it.

He smiles and shouts for Draco. 'Let the men go. Come with me. I know where they are.'

174

The wall torches are few and far between, the maze of passageways cold and heavy with the smell of damp and death.

Caitlyn clings to Gideon as they run. She prays that he

knows what he's doing. Fresh in her mind is her own futile escape attempt.

Something seems wrong to her. They're heading downward. Running deeper into this horrible place rather than up and out into the safety of the outside world. 'We're going the wrong way!'

'Trust me,' shouts Gideon, short of breath.

Caitlyn knows she doesn't have a choice.

As they run down the darkened corridors, he frantically tries to picture the twists and turns of the Sanctuary. In his mind it is like a buried pyramid, only dome-shaped. He sees the upper levels, the modern operational area. The carefully constructed weight-relieving chambers and corridors. Under them the Master's chamber and the Great Room. He sees the Ascending and Descending Passageways east and west of these. Pictures them all built around the central star shaft. The corresponding points of the compass and constellations.

Now he envisages the eastern passageway. The access to the lowest level. The Crypt of the Ancients. The place they are heading towards.

The twisting and tilting corridors remind him again of Egyptian tombs. The kind of places that hold architectural secrets. He sees Khufu's Great Pyramid and remembers its hidden chambers and passages.

He prays the Sanctuary has its own secrets. The star shafts, the varying heights in the corridors, the Ascending and Descending Passageways, and the geographic alignments. They are all clues that he's right.

They slide to a halt in front of a locked oak door.

'Quickly,' he says, pulling a breathless Caitlyn tight to the wall. 'Sit down. Sit here and stay here.'

He backs off several metres, turns to look at her. 'Further forward. Come towards me half a metre.'

She slides along the ground, pulls her shaking knees up to her chest, rearranges the loose sacrificial gown.

'Okay. Stop.' He backs off further, rounds the corner of the passageway behind them, then reappears, looking hard at her.

'Stay here. Don't move. *Whatever* happens, even if you see them coming for you, don't move.'

175

Caitlyn sits shaking on the cold floor, caught half in the light of a flickering wall torch, half in the long shadows of the high passageway leading to the Crypt of the Ancients.

Gideon has vanished. She is alone. Her mind drifts. Back to when she was a child, playing hide and seek with her parents. Only she hides so well neither of them can find her. She waits and waits and waits. Fears they'll never come.

Is he gone for good? Has he left her as a decoy?

There's a noise. Footsteps. Someone is approaching. The waiting is over. Muffled voices. They are coming for her. She remembers what he said: *don't move . . . whatever happens . . . don't move.*

Caitlyn holds her nerve. They're close now. Very close. Footsteps so loud that she knows she is only seconds away from discovery.

She sees them. Two men. One old. One younger. Caitlyn screams. One of them moves to grab her.

The corridor fills with a ball of noise. A sound so loud she flinches in shock. Painful ringing erupts in her ears. The man in front of her clutches his chest. His eyes are wide, his mouth open. He lurches to the side, falls to his knees.

Gideon steps from the shadows. He levels a shaking gun at the older man in the red robe. 'Father—' He spits the word out.

The Henge Master glances at Draco on the floor, his blood leaking onto the stone. 'What have you done?'

Gideon waves the gun. '—I need the key to the Crypt.'

The Master lifts the string from around his neck, his face full of contempt. 'I knew you wouldn't be able to leave without stealing something precious. You're just a grave-robber like Nathaniel.' He throws the key into the pool of blood near Draco.

'Get it,' Gideon says to Caitlyn, the Glock still levelled at his father.

She bends to pick it up.

Draco grabs her by the ankle, pulls her over.

The Master charges Gideon like a bull elephant, crashes him into a wall.

There is another deathly explosion.

176

The two men slump to the ground. Locked together. The Glock clatters over the blood-spattered stone slabs.

Caitlyn's survival instinct kicks in. She stretches her arm through the cloying pool of Draco's blood and grabs the fallen weapon. He's still pulling at her. Strong hands moving from her ankle to her knee. She twists around. She has no choice but to go with the thought in her head. She pulls the trigger. Shoots him in the face. Point blank. The report is deafening.

Blood and brains spatter her. She drops the gun and holds her crimson-soaked hands in horror. She sits frozen until Gideon gets to her.

'Come on, we have to go.'

Caitlyn can't move. Multiple images of what she's done are already branded in her mind. The way he looked at her, then the blood-red mist, flaying skin, saliva, flying bone. He's dead. She just killed someone.

'Caitlyn! Get up!'

She feels Gideon grab her hand. It's wet with blood and brain. He is pulling her along, the stones feel soft beneath her feet. Her vision blurs. She stops and retches. Heaves the last specks of moisture from her empty stomach.

'Come on!'

She retches again and looks to the side. Gideon is unlocking a door just a few metres away.

He rushes back and gets her, drags her with him through the new opening.

Blackness. Total blackness.

She stands shaking while he searches. The blood red mist sprays up before her eyes again. Flesh. Saliva. Bone. The final, frozen look in his eyes. Like a broken doll.

Light. A wall torch finally starts to burn close to her. Orange. Orange not red. Gideon has lit it. He leads her by the hand, lighting giant candles around the room. The blackness dissipates, dribbles away like water on hot sand. The room tilts. Her knees buckle and she feels a sickly warmth course through her.

'Caitlyn!'

She hears his voice, tinny and distant, a shout from down a long, dark tunnel, as she falls.

177

The bullet from the Glock has gone straight through the Master's thigh. He's lucky. As a career soldier, he knows two simple truths. First, there's no such thing as a non-fatal shooting. Let any wound bleed long enough and you'll die. Second, unless you shoot your enemy in the skull or the spine, you're not going to incapacitate them with a handgun. They're going to be shocked to hell, but once they're over that, they're going to be up and at you again. And that's what he's going to do.

He wipes away the blood and examines the entry and exit points. Clean. He feels tentatively around the traumatised skin. The bullet was low velocity, so it's a straight hole. Little effect on the surrounding tissue. He presses and watches the cavity fill. If it had been a high-velocity rifle, the injury may have been much worse.

He probes and pokes until he's sure there's no fragmentation in the wound, no shattered bone that has ripped up masses of muscle tissue. He tries to stand, but it's hard to balance. Difficult to straighten his leg and painful to put any weight on it. He leans against the wall and pulls the cord belt from around his waist. He loops it around and pulls a tight tourniquet. It's a temporary fix but good enough for now.

He's risking nerve damage. Better that though, than to bleed to death. He looks down and sees the sticky puddle of blood and brain matter that has seeped from Draco. No point even checking for a pulse. In his peripheral vision he notices the flickering lights from the candles in the crypt. He hears his son shouting. Shouting to the woman to hurry up.

He dips in the deep pocket of his robe. Feels the sacrificial hammers and the ceremonial knife.

Enough to stop them.

Enough to fulfil the ritual.

178

Gideon reluctantly leaves her slumped and twitching in her faint. He carries the torch high and quickly makes his way around the crypt. He has to find the clue. Some proof that he hasn't made a fatal mistake.

From the dozens of inclined coffins, empty eyes in skin-less skulls seem to follow him. They trail him like ghosts. He can feel their wispy hands on his neck, cold like a dead-of-night shiver down his spine.

Egyptians ensured the dead who they honoured were surrounded by their most prized possessions. From what he can see, it seems to be the same with the Followers of the Sacreds. But the Egyptians equipped their tombs with something else. Secret passages into the afterlife. Long tunnels that allowed the reborn kings to rise again and rejoin their people.

Gideon tries to think of everything he knows about the pyramids. Of the modest structure honouring young Pepi II. The stepped Pyramid of Djoser. Sneferu's Red Pyramid. And Giza – built two thousand five hundred years before Christ, around the same time as some of Stonehenge, and just after the completion of the Sanctuary. The Great Pyramid had chambers similar to those now surrounding him. Mysterious shafts stretched from the King's and Queen's chambers to the outside world. Secret corridors allowed freed spirits to escape to the heavens.

Gideon moves the coffins. Stirs the dead. Hears their bones grumble discontent. Cobwebbed skeletons creak and crack as he searches behind and beneath the caskets for trap-doors or concealed passageways. There are none.

He hears Caitlyn moan and walks over to her, stoops and holds the flame so he can see her face. She is coming round but she's deathly pale. Glassy eyed. Her energy is spent.

He touches her shoulder reassuringly. 'You're all right. You fainted.'

Her eyes flick from him to the horrors of the room. Coffins. Skeletons. Candles. Her nightmare isn't over.

He thinks back to his studies, to the dusty files of his research, his academic past. His mind tries to see beyond the obvious. A fleeting memory of a massive maze. It is that of Amenemhet. Reputedly an architectural work that surpassed the great pyramids, hundreds of rooms, passageways, corridors, false chambers, star shafts and hidden trapdoors.

There had been a hidden exit in the ceiling. Concealed by a stone trapdoor. A small hole opened up into a series of hidden rooms and passageways. An exit route filled with decoy chambers and deadly shafts. But still an exit route.

He remembers Scandinavian archaeologists discovered that the symbol of the maze represented the spring equinox, the time the sun was supposed to escape from the winter's blackness. He looks up. His gaze drifts to the top of the giant cube of artefacts in the room's centre. Even if they climbed it, they couldn't reach the stone blocks above their heads. But it looks like the only possible way out.

He hopes Caitlyn is strong enough to make it.

'We have to get moving, come on,' he grabs her wrist and leads her to the giant stone block. Gideon starts to climb and then pulls her up the first set of stone shelves.

'Hang on.' He places her fingers on the edge of the giant sandstone cube. 'Grip tight. I need to climb up another level, then I'll—'

The words shrivel in his mouth.

He can see what she can't. See the shape behind her.

179

Gideon moves too late to stop the stone blade slicing into Caitlyn's calf.

She screams and almost loses her hold on the giant sandstone cube. Gideon grabs her arm and hoists her up a level.

The Master sweeps the knife again. Too low. It misses. He pushes himself closer. Slashes again. He's closer now but not close enough. He ignores the pain in his leg and hoists himself on to the bottom layer of the archive cube.

Gideon is pushing Caitlyn up and around the side of the block. Edging her out of harm's way. He's looking the wrong way. The knife slices into his shoulder. He tumbles from the cube.

The Master lurches after him. This is personal. Pride.

Honour. Everything to live – and die for. He attacks again with the blade.

The gun is back on the cube and Gideon has no chance of reaching it. His eyes are locked on the lethal blade in his father's hand.

The Master hobbles and stabs. It's an unbalanced lunge that falls short of its target. Gideon sees the weak spot. Blood is dribbling down the Master's right leg. He launches a wild kick.

The Master howls with pain. The knife drops. Gideon could finish him. He could go back for the gun and shoot him. He doesn't.

He turns and climbs up towards Caitlyn.

'You're a fool!' shouts the Master, lying on the stone floor clutching his leg. 'There's no way out. You can't get away.'

Gideon pulls himself up on to the top of the centrepiece and helps Caitlyn climb the last half metre. As they stand on the apex of the giant sandstone block, he sees that his father is right. There is no way out.

180

The Master hobbles back from the Crypt of the Ancients. He knows there is still time. If he can reach the Bearers, the Lookers, then the sacrifice can be recaptured. The hour is late but it is not yet impossible to complete the ritual.

He's weak, dizzy, losing too much blood. His thigh is twitching and cramping. He stops, quickly refastens the tourniquet. Already nerves are deadening. Every step up the sloping passageway is a form of torture. But as he reaches the middle landing, he sees Grus with three Lookers.

'Here! Over here!' It's the best he can manage as he slumps to the ground.

'Get a medic, quickly,' shouts Grus. He turns to two of the men. 'Help me get him to his chamber.'

'No,' protests the Master. 'My son and the sacrifice are in the Crypt of the Ancients. Get her. Get her now.'

'Watch him,' says Grus to one of the Lookers. 'Don't let him pass out.' He looks down at his friend. 'There'll be a doctor here any minute.'

'Go!' shouts the Master. 'They were climbing the centrepiece. Do whatever you have to, to bring the girl back.'

181

The Master is laid out on a stone table in his chamber.

'You've lost a lot of blood,' says the man tending him.

'I know that,' he snaps. 'Just fix me.'

The medic nods. He waits for the ice and alcohol to come from the fridges in the operational area. He's going to have to cauterise the wound with heated metal. Battlefield improvisation. Something he's done before.

The Master's mind is elsewhere. If he can't complete the ritual, there will be repercussions. The power of the Sacreds will wane. Perhaps critically. It will be disastrous for so many people.

But if the sacrifice and his son escape? He shudders.

The Craft will be exposed. He cannot let that happen. He will have no option but to take the ultimate sanction. One that has been prepared. One that only his word can execute.

182

The top of the centrepiece in the crypt is solid. Gideon feels no break in the giant sandstone except for a thin square shaft that runs straight down the middle. He can see no obvious use for it. Was it designed to let something out? Drain away water or gasses? Or let something in?

He looks down the bottomless hole. Did it once house an even taller centrepiece that connected to the roof of the crypt? The shaft is about the width of a waterwell. It's barely wide enough for him to fit into. But it's all there is. There's no sign of anything else that could constitute an exit.

At the edge of the block, Caitlyn sits nursing the gash to her leg. He looks again down the shaft, down into the terrifying darkness. The Lookers will be in the room any second. He sits and dangles his legs into the void.

Caitlyn stares at him incredulously. 'What are you doing?'

'I don't know. Ancient structures seldom make sense. You just have to feel your way around them to discover their purpose.' He lowers himself into the hole, so he is resting on his elbows. His gashed shoulder barks pain.

Gideon scrapes a foot against the wall. He can feel something. A tiny foothold. A gap in the sandstone. He wriggles his bare toe in and stretches his other leg down, searching for a second foothold. After arcing it back and forth, he finds one.

Caitlyn watches him disappearing into the shaft and drags herself over. She's not going to be left here alone. Only his fingers are now visible from the top. He calls to her. 'There are cut-outs in the side of the walls. It's like climbing down a ladder. Feel your way down.'

His hands disappear and in the dim light she can only just see the top of his head. She gets on her knees and lowers herself into the blackness. Back into the dark hole. Her mind rebels, her body freezes. She can't do it again. She can't go into the hole.

But she has to. She has to follow Gideon. Has to trust him.

Her once-beautifully manicured toes rub against the rough sandstone until she finds the gaps and descends into the dark unknown.

Her left foot hits an unusually solid foothold, a knob of stone that protrudes from the wall. It enables her to shift her weight from her gashed leg and move down more confidently.

As soon as she's done it, there's an awful noise. A sound like a train trundling through a tunnel above her head.

'What's that?' Gideon shouts from below.

She has no idea. She looks up.

Something is sliding across the top of the shaft. A stone disc cutting off the remaining light. Caitlyn watches it fill the gap above. There's a clunk. A deathly halt.

They are sealed in. Trapped.

183

As the medic ties off a wrap of elasticised bandage around the Master's wound, Grus repeats his awful news: 'The crypt is empty. We searched it from top to bottom. If they were there, they're not now.'

'They were on the centrepiece.' His voice is thinned by pain. 'They were in there, I saw them climbing it.'

'Do you think I ignored you?' says Grus. 'We searched everywhere. *Including* the centrepiece.'

'I climbed it, Master,' adds one of the Lookers. 'To the very top. The roof above is unreachable. There is no way anyone could have escaped from up there.'

The Master swings his legs down from the stone table and sits up. The rush of blood makes him dizzy. 'Then they're still in the room.'

Grus leans close to his old friend. 'Believe me, they are not. We would have found them.'

'Then they must have slipped out of the crypt behind me.' He stands down and flinches.

'You should really rest,' says the medic. 'The cauterisation is fresh and you shouldn't traumatise the wound any more.'

The Master ignores him. 'Sweep the area one more time. Once more and then we are finished.' An expression of defeat washes over his face. 'Grus, you know what must be done, don't you?'

He nods. He understands. Understands perfectly.

184

For a few seconds neither of them move. Frozen in the suffocating dark. They can see nothing. They hear nothing in the hot, still air. Only their own stilted breathing. The scrape of their feet on the stone.

Caitlyn starts to panic. 'We're going to suffocate. Oh Jesus, no!'

'Stay calm.' Gideon climbs up several notches in the stone well. 'Caitlyn, stop it.' He reaches out, finds her foot with his hand. Touches her. Makes contact. The shaft is too narrow for him to get any closer. 'Please calm down. We have to think our way out of this.'

She shuts her eyes. Tries to squeeze out the stinking blackness of the shaft with her inner blackness. She breathes in slowly through her nose. Out slowly through her mouth.

Gideon hears the deep rhythm building above him. He waits, then asks, 'What happened? Did you pull something, stand on anything?'

'I stood on something.' She sounds tearful. 'I'm sorry. It's near my knee now. It was some kind of ridge that stuck out.'

It figures.

He knows ancient tombs were often rigged with devices to stop thieves plundering them. He pulls himself up a little further and feels for the ridge. The stone is smooth. Innocuous in size and shape. It's a strategically placed block counterbalanced by another lodged deeper in the structure. Any sizeable pressure on it, such as a person, shifts the counterweight, which in turn slides the stone disc above across the mouth of the shaft. Simple. Simple and deadly.

'We're trapped, aren't we?' She is trying to sound calm but shaking with dread.

'There's no going back, that's for sure.' Gideon doesn't give her time to dwell on it. 'We need to continue downwards. Don't tread on anything else that sticks out. If you feel another of those trigger ledges, tell me. Okay?'

She takes another deep and calming breath. 'Okay.'

She feels and hears him moving away from her. Finds it hard now to hold on. Knows the strength of her limbs is giving out. She's losing the ability to grip securely.

'Stop. *Stop!*' His cry halts her in her tracks.

'I've found another one.'

He runs his toe across it. There's no doubt that it is a

trigger ledge. But what exactly does it trigger? An opening? Or another seal? Perhaps one that will trap them in the shaft for eternity.

Or is it just a decoy?

Should they ignore it and press on? But then again, doing nothing could prove fatal.

Gideon's mind spins. The very bottom of the shaft may also be a trigger plate. It's not impossible that standing on it could unleash an avalanche of hidden sand, lime and chalk, or even rocks.

They could be buried alive.

185

'Nothing,' says Grus. 'They are nowhere to be found.'

The Master sits with his wounded leg elevated. 'You are sure?'

Grus nods. 'We have swept it systematically, chamber by chamber, passageway by passageway.'

'Then they are gone,' says the Master. 'That can be the only conclusion. They must have somehow slipped past the Lookers on the surface.'

Neither of them can see how that can possibly be, but there is no other logical conclusion. Grus is reluctant to say what's on his mind, but he has to. 'We are out of time to complete the ritual. We must give instructions to disperse the Cleansers, the Bearers, the Lookers. Our foreign brothers must be alerted. All precautions have to be taken.'

The Master struggles painfully to his feet. 'You are right. We have failed the Sacreds.' He corrects himself. '*I* have failed them. Failed you all.'

Grus knows there is no time for reassurances, forgiveness or sentimentality. 'Do I have your permission to cancel all other activity and revert to the back-up protocol?'

'You do.' He opens his arms to his friend and they embrace. 'Make sure the Sanctuary is cleared within the next ten minutes. I will attend the Sacreds, then use the passageway.'

Grus nods. 'It is the only way.'

186

'What's happening?' shouts Caitlyn. 'What are you going to do?'

Gideon doesn't know.

His heart is beating way too fast.

'Just taking a breather,' he lies as he slides his toes away from the trigger ledge. He finds another foothold and relaxes a little. 'Be careful coming down, there's another one of those traps.'

'Okay.' Her fingers slip. She leans back against the side of the shaft and jams herself against the walls before she falls. All that time immured inside the Sanctuary at last has some use.

'You all right?'

'Lost my grip.' She feels the walls and is relieved to find another finger hold. 'I'm fine now. It's all right. Go on.'

He can't.

Gideon has reached the bottom of the shaft. He pulls his foot back.

Uncertainty hits him again. He tries to calculate how far down they have climbed. At least five times his height, that's five times 1.8 metres. They're a good nine metres down. From what he can remember, the centrepiece was about five metres high, so they are already well below the floor level of the crypt.

The thought gives him comfort. Enough for him to put one foot down and then the other.

Nothing happens.

It's safe.

But there is no way out that he can see.

There is a noise above him. Suddenly, he feels a crushing blow, a great weight thudding into his shoulder, driving him down the thin shaft, making his legs give way. It's Caitlyn. She's fallen on him.

The ground beneath him has opened up. The extra, sudden weight has triggered another trap. The stone floor slab tilts and falls away, and they slide entwined down the slope, sandpapered by the rough surface of the rock. For a few heart-stopping seconds they drop into nothing. Then the slope bottoms out, they slow, then stop.

They're still alive. Alive and excited. There can only be

one reason for the final drop. It is a passageway to the outer world. Gideon suddenly understands the centrepiece. It was designed to be filled with the spirits of the ancients. When the shaft was full enough with the weight of the spiritually reborn, it would trigger the opening to a final passageway that would allow them to exit.

Caitlyn groans. Tries to move. Gideon listens to her heavy breathing. He can tell that she's exhausted. He puts an arm across her. 'Rest a minute. We're going to be all right now.'

187

The Apache crew scrambles within five minutes of the call from base.

Tommy Milner had been beginning to think the night time operation wasn't going to happen. It seldom does. A routine seek and destroy, something he could do in his sleep. The four rotors lift them high into the black night sky and out across the range. In the distance they see the lights of vehicles clearing the range. They'd been told there'd been some secret recon done out there while they had been stood down.

Milner's radio crackles into life. 'Range now cleared for manoeuvres. Confirm when you have target in sight, Apache One.'

'Affirmative base, we're airborne and beginning our approach.'

'System lock,' announces Charlie Golding, the Longbow fire control radar at his fingertips. 'Within range and ready for fire command. Over.'

'You have authority to fire at will, Apache One.'

Golding checks his helmet display. From up above the main rotor, the fire control radar relays data to a matched millimetre wave seeker in the nose of the laser-guided Hellfire II missile. In the middle of his display, Golding sees the first of the enemy tanks that they have been instructed to destroy.

In the dark Wiltshire night there's a blinding flash and an explosive roll of thunder. The ground trembles and groans as it sucks up the brutality of the bomb. Beneath two old Chieftains, the dome of the Great Room cracks like a boiled egg. The Sanctuary's passageways disappear like shrivelled veins and the Crypt of the Ancients is buried under thousands of tonnes of sandstone, earth and rubble. It's like it never existed.

188

Caitlyn and Gideon feel their way through the pitch black passageway. It's getting wider and higher now. They're able to walk side by side. She leans on him to ease the pain in her injured leg.

Gideon is still fearful. The ancients protected the shrines ferociously. There could be more surprises. The whole thing could collapse on them. Or underneath them. He stares into the murk, at the floor, the walls, desperate for any telltale signs. Anything unusual.

He uses his left hand to feel their way along the rock. Holds it high, in case there is a support beam or something worse threatening to smash into their unsuspecting skulls.

From the strain of his knees he can tell they're climbing. Hopefully *up* means *out*. Bearing in mind how deep below ground the Sanctuary was sited, he guesses they still have a long way to go.

Caitlyn says little. The trauma of the last few hours and seven days without food have taken the last of her energy. It's a miracle she's still putting one foot in front of the other.

'Do you want to stop?'

'No. No. Keep going. If I stop, I might not be able to start again.'

They hobble on. A deafening noise erupts somewhere behind them. The ball of sound rolls through the passage. They can't see anything, only hear and feel the shockwaves. The ground beneath them shakes. The walls too. The air fills with dust.

Gideon knows what's happening. A cave-in.

'We have to run.' He grabs her around the waist and gets her moving. 'The tunnel's collapsing.'

It sounds like a giant subterranean beast has woken and is thundering after them, growling and biting at their heels. They charge in a blind panic up the darkened passageway, the jaws of the animal snapping at their heels.

Gideon runs smack into a stone wall. A dead end. The blow knocks him flat. He brings Caitlyn down with him. She tumbles sideways into the blockage and cracks her hip.

There's so much flying dust and rubble she can hardly breathe. The passageway is filling with soil and debris. They're being buried alive.

'Where are you?' She has lost him in the darkness.

She feels soil and stone flow like a river of dirt over her bare feet. The tide of death is coming in.

'Gideon! *Gideon*, where are you?'

He is face down in the gathering debris. His chest feels like it is filled with wet cement. There is a pounding in his head and his nose is broken. It takes all of his energy just to get up on his hands and knees.

'Gideon!' She shouts in desperation more than hope.

'Here,' he says. 'I'm over here.'

But she can't find him. 'Over here! Gideon, I'm over here!'

He stumbles towards her voice. His outstretched hands finally find her. Dust is swirling, spiralling above her head.

'Put your hand up! Lift your hand *up*.' There's excitement in her voice.

He does as she tells him.

His fingers find a thin ragged hole. A hole in an exit shaft through the tunnel ceiling. He links his hands together and presses them against her. 'Put your foot in my hands. *Climb*.'

She'd laugh if she had the energy. It's a shaft.

If it's the same as the other one, Gideon calculates they're just nine metres away from escaping.

Nine metres from freedom.

189

They haul themselves upwards using the last of their strength.

'*Stop*,' she shouts. 'It's another switch.'

'Work round it,' he says. 'Don't put any weight on it.'

Caitlyn shifts slowly around the trigger plate. But she is high in the shaft. She looks up, hoping to see some light. A glimpse of night sky. A sparkle of stars or fresh breeze. But there's nothing and the air is still rank and fetid.

She climbs, thinking now about her parents, about making up with her mum, holding tight to her dad, saying a long and heartfelt sorry to Eric.

There are no more finger holds. She has run out of space. Reached the top of the shaft. She bangs it with the palms of her hands.

'It's blocked,' she shouts down, dregs of panic already filtering back into her voice. 'There's no way out. It's all sealed off.'

Gideon wishes he was in front and could explore whatever it is she has found. But the shaft is too narrow to swap positions.

'What do I do?' she shouts. Impatient. Frightened.

'Wait and think.' He tries to imagine the layout of the crypt. They climbed five metres up the centrepiece. They descended a total of nine metres. So the escape tunnel was four metres below the floor level of the crypt but probably rose by the same amount as they made their way along it. He reckons that since entering the second shaft they've only climbed about two metres. So the surface could still be at least three or four metres away.

'Keep your hands off the roof of the shaft,' he calls. 'I'm going to try something.'

Caitlyn crouches low and waits.

He steps across the hole and deliberately puts his weight on the trigger ledge near his right foot. At first nothing happens. Then the stone disc above their heads slowly starts to slide back.

'It's moving. The thing is opening up.'

Her excitement quickly dies down. There is still no glimpse of sky. Just more shaft.

'Keep going up,' he urges. 'After about a metre, you'll find another trigger plate on the right. Don't stand on anything on your left.'

She finds it. Tingles with anticipation. 'What do I do?'

He hesitates. There's everything to gain and everything to lose. He closes his eyes. 'Step on it.'

Caitlyn edges upwards and leans across on her right foot. Nothing happens. She slides her other foot across. All her weight is now on the ledge. Soil and stone rain down on her head. She gasps with shock and fear. Turf and sand fall in on her and cascade down on to Gideon.

Fresh air. Caitlyn feels it for the first time in a week. She all but scampers up the last metre. Her fingers touch wet grass. She can hear the sweet sound of outside, feel freedom.

She hauls herself out of the hole and rolls on to her back. She's still laughing as Gideon crawls out of the shaft and collapses beside her.

A cool wind floats across the bomb-blasted fields. They lie there panting and breathing in the early morning air. Neither of them notice the open-top Jeep heading their way or who is in it.

190

'Stop in front of them,' Grus calls to the staff officer at the wheel. He and Aquila ready themselves. Both are still dressed in the Craft's sackcloth robes. The Jeep's bobbing headlights cut through the grey twilight and fall on Gideon and Caitlyn's wasted bodies.

Everyone had deserted the Sanctuary just minutes before the Master emerged and phoned the military base. In his capacity as lieutenant colonel, he'd given the command for the Apache air strike to take place and had then made his own escape.

Grus never expected to come across Gideon and the sacrifice. He was simply trying to get to his car parked just off the Imber range.

Gideon turns towards the blaze of light. Help at last. He shields his eyes from the glare and is about to shout to the driver when he makes out that the man approaching him on foot is carrying a gun. Even if he had the strength to run, there is nowhere he could hide. No escape.

Grus lets out a shallow laugh. 'One last gift from the Sacreds. The treacherous son and the woman that ruined everything. Looks like she's going to die after all.'

He slips the safety catch off the pistol and walks closer. Night sun lamps from the Apache suddenly unleash a torrent of blinding white light. A megaphone message echoes out of the surrounding field. 'This is the police. Drop your weapon. You are surrounded.'

Grus's face says that's not going to happen. He recognises the voice. It's Jimmy. His own son. He glances to the side and in the half-light beyond the search beam catches a glimpse of men in black uniforms, no more than fifty metres away. Tactical support. They're running low, dropping into the grass, sighting their weapons. He knows the drill.

The light from the Apache burns brighter and the copter hovers lower.

'Armed police, drop your weapon!'

His son's voice hangs in the air. He's out of time and he

knows it. Grus raises the pistol, jams it in his mouth and fires.

The idling Jeep instantly kicks up grass and darts away. Gunfire blazes from across the field. The headlights of the Jeep go out. More shots. This time returned from the speeding vehicle. Sniper fire barks back from the grass, short growls like feral dogs.

The vehicle swerves viciously. It flips on its side. Cartwheels like a clumsy gymnast. Crashes upside down, spilling ragdoll corpses. An eerie silence ensues. No one moves.

Only when birdsong fills the air does one of the firearms team signal that it's safe to move in. Gideon and Caitlyn struggle to their feet and hold each other. The new moon fades in the morning sky.

Dawn finally breaks over the flat Wiltshire plain.

191

MONDAY 28 JUNE

News of Caitlyn's safe recovery is relayed to the suite of Kylie Lock at five a.m. By six, the Hollywood star has sobered up enough to speak to her daughter and to tearfully relay the good news to her father.

Jude Tompkins has a full crime-scene team working on

site at Imber by six-thirty. By seven the bodies of James Pendragon's driver, Nicholas Smith, the Deputy Chief Constable, Gregory Dockery and Inspector Adam Stone have all been examined in situ by a Home Office pathologist and moved to the county mortuary.

By eight a.m. Lee Johns is being formally interviewed in Devizes by Jimmy and by nine he is the first to be charged with kidnapping and manslaughter.

By ten past eight, the media has the story. Newsflashes are filling every radio, television and web bulletin across most of the world.

At ten a.m., Chief Constable Alan Hunt fronts a hastily called press conference in Devizes, congratulating his officers and thanking the Home Office, the FBI and the public for their support.

By eleven, Josh Goran has given the first of what he intends to be many TV interviews, telling how he was responsible for leading the police to Imber and how he is now going to sue the army for the ten million dollars reward that he thinks should rightfully be his. He also shows reporters the fox holes that he and his men dug to escape from army patrols.

By midday someone at the barracks in Warminster remembers they still have several of Goran's team in their cell block and grudgingly releases them.

A little after one p.m., Megan is at her parents' house hugging her daughter Sammy and wondering how to tell her that she'll never see her father again.

Just before three, Gideon wakes in the recovery ward of Salisbury District Hospital, the same one he was in after being attacked in the house of the man he'll always think of as his father. His real father. Professor Nathaniel Chase.

At five p.m. Gideon receives a call of thanks from the Vice President of the United States and a fax from the office of the President.

At six p.m. security teams strip the black plastic sheeting from the fences around Stonehenge and prepare it for a public reopening the following day. By the time the workers have cleared the site, it's twilight again.

Police reports show that no VIP party had taken place after all. There were no crowds and no sacrifice. Nothing out of the ordinary happened. Except for one thing. In the pale light of that busy morning in Wiltshire, there was a solitary visitor to the henge. A tired-looking, grey-faced man entered the circle. He spent a solemn time on his knees, embracing each and every stone.

No one seems to know his name.

And no one has seen him since.

ACKNOWLEDGEMENTS

First and foremost my consiglieri and spiritual bodyguard Luigi Bonomi – agents don't come any better. The folks at Little, Brown/Sphere have been amazing – this is as much Dan Mallory's book as it is mine, maybe even more so, and it's been an honour to write this with him. Big thanks to Iain Hunt for all the heavy lifting he did on draft one at short notice. Kudos to Andy Hine, Kate Hibbert and Helena Doree in international rights, you are all goddesses. Thanks to Hannah Hargrave and Kate Webster in publicity for spreading the word. Scary Jack, big thanks to you too. Mrs M, I couldn't have done this without you x

The Stonehenge Legacy is purely a work of fiction. Scholars will note that while much of it is based on astronomical, archaeological and historical fact, some of those facts have been used in ways to purely enhance the story and don't purport to form a collective truth. That said, despite centuries of research, there is still no indisputable answer to the big question: why was Stonehenge built?